# CLEM ANDERSON

## A NOVEL

# R.V. CASSILL

# BOOKS BY R.V. CASSILL

## Novels
The Eagle on the Coin
Clem Anderson
Pretty Leslie
The President
La Vie Passionnée of Rodney Buckthorne
Doctor Cobb's Game
The Goss Women
Hoyt's Child
Labors of Love
Flame
After Goliath
Jack Horner in Love and War

## Short Stories
15x3 (with Gold and Hall)
The Father and Other Stories
The Happy Marriage and Other Stories
Collected Stories
Patrimonies
Three Stories
Late Stories
The Castration of Harry Bluethorn and Other Stories
The Man Who Bought Magnitogorsk and Other Stories

## Other
Writing Fiction
In An Iron Time: Essays

Widely recognized as R.V. Cassill's masterpiece, Clem Anderson is the story of an author whose astonishing talents are outmatched only by his capacity for self-destruction. Arrogant, untrustworthy, moody, and narcissistic, Clem Anderson is also a brilliant artist capable of astonishing feats of alchemy: with his pen, real life is magically transformed into the stuff of great literature. But the rising tide of literary success is dangerous ground for a personality as unstable as Anderson's, and when he dies at the age of forty, alone and disgraced, it is up to his few remaining friends to pick up the pieces.

"The best novel I know of on the subject of writing, or on the condition of being a writer."
   — **Richard Yates**

"A brilliant satirical study as well as a masterful piece of comedy. There is running commentary on the whole post-war generation that gives the story a unifying resonance rare in most novels . . . Cassill is a master at showing us how. It is this fascinating how that makes Clem Anderson a major novel."
   — **New York Times Book Review**

"The best of the 1961 novels I have read. Clem Anderson deserves the National Book Award."
   — **Los Angeles Times**

"Clem Anderson is that much-cited and seldom-seen phenomenon: a major novel."
   — **Atlanta Journal & Constitution**

"A massive, significant work . . . a gifted novelist."
   — **Chicago Tribune**

"Vivid, soaring - by any standards this is a notable novel."
   — **Saturday Review Syndicate**

This book is for my father and mother, who were educators.

Strong the gier-eagle on his sail,
Strong against tide, the enormous whale.

—CHRISTOPHER SMART, A Song to David

# CLEM ANDERSON

# I

## THE PASSAGE OF A FAUN

*Life, our present life, is scarcely possible of scenic representation, since it has withdrawn wholly into the invisible, the inner, imparting to us only through "august rumors"; the dramatist, however, could not wait till it became showable; he had to use violence toward it.*

— RAINER MARIA RILKE

# 1

AT THE BLACKHAWK RAILWAY STATION, where Janet and I picked Clem up, we found him being helped from the train like an invalid V.I.P. by a porter twice his age. Clem was drunk—"Already," Janet whispered. In that moment of seeing him come back to us like a battered refugee from time, it seemed to me no early indulgence that we were witnessing. "Still," I said.

"Fat, too," she had time to say before he saw us hurrying down the platform to rescue him from the solicitude of the porter. Evidently Clem had added twenty pounds since we had seen him last, two years before. In his blue flannel suit, blinking in the warm April sun and rocking gently, he looked like a roly-poly toy in exile from the nursery where it is at home.

He could not have heard her. Nevertheless, his first words of greeting to us who had known him through the string-bean days of his poverty were a direct response to her observation. "Fatness has come on me, cried the Lady of Shalott." Turning once more to the porter and giving him a dollar, he identified himself otherwise. "W. C. Fields to you," he said, clapping the man's shoulder. Then, raising his fat-softened muzzle to the academic sky that he saw spread over us, lifting both elbows so that Janet and I could get the necessary purchase, he gave the stage direction, "Here comes Oedipus, poorly led."

"Thank y', Mr. Fields," the porter said. He scampered back onto his train with an alacrity that suggested all his gladness in passing this torch of volubility on to us.

It fizzled quickly enough in our hands. Or else the implacable fact of arrival settled its melancholy on Clem at once. He blinked at us several times, suggesting we had been much nicer people in his anticipation than we appeared, in daylight, to be. While Janet was still hugging him—she had refused his offer that we take hold of him like a wheelbarrow—his hands were already anxiously busy inside her embrace. He was searching his inner pockets for the paper he had come to read that night before an audience of Blackhawk University people.

Since I had sponsored his invitation and would be in about three hours on the platform with him, introducing him to my colleagues and students, I was almost as relieved as he when he had nudged Janet back and produced the tattered, dirty envelope that contained his talk. I

1

didn't doubt his ability to improvise if necessary. I was merely afraid of it.

Relieved to find it he was. Yet the relief itself reminded him of the ordeal to come. Mutely he handed the envelope over to me for security, but with such a look of the disgraced Soviet official handing himself over to a Siberian welcoming committee that I could not help a slight feeling of injury.

"You've landed in the U.S.A.," I said to his fogginess. It was like calling out the window into the night on the presumption that your listener is out there somewhere. "Mrs. Hartsell and I are going to take you to our president."

He nodded raptly and stared past me at the half-leaved gold and green of the trees by the end of the station. Mirrored in his slightly protuberant eyes I saw the silhouette of this residential part of our little town. "Those are trees you see," I told him.

"Trees I can recognize. I believe that they require oxygen to do their part in the scheme of things. So do I. I'd be obligated, Dick, if you'd take me where I can get some."

Our little whimsies of greeting all ran down while Janet and I drove him to our home to leave his bags and then to the highway restaurant where we had planned to eat before his scheduled appearance. He continued to concentrate powerfully on something besides us or what we had to show him—perhaps on the talk he was to give, on what W. C. Fields had said to the porter on the train, on the kindly city of New York that he had so ill-advisedly left last evening, or, for all we could get out of him, on his cloaked and sweaty navel.

He hardly seemed to notice that we left the car for a few minutes at our place. He looked outraged when Janet asked if he wanted to wash or change his clothes or lie down. Had she forgotten how his strength deserted him in contact with water?

When we explained that we were not going to eat at home because we wanted to escape, one evening, from the children, he smiled sociably and looked behind him, as if we were addressing some other guest whose presence with us he had not noticed yet. We said that after all there was so much to catch up on. We said that his visit was as much an occasion for us as it was for him. He went on smiling sideways.

I thought that while we drove up the highway north of town he was putting us off so that he could concentrate on the loveliness of the evening. It was wonderful, with ranks of silver-and-blue clouds diminishing away into the sundown, columns of showers standing here and there among the velvet dark clumps of half-leaved trees like a

Rubens landscape or something by an English water-colorist of the eighteenth century. This was nearly home country for Clem. We were two states away from the town in which he had grown up, but it must have been a long while since he had seen the Midwest at its promising best. Well, whatever he was taking in, he was giving nothing out. We asked him about Sheila and their children, Jess and Lulie.

"Fine, just fine," he said.

We asked about the rumors that his play *Death and the Devil* was at long last scheduled for a Broadway opening in the fall. "True, that's true," he said, staring through the windshield as if I were driving recklessly through a mine field.

I asked about his friend Terry Burbidge, though I had a suspicion that he and Terry had fallen out for reasons I could not know. I withheld any comment about the prize given Terry's new book of poetry until I should have the chance to sound Clem's present sentiments. I supposed he might be somewhat embittered by the success of a man who, not many years ago, had frankly recognized Clem's superiority to himself. Clem in his old days had been a fierce literary competitor.

"Terry deserved the award," Clem said.

Altogether, by the time we had parked, Janet and I had pulled as much information from him as he might have put on a postcard. That was some accomplishment, I supposed, since we had not had a postcard from the Andersons for more than a year. Clem's letter accepting the invitation to speak had said nothing about his private fortunes or opinions.

Once seated in the restaurant, where he could peer like Narcissus into a crystal martini, we got a little more from him. Overheard it, I felt.

He told us that Sheila had, since we saw her, written a children's book scheduled for early publication. "It's called Beauty Bear," he said. "The idea for the title is mine—you know, from that breathless line of Edgra St. Whipleash McTate about who's the lucky individual that's seen bareback loveliness—and it's, her book, a true-life portrait of an unfortunate friend. There's more ambiguity in children's books than meets the adult eye, the cunning little bastards. Every one of them a world of delight closed by our senseless five." He laughed into his ginny reflection, shaking like a bowlful of wicked jelly. "I'm working on '*The Skeleton Key of Beauty Bear*,'" he said.

After another martini and a few bites of steak, he volunteered that he didn't mind Terry Burbidge's getting the National Book Award, since some people he didn't like were running Robert Mingus and

Edgar Tobey against Terry, and Mingus was queer as a three-dollar bill—no disqualification in itself, we were to understand, but the queers in this country owed it to the young to reveal themselves, like Gide, not play hide-and-seek-I'm-a-misunderstood-straight-boy-like, and Tobey would be a better poet if he spent less time on the road organizing his reputation.

"At least Terry's honest," he said. "If he wrote that his heart ached and a drowsy numbness pained him, you know, I'd believe him. Who cares who gets the prizes anyway, except it catches the academic boobs who still believe in standards." That was me he meant. "It's all huckstering anyway, and in a couple of years I'm going to straighten out their curves, Dick. I've got a tremendous long poem going. I call it 'Prometheus Bound.' That's a title will stick in your mind. You like it, Janet? My agent forbids me to tell you the real title, but it's the logic of my life. The everything. Then the crumbs will all shake out. They'll have to invent me a new prize, you know. Knight's Order of the Two-headed Vulture with rubies, silver-on-gules ribbon that will cover me from armpit to armpit."

We were starting to laugh with him at this when, abruptly, he jumped up and started for the men's room. Our laughter died thinly before an obliging waiter caught his arm and guided him in.

I looked at my watch. I looked at the brown-and-ruddy steak on his plate from which so few morsels had been cut and fewer eaten. In less than an hour he was supposed to speak.

"He can't go on," Janet said firmly. "Call the department secretary and have her announce that he's sick. Poor Clem."

No doubt I should have taken her advice. I had nothing to lose if he missed his engagement. I might be embarrassed for a few weeks by those who guessed why he was unable to appear. In some intangible matters of prestige my rating might swerve a bit downward, but I had tenure now and was bucking for exactly nothing except peace and security in my middle age.

Nevertheless it seemed to me at the threshold of this decision—and the intuition was odd enough—that the only hope we had of continuing our thin-worn friendship with Clem was to bring him through what he had undertaken to perform. I was shaken by the evidence of remoteness that had grown between us since our last meeting. I didn't like his reticence or the egocentric brashness of his talk when it came. (The talk about "running" poets against each other for a respected prize, as if they were horses doctored and doped by a crew of cigar-sucking gamblers, had seemed pitiably offensive.) I was angry enough to assume my right to know what he was really thinking—where, in his view of his own field, he had come to by now.

Let me say at the same time I was not forgetting Clem's old complaint, "Everyone that Sheila and I make friends with thinks he's our best friend. How can you have so many dozen best friends?" It was the understandable plaint of a man who had traveled far. He had met an absolute swarm of nice people to whom he had given more encouragement than, perhaps, he realized. I remembered and respected the warning, even to Janet and me, against presuming an intimacy that might be onerous to him. Still the case seemed different with us.

Academic boob though I might be—and my poor wife dragged down to my level—we had known him a very long time. Over fifteen years. So much of what had happened to him had involved us that I could not quite bring myself to accept the alienation I felt now. I told myself that after his talk was out of the way we could be easy together again.

So I said, "He has to go on."

My hand flew to my breast pocket to touch his envelope. And I have thought since that my own anxiety should have been another warning, another chance to turn him back. He should have gone home to bed, not to another public trial. Strangers, I have accused myself, would have known that better than old friends. Strangers would have been kinder. I think of that when I think how, finally, he turned entirely to strangers.

In any case it may have been Clem who made his own decision. Just in time he came out of the men's room emanating a reasonable appearance of jauntiness. His plump face was white, but his hair was neatly slicked down with water.

Watching him come toward us, I said to Janet, "Nonsense. He'll win all hearts. What's there to be afraid of?"

Clem said, "Avanti. I go to face the jury of my pierce."

I announced that Clem's topic for this evening's Falmouth Lecture was "Why Is the Play the Thing?" When I had extended the lecture committee's invitation to Clem there had been no specification as to his topic except that it ought to spring from his experience as a writer. He could have chosen poetry or fiction and satisfied our requirements as well, but, as he had blurted while we climbed the stairs that night to the Winslow Memorial Chamber, he had thought he would "draw better" if he spoke as a playwright. "Bigger money in theater," he said.

As he rose to speak I took a chair at his left hand on the dais, breathed easily at last and gratefully heard him raise his voice to a performer's pitch. Though he had put on glasses and was reading closely from his typed manuscript, his tone was strong and flexible. Like many poets, he knew how to use his voice professionally.

Now I could take a good look at our audience and count the house. I was not a little pleased to see that at least three hundred people had turned out, literally crowding the wide, shallow room from the Victorian busts on the right to the huge portrait of benefactor Winslow on the left. Under the chandelier in the center I saw Drs. Weisdrop and Banning, both professors emeriti with bald heads so shining that on them each I could make out the individual reflections of every light in the room. Around them colleagues, faculty wives, librarians, the younger faculty, and students from both the English and the dramatic-arts departments were listening raptly—as for the time I was not.

Truthfully I must admit that for many minutes I did not follow the tendency or catch the major points of Clem's talk. For one thing, I felt I had finished a tricky mission merely by getting him up there. A fixed smile of inattention on my face served as a kind of screen behind which I could first congratulate myself for overriding Janet's doubts (I saw her out there in the audience, her brow beginning to smooth at last) and presently select bits and morsels from the flow of all he told the rest. It was rather as if I were reading a page covered with another blank sheet in which certain holes had been cut so that the messages I received were essentially different from those heard by the group at large. And by this artifice I got a sort of substitute for the frankness he had been withholding from Janet and me since his arrival.

"It was my little boy Jess convinced me that I ought to try my writing hand on plays," I heard him say. "Jess and I communicated well before he knew words. If I cocked my ear he would listen—for Mama or fire trucks or the postman putting checks in our mailbox. If I cooed or simpered he lifted a skeptical little eyebrow. He reached up from the mire of his soiled diaper like a baby Lear welcoming Cordelia home when his mother came to change him. With us the transition from signs to sounds was unbroken. So, when he could talk, the words had grown naturally out of a more primitive communication, and the words were twice as good because they grew stage by stage out of the mystery of silence and noncommunication.

"And the way it was between me and my boy is the way I want it to be between you and me, between my sad and funny characters and whatever audience I can lure into the theater from the business of the street. The reason I'm up here tonight—sweating, mind you—" and here he made a little comedy business of tugging at his ugly jacket—"'is so you'll know what I mean better than if you read these sheets instead of me, which," tongue in plump cheek he said, "I imagine most of you would be able to do. This—this you and me—is a kind of theater, too."

And what had I screened from such a passage as this for my private information? Jess's cocked eyebrow and the "mire" of his diapers. Primitively communicated to, I heard the good note of Clem's love for Jess and cut off, letting our speaker run on to tell the others what he had made, in art, from the exploitation of his love. I let go the sound of his voice so an image of Clem and son could expand at leisure in my mind.

The last time Janet and I had been really close to Clem was in the summer before Jess was born. Since then I had seen Jess once briefly in Paris. Janet had never seen the boy, and we had often wondered together what kind of father Clem would make. Knowing Clem, we could hardly have doubted that he would love the boy deeply. But constantly? And wouldn't a child, above anyone else, suffer the bewilderment of expecting a best friend to stay always as close as he had come in his closest moments?

Now, in Jess's fifth year, I believed I heard the note of constancy and was a bit humbled for the impatience I had felt in not being assured of it in private conversation. Leave it to Clem, I thought. In his own way, in his own time, he'll answer everything.

I returned from this private reflection to hear him mention Sheila again—working a laugh from his audience, something more deeply glad from me.

He said, "If there's one thing worse than being the wife of a writer, it's being the wife of a playwright whose play is in trouble. In the first rehearsals I put my wife in a lead-lined room to protect her from the fireball—actually I staked her out on a farm in Rockland County—but she still took everything harder than I did. She thought they were cutting off my fingers and toes every time lines were dropped from what I'd written. Now, a playwright who expects to keep his original lines intact is a species of egomaniac who …"

I stopped listening to consider Sheila and the unchangingness of her loyalty to what Clem did. He could have stopped talking then for all I cared.

But this time when I came back to awareness of what was happening in the room I became—by primitive communications— aware of something incongruous and, to put it as mildly as I did at first, equivocal.

There was no doubt by now that he was carrying, "taking," his audience. Faculty parents had beamed when he used the superficially homely illustration of familial communication to typify the birth of the drama. Graduate students were assenting to his literary allusions. The boys and girls from Dramatic Arts would have been admiring his excellent voice and "projection." Librarians and professors emeriti would have been satisfied that another Falmouth Lecture had brought them solemnly together at the feet of a man "one has heard about."

But as I listened more attentively and watched I couldn't doubt that he was building his rapport with them in two distinct and antithetic ways. He entertained them. Glibly almost. But at the same time he was communicating to them a primordial smell of fear—his fear—like the victim of a genuine saturnalia romping through those antics of a king that everyone dimly knows will end in his sacrifice.

In anticipation of what I know as I write this I see that I have already overstated what I knew then. No one knew—not yet, not in any part of that night still far from a peaceable end—what they were watching. I think I could not have identified as simply as I do now the smell of fear that was playing such an eerie counterpoint to the confidence of his words. But, without the language to describe it, I knew something was loosed among us that should not have been.

He had told them he was "sweating." I saw how much of an understatement this was. I saw his hand tremble when he lifted it from the side of the lectern to turn a page. I watched it fly back, grope for a hold and cling so desperately that it seemed he was afraid of falling.

His left leg, mercifully hidden from the audience by the lectern, but fully visible to me, began to pump and jerk like the uncontrollable limb of a spastic. Involuntarily I cleared my throat, and he spun halfway toward me as though I might be an expected assailant coming on him through the woods of Nenni with my club. Recovering, he turned to the last page. His nails scratching at the top of the lectern found only polished wood beneath this sheet and in this relief he gathered presence and charm for an effective conclusion.

With winning, winsome melancholy he said, "I hope I have not left the writing of poetry and the writing of fiction permanently behind me. Poetry was my journey to the wars and fiction was my coming home to peace, and when I'm older and maybe wise again I want to write a novel as long as my arm, and before that a big poem as deep and rich as a Texas oil well. But for the time being I've found my love in the theater. I mean, you know, I write plays. And I kinda, you know, like—hell, I hope I kinda tonight explained why."

So, with an easy-to-love stammer and the blush of a modest child finishing a declamatory reading, he walked stiff-legged to his chair and fell into it. The applause started, thin at first, then swelling to something more than polite, something unmistakably charged with emotion, hungry, anxious or loving. He poured a huge glass of water, slopped half of it on the carpet in trying to raise it to his mouth, and the audience clapped harder, laughing now. He had got through—free style, Clem style, but at least he had made sanctuary ahead of the pack.

Thanking the god of time that Clem was safe, I stood up to conclude the program. I found myself shaking miserably with the contagion of his stage fright. Now it was my hands which were sweating coldly as I clung to the lectern for dear life. But I was practiced in the formalities of my job—and made the mistake of asking for questions instead of sensibly bidding everyone good night.

Out in the center of the chamber under a chandelier that I saw shimmying like a grass skirt, old Professor Banning was rising slowly with his hand in the air. His face was kind and sleepy. His mouth was pale pink as the rose of late-nineteenth-century poetry, and I gratefully assumed he meant to ask Clem what he thought of the drama of a young Britisher named Somerset Maugham.

I aimed my forefinger at him. As I nodded an invitation for his question a dark, unpleasant voice called from one of the doorways at the back of the chamber, "Anderson. Mr. Anderson!"

This voice, I made out, came from a boy who I would probably have said was a dramatic-arts student. He was tall, thin, sallow, with a forelock of hair pulled down to his right eyebrow. Over his folded arms he carried a dirty trench coat.

"Mr. Anderson. Sir!" While I wavered in uncertainty and hoped he would shut up, it struck me that I was still hearing Clem's voice, or, more precisely, that someone was personifying the fear that Clem had communicated only by his weird trembling and aura. The voice was strident and aggressive, at the same time slopping over with a note of terror.

"Mr. Anderson!" the boy called—or commanded—again. He took a few shuffling steps into the room. His hand found a chair that had been vacated by someone departing promptly. He flopped, just as Clem had at the end of his talk, but shouted once more, "Mr. Anderson!"

"Dr. Banning has the floor," I said. But already, with the boneless gentility of the old, Banning was bowing and yielding to the boy's importunity.

"All right," I heard Clem say beside me. I stepped away to let him resume his place at the lectern. "You want to ask me something?" Clem queried.

"Yeah, man. I mean all this like crap you were saying."

There was in that room the almost tactile shock of the totally unprepared. Necks were twisting, for the boy remained seated. We could not believe it yet, but plainly he meant to go on speaking.

"I mean, you, uh, you say you wrote some poetry. You used to write a little bit of poetry before you, uh, got wised up like—I mean, gee, that's pretty decent of you to, uh, like even condescend to make the goddam scene with it, to mess around with like what Donne, and Whimman, and Tiss Eliot'd waste their goddam life on, huh? Huh?"

"Go on," Clem encouraged him.

The boy licked his lips with a long tongue. It moved around his mouth like some marooned sea slug searching a hot rock for moisture. Obscene and pitiful—but it should not have been both at the same time.

"Wait," I shouted. I meant to answer this hoodlum for Clem, to shield him from a rudeness that he was under no slightest obligation to accept. I even put my hand on his shoulder, meaning to urge that he leave the stand to me until I had restored order. In a peculiarly nightmarish indecision it seemed to me that I must not deny him the physical support and coverage of the lectern.

"Go on," he said in a low, fond voice.

The boy pushed up his forelock with a Brando gesture. He tried to get to his feet, but his nerve failed him. Flopping in his chair, he shouted, "What are you trying to make out, Anderson? You know damn well you're writing this glug for Broadway to make a buck and flopped with your novel and who ever reads like your goddam poems? I read one of them it went like, 'Soldiers are Boy Scouts at twelve.' It was lousy. What d'ya mean by crap like that? Whyn't you write for us kids, man? I mean like we'd like to know what you got to say, man."

In some other kind of gathering at this point, surely, someone would have yelled at the boy to shut up. But we are an academic community and our oddly characteristic response was best expressed by Dr. Clarence Coleman's climbing onto his chair and shouting across many embarrassed faces at the boy, "Shame! Shame! Shame! Shame! Shame!" He was clutching his Phi Beta Kappa key as a small child might clutch its genitals. His reedy, English-accented voice was the only articulate protest against the assault.

Over it, Clem repeated his invitation. "Go on."

But now that the boy had discharged his mud, he threw his arms back and slumped as in some deposition from the Cross. A sick, catatonic grin spread across his face from ear to ear. Those nearest him were muttering rebukes now. I am convinced that he heard none of them, being so inwardly concentrated on his ideal image.

"I'll try to answer that—question," Clem said with a white smile. There was a titter of alliance and encouragement at his ironic emphasis. Then Clem hung on the lectern for a terribly stretched period of silence. If, before, the audience had missed what I caught of his fear, now they were glutted with it. Two or three times he opened his mouth—but he too tried to moisten his lips with his tongue.

It came to me with perfect clarity what I was afraid of. I was afraid that Clem, being Clem, was going to try to answer honestly. The boy had challenged him, as poet, to show the "foul rag-and-bone shop of the heart." Clem might have been fool enough to show it, and I realized how such foolhardiness might show us all, too brutally, the thinness of the ice on which we had gathered.

I said to Clem loudly, "In the name of the university, I want to apologize."

He nodded. At last, with a soft, dismissing wave of his hand, he said to the boy in back, "You may be right." I am afraid he would rather have talked to that boy than to any of the rest of us.

Then, with a consummatum est blankness, really tragic and indescribable, on his face, he turned and plucked at my lapel.

"Lead me," he said, trying to grin. "You play rough out here in the colleges. I guess your buddies saw right through me, huh?"

Of course we did not even want to look. But he believed we did. I was going to have a hard time demonstrating to him how harmless, utterly harmless, we were.

That is why, with alternatives still open, I led him as quickly as I could from that chamber where several were waiting to congratulate him and presently made up my mind that the dean's party was our next stop.

When Clem, Janet and I walked into the buzz of the dean's living room and while Clem was receiving the dean's congratulations for the lecture, "which I'd very much like to have heard," I congratulated myself for steering him well.

For the first hour of our stay, it seemed to me that he was recuperating nobly. The dean's wife had disengaged him from Janet and me to introduce him to their other guests. As far as I could tell he was lighting up for these strangers in sharp distinction, I recalled ruefully, to his reticence with us before the talk. He seemed to be gathering new friends like a sow finding truffles—sniffing hearts under the stuffing under the shirts.

Even at his present age of thirty-seven, when the shaded lamps showed up the bloaty softness of his face and the bat's-flesh bags under his eyes, and his posture was that of a deflating aquatoy, he could project himself as a deserving youth. His cheeks were abnormally pink, a pinkness rather scary by the daylight in which we met him. His eyes could look boyishly eager when he had the control and the motive for peeling back the upper lids, as he did now. And around his remaining good facial features he could organize the illusion of a promising orphan who meant not to waste the wisdom and affection that so many people seemed glad to shower down on him. The dean's guests were no more proof against this charm, now that he had cut it loose freely, than, say, his bar companions in New York or than Janet and I and his other caretakers in college.

I saw him once that evening wedged between Gladstone, head of the English department, and Mrs. Bellegarde, whose husband had been Blackhawk's great historian. The three of them made a curious group in front of the dean's mantel, where a bust of Dante and some massy candlesticks loomed dark against the dark wood paneling of the wall. (This house had been built by a long-bankrupted fraternity, hence its air of an Oxford commons and the clublike spaciousness of all the rooms on the lower floor.) Clem looked like a hillbilly relation who had drifted into a Tidewater family seat, worth the lore sifted on him by these two family eminences only because still so obviously unformed, so intent on adding an extra luster of value to every pearl they let fall. He made listening a positively vigorous art. In all seriousness they were giving him the best they had. Then, setting a tiny cigarette butt in the corner of his mouth and squinting against the hot smoke from it, he made a three- or four-word quip that dropped those two like a brace of venerable ducks falling on each side of a hunter's boat, both of them literally staggering with giggles.

He was doing so much better, even, than I had expected that I wondered if I had not overdone my earlier worries about him. I turned my full attention to Mrs. Manson, with whom I had been carrying on one of those numb conversations that no amount of deanish bonded can liven up at an essentially deanish party.

She was a hard, bright bitch in her early fifties. Her husband published our state's leading newspaper, which accounted more than amply for her being among the guests that night. She hadn't, she told me, attended Clem's lecture—I gathered that she had dined here with the Hagerstroms and the dean of the medical school, among others. She called Dean Hagerstrom "Willy." By tone and implication she made it clear that she didn't go to any speeches of less weight than major political addresses. Lecturers came to her, she made you know, to deliver the inside story they couldn't give to the Consuming Classes. She didn't care boo about the drama of Chekhov, Shaw or Brecht, or any comments Clem might have made about it tonight. She was hungering for the latest theatrical gossip he might have brought from New York.

The dean's wife had told her that I was an old friend of Clem's. Ergo, I must have, already, some choicely chewed worm bits I could relay, like Daddy bird, into her waiting maw. She wanted to know who was putting up the money for this second try at getting Clem's play to Broadway. (The first mustering of a cast for rehearsals and a week of tryouts in Washington had somehow shoaled in a Second Avenue theater. The reviews last winter had been good, but the production had failed, after four weeks, to meet its overhead. Mrs. Manson seemed to understand this process all much better than I, but she hungered for more details.)

I felt in her attitude an exact calibration of Clem's rank as a writer—something I was far from sure of, if I had ever worried much about it. I was to understand that Mrs. Manson came early to any success. Still, she hadn't the faintest notion that Clem had written anything before this play. She managed a half-disparaging, polite "Oh" when I mentioned the novel, the short stories and the poems he had published since 1938. But she wanted to know if it was settled that the producer was bringing Barbara Dunne Martin in as a star to replace Joan Marian now.

When I confessed ignorance of this, her micrometer eyes screwed a little tighter to my diminished measurement. It was becoming evident to this she bear that I was only a former acquaintance whom Clem was using for bed and board on this lecture stop. In my uncertainty, I thought she might be right.

However, even as pretended friend or coattail-hanger, I would serve to bring Mrs. Manson into what I suddenly must think of as his presence. She went to him then like a battleship through a harbor of flat civilian hulls, and I was brought along to give her name—which she had somehow neglected to have emblazoned on her bows.

13

"I've been betting on you from the time I saw your stories and poems in print first," she said to him, as if for this he owed her two thousand dollars.

He stared at her in pure, alcoholic bewilderment, let his eyelids slide over his startled eyes a couple of times and asked, "You mean those in *The Southern Review* and *Prairie Schooner*?"

"Yes," she said gamely. I would have bet on her that she thought The Southern Review was starring Lena Horne. "And I really liked *Angel at Noon* better than any first novel I've read since the war. You may consider it embarrassing juvenilia and all, but I thought it was warm and full of zest."

"You did?"

"Yes, I did."

"That's good."

"Well, I really did."

Clem was staring hypnotically at her white bosom as though he wanted to put his head to rest on it, but with a great shudder he recovered himself, smiled and said, "It's a great thing to find someone who's read it. May I have your autograph?"

And at that point, perhaps thinking that she served him right for some of the concern he had given me, I unhooked her on him while I headed for the martini pitcher.

I found Dr. Gladstone there, enjoying the potion and ready to draw morals from it. His moral was that, after all, life was not so constrained here in the Midwest as the carpers made it out to be. He cited—directly into my ear, in a cautious whisper bubbling with chuckles—the liberality with which hard liquor flowed in the home of an old hard-shelled Baptist like Dean Hagerstrom. I admitted that I had never seen a teetotaler who served a drier martini.

"Do you think he likes it here?" Gladstone asked, nodding back toward Clem.

In view of the liquor supply, I said truly that I was sure he did.

"And I expect he doesn't find any more liberality at the parties he attends in New York, does he?"

I said brazenly that I doubted it.

The point was that Gladstone was quite taken with Clem. He, for one among them, had heard Clem's lecture. And to his undying credit let it be said that he had read a good share of Clem's published work—just before Clem's arrival, it is true, but even that was something, since to my knowledge Gladstone had read little else more modern than William Dean Howells.

We even chatted there for a moment, above the exalting dead-pale glitter of martinis, of the possibility of bringing Clem back sometime as a teacher. "He'd be very good for some of our bright graduate students, who are ready for him," Gladstone said. "I'm afraid he might be too quick, too devious, for the undergraduates. His humor is ... it's sly." All at once Gladstone looked frightened by his own epithet. He did a double take and twisted his neck to look at Clem again, as though he had just now realized the possibility of deception in whatever Clem had said to him a while before.

But Clem was reclining innocently on a sofa, with Mrs. Manson leaning over him, and it looked as if the worst he was capable of was falling asleep under her. I thought she might have her jaws in the scruff of his neck to shake him if that happened, and I went back to them, meaning to lead him home.

"Art," Mrs. Manson was telling him as I came along, "is just a matter of applying imagination to the experiences of everyday life that we all have." She was pivoting on her hard right haunch to drive this epigram home, and she followed through, when Clem failed to say "Yes, ma'am," with a sweep that presented the question to a visiting cellist named Horlock and my wife, who also meant to snatch Clem away from her and take him where he could rest.

"Isn't that so?" Mrs. Manson demanded of Horlock. He closed both eyes and nodded his handsome head.

"I'd certainly agree with that," Janet said. She braved the thirty-two Manson teeth and reached in to shake Clem's shoulder. He had—as usual—a dying stub of cigarette in his mouth. The ashes from it spilled down his tie when he twisted like a sleepy baby to get away from her hand.

Eyes opening, he leaned very close to Mrs. Manson and answered her in such a falsely cute, babyish tone that I was sure he meant to make her the butt of a joke, now that he had an audience for it. "You know how I found my vocation in art ... well, it was ... the aht of medicine ... like Faustus, I ... but same thing, like the experiences of ev-ree-day lah-eef."

"So? Oh?" Mrs. Manson said. She wasn't born yesterday and she wasn't about to be the end man for any routine he might have in mind. "I meant that perfectly seriously, and I've heard no less a person than J. P. Marquand say it himself."

"All right," Clem said. He skinned his eyes again, saw the white cliff of her bosom and announced—in a shockingly clear, rather beautiful voice, only most terribly inappropriate there and then in whatever was happening, a really somnambulistic storyteller's voice, earnest as the sourceless speech in a dream—that his vocation had been revealed to him at the tender age of four. "At a family reunion in Boda," he said. "Aunt Alice, Aunt Veda, Aunt Mary Dolores, Aunt Callie and Mama were doing dishes in the kitchen. Uncle Raymond, Uncle Harvey, Uncle Sewell, Uncle Cole, Great-Uncle Finch …"

Strategy or confusion? Had he really gone to sleep, or was this some utterly smug game of mockery? Not exactly any of these things, I suppose. As nearly as I can characterize this inappropriate declaration he had begun, I would say it was a response to the boy who had heckled him at the lecture. Just that. I think, grotesque as it may seem, that it made no difference that the persons confronting him had, to put it mildly, changed. Neither he nor the dean's liquor was, any more, a respecter of persons. The mind went on turning a subject that had been called for elsewhere. The mouth let out what he had been cudgeled back to think about.

I could see Mrs. Manson's eyes contracting with each meaningless name added to his Biblical or Joycean catalogue. She was a person requiring respect. Every name struck her as an ambiguous personal affront. Whether it was his intent or not, she knew that what he said mocked her. As indeed it did.

"Control yourself," she bade him, poking him away from her with red fingertips when he seemed likely to spill like Jello on her front.

But his elevated voice rippled around hers as he went on to describe how he had toddled down to the barnyard, that day in Boda, following the adults who had taken the .22 to shoot pigeons. His stiff, plump fingers toddled down his thigh, hit his whiskey glass and jiggled drops from it. I saw that Horlock was watching and listening with undisguised fascination. The glaze of boredom he had worn through the evening was gone. Whether he was fascinated by the antisocial antics of our drunken friend or by some note of aboriginal—musical—truth, I can't, of course, say.

Now Clem's baby fingers were holding up a pigeon that his Uncle Cole had shot from the ridge of the barn, and its blood was running down onto the clay of that vanished barnyard … or onto the immaculate Manson lap.

"Then, all at once," he said, "there's this hell of a commotion back at the house. It was little Cousin Evelyn, Cousin Billy, Cousin Waldo, Cousin Al and Cousin Mark all screeching together. I go toddling back like it's my duty to visit all disasters that day. Maybe scared, maybe excited, knowing I was about to learn it. Hermetic secret. I peeked in

16

through the kitchen screen door, brushed away the flies, saw around the curve of my mother's butt that all those grown-up sisters were glaring down at little Cousin Mark. Who looked like those Sunday-school-card pictures of Christ confounding the doctors in the Temple.

"'We were only taking her temperature,' says smart-aleck Mark.

"'But that's not the way to take her temperature,' says Aunt Veda, holding Evelyn in her arms and rocking her to make her stop bawling. 'That's not the way we take her temperature even with a real thermometer, let alone an old Fudgicle stick.'

"'That's the way Mama takes mine,' Mark said. So his mother slapped him and he began to bawl, too. Said, 'I thought you wanted me to be a doctor when I grow up.'"

At which point in his story Janet laughed, a painful, short laugh like a groan, a willing-unwilling sound, as if the conflicting impulses to listen and to rescue him were strangling her.

Mrs. Manson took the laugh as the irrepressible snicker of someone who has witnessed a shameful performance. She laughed, too, a single hard "Ha," and said with a voice like a scythe, "That's very interesting." Her eyes glittered and she had a victory smile all ready for the moment when she would stand up and stalk away from this disgrace. She had seen—and we had seen the same thing—a demonstration (her demonstration?) that underneath the pretense of success that was Clem's passport among us there was a bloody, stinky, drunken mess. She said in a trilling, frigid explanation, "They'd taken the child's temperature down there." To all of us except Clem she said, "I've never understood why so many writers feel the compulsion to be dirty. Great art doesn't have to go to the gutter." She looked at Horlock for confirmation. He looked blank.

"Then why are you sucking around me?" Clem bellowed at her. Now we were beginning to attract attention from around the room. I don't think anyone moved toward us. They weren't the kind of people who would have done that, and I'm sure they tried to go on with their conversations. But we felt them closing in to witness. For a second all I saw was the pain and pity on Janet's face, and her straining to comprehend.

"Oh," Mrs. Manson said, using her nostrils like clarinet pads so that the sound was a slurring rise and fall. "No one's ever talked to me like that before."

"More's the fucking shame," Clem bellowed. Caught in the slamming hush that followed, I had the notion that he had calculated this effect long, long before he had used it—that this was what he had been meaning to slam us with all evening. And, perhaps worse, I had the feeling that it was not Mrs. Manson, nor us, whom he meant to degrade by his grossness. It was himself.

Everyone seemed petrified. Certainly I should have tried some diversion to cover up what had happened, and I should have tried bodily to get him quickly out of that place. I couldn't quite stop the spin of emotions that he'd so intolerably broken out of the secrecy where they belonged.

It was Gladstone—good, practical, timid, shrewd Gladstone—who broke what I'm going to call, perhaps melodramatically, that moment of horror and enchantment. Gladstone mentally calculated the number of those who had heard (this obviously included Dean Hagerstrom and his wife). He calculated the degree of shock and disapproval and outright disgust that each one would feel, and corrected this calculation with the variable of their importance in our little academic world. (Mrs. Manson weighed heaviest. The newspaper had to be favorably disposed toward the university or the spring budget would go down in shambles. Horlock might report the incident at other places where he was scheduled to give concerts. Mrs. Bellegarde would accept it with the same equanimity with which she accepted Belsen and Hiroshima, events in the endless march of history. And so on.) He completed this incredibly agile calculation, and when it was all done on the clean white sheet of his mind he lifted his arm like the accuser in an old melodrama, pointed at Clem and roared what I have come to believe were exactly the right words:

"This man is drunk!"

He did not spoil the Old Testament finality of his judgment with another word. He let it ring and settle, and in its Hebraic echo poor Janet and I both bowed over Clem and tried to wrestle him into a standing position.

"I'll come," he said, as quietly as Joseph K to his executioners. "I've insulted Mother Hood and it's time to go."

That night—which so often in my memory has returned like the animate personification of a riddle, intent on snaring us all in the same limed cords of embarrassment—had at length trussed us neatly and would now let us dangle in peace.

Naughty Clem appeared serene enough in his silence as we took him home. In his head—that "hive of subtleties," as he sometimes rightly called it—I fancied he was making a satisfied comparison between his fireworks and those of the boy who had heckled him after his lecture. "Now you see, kid, how an old pro does it. Anderson, for social chaos, remains the champ." If Janet and I had pressed for "communication" with him, well, had he not just given us the ultimate sign that he was still our Clem, irretrievable and constant?

Behind us the dean's porch light shone like the angel's fiery sword barring our return to the complacencies with which we had anticipated Clem's visit. But all was well and fair. Did we not have instead the full April moon over us and some sense, however fugitive, that our boy had knocked down a wall for us that was shutting off air? We could laugh together now, and Janet—as if fifteen years had been smashed to nothing—flung out her arms and shouted, giggling, "'This man is drunk,'" as we walked up the slope of our lawn to the house. "Clem, angel, come in and tell us instead of Mrs. Manson."

"The man was right," Clem muttered. He embraced our hickory tree beside the path and vomited. That too a symbol for the purging of all the cant that the dean's guests used to stiffen their decency? Romance's rebellion of the flesh, spewing them (us?) out of his mouth for being neither hot nor cold? Mere mess on the lawn past which our prim daughters must walk on their way to school?

"Oh, Clem, come in and rest," Janet called to him in pity and love. "Sleep a long time, good boy, and when you've wakened you can tell us everything. Tomorrow is another day."

So we gentled him to bed that night, unpacking his bags and loosening his tie, bringing him a cold open beer to sit on his bedside table. This was his one demand on us, and explaining it he lost me in some muttered, owlish references to the animals (or did he say "alternations"—animal alternations?) that would come on him if he woke before morning with the shakes. They had been coming on him since Kansas, he said, and it would be appropriate for us to respect them.

Respecting our own animals and shakes—and the fact that, after all, I must appear to teach a freshman class on the following morning— Janet and I lay down to sleep without much talk of the evening's disasters.

She said she thought that, really, Gladstone wouldn't hold this against Clem, and I said, No, I thought he wouldn't either. And if anyone did, *tant pis* for him. It was nice to think that Clem had risen beyond the effective range of any local disapproval. I supposed that meant even ours.

Still, I went to sleep with boulders precariously balanced in my head, ready for avalanche. At two o'clock the world I was used to seemed unworldly enough, strange as a new planet whose ways I would have to discover all over again.

## 2

TOMORROW IS NEVER ANOTHER DAY. It is only a new vantage point from which memory and premonition widen their perspectives under the merciless neutrality of light.

A foul depression was riding me when I got up the next morning. From the bathroom window I saw fog among the dripping evergreens of our lawn, and behind it I sensed, or imagined, that dank stones had been planted in the night to bar all exits from the labyrinth my bad dreams had guessed. The customary morning peace of our big frame house was ominously compromised, but by nothing I could lay my finger on as a real threat. I heard the automatic stoker come on in the basement, the little stir as my daughters got up to close their windows and bounced back to bed, the slap of a newspaper hitting the front porch. And none of these comforting sounds had the power to balance my thoughts. The selfish instinct that might have seized me during a shipwreck pressed me to leave the house as early as I could.

Meeting my class of freshmen at ten did much to domesticate my moods. Is there any horror or exaltation within the scope of experience that cannot be neutralized by one hour's exposure to youth, apathy and imprecision? Whatever paradoxes Clem proposed, their power to shake me faded fast.

Then after class when I was heading down a long corridor of Bierman Hall toward Gladstone's office, Calvin Stipe fell in step with me. I had been directing Calvin's thesis on George Herbert for the last two years, and a considerable familiarity had resulted.

"Dick," he began, with an unmistakable trill of glee in his voice, "what really happened at the dean's shindig last night?"

Apparently the story of Clem's misbehavior was abroad. Or some of it was. It was hardly my intention to leak more. "What did you hear?" I asked with an affectation of surprise.

"I heard our friend Anderson told off Gladstone and the dean in the only language they understand." His face was blooming like a poppy field. "That boy doesn't roll any BB's on the drum." He cracked his fist into his palm, winked and said with dismaying volume, "'Fuck you, fuck you, fuck you.' That's what I've been meaning to say to Gladstone ever since he spoiled Chaucer for me when I was a junior. All we ever needed on this campus was a man like Anderson. 'Fuck you.'" I had not realized since I left the Navy the peculiar joy of release that lies in that word.

"Quiet," I said sharply. A cluster of undergraduate girls was passing us, and their eyes were round as pistol targets as they overheard him and—some of them—recognized me.

"It lets in light and air," Calvin said. "That one declaration is worth all his verse, which I frankly think is second-rate anyhow, not to mention his play, which is pure trash. But that. 'Oh, set it down in gold on lasting pillars' ..." He got ready to say the word again, and I thought I would put his tie in his mouth if he did. Happily, his spurious heroism failed him right there. He only demanded again that he be given the true, inside story. He knew there had been a collision, and he so badly wanted to believe that Clem had struck a blow for liberty that from his will to believe I got a preview of the myth being born on the campus. "Back in 'fifty-three," they would be telling it, "the president of the university came out with one of his customary banalities and the writer Clem Anderson answered him to his face ..." The truth would have to pant to catch the spreading apocrypha.

After assuring Calvin that some bearer of wicked tidings had been exaggerating grossly, I went on to the English office with a rather firmer step. It was as if Calvin had reminded me that I had marching behind me the invisible army of the outsiders, the anarchic mob in whose name I could plead license for Clem's default.

Actually I had to make no plea at all to Gladstone. He gestured away his blond secretary, motioned me to a seat and began almost at once on a monologue that seemed to bear—very indirectly—on Clem's case.

This was, he said, a "hideous epoch" (Churchill's phrase) and for his part he saw very little hope in it. He could not look at a morning paper without being reminded of the fragmentation of our social values, the interpenetration of vulgarity and power. (A reference to Mrs. Manson and her husband's newspaper, on whose favor we depended for the occasional egg in our faculty beer?) There was no continuity of manners by which the poetic spirit could be infused into the general social commerce. In Geoff Chaucer's day when the wine and mead went round it was to the accompaniment of inflated spirits to which the ingredients of wit and fantasy were as necessary and welcome as the fire on the hearth. A man of letters (himself in the gown of Erasmus, Clem with a freshly sanded *chanson de geste* under his arm) was at home in any company. But the Time Spirit had dealt uncharitably, to say the least, with those of us who valued the life of literature. Isolation

22

and friction were the lot of those who might in better times have entered naturally into the comity of learning. It was still the time of the *poètes maudits*, though of course that term probably hadn't had much currency since he was a young fellow. Cursed poets and a cursed populace, deprived of and even antagonistic to the civilizing arts. "I realize your man Eliot has had some popular success, but I get the impression that a good many young people have taken him on as they would some movie star or—or crooner, or some other sort of idol rather than as a poet, 'a man speaking to other men,' as old Wordsworth had it."

As I listened along, grasping generally that all this talk about the poet's place in the age had something to do with Clem, it seemed to me that by a quirk Gladstone had fallen into an identification of Clem with Lord Byron, somehow blowing him up in size until he was like heads in movie closeups, so much bigger than the scale of people that one can never feel of them that they are older or younger than you, or wiser or duller, or stronger or weaker, but only that they are, and that they obey the laws of the projecting machine rather than the laws of humanity.

Naturally I wondered why Gladstone was making this humble reverse from the indignation I had expected, and particularly why he was hauling out such heavy cannon to shoot a pigeon. (Old Wordsworth and Geoff Chaucer indeed; it was hardly necessary to cite such company to suggest there might be a jewel in Clem's forehead that we shouldn't trample underfoot.) Then it came to me that Gladstone must be recalling, more vividly and painfully than any of the rest of us would, the moment when he had been forced to pronounce anathema on Clem in a company whose good opinion he must think Clem valued. He had been caught in the middle.

Obliquely he was hinting that he wished to apologize to Clem. Just as obliquely, as I prepared to take my leave, I hinted that an apology would be too great a shock for Clem to stand.

"Wait," Gladstone said, calling his secretary. "Didn't some mail come for Mr. Anderson? And has his honorarium come from the treasurer's office?"

There was a thick gray envelope from Sheila and a letter from Clem's theatrical agent to put in my pocket with the check for his lecture. I was glad enough for everything I had to take back to the house I'd left so dismally. Time was moving again. Gladstone and Calvin Stipe had reminded me how wrong the expectations of bad conscience can be. The sun was out. Up some budding alley, just out of sight, little David Clem had put the stone between Goliath's eyes. Pippa Hartsell was coming home with goodies and a message of joy.

Grace of those powers I sometimes pretend to understand, spring was on us again, gibbering its cries in the blood and pushing grass as green as money up through the burned patches in the slope of our back yard. When I stepped down from the car, our youngest, Beth, was at the bottom of the lawn pursuing the dachshund and Clem was standing by the back steps watching her. Beth, who was only four but massive and obviously dangerous, leaped on the pup with a carnivorous growl and lifted him triumphantly by the tail.

"Hey, Owl, for Christ's sake, let that animal be," Clem called. He trotted down the slope to liberate the dog and persuade Beth to come at it in a gentler manner. I thought as he panted back up, with a golden glass of beer in his hand, that he didn't look too bad. All things considered, not too bad at all.

"The function of the dog is to keep them from turning on their parents," I said. "It actually reassures me to hear him cry out in pain. Poor mutt."

"I know. It's a funny thing how us kids keep going the limit to find out what pain is—in something besides ourselves. The primitive curiosity." He squinted at me seriously and said, "You've been out in the world this morning. What'd I break last night?"

"Nothing. Get used to it. You're a wheel, and the things they used to whip you for are all dumplings for the legend now. Everyone thinks you were pretty funny."

"Nothing? I dreamed I pinched the Sphinx's tiddy at this party last night. There she was on top and asking questions, and zip, just like Beth and the dog, I had to find out what hurt her."

"That was no dream. But you got votes from it. A boy you'll meet this afternoon thinks you said it to the dean himself."

"Said what?"

"If you don't remember, never mind. You got some mail and beer money too." I gave him the check and the letters.

"Oh, from Sheila," he said.

"Why not from Sheila? You expecting bad news?"

"No, no. Look, is it all right if I sit out here to read it? Feels heavy."

I left him to go inside. Janet was in the kitchen, clearing away the scraps of the breakfast she had fixed for him and starting on lunch for all of us. She had our old-fashioned range going—it must have been chilly when she got up—and was putting biscuits in the oven. Pink

24

from the heat and with her dark hair caught back in a rubber band, she looked very good to me. I stood admiring the country-girl authority with which she commanded her kitchen, thinking fondly, and with a lapse of sentimentality that Clem's presence must have set off, that she had not changed greatly since the time fourteen years ago when she was "everybody's girl"—the only girl we knew who was not a student and who actually earned enough money to live in an apartment of her own, whom no dean of women could ever discipline for entertaining men in her place, so that Clem, Jack Miller and I could go there together after the library or the beer joints closed to talk or neck with her in a chair called, for vanished reasons, "the Tiger." I thought, She makes everything around her as sure and certain as her own elephantine heart, and I thought of her heart just then as like the biceps on a circus strong man.

"Clem got a letter from Sheila," I said.

She let the oven door slam shut on her biscuits and said, "That's dandy."

"What's wrong?"

"Nothing's wrong." But the pathetic aggressiveness of her tone jolted me badly.

"Have you and Clem been fussing? Is he still playing hush-hush-I-have-a-secret with us?"

"Oh, he talks," she said. "Your friend Anderson has news for you. You'll have to congratulate him."

"What's all this?"

She tried to brush past me on her way to the sink. I caught her shoulders and held her still.

She wouldn't meet my eyes. With sly sarcasm she said, "Ask him. He and Sheila have split up. I think he's ditched her—and the kids. Anyway, she's been at home with her folks for a month."

"That explains why he was so owly yesterday."

"Does it explain …?" In outrage she ticked off the things that it did not decently explain: the pious references to family in his talk, his callous self-concern when he knew that Sheila was as dear to us as he, his refusal even to attempt justification of a circumstance that would certainly seem to us nearly unjustifiable.

I could have recited these complaints as well as she—and yet the verbalized complaints seemed a mere threshold over which I peered at more wretched losses. "Poor lost souls."

"Go Weltschmerz with him—I don't have much sympathy right now," Janet said. "He's being a fool and that's too bad, but he's a

25

bastard too, and that's not just his chemistry or something he can't help. Go on. Shoo. Jill will be home from school in a minute and we're going to eat out on the lawn, the sun's so nice."

"Did you tell him this—what you thought of him?"

"And he shrugged at me," she said, fighting to swallow her anger. No one shrugs at Janet with impunity.

That lunch under the greening willow tree sticks in my mind like an odd memorial service, a wake for the lost times to which we had all committed so much that, with them faded, even memory would remind us we would never be quite whole again. Though I thought it wiser not to raise the subject of Clem's separation, Sheila's presence was more poignantly evoked by the news than if I had been told of her mortal illness. Sheila, one could not help remembering, had always been so fond of picnics or any kind of alfresco eating and drinking in the good seasons. I thought of our slow summer in Mexico together, at Acapulco, the long lunches in the Pacific light, when she had been first pregnant but still nimble and kittenish, tickling Clem in his somnolence, juggling the balloons of his wit to show them off better, and above all was "good for our Clem," as we said, yielding our worries into her hands, watching him regain what he had lost in the war and the weeks in a psychiatric ward just after it was over. Where now the painfully won confidence of those days? Seven years had made a wry thing of our hopes, had betrayed us subtly in giving us so much of what we had wanted. We had been frank—the war, whatever harms it had done, had won us frankness that year. Now we had to be circumspect, cautious, not quite hostile, but, as it were, afraid of hostility that might animate us against our own will.

Jill had come home from school evidently intent on showing Clem that there were now two geniuses beleaguered in our Philistine household. With more than her usual eleven-year-old's passion to compete in an adult world, she hunted for intellectual topics that would involve him.

Just as Janet brought the tray of food out, Jill raced to Clem with her gem book and cigar-box collection of semiprecious stones. Since he had Beth on his lap then and was reading Pogo to her, the competition for his attention sounded like a badly managed seraglio.

Beth: "Why is Owl in the water?"

Jill (holding a gravelly chunk up in his face): "Here's chalcedony."

Janet: "You can show him your rocks after we've eaten. Beth, get off Mr. Anderson so he can breathe."

Jill: "Not rocks, Mother."

Beth: "I hate Pogo. Read Dennis. Dennis the Menace."

I (to Jill): "All right, honey. Mother didn't mean to belittle your collection. Gems." An aside to Clem, fumbling his judgment of Paris among them: "You'd be surprised to learn that our continent is practically bedrocked with gems, according to the tolerant definition in this book of Jill's. We've found all these in local creeks, haven't we, Jill?"

Jill (misusing my soothing oil as support for her aggression, thrusting the open gem book over the comic page): "'Beryl. A silicate of great hardness, commonly green or bluish green. Aquamarine and emerald are varieties of beryl.' Beth! Mother, she knocked my beryl down in the grass."

Beth (intoxicated by her whiff of successful malice) "I hay-yut Dennis the Menace. I hay-yut my home. I hay-yut Daddy, Mama, everyone."

Janet: "If you girls can't let Mr. Anderson eat in peace, you'll have to go inside." Then, to Clem as the din subsided, "Have you seen anything of Wadleigh Hertz at all lately? He's around New York, and I believe Sheila mentioned him in a letter." I thought the comment was many-edged as broken glass. Sheila hadn't written for more than a year.

"I'd like to see the old guy," Clem said. "One way or another I've lost touch with everyone. It's so funny to think of him selling insurance. His pays off in rubles in case of reverse rollback?" Wadleigh was our college friend who "dedicated himself to socialism" and it was more funny than sad to think of him in the insurance game. But sadder than funny was the way Clem sparred off all such references to Sheila. Surely he heard, as I did, the memorial sound of the willow recite the absence of her voice. "I don't forget people, but I don't keep in touch," Clem said. "I'll never forget Wadleigh and me stealing the Venus de Milo from the art department and setting it up on the Kappa lawn. Wadleigh wanted to hang a red lantern on its neck. Proletarian hatred for that inaccessible gash."

"What's gash?" Beth asked, gimlet-eyed, expecting a lie. I had the quicksand premonition that Jill knew.

"It's what changes a man," Clem said, puzzling and satisfying Beth, proving that poets need never lie. "Poor old Wadleigh must have changed a lot by now."

"Our brief against him is that he hasn't changed," Janet said. "Never grew up, just kept identifying himself with the latest generation, and now it's all hipster talk with him. 'Man', 'you dig that, man?' and he gets in a regressive state and begins chewing his fingernails. He spits them on the rug, curtains, upholstery. Oh, yes, he stopped to see us last year on his way to Chicago. I think he pushes marijuana when the insurance game is slow."

Clem laughed. "Well our landlady used to say, 'Mr. Hertz is a nuisance to himself.' Old Emmy Polk."

"Not merely that," Janet went on maliciously. "He was here in October and it was cold, but one afternoon he went parading out here on the lawn in his underwear with a bottle of beer. Goodness knows the neighbors are shocked enough by us without that." Her "that" was ample enough to refer to all the misbehaviors of our ancient friends come visiting. Clem could hardly have missed the fact that he was included in her rebuke of those who fell into regressive states. He had been so much her boy at one time, and, beyond any fondness or compassion for Sheila, she was angry that he had failed her, had disappointed her by his break with Sheila.

Evidently he had taken more of her lightning than this before I came home, and, muttering only, "*L'enfer, c'est les neighbors,*" he went on eating imperturbably.

"Not merely that," Janet said. "I made Jill lock her door at night while he stayed."

"Botemntin," Jill said, looking up from her book, still chewing rapidly. "Let's all go to Arizona."

"And locked our little dog in the basement," I said. "Now, Janet. Wadleigh wasn't such a disaster as that. We need stirring up once in a while."

"Well," Jill said, "if this Botemntin stone can only be found in Arizona and it's more beautiful than any other one, why are we sitting on our big fat duffs here?"

"You asked the right question, honey," Clem said.

"I mean it," Jill said. She looked at each of us grownups in turn. Very small and pale tears began to slide down either side of her nose, but she would not blink, and it seemed to me that she hated us all for the failures of loyalty that winked in and out of our conversation like the blue sky winking through the moving branches of the tree. "You tell me one time that it's very important for me to study this book and find the rocks. Then you laugh at me when I want to go to Arizona to get the best one of all."

"No, honey, no," Clem said. "No one's laughing at you. Them you see are tears. If I could, I'd pull stakes this very afternoon and head for the Potemkin mines with you, but I've got to go with your dad and meet some people. Isn't that so, Dick?"

"At four," I said. "Everything ought to be much more tranquil than last night—unless that J.D. brings his friends back for a rumble. No. You can sit in an armchair and the students will sit quietly at your feet."

"Stop laughing," Jill charged us.

"Of course we're not laughing at you," Janet soothed. "Maybe we'll take you to Arizona some summer."

"When Easter comes on Tuesday," I said. "Your emotions are running away with you, Jill. Dry your face and let us aged persons talk."

Her unyielding eyes reminded me that we were—mostly— avoiding such talk as might have counted; skipping, evading, and making noise against the heaviness we all felt. Then quickly she jumped back from the table and ran to the bottom of the lawn. She leaned on a fence post there and stared at the trees looming on the opposite hill.

Seeing Clem start up to go comfort her, Janet said, "Let her alone. It's only nerves, and she's better when she has time to soothe them herself. You can't help, Clem."

"All this is a bit artificial, too," I said. "Look. It's Lillian Gish at the pasture gate."

"It'll pass," Janet said. "Thank God, at her age everything passes quick." And that, too, reminded us that Sheila was thirty-six.

It was just about then that the phone rang in the house. At least I remember we were still reassuring ourselves against Jill's repudiation of us when I went in to answer.

First the operator said, "Denver calling," and then a female voice that seemed all treacle and bubbles said, "Clay-em? Clay-em, listen to me, darling, can you get away from that awful place this afternoon, I mean right now, and meet me in Chicago. I'll get us reservations—"

"This isn't Clem. I'll call him for you."

I could not resist saying to Clem that a girl with venery in mind was asking for him. Then, because I did not want to go into explanations with Janet, I walked on down the lawn to Jill.

She wouldn't answer when I spoke her name, nor show by a single flinching of muscles that she recognized my presence.

"Jill?" I touched her shoulder. Her rigidity shocked my fingertips, so excessive it seemed in view of the slight rebuff she had felt herself to suffer, and yet so female and so knowing in that knowledge of corruption that frailty can apprehend better than the fortified adult

29

mind. It's a large-scale experience any time to encounter one's child as a woman, and worse to find her in the knowledge that her sex is a deprivation she must endure as she has, too patiently, endured childhood.

"What's the trouble, darling?" I asked, as if I did not know.

"I only want to get it straight, once and for all," she whined. "What's important and what isn't? Once and for all you better tell me. You'd better!"

"That's kind of hard," I said.

Too hard? Her eyes flamed a destructive triumph. Her arm lashed back behind her head and she threw the damp handful of stones she had been clutching into the weeds beyond the fence. Now she could smile spitefully.

"Honey," I said. "Oh, honey. It's taken you so long to gather them."

Women. Sheila, Janet, Jill, and presently Beth in her turn. Oh, my ladies, do you have to ask so much?

The goddess had summoned Clem, using the Bell telephone and the voice of Susan Butterfield (or Cindy Hunt, as she was called professionally). Returning to our maudlin picnic, he told us, "She's wangled a compartment on the Pacemaker and wants me to ride in to New York with her. She's flying in to Chicago from the Coast and has a lot of problems on her mind. I couldn't very well tell her I was this close and wouldn't meet her."

"Nor say you were scheduled to meet a bunch of our students this afternoon and let them whiff success," I reminded him. Until that moment I had counted heavily on that afternoon meeting. I had some notion that the "real Clem" would emerge in an atmosphere of informality to redeem the misleading appearances thus far spread by his visit.

"I forgot about that," he said, honestly contrite, as far as I could tell.

"They'll be disappointed, but that's good training for those who think they may become writers."

"Damn it," he said. "She was between planes at Denver. There's no way to call her back now."

"Send a wire to the airport in Chicago," Janet suggested. "Or is this someone so important you have to see her?"

"No, no," Clem said. "Not important. But I promised her. How do you deal with a conflict of promises?"

"Yes," I said. "Tell us. Did you also forget that there might not be a train or a bus out of here that would get you to Chicago before midnight? There isn't."

"Well," he said sheepishly, piling on just a bit too much of his bad-lovable-boy act without managing to hide the genuine misery that underlay it, "I did remember that. So I told her my great good friends Dick and Janet would disregard all other obligations and drive me in. I thought we'd have our chance to talk. We haven't had yet. It's a keen day for a ride." He inhaled the air as if trustingly. He beamed at us to encourage us to breathe deeply with him.

"I can't go," Janet said, planting the lead basketball squarely in my hands, wanting me, evidently, to say I couldn't go either. It wasn't an easy choice to make. There is a certain solidity to gestures that words can't refute, and I didn't want, any more than Janet, to make any gesture of approval for the assignation he'd arranged.

"We'd have to start pretty quick."

"The train doesn't leave until seven," he said. "We'll have time for a couple of beers on the way."

"Take him if you want to," Janet said in a tone that implied she would expect no more from men, and imperceptibly the thing seemed to have been arranged.

Once we were on our way and Clem had, finally, begun to air the corpse of his secret, I was glad that I had come. I won't say he talked frankly that afternoon, because when situations reach a certain complexity it is ridiculous to assume that frankness about them can be achieved by mere intent, as it would be ridiculous for me to think I could tell the "truth" about Clem Anderson (to Calvin Stipe, for example) by mere honesty.

"Things had got to the point where Sheila and I were each other's sickness," he said. "She's better off turning in her suit and getting out of the Anderson rat race. The kids are, too. Whatever we've meant to do, we've been killing each other these last eighteen months. My slogan for the past year's been 'Who will deliver me from the body of this death?'"

"And Cindy delivered? Am I wrong in supposing she might have delivered without breaking up your marriage? If I can judge by her voice ..."

"Go on. Judge."

"... she would deliver most readily, easily and happily. On demand."

31

And had, too, he answered without the slightest trace of resentment or prudery (or bragging either; I would like to convey that he had seemed to suffer through to some plateau of honesty where he was beyond reach of my prejudices). She had delivered for him the afternoon he first met her, going to a hotel room in Washington with him as casually as he had given the invitation. They had, on that occasion, enjoyed each other "like puppies," enough to want to repeat the experience when he was back in New York and she had returned from a few weeks on the Coast. Not so much, though, that either had made any demands on the other at first. Oh, Cindy would deliver. It was the obligation of her youth and beauty to do so, and she did not funk it.

But "deliver"—my pun, he thought, obligated me to understand how complex this word was. He was to be delivered, too, from the shame of his infidelity to Sheila! Now, plainly this formulation takes some unraveling, and it was days later before I could be sure I knew what he had meant.

It was approximately this: Whatever hidden strains or fissures had existed in his marriage to Sheila, he had considered them sexually indissoluble until he had been unfaithful to her "for the first time" two years ago in Kansas.

I answered with considerable patience that I knew of previous instances. There were Cecile Potter and Venetia Pogorski, for example.

Those women were not examples. And besides, five years of literal fidelity, as it can, had canceled out those almost unintentional slips. But at last, in Kansas, he had really gone off the sexual wagon. Whether he had enjoyed the many liberties afforded him there and those that seemed to follow, as if in a compulsory series, when he had gone back that time to New York—well, that was a dark secret into which he needn't pry to make his point clear. (He said "clear." If it is still muddled in my reconstruction, not all the fault would appear to be mine.)

The point was that he had been, after Kansas, many times unfaithful to Sheila, and couldn't I understand that his "special bonds" to Sheila were such that it might become intolerable to live with her after deceit had compromised the very essence of their relationship? If he had not, truly, loved her so much, he would have felt less guilt for infidelities and therefore could have "lived more equal to" his love.

He could have stopped this string of infidelities. Surely common sense had suggested that.

Of course it had, and I must not think he was either so giddy or so sensual that he could not resist "the propinquity of skin" in theatrical circles. In fact, I must understand that the sexual act was as often as not repugnant to him. He would not offend me with illustrations, but if I had ever been blown by a seventeen-year-old dancer in an elevator in an East Side apartment house I would understand his meaning.

I said I fairly grasped it anyway.

But, enjoying his nondomestic dalliances or not, he could not think of sex as very important "except as the perfect litmus paper"—blue or red signals, I supposed, indicating states of the psyche and the soul for which there was not, even for him, another language. The girls, the many girls, had signaled Condition Red. That being known, he must find the means to spare his family.

And there had been other signs—barometric, one might call them—that confirmed the readings on the litmus wick. In a breaking voice he told me about buying the kids a dog for Christmas last year. Sheila and the children were then on the farm in Rockland County, and the pup—ridiculously incapable of such a task—had been intended for a watchdog as well as a pet. A bumbling, annoying, loving, importunate, lovable black-and-tan creature, its chief accomplishment at three months was to determine Clem's intended path and to prance underfoot exactly where he had to step. His patience wore out quicker than his affection, so that his relation with the animal was always ambiguous, and one weekend while he was at the farm he killed the dog with an unintentionally hard kick. He knew while the little beast was still spinning in mid-air across the front room what he had done, but nevertheless the dog was a long while dying. He wrapped it in his jacket and carried it to the woodshed, where he sat with it in his lap through half a morning and nearly all the afternoon until it died, at four-thirty. Sheila had tried to coax him out of the woodshed to eat something or to rest, and Jess had come to stand in the snowy doorway wide-eyed and horror-stricken, watching him cuddle the dying pet. But he would not accept their consolations, for he was not only tending his victim but "thinking it all out, discovering what it stood for."

To simplify—as of course he did not—it stood for a monstrosity in him to which he dared not continue exposing those he loved best. Dared not expose himself either. For everyone's sake, in the long run, he had to find the shelter of circumstances in which he could function. In the snow-swept, love-swept shed in Rockland County the dog had whimpered on his knees like Desdemona unjustly slain, had drunk like a vampire from his pity, had seemed synecdoche for all suffering, and he had felt, unarguably, that his remorse was unequal to his guilt. But the very next night—what did I make of this?—in that elevator of the East Side apartment house, in medio fellatio, the thought had come to him, It was only a fifty-dollar terrier and I can buy another.

I made more of it than I cared to or knew how to say, but failed to see in it grounds for divorce ("Not grounds. Isn't it already, in itself, divorce?") or even a reason why he must continue a sexual rampage he characterized as repugnant.

Well, the reason the infidelities had to go on was that they had begun.

Once Sheila and he had sat on a stone and made it theirs (an actual stone, if that would help me visualize better, a dragon showing its stony back out of a Wisconsin hillside; Sheila and he had found it fifteen years ago, literally sat on it, figuratively lugged it with them afterward). Every hunk knocked from this stone of fidelity dropped in Clem's path to trip him again. He could not—being himself, and who else did we expect him to be?—help feeling that if he kept on breaking off bits, presently there would be nothing left of the relationship that above all, in his whole past life, he valued more than anything, more even than his gifts.

"So the reasonable thing to do was to smash it quickly?" I said.

"Don't you understand that impulse?" Hadn't I understood Jill when she threw her gems into the tall grass? I would have been stubborn to deny that I was following. But ...

"Let's try another way of putting it," he said. "I wanted to put Sheila and me—what we'd been—in the bank. Where mothy dancers and rusting Anderson could not corrupt. Out of the loud world. Where the pilgrim's journey is done."

"Wanted," I said in a grief of comprehension. Desired, yes, but ...

There was much more of what he was willing to tell me that represented merely a deeper harrowing of the same ground. I began to see what he had meant by "the body of death," the gradual and irretrievable wastage of a love that he had not for a second denied. What I could not understand, or allow, of course, was the daring of his refusal to wear this common garment of mortality out to its natural end.

Beyond the comprehension of his all-powerful wish, I could make no sense of what he meant to do now that he had stripped himself and banked his valuables. All he had said amounted to an intense poetic conceit. It would not do for life. It offered nothing to go on from—and both he and Sheila had, somehow, to go on.

All right, I said, he had shown me, vaguely, how he had used his harem of doxies to achieve a freedom that might be worth the awful cost. They had delivered him by delivering for him. What in the hell did he propose to do for a life in the future?

"Oh," he said, not quite glibly, but with that smooth assurance of utter conviction, "it's more important to take care of the past than the future."

I think I never understood my poor friend or his divorce from our general reality better than when I heard that unhesitating belief. I had to laugh as well as groan. "On to the open road," I said. "Tonight you'll pay off Cinderella for her services. Tomorrow green fields and pastures new. I wish I envied you, boy."

"Oh, no," he said. "It won't be like that. I'm going to marry Cindy Susan."

The utter preposterousness of this announcement, coming on the heels of his fine-drawn explanation for ditching Sheila, forbade even an exclamation of surprise. All I could do was waggle my head in disbelief. What about the other women, the nameless gash that had changed him? Why should the series stop with Cindy Sue?

I should have figured out the answer to that one, now that I was sufficiently reindoctrinated in his peculiar fashion of reasoning.

Infidelities to Susan would be less important—neither of them would care as much as he and Sheila had—therefore infidelities were less likely to take place. Faced with this ominous ingenuity, I gave up argument and merely listened.

"You shouldn't be automatically supercilious just because she's a Hollywood person," he said. "There's more to that tricky little being than meets the eye. I like her pretty well." Pensively he reconstructed his estimate of her, nodded to himself and said, "She'll do. She's odorless. Mentally she's not a slob, not quite your stereotype of an actress. As a matter of fact, Sheila met her once or twice a couple of years ago—before I knew her—and liked her. As a matter of fact, Susan is probably the original of Beauty Bear. You know, Sheila pumped her and then made her story over cute."

"Sheila liked her. I'm comforted. Does that comfort you?"

"Nothing much does when I think. But Susan does when I don't. Like the juvenile in the elevator. Susan's a born survivor. You'd be surprised what she's been through in her short life. Cinderella indeed. Her cruel stepfather tried to rape her when she was eleven—no one's ever blamed him much for that—and her mother is a pure psychotic who dragged her all over the country from one slum to another. She was married first when she was fifteen, to a part-time pin setter in a bowling alley, no less."

"I must read Beauty Bear."

"You won't get the whole story. It's a real American saga. Anyway, she's a perfect dog under some of her coo. A silicate of great hardness. She came through it all unscathed, somehow. She teaches me how to be a dog. It's time I was one if I'm going to survive. And there are reasons why I should, Dick."

"Yes."

"I could have told everything I told you today differently. I don't know why I'm doing this. I've mostly given up motives. Every act is an *acte gratuit* from here on out. The main thing is, it wouldn't be right for me not to marry Susan now, after what I've done to Sheila."

Who invented that fastidious, absurd morality? Useless to ask, for I knew all too well who had invented everything that Clem had ever lived by. He had invented himself from the time I first knew him, had to a great extent invented Sheila out of the fragmented eyes and arms, hair, sweets and tenderness of all his childhood loves. Had merely expropriated from reality what he needed to invent his own despair and its antidotes.

It was vain to suppose that at any point I might ever exceed his insights into himself. He gave me no occasion for saying anything to him that he had not already thought of. If that long afternoon of contention satisfied me at all it was by confirming my suspicion that I could do nothing for him except to watch through seasons of envy and pity.

Yet just before we came to the station in Chicago, he contrived a moment when we might have been keyed to a single pattern of reality and might have shared some truth invulnerable to the confusions of circumstance. Soberly, almost sternly, he said, "Dick, I didn't come all this way out here to give a pompous lecture and insult the queen. I only came so you and Janet could tell me I was doing something wrong. I don't know anyone else who would tell me that. They all take the attitude that it's my own business and I must have my justifications. You know I haven't. So tell me."

"Janet already told you," I said. "You'd do what you're going to do whatever I said."

"Yes, I'd do it—but what I do isn't all that counts."

I shook my head in refusal. "You've mixed me up too much. I don't know what to say except 'God bless you.' I wouldn't dare. I thought I was protecting you when I steered you to the dean's party."

"From the boy who spotted me for a fat merchant?" His quickness in taking my thought in this case suggested that on other points we had been in closer communication than I feared. But immediately he dispelled this illusion by citing a connection different from the one I still had in mind. "When he first came on I was sure he was the same black sprite that got up to heckle me the summer I was in Kansas at the writers' conference. But they liked me there. I've kept in touch with some of them. The boy from there. He's good. I've done a lot for him. No one will keep in touch after this. Sic transit," he said mournfully.

"We liked you here. Would have liked more if we had seen more."

"Don't get browned off that I didn't meet your students this afternoon. They'd have seen through me, too. That always happens now unless I'm given the advantage of some aerial perspective. I'm really better at a distance. Anderson, *le vrai* Anderson, is not to be comprehended through his presence or his actions. The only way you'll get me is by thinking about me."

"You've made sure we'll do that."

"It's the one trick I have left. And remember ..."

But what, specifically, out of what had been said and done I was to remember was left undefined. I swung into a parking place then, and we hurried for the station. There would not be much from his visit I could forget—but neither could I make from it nearly enough to still the ache I felt. A drowsy numbness pained me, sure enough.

My only glimpses of Susan that day were of her face inside the compartment window—first as Clem and I hurried down the train with his bag. Against the dissolving brown-green background inside the car I saw her face as sharply outlined as a piece of white paper. Her mouth could have been that of any woman with the price of lipstick and the confidence to spread it on thick. Only her wide gray eyes that lightened with relief when she saw that Clem had made connections after all indicated anything human or personal about her—otherwise she was the simple incarnation of every blonde on the placards they put out to advertise B movies. She seemed to me pretty, vivid and heartbreaking, for all she suggested of what we have come to expect of women.

After Clem's unexpectedly crisp wave of salutation and reassurance to her we hurried on to the end of the car. As I handed his bag up to him, Clem said, "Dick, one more favor. Will you write to Sheila? She's home with her folks. You have the address."

"Sure. We'd have written anyway."

"You can tell her I broke the news to you. Dick?"

"Yes?"

"Don't go light on me. Don't try to defend me to her."

"No." The conductor was shouting down along the train, and some late visitors brushed out past us. "Good luck, Clem."

"Oh. Yes, I'll need that too."

As the train began to move I saw him throw his shoulders back like a little soldier and march down the corridor toward the compartment. He had not yet reached it when its window passed me.

Susan, warranted to be hard as beryl, was still peering lornly from its shadows. When she gave me a timid little wave, my heart failed with the doubt that she would be hard enough to bear what lay ahead. But silently I wished her good luck, too.

Clem was our proxy to success, our representative sent up to the capital of the world—oh, even that figure from the Platonic myth who leaves the shadows of the cave to adventure in the light, then comes back to tell us all. To tell us—as if that superior light were no more than the heart of darkness and he had seen exactly what Mr. Kurtz saw—of the horrors waiting for us if we should be unfaithful to our shadows.

As I drove home through the eloquence of the prairie night I heard it ask with a thousand voices if this was all the years could come to. Some high-school kids in a hot rod gunned past me as I was nearing Blue Hill. The girls waved their arms in my headlights. Maenads on their way to what grove or cemetery where the sweated blankets would lie presently under banal headstones? (Or was all erotic adolescence different now than it had been in Clem's youth and mine? His allegory of the elevator had—as it was no doubt intended to do—erased some of the indulgence with which I viewed the postpubescent female.) In the road ahead a young farmer stood at the wheel of his tractor as he raced it toward town. I heard him singing over the tractor's clatter as I swept past. (Will no one tell me what he sings? Of Hollywood gash and tailfins as tall as a bomber's? Or some more familiar lay? The brute frustration of envying the names in slick magazines, the men of paper distinction, the boys upstairs in a house that has no upstairs to go to?)

Once upon a time (my fairy tale went) Clem and company would have seen the same land and these very people better (if not more truly) than we would ever see them again. Once upon that time such girls in an open car, the farmer on his tractor, and all the little towns with names like Blue Hill, or What Cheer, Nebraska City or Shiloh would have roused such a hot love in Clem that, if he could not literally follow them and find them all, at least he would have followed as best he could—with his art, by the way he had tried to marry the one girl who represented it all. Once upon a time the real Sheila had brought the myth to bed for him. (I remembered all too vividly the way he had talked of her in that unquiet summer before the war when they got engaged. She was his girl from a family of builders whose monuments were the clean schoolhouses, the county courthouses, the bridges and the back-yard barbecue pits. She was Hygiene and toothbrushes and faith in the value of education, ice-cream socials and dances at the country club, the child born in a hospital and fed three thousand calories a day, the girl who read movie magazines at twelve and put them away forever when she passed fourteen, who respected her professors and newspaper editorials, who would persuade him to go to war "when his time came" for no more complicated reason than that Hitler was "a bad one." Who would laugh in his face at his arty pretenses and hold her hand in fire to maintain his right to be a poet if that was what he wanted most to do.)

Well, then, he had married her for her mythic value, since there was no legal and practical way for him to marry that national virtue he tried to wrap in her skin. And he had got good use of her, too, in that way. She had sent him off to war and brought him home. (I remembered him on the red shale north of Acapulco, watching the void ocean and the constantly circling vultures, trying to decide, as he put it, whether to have the child that was already quick in her belly. She made that decision for him—and not only by blind physiological processes either. She let him watch the vultures, listen to our nihilistic friends the Pogorskis, and weigh as long as he wanted the losses of the war. Then somehow—she would know how—she told him, Come, it's time to start believing all over again. She brought him through and back from the private madness and breakdown with which he had tried to match the external madness of the war. Gave him impetus from all the past that he believed invested in her.)

And now the impetus had carried him over and beyond, so he could at length lay hands on another American dream personified—the Great Blonde. Out of the crackerjack box, some prize!

I was spared the pain of announcing to Janet that Clem meant to marry this Hollywood Person.

I came home to find that Clem, in his rush to pack, had left Sheila's letter in our guest room, and furious Janet had read it. I suppose every woman can hear echo in her soul the rage of Medea deserted and instinctively appropriates from that rage the right to shatter conventional niceties. She read the letter because it was the only means at hand to get back at Clem.

The sheer brazenness of his conduct—he had satisfied her no more than he had me with pretenses that he had fallen out of love and into love again—called her own life into question, even if in no practical way. When morale is touched, the future is in question, and Janet's morale is not something that can be sustained by the promise of old-age benefits and a man with whom to discuss the problems of child raising.

She gave me the letter with a chilling "Here's the side he didn't dare tell us."

I read it with less justification than she had had. I had no anger to vent and could not imagine that my compassion might in any way help Sheila. I read it because I had watched Clem get on the train with his blonde. Having watched that, I could watch the antithetic shadow that fell so grimly from it. After such knowledge, what forgiveness? I must have asked myself, beginning to read.

DEAR CLEM,

I promised to let you know regularly how the kids are, so I'd better tell you right off that Jess sprained his wrist falling out of the car. He'd been downtown shopping for dinner with Dad and tried to get out with his arms full, that is all. We think he stumbled on the curb and anyway there was milk and eggs and broken ketchup all over. Mother thought it was blood. You know how silly she gets. But it's really nothing. We wrapped him up but didn't even take him to the doctor. Lulie is all right.

It's when I go to bed at night, like when you were in England during the war and I was still in Washington, and when the mail got mixed up and I knew you were in the hospital and didn't know it was only your damn brain for a month. Otherwise I get along all right.

You're such a dirty bastard you don't even care, but I spend all my time here trying to "explain" what it is you think you're doing, and I'm damned if I know. Is she that good? I didn't know you were that lively in bed any more.

I'm sorry. I do know that you have to do what you have to do, but it is very hard for me to follow your reasoning sometimes. It's like the time you were on your mystic kick and ate vegetables, which was hard to understand. I ought to be smart enough after all these years wasted at it to know that it is different for artists than for other people, and that they have to listen to their demon or wrestle with their angel and all that other shit you tried to foist on me for so long. As I say, that's what I explain to the folks all the time. Mother makes me so mad because she wants me to tell the family that it was I who left you because you were an alcoholic and were ruining the kids. Which, of course, is true, but you know that since hell hasn't frozen over yet this winter it wasn't I who left. I am not a quitter. What am I, a jerk?

Somewhere I failed and I don't know just when or where it was. I knew you weren't happy any more, but I didn't want to poke in too close when I thought you were trying to work it all out in that pointed little head of yours, and all you were doing was getting into the pants of that Hollywood idiot behind my back. Do you think I cared about that? I wouldn't have said a word if you'd just gone and done it and let it go. But oh no, not you. You'll find out, though, when you realize all the other things there are that go to make up a marriage.

Incidentally, took Jess to see your inamorata's latest film, which is Attack at Hell River. I have to admit that just as you say she can act well enough so that they ought to give her better parts. She holds a horse and is on screen for all of two minutes (different times) and I must say I've never seen any one do it more like she is used to it. It's a real triumph for the Stanislavsky method.

Can't you understand that people will laugh at you if you tell them that she can act and you will probably let her talk you into giving her a big part in your play. But as there are no horses in it, what can she hold? That will be the end of you. You are not so big as you think you are. Gorman will drop you like that and you know very well that any money you've made you made because you sucked around him so long. You're going to be pounding the pavement old boy with no one to work in Macy's to support you.

Oh darling, I worry so much about you all the time. I want you to be happy however you work things out, but I don't think you can be, this way. Why the hurry? Wouldn't she wait a year until you knew your own mind?

Dad is worse than Mother is, since she never liked you anyway and always thought your stuff was morbid and says she never expected anything much different. He is only sorry he didn't whip your tail when you were around and he could get at you. It is awfully hard to keep him from saying anything about you in front of the kids, or at least referring to the way you let them live around New York, or out on the farm, which you'll admit was pretty shabby.

I wish I had had the guts or money to go somewhere else besides home here. I wasn't thinking very clearly when I came. If I kill myself I don't want to do it here, because that would be too much to ask them to stand, when my whole goddam life since I met you has been such a worry to them anyhow. But I chose it, and if I had it to choose over again, I guess I'd bitch myself and throw it away again. They can't take it away from me. But it isn't there any more. Where do lives go?

I hadn't meant to worry you with this letter while you are out there lecturing, because I know how hard it is for you anyway to have to get up in front of people. But you asked me to write now and then and I got so nervous with Jess that I had a few bad nights.

I wish I could see Dick and Janet. Will you tell them hello for me, but I don't suppose I will see them again because one thing I won't do is try to take your friends away from you when you are going to need them so badly.

Burn this.

Sincerely,
SHEILA

P.S. I tried to sit down and write a play about the whole stinking mess. It turned out lousy. I only wrote two or three pages of it. You're the author for it, but it's too melodramatic and true for a highbrow like you and I suppose it won't ever get used. Beauty Bear will have to do.

I finished the letter and leaned back to meet Janet's eyes. "Well," I said. "It certainly is a Sheila letter, isn't it? Not entirely grammatical, but expressive."

"How could he go meet that floozy after he read this?"

I couldn't have put it better. Yes. How do you carry such molten stuff safe in your head when you let the belt buckle loose and climb over the edge of a berth? I had asked for, and now I had, a double vision of Clem's trip. "Those Marches are certainly never let off anything, are they?"

"I don't know any Marches and I'm too headachy to joke about it," Janet said.

"All right. Let's put it in the cupboard for tonight. There's nothing we can do. It's time for us to sleep."

"Now," she said. "Now when Clem's got it made, people know who he is and they could have lived a little better. Now, after all she's given him, he puts her out."

That was the truth for her, and it had to be. She had long settled to the conviction that Sheila had "saved" Clem from the excesses that were beginning to spoil him when we knew him in college; and, as a matter of fact, it had been Clem himself, in some earnest long-ago palaver with her, who had planted this idea of Sheila's contribution. It would have been sinister if Janet had interpreted his action otherwise. Still, I saw something else: the lifted, demanding thighs, the iron jiggling of the train, the photogenic belly like an anvil under the intolerable hammer of memory. It was not Clem's luck to ever forget anything. "I wouldn't say he had it made."

"He has what he wants," she said furiously.

Maybe. I didn't know. It might have been that he was riding his guilts home, "the strongest boy in Boda" dauntlessly up there on the surf board, untouched by the churning belly of the wave that carried him. It was Clem's trick to nourish himself on disaster. "If he has what he wants, that's something for Sheila. She would want him to be happy," I said.

"I don't."

"Well."

"I want to howl."

"Well, now, darling …" Oh, my ladies, my darlings, what are you going to have of us? Only that once and for all we tell you what is important and bide that guess out to the end of time?

# II

# THE SHAPING OF A MASK

*Our Childhood sits,*
*Our simple childhood sits, upon a throne*
*That hath more power than all the elements.*

—WORDSWORTH, The Prelude

# 3

AT THE HAPPY MERIDIAN of their marriage, in Paris, where I spent some days with the Andersons in the summer of 1950, I had found Sheila entranced in reading an advance copy of *Angel at Noon*. It was Clem's first book of fiction, and though she gave lip service to the superiority of his verse, clearly the prose medium wove a tissue as attractive to her as wool to a moth.

It was a joy to watch her reading. Shadows and lights played formlessly on the near-translucent skin of her face as if an actual persona moved within her, illumined by some unguessable globe of brilliance. Her wren-colored brows worked like a puppy's jaws when he lies oblivious with a bone. If what she read was not quite the nourishing substance of truth, at least it had that superlative ingredient of the true, presence. And might one not add the corollary, that by its mere absence the nonfictionalized past became progressively false?

Rarefied speculations, and we will have many of them before we know Clem by "thinking about him." It is enough to say that the old dialectic battle between truth and fiction was pitched in Sheila's reading. Now and then, I remember, she would look up quizzically from the book to demand of Clem or me whether something hadn't been put in the wrong place. (Truly a moral question, this one that queries the propriety of place. A flower in the wrong place is a weed, an assault on the wrong shrine of the singular goddess of love, adultery.) Both she and I had read the novel before in its much longer manuscript form, so I might have been of some use in helping her sort out the changes, the "misplacements." But since Clem refused to answer such queries, I thought I should not either. It must stand as it is in the book, I thought then.

But she persisted in her dissatisfaction. "'We lived through it, all right,'" she read. "'What else do we have to say?' That isn't my line, Clem. That's Lucille Zachary's line, I think. But you've got Melissa saying it in a letter after the war." She wanted, to the utmost, to enjoy a changeling's dream as she read and see no bothersome distinction between herself and the character Melissa, none between Clem and the fictional Harry Rinehart. Recollections that things had been otherwise—even if that otherwiseness lay in another fictional draft and not in actual circumstance—watered the intoxicating illusion of *temps retrouvé*.

Of course she was partly joking when she instigated these examinations into the devious interweaving of fiction and fact in what we were ever to know of Clem's life. But perhaps it is only through such jokes and finally unmanageable circumlocutions that we can sniff all we might know of the history of a consciousness. And a writer's past is, after all, not exactly of the same order as that of a stone where one can read the reliable history of fact in scratches made on its surface. And no one's past is that simple, in spite of the workable fictional pretense that it is so. As soon as one tangles with the formula, "I remember remembering remembering"—on to whatever power you might wish to carry it—the essential mystery of our conscious nature is encountered in much the way Sheila encountered it, enchanted and frustrated with Clem's book.

I remember (and remember remembering) her pale head bowed to the mystery of her husband's book (so much more puzzling, really, than the pretty children who had come from her body so naturally). Sadly I recall the cloud-and-sun transformations on her face as she tried to milk it for more, perhaps, than a poor thing of glue, paper and ink will ever yield. ("She reads like a stone trying to read the inscription carved on it," Clem said once, chilling me with the brutality and pertinence of his insight.)

She said in lovely abandonment, shivering with pleasure in the book, "I always wondered what happens to people in books after I stop reading. And here we are." She shook the café table that was in front of us and watched the white wine ripple in her glass just as it might have been described in a golden novel.

So what had come back from the past in a red, white and blue dust jacket enchanted her—but did not entirely please her, either. When she had finished reading it and turned back to the opening page like a bereft amputee searching for her limbs, she said with uncharacteristic bitterness, "I'll cut his nuts off, if any." Whether she wanted to assault Time, who had gathered so many alms for oblivion out of the "true" past, or Clem's editor, who had pruned off so much of the book, I did not          then          or          now          inquire.

But here I can brush off the problems of fiction and truth, truth in fiction, to record the simple truth that Harvey Plankton, Clem's editor at Parsons, Lord and Overholt, abolished some two thirds of the autobiographical material from Clem's first mighty drafts.

That summer in Paris we talked considerably about the proprieties of such editing (the morality of submitting to it, too) and I saw most of the correspondence between Plankton and Clem. One of Plankton's letters read in part:

I've been working over your manuscript for the last three weeks while I was on vacation in Bermuda. I believe that I have worked out a plan for saving it. Out of these eight hundred inchoate pages I see a tight, hard story of about three hundred pages emerging. It is the love story of Harry and Melissa. Most of what precedes their meeting in Washington is irrelevant and frankly dirty. Further, it is the kind of autobiographical detail that can be found in a thousand first novels and consequently boring. I can foresee what the critics would say of it, Clem, and I don't want to expose you to them.

Because the house has published a fine volume of your poetry [*The Throne of Oedipus*—D.H.] I know you are artist enough to drop these passages and cling to the story line that will permit the warm, liberal, engaging personalities of your central characters to come home broadside to your reader. Remember that a story line is like a skeleton for your book. Remember that a sympathetic character is one that you would want to have to dinner in your own home. Frankly I would not want either Lucille Zachary, Jack Wagner or Dr. Store to come to dinner in my house, though you evidently intend them to be sympathetic characters....

As for the episode of Harry's masturbating in the snow while delivering newspapers because his mother is unhappy over his father's inexplicable and frankly boring behavior and he dreads to go home, it is incredible in motivation and in the worst possible taste. In fact all the scenes of Harry's masturbation could go out in favor of the general credibility of your character....

The Lucille Zachary of the novel, Clem told me, was Irene Lacey in Boda, whom he got pregnant when he was fifteen. Dr. Store was really Dr. Wickham, who gave her the abortion. "It's all been a long time ago," Clem said wryly, "and I don't know if I would want to have Irene to dinner in my house any more or not, considering how hard it is to raise the loot for an extra pork chop chez Anderson, but I would refuse to go to heaven if Irene missed her passage. As for Doc Wickham, I'm beginning to see his need better than when I wrote about it. Why shouldn't he help himself, as long as the damage had been done her? He was a man of good appetite, no sadist. I don't think he hurt her or her feelings any by collecting his fee in the only form she could pay. And no masturbation would make Harry more credible. Is Plankton insane? As a matter of fact, it wasn't so pitiful beating it off in that stockyards shed as I made it sound. I could see the snow coming down past the cracks between boards—pretty, pale rainbows of the stuff falling on the wind with the street light on it, you know. I always wanted, afterward, to find a woman with skin that pretty."

Much of the "irrelevant autobiographical detail" of which Plankton complained had been, I knew, chosen with great finicking in an attempt to shape the novel into a prose paraphrase of the long poem The Throne of Oedipus. The book to which it gives its title had indeed been published by Parsons, Lord and Overholt, but another man had edited it, and Clem was convinced that Plankton had never read it. I might point out here that the poem is a Freudian-romantic speculation on the royal power of childhood experiences to define the shape by which love grows. Clem said, "I tried to tell Plankton that I'd set up this beast-marriage part, the eroticism in the greenhouse and the sexual ambivalence in the Lucille Zachary affair the way Mann sets up preconditions for the birth of reason in The Magic Mountain—so that the bedding of Harry and Melissa wouldn't be just another draftee making out with the little old college sweetheart before he goes off to fight the enemy across the water. That marriage of true minds was supposed to have been begun long before he saw Melissa, even. She was supposed to take bridal shape for him out of everything that had ever excited him, from the white dog on. She to be the last incarnation of an evolving series. But when I said this to him, Plankton grinned— one man of the world to another, y'know—and said, 'Well, Mann, Thomas Mann, with his reputation, can get away with that kind of thing. But you've got a crackerjack war novel here, whether you know it or not. There hasn't been anything else out yet about the Signal Corps. Now don't spoil it.'"

Clem must have been once determined to fight to keep the novel intact. During the previous winter he had flown from Paris to New York, no small expense for Sheila and him just then, to thrash the matter out with Plankton. He had lost his argument, hook, line and sinker, to Plankton's superior familiarity with production costs and the tricks of eliciting interest among the book salesmen and library reviewers on whom success depended. But when I saw Clem, some five months later, he expressed regret for nothing except the wasted passage money.

He had no concern with the printed book, he implied. If something was lost it was not his loss. He had got the good of it in the writing; and the chance to take off Plankton's manner and speech, which he did with a spiteful, jolly brilliance before friends who would understand, was all the compensation he wanted for losing the practical argument on the book's length. Had Plankton really destroyed a form by insisting on the abridgment? Sheila, who wanted no less than to nail Plankton's hide to the wall, insisted that he had. Clem annoyed her by arguing on either side of this problem. He wouldn't say what the form of a novel ought to be. True enough, some things had once been included to round out a "poetic" idea of form, but other things had been written in because of an antithetic conviction that a novel was "a book of life" where anything might go on the bare excuse that it had happened or even had been compulsively imagined. If a novel should approach its Platonic perfection in becoming as indiscriminate as life, then wasn't Plankton's word "inchoate" the perfect epithet for it? And one—anyone, even anti-Platonic Plankton—was justified in slicing the inchoate wherever convenience dictated, no?

Sophistry, Sheila hooted. He could afford to talk like this only because his affections were all gone over to the play on which he had worked for the last many months. For her part, she would never yield up an old love to the Planktons of this world, or certainly never make up for them yellow-dog arguments that they were too stupid to make up in defense of their depredations.

It wasn't quite, Clem conceded, as if he had been entirely callous about the fate of the novel once he put it away from him. But the worst was only that he missed having it around, loyal as a wife or a wastebasket into which he could toss all those wonders that refused to jell for poetry or crystallize into drama. Published now, the old bawd novel was dead. What would he do with his pretty thoughts of little girls?

"You can tell your stories to me." Sheila laughed. "You've still got me, though you deserted your poor, poor novel."

What's left of the long draft of *Angel at Noon* exists now in the truly inchoate carton of manuscript which Sheila recently pulled out of the attic of her father's house and sent to me. The remains in the cardboard box show no formal resemblance to The Throne of Oedipus. With dozens of alterations and revisions, and the absence of whole passages thrown away here or there, the pile of manuscript pages has become a mere scrap heap of fictionalized autobiography. It would be absurd for me to attempt a reimposition of the design that may once have ordered it.

And yet for my need it is perhaps just as autobiography that the remains are most pertinent. My task is justly to represent a man who deserted his wife and children—not to justify a fictional mask named

Harry Rinehart, who found his happy marriage with Melissa out of the grief and fantasy that attend the birth of love.

Lives turn—even those that have solved the Sphinx's riddle of childhood, as Clem's did—and it is the painful obligation of the scholar to deal always with what happens after the fireworks of success are shot away. (For "scholar" read "man" if you like; and for my morbid preoccupation with the afterward read a curious sense of failure, for I have that when I compare my stable life to Clem's, and a feeling that if I had dared to burn myself away clean out of it with his recklessness, I would not be here at the Sisyphean job of dredging again—and how many times again?—through the rubble of his wastebasket, looking for the assurance Clem wanted us to keep when it no longer sustained him.)

There was a time when Clem thought that his high-school affair with Irene Lacey had been the blundering, comic preparation for his successful marriage with Sheila. More than that, it seemed like an early, unrecorded voyage of Gulliver, sailing among the islands of adolescence to discover all he would ever find in subsequent explorations, though here the intellectual forms appeared in disguises of Lilliputian sexuality.

Typical of the whole novelistic progression (in its pre-Plankton form), the infatuation with Irene blurs over from an immediately preceding infatuation with another girl, as that had blurred over from the one before, and on back through a series of love objects almost coincidental in origin with the ability to distinguish objects visually. ("My God, I was always in love," he said once in a tone of astonishment. He had come straight from working on a poem, and it was as if the words, appearing on the page under his pencil, had all at once spelled out this revelation for him.)

The episode, as I have reassembled and edited it, begins this way for Clem (appearing under the name Harry Rinehart):

… She has no one to blame but herself, Harry thought, dragging himself through the ditch bottom, closer to the Everling house and to the lighted window behind which he supposed his girl Con Everling was getting ready for bed.

He clutched his bakelite field glasses in his left hand and gritted his teeth in satisfaction at this way of paying Con back for her refusal to let him walk her home from Luther League. It was only a three-block walk he had asked for. He knew for a fact that she had let Roy McCune feel her breasts and Sidney Beerman put a hickey on her neck.

Behind him in the tickling weeds his friend Mark grunted and whispered, "Near enough."

Harry stopped. In the best traditions of scouting he eased his head above the edge of the ditch, set the field glasses to his eyes and reconnoitered the porch of the Everling house. On the porch he could see the pulsing glow of the cigar Con's father was smoking as he rocked. Through the bay window Con's mother appeared, folding laundry on the dining-room table.

A scout no longer, he tipped the glasses upward, fingered the nickeled lever that was supposed to adjust the focus. I'm going to magnify her, he thought vengefully, and it didn't have to happen this way if she'd only been decent.

"She's not up there," Mark breathed close to his cheek.

"I can see that."

"Even with them dollar binoculars?"

"Wait!" Harry said. "Look at that shadow moving on the ceiling. Look! It's her shoulder."

"Whoo-ee," Mark said, "a shoulder shadow! Just don't get so excited. Give me a look."

Harry passed the glasses and gripped the weeds around him with both hands. He began to worry that he would sneeze. The weeds were thick with August dust, and the smell of pollen tickled his nose. He would sneeze and Con's father would come baying down from the porch and catch them there. Let him, then, only not until I see her enlarged, Harry prayed, not until she passes that window squarely.

"You smashed a bug on the glass," Mark whispered. "I can't see anything but that bug." He started to polish one of the lenses with his shirt tail.

"There she goes," Harry said as Con passed the window. He grabbed wildly for the field glasses.

Mark wrestled them out of his reach. "She'll come back. Don't run amok on me."

"She's down to her slip and you had to be wiping bugs off my glasses."

"Take them," Mark said. "Jesus Christ, doesn't friendship mean anything to you?"

"All right. Keep them."

"Hell with them. I can see better without. Hey, there she is again, but she's got more than a slip on. Aaaah. That's the dress she had on at League."

For a dozen heartbeats Con stood at her bedroom window with the light behind her showing her in gray silhouette. Pearl gray, Harry thought, like the inside of a clamshell, laced with iridescence through its dappled paleness. If she was beautiful or not, if she was the prettiest of the sophomores or not, if she was not even so pretty as her married sister, didn't matter at all, any more than, probably, her being female did, or the decent dress from Penney's that hid the roundness Roy McCune described. What mattered was that through the field glasses, got by fraud and selling a few Collier's subscriptions, she was there on the moon-round field of vision like a goddess stamped on a coin, the Diana of his despair with the common world. His heart thumped against the dirt bank of the ditch as if it might be saying, Now it is fulfilled and now not even death can matter.

Con turned from the window and put out her light.

"Whoo-eee," Harry whispered, trying now to perpetuate the awe of what he had glimpsed, feeling it elude, sift out through the hugeness of the night.

"Does that moron sleep with her clothes on?" Mark asked in disgust.

"I'd've given you the glasses in another minute," Harry said. "I didn't mean to be selfish, but my hands got paralyzed when I saw."

"Don't snow me, you didn't see a thing."

"Nipples," Harry said. "The shadow of them. You couldn't see because you didn't have the glasses. Her belly button. It looked like an eye socket. No kidding."

"They ought to lock you up, with an imagination like that," Mark said. "They ought to have you in a padded cell."

"'How da-dum-like I see thee stand, with an agate lamp within thy hand,'" Harry whispered reverently, lifting his face toward the moon, calling it now the girl's name with his tongue, naming its profaned whiteness. Diana. And the horns sprang at his temples. Ahead of them the Everlings' terrier began to bark.

"An eye socket." Mark laughed. "What'll that boy think of next?"

To their left another dog began to bark. Above the lip of the ditch there was a sudden pattering of feet as the terrier, reinforced, made a pass toward them. They've got me now, Harry thought. He was on his feet and with a deer leap had plunged across the garden toward the railroad embankment, tumbling to all fours and bounding up again before he even heard Mark yell, "Split up." Thinking, It won't be so bad if they catch Mark, since I'm the one who used the glasses on her.

Between the garden and the embankment a swale of brown grass gave him a surer footing. Veering on it, because his one talent was for speed and he thought the dogs would have him if he tried the embankment, he raced down parallel with the tracks toward the stockyard, meaning to lose himself among its pens. If there're cows there I could even stand among them, he thought. No one would think of looking for him at the center of a herd of cows and surely their smell would throw the dogs off his trail.

He was thirty yards from the loading chute when he saw the black shape of the car parked just beyond it along the tracks; fifteen yards when its headlights whipped him square in the face, and too exhausted to run any more when a head leaned out and a man's voice commanded, "Come here, you."

Slowly, with his head bent heavily forward, Harry moved to the side of the car. A hand swept out to grab the leather bootlace from which the glasses hung around his neck, jerked it and let it go slack. "Caught you, didn't we?" Then he recognized Jack Wagner's voice, and as his eyes grew accustomed to the dark again he saw Lucille Zachary on the other side of the front seat. In the back seat was another couple, visible only in silhouette.

"The way you were galloping, you must have done something pretty mean," Jack Wagner said. His big hand, blond-glittering in the moonlight, lifted the cheap glasses, seeming to understand them only by touch. "What you got these for, Harry? Not much to see out at night, is there?"

"Looking at the stars," Harry said. He wanted to strike the big hand away from his glasses, and yet to be held this way by them with a leather thong around his neck seemed a curiously natural and acceptable punishment for what he had done. As he stood in the tether, neither his courage nor his will rose strongly enough to resent it. His breath still whined and he submitted.

"Not much to see but people's windows," the man in the back seat said. It was Sid Beerman's brother Lloyd.

"Oh ho, oh ho," Jack Wagner said. "So you been out window-peeping, Harry? Who was it up that way? Nancy Mosebach? I'll bet it was that little Everling girl. Now, you're not old enough for that, Harry."

"Let him alone, Jack," Lucille commanded. She leaned over to look up into Harry's sweating face. "Let him go. It's no fun to be stag on a night like this. Is it, Jack? Is it, huh?" She pulled the hair curling from the neck of his polo shirt. "How would you feel if I walked off with Harry now and left you alone?"

The illustration was too farfetched. It only brought a grunt of contempt from Jack.

"Let him go, you dumb farmer," she commanded. "Pick on someone your own size."

Jack's hand opened from the leather cord, and with a movement almost swift enough to be a blow he put it on Lucille's face, pinching so that her mouth (black in the moonlight) was higher than it was wide. "You about my size, honey? You about my size?"

The last thing Harry saw before he started to run again—on down the tracks and out of town before he circled toward home—was Jack leaning to kiss that distorted mouth.

Two days after that, Lucille detoured through the Harrisburg square to speak to him. He and Mark had parked their bicycles against the bandstand and were waiting for the afternoon bus to bring Harry's papers from the city. They were using their time to perfect one more plan for hitchhiking to California after robbing the grain-and-feed company, for defrauding Crowell-Collier's of another premium for junior salesmanship (after the field glasses Harry wanted a set of camp cooking equipment or a model P-12), or for filing out a skeleton key that would let them into any house in town.

Lucille not only interrupted them, but stood there as if she wanted something, as if they were supposed to be interested enough in her to try to figure out what it was. She was five years older than they and had graduated from high school the year before they started. Mark, at least, had known her all his life and was committed to the judgment that "any woman who runs with Jack Wagner will do anything." It was hard for either of them to get the idea that she might have come over to them because they were boys. She wore a white cotton smock for the heat, and the matronly figure beneath it struck them as bordering on the repulsive fatness of Mrs. Chader, Mrs. Bloomquist or other wives of the town.

"You want us to do something for you?" Mark asked warily.

"I thought maybe one of you would pump me home on your bike," she said, beaming the request at Harry.

"I've got a low tire," Mark said. "Anyway I make it a practice not to give people rides. Nothing personal. I like to stick to principle."

"I could ride on the handlebars," she said to Harry. "I've done that lots of times. When my brother had a bike he took me everywhere."

Mark said, "You're not dressed for it. What you got on under that kimono?"

"I guess I could do it," Harry said. "I've got to deliver my papers, but …"

"They'll be here any minute," Mark said.

But Lucille was already hoisting herself onto the bike, her haunches bulging like white sails, entirely filling the space between the grips of his handlebars. As he shoved off and began to pedal, Mark called once more in a tone of self-righteous admonition, "You want me to deliver your papers, then?"

"Yes, deliver his papers," Lucille shouted back. "Get up some steam," she said to Harry, "or we're going to end up in a flower bed." Under her weight the bike was wobbling crazily. He rose on the pedals and with his cheek against her shoulder, blind and obedient, he straightened on his course.

When he caught up with Mark again that evening—two hours after the last paper had been tossed onto porch roofs or lawns—and tried to make his peace, he found Mark still more in grief than anger. "I thought you had some standards," Mark said. "You talk so big. I thought I could count on you not to go any lower than Con Everling. So you go pumping away out to the Grove with that cow. She might at least have the decency to wear a corset."

"We didn't go to the Grove," Harry said.

"Wherever you went."

"We went to her place and sat in the yard talking."

"All this time? Yeah? What were you talking about? What old Jack Wagner does with her three nights a week, not to mention that bald-headed Farm Bureau agent, Lloyd Beerman, and the whole softball team from Elder?"

"That's all lies," Harry said. On the lawn of the Zachary house, where Lucille had spread a quilt for them to sit on while they drank their lemonade, he had sat in a swarm of feelings so new to him that he could not yet defend them, even to himself. He was not even sure what all their talk had been about as the sun went lower and threw the geometric shadow of the grain elevator and then the fringy shadow of dark elm trees over the Zachary lawn. He had got from it a refrain of longing. Lucille felt she had been getting farther from all she wanted in the two years since she had graduated from high school. She hardly ever played the cornet any more and she felt out of things when her younger brothers and sisters came home with stories of school picnics and parties or "just what they're learning—I've forgotten lots of things."

She wanted to go to college and her older brothers in the Army had promised to help, but somehow each year that had got put off. Her father had had a time with his back and couldn't work at the garage as many hours as he needed. Her mother had had an operation for goiter. "And there's nothing in Harrisburg except to get married," she told him. "I don't want to marry Jack. What does he ever think about besides playing ball or tanking up on three-two on Saturday nights?" Harry had nodded sympathetically, flattered to think himself the ideal male with a treasure house of thoughts on all subjects that he could pour out for her—if he chose.

He hadn't chosen. He had kept mum and let her spill her soul. But he had felt pity for her, as he had felt sometimes for his mother, and had thought how great it would be if he could take all the women who counted on him to California, where they would never have to carry coal in the winter and where they could have interesting thoughts all day long in the sun.

"What's more," Mark said, "you hadn't been gone more than two minutes when old Jack came out of the pool hall right across there and stood with a beer bottle in his hand looking up and down the street. I about crapped. I thought he'd seen you pedal off with her, and boy, he's not letting anyone else get at her while she's his girl. You saw him beat the devil out of Larry Michaels for even telling that story about her and the softball team."

"Was that what it was for?" Harry asked, weakening. He had seen Jack whip Larry in the school yard. He and Mark and Roy McCune sat up on the fire escape that day and watched Jack run poor myopic Larry Michaels down three blocks from the cream station, catch him among the swings and teeterboards, and hold the boy on his knees while he alternately slapped him, lectured him, and hit him in the forehead with his fist. In spite of himself Harry had enjoyed the display of dominance. He despised Larry Michaels and believed that everyone else in town shared his own admiration for Jack as an athlete. He had laughed when Larry kept trying to put his glasses back on for protection, and he had trembled to the thrill of watching Jack's blond arm lifted to strike. (When someone asked Larry how he got Jack to stop when he did, he grinned foolishly and said, "I kept telling him what a swell right-hand punch he had"—duplicity which lowered him even further in Harry's eyes.) But now those chickens were coming home to roost and Harry said, "Good Lord, Jack must know I wouldn't try anything with her. I'm not the kind that would take another man's girl."

[NOTE: There are breaks in Clem's old manuscript here and a considerable diversion, among the fragments that remain, from the Irene-Lucille story. The fat-in-the-fire encounter with her took place during the same summer as the suicide of Clem's Uncle Cole (of which he made the story "Spider on the Rope," published in 1941).

There also remains a catalog of various athletic specialties to which Harry—or Clem—devoted himself that summer and in the early fall. The athletic interests were: weight lifting, the snatch-and-grab of a fifty-pound bar bell (he made the bar bell himself out of an automobile axle and weighted wheels); something he calls "the Greek press" (of which I have never heard, and to which I can find no reference in the standard literature of gymnastics or weight lifting); and several exercises in Dynamic Tension, which of course were part of the training offered by the Charles Atlas Company. It is on the basis of superiority in these trials—which naturally no one else in Boda (Harrisburg of the novel) would have been caught dead engaged in publicly—that Clem took for himself the sobriquet "the Strongest Boy in Boda."

The skeleton story line goes on with the Irene-Lucille affair.— D.H.]

Marked in pencil as the beginning of a chapter:

He had no intention of going back, ever, to repeat the intimacy he had shared that afternoon when he and Lucille drank lemonade on the quilt. Con Everling was his girl, and if she didn't know it yet, she was going to know it, just as the world at large would be forced, in awe, to recognize his still secret wiriness and strength. He had put on weight that summer, his footwork was incredible. There was no doubt at all that he would make forward on the basketball team. He had learned to punt a football so that it usually spiraled like a pass instead of tumbling end over end. His kicks outdistanced Mark's by an average of five yards. And Con Everling was going to learn the difference between cosmopolitan repartee—as in the Collier's stories by P. G. Wodehouse—and Sid Beerman's stock of moron stories that everyone had heard so many times. She might also learn the difference between a gentleman—who never told his successes—and a jerk who would boast at the cream station that he had broken both her brassière straps on a recent Sunday night.

When Lucille resumed practicing with the high-school orchestra and sat beside him, since they both played cornet, he made up his mind to treat her with merely professional crispness. If she had questions about difficult musical passages or about Miss Fleming's instructions, he would answer her courteously, but he was not going to take the slightest risk of encouraging her. That would be hardly fair to Jack Wagner—or to her, for that matter.

As a cornet player, Lucille was five times as able as he. She showed him how to tongue the staccato passages in *"Oenone's Plaint"* that he had always slurred and lost the beat on, and she soothed his astonished pride once when he played right through a rest and got "Well, Harry, really!" from the disgusted Miss Fleming. Further, she broke into warm, contagious laughter when he tried to be crisp with her, and thought it was an act he was putting on to amuse her. She always got his wisecracks, where a lot of people fumbled.

So when the orchestra began practicing at night in preparation for the Harrisburg Corn Festival it seemed natural enough (and no harm) that he should walk her home afterward. Jack Wagner, she told him, thought she was nuts to waste her time going to orchestra practice.

"He's right," Harry said. They were walking down the dark block past Will the druggist's house, their cornet cases clacking decently together between them—he did not mean to walk close enough to touch her. "I wouldn't come if my folks hadn't bought me this horn. I tried to tell them not to, but they had a big tissy, so here I am."

"He's wrong," Lucille said. "Now it may not mean much to you. When you're as old as I am you'll be sorry you didn't practice more. You could be a good trumpeter."

Owlishly he weighed her comment. Yes, she was old enough to know what she was talking about, and still not so old that she couldn't understand that athletics, for example, were really more important for someone who had strength and talent than music could be.

"How good?" he demanded.

"You wouldn't make a Harry James," she said. (Then where was the point of it? he thought.) "But good enough so it would be some satisfaction. Look, I could teach you a lot of things. Tonguing. You don't know anything about that."

"I do too."

"Show me." She laughed oddly (a little crazily, he thought) and put her free arm around him. For a minute she held her lips waiting for him, then kissed his mouth. The cornet cases knocked hollowly. "Well?" she said. Then to his disgust and before he could prevent it, her tongue slipped past his lips.

"Please don't," he said, wondering how a Wodehouse character would have squelched her in such a circumstance. He could remember reading nothing similar to this in Wodehouse.

"You little bugger," she said. "All right for you. You can bring the horse to water but you can't make him drink."

"What, exactly, might that mean?" There was the upper-class British frostiness he wanted.

"If you don't know, little Lucille isn't going to tell you."

Slowly, slowly the street lights parabolaed over their heads as they walked the remaining blocks to her house, and, slowly as the stars swung their drunken circles through the blue night, the vastness and the enormity of what she meant circled and came home to him. She had offered him her body. His knees began to tremble and his mouth went dry. She had offered and he had refused.

When they went up the sidewalk to her porch, she was chattering about nothing—about some car that had been brought in smashed to the garage where her father worked. She opened the screen door, leaned bosomy against it and said, "Good night."

He did not answer, but stood there with no sign of turning to go.

"Did I forget something? What is it?" she asked.

"Please," he said.

"What? Oh, Harry, don't be silly. Run home like a good little boy."

He ran from her house that night, just as she told him to do. He did not believe he ran because she had commanded it. In those days he was always running.

He would run part of the distance of his newspaper route. He ran the seven blocks uptown and back when his mother wanted something from the store. Sometimes he ran out to the grove at the intersection a half mile north of town. He ran because it seemed to him that he could think straight only while his legs were pumping under him and his heart was thundering in his chest. When he slowed down his thoughts knotted with the absurd conflict that had come into his life.

He still hoped to take Con home from the corn festival. At last he worked up his nerve to waylay her at school one day between assembly and the ancient-history class. Might he count on the pleasure of her company after the festival?

"Yah," she said.

He put aside a dollar and a half to take her out for hamburgers on their homeward walk. Hamburgers probably meant sundaes and soft drinks as well, since she was said by the other boys to be a spender.

On the other hand, wasn't he now committed—involved, sworn, pledged—beyond the possibility of retreat with Lucille? These nights after orchestra practice they were kissing so much he thought he might be ruining his lip for the cornet. In the black corner of Chader's hedge she had let him pet her a little. Now he knew what a nipple felt like through cloth, unless it had just been the stitching of her brassière. Solemnly he recognized her claim on him. He would have felt like a dog if he refused to walk home from the corn festival with her— provided that could be arranged so Jack wouldn't see them.

Two days before the crisis smote him, Lucille announced she wouldn't play with the orchestra on the big night. "I'd feel silly sitting up there with you when all the rest of you are still in high school," she said. "Miss Fleming was nice enough to say it would be all right for me to sit in, but I said I'd rather not. So I'll stay home by my lonesome."

"I can see how you'd feel," Harry said, so moved by relief that his compassion felt genuine.

He was not sure that he was fooling her. She grinned slyly and said, "You could come and visit me after the doings. I really will be all alone except for the little kids. Dad's going into the hospital again tomorrow. Mother and Willis and Jane are driving him in to the city and they plan to stay aw-uh-ull night."

"That's too bad about your father," Harry said.

"Will you come?"

Twisting and writhing with embarrassment, sure that even his silence would not hide the compromising truth, Harry avoided an answer.

"I wish you would," she coaxed.

He had to run at top speed for half an hour after he left her to burn the same impure wish from his treacherous limbs.

Was he really sure that he had a date with Con? Her "Yah" echoed faithfully in his mind, but he also recalled that he had kind of caught her by surprise when he uttered his invitation, coming up behind her so fast in his tennis shoes and beginning to speak before she had turned to recognize him. She couldn't have thought he was asking for after Luther League next Sunday? She might have, damn her. She might have.

On the night of the corn festival he arrived at the opera house early, convinced that he should have fixed some definite point of rendezvous there and a specific time when he would meet her. He found that in spite of the rain that had persisted all day there were already more than three hundred farmers and townspeople in the building. They were milling around the church booths, clotting the displays of corn, vegetables, baking and handicrafts like damp clusters of flies after the goodies. He could not find Con among them.

He lingered by the entrance as long as he dared, hoping that she would arrive before he had to take his place with the orchestra on stage. At five past eight, when Reverend Olsen rose to open the program with a prayer, she had not yet appeared.

He played through the first number without bothering to tongue a single passage, though it was, according to Miss Fleming, a "sprightly air." He watched the crowd more than he watched the music on his rack.

The mayor made a speech of welcome to the former residents of Harrisburg who had come back for the night. Miss Fleming announced the orchestra would play a march, "El Capitan."

Con came in then. With her raincoat belted, her tam perched on the side of her curls, and her green umbrella still haloing her, she looked to him like spring come to see what had grown from her sharecroppers' planting. He thought that she nodded an affirmation when she glanced up at him. His tongue vibrated in the nickel mouthpiece and his soul marched as he blasted the glory of El Capitan.

Then, as the school superintendent began his long rigmarole preparatory to awarding the yield and best-ear prizes for the corn, Harry noticed that Con had found a seat by Roy McCune.

Well, that didn't mean anything. Well, the crowd was large and seats were scarce, and naturally that dirty sneaking bastard, too stupid to play an instrument in the orchestra (alas, too wise) had beckoned her over to a seat that in his sneaky way he had been saving for her. That still didn't mean she had forgotten her solemn promise, that inconsidered "Yah."

Harry felt the sweat start on his face. How could he get down from the stage in time to save the evening? Well, he might puke in Larry Michaels' French horn to signal that bad health would not permit him to continue in the position of second cornetist. Yah, that was a brilliant scheme, all right.

He had to sit up there and endure everything, every word his stupid elders could think of to say about corn and home-town loyalty. How much banality does it take to kill a man? he wondered, not daring to look down and see Con and Roy snickering together as they watched his discomfort.

He tried to bolt the stage ahead of the speakers and the corn judges when they were finally done. Miss Fleming pinched his arm and thrust him back with the whisper, "But we're the orchestra, Harry."

With her interference and the slowness of old Mrs. Gorley on the steps ahead of him, he did not get to the front door of the opera house until Con had gone out. When he stampeded through the umbrellas and bodies clogging the doorway, she was already walking away into the rain. And Roy McCune was close beside her.

"Con." Harry's shout sounded even to him like a cry for help. He was furious with himself for being unable to control his voice. But at least the shriek had stopped her.

She and Roy turned and waited for him to come up. Roy shrugged his raincoat collar high, averted his face and began to whistle.

"Hello, Harry," Con said. "Isn't this rain awful?"

He was afraid to try his voice for a minute, almost frenzied that he couldn't answer such a simple question. "Thought we had a date," he growled.

Roy whistled. Con looked blank. "Now? It's so rainy tonight. It's awful. Roy ..."

"Yah?"

"Roy, I did say something to Harry the other day about going home with him."

Roy started to whistle again.

Harry said, "I suppose I speak the English language sufficiently that persons of ordinary intelligence can grasp my meaning when I ask them a special question."

"My, my," Roy said.

"I don't know what that means," Con said.

"I asked you in so many well-chosen words of the English language if could you would me take home tonight." The words sounded screwy to him and he heard only their betraying falsetto that rose in spite of everything. The rain seemed to sizzle on his face like grease in a frying pan.

Con shook her head in puzzlement and something like contrition. She lifted her hand to pull Harry's jacket tighter against his neck and let her palm lie fondly against his chest. "I'm sorry if there was a misunderstanding," she said. "Couldn't we all three of us go down to the Hamburg Heaven and talk it over out of this cold rain? Brrrrr."

"Brrrrr," Roy said.

Fondly, falsely, her hand lay on his chest. Harry slapped it away. "I'm not going no goddam where and talk anything over. You promised me and now you big whore you're ratting out of it."

"Now, listen," Roy said. He took his hands out of his raincoat pockets.

Harry put both hands against Roy's chest and shoved. The fury and surprise of the onslaught worked. Roy went sprawling out among the parked cars.

"I spit on you," Harry shouted at Con. "I spit on you." He meant to do it, too, but in all the moisture of that night his mouth was like Sahara in August. Before he burst into tears, he cut ignominiously through the parked cars and began to run.

In that October rain which matted his pompadour and soaked the jacket his mother had pressed for Con Everling's sake, he knew for the first time, surely, that he had no home. When he took shelter on the unlighted porch of the Baptist church and huddled against its kellystone wall to think, it was as if the shrouding rain itself had orphaned him. He felt it strike the brown grass and ooze downward into the loam where all his fathers were buried. Eyeless they lay beneath its insulting fall. Nothing watched him. In the Halloween of rain the church was his to despoil, and he felt he could not go home until he had committed some avenging sacrilege.

Con's family had been Baptists until the pinch came, and this church had failed two years ago, overcome like the town's second bank by the depression. Now the Everlings claimed to be Lutherans, which showed how good their word was. Anyway, it was in this building that he had first seen Con, not so long after he had moved to Harrisburg. She was wearing a green-and-white dress that day, he remembered, and her hair was pageboy then. He could even have described the shoes and socks she had been wearing if anyone had asked him. That there was no one to ask him filled him again with sentimental rage, and he hissed at the dark bulk of the church, "I spit on you."

He began trying the basement windows. On the side that faced an alley he found one unlocked. He pushed it open and dropped to the invisible concrete floor inside. Around him was a smell of dankness from the damp concrete, of unpainted wood from the floor beams, and—after all this time—an undefinable essence of cookery from all the chicken fried here in the epoch of Coolidge prosperity.

He found the stairway and mounted, coming out in the Sunday-school rooms behind the pulpit. He heard mice skitter back to their hymnbook nests as the floor creaked under his weight. "Fly, mice," he said in the tone of Fu Manchu.

In the wide, vaulted space before the pulpit he felt a pang of uncertainty from the mere sensation of standing alone in so much emptiness. He fought it down with a reckless commitment to blasphemy. "Boo," he shouted. God did not answer the insult.

He heard the rain gust against the imitation stained-glass windows and thought, Even the building won't last long against that. The Chinese water torture. Even Inspector Nayland Smith couldn't hold out against that when old Fu Manchu put it on him. Nayland Smith and the burden of empire, indeed. If he had old Nayland Smith here he'd put him on that altar and cut his gizzard out. Him and his smelly pipe. If Smith got the better of Fu Manchu so often it was only because Smith had all the sneaky, McCuney cruds on his side. At least Fu was a man. Fu always came back, with his whips and his tortures and his admirable contempt for the cringing weakness of the whites.

Then Harry's thoughts seemed so ludicrous to him that he tried to laugh. It was no good any more to go around hissing contempt like Fu Manchu and thinking that that meant anything in the real world. Father Fu was under the rain like the other fathers, and with him had gone all the comforting nonsense of childhood.

The oleographed pageantry of a thousand Sunday-school cards still swum around him in the dark of the church. He could still sense what he had intuited before, the tang of the Orient and its vices mingled with an austere Midwestern piety—Joseph's tricky coat of many colors, the female, dagger-hiding robes of the Biblical hordes, the saw teeth of palm trees, the insidious faces of the camels that brought Wise Men out of the East. But even these intimations had lost their power to awe him. The sacrilege he needed could not be found here.

On the instant he realized this he remembered where he must go to find it. He would wallow with Lucille. Now neither loyalty to Con nor respect for his own athletic nature would restrain him. At the very moment Lucille soiled his flesh he would laugh his contempt for the treacherous Everlings.

He was drenched to the skin and cold when he slipped through the mulberry bushes at the corner of the Zachary lawn. (Harrisburg being what it was, there was no use risking talk by getting too near the street light by their front walk.) He saw no light in the house and debated which door he should go to to knock. The back door was the logical choice, even if it might be closer to the room where the little kids were asleep and he might wake them. It would be Lucille's problem to get them back to sleep. On the other hand, there should be still some heat from the kitchen range and he needed to be close to warmth when he shucked out of his wet clothes.

He had come to Lucille with faith—as he had never, really, had faith that Con would keep her promise to him. The faith had been as sustaining as certainty, and yet, he was not really surprised when he saw Jack Wagner's car parked in among the bushes near the back door. On the contrary, he was almost glad. For one thing it confirmed his cynicism about the world—there wasn't a bitch of them you could trust. For another, his excess of emotion had worn him out. And finally—why not admit this, since he had already admitted there was no God, no laws, no responsibility?—he liked the idea of Jack's being with her more than the idea of his own success.

In the shelter of the eaves, he stood outside the back door listening. Presently he heard cinders fall softly in the range, what might have been a voice, then silence again. The one question was whether he dared to sneak in. He tugged at the tar-papered screen door and found it unlocked. With infinite slowness he turned the knob of the inner door and thrust it open an inch. Now he could hear something—creak of springs and two voices. Jack's was dark and low. There was no making out what he said. But, listening painfully hard, Harry made out Lucille saying, "I've told you so many times, Jack, I just don't want to any more." Ha, he thought cynically, if she means that, why aren't there lights and why are the springs squeeching?

A bright flash of lightning threw Harry's shadow inward onto the kitchen floor. After the following thunder he heard Lucille demand, "What was that?"

Then he heard one intelligible word from Jack as he answered, "Nothing."

The springs banged devilishly as she seemed to be trying to fight her way from the couch. (Harry had placed them now in the house's geography. He had seen the couch through the front door once.) Perhaps she meant to come investigate whatever she thought she'd heard; maybe she was only trying to get away from Jack. In either case, Harry thought, he won't let her go. And he exulted, He's too strong.

The idea of Jack's strength emboldened him, as if it were his strength too, as if Jack really meant to do this for him. He stooped to pull off his squishy shoes and then entered the kitchen. The coals in the stove glared like jack-o'-lantern eyes and it was hard to see past them, but he made out that the door between rooms was open. He asked for lightning from the window beyond them to define them to his straining eyes.

The struggle on the couch was more violent now. An elbow crashed against the plaster of the wall. The sounds described a body turning and Lucille said, "Don't make me hate you, Jack."

"Stop your goddam tricks. Roll back." Another flurry of struggle and Jack said, "All right, bitch. One way or another you're going to take it."

"No." There was a sound like a boot hitting a pumpkin and Lucille moaned, "Don't." A thousand devils in Harry's mind howled Do.

And now with the stallion thrash of a table being kicked over, lightning blasted the rectangles of window and door, and in the patterning of white against white, black against black, Harry saw one crescent thigh repeat the crescent beneath, as if while he were watching a half moon he had taken a blow on the head that made two exact and overlapping images profiled together against the flat infinite line of the couch's blackness, saw her knee on the floor beside the couch and thought, Not just for me, to me, while the aftermath of thunder growled that it would not be mocked. Harriet crouched while Harry panted, felt the double blossom and remorse of sin.

"That's quicker'n other way," Jack said in a tone so shabbily apologetic that Harry hated him. Too quickly lost. No lightning came a second time to create the scene again.

From the second story came the sound of a door opening and a child's voice calling, "Lucille? Lucille?"

"You had to kick that end table over to wake them up," Lucille said crossly. "It's nothing," she shouted. "I bumped something. Go back to sleep."

"Why isn't there any light, Lucille?"

"I'm trying to sleep down here. Please get back in bed."

"Can I come down to the kitchen for a drink of water?"

"There isn't any water. You're not thirsty. Go back to bed."

"I can't."

"The bucket's dry and I'm not going out in the rain to fill it."

"Come up here, Lucille. We're afraid of the dark."

"I can't come up. Don't you think it's dark down here too? I'm not afraid."

"Why doesn't it stop raining, Lucille?"

"It's got to rain. Now, please, go back to sleep. Try to sleep and I'll come up later."

"Can I turn on the light?"

"Only in your own room. I don't want any light down here. I'm trying to sleep."

"Good night, Lucille."

"Be a good girl and only leave the light on a minute."

"I will be. Good night."

"Good night." And then a long, frail silence before the springs creaked again and Lucille said, "Well, you did it, didn't you? And I've got to start all over again."

"There's no use talking like that," Jack said. "You got what you bargained for. How come you had no pants?"

"I wasn't going out on a night like this. Why get dressed up?"

"Maybe you were expecting someone else."

"I wasn't expecting you. I truly wanted to go to sleep early."

"Maybe little old Harry. I hear you've been walking home with him from orchestry practice."

"Who told you that?"

"The birds. I may have to whack him around a little."

"Don't be so silly. Harry hasn't got anything."

"If I promise to be nice and not whack Harry around will you be nicer to me?"

"I don't care about Harry."

"You better answer me nice and straight when I ask you something."

"You can do what you want with Harry."

"That's not my answer. You gonna be nice to me?"

"Yes."

"Whenever I want?"

"Yes."

"Whatever I want?"

Yes, Harry thought in the silence.

In the following golden days of November a worse restlessness than he had ever known settled fast on Harry. Nothing that he could think of, or that he usually counted on, would satisfy him. He went on long hunts through the woods with Mark and sometimes Jimmy Store. The crisp fall weather and the satisfaction of physical fatigue afterward could not touch the core of change he felt gnawing within him. Killing squirrels and rabbits with his Stevens Crackshot was good as always. It was simply not enough.

Nothing was enough. When the basketball season started, he went into the first game as forward and scored fifteen points against Bremerton. He was something of a hero around town after the game.

Doc Store stopped him on the street to say, "Don't let them tell you because you're light that you aren't damn good athletic timber. You've got a fighting heart and—and a tricky little dribble. Keep going and we'll get the county championship." Doc Store said about the same thing to the rest of the team—except Mark, who had gone in as a substitute and let the Bremerton forwards make eight points against him before the coach could get him off the floor. But anyway, it should have been all the reward he needed. It wasn't necessary to poke fun at Store for having got drunk and smashed his Buick, or to tell Jimmy Store that his father was known to be messing with a married woman in the city—this spitefulness because Doc's praise hadn't been enough.

The great thaw took place when his twelve points helped the team nudge out Oxley 31-30 and Con Everling arranged to ride back to Harrisburg with him in the school superintendent's car.

"'Frailty, thy name is woman,'" he said to Mark later. "Here it hasn't been a month since I called her a whore in the public street and spat in her face and I climb into the car with her and Beuleen Chisholm and find her actually smiling at me."

"So?" Mark said.

"So I made the most of it."

"Whatever that might mean."

He could have told Mark he had cupped her left breast in his hand. That meant—far too little.

Because nothing would salve Harry's itching dissatisfaction, he led Mark and Jimmy Store into trouble that they would never have touched without his daring them. One night they went into the building of the defunct State Bank of Harrisburg and carried off a gunny sack full of old business papers from the files. They hid them in the furnace of the Baptist church. On Sunday mornings they would go to read through them—the papers had to yield some good, since they'd had the trouble of stealing them—for the scant bit of dirty light they might shed on the lives of Harrisburg people. Mark found a letter from Con Everling's father promising "immediate restitution" of the eleven hundred dollars he had evidently appropriated to use on the grain market back in 'twenty-four. It was fixed with a notarial seal applied by an out-of-town notary, and the fussy language sounded "like a Jew lawyer," Mark thought. It made Hubert Everling's reputation as "the one honest man" in the failing bank look pretty bad, and the boys talked of using it to blackmail Con into meeting them there in the abandoned church basement. The scheme petered out from sheer impossibility, of course, but also from Harry's lack of enthusiasm.

He dared Jimmy Store to swipe his uncle's .32 pistol from the glove compartment of the car, the theft to be staged during a basketball game so that the uncle would think the boys from Oxley had done it. They kept the pistol too in the Baptist furnace, between their hunting excursions with it. The times they took it out into the country to fire had some special quality of farther-ranging, of the exploration of a strangeness that was more than geographical. The only thing they ever killed with it was a rabbit that they had driven into a culvert. Mark held the pistol inside the culvert and shot blind, automatic fire, and when they pulled the rabbit out with a stick its head and front feet were a pulp of brown hair, blood and white bone splinters.

He and Mark hitchhiked to the nearby city one day—and ran into Lucille on the street there. Harry thought that her face looked worn and older than he was used to thinking it. The scarf tied around her head was pulled so tight that she looked like the pictures of European peasant women.

"Mark and I are going to see I Am a Fugitive from a Chain Gang," Harry said. "Come on and go with us."

"That ought to be a pretty good movie. But I can't," she said.

"We can go back on the evening bus," Harry said.

"No, I couldn't do that."

"Paul Muni's terrific," Mark said. "It's a better film than Scarface."

"Oh, how do you know?" She laughed. "You haven't seen it. Little boys have such big imaginations."

"Little boys, hell," Mark said. He pinched her breast hard with his left hand, smiling. "Any time you want to find out, Grandma ..."

"That hurts, you dope."

"Then don't call us little boys."

"Oh," she said. "I guess that hurts, too, doesn't it? I'm sorry." She made a mock curtsy of apology to both of them. "I wouldn't think being a boy was the worst thing in the world."

"Walk on a minute," Harry said to Mark. "I want to talk to Grandma."

"That hurts, too," she said.

"Why can't I ever see you any more?" he asked.

"I've quit the cornet," she said in an attempt to joke. Then said, "I guess you know why."

"Jack?"

"Him."

"You told me you'd thrown him over."

"I lied. I tell a lot of lies, Harry. So do you and you ought to stop it."

"I don't know what you're getting at," he said. He felt the hot cud of danger cutting down his breath. Did she know he had been in the kitchen that night? She couldn't know. But if she knew, how more desirable then. "It's the truth that I love you."

"Oh, please," she said, jolted into laughter again by the sheer surprise of his declaration. "Run on and see Paul Muni in the chain gang. I've got to meet Jack down at the tavern by the bridge. I'm already late."

"When?" he called after her retreating back.

"When what?" was all she answered.

As they were coming out of the movie, Mark said (in imitation of Helen Vinson as she had appeared five minutes before) "'What do you do for a living, Harry?'" And he, as Muni, vanishing into the night, said, "'I steal.' The End. Listen, did you ever tell a girl you loved her?"

"Were you sitting in that movie thinking about yourself?" Mark asked incredulously. "Haven't you got any soul at all? Here's this poor sonofabitch gets trapped onto the chain gang for what he didn't do, and you sit there with your little personal problems. Kay-rist."

"I mean it seriously and I expect a civil answer. Did you ever tell a girl—"

"I tell them all that. You've got to. You mean did I ever use those words? Naturally not. I'd feel like a hypocrite if I did and maybe laugh. What you have to do is make them think you said it when you really said something like 'It's not hard to think of loving you.' That's my line and I'm giggling inside whenever I use it."

"Does that work?"

"Of course not," Mark said. "We've still got an hour before the bus. Let's go down to the dime store and steal something. 'What d'you do for a living, darling?'"

"'I steal.'"

Among other objects that he lifted from the dime store that afternoon—a stocking cap, a palm-sized flashlight, and a screwdriver set—Harry stole a little blue-covered book of poetry on sale for twenty-five cents. It was the most feverish tour he had ever made of the counters. Usually he rationed himself to only one pair of socks or women's garters, or a single piece of fishing tackle.

The loot was deposited in the Baptist furnace with the other junk they had stolen that fall. Mark was going through it one day when he paused to read the book.

70

"What did you take this for?" he asked.

"Present for a girl," Harry said. "I told you I was in love."

"With who? Don't pull that stinky line on me. With Con? With Lucille? Don't give this to that cow. There's some good stuff in it. There's one by John Crowe Ransom about blue girls and there's something else by a Joyce that I really like. 'Wind whines and whines the shingle. The crazy pier-stakes groan ...'"

"Do you have to whine when you read it?"

"'... and in my heart how deep, unending, Ache of love,'" Mark finished. "Why not whine? It's onomatopoetic that way."

"I'm going to give it to Lucille," Harry said grimly.

"You'll end up marrying that cow and living your whole goddamned life in Harrisburg," Mark said. "And you'll get your head beat off besides."

"I don't give a damn for Jack Wagner," Harry said, against the hot knocking of his heart. "He's a goddamned bully. If he tries anything with me, I've always got the pistol."

"Hey," Mark said. "Take it easy."

"I mean it," Harry said. "Things can't go on this way."

Lucille was more pleased by his gift than he had expected. It had seemed only like an excuse for talking to her again, for however short a time. But when he knocked at her front door and whipped the blue book from under his leather coat, tears actually came to her stupid eyes.

"You bought it ... for me?"

"There's some good stuff in it," he said. "James Joyce and Johncrow Ransom."

"Well," she said. "I'll ... read it. Do you want to come in for some coffee or something? Isn't it starting to snow?"

He saw her father hoist his spectacles up his nose and peer at them from the living-room couch. Her two younger sisters crept down the stairs like big-eyed mice. Her mother's face shuttled across the kitchen door and returned to hang stationary, like a pot suspended from the lintel. His heart failed him. He couldn't go in and make like a boy friend with a girl as old as she.

"When can I see you alone?" he whispered hoarsely.

"Oh." She closed the door behind her and stepped out with him onto the wind-whipped porch. Her arms were bare and she hugged them with her hands. "I don't know, Harry. You know how I feel about you. I never could hide anything."

"Tomorrow night there's a movie at the opera house."

She shook her head. Flakes of snow were beginning to lodge in her hair. "Jack would see us. He's always hanging around uptown."

"All right. Meet me by the stockyards. Where you were that night—"

"I know," she said hurriedly. "O.K. Eight o'clock, and I'll tell them I'm going to a movie."

"Goodbye now."

"Can't you come in even for a minute?"

"I got to run and get my papers," he said.

She left a track in the new whiteness of the snow as she turned from the sidewalk to walk toward him. From the boxcar where he watched her approach Harry thought, That's bad. The snow was a bit of bad luck he hadn't counted on. Anyone might come along and see the tracks where they had no business being and investigate.

"My feet," Lucille said, as he helped her climb into the car. "Oooo, they're frozen. I had to wear decent shoes if I was going to a movie. I couldn't very well come out in Dad's four-buckles."

"I'll warm them," Harry said crisply. He rolled the boxcar door shut with little noise. One good thing about the snow was the way it muffled sounds. "Take your shoes off."

"Right," she said obediently. She sat on the gunny sacks he had brought and let him take off her shoes. Silently he chafed her feet. He tried to put his hand straight up under her dress.

"Hey," she said, laughing and putting her forehead against his cheek as she grasped and forced back his arm. She smelled of powder and a recent bath. Her cheek seemed to smell of the snow. She seemed very glad to be with him, strangely gentle in spite of the power of her grip. But she said, "Hey," and twisted him into a seat beside her.

"I might as well face it—I love you," he said. (None of Mark's ineffectual compromise now.)

"You don't love me. Any more than I love you," she said gaily. "We like each other quite a lot, though, don't we?"

"It's not hard to think of loving you," he said. (Maybe the tricky approach did work better, after all.)

"Hey," she said, rejecting his hand once more. "I read your book and I liked just what you did. 'Blue girls, under the towers of your seminary ...' I like it better than Shakespeare. Well, not really, but I like it so much."

"It's not bad," he conceded owlishly. He had not read the Ransom poem, but since there were Mark's coal-smudged fingerprints in the book (from the Baptist furnace) he had to keep up the pretense that if anyone had read it, it was he.

"I lay in my bedroom upstairs all afternoon reading them," she said, "and watching the snow come down over in Halvorsen's pasture, and I guess some of them stuck. They're all beautiful, even if I like some better than others."

No doubt they were. No doubt in their own place the labors of Ransom and Joyce were deserving of praise. But Jesus God, why did it have to be here? This boxcar should have been consecrated to some other brightness than that of verse.

The evening ended with her tongue in his mouth and the feel of her mounded coat tingling against his fingers. That—more than he had ever got from anyone, but so terribly not enough.

His next move was an attempt to spy on her with Jack again, but he came so close to being caught by a neighbor that he was really frightened. And if Jack had caught him? His talk about the pistol lying among the papers, candy and socks in the Baptist furnace did not seem so easy any more. But if Jack caught him? If it wasn't the black pistol he worried about it was that unspeakable moment when he had seen the double curve of buttocks and had thought, Mine is like hers, which, when he tried to recall it, scared him worse than the gun. What in hell was he, a maphrodite who wanted to be a good clean athlete? No. If Jack laid a hand on him he would kill him.

The hidden evening rendezvous with Lucille went on past Christmas, and gradually he forced down and destroyed the gay lightness he had felt that night in the boxcar. She wanted to talk to him. It made her feel his age again, not already old and spoiled. He knew this and grimly made the barter that both of them at length accepted. He would talk and she would endure the wrestling that he wanted in exchange. Maybe she even liked the hours of kissing that they found together. (She would say sometimes, "Oh, I want to, but it would ruin things for us. Let's not ruin you and me, Harry." "But you've done it." "Yes, I've done it." "You're still doing it with Jack." "He makes me, and you can't. I didn't mean that. I love you and not him." So it was love now, he thought sarcastically. Love was so cheap; what he wanted was so desperately beyond even imagination—except by that one act where the union would take place that must never take place otherwise, the lightning-illuminated identification of his father-mothering flesh known once with such damning briefness.)

The stalemate ended with the exhaustion of her need for a compensating drama of Virginity Recaptured. It ended, in any case, with her decision and to Harry's surprise.

One thawing Saturday in late January she met him on the street as he was going about town making the weekly collection for the papers he delivered in the evening. It seemed that she had come looking for him. It was clear enough that something bleak and painful had come up to worry her. "I want to see you tonight," she said with a failing attempt at lighthearted coquetry. Whatever her misery might come from, the fact of its existence was as clear to the eye as the wisping cloud of her breath in the winter air.

Moved a little by pity—but annoyed, too, by the impulse that muted the pure savagery with which he wanted her—he said only, "Yes. What about Jack?" Thus far all Saturday nights had been Jack's, with what other times he might demand.

"Don't be so afraid of Jack," she said with a small, wry twist of mockery in her voice.

He jingled the small change in his canvas collecting sack and asked, "Where?"

"I don't know," she said. "Can't you even think of a place? Oh, Harry, I can't count on you for anything. You can't even drive a car so we could go out in the country. Harry, what have I got myself into with you?"

"At the Baptist church," he directed. "As soon as it gets dark. Go around the corner by the alley. Push the second basement window."

"Harry! We can't go in there."

"There isn't anyplace else."

She looked away for a long minute, up the ice-bright ruts of the street toward the central square. A farmer's wagon mounted on runners for the winter went past them. The steel-shod runners shrieked on gravel exposed by the thaw. "All right," she said, "but not until after supper."

"Not after eight," he said. "What's eating you? You act so funny today. You had another fight with Jack?"

"Oh, no," she said. "I haven't seen Jack all week." She stared him down in his effort to read her secret in some betraying waver of her eyes.

He went hunting, alone, that afternoon, driven on and on under the clearest of winter skies by some imminence that seemed to hover always behind the back of his head. As he slopped through decaying snowbanks five miles from town, sick premonitions told him, too, that

74

his long stalemate with Lucille and Jack was ending. But as if he were only partly himself and already partly the wise, insatiable nemesis that sat out of sight behind his ears, the intimation came to him that he was elected the victim of the change. And it was as if the nemesis had already been directing things when he had blurted out his suggestion of a meeting place, as if it had known with perfect lucidity what he thought he had forgotten—the pistol was hidden in the furnace there. With the pistol he could force her. Yet he could not bear the idea of thus using the pistol. To drive it out of his mind, he ran at a dead run up the whole drift-covered slope of a long hill. Running, he held the Crackshot in front of his breast with both hands as the Marines charge in the movies when they break up over the sand and into the jungle to rescue the frightened blonde who is about to be raped by greasy revolutionaries. For England, home and beauty he put the last painful ounce of his energy into the daredevil attack. And when he stood on the crest of the empty hill and looked down into the blue snow shadows of the next valley, the filthy determination to use the pistol if he had to crept back like his returning breath. I won't really shoot, he told himself. I'll make sure the safety is on and just put it behind her ear and tell her coolly what she's got to do. But—damn her—she had acted so unhappy about something that she just might say, Go ahead and shoot, Harry. What if she said that, Little Harry, Lighthorse Harry?

He charged down the hill, falling where the run-off of snow had begun to freeze again. In the willow-furred ravine at the valley bottom he pulled up, staring at a stone girdled with a frilling lace of ice, thinking, It can't go on this way. It's got to end.

At six that evening he entered the Baptist church basement. Huddled into a ball for warmth, he ate some of the candy bars that he and Mark and Jimmy Store had cached there. ("It would be wrong to steal them if we weren't going to eat them," Mark had said in their first gorging after the theft. "It would be un-Indian. The red man never kills more game than he needs.") But the bars were stale to begin with and most of them had lain too long with the other junk of that magpie's nest.

When he had finished eating, he took the pistol from the furnace and went upstairs. Selecting a bench near the center of the main room, he put the pistol into the hymnbook rack of the bench ahead and lay down to wait. He did not particularly feel cold any more. He did not feel anything. He heard a few cars pass outside as the farmers began coming into town for their Saturday night, and with a weary, detached amusement he thought of what they might soon be doing. The women would be going into Finley's store to sell their eggs, shop for groceries and finger the dry goods while they waited for the men to come back for them. The men would stop by the cream station for a little gossip. Some would go to the pool hall, and some of the younger ones might go up to the dance. They would stomp around to the hillbilly music, and ... and finally everyone would go home. Out there was the world of people who went home. He was alone in the vigil of those who could not.

His watch said seven-thirty when he pulled it from his pocket. He dangled it by its chain from the hymnbook rack near his head. He watched each of its luminous hands move (he was sure that his filed senses caught the movement of the hour hand too) and thought that they were closing a final lock, turning the way a key turns in the door of a death cell.

At a quarter of eight he went back to wait by the basement window. When Lucille knelt to push it open, his face was so close to hers that she ducked back in fright.

"Harry?"

"Sure. Come in."

She giggled as she dropped to the concrete floor beside him. "I never thought I'd be breaking in here," she said. She kissed him wetly and said, "I never thought I'd be making love in church, but if you get married here, why not?"

"I never believed in marriage," Harry said. "The way I see it, if two people feel they're married that's a lot more important than having a dumb old preacher say some words over you." He did not know what he believed, or, just then, what he was saying. The words were a gambit to divert her attention from where he was leading her—up the stairs and back to the selected worshipers' bench.

She let him seat her on the bench and then she laughed again. "Well, start the sermon," she commanded into the dark. "What he's saying now is, 'Those highfalutin scientists will tell you they can look at some bones and tell you how old the world is. They think they can prove there's evolution that way. I want to ask you, could those scientists go out in your pasture, look at the old cow's bones and tell you when the old cow died?' Oh, Harry, preachers are all so silly, just like you say." Her gloominess of the morning was being swept away on the tide of her amusement. This was adventure.

He heard her gaiety rise far away. He put his hand out to touch the pistol butt and wondered, Now? Or shall I give her a chance? The touch of cold metal sickened him. He felt the hard ball of candy thrust out against the walls of his stomach and he realized he had broken the athlete's rule of eating light before a game. He had better give her a chance. He kissed her and began to unbutton her coat.

"It's so cold in here," she said. "Brrr. Wait a minute. You and I think a lot alike, Harry. What difference does it make whether some stupid preacher mumbles a marriage ceremony? That doesn't change … what's happened."

"Or what's going to happen," Harry said.

"Or what's going to happen," she agreed philosophically. "Marriage is strictly immaterial to a thinking person," she said. "Guess who just got married?"

"Dunno."

"Jack."

"Who?" A strange, wild singing had begun in Harry's ears.

"That idiot Jack Wagner. He married some slut from Oxley whose family hasn't got a nickel and so now the lazy bum is going to have to go to work. I think her father's a miner and they may have him down in the mine shoveling coal, which would serve him right. They're Catholics too and I'll bet a dollar that the reason he married her was she wouldn't give in to him otherwise; though Jack takes what he wants, so I don't know how it happened. But I heard about it and didn't even cry. I'm a thinking person and was glad enough to be rid of him if he's as stupid as he seems. But my family—oh, Lord. They're disgusting. You'd think I'd brought some terrible disgrace upon them instead of keeping them from having a moron for a son-in-law. You see, some of the times I've been meeting you I've told them I was with him, and Mother notices things—spots and tears, when there's straw from a boxcar or stuff. The old biddy will probably find a hymnbook page in my pocket tomorrow, but I don't care, after what they said to me since they found out he's married. My own damn parents."

He's gone, Harry thought, we've lost Jack and she can only think about what her silly folks said to her. "I didn't think he'd get married. A guy like that."

Lucille clutched the sheepskin collar of his coat and then buried her face in it, next to his. Then he felt her tears sliding against his cheek. "They've been so devilish with me I haven't had any time for myself," she whimpered. "Don't they think a person has any private thoughts on a thing like this? Maybe I loved him, but all they can think about is, Why didn't I hook him?" Her strong shoulder trembled. "Harry, you didn't hate Jack, did you?"

"No." He felt cleaner, purged, now that he had been able to utter this declaration—not of love, maybe, but of the lightning-colored desire that had flickered so long now in the cave of his dreams.

"I know I double-crossed you with him, but you didn't hate him?"

"I thought he was a pretty swell guy."

"Harry, this is why I can talk to you. You don't see just your own side, like everyone else in the world does. You're ... decent."

On the sweep of this praise Harry said his love words incautiously. "He was good-looking. Strong. I can see how you loved him."

"I guess I did," she said. "No, I didn't, either. I'm not much good. Harry, would you hate me if I told you a secret? The only thing I loved about him was ... what we did. He was such a dog otherwise. Do you hate me for saying that?"

"No."

"Harry, I've been so bad to you, and you're so decent. You are, you are. You're better than Jack. We're going to forget all about him. I'm going to be better to you. Really, really. I'm too tired to fight any more. I don't want to fight you, Harry. Harry, I can't fight you too."

He lay on the straps of her garter belt like a dead fly on a white web, and she said, "Never mind. It's all right. You'll do better next time."

"It's not all right," he said, choking with a failure she could never help him now to understand. "It wasn't like with Jack, was it?" he said with plummeting bitterness, expecting no remedy of answer, since it was himself who would have had to answer if either of them did. He had expected the instant of contact to recover for him the total vision that had branded him in the lightning glare; had crouched waiting for it like a child fishing over mossy water who sees the bright scales and then the form itself for an instant clear in the depths, rising, swimming toward his hand; had grasped for it in the total physical convulsion that sent the bright spray geysering around him, all gasp and rainbows; and had driven both scales and form forever out of sight, himself on shore again and, for his pains, merely wet.

The two of them lay there, both doubly bereaved of each other and the faithless Jack. Because they had to get up, both go out from this sacrilegious encounter of which they had expected so much, each had to invent a way to go.

She said, "I never knew I loved you this much. You'll do better next time."

He thought, She only wants me because she can't have him. Con Everling wouldn't have done this unless she really loved me and probably after we were married.

Covering her against the vicious cold to which he had exposed her, he said with a pretense of solicitude, "I'm sorry your folks are giving you a bad time. It's a tragedy all around that you and Jack didn't get married."

"It isn't. I'm so glad it worked out this way. I'm going to make you happy."

"Oh, I'm happy enough," he said. "Brrrr."

Silently they retraced their steps to the basement window. Before she let him open it she said, "You don't have to marry me, you know. If that's what's worrying you."

"I'm not worried. You go on ahead. It will be better if we don't go out together, and I've got to go back upstairs to get something I left."

"Oh," she said. "My word. Yes, you'd better. People would really hit the ceiling if they came in and found something like that left lying around a church."

He thought she too meant the gun, and he was quite a little shaken to think that she had noticed it. But he comforted himself by believing she thought he had put it there for their protection in case they were caught.

He went home from the church that night with hardly a thought of Jack, as if by marriage to the miner's daughter the bright lawless figure had been condemned again to work those invisible tunnels of darkness from which he had risen. "They may have him down in the mine shoveling coal," Lucille had said. Let him stay there, Harry thought.

He had other worries now. Time, which had narrowed to the black wedge described by the hands of his watch, was unfurled in the whiteness of snow that seemed to loop outward from the town over all the hills to the world's end. In the reprieve of time he could think soberly—he had better think soberly if he didn't want to be stuck down in the mine, so to speak, himself. She had said he didn't have to marry her. O.K. In the past months she had said a lot of things and then changed her mind. It seemed to him that she had a good claim on him now, or could have if this went on. He did not mean to spend the rest of his life in Harrisburg, working for her. Out and over the icy slopes of time his imagination skied. He had far to go, and if a woman went with him it would be Con Everling, who knew how to wait.

He was in full rebound toward Con in the days that followed. He dated her for the county basketball tournament and bought her for

Valentine's Day a vast heart-shaped box of candy at Will's drugstore, though he knew where he could have stolen one almost as good. He shared a hymnbook with her each Sunday night at Luther League. Her parents and her married sister began to tease him suggestively, and one night old man Everling got him in a long discussion about going to college. Though Harry argued stubbornly that he was going to be a world traveler like Floyd Gibbons as soon as high school was over, Mr. Everling was good-humoredly sure that he would go to college and make something of himself. They had been thinking of sending Con down to Stevens College, but she preferred to go to a coed school.

"So you finally got burned on that cow Lucille?" Mark asked, observing the change with unaltered cynicism.

"I play the field," Harry said. "I'm not a one-woman man."

"You will be when that Everling gets through with you. She's the kind that knows how to put a price on her cherry. When you make out with her they're going to be singing hymns over you and throwing rice. Gaaa, it makes me sick. Oh, she'll pet a little, but let me tell you the truth. You aren't going to get paid for the time you put in, let alone the money you sink on her."

"I don't care about that. You don't seem to understand decent feelings."

"From you," Mark said, "no. I figure you spend more time worrying where to get in than anybody I ever heard of. You'd take on a snake if someone would hold its head."

"I get all of that I want. Anyway, it's not what it's cracked up to be."

"You're lying."

"I'm not lying. I get it once a week—if I want it."

"Not from Con?"

"Not Con. I told you I play the field. I've got my stock lined up."

"Boy, you better watch out," Mark said. He was envious, all right—but, beyond this, disapproving and honestly worried for Harry's sake. "I hope you're using a good brand of protection."

"Na," Harry said, feeling fear and guilt and a more generalized remorse shake him, trying to cover it with a stupid veneer of acting tough. "I don't use anything. It's the babe's worry. She wants it. Let her look out."

"Here's my jackknife," Mark said. "Since you want to cut your throat, go do it the easy way."

He laughed at Mark's warning—to Mark's face. He could hardly laugh at the continuing situation that he dragged along with him. For if he had rebounded again, it was not with the simple billiard-ball ricochet that had sent him from Con to Lucille in the first place. He had not broken with Lucille, not even emotionally, as he had once broken with Con; and if he talked like Jack Wagner about Lucille (and sometimes thought of her, too, I spit on you) it was no longer because of adulation of Jack's way with her. Rather, this brutal talk was a way of punishing himself, a self-degradation performed in contriteness for what he felt her to be suffering. He pitied her now. Was it pity that her loins had been unable to bear for him the total, perverse pleasure he had once demanded? Was there still at least a taint from that impossible expectation? It did not matter. He pitied her that she too had wanted so much—her expectation no less impossible than his—and got nothing for her pains except to be tossed from one pair of faithless hands to another. Now, in the unleashing of time and in the growth it had forced on him, pity was no longer antipathetic to desire. He could see her now as doomed and hurt by the female condition from which he had once dreamed so fiercely of liberating his mother—and in the sweeping current of his pity would feel desire for her waking once again. He would arrange meetings with her then in spite of his resolutions. On the couch in her living room and, when the weather was milder in the advance of spring, in haymows and finally on her back lawn (always in the dark and always with a panicking haste) he tried to appease them both with what both knew was an inept sin.

"I told you it would ruin us," she used to say quietly afterward.

If you knew what I didn't, he thought mournfully, then why did you let it happen? "We're not ruined," he said doggedly—so many times. And she would think about this a while as if he had delivered a careful opinion and agree, "No, I guess it's just fun as long as we're careful. You are careful every time, aren't you?" "Yes," he said, because in the mire of his own guilt and pity for her he could not bear to admit his trickery or to make her worry. "You're getting better," she said. "Maybe we'll turn out all right." If we could just quit this, he thought. If I was man enough to stop.

Then, in May, she did not come to him immediately when she believed she was pregnant. He, in the exultation of the weather and some heart-to-heart talks with his real girl Con, believed that at last Lucille had understood what he never dared tell her, or that she had another convenient boy friend. (He had tried to interest Mark in her once. Mark was too smart. But there were plenty of young men in town looking for what she had too much of, and it seemed to him that some of them might be more fun for her than he was.) It even seemed possible that Jack Wagner—five months married now—might be ready to resume his office. Well, let poor dumb Jack take over.

He could not quite afford to give up his imagined solution even when she told him the truth. Particularly because she was so calm, the temptation remained to think, She's not sure.

"What are we going to do?" he asked, imitating her calm.

"Wait another two weeks," she said. "Can you think of anything else to do?"

"We could get married," he said.

She laughed in his face. "You lied to me, didn't you, Harry? Were you ever careful?"

"All but once."

"Oh, no. But I knew you were a liar. I should have known this would happen. At least a man would have been too scared to—"

"O.K. I'm not a man."

"You're my bargain, Harry. Don't worry. We'll wait."

That very night, after the dance at the opera house, he walked Con Everling up to the highway viaduct that passed over the railroad tracks, and under the benign stars he asked her to marry him. It seemed to him the ultimate of recklessness, and now he felt himself committed to recklessness. In the simple justice of retribution he had to take all the chances there were.

Con laughed mournfully. "I wish you'd waited a little longer before you asked me, Harry."

"I can't wait much longer." The luminous constellations moved like watch hands, narrowing his time again to the black wedge where all sin is done and where it must be paid for.

"Silly. You could wait two more years at least. No one gets married any younger than that." Two years—time enough for dinosaurs to hatch and glacial icecaps to creep down from the poles to chase them away. Time enough for Lucille's child to recognize its daddy.

"I can't wait that long. You don't know what goes on in my mind."

"I know you have a busy mind," she said. "Buzz, buzz, buzz. It's running all the time. But that doesn't change anything."

"I think about my uncle," he said. "Maybe he was right to take the old rope. I don't think it's the coward's way at all. It may be the bravest way."

"Harry!"

"Look down at those rails," he said. "You stand here until the engine is twenty feet away. Then alley-oop." He feinted a vault on the viaduct rail, thinking, as the sweat crept in his armpits, But I'm not really kidding this time.

"If you talk like that I'm going home. Don't spoil it, Harry. Tonight started out so perfect."

"Oh, deary dear, I'd hate to spoil a perfect night."

"Harry, what have I done that makes you this way?"

"I asked you to marry me and you say I'm not a man yet."

"I didn't say that." Her soft small fingers moved cajolingly on his neck. "Harry, look at the stars. It always helps to look up when you're feeling low. Harry, I know what you mean about getting married. Don't you think I have my dreams, too? It isn't so hard to think of loving you."

"What?" He jerked away as if a bee had stung him.

"Harry! You're crazy tonight. If you're not nicer to me I might as well go home. That's better," she said as he kissed her and put his hands around her waist, "ever so much better. When you're good, you're very, very good and when you're bad you're—Harry."

"There's so many things you don't count on in this life, Con. You've got to believe me. It's all fun to sit around and talk about maybe we'll go to the same college. It can't happen. It can't."

"I see it in the stars."

"You've got to realize I'm serious. Just do one thing for me, huh? Give me an answer. Will you marry me?"

She looked very solemnly at him. He could see the whites of her eyes enlarge. She said caressingly, "Yes, Harry, I will."

"All right. There's just one other thing. You know how I think. I'm a lone wolf and I don't have a lot of use for formalities and ministers saying a lot of blah over you, and there isn't time. Did you hear this radio program where the girl died of appendicitis before she could marry her sweetheart, and afterward it comes out that they'd spent a week together at a cabin camp when her folks thought she was visiting her aunt …"

"What on earth are you talking about?"

"… and the point of the whole thing is, her father's glad when he finds out about her lying, because even if she's dead nothing can ever take away from the sweethearts what they've had together."

"Harry, I'm afraid of you when you talk the way you have tonight. You've spoiled everything."

"Yes. I spoil everything," he said. "It's nice tonight and the stars are fine and I spoil it all."

"Oh, don't think you're so important," she said. "It's late. Walk me home."

He woke at five-fifteen in the morning when he heard the milk train rush under the viaduct. The first streaks of dawn were in the sky. The smell of greenery was in the breeze. Intermittently a rain crow called from the direction of the railroad embankment. Now the light came in to touch the red feathers of his hunting arrows and the whitish crescent of his bow, hung above his worktable with the pictures of Jimmy Doolittle, Frank Luke and Cotton Warburton. A little spider dangled from the filament it had spun down from the window curtain. It swayed with a joyous ease back and forth. Like a hanged man in the antic of death. "I spoil everything," he said.

The streets of the town seemed swollen with Lucille's presence. He did not know as the deadline ending the two-week wait approached whether he was avoiding her or looking for her as he rode his bike around or went delivering his papers or ran home from school. He did know that she was hinted everywhere in the green fecundity of the season. The lilac buds swelled. The neighbors' cat bore a stunning number of kittens. Hap MacDougall's wife went around looking like she had a basketball under her dress. Jack Wagner announced to his cronies at the pool hall—and Harry heard it secondhand from Mark— that his wife was going to show how good a Catholic she was in September. Hens seemed to cackle all day long in everyone's back yard. Two dogs were led to couple one Saturday night in the cream station and then scampered, wild with terror and still linked back to back with a horrible ligature, from one side of the room to another while Don Alpen sprayed them from a hose and the crowd of men roared their amusement.

The human heart could not stand two weeks of this waiting. But two weeks was very short. He had not actually seen Lucille for half of that time when she sent him word through Mark that he was to meet her one afternoon by the bandstand. He was to ride his bike there and go ahead with the delivery of his papers if she didn't show up.

"What's going on?" Mark asked in honest grief. "I never heard of anything so spooky. Is she trying to blackmail you?"

"That's nobody's business."

"Look. We can use Plan A and hit for Colorado now. I won't even go home for clean clothes if it's that bad."

"Let's cut out the kid talk," Harry said.

"All right. It's your funeral."

The ultimatum was ready for him and he could not face it. He sat from eleven in the morning until four-thirty in the basement of the Baptist church with the pistol at his feet. He watched the shadows of branches and low-growing shrubs move on the frosted glass of the windows so that he would not have to look at the gun until the last minute. He tried not to remember the coupled dogs shivering under the onslaught of water, but it was all he could do to keep from barking his terror as they had barked.

He picked up the pistol and looked down the barrel. It was like everything he had seen before rather than like a gun. Like the reflection of the day moon in a cistern, he could see the copper-tipped end of the bullet when he held the pistol in a certain light. Moon in the cistern, fish in the moss-dark pool, it was what he had wanted. All he had ever truly wanted.

He felt very sleepy as he watched the fish (or the moon) seem to enlarge as if now it were truly coming to his hand. Sleep now, dream now, find it now.

With a jolt he shook himself awake. There was no use rushing it. He put the gun back on the floor. It would be there when he wanted it, and in the meantime he had to examine every wonderful flaw in the cement of the floor, every wave in the uneven surface of the window glass through which he saw the shadows, every splintery miracle of the raw lumber in the floor over his head. Between sleep and full consciousness he begged, Let me stay here, and now the church, which had seemed so empty of everything except the phantoms with which his eroticism had populated it, seemed full of Gracious Ones who could stoop to save him if they chose. Even if it's dull as a sermon, he begged them, let me stick around and hear it all. The leaden minutes filed up through the hollow handle of his world, gleamed, and pierced his eggshell skull. They all hurt, but what hurt most was that one of them would be the last.

No, he said.

The silence in which no one came said, Yes.

Let there be some mice at least, he prayed, anything at all for company. But it was broad daylight and the mice God might have sent him by night stayed hidden in the walls.

No, he said. I won't do it. The silence said, No one else is going to and it has to be done. Thy will be done, Harry. Thy will be done.

His watch said four-thirty. He was already late. By now if he had not been a coward he would have been at the bandstand to hear the news.

He took off his shoes and began running silently from side to side of the basement, returning always past the stuffed belly of the furnace and the one black item that counted from all his pilfering. I won't do it until I've worn myself out, he thought. There's no use wasting all this energy that I can use.

His breath grew short from the running, and then he wanted to sing. With the first gasping note he got out gagging, he heard someone tap or kick against one of the windows. They've come to stop me even from this, he thought. He quit the song and walked dutifully to where the pistol lay on the concrete. Before they interrupted he had to finish the business that was private, between No God and himself. He thumbed the safety off and stared right down the barrel. The angle of light was wrong this time, and he saw no moon-shaped curve of the bullet's nose. It would come out of the dark.

"Harry," Lucille said. "Harry, be careful."

"How did you get in?" he said. Sluggishly he recognized her, though she was dressed in Sunday clothes and seemed so unlike anyone he had ever been in the basement with before.

"Harry," she said cajolingly, coming like his mother to take something dangerous out of his infant grip. He let her take the pistol. She laid it on the floor before she took him in her arms to cradle his head on her breast. "Harry, Mark said you might be here. It's all right, Harry. Everything's all right."

"I spoil it all," he said from a dry mouth.

"Harry, why I wanted to see you was to tell you not to worry."

"Did you see them laugh at those goddam dogs?"

She shook him roughly and said, "Harry, Harry, wake up. There aren't any dogs."

"What are you doing here?"

"I came to tell you, is all. I'm not going to have a baby."

"Why'd you tell me you were?" He began to blubber awfully.

"Because I was," she said. "Now I'm not. It's all right now. That's what I wanted to tell you, Harry. Now you can go out and celebrate with Connie."

"I don't want Con. I don't want anyone."

"Hush," she said. "There's no use crying. Hush."

"But I did such terrible things."

"I guess we both did. Maybe some old preacher would think we ought to go to hell for it. I never had a lot of faith in what they said. We lived through it all right. What else do we have to say?"

Now laughing, crying, he hung with his arms around her neck, against that good, sturdy body dressed in its best clothes. "But I was so goddam dumb," he said, not loudly, but with his breath roaring it, cascading it out of the full treasury of his relief.

"Well, I wouldn't argue about that," she said.

Gently, firmly she thrust him back from her. "Now stand up by yourself," she commanded.

It was over, but the cleaning up remained to be done. "Old Mrs. Chisholm was out in her back yard and saw me come in here," she said. "We can't hang around much longer. She'll call someone and they'll be down to investigate."

"You didn't have to come," he said in stupid gratitude.

"Mark said you looked scared to death." She made no reference then or ever later to the gun she had found in his hand—only to his fear.

They dropped the gun down between a wooden wall and the stone foundations. Quickly he went to the furnace and set a match to all the loot that had been accumulating there through the winter. This was the emergency evacuation plan he had worked out with Mark and Jimmy Store. "Someone will see the smoke," Lucille protested, but when she glanced inside at the bank correspondence, the stocking caps, the fishing tackle and the candy boxes she fell silent in agreement. Only she said, "I'm getting out now. I'll walk right out the basement door, since it's only bolted. And if anyone sees you go out … I might just go to your folks and tell them everything."

"Goodbye," he said. "I'm sorry."

"Goodbye was all you had to say."

An hour later he sat on a hill just outside town and watched Mr. Everling, Tim Carey and Waldo Smith arrive separately, but within five minutes of each other, to enter the church and see why a plume of dun-colored smoke came from its chimney on this mild May evening. They won't find anything, he told himself. We were careful about that at least, and all there is left to show is the smoke.

[NOTE: Here the chapter and the main part of the Irene-Lucille narrative ends. Insofar as the Clem-Harry story touches on the two years following, the center of interest is displaced to Con Everling, Mark Fuller and the comic squabbles between Harry's parents. The times Clem referred to Irene-Lucille later were invariably colored by the sense of debt to her which was perhaps a product of the rethinking of the past that went into its composition. Insofar as I can grasp her role in his life, it is as the retreating, backward-smiling figure of three more short passages—D. H.]

The first:

Harry knew as soon as he heard Jack Wagner talking that he was telling about Lucille's troubles. And he knew that it was his simple duty to shut Jack up.

The five men in the cream station made a loose ring around its walls. Harry was in the ring when he dropped his paper sack and sat on the scales to listen. "Damn right she'll have the kid before September," Jack Wagner said. "And the reason I know is she went back to the same place she got the first one knocked last spring—which is where I told her to go when she came whining around me that first time telling me she's in trouble."

"That doctor in Bremerton?" someone asked.

"Ho ho," Jack said. "Ho ho. He'll do it, but he works for cash and nobody pays Lucille. She's lost everything but her amateur standing. She works for fun. No, I'll tell you if you all won't ever tell anyone else. I mean you too, Harry."

The reflections in his blue eyes looked like nail points. Harry met the stare without a word.

"It was Doc Store. They went out of town to do it, but it was good old Doc Store. So when she's damn fool enough to let it happen again she goes back to the Doc and asks him will he fix her again. And what he said to her, what he said, was, 'I guess I might be able to do the job for you, but I'm damned if I ain't too worn out to take my pay for it again,' and he talked her into getting married this time. As he says, it would just go on happening, and it would kill him if he had to let her pay him off for it every time."

"And who's the guy?"

"It's that Farm Bureau agent she used to monkey around with."

"Wall, now, is it his kid, Jack, or is it yourn?"

Jack snapped his gloves against his knee, stood up to go and said, "We'll have to wait and see about that. But I'll tell you one thing, I sort of helped Doc Store save himself from taking all them payments. We sort of got to help our fellow man out in a town like this, ain't that right, Harry?" He tapped Harry's stocking cap with his gloves as he paused by the door to end his joke.

Harry was on his feet, taut and glaring, stopped from the pure, justifying disaster of striking and being smashed only by starting to think too quickly. He might be on the verge of letting go a secret that was not his to open.

"Whatsa matter, Harry? You nervous?"

"I happen to be nauseated, Wagner. Permit me to depart?" He stepped in front of Jack—then, halfway down the block, cursed himself wild as he realized that Jack might not know what "nausea" meant.

He got some tiny fragment of honor back a week later, when he stopped to watch a horseshoe game behind the garage. A stray dog had wandered near the pitchers and Jack kicked it in the head. With no lapse for thinking this time, Harry swept a stone the size of his fist from the ground and slammed it into Jack's ribs. Jack went down.

Ashen-faced, maybe still more surprised and scared than angered, Jack said, "Why'd you do that? I think you broke my ribs."

"Go get Doc Stone to fix you up, you whore," Harry said.

Now Jack was on his knees, supporting the weight of his shoulders by resting on his knuckles, and he was smiling whitely through the pain. "I heard that," he said.

"All right, boys," Tiny Overst said. He was one of the farmers who had been pitching horseshoes. "Wagner, I guess you had it coming for kicking the kid's dog." Tiny was getting up steam slowly as he spoke, and when he had finished he was bouncing his three hundred pounds lightly and furiously on his toes. His face looked like raw beef. "There was no call for you to kick his dog," Tiny repeated.

His brother came up to grab his arm and whisper eerily, "Don't kick him, Tiny. You'll kill him. He heard you."

"I didn't know it was his dog," Jack said.

"Well," Tiny said to Jack, "you know it now."

Suddenly Harry owned a dog.

The second:

Harry had begun to read books again—as distinct from either Collier's or Liberty magazine serials or the texts he was assigned in school—for the first time since he had finished the Tom Swift books and the adventures of the second-generation Rover Boys. From the tiny library shelves of the high school he read *Ramona, Ben Hur, The Long Hunt, Main Street, Scottish Chiefs, David Copperfield, Winesburg, Ohio, So Big* and *The General* (illustrated with stills from the Buster Keaton movie).

In reading *Main Street* he made a strong identification between the heroine, Carol Kennicott, and Lucille Zachary Benson. Both of them had wanted so badly to move out of the trap of small towns. Both of them had some pitiable letch for culture and the finer things. (He remembered Lucille's cornet and the blue poetry book and cried a few maudlin tears.)

89

It came to him that he could identify most of the people he knew with characters from *Winesburg* and *Main Street*—and this of all things was most strange, to see people simultaneously in two ways. They remained themselves, but through fiction became someone else as well. It was like looking into a goldfish tank from a certain angle and seeing, by the refraction of the water, the top of the fish at the same time that he saw its profiled side.

He talked about this discovery a little bit to Mark, but he needed to talk it over with a girl. More and more since the day when Mark had broken the code to send Lucille after him, they had to talk to each other about serious subjects with a cynical, even cryptic, irony. He thought that Mark must know he had been about to kill himself, that Mark was both frightened and disgusted by the knowledge. At any rate Mark blocked the way to a broadening discussion by saying, "O.K. Lucille is Main Street Mollie and naturally you're the hero?"

It was no use trying to talk about it with Con. He dared not let slip to her a hint of how his emotions could still flare out toward Lucille. And Con's line was "Don't you get enough of books in school?" She was trying to teach him to dance and was impatient anyway with his lack of progress. "You think you're such an athlete and you can't even control your body!" She didn't seem to think it made any difference, even, when he told her she was Helen White, the banker's daughter in *Winesburg*. Maybe she felt this was a cutting reference to her father's role in the Harrisburg bank's failure.

The simple truth was that he wanted to talk with Lucille about the implications of his discovery. He thought of all that he had wasted in the passionate times they had been together. He was far along now in the process of forgiving himself for the worst he had done to her. He could have returned to pick up where they had once gone astray—if by this time she hadn't married, moved to a neighboring town and produced a baby.

The strangest thing of all would have been to make her say, in understanding, "Yes, I am Carol Kennicott, but at the same time am Lucille Zachary Benson." That would have been to replace himself as observer of the goldfish in the bowl with a third image of it. If he could do that, his eerie thought teased him, then he, Harry, could step back and take his hands off and something would begin to work like a perpetual-motion machine.

When he went hunting with that stray dog he had been forced into adopting after he had slammed Jack, he was no longer so interested in finding rabbits or squirrels to kill. (The dog wouldn't track, anyhow, its sole utility was to keep up the alliance with Tiny Overst that protected him from Jack.) The trick of the three goldfish, or some variant of it, often absorbed him as he walked. He still believed then that if he had not thrown away Lucille's help he would know already how to make it work. And from the despair with his own compounded folly he made a slogan that was for Lucille if it was for anyone besides himself: "The worst thing about books is that you always find them after you've lived through them." If he had known she was Carol Kennicott he would not have dared to hurt her as crassly as he had.

He had seen Lucille not more than a dozen times since she walked out the front door of the church basement almost two years ago. From a distance he had seen her swollen with pregnancy at a Lutheran Easter service. The fact that she looked happy had done nothing at all to quell the sudden horror of seeing her appear that way in public. Now and then on Saturday nights (and sometimes when he was with Con) he had seen her sitting in a car parked on the square, holding her baby. Then his puzzle of the goldfish would become intolerable to think of. For if, through the medium of fiction, there might be a way to father that third image over which he puzzled, could there not also be a way to show his parental kinship with this child, which only in fact was not his own?

He had spoken to Lucille exactly once. At Christmas time he had bumped into her on the post office steps. She was holding her eight-month-old child against the same cloth coat that he remembered so well, protecting its face against the chill of fog with a swaddling of blankets that seemed likely to smother it. "Uh, hello, Lucille. Don't see much of you these days," he said.

"No. Don't get back to Harrisburg very often," she said. Then from ear to ear, all sunlight, June and flowering shrubs, her smile spread. An irrepressible giggle burst from deep within, as if she had tricked the ultimate powers of winter itself. She peeled the blankets back from the squinching red face.

"Here's our boy," she crowed.

The third:

On the night of the senior party in the schoolhouse, he and Mark were sitting in the superintendent's office. They really weren't supposed to be in this room, and lately they had been very cautious about entering where they were not supposed to be; the time of the skeleton keys and the constant pilfering was long gone. But in the May night and the licensing sense that something truly would end with their graduation, they had withdrawn from the main party down in the gymnasium and had found this unlocked door. Con was dancing with someone else, and Mark's girl, Beuleen Chisholm, was making a damn fool of herself flirting with the basketball coach.

They threw open the office windows and perched on adjacent sills.

"I'm going to smoke," Mark said. "To hell with it."

"Me too. Pass the Bull."

They each rolled cigarettes and sat at ease blowing smoke out among the rain-dripping leaves.

"What a bunch of crap they hand you when you graduate," Mark said. "All this about high school being the happiest years of your life. What they don't know. It's got to get better than this."

"I don't expect much," Harry said.

"Christ, neither do I, but whatever they hand me I'm not going to piss and moan about it. At least it will be going somewhere. The one thing I wouldn't stand is if some god would say to me I had to go back and live through anything again."

Passing under the street light on the corner, a girl in a belted coat with a green tam on her head and an open umbrella hurried toward them.

"Would you live through it all again? All this crud?" Mark asked.

"Hell, no," Harry said.

The umbrella shadow lengthened ahead of the girl and moved away from her face. He recognized Lucille and his breath caught in surprise because the girl had looked so young in the rain, younger than Con on the night of the corn festival.

Impulsively he whistled, and when she stopped and lifted her face toward his window he called, "Hey, Lucille, come on up a minute. The door's unlocked. Come sit a while."

He could see her shaking her head, and it seemed to him she must be whispering an answer he couldn't hear.

"Don't be afraid," he said. Then a little more anxiously, coaxingly, as she edged down the sidewalk, "Where you going on a night like this?"

"I'm not going anywhere," she called back over her shoulder as she walked on.

"Bitches are all alike," Mark said. "You wouldn't want, for example, to get involved with her again, would you? I've made up my mind. I'm going to take my Navy physicals next week. No sense waiting. And I'm going to apply for duty as far away from this burg as they'll send me. You're not listening."

"Yes I am," Harry said. He heard the rain drip on the gravel of the schoolyard and on the homely shingles. The rain made everything so small, he thought, all space so tiny you could touch its edges with your outstretched hand. And yet in this smallness that he and Mark and Lucille and Jack and Con had sifted so fine was lost the one round coin they could not afford to miss. "You said you wouldn't live through all this crud again and I agreed with you."

"All right. So come with me when I take my physicals. If you go to college you'll always be coming back here. Cut clean and see the world."

"I don't know," Harry said. The small rain fell. Lucille had vanished past the third street light. The superintendent's clock ticked. His heart beat again, again, again, again, again.

The editor Plankton asked, when he was working with Clem on recomposing the novel, "Just how much of this is autobiographical?" after he had made the point that autobiography was a dirty word in the best book-reviewing circles.

By his own account, Clem answered, "Well, if you take into account the style—"

"I'm not interested in style. Isn't it, after all, mostly your own reminiscences? Now this stuff where Harry thinks about the books and the goldfish—that may have been very important to you, Clem Anderson, in your own life, because you're a poet. But your character Harry isn't a poet, he's typical. And anyway, the goldfish don't come through to me. What have the goldfish got to do with it?"

Sweating, Clem said, "Well, the kid thinks if he can just get three goldfish to do by themselves what he has to help them do—that is, be seen—he'll have achieved art. It's like Joyce saying an artist ought to set his art machine in motion and then let it run while he sits back like a god paring his fingernails. Harry's got the same nation in a rudimentary, nonepigrammatic form."

"Mmmmm. But Harry's not an artist."

"That's true," Clem conceded, "except in the sense that everym—"

"So that part ought to go. And all that stuff about Clem—I mean Harry—banging this girl at such an early age is going to make him come through very untypically for the average reader."

This was before the days of the Kinsey report, and Clem had no answer. ("Except," Clem said in recounting this conversation, "what if I'd told him about Ruth Nielson, Vonnie Searles and Betty Otis, not to mention the romantic places my mother found the lipstick traces?")

"So it ought to go," Plankton said, dismissing seven hundred pages, "and we'll come in where Harry gets his draft notice. Having him mixed up with two other girls before he finds Melissa is going to tax the reader enough."

"If that's the way you want it," Clem said.

"That's not the way I want it," Plankton said. "This house never dictates to its authors."

"No offense intended."

"It's merely that I see a fine book in all this, Harry, and I don't want you to run your colt under wraps, so to speak."

"All right," Clem said.

"I think so, too," Plankton said thoughtfully. Then, more at ease, he threw himself back in his swivel chair, removed the felt hat he usually wore for serious work and smiled. "For curiosity's sake, though, would you mind telling me what Harry saw in that darn kitchen?"

"That's not autobiographical," Clem said. "It never happened, and the bit about the near-suicide didn't really happen either, though we had a gun and a pregnancy is a worrisome kind of occasion."

"No doubt," Plankton said sympathetically, then pursued, "Well, what does he think he saw?"

And Clem said, "It's a Creation fantasy, in which Harry, after he's repudiated his actual father and even the symbolic fathers of his remote family and the church, sees himself in the avatar of his hypothetical mother enduring what must have been done in that flash of light and heat which, as Jung would say, is our racial memory of the first explosion from which the universe is still expanding away. His, Harry's, uneasy compulsion to repeat the knowledge of that initial élan, explosion, is his lust for the knowledge of good and evil copulating in himself, which, like God, or anyone else sensible, he would rather see objectified in two bodies, or three bodies, if you can imagine a sandwich, than merely have giving him fits in his dream life. Like any other expelled male mortal he suffers the hope that if he gets past the ice-girt stone of chastity at the vaginal gate, he can return to the three-in-oneness which he must not only have experienced in the instant of his conception, but have seen re-enacted for him by these particular people, Jack and Lucille. He wants to be father and to be had by father, to be mother and to have mother.

"The water, the stone, and the stolen pistol are the key symbols found in the objective world by which he must solve the problem he finds scribbled on the slate of his subjectivity. The images of white-underwear frills of frozen water around the quintessential stone and the rain water which will not slake thirst suggest the tricky ambiguities presented by water from the source, the mossy pool, or the cistern in which he catches the garter snake, he a garter snake of another stripe himself, his green swimming brother recognized and drawn forth—and by the way, once I was looking into our cistern, at the reflection of the day moon this time, when my father whacked me on the side of the head for some reason, an error and he said he was sorry—that mythic cistern of the giant woman in which he fishes for the phallic-formed gilled thing that will emerge into daylight only as the boy baby that Lucille presents jokingly to him, the significantly fictive father, thus satisfying in ideal terms the search for happiness in trinity that he could never glimpse with his senses but only intuitively recognized at the moment he calls himself Harriet, and the only other way to have been satisfied would have been to arrange a sandwich, which for an uninstructed boy in a Midwestern town is not easy."

Plankton said, "Wow." He smiled around the tall bookshelves and the Babel tower of manuscripts in his office as though projecting himself to the audience of a TV quiz program. "Admitting—all—that," he said, "what—did—Harry—think—they—were—doing?"

"That Jack is doing?"

"You tell me," Plankton said. He began to polish his glasses, slowly, deliberately.

"Cornholing," Clem said.

Plankton lifted the glasses, squinted through one lens at the holiday decorations outside on Madison Avenue. Sulking over one more evasive answer, and no doubt bitter that he was here called on to deal with a poet and amateur rather than with a professional novelist, and yet determined to keep patience in the hope of learning by patience alone what strange crops grew on those lank, far fields beyond the Hudson, he said, "I see. Planting corn."

# III

# AN HEIR OF THE DRAKE ESTATE

*How exquisitely the individual Mind*
*... to the external World*
*Is fitted:—and how exquisitely too*
*The external World is fitted to the Mind.*

—WORDSWORTH, The Prelude

# 4

IN THE AFTERMATH of Clem's lecture and brief stop with us in Blackhawk, both Janet and I wrote to Sheila. We sent separate letters, but each of them was trimmed and recast many times and probably made unfortunately artificial by the discussions we had before we put them in the mail.

Janet's letter was incautious, I felt. She had written from a fury that seemed to find its reasons from the very arguments I made to temper it. Partisan, unconditional, she had ended by blaming Clem for what seemed in the light of hindsight to be a lifetime of duplicity. She apologized for ever having taken his part. She had been "an idiot" gulled by his false air of dependency, his earnest pretenses of following the crooked, hard road to goodness. (Reading these sentiments, I argued that one can't be mistaken about a friend for fifteen years and then be suddenly "corrected" by the revelations of a day. No? Well, I hadn't heard his great line, she said. No, I hadn't been in the room when she asked him, "What is it you intend to do with this girl you're meeting in Chicago?" He had answered in language poetically calculated to offend what Janet had become as well as what she had been. "Don't you know, Janny? We're going to fuck till we scream." Surely that offensiveness gave her the right to revise the ancient loyalties and re-examine all she had thought most settled in her attitude toward him.)

Incautiously she had invited Sheila and their children to spend the summer with us at our habitual retreat in Colorado. It could be like the good summer we had all spent in Mexico years ago. (I pointed out that we would not "all" be together again if Sheila accepted. Attempts to relive a past from which Clem had been willfully erased might boomerang unpleasantly, for Sheila as well as for us.)

On the other hand, I must grant Janet's criticism that my letter was "pedantic" and "cool"—even more so than I am, she implied. Every attempt at expressing a natural feeling was met and blocked in my mind by a plethora of conditioning memories that throttled it before I could get the words on paper. How should one address the faithful Desdemona in the kingdom of shadows? "You had bad luck, honey— next time you marry, be more careful and it may turn out better"? I could not think that one should address love in this way, though love had miscarried, and it was impossible to think I was addressing less. Of

97

course I did not literally see Sheila as Desdemona, but the dismaying similitude between this separation and a death continued to haunt me, and I would have expected that Sheila, if asked who had done this to her, would have answered, "No one. I myself."

So, poor back-broken things, neither honest nor just, our letters went off to her within a few days of each other. I could not remember mine without a shudder of disgust—and a sense that it fairly represented my inadequacy to face the magnitudes of tragedy.

She answered from the far side of the moon. She was glad Clem had told us "the news" and apologized for "procrastination" that she had not done so herself. It was one's duty, she felt, to keep old friends informed when "changes" were in the wind.

She appreciated our invitation for the summer, but she was too busy with new plans to think of coming to us. She would be back in New York soon for the divorce hearings. She had to keep her lawyers from taking Clem's pelt altogether(!) and at the same time make plans for the children. A New York friend had suggested she might do a column of theater gossip for a Village newspaper that was being organized, since she knew "now" so much of the inside story of that crowd, and she was trying very hard to work up some samples before she flew in to the city. Had Clem got around to mentioning Beauty Bear? (Had he not!) She would send us a copy when it was off the press. Her children sent their love to our children.

At a mean and practical level her letter was a relief. Cosmetics hid the skull. Desdemona hath acquitted herself like Maggie Verver, I thought, grateful for the less than heroic ruses that get us by the dark gates so many times. We could tell ourselves we had done what we could. Nothing.

Or nothing but think—as many others besides ourselves around Blackhawk were thinking. Clem had impinged somewhat below the superficial order of the spring semester.

One current rumor had it that he had "blown his cork" at the dean's party. An ambulance had arrived to take him away. He had been smuggled out of town under heavy sedation. (True in a way, I thought. Berthed with a popular opiate, cork-blown Adonis dreaming himself a dog's life.) In New York, it was said, he was once again under the constant psychiatric supervision that he should never have tried to do without. His nervousness on the platform when he read was cited to support this story. I had, though, to debunk all this explicitly for Calvin Stipe. He might have needed sedation if he had thought it true, for it conflicted with his image of Clem as dean-smashing iconoclast.

A filthy and bespectacled undergraduate was overheard in the men's room of the library declaiming, "The law, like Noah's rainbow, bends from earth to earth" by someone who recognized it as Clem's verse.

The campus bookstore got a belated rush of orders for *Angel at Noon*, *The Throne of Oedipus* and Clem's first volume of poetry, *Sugar Oboe*. Mason Forsberg, who teaches contemporary lit., told me that four of his students wanted to do papers on Clem's work.

Then one fine May day a freshman girl named Bonnie Waller came into my office wanting to talk about him.

I recognized her from her picture in the college newspaper and had talked about her with some colleagues of my own age and with Janet. She had been the entry of the Jewish sorority in the contest to select a campus beauty queen—hence the photograph. Her last name struck an echo.

Her stepfather, Stewart Waller, had been one of the publicized figures of the New Deal in its early days. When Clem and I were in college he was already beginning to fade back out of public prominence, but just at the outbreak of the war he had come back as a member of Willkie's entourage. He had been one of those who spoke out most powerfully for intervention against Germany, before and after the blitz was put to Poland. In 1942 he had married the refugee widow of a German Jew who had been turned over to the Gestapo by the French police. That was almost the last one had heard of Waller—as it was the first one had heard of Eric Stein. In 1933 Stein had been on a rubber band that he could stretch to get away from Germany but that always pulled him back. He had gone to Czechoslovakia and had tried to settle there. Then Holland, from which he had sent his family to the States before he went to France.

The sheer cynicism of the French in handing him over to the Germans brought him finally to the world's attention, and for a few days a great deal was written about him in the world press. It was said then that he had remained in Germany after the revolution of '33 to fight Hitlerism and to help other Jews escape; that he had been mutilated in a concentration camp by Streicher's bullies; that he had gone to Czechoslovakia as a secret emissary to warn Beneš of the Munich deal already known to be cooking among the Cliveden Set; that the French police made a special effort to hunt him down because he had beaten a Doriot thug whom he caught abusing a crippled Jewish veteran. All those things and much more were said of him in a time when the slogans were different. They may be all true, or not. What is certain is that he was a Jew who did not run far enough and fast enough, a Jew who did not live to see his daughter become a beauty at the end of her teens.

The photograph had not quite prepared me for Bonnie. With her clear skin, blue eyes, good teeth and black hair, she was better-looking than I would have expected. If I said she had the coloring of everybody's stereotype of the Irish girl, that would be correct but would still leave unsaid that the ultimate finesse of complexion, teeth, hair and figure came almost visibly from American diet, dentistry, exercise, good habits and cosmetics. When you looked at Bonnie Waller you saw all those barrels of milk she had drunk, all those summers she had vacationed in the sun.

But I saw also, or thought I did, a certain vacancy in her eyes that put me on guard.

When she had introduced herself timidly, and I had with some curiosity asked her to sit down, she showed me the two books of Clem's poetry she was carrying, still in fresh dust jackets from a bookstore. "How do you read this stuff?" she asked. Only a slight twisting of her shoulders seemed to apologize for the rudeness of her phrasing, as if to say she would have used a better word if she had had one.

"Modern poetry is difficult ..." She wasn't listening. She wasn't quite there, behind the cornflower eyes, and in their blue reflection of the day neither was I. She wanted a Voice to answer her, I thought irritably, not a teacher.

"Why do you want to read them? If you want to read anything of Mr. Anderson's, why don't you start with his novel? It's easier."

"I've read that," she said. "It doesn't tell me ..."

"What?"

"I don't know," she said. Her eyes created me again, as if they were magic lanterns throwing me two-dimensionally on a white wall.

"Then you're in trouble, if you don't know what it is you want to be told."

"Yes. Trouble."

Uncomfortably I made the professorial chuckle and tried again to get with her in whatever dimension she was listening. "If you're looking for a message you may be disappointed. Modern poetry doesn't exactly specialize in messages. It's neither a sermon nor a how-to-do-it series."

"I know that," she said. A frown brought her black eyebrows close together. "I've heard that said in class. I've copied it down in my notebook three or four times, I suppose, but that isn't what I mean."

"You don't know what you mean, isn't that it?" I said severely. I wanted at least to ruffle the composure with which she was confronting me, like the surface of a perfect sphere. "Or you won't say."

"Maybe that's it. I won't say." She laughed. She was unruffled in her perplexity. I should have known that it was beyond my pedagogic power to disturb a young woman wrapped in so beautiful a sphere of confidence that even football heroes liked her just as she was.

"If you won't say—or ask more explicitly—then we'll have a pretty silly conversation, won't we?"

"Why didn't he come to the Union to meet the students? There were a lot of them there who wanted to see him."

"The English secretary was supposed to announce that he'd been unexpectedly called away."

"Oh, she did. Everyone who had come was disappointed."

"I don't doubt it."

"I was. Awfully. I wanted to be near him."

"So that he'd tell you what it is you want to be told, even if you're not sure just what it is? I'm afraid you'd have been disappointed there, as well. He wasn't going to say anything as carefully thought out as what you heard in his lecture."

"Not to hear him say anything. I wanted to be near him because … I'm afraid for him."

Her voice was still almost casual—soft and very private. Shadows walked in it, and (of course because of the associations I made with her past) they seemed the shadows of Gestapo agents descending the stairs toward the concrete and silent torture chambers. It is not easy to accept the echo of Kurtz's whisper, "The horror of it, the horror of it," during the middle of one's office hours and during an unscheduled interview, but I heard it there. I knew what she meant, and I could not admit it. I swept it away with an ironic thought of Clem's blond mistress ("… till we scream") and said, "Now, now, my dear. I'm afraid you have a highly romanticized notion of poets. Mr. Anderson is young and spry, not even forty yet, though fat. He doesn't need a bodyguard."

She looked at me as if I had said something unforgivable. "I know that. I know I couldn't help him." She shook her black hair and gave up whatever it was she had been trying for. "I didn't like his novel and I can't make sense out of this poetry. The novel was too sarcastic. He didn't love his characters."

"That's what some reviewers—and his editor—felt."

"Is he like that? Sarcastic?"

"Ironic? Yes. Modern poetry, like metaphysical poetry, for example, is often highly ironic, and Mr. Anderson isn't exceptional in that way. As for his character, he is a monster. If I had my choice of being near him or being near a king cobra, I think I might elect the cobra."

"Oh," she said, wreathed in coed smiles and favoring me with a sultry look, "you're joking with me now."

She shouldn't have bet on that.

Ironic? Clem had achieved some ironic distance the hard way. Janet and I had often thought that it was Sheila who had finally made irony possible for him. Certainly the Clem we knew in college had wit of a savage kind, that could be turned against himself as well as against anyone else; perhaps it was more frequently so turned. But it had no ironic tolerance in it. His jokes had what we called the "death sentence" ring about them. He could joke about his own absorption in himself when people pointed it out, as they often did. "You say I take myself too seriously? It is impossible to take me too seriously. Do you think that heaven and earth were created in jest?" But we never knew whose cheek he had his tongue in when he talked like that.

If there is irony, and even an overabundance of it, in *Angel at Noon*, the irony is a matter of style. I don't have the faintest idea of how to escape the problem of style and truth in the autobiographical passages of the novel. I am inclined to believe that both what happened once and the stylistic reorganization of the event are elements of the truth about Clem Anderson. ("I never asked to be temporal," he bellowed once. Now, in my pages at least, he can have his way.) But when I remember the temporal stations, trying to project what he was at one time from what I know him to have been at other times, as one recreates a line from three known points in space, I can't believe that Clem had the slightest freedom of irony when he came to college. In his amused reportage of the times before I knew him I try to gauge the deflection. I allow for windage.

Later he told it like this:

When he came down from Boda to the university in the fall of 1936 he had no more to indicate his future as a writer than an irresponsibly fictional notion of himself as football star material.

In high school he had identified himself with Cotton Warburton, the smallest man ever to make All-American, and though he weighed fifteen pounds less even than Warburton, he actually thought he could make up this weight differential and the greater one that separated him from the 180-pound average of our squad, too, by speed, wiriness and "cunning."

"And I had the sobriquet 'the Strongest Boy in Boda,'" he would say. "That wasn't easily come by."

He had it on authority that he was "good athletic timber." In Boda Dr. Wickham, a sports lover in whom he had a secretive, obsessive faith, had told him so. He had two basketball letters from Boda High School and a track medal won for the fifty-yard dash at a Cub Scout jamboree years before. (I saw the medal in his wallet as late as 1950, a tarnished little disk, olive-wreathed, with his name engraved on the back in Roman letters: "Aaron Clement Anderson, First Prize, Junior Competition.") Onto this background of public recognition he had pasted up an elaborate collage of wishes that made the image of the "even smaller" All-American he meant to become. Into it went the hip-swiveling runs he had made across the pastures around Boda on football afternoons (alone, of course); the cunning of football strategy that he had gleaned from stories in Collier's and The American Boy, "where it was always a dandy idea to drop a couple of important passes and get the crowd booing you and your girl about ready to faint with shame before you jumped eight feet in the air to snag the one that counted." Crowds he could dub in from the memory of the crowds roaring over the dirt track races at the state fair (since he had never really seen a big football game before he ushered at one in his R.O.T.C. uniform in his freshman year); his natural modesty would carry him through when the old grads came pouring down out of the stands to thank him, through tears, for the heroism he had displayed against odds. ("I used to practice phrases for answering them," Clem said, "and I meant to pass the credit around for all my teammates and even back to my coach at Boda, though he was a turd.")

He foresaw it all, he explained, and it seemed all the easier for him to execute because he had never played a game of football with more than four kids on a side. The little high school at Boda had a basketball team and, in years of peak enrollment, a baseball team, but there was neither a field nor equipment nor enough physically fit boys to make up a good football squad. With this handicap, it appeared merely natural to him that he had won no football laurels before he went to college.

His illusion had been hardened through countless afternoons while his father and sister listened to games on the radio, they content with the disappointments of reality while he lay belly down on the linoleum behind the heating stove and imagined how it ought to be. The illusion had to be hard to carry him through as many as three practice sessions with the freshman squad at the university.

For, first of all, the athletic department did not even bother to issue him the one set of shoulder pads small enough to fit him (these originally a gift from a sporting-goods company to the coach's junior-high-school son, left in their inventory when that coach had gone after a bad season, squaring in perpetuity the books so that alumni vengeance would never catch him in the Methodist college to which he had descended or call him back to suffer for bribetaking, since no court would really convict him for his ultimate crime of having lost even to South Dakota). They wouldn't issue Clem the pads for the simple reason that "those mutts would kill you if I let you scrimmage," as the freshman coach told him.

For three days he made the quarter-mile run around the field with the rest of the squad in a numeral sweater that hung to his knees. "Number one-nine-one," he recalled it. "They retired that number when I left the squad. Among their cloudy trophies hung, a backdrop for all the gold footballs of all their Big Ten championships, pointed out to all comers as the one numeral that would never be replaced." "They hold the squad to one hundred and ninety people now," Sheila said.

He learned to recover fumbles in a smashing dive that ended with a roll onto his back. "'Don't pull your legs up like that,' the coach would yell at me. 'You look like a rat stealing an egg, Anderson.'"

He sent his punts arcing away with the best boots of the monsters from the city high schools—punting and passing he had practiced hard in high school, though he had modestly decided to tell the coach, "I've got everything to learn"—but they fell twenty yards short of the average, and the coach hurt his feelings by yelling, "Use one foot at a time on them punts, Anderson. You'll bust the ball that way." Then he took to using Clem in his demonstrations of blocking technique. Clem was light enough for him to push around without getting a sweat up.

"So I thought, Let them pay off their own damn mortgage on the stadium," Clem said. "I saw I was letting Boda down and that gave me a way to soothe myself. If there'd been kudos I'd have collected it, but when it was plain that I'd fizzled I converted what might have been a very traumatic loss of confidence into altruism and pity. I felt sorry for Boda because now they'd never be able to boast that they'd produced the littlest All-American, and they'd have liked that so much. For my part, I decided to put on weight and become a poet."

Was the decision made like that? I like the explanation enough to believe it, though of course there is more to say of it, and in any case it would be necessary to suspect its lightheartedness. Clem never took anything lightly while it was happening.

He did not settle to poetry in that year because he liked to write. After all, he had never written anything. I think that just as his account implies, his motive must have been, from the first, a competitive one. Why he or any boy from such a background should think poetry an area of competition more open to him than football is a question for which I can only conjecture a serious answer.

First to take into account is his loneliness. Even when I met him, two years after his try at football, I thought him psychopathically withdrawn. He was—in a term that recollection permits me now, though twenty years ago it would have been unthinkable—a beautiful boy. He had a kind of English complexion, cheeks that were usually bright as arterial blood, creamy pale skin, and darkish hazel eyes. His mouth was large, his lips were full and inclined to pout like a girl's. His hair was dark brown and usually so wavy that it tended to pile up thick and loose.

If I digress a moment to speak of his consistently atrocious haircuts, my reason is a wish to illustrate a general presumption, for his difficulties with barbers always stood in my mind as a token of his difficulty with all uncomplicated artisans.

He complicated them. I watched him once talk a barber into follies that would have been perpetrated on no one else. Up to a point the barber had done a good job. Perhaps a job he was proud of. Then he held the mirror up for Clem's approval.

"Fine," Clem said. (Nothing wrong with that. A reasonable answer. A common answer.) Then, unable to leave well enough alone and perhaps fearing that the single word might be taken for an unconscionable pride in the shape of his head or the texture of his hair, he added, "I mean you did a fine job. My hair looks like hell."

"What do you want me to do?" the barber asked. His foot began to tap rapidly.

"It's not your fault."

"I been cutting hair twenty years. I don't get many complaints." The barber moved his razor farther away on the shelf beneath the mirrors, as if removing temptation.

"It's fine."

"Want some more off here?" Compulsively the barber began to shear again. After one bold swath he said, "I want you should be satisfied."

"I am satisfied." Clem tried to climb out of the chair.

"Can't leave it like that. It ain't even."

"You did your best."

"I'm not through doing my best."

Once the unfortunate rhythm of dialogue was begun, there was no turning back. "Finish it however you want," Clem said, "I like it however you like it."

By this time the barber was twitching and trembling badly and perhaps he saw the hair under his hands as only the bristly miasma that kept his honest thought from penetrating the skull beneath. "Nearly every customer I ever had is satisfied. People come in here, like once the State Treasurer of the state of Nebraska came in here, he's on vacation and he says he couldn't have got a better haircut in the capitol barbershop. Some people's hair is just harder to do than others. The shape of the head can vary from like a potato to like a volleyball. I can't do miracles"—gouging a white spot the size of a silver dollar above Clem's ear.

When we left the shop, Clem looked like the victim of some Asiatic disease. Dark tufts erupted from the rat-gray splotches shorn nearly to the scalp. His ears seemed to have slipped two inches down his neck. But now that it was over (consummatum est would hardly be too exaggerated an expression for anyone concerned about his appearance) Clem seemed to feel that everything was all right again. (And was it not? In two months he would again have a luxurious crop standing four inches straight up above the hairline; even his temples would be covered again.) All he chose to remember of his session in the chair was something he had overheard from the customer seated next to him—"They tell me a cuppa this concentrated water will float a ship."

If it weren't for all this fooling with his hair, Clem would like to spend lots of time in barbershops.

I saw it done to him only once, but, on the evidence, all barbers responded the same to him, doing their office in blazoning the sign of his difference from others—a warning or incitement for all who saw him. Once he got into a fist fight with a fraternity boy who had been playing catch in the frat yard as Clem passed. The boy yelled, "Hey, you with the cap, you wanta snag that ball for me?"

"I wasn't wearing no cap," Clem said. "Dumb sonofabitch."

But when others didn't notice his hair, he never did.

I won't say that loneliness or alienation makes anyone write poetry, though I have elsewhere written of Clem,* "Such loneliness as his, inconceivable for the majority of us who have learned to identify ourselves as members of the lonely crowd, produces in the passionate individual an undischarged potential of responsiveness that might be likened to the critical mass required for atomic fission, or to Blake's 'overflowing fountain.'" In the same article I quoted an excerpt of tongue-in-cheek autobiography from one of Clem's letters to me. "The old she-devil of loneliness sang in my ear, and what I thought she sang was, 'You're an artist.' Since I had nothing better to believe, I said, 'Why not?'"

At home in Boda he had had friends and girls. And it should have been easy enough for him to replace at least Margaret Shea (Con Everling of *Angel at Noon*) with someone like her, if he had wanted to. In his first two years of college he certainly could have replaced Mark of the novel (by a not insignificant coincidence named Harry in real life, Harry Rinehart) with an equally close friend. So I am tempted to think that his loneliness of that period was chosen, if not consciously, then by accident and the unconscious design of whatever knew better than he why he must become a poet and was preparing him for it.

That reinforced and expanded loneliness, then, I take to be one condition for his swift discovery of his vocation. Second, there was his reading, which from his first year in college was altogether different in scope and import from the reading done in high school. That earlier reading had been exciting, in a sense, to his eye. It was a big discovery to make for oneself that there could be resemblances between the people in books and the people he knew in his home town. Now, in a number of ways, he was brought to the greater discovery that some books struck below the level at which the eye and the ear could recognize resemblances, that they touched a mythic level, that they were about himself. This is not to say that he came suddenly on better books, but suddenly on those great moments of a reader's life when he finds the books which will make all books he reads thereafter better.

As a matter of fact, the books that Clem blooded himself on (and remembered thereafter with a special weakness that blinded him critically) compose a most peculiar list. They were *The Picture of Dorian Gray, Crime and Punishment, Salome, Thurso's Landing, Sons and Lovers* and *The Sound and the Fury*. I have speculated that there may be a common denominator of romantic violence in these books which made them ring like an echo chamber for the experiences he had acquired in his affair with Irene Lacey. (One sees that she was not exactly to be fully accounted for by matching her against the heroine of Main Street, as Harry had matched Lucille in the novel. There were darknesses and an aboriginal depth in her that one looks for in vain in Carol Kennicott.) And if one could not be Cotton Warburton, one could be, one was, the sexually bemused boy of Lawrence's novel and in being so could hear the echo of another kind of heroism, more familiar and vastly more important than the heroism of an All-American quarterback. Down in the dark world slam-banged into by way of a high-school sex jag the great heroes began to show some outline— Oedipus, Odysseus, Herakles, Orpheus. He caught the intimation, from Lawrence's novel at least, that being crucified into sex was a more heroic (if more common) experience than razzle-dazzling a football before great crowds.

But at any rate, whatever subprivate alchemies resulted from Clem's private encounter with the pages of these or other books in his freshman year, something needs to be said of the mentor who put these particular romances in his way.

H. Warwick Lloyd (as he signed himself, preferring to be called "Warry") was a professional student and latent homosexual who happened to be in Clem's R.O.T.C. squad. He was on his fourth college and his sixth year of attendance then, finally forced into R.O.T.C. drill if he hoped for graduation. It may have been his refined, frustrated homosexual eye that picked Clem out for special attention and friendship. ("He used to admire my build," Clem said. "That made up to me for the absolute contempt of the football coach.") But Warwick's line, from the start, was that Clem looked like a poet—for which acuity I must credit him, whatever his suppressed motives might have been.

It was on a day when the drill instructor had fingered Clem's neck and ordered him to get a haircut that H. Warwick opened the acquaintance. Walking out of the armory with Clem, he said, "I've had experience with the type before. When I was at Illinois one of the beasts had the audacity to touch me. I was standing at attention or whatever they call this ridiculous position where you must arch your back and not breathe, and he was measuring the length of my hair with extended forefinger. I turned and jolly well bit it. To the bone. I was threatened with summary court-martial. Can you imagine? I fancy they may have planned to hang me as a mutineer for part of the Homecoming ceremonies. 'Upon a day of dark disgrace, Upon a gallows high.' Do you know Wilde's poetry?"

Clem said he didn't.

"Magnificent. I was reminded of my own tribulations when I saw this fat martinet toy with your curls this morning."

"I'm going to get a haircut this afternoon," Clem said. If even a sympathizer could speak of "curls" it was time to take action. "What did they do to you?"

"Pardon?"

"At the court-martial."

"Of course that was an empty threat. They wouldn't have dared. I'd have turned Communist. There's a very strong movement on the Illinois campus and if there is one thing the Communists hate above all else it is the R.O.T.C. If I had given them my grievance, I think they might have marched on the field house. However, I was sent to a psychiatrist. Actually, I rather enjoyed that. I fancy knowing what's wrong with me. Rather delicious to know about all the Teddy bears one has tucked away down in the id. I'm Oedipal as hell. I suppose you are, too?" Another might have asked as hopefully, "You're Sig Ep, aren't you?"

"They turned you loose?" Clem said.

H. Warwick was delighted with Clem's naïveté. "They had no recourse. I even resumed—now and then—attendance at drills, though I was shuffled to another squad. Apparently the word had come down through administrative channels that I wasn't required to get a haircut. I looked like Yellow-Hair Custer by February, out of pure spite." He put his gloved hand coyly to a frail, pimpled cheek and said, "Don't you think I rather resemble Custer anyhow? My ancestors distinguished themselves at Bull Run. For the Confederacy, naturally, believe it or not, though the blood is terribly degenerate by now.

"But you want to know how I fixed them? Every spring they have the silly old Governor down for a silly review and you're supposed to prance by him like a bunch of chorus girls. Well. I think the colonel meant to omit me from the review. I could see he had his brutal eye on me for weeks in advance. So. I got a Prussian haircut and practiced arching my silly back, though I have a slipped disc, and I suppose the idiots thought they were making a soldier out of me. I want you to know that I was commended for the thump I made when I 'grounded my piece.' The fools.

"I was ideally located in the center of the third squad of the column on the great day. Just before we came abreast of the Governor, and just as we were given the command 'Eyes right,' I uttered a piercing scream and dropped my piece in such a way that the idiots on my right and left both tripped over it, as did I." Tears of joy were streaming down either side of his thin nose as he went on. "Not only did I create local confusion, but when this happened, all down the ranks behind me others began to throw down their rifles. It developed later that there were many Communists in the ranks and they took my deed as a signal for a demonstration. Nothing, nothing I have done in my whole dilettantish life has given me more satisfaction than that day— though I was expelled afterward. Even the psychiatrist refused me sympathy."

Clem said he didn't think he would have the nerve for any rebellion like that. H. Warwick patted his shoulder. "I can see that you're very sensitive and aloof. And by the way, you told me you hadn't read Wilde. If you'd care to stop by my digs, I'll be glad to lend you what you wish. You must promise to be very careful of any Wilde I give you, though. I've had it done in full calf."

H. Warwick was a complete Anglophile and, insofar as possible, attended (at whatever college he was actually enrolled, even presumably at Black Mountain, where he had found admission after being expelled from Illinois) Oxford. Inside the Methodist and Sears, Roebuck austerity of his rooming house and to the awed derision of the six other students who shared the bathroom on his floor he recreated something like Balliol on the prairies. He brewed tea each afternoon on his "spirit lamp" (sold at the student co-op as an alcohol burner), kept Scotch-type whisky in his cupboard, "tutored" with a Jewish boy from Brooklyn (actually the boy ghosted all his science and math work), and "sported the oak" when, as Clem conjectured later, he required a session of masturbation to the tune of Beardsley illustrations.

When he learned that Clem was working as a dishwasher in the Hamilton Hotel, he took to eating his Saturday and Sunday dinner in the hotel dining room. It gave them a subject for the conversation of courtship. "I found the chop excellent tonight, though the service was not up to par. I had to ask that redheaded servant twice for a bit of Worcestershire sauce," H. Warwick might say when they rendezvoused later, after one of them had eaten the hotel dinner and the other had done the hotel dishes. It repeated—in a new form—that double vision of experience which Clem had thought of earlier when he saw the goldfish simultaneously in profile and from a top view. The swinging door of the kitchen served, that is, like the right angle of the refracting water. Inside, the redhead was Alice, who talked about her husband's becoming a third-degree Mason and studying business law by correspondence, who scratched her crotch contemptuously in front of the dishwashers. Outside, she was the Servant Girl, swift to do Master's bidding, one of the Lower Orders. Outside, the mutton was a chop sizzling under a sprinkle of parsley, to be seasoned with sauce that bore a name out of Shakespeare, while inside it was a piece of meat that the cook Bartolomeo had snatched away from the year-old pointers (owned by the hotel manager) who frequently roamed the kitchen and always ate better than the help.

(If I seem to be here overemphasizing the educational importance of a dining-room door, or to be overstating the simplicity of Clem's mind at this period—when, God knows, it must have buzzed with complexities and ironies that his art would never have time to recreate—I plead merely that doors, like other commonplaces, mean as much as the observer can make them mean, and that the observer here was Clement Anderson, not you or I. For my part, there is a need for anchoring symbols when I approach the problem of his life, just as, I suppose, the artist must find his symbols when he essays the mysteries of consciousness in general.)

Whether it was the Hamilton dining room or another "holy counterfeit of life" (Clem's phrase) that H. Warwick occupied on the other side of Clem's daily experience, the half-separated equilibrium of their relationship was an essential phase of the poet's growth.

Like many first-rate writers, Clem had a high conversion rate. He could make a great deal out of a very little. ("I saw my duty to have responses disproportionate to the event," he said once to a, presumably, bewildered TV audience, while being interviewed to promote *Death and the Devil*. "I'm not the objective equivalent of anything except what I think." "And you've certainly had a varied life, Mr. Anderson!" the interviewer said. "Dishwasher, roustabout, postal employee, hitchhiker, aviation cadet, counterintelligence agent, steamfitter in the shipyards, poet, Marine raider, night clerk, teacher, student of Yoga, translator, bullfight aficionado, and novelist"—thus sketching the subjective equivalent of Clem's intense fascination with other people's photograph albums, as well as his Willingness to Lie Where It Doesn't Count.)

Like Utrillo, who produced fine landscapes by copying cheap and tawdry postcards, it was Clem's gift to make something true out of the phony Anglophilia and the sophomoric decadence of H. Warwick's posture. If H. Warwick spoke of himself as a "sybarite" because he had gorged on the $1.35 blue-plate special at the Hamilton Hotel—in that word and circumstance, however punily caricatured, there lurked the embryonic image of Proustian languors and the extravagance of Mitya

Karamazov flinging his stolen money to the gypsies. Time and Clem would find them.

Would also, when he went to England during the war, greet the Potters and their friends as old familiar faces, be terribly at home in Oxford, and slap the Empire on the shoulder because he had already seen them (all they could be) in H. Warwick's affectations.

But in the time of which I am speaking he had yet to catch up with his teacher. It was marvel enough in the college years that he sifted the usable hints from the ridiculous distortions H. Warwick had fixed them in. Getting Ariel out of the tree is the crucial test for young magicians.

"Warry read Oedipus Rex over and over because it explained him," Clem remembered. H. Warwick was fond of quoting Nietzschean epigrams, but with a bony finger to his bony nose regretted that they could not be attributed to Wilde, for "Wilde was a gentleman and Nietzsche was, except mentally, a boor." He recommended Jeffers because "the Californian is so deliciously morbid." Lawrence "demolishes the pretenses of the rational mind"—and, no doubt, the smug pretenses of all those science and mathematics teachers who expected the impossible from H. Warwick's facile aestheticism. The Sound and the Fury "utterly destroys syntax; only in Lewis Carroll will you find such creative nonsense for its own sake." Hemingway's great value lay, he thought, in "having exploited the staccato." Crime and Punishment—I wonder if he had not recommended this novel to Clem because the inspector's patient stalking of Raskolnikov reminded him unconsciously of his homosexual stalking of Clem.

No doubt both of them would have cut and run if there had been any overt expression of the sexual in their relationship at that time. "I never even saw his genitals," Clem said a year or two later, when he was very knowing about and stably superior to the slippery places he had trod. "The one time we ever went swimming together, he went into the can to put on his suit, for Christ's sake." By that safe time, Clem was in the habit of leering when he spoke of H. Warwick, calling him "the friend of my youth," and implying that he had always known Warry's true objective.

I wonder if the suppression of overt sexuality required by the delicate relation between them was not, in its season, valuable. The rib had been torn from young Adam in his high-school days, and God might have said, "Let him miss it a while so that he will know how to value it when I give it back. Let what happened become important to him, since he chooses to be a writer. Things are not always most important at the time they happen." The premature consummation of experience had to become equivocal, frustrated—had to become past before it could become art. (And what else was there to make into art except the erotic trial of his high-school days, repeated in variations like the variations of a musical theme, his litmus-paper way of testing the inherent form of novel situations, his Italian music to be played in the Dakotas that time would open for exploration, "strangely fitting, even here, meanings unknown before"?) He had chosen, in choosing to write, to woo "the otherness," and for a small town Midwestern boy the homosexual is apt to be more "the other" than a girl could be.

Ever afterward Wadleigh Hertz would say with satisfaction, "Clem was queer as a three-dollar bill before we took him over." Wadleigh meant that he, Jack Miller and I wised Clem up, gave him a manly taste for alcohol and making out with student nurses from the university hospital. But I guess that Clem was wise, instinctively, intuitively right, in lingering equivocally a while in sterile dalliance with H. Warwick. When he was ready for us he found us.

Jack Miller and I might as easily as not have been his friends two years before we were, and we might have shortened his path to some graces unknown in Boda. At least we would not have told him that *The Sound and the Fury* had anything to do with the brillig waves or (another favorite of H. Warwick's) Winnie the Pooh. We could have told him that muscatel in the afternoon and apricot brandy at night are not the drinks for gentlemen songsters. (Poor H. Warwick had no stomach for sherry and lapsed his Anglophilia to accommodate sweet California wines.)

But Clem needed the time to perfect himself in equivocation before he encountered the unequivocal certainties that the rest of us held then. Jack Miller was sure that "stopping Hitler" was the only necessary precondition for an era in which all states would wither away. Wadleigh Hertz was sure that his "dedication to socialism" could never lead him up the garden path to insurance selling and middle-aged hipsterism. I was sure that the open road for literature was up the way opened by Joyce, Pound and Eliot. Sheila and Janet, entering the cast a little later, were sure that love was not love that did not guarantee its own endurance. To all these certainties, Clem had to say No. H. Warwick, holding him to the crooked unimproved roads, prepared him to say No to anything.

Third, after loneliness and the seminal books Clem read at H. Warwick's prompting, one looks for some root of practice in writing from which his subsequent craft could grow. In vain. (Clem told the TV audience in 1953, "I wrote my first novel at seven. It was about a boy at the Battle of Bull Run. I composed it standing on our front porch wearing some gloves that had belonged to my great-grandfather when he rode in Sheridan's cavalry. Madrigals and sonnets. By twelve I was turning out a sonnet a day." "You certainly were very young to be so precocious," the interviewer said. Very old, one might say, to be so free with the truth. Not one of Clem's great-granddaddies left Europe before 1870. Before college the extent of his literary composition, exclusive of high-school assignments, was an essay for entry in a contest held by the American Legion, subject: "Liberty and the WPA." Clem had sycophantically exposed the WPA as a cruel cancer attacking American Ideals, but he had won only an honorable mention in the county contest.)

Clem began to write during his first year at college. Began from scratch. But at this point the university did for him what we hope for when we pay our taxes—it gave him Felix Martin as instructor in freshman composition.

Felix was the type of graduate assistant more common twenty years ago than today—the already middle-aged, outwardly dry-as-dust candidate for a Ph.D. who had taught in high schools and small colleges for half his life, returning only at forty to perfect himself for his comprehensives and to prepare a thesis. The gaunt son of a Nebraska minister, his appearance suggested that he would have welcomed the grind toward examinations for its own sake, just as his Baptist father and more remote pioneering ancestors might welcome God's test in flood, drought, dust storm or other prairie affliction. There was a John Brown sparkle of fanaticism in his lead-colored eyes, set deep above a leaden, ineradicable stubble of beard. An absolutely born cleric and ascetic, he was of the kind who are apt to show up as worker priests, slum missionaries or chaplains of leper colonies.

He called himself a Humanist, but he was without that High-Church and reactionary smugness that distinguished so many of the followers of More and Babbitt. His keen sense of hierarchy made him humble where it made some snobbish. Just because he revered Sophocles, Dante, Shakespeare, Racine and Goethe he could avoid the moldy self-righteousness of those who thought themselves anointed for preferring Dante to Dreiser. In my first year of graduate work I tangled with Felix once on the subject of Pound's erudition in classic and Far Eastern cultures—and never afterward respected quite so much either Uncle Ezra's or my own. I remember ridiculing Felix once when I found framed above his desk the motto, "Gladly wolde he lerne and gladly teche." I thought I had smelled out his vanity at last. Now I think he deserved it on his office door if any man I have known ever did.

Unerringly he spotted the slips of virtue in the garden of weeds that Clem offered to view that year. I can hear Felix's tongue clicking like a beaver's tail sounding alarm when he first discerned Clem's melodramatic vision of himself as either quarterback or marvelous boy. The echo of H. Warwick's bargain decadence would have chilled Felix to his Nebraska marrow.

He never flinched. First he set himself the ungrateful task of teaching Clem what a sentence was—not merely how to make one ("though for me that would have been an advance," Clem said) but its nature, "that lovely postulation of substance in a dimensional world where, according to its qualities and degree of abstraction, it moves or is moved through time and space." Discovering (slowly, cautiously) the boy to be teachable, Felix did not fail to understand how high the grains of learning might grow. In the very opacity and confusion of Clem's themes Felix deciphered the mad conservatism and the simultaneous open breach by which genius works.

Felix said, "But of course the sign by which I recognized Clem was his overwhelming arrogance. Modesty would have become him then, but it might have misled me. When I suggested he try exercises in imitation of great examples, his most obvious accomplishment was to butcher the syntax of the original. He didn't know that Shakespeare's or Milton's sonnets were composed of sentences. I tried him on the first stanza of Yeats's 'Sailing to Byzantium.' He could not find the verb in the second sentence, and when I pointed it out to him he thought it was in the imperative mood, which he could not define precisely or name.

"Yet he had written a free adaptation of the poem—having read somewhere that it was greater than I had represented it to be—which he felt to be superior to the original."

It had never before occurred to Clem, still mythologized by tales of sport, that it would be "fair" to model his work on famous examples, or perhaps even to learn from criticism. Poetry was a man-to-man competition. You went into the ring stripped to your poetic buff. Let them report how a Boda boy was slain, if they must! Never let them report he had used someone else's gimmick or profited from criticism!

Felix gentled him beyond this valorous stupidity. Going beyond was, once more, a plunge into excess. Besides the imitation Yeats and a few Shakespearean sonnets, Clem wrote that year a nine-hundred-line imitation of *Thurso's Landing*—set, of course, in Boda. "I can see now that I didn't understand exactly what the characters in *Thurso's*

*Landing* did to each other when they did something, but I'd caught the tone, and I knew something mighty happened when they screwed," Clem said in recollection. "I worked from that. Felix was astounded and patient."

I believe no copies of this hairy mammoth exist. Sheila never saw it. Clem's mother does not have it in the trunks full of books, letters from Harry Rinehart in the Navy, stamp collections, bow, pistol, first baseman's mitt, Margaret Shea's scarf, photograph albums, a shield hammered out of a five-gallon oilcan (bearing, for no reason, or an inexplicable one, the device of Gawain's shield) and some copies of the Southern, Kenyon and Sewanee Reviews and Accent of the early Forties—all the embassy bequeathed her by the son "who might have come out all right if he hadn't got mixed up with those New York people."

But I think both Clem and Felix remembered it, with whatever ineptitudes, better and perhaps more tenderly than many of the things he did later. It may be that this lost poem was the first recognizable incarnation of all he had to declare—that "missing link" of popular science jargon, the heroic monster that bore the anguish of change from brute to human.

Once Clem quoted from it: "... as if their farmer's blood had swarmed the Atlantic westward to scythe immortal harvest in Wisconsin fields," and a most queer, stricken look softened his face. He shook off his nostalgia with a remark to the effect that we hadn't time to hear the rest—"which is much, much, much more of the same. But Jesus, it seemed great when I wrote it. I thought I'd been occupied by the Muse, since clearly no Anderson could write anything like that. Felix pointed out that was right, I couldn't have—I'd stolen everything I knew how to carry. What's more, he said, what I'd lifted was a 'barbaric yawp.' I didn't get the allusion, but it sounded like I'd carried off the checkbooks and missed the cash when I robbed a bank. My feelings were really hurt."

While it is hard to think a Humanist would approve "barbaric yawps" from any source whatever, Felix had advised imitation. He, for his part, was not dismayed by the consequences. Anyone skilled enough in the astronomy of the spirit to infer from Clem's mere themes the existence of an invisible magnitude undoubtedly saw evidence enough here that this magnitude might discharge its force in language. After discipline, of course.

Before the year ended Felix had buttered the hurt feelings. He leaned over backward to restore the arrogance that he sensed to be

116

Clem's only solid capital for the time being. "I think if I hadn't praised his sensitivity shown in phrases and the choice of individual words he would have lost confidence in me completely," Felix said. "But then, if I hadn't, I should have lost confidence in myself. Some unaccountable principle of selection guided him. I'll call it his innocent ear, at the risk of anomaly. I noted such things as this: While he was then completing his first year of French, and while his pronunciation was inadequate, to say the least, he'd picked up some real gems from casual browsing. I think he may even have gleaned them from reviews in Poetry magazine—he had read very little modern French poetry in class or elsewhere, as far as I knew. I suppose he picked them with the natural discrimination of a child choosing his daisies out of an endless field. '*Dans les eaux des beaux mois*,' for example, just that fragment, which, all out of context, 'made him cry' he said. '*Vers une cimetière isolée, mon coeur va battant comme un tambour voilé.*' Or '*Ses ailes de géant l'empêchent de marcher.*' He barely knew what they meant in a literal sense, but they were his. He recognized them as if he had heard them a thousand times before.

"I told him that whatever else he'd done in his monstrous poem, whose *ailes de géant l'avaient empêché de marcher*, he'd made some glittering images. I consoled him thus. But, I suppose, the most glittering outrageous image he had created was of himself. He knew very well that he was a little past the age of Rimbaud when Rimbaud had been first acclaimed in Paris. I think he was capable of pitying me, all of us, for being so provincial we could not recognize who had come among us.

"When I had the temerity to suggest that there were other gifted students on the campus whom he should meet with the end of learning from their trials and errors, he greeted my suggestion with, uh, smirking condescension. He knew he would be an eagle among crows. Too bad for me if I knew it not. I've never known anyone who had so little doubt, *ab initio*, of his vocation."

With skeptical amusement I tried to scramble Felix's conviction of original certainty by tossing in what I knew of Clem's prior dreams of athletic glory. Felix shook his head. "Under the cloak of appearances, it may amount to the same thing. A poet can conceive himself a quarterback, though a quarterback might not wish to see himself as poet. Of course, Dick, we'll never unravel the mysterious origins of a vocation, for Clem or the multitude of others called to the world. I wonder—it may be that the quarterback is a station of the spirit from which, in embarrassing profusion, poets may someday emerge. Yet not an equivalent station. We can imagine a quarterback becoming a poet, but not a poet becoming a quarterback. The process of obtaining a finer identification is irreversible. I see the law in this, whether one calls it the second law of thermodynamics or the birth of the poet's mind. And it's tragic, too. If his wings hadn't grown for another year he might have got great pleasure from football. At least as a fan."

* In an article that appeared a few weeks after his death. The still persisting shock of this event may have led me to overemphasize the painful elements in his life and character, confusing them with the broader aspects of his personal tragedy.—D. H.

## 5

CLEM WOULD GO HOME to Boda for that summer vacation when he was eighteen, no doubt with a sense of things previously unfinished that in his new estate he could master. The mystery of Irene Lacey's double existence as particular and type could be solved Q.E.D.—as Nayland Smith was wont to solve the mysteries of the inscrutable East. Or at least the mysterious self of high-school days could be articulated, now that he had a language and a beginner's license to use it poetically. If there had been someone there who understood what he was saying, now that he knew, a bit, how to say it … But Harry Rinehart was gone (the real, original Harry, that is; the fictional one had not been born yet), Irene Lacey was married and had moved away. Even before they both went to college he had found Margaret Shea a less than adequate confidante. The college year had separated them immeasurably.

Still, Margaret had come home from her girls' college groomed and aromatic as never before. When he first saw her at church—he had gone just once because his mother wanted it so badly after she heard some of his "college ideas"—saw her in a green dress, crisp as a brand-new dollar bill, he told himself that even a decadent *aux ailes de géant* might find in her an antidote to the longueurs of a Boda summer. I think he had bragged to H. Warwick of the Edwardian sins that could be found in this little town "a hundred miles from Milwaukee and right next door to nowhere." In bragging he may have convinced himself that this summer when, as Salome, Margaret stooped to kiss those finely chiseled lips on Herod's platter and they said, "Make it French," she would accede with rapture. Girls didn't go to Stevens College for nothing!

The first time he talked to her she reproached him for not having written to her all year. But then—smiles—it didn't matter. Nothing mattered! She was engaged to a Deke pre-Dent from the University of Missouri! She wanted still to be friends with Clem. She hoped to see a lot of him this summer, a really lot! But in a short enough time it would dawn on him that his value to her as a summer companion was that, since he had been away to college, too, he could help her advertise the value of a Deke pre-Dent to their stay-at-home friends. As local satyr, might even serve for contrast to the absent Hyperion.

Between the kisses and the wine—between Bulie's drugstore fountain and her porch swing—he had hoped to purge her from his mind so that it might wing after less earthly Cynaras. It seemed to him, then as always—this was the very trap that finally took him—that he must not quit until he was ahead of the game. That meant he had to score with her, then break from her entreating arms like that natural-born hunter, Adonis. Now to be relegated to the office of foil, of her public-relations man ...

Unthinkable. He began to talk threateningly to his parents of hitchhiking to California. They took his threats seriously even before he did. (He might never have gone if he had not put himself in the position where he would seem to himself a fourflusher if he didn't.) They recalled with worry that Harry Rinehart was stationed in San Diego. Wouldn't it be just like Clem to go out there and ruin his chances by signing up in the Navy as Harry had? (One wonders, marveling, what chances they visualized. Surely not those that Clem would seize as his own.)

Clem's father came in to talk to him one hot morning when Clem was still in bed. He wanted to offer Clem the opportunity to make a solid summer wage, he said cheerfully.

The proposition he offered was prosaic enough on the surface. That year Mr. Anderson had gone into partnership with Edison Graber to make steel-plate burial vaults. The plates came, already cut to size, from a company in Milwaukee. Anderson and Graber welded the plates, ground the corners smooth, bronzed the finished shell and added whatever ornament might be chosen by the bereft family. They were willing to put Clem on the payroll as the full-time bronzer, paying him what they had paid Keith de Leo before the paint began to "get" Keith's lungs.

But perhaps Clem's father was not the right person, after all, to sing the siren song of stability. During all of Clem's early years their petty fortunes had been tied up with Mr. Anderson's investments in the Drake Estate.

The Drake Estate was one of those bubbles of the Twenties that took in a good many Midwesterners. Certain promoters were in the field bearing tidings that practically all of North America belonged in title free to the heirs of Sir Francis Drake. The whole goddam continent. And lusty Drake had left many descendants. All that was required of them was faith and investments of cash that would enable the case to be fought out in the courts. The usurpers would be evicted from cities, plains and mountains—or at least reduced to the status of renters, paying their incredible revenues to the Anderson family (in direct descent from Sir Francis through the maternal line) and some hundreds of others who had known how to stand up for their legal rights.

From as far back as the time they lived in St. Paul, Clem's father had been putting money into this marvelous fiction. He had mortgaged and lost a farm bequeathed him by his father, in the vain intent to see that legal fees were not wanting. ("Naturally the opposition"—which seems potentially to have consisted of one-hundred-forty-odd million citizens of the U.S., not to mention Mexico and Canada, all threatened with dispossession—"meant to make a big fight of it.") He had skimped his children's Christmases and dressed his wife in family hand-me-downs for the great dream, the main chance. He had bled away the honest wages of his young manhood and had foregone the modest intoxications of security, pleasure and ease of mind for the sake of the incredible intoxication of some con man's fancy. Naturally, once Mr. Anderson had started to pour money into the scheme he had to go on. (It continued because it had begun—how familiar the echoes are, generation after generation of the race of visionaries.) Only the depression, only the sheer and absolute grind of necessity and the great showdown of humiliation that left him something less than a man had at last forced him to stop throwing his money to the blue winds of faith. Even when the promoters of the Drake Estate were arrested, Mr. Anderson had contributed money to their defense, saying in an extremity of bitterness, "This shows what lengths people will go to prevent simple justice." In later years Clem vaguely suspected that his father had driven through the Midwest trying to incite other investors to make an armed raid on the jail in Chicago with the object of freeing the incarcerated promoters.

Clearly such a man was not a good apostle for the cause of industry and modest goals, though on the morning he came to talk to Clem he spoke as passionately in their behalf as he had spoken for "the right" and his rights to a big share of North America. He talked of making burial vaults, and particularly the tasteful bronzing of their exteriors, as if it were a priestly calling.

Clem said politely that he didn't see any use in an occupation like that.

Any use? Any use? Well, it was pretty good money considering the times, and Mr. Anderson thought he could surely use a little folding money if he meant to go back to college next year.

121

Languid Clem replied that he could step into an assortment of jobs in California at a dollar seventy-five a day. (Poor consumptive de Leo had sniffed his overdose of bronze at a dollar ten.) But the main thing was that he didn't believe in the vaults.

Didn't believe in them? Why, they kept people's loved ones from getting wet in the rain. They kept sewage from seeping in to ruin the satined coffins inside, which, as anyone knew—or would know if they ever dug up a grave—ordinarily went to pieces in a month.

Clem said that if anyone ever dug up a grave they would probably find that the bronze came off an Anderson-and-Graber vault in a week, since it was only putty with bronzing paint sprayed over it. But that wasn't the point. The point was that he believed in letting the dead rot punctually, returning to nature in the first rains, *dans les eaux des beaux mois.*

Mr. Anderson stomped out, declaring that if this was a sample of the atheism Clem was picking up at college he saw no point in helping him return. He withdrew his offer. De Leo could still stand to work a couple of hours a day and would probably be more valuable, even in his condition, than a boy who thought he was too good to help his fellow man in the hour of sorrow. Clem could go to California for all he cared.

Clem began to pack. Since they had dared him to go, he would. Seeing him gather fresh T shirts and socks to fill his laundry case, overhearing his questions about the Lincoln Highway put to a neighbor, his mother arranged concessions to keep him home.

Even though he wasn't a very good driver (something in Clem long resisted all mechanisms invented after 1850) he could have the family car whenever he wanted it, providing only that he pay for the gas himself. And they supposed that if he didn't want to work for Daddy he might at least earn some money for gasoline and dates by working for one of the farmers as he had done in past years.

Clem did not even bother lifting his hand in labor until he proved how their offer might work out. Sinking a borrowed dollar in a pack of cigarettes, a pack of condoms and two gallons of gas, he called Margaret Shea to ask if she would like to ride out that night and "get some fresh air."

If there was one thing little Boda had in profusion it was fresh air, so there is no reason to assume that Margaret, changed as she was by her year of college, misunderstood the Aesopian language of the invitation.

But she chose to. When he swung the Chevrolet into the yard of a country school five miles from town, missing the culvert and tearing the rear bumper loose on the stony edge of the ditch, she simpered with collegiate poise, "Dearest, it's too hot to park. We'll smother if we don't keep riding, riding."

Smother, would they? *Tant mieux*. He had counted on the day's oppressive heat as an ally. From so long ago that it seemed in another life he remembered Harry Rinehart's saying, "If you can work them up to a real, old-fashioned sweat, no girl can resist you. Something goes to pieces in their chemicals."

As he got out to examine the damage to the bumper, he felt the running sweat on his back, his chest, his calves. The sky itself seemed oppressive as a sagging canopy of hot black velvet. The outline of the one-room schoolhouse was hardly visible against the stars. Smothering. Good. Not poppy or mandragora but good old $CO_2$—plus the chemical-deranging sweat—would lull the hapless girl, ready her for le vice anglais. He was ready to punish her now, punish her for not having suffered as he and Irene had suffered in high school, punish her into life.

Was anything damaged? she asked when he re-entered the front seat. The rear bumper looked like a total loss, he muttered, intending that she understand him to mean it was well lost for such purposes as he had in mind.

But then, in a wild transformation as he tried to embrace her, she began to babble about her French fiancé. The Deke pre-Dent bore the surname Dull B A (Dolbier), she confessed lyrically. While Clem felt the sweat trickle to the elbows with which she fended him off, his Boda Salome made everything (all her sublimated and unreachable passion) French. Dull B A got whatever profit there was from her sweat-slick undulations as Clem the Baptist pursued her back and forth across the wilderness front seat in his mission of punitive salvation. There might as well have been, literally, a third person there with them. When she panted, it was for Roger (Row J). When she scootched to cover it was under the steering wheel of Roger's coupé. When Clem tried to claim even his ancient rights of domain on her right nipple she took this as occasion for telling him that only Roger had ever touched them both at the same time, once when they made what she called "bare-chested love."

She would not stop talking even while, playfully and for old times' sake, she accepted a few kisses. Through his Eustachian tubes he heard liquescent, bubbling praise of French subtlety and savoir tickle. It might have been Roger (momentarily materialized) who kicked him off her finally. In that tangle of arms and legs—they were on the floorboards and the brake pedals, with the gearshift set in low gear between them, she still talking as briskly as at a Stevens College tea party—it was dreamlike hard to tell whose sandal caught him in the Adam's apple and sent him toppling out of the car to gasp for breath on the ground. Watching the grease-droplet stars settle back to their equilibrium in the jiggled sky, he was already trying to catalogue what he had been able to touch in the last spasm of their wrestling, as if he already knew that never again would he reach for the trinkets he had missed in high school. What was already fading from the memory of his fingertips was all he could take with him for talisman when he went west tomorrow.

Margaret had put on the dome light in the car. Stretching to the mirror, she was mopping lipstick from her wet cheeks. The bodice of her dress was sweat-stained dark, like a dancer's briefs. "I might as well tell you," she said through the pucker of her lips as she repainted them. "Row J has still touched me where you haven't."

"You went all the way with a Frog," Clem accused, half-dreamily wondering if that, indeed, wasn't what he had just been trying to seize, like a rat trying to steal the eggshell wherein love was complete.

"Clem! What do you take me for?" she asked with a flattered laugh. "Just because you've found some coed who'll ..."

"Sonia," he said. "Whenever I want."

"Tell!" Margaret commanded after a moment when he felt her curiosity strain through the hot silence.

Like a breath of cool mountain air he felt the impulse to tell her that of course Sonia would serve him whenever he had a ruble to spare, since Dostoevsky had made her a prostitute. Sweet mountains of fiction. Sweet schizophrenia.

Or suppose he told her now, finally, in this last of all meetings, how her image had risen like Cynara's once upon a time when he lay with Irene Lacey. But it struck him that all his past was as fictional now as Dostoevsky's novel, that Margaret was no better equipped (by Stevens College or her naturally mediocre I.Q.) to separate truth and fiction in one than in the other. Further, she had lost her rank as Cynara. Woman of clay and sweat, she had thrown herself away on a mortal Deke.

Yet, in one last reversion to playing Harry Rinehart, or in anticipation of an invention still to be made, he had a last gambit to try with inconstant Margaret.

He gloomed histrionically while she finished her repairs, would not open his mouth to lie about Sonia, and then, starting the car, said, "It's no good. I can't love anyone but you, Margaret. If I can't have you, the frog won't. I'm going to kill us both."

He gunned the motor. The car went lurching, bouncing, accelerating toward the brick schoolhouse. She thought he was playing. So did he, until she screamed.

Well, Clem never did handle machines adequately. He threw his weight on the brake and probably on the accelerator at the same time.

The car hit the schoolhouse hard enough to break seven windows. Margaret was thrown against the dashboard. She was not seriously hurt, but real blood began to drip from the corner of her mouth. Very like a scared vampire she looked for a few minutes while they wandered in the headlights assessing further damage.

Besides the windows and the rear bumper, now Clem saw that the front bumper was a total loss, too. As he raced the car back toward town he heard the bumper wail like a siren as it rubbed the front wheels.

It was not the next day but two weeks later that Clem left Boda for the fictive West. He spent those two weeks working for his father, in honest contrition wanting to pay for the cost of repairing the car. (Why did he not add "vault bronzer" to the list of occupations he gave the TV interviewer? Perhaps because, being true, it would have been out of place on that ritual list.)

On the great day of his departure his father, mother and sister drove him to the arterial highway nine miles south. The bumpers still dangled on the Chevy. Clem's father gave him the eleven dollars cash he had earned, told him, "You wire us if you get in any trouble, son," and then gave him another dollar, in small change. His mother cried, and in his sister's round, scared eyes he saw himself diminishing like a Theseus walking into the labyrinth.

A black Essex stopped to pick him up. And he never really went home to Boda again.

A few years later Clem wrote some stories and a few poems based on his hitchhiking that summer. (One of the stories would begin, "The rising sun bronzed the vault of the sky. Lefty watched the road where nobody came.") Most of what he wrote, when one reads it now, seems to have been stifled by certain paralyzing conventions of the Thirties. The standard regional events and proletarian figures are there. What is missing from them is just the thing one wants most—some token of the shape they took in his not at all standard sensibility. He had not yet found himself amid his material. Or it is as if he truly didn't know who he was in that transitional summer when he saw so much.

In his stories it is only someone who rides on top of a boxcar from North Platte to Cheyenne. The anonymous innocent of a thousand American short stories "wants to know why" the bum who befriended him and shared an onion sandwich in the glory of dawn can betray the Huck-Jim relationship by dogging after a whore when the train rolls into Cheyenne. Or the same innocent sits all day at a crossroads west of Lincoln wondering where the pretty girls are going in the tourists' cars.

In some frustration one thinks, But this was Clem and at that age he was probably more visionary—and, in the sense Freud intends when he calls children "polymorphous perverse," more corrupt—than ever again in his life. He did not necessarily see bodies or faces when he looked at people. The bums he met and rode with probably looked to him more like Crane's "blind fists of nothing, humpty-dumpty clods" than they looked like the photographs in the sociopoetical books of the time.

And, as for sitting all day watching the tourist girls fly past like the tragic division of forces on their way—well, he tried once to explain the most memorable and poignant of his sexual experiences that summer. One day in Nebraska, he said, he wandered into an enormous cornfield. There was no female there, nor did he imagine one. The tough green arches of corn leaves, the hot sky, the intricate, dry crumbling of the soil underfoot and the mournful endlessness of the repeated patterns stirred him to a sensuous ecstasy. The cornfield itself, needing no interpretive additions, was the bridal shape to which his senses responded. That was all there was to the story, at that time. But what happened there? I asked in frustration. Nothing, except an intensification of mindless joy that had resulted presently in a spontaneous orgasm. He explained that he had had the same "knowledge" two other times. Once when he was studying Yoga from a New Jersey guru, and once when he stood with Cecile Potter in the bombed ruins of Coventry. It would be repeated a third time, after his attempt to explain—in Kansas, when he was there to lecture at a writers' conference, and presently I will give a full account of that. That such powerful intuitions came to him can mean little except in the full context and the repetitions which I have to present. Say for now that it means nothing. The third repetition may have some magic to it. Then or never we'll know what it means.

Say it was his final disappointment with Margaret Shea that cut his tie with the realities of home and let him go wandering off to a demented vision in a cornfield. He was surely not less than demented that summer, and the whole mythical West was the landscape of his insanity. He didn't know where he was going. "California" was merely a conventional name for his destination, a sop to keep his folks from worrying. He was looking for himself and he thought the granite mountains might have news of him. Maybe he was wanted at Little Big Horn to turn the tide of defeat into victory. Or Sutter had found traces of the philosopher's stone in the millrace of a common workaday gold mine. He went to survey the Drake Estate. His love had died up in the Donner Pass and he must go hide her bones from the timber wolves. Hickok wanted to hire a new gun. The girls at Chinese Kate's were spreading slanders about his masculinity, and he must ride over the mountains to hush them. Beryl in the beryl mines was changing from a silicate of great hardness to a green substance like Jello. Is there an alchemist in the country who will save the vital beryl industry?

Say all the most fantastic things about why he went west that summer and you'll have some chance of reaching the truth. When he came to a junction he flipped a coin to see which road he should take—as long as it went west. He meant to head for Albuquerque and found himself in Yellowstone Park. He thought he was looking for work, but when a Salt Lake garage owner offered him two-fifty a day to handle the service station, he refused on grounds that they were paying three dollars for harvesters in the eastern-Colorado dust bowl. A homosexual truss salesman offered him a ride all the way from Grand Junction to Los Angeles. Before they had gone fifty miles Clem discovered that he was supposed to earn his passage, and he walked most of the way back through the desert. He went up to Taos and was no doubt surprised to be told there that D. H. Lawrence had moved away and died. Mrs. Luhan was not receiving beardless geniuses.

He worked four days in a restaurant at Grand Lake and came down out of the mountains with exactly the sufficient sum his father had given him when he left home. With his eleven dollars and change he settled in Boulder.

At this point he returned, as it were, from a mental fugue to a perch on the flatland of reality. Only a perch, where he rested on one foot, ready to fly away again on his *ailes de fou*. But at any rate one can here recommence to conjecture his motives in terms somewhat short of fantasy.

He settled in Boulder for almost a month "because there was a university there and a nice library." That's a good enough reason—for Clem. It proves he knew who he was, at least better than those who had sought to entice him with perversion or honest employment did. He was, by the skin of his teeth, a poet. If the library hadn't stopped his wanderings, heaven knows what could have.

He took a room for three dollars a week, stocked up on bread, peanut butter, fresh tomatoes and milk and began to read. I never asked how he got his library card. It is unlikely that it was honestly come by, and somehow the picture of him as an illicit reader is appropriate.

His money ran out and he was still not through reading and thinking. (He thought when his eyes were tired, lying on the same cot he used for reading, hearing the same nearby church bells strike the hours, so that the substance of reading and recollection took on a seamless unity as it never had before. If his mother could have seen him there she would have said, "But Clem, you didn't have to go all the way out there and worry us all so much just to lie around and read or be lazy. You could have done that at home." She would have misunderstood grossly. The distance of that room was just what gave it its necessary quality. It had to be three thousand miles from home—not three thousand miles as the crow flies but as the blind or the saintly wander—to permit him, for the first time in his life, to taste there the equivalence between subjective loneliness and the outlaw liberty of unconstraint. He had fled away from reality or been banished for having the temerity to call himself a poet, had even committed his symbolic suicide on the eve of making the break. Sooner or later he had to come back inside—still calling himself a poet—and that was a much tougher nut to crack. He had to temper the idea in himself for a while. That is what he was doing as he lay in Boulder. "Between that room and the street there was no joint," he thought later, paraphrasing Sweeney Agonistes. "I've never been so drunk as when I lay up there with nothing to drink but milk, and that running out. I've never been a better poet than while I was in that room. Everything came through my mind, and the hungrier I got the clearer it all was.")

The obvious joint between that room and the street was that the room cost three dollars a week, and his landlady told him that if he did not pay up soon he would be on the street again, before he was ready. He gave her sweet promises. She liked him well enough to believe in them. He worked one day spreading asphalt on a tennis court for the university, invested all his money in food, got more books, gave the landlady more stringent promises.

All he thought, or what poetry he may have advanced toward form as he waited out the summer weeks in that room, is of course a mystery of the same order—no more, no less—as what he "knew" when he had his vision in the cornfield. "I thought about every bit of my past life and every bit of the future," he said, half facetiously, again shrugging away the truly incommunicable. "Well, you know, I thought about where I'd just been hitchhiking. I read Hesse and Mann and Laforgue and Corbière, Whitman, Eliot, MacLeish, and I reread *Crime and Punishment* after I decided I hadn't gotten it the first time through. I recalled that I had so touched Margaret Shea's never-never bristle that night on the floor of the car. Things like that I thought about."

And when his landlady at last became more adamant in her demands for payment, he merged reading and thought into the question, "If it made a better man out of Raskolnikov, why not out of me?" He said he spent many days lying alone wondering whether to kill his landlady with an ax some Friday after the stabler tenants had paid their rent. "I don't know if I seriously meant to do it. It was an artful thought, and you tell me that art is always serious. I suppose if I'd tried it, really, she'd have taken the ax away from me."

Then one day it came as a great shock to him that the landlady whom he might have laid open à la Dostoevsky had both the power and the wit to evict him before he could get to her. She showed up in his room that afternoon with a burly tenant who had offered to settle her problem. The tenant was all for holding Clem's T shirts and blanket roll against the unpaid bill. The landlady said, No, if Clem would permit them to search his pockets to make sure he really had no money he could take his possessions.

Junior Raskolnikov agreed to the search, but hid his last dollar thirty-five in his shoe before the search began. ("While I was in the bathroom hiding it, it occurred to me that a body orifice is the traditional place to cache the loot in such a case; but then I realized my tennis shoes were nearly as offensive a place to search.") So he left with only a few dollars' worth of default on his conscience instead of a split head—and yet a sense of having "been there and back," of understanding at last fully the utter freedom of a criminal. Good preparation for a creative man. His luck was running full and strong.

With his dollar thirty-five he made his way back east. Not to Boda. Boda was twice as far behind him as the Rockies. He came back to the university, where he worked in the kitchen of the university hospital until school started.

He explained this action by writing to his parents that he felt he was ready to work seriously now. They took this as evidence of zeal to pay his own way through college. He took it to mean that he would write poems, novels, short stories, epics, sagas and dramas. For the time being the ambiguity satisfied all parties.

# 6

ABOUT THE POEMS Clem wrote that summer, H. Warwick pronounced that they lacked sensuality—by this pronouncement voiding any claim to Clem's respect. Clem might pity Felix Martin for being blind to his merits, but at least Felix could point with a certain precision to remediable flaws. H. Warwick's impressionism had no such utility. While he flattered he would be listened to. When he offended he was talking to a deaf ear. Henceforward he would have to pay his way in Clem's tolerance with his gifts as a clown or by sheer practical usefulness.

Usefully he found rooms for Clem and himself in a small house several blocks from the campus. There was a ten-dollar-a-month cell at the back of the second-floor landing for Clem. For himself H. Warwick took the comparatively grandiose front room. Ordinarily it rented to two students, but he needed breathing space for his calfbound books, the reproductions of Whistler etchings he had "picked up at a ridiculously low figure" at his home-town bookstore, and the Black Masses that he constantly threatened, with a whinnying giggle, but never dared perform.

The tiny room was exactly what Clem needed to work in. It isolated him nearly as well as his room in Colorado had. When he wanted to relax sybaritically and traffic with a confessed Satanist, he was always welcome to journey down the hall to Balliol, tea and the aphrodisiac smell of incense.

Aside from the relative seclusion of the yellow house and the happy proximity it afforded poet and friend, there was another "utterly delicious" recommendation for it, H. Warwick confided even before they were well moved in. Emmy Polk, their landlady, was quite, quite mad, in the English style. She really confused day and night. With no trouble at all Clem could "sneak his girls in past her whenever he wished."

A rare opportunity—if Clem had had even one girl. He didn't know a single girl at college who would go to the movies with him, let alone any who with purpose predestined would tippy-toe up Emmy's stairs to ease him. He sensed that his life with women was forever behind him. But for obvious reasons he hardly dared admit this to H.

Warwick. Better to let Warry go on believing him the insatiable heterosexual, like Wilde in his early days.

Clem was getting a little weary of the insistent identification with Wilde as well as being annoyed with H. Warwick for other things, "I signed up to take my phys.-ed. credit in boxing that semester," Clem said. "When Warry pointed out that Wilde too had been handy with his dukes and had once whipped some roughs who called him a lily sniffer, I changed over to badminton. Dukes to marquises all too short a way."

But he took the room so latent with fictive opportunity. After all, someone had gone to the trouble of finding it for him. He had the real prédilection de l'artiste for letting people wait on him. As the courtship became more hopeless H. Warwick would be increasingly zealous to flatter, make loans, even provide a girl of sorts. Didn't Clem foresee this when he moved into Emmy's?

The house might have been chosen for illicit privacies; alas, they were watched with more cynical suspicion than they ever deserved. The eye that watched Satanist and poet slip or scamper to each other's room was that of Wadleigh Hertz.

Wadleigh was sharing the third room on their floor. When his door was open—and Wadleigh was not a man to close his door—he saw everyone who passed in the corridor or on the stairs. Wadleigh's Marxism was burning then with its hardest, most gemlike flame. His favorite literary critic was Mike Gold of The New Masses et al, and I suspect that what endeared Gold most to him was Gold's habit of denouncing bourgeois books and writers as fruity.

When Wadleigh learned—by listening at the door and by subjecting H. Warwick to inquisition in the bathroom—that Clem was "a writer and a most promising one," a complete set of stereotypes must have fallen clattering into place.

One imagines the interrogation in the bathroom. Wadleigh Hertz Gold, bearish and stripped to the waist with his galluses hanging, would be standing before the mirror above the sink, manfully and expertly shaving with a foot-long straight razor. Willowy and smirking, swathed in a red silk dressing gown, H. (Fruity) Warwick perched on the edge of the tub, unable to meet those black eyes fixed on him with such steadiness they might have been pistol targets pasted to the glass.

"And you say his folks are working-class people?"

"Oh, I would hardly characterize—"

"You know what the working class is, don't you?"

"The lower classes, certainly. But I fancy there's a bar sinister in Clement's family. Blood will tell. Ha ha, you've cut yourself."

"I never cut myself," Wadleigh said, stanching the red flow with toilet paper. It was the capitalists who had done it to him, as it was the capitalists who made him fall on icy sidewalks, catch body vermin from a rich sorority girl and flunk political science in his senior year. "He is from the working class. He better not forget it."

"I picture him sprung from a mixing of the orders, like little Hyacinth in The Princess Casamassima." (One thing you have to give the fruity aesthetes. They read everything.)

"Hyacinth? Hyacinth? That's a name?" If Mike Gold Hertz had met a living creature named Hyacinth he would have trampled it like a grub on the sidewalk.

Frightened by the rumble of wooden shoes on the stairs, H. Warwick modulated his teasing. "At least he's not bourgeois. Aristocrats and the lower classes have more in common, I find, than either have with the middle classes."

"How come he calls himself a writer if he hasn't even published anything in the college magazine?"

"He doesn't feel ready to publish yet," H. Warwick defended. "I approve. Too many immature writers are rushing into print these days."

While, in the mirror, the razor scraped away the affectation of H. Warwick's clichés and slopped them into the sink, Wadleigh would have been deciding, I owe it to the Movement to put this Anderson straight. What was the kid? Only a sophomore English major, nineteen years old and looking about sixteen. But—theoretically and just supposing—if this one should break through the evil competition that capitalists set up to smother writers, well, it was Wadleigh's duty to see that he didn't turn out to be a Thornton Wilder, a Scott Fitzgerald or a James For-Christ's-Sake Branch Cabell.*

A few days later, his deadfalls laid and his petard fused, Wadleigh intercepted Clem as he returned from classes. Through the never-closed door Wadleigh bellowed, "Come in here, Anderson. I got two quarts of beer."

Of course he intimidated Clem at once. Wadleigh intimidated everyone he met in those days, from the dean of students (whom he had called to his face "an instrument of reaction"—he would have been expelled if he had used the word "tool") to poor, senile Emmy Polk (who doted on him anyway and would have given him his breakfasts free even if he hadn't bullied her, but if they had seemed like charity he might not have been able to choke them down). At twenty-two he had the air of a working-class Pilate, disillusioned, impatient and not so much cruel as resigned to the cruelty with which history would deal with fools. He knew that if capitalism set the dean in a position of temporary authority and gave the uninfected sorority girls to "sons of decadent families," this injustice was only for a day. From the pinnacle of historical inevitability he could thunder anathemas like Moses from the slope of Sinai.

But he did not intimidate Clem so much by the superiority of his dialectic as by the fact that he seemed to Clem a startling reincarnation of the men who used to hang around the cream station in Boda—the sports, the hunters, the former high-school athletes, Jack Wagner and all his buddies—who had for so long been his bullying arbiters of manliness, and from whom he thought he had escaped when he came to college. Fierce as a censor of the conscious, here was one of them between his room and H. Warwick's. He had better match this man drink for drink or be thought a sissy. (He did not know then that Wadleigh was prepared to think him worse than that.)

Over the swiftly disappearing beer Wadleigh began the inquisition on literary lines. What did he, Anderson, like?

When Clem said that D. H. Lawrence seemed pretty great, Wadleigh roared in pain. Lawrence was a premature Nazi, with all his bullshit about thinking with the blood and trying to solve the contradictions of capitalism by having a workingman and a highborn lady go off at the same time. "You think you can think with your blood? Go ahead. Think something," Wadleigh commanded. Clem couldn't.

But if his blood was too base to form ideas, his brain was busy with them. He had just learned, somewhat inadvertently, that women could have orgasms. At least some women could. English women. English women in fiction. A dandy idea, just revolting enough to prepare him for accepting Wadleigh's implication that working-class girls were too pure to worry about whether they came or not. Maybe he wasn't through with women after all. There were still possibilities to experiment with. And if Nazis like Lawrence knew more of these possibilities than he did ... "I kind of favor the Nazis," he said.

"What?" This conversation was taking place in the fall after German planes bombed Guernica. How could he, Wadleigh, sit still and listen to a small-town punk not only admit coolly that Lawrence was a Nazi but drink his, Wadleigh's, beer and go on insisting that Nazis were right in valuing war, violence, blond beasts, splitting open the heads of pawnbrokers or landladies with axes, and the dictatorship of a fair-skinned elite.

"Do you have any idea what war is?" Wadleigh pleaded. "Do you want to die? Be burned alive? Gutted? Choked? Mashed by a tank? Blown up by a man you can't even see?"

The Boda hero shrugged coolly. A smile played on his stern lips. His quart of beer was gone and he was thinking on loftier planes than poor Wadleigh could guess. He thought he heard Sherman's ragged veterans sing "Marching through Georgia," and he hummed a little bit along with them to show Wadleigh what he meant.

Wadleigh drowned him out. "I hear that you read a lot. Haven't you ever read anything about war? Not even Dos Passos or Under Fire or Paths of Glory or The Good Soldier Schweik? Not even All Quiet on the Western Front?" Wadleigh pleaded.

"I saw the movie." Clem began to imitate the thrilling aa-aa-aa-aa-aa-aa of machine guns.

"War is a bunch of idiotic, fat, half-assed generals working up their pitiful egos by slaughtering saps like you. 'War is the health of the state.'"

Clem tried to placate his new friend by saying that he was in favor of health.

"Health of the state, I said. That means the big guy—"

"Better live big and get it over with."

"You're mouthing Mussolini," Wadleigh yelled, clutching his groin. "'Better one day as a lion than fifty years as a sheep.' The sonofabitch. You know what Mussolini does to the opposition? They force castor oil down you. They force it down women. Now don't sit there and tell me that's any way to run a democracy. You sit there and pretend to be so literary and you don't know what the hell you're talking about. You ever read Malraux? Briffault? Romain Rolland? Steinbeck? You got to read In Dubious Battle before I can talk to you. To Make My Bread? See you haven't read anything but Nazi, fruity stuff. You haven't read Auden or Spender. Those guys are poets. They don't waste their time on a lot of fruity sentimentality. For Christ's sake let me give you some books. Here, start with Man's Fate. Listen...."

In the weeks and months after that Clem listened a great deal to Wadleigh. He had to. Wadleigh doted on him for his loathsome intellectual sins and heathen taste.

In fact, from that first afternoon when he had merely intended to nudge a boy with pretensions onto the correct and leftward path, Wadleigh was a victim—as so many other people would be—of Clem's peculiar mixture of charm and wrongheadedness, purity and perversity.

Hoist high on a petard he had trusted as he trusted the eventual triumph of the revolution, Wadleigh would never be his tranquil self again.

Now he was in competition with H. Warwick in courting the boy, a situation that Clem exploited by snickering over H. Warwick with Wadleigh and snickering over Wadleigh with H. Warwick. Like D. H. Lawrence, whom he considered turning into that year, Clem liked to talk about people behind their backs. "It encourages profundity," he always said. "How can you talk seriously to someone's face?"

In this new competition for Clem's allegiance, Wadleigh had one telling advantage. While H. Warwick had talked aphrodisiacally about the girls Clem might or should be bringing to his cell at the end of the hall, so far he had managed only one introduction, of dubious worth. He had introduced Clem to a girl named Marienelle, who, alas, had H. Warwick's scant and pimply face, evasive eyes, and the Pardoner's hair. She was tall and gaunt. Her long nose dribbled excessively in cold weather, just like H. Warwick's. She told Clem on their first date that she was a Lesbian, had been expelled from Barnard for seducing a Georgia girl. Like H. Warwick she drank gallons of tea, loved English things, and reread Winnie the Pooh each year at Christmas time "as a special holiday treat for myself." She valued Clem's intellectual companionship, his interested and submoral attention to her accounts of the tangled web of the gay life. When he, who had bided his time, at last desperately suggested that they liked each other enough to go to his room, she tittered and said, "Dear boy, don't you understand?" He said he understood but it didn't matter. She said that much as she cared for him, she could not yield on an issue involving principle. "You might have my body," she said carelessly. "That would mean nothing to me, but I am afraid that my awareness of the act would violate my immortal image."

On the other hand, there was suitor Wadleigh, who valued Emmy Polk for reasons not very different from Warry's, but who also knew some girls who might make the mischievous hypothesis into reality. Working-class girls. Nurses and student nurses from the University Hospital. Lots of them. Clem had heard their working-class glee in the middle room on some rare occasions when Wadleigh's door was closed. Since he had seen Wadleigh dosing himself in the bathroom with Larkspur Lotion, he reasoned that the bark of Wadleigh's innuendoes represented the bite of true accomplishment.

It was against Wadleigh's code to announce openly that he had ever succeeded with any girl. When asked directly, he would reply with a roaring quote from Hemingway, "'Watch thy mouth!'" Clem learned later that it had been during a humiliating and incomplete connection that Wadleigh had caught the vermin for which he was treating himself, but at this time Wadleigh's reticence merely glamourized him. The bluntness of his literary and political opinions threw around the undiscussed sexual adventures an aura of stallion force. Wadleigh spoke often of "effete capitalists" who didn't know how to value women as women. He cited passages in Man's Fate as evidence. "Capitalists only want to degrade women by sex," he told a rapt Clem, implying that he had learned somehow the trick of exalting them by putting them on their backs in a proletarian manner.

If Wadleigh had come through that winter, as he seemed to promise he would, with girls (even one would do), Clem felt the world might have been enriched with one more proletarian writer. ("It's funny how you need to have a woman who belongs to it to make each new part of your life real.") This new self who had come back from hitchhiking in the mountains was not quite real yet. Some husky, gap-toothed nurse in training might well have helped him realize himself as A. C. (Jack) Anderson, the Jack London of the prairies—just as Marienelle, had she been short of Lesbian principle, might have realized him as A. Clement (Pix) Anderson, aesthete and university wit. As things fell out, a fortunate ambiguity was perpetuated.

One icy Saturday night a week or ten days before Christmas, Clem was alone in his tiny room working on a short story. He had recently heard from Harry Rinehart in San Diego. Better than news, the letter brought literary raw material, of the sort more suited to Jack than to A. Clement. On leave in Los Angeles, Harry had been picked up in a bar by a young civilian who he thought at first was a queer. "I figured as long as the nut was buying me drinks I'd play along with him," Harry wrote. "And if I'd had you here we could have rolled him, but I do not have any buddies in the service as criminal as you. I still wake up sweating when I remember that pistol you kept in the Baptist church basement. It's a wonder we didn't all end up in the chair. You first. Anyway this pogy finally asked me to go home with him because his wife was waiting and we'd have more drinks there. I figured he was lying, but when we got there his woman was waiting, all right. They lived in a crumby apartment up on the Hill. There was a bare light bulb and green shades in the kitchen. The guy got to fooling around with his wife and the first thing I knew—or the second, because I was watching it all—he had got her completely stripped and then he wanted me to take her on because he couldn't satisfy her any more. Boy! I reached down and grabbed an empty milk bottle and told them to stay away from me and I got out of there. I don't want anything like that."

There, Clem had gloated, was the raw and dripping stuff of life itself. Let's see how the bourgeois like that when I slap them in the face with it, Jack muttered through white lips.

He could give it what Harry had failed to provide (though lucky and dumb Harry had lived through it, right up to the unsatisfactory ending). He had never seen Los Angeles or even an honest-to-God slum district resembling the Hill, but he had given the story a setting of sights, sounds and smells. In the letter there was no concreteness except the green blinds in the kitchen, the bare light bulb and one milk bottle. The bar in which sailor and civilian met had been described now and peopled. (Blunt, mahogany-colored pillars framing the mirror behind the bar, stamped tin on the ceiling, beyond the sailor a thin man wearing glasses who carried in his pocket a worn, often refolded prospectus of the Drake Estate. Before the young man intruded, the man with glasses had tried to interest the sailor in investing some money in the inheritance of Sir Francis—"Drake was a sailor, too.")

In the story Clem was writing there was now dialogue to express the loneliness of the sailor, separated by mountains and deserts from his home in the Midwest. There was the young civilian's affectation of culture and worldliness, very fruity and not unlike the speech of H. Warwick Lloyd.

All this Clem had spun together in a week of fascinating, demoralizing effort in time stolen from his classes. He rather liked the feel of risking his grades in botany, philosophy, economics and survey of English literature for the sake of his story. It made him feel like a real artist—like Gauguin turning his stockbroker's uniform back to the Bourse, like another Anderson telling his secretary he was "walking in the bed of a river." Yet this flirtation with guilt had caught up with him this evening in his despair at how to finish the story.

It was something that happened, that was all, and it had no meaning. It had happened far away in Los Angeles, far from the bourgeois conscience it was supposed to affront. He had made it happen here again in Emmy Polk's nine-by-twelve room with browning roses on the wallpaper. He had seen it all, and he could see it all again now as he stared over his typewriter at the black, frost-rimed window. He saw—and had described—the shamed smile of invitation from the denuded woman, the blunt, honest hand groping for the milk bottle. It was all there, all written on fifteen typed and many-times-corrected pages stacked on his study table. And "I don't want any of that." The reader—Clem himself, and he knew it—rejected the sorry episode just as Harry had. Common sense and common decency both rejected it as meaningless. Such things happened all over the world. There might be prophecy in the violence itself, in its very meaninglessness a threat to annihilate proletarian with bourgeois in some absurd holocaust of fire. He vaguely sensed that this was what it did mean, and the icy black of his window seemed mutely to confirm his intuition. Yet, if that was what it truly meant, what was the use of writing? If the promised end was fire, blank paper would burn as well as a perfected story.

And, goddam it, he told the rattling window, he wanted to write and have it mean something, and maybe the writing itself could alter the predetermined triumph of the void. But it seemed to him the window watched him cynically. Its black silence said, Hurry now; if you want it to come out right, you'd better think fast.

He had already tried fitting a half-dozen invented or plagiarized endings to the brute material.

There was a bloody Jeffersian ending. The woman killed both her husband and the sailor in a bacchantic frenzy. They had been unworthy of the divine female principle that she represented. Proudly she waited for the police to come.

(That's more optimistic than I'd write it, the window said. I'd leave out the pride.)

Why not a good proletarian ending and have the sailor walk out in revulsion against the couple's bourgeois decadence? But, damn it, that meant setting the whole thing in a Santa Monica beach house rather than a ten-dollar-a-month fleabag on the Hill. If he meant to be honest he had to show the poor devils as being more proletarian than the sailor.

(Why be honest? the window asked. But if I were writing it I wouldn't even give them the dignity of the proletarian label.)

There was the Ballad of Reading Gaol ending. After the sailor was gone, the poor perverted husband knew he had killed the thing he loved—not with a sword, but with a word.

(Ha ha, the window said.)

There was the clean regionalist ending. The sun was rising as the sailor left the apartment building. He purged himself of his glimpse into hell by vomiting in the gutter. Then, wiping his lips and thinking of Sally May back home, her lithe body brown as an oak bud, already carrying water to her father in the fields, he would throw his shoulders back and proceed to duty on the white ships of the youngest, most wholesome country in the whole world.

(They're my ships, it's my country, the icy, brittle window said. I made up all that crap about wholesome Sally May. She sweats apple cider and comes like a thunderclap. Huns, Frogs, Japs, Communazis and other species of internationalist will never spread that berry-brown body. And neither will you, son. Neither will you.)

There was—when nothing would hurry and disgust with himself was making laps on the vicious circle like a racing cyclist—an O. Henry surprise-type ending. The woman stripped by her husband turned out to be Sally May. The sailor recognized her by a mole on her shoulder. Or she was Lorna Doone. She was Madame Sosotris. What the sailor grabbed when he reached down was not a bottle—Oh, hell. Throw the whole thing away.

(I'm willing if you are, the window said.)

Once that year the landlady Emmy Polk wandered into Clem's room at night and found him so entranced that she got scared. She asked him what he was staring at when he couldn't see anything but maybe his own reflection on the dark window. She always remembered—without knowing whether to believe him—that he told her solemnly the Devil was out there waiting for him. It must have happened often.

But on this particular night, just before the Devil got in, Wadleigh Hertz came pounding on the door. He pushed his way in without waiting to be asked. He was benignly drunk.

"Jeez, didn't you hear us?" he asked.

"Hear who?"

"We're having a party in my room. Lotsa people are." Then with some unusual impulse to flatter he said, "I might have known you're the one person of my acquaintance with enough dedication to be hard at it on a Saturday night. But, goddammit, Anderson, the bourgeoisie will grind us down if we don't relax now and then. Come on with me. We're really beginning to soar. And the reason I particularly thought of you, friend, is that there's the hottest little ginch I've met for a long time who's with nobody yet. I mean this girl won't leave us guys alone and we've all got dates. So I thought there might be a chance you weren't dated up for later. Come on."

Clem said, No, he had to finish his story. Fifteen minutes after Wadleigh backed out he was at Wadleigh's door.

The "hot little ginch" was Sheila Golfing, more bewildered that night by what she had stumbled into than Clem was. This was her first year in college. She lived in the women's dorm. Ordinarily she kept pretty sedate company. She still went to the once-a-week social evenings of the Epworth League, was still mindful of her mother's admonition that she ought to "find out a boy's background" before accepting a date with him. ("Only, Mother was very vague about what I was supposed to find out," Sheila said later. "Maybe I was supposed to inquire if they had descended from a long line of sex fiends, or maybe just make sure that they weren't Catholics, Jews or as poor as Clem.")

On this particular night a girl from her home-economics class had called to ask if she would accept a blind date with an "awfully nice boy." Sheila, agreeing, had been a little stunned to find that she was to meet this nice boy in a men's rooming house, stunned again when she, her classmate and a third girl they had picked up on their way encountered mad Emmy Polk at the front door. Emmy barred their path, told them they certainly could not go upstairs. But they were Mr. Hertz's sisters, Sheila's classmate explained. Then Emmy seemed to recognize them. Oh, yes, oh, yes, they had been here before. Oh, yes, they could go right on up.

Surprises continued. Wadleigh Hertz's room was not the rendezvous from which the evening's excursion would proceed (Sheila had been given to understand that they would probably all go to the movies) but the site where the evening was to be spent. And one more thing—there were four couples besides herself gathered into the modestly spacious room, but no extra young man waiting for her.

She was on their hands and, while no full-blown saturnalia was in prospect, they could not very well carry on with their usual freedom under the disapproving eyes of a girl who looked like everyone's little sister. Wadleigh, a man who always meant to kill two birds with a single stone and hence hardly ever got one, brought Clem in to distract her. If Clem was pleased, so much the better.

At the moment of Clem's entry the phonograph was playing "Strange Fruit." A bearded art student—Jack Miller—was crouched close to the machine, his eyes and teeth glittering. Wadleigh's roommate and his girl lay companionably on the bed opposite the one on which Sheila sat alone. Their heads were together as if they were plotting something, but there was as yet no unchaste bodily contact. Sheila's classmate had just complained to Wadleigh that they couldn't dance to "that record," and he was condescendingly explaining that it was "a blow against Southern fascism"; once it was struck, Goodman, Ellman and the Duke were coming up. Not a saturnalia at all—but it looked like one to Clem. He must have been drunk from the moment he crossed the threshold and saw his true love sitting prim as a little Dutch girl on the bed of his naked desire.

141

It was Sheila's first impression that he was far gone before he came into the room. When he approached her, leering, asking with a thick tongue if she would like a beer, her gaze took in the thorny mass of hair so precariously stacked over his nude temples, the loosened dirty collar of his shirt and the askew fierceness of eyes that had been staring at the night. She thought that whoever gave intoxicants to such an urchin ought to be darn well ashamed of themselves.

"Beer?" he repeated lasciviously.

"No, thank you," she said again.

He helped himself from an open case and perched beside her on the bed, still not seeing her, blind to everything but his intemperate expectations. He was only searching for the proper swaggering phrase to suggest that they toddle down the hall to his crib and get at it—maybe wondering whether it was necessary to say anything at all to a girl of her type. But she sat there so stiffly (after all, no one had given her this boy's background) that he began to worry. He drained the bottle in two fearsome gulps.

"You're from the hospital?" he asked.

"Me? No. No."

"Where do you work?"

Sheila laughed thinly. "I'm afraid I don't. I'm in school, though but a freshman."

He looked disappointed, almost as if he had been given an answer that would drive him away. She asked, "Are you in school? You see, I'm afraid I don't know anyone here except Eloise and Bertha, and ... and ... what are you all?"

The question and her bemusement, as of a stranger on their queer planet, had its humor, and when he remembered their meeting it was this query that seemed funniest to him. But not then.

Dead drunk on his own seriousness—he was in full campaign and he had not expected to have to say more than Napoleon in a similar press, crying "Déshabillez-vous!" to the woman provided for his refreshment—he lost his way in rambling, plaintive frankness.

"I'm killing time in school," he said. "But I may join the Navy any time. Sailors' lives are ... more real than this. And why the hell not? There's going to be a war anyway. May as well go out and meet it. War is the health of the state."

"Oh," she said, pitying him more for his present woe and intoxication than for the remote likelihood of war. "Oh, I don't think you should."

"I may go to Spain with the International Brigade. 'The horn of Roland in the passages of Spain … Against the silent ground the silent slain.'"

"What on earth are you saying?"

"I'm tired of life. 'Of what is it fools make such vain keeping?' Huh?"

Sheila pinched herself to make sure that she was awake, alert and not missing any of the connectives this weird boy might offer to link his incoherences. "Of course that's poetry," she said, as if mere identification might help her snag a branch of meaning. "'The silent slain' and 'Spain.' That rhymes, but—Are you really going to join the International Brigade? They're Communists, aren't they?"

"We're all Communists here," he said with a deranged smile. "Except me. I'm a fascist by temperament and tradition and intellectual choice. Like Ezra Pound. Jefferson and/or Mussolini. But Franco's a bad fascist. You know what the bastards did to Guernica."

"No, I don't," Sheila said in alarm. She did not know what Communists and fascists did to little girls from Indiana, either, but she was beginning to guess that it might be something her mother wouldn't approve, and it had occurred to her that Clem might be telling the truth about these people in the room. They might well be Communists, since they bore so little resemblance to the students she had met at Epworth League. If this one was only a fascist, maybe she would do well to play up to him until she could persuade him to get her out of here. "That poetry about Spain," she asked. "Did you write it?"

"MacLeish," Clem said. "'Is it like this in death's other kingdom? Waking alone, at the hour when we are trembling with tenderness. Lips that would kiss form prayers to broken stone.'" He had such a compelling vision of death's first kingdom twitching around him to the rhythm of Ellman's horn that he nearly wept. Armoring himself with snideness, he said, "I didn't write that either, to tell the truth."

"I know you didn't. That's T. S. Eliot," Sheila said. "You seem to know so much more poetry than I do, but Mr. Martin read us that, and the part you quoted stuck in my mind. 'The hour of tenderness …' That's awfully touching."

Now he glared at her as if she had insulted his mother's cookery. "Between the noit and the dayloit, when the milk is beginning to sour, comes applause for the day's palpitation who is knowed as the chilling power."

"Longfellow!" Sheila said, gulled further into thinking that this was a gentle and sympathetic fascist, after all, who knew such sweet melodies. Longfellow had always touched her.

"It ain't Longfellow," Clem snarled, "and 'the hour of tenderness' ain't Eliot. You make Eliot sound like Longfellow, is all I meant to illustrate. Don't you have any ear for meter? Longfellow stinks."

"I'm sorry. Mr. Martin tried to teach us to scan. I was taught it in high school. I never believed in it, I guess. Maybe I'm just dumb."

"Aw.... So you're in Felix Martin's class?"

"I think he's fine, though a lot of his students make fun of him. He does look like a mummy, sort of. But what difference does that make? He's a good man."

Tuned tight as a piano string, Clem thought a comparison had been made, and through his failing arrogance he felt well up a horrid wish to concur in it. "Felix is good, and I'm no good. He could teach you about meter and I just make you feel bad. I'm no good. I tell lies about myself and pretend that I'm some great writer. My poetry stinks and I can't even write a short story that doesn't sound like someone else's. If I ever got to Spain I'd hide behind a tree like a yellow dog. I'm not a fascist and I never read Jefferson and/or Mussolini. I keep using the titles of books I've never read, and Felix has read them all. Even that goddam Longfellow is probably a better poet than I."

Now, if he had only known it, he was winning her. In voiding his lies and ripping away the scaffolding of pretense he had needed this long, he was showing her a person no one had seen before. In some magic of sympathy she seemed to recognize this. She put out both hands, as if intending to protect him from scoring himself physically. ("I never had any defense against Clem when he was being a wet dog," she said later. "Not even that first time I saw him and I was such a little fool and he seemed so peculiar to me.")

She only touched him with the back of her nails. He could hardly have felt the touch any more than he could have missed knowing some part of what it meant—at least recognizing the gesture as the dumb and still swaddled equivalent of his need for it, a mirroring of his shyest secrets, secrets so shy that he alone could not coax them into the light. It was the touch of Eve or Miranda discovering in the brutally different body of the male the wondrous tender reality of Adam or Ferdinand. Force majeure. What had been in this trivial moment revealed could never be hidden again in doubt, this meeting never sundered, though it might be hundreds of times betrayed.

The first betrayal followed almost instantaneously. Why? Clem thought it was because, just then, a girl named Dodie sat down in Wadleigh's swivel chair and all the young men—there were more of them in the room now, from somewhere—were taking turns at sitting in her lap and kissing her. The beast slobber on her chin glittered in the light and Clem thought it utterly devalued the little touch he had exchanged with Sheila. He was challenged to competition. But more than that, first and last, he couldn't let well enough alone, let love enough alone.

When Sheila said in all good faith that if he was a writer he was probably a pretty honest one and that she'd certainly like to read his stuff, he proposed that they go down the hall to his room. This very minute, he promised, she would hear some of his poems.

Faithfully she let him guide her out of the noise in Wadleigh's room and down past the bathroom door to his own. She simply believed that he meant to read verses to her. And he, that she was stepping into his trap. If she wasn't ready yet, if she didn't go straight for the bed, he would read her bits from the story he was working on. It ought to have on her the aphrodisiac effect he felt so powerfully each time he typed or read those scenes of twisted passion on the Hill. She liked him. She was weakening. If the fine hopes with which he began the story had failed, then, *instrumenti diaboli*, all his sweat on it might come to another kind of profit. Why shouldn't it be the straw to trip her?

She stepped aside in the narrow hall to let him open his door. In the poor light he saw that she was smiling encouragement. He could not meet her eyes as he put his hand on the knob.

The door was locked. His door was locked.

He would not, could not believe it. He never locked it when he went out, in fact had lost the key. The door could be locked only from inside. It took his hot brain a minute to transpose the idea that he wasn't inside to lock it into its correct form: It wasn't he who had locked it from inside.

He tried to pull the door out of its frame by sheer force.

"Never mind," Sheila said. "You can show them to me another time."

"Now!" he said with a furious whistle of breath. He took a bottle opener from his pocket and began prying the stop molding off the doorframe. Nails shrieked in the wood.

And from inside, like an echo, but unmistakably not an echo, came the mocking, punished squeak of bouncing bedsprings. Then a cry like that of a mortally wounded rabbit.

It took Sheila just three seconds to interpret these sounds. Then she ran for her coat.

Clem caught her as she was going out the downstairs door. "Please," he said. "I didn't know there was anyone in there. They shouldn't have been in there."

"They certainly shouldn't."

"Please come back to the party. We can go in the front room and see my friend Warry. He doesn't fool with girls. He—I'll recite you a good poem. Not one of mine."

She pulled her sleeve free of his grip. "Good night. I'm sorry about it all. I shouldn't have come here. I'm not used to you ... you Communists."

She walked out into the snow that was falling so densely and wetly around the shabby frame buildings of this block. As Clem followed coatless, he saw that her tracks were the first in this fall of snow, as if she were venturing into a brand-new world. He could not bear to let her go without him. He would promise anything, lies or the truth, whatever she required.

All she would admit wanting was a cab to take her back to the dorm. He did not know if he had money enough to pay the fare, but recklessly he ran ahead of her to Marshall Boulevard and leaped into the middle of the street to flag a cab.

She did not care to discuss what might have been happening in his room. He may have said it was surely more innocent than she thought—and otherwise have worsened what he was trying to mend. She would not let him put his arm around her. She would not even tell him what she liked to read. She would not—now—be impressed that Felix Martin, whom she had called a good man, was interested in Clem's writing.

Leaving the cab in front of the women's dorm was, as far as she was concerned, the end of what might have been a friendship. "Goodbye," she said when he said good night.

Paying for the cab took all of Clem's money. He was coatless, a mile from home. The snow was falling more heavily than when he had left the house. On his bare head it felt like refuse flung by a universe bored with the farce of his intentions.

Too restless to walk and too worn-out to run, he jogged. If and if and if, he jeered at himself, if things had been what Wadleigh had led him to believe, he might be panting with pleasure now instead of trying to fill his lungs with this frosty slop. If and if and if he might have caught on quicker to what kind of a girl Sheila was, he might have had the sense to go more slowly with her. He wasn't stupid. Why did he do such stupid things? Something intended always to offer him his good breaks at the time he was bound to mishandle them.

But as he went on, he began to understand that the injustice was not in things around. Even the tormenting snow began to seem more benign than the terrible contradictions in his heart.

Earlier in the evening, when he had sat in frustration over the story that would not mean what it had to mean, he had stared out at the night and believed that the void was out there—a natural enemy that might erase him at its will. Now he was out there, looking back as if at himself crouched over his creations, his imaginings. He knew there was nothing to be afraid of out here. The Devil was not in the dark. And in knowing this, he knew how to finish the story by fitting it to a theme he could not have grasped familiarly enough before.

He couldn't finish the story all at once. Not that night and not for many days afterward would it come out as he could see now that it must. Every page he had done so far would be thrown away, the material itself thrown away—so that it could come back to him all changed from those recesses of interior darkness where nothing is ever really lost. Changed but more itself than before it was discarded. The form into which labor would press the changed material was his gift from the hard trial of the night.

He was still half drunk when he got back to Emmy Polk's house. He did not pause to look in at Wadleigh's party, but went straight to his own door. It was still closed in his face, but now he was ready to do what he should have done while Sheila was there to see him do it. He braced his back against the opposite side of the corridor and kicked with all his might.

With a splintering of wood the screws holding the lock ripped loose and the door flew open. And still he was being mocked, for this time it had not been locked at all. The room was empty. No lifted thighs of a joy-tormented girl. No romping Wadleigh Hertz or Jack Miller. Only the crazy-quilted bed on which he could lie down alone and see how things might have been.

He heard a mousy stirring at the door. H. Warwick's thin nose poked in. "Are you all right, Clem? I thought I heard some of Wadleigh's roughs pounding at your door. My, my," he said, fingering the splinters where the lock had been. He inclined his head toward the sound of the phonograph, the babble of voices. "It's still going on. I thought if you wanted to work you could come in my room. I shan't disturb you. I feel a cold coming on and I've curled up with Proust."

"Get out," Clem said.

"You want to be alone?" H. Warwick shrugged cutely and blew a good-night kiss as he left.

No, Clem thought, he didn't want to be alone. But was. And not by accident. He threw himself down on the bed without taking off his wet clothes.

Here he was, as if he had wandered out of a party where the promise of joy waited and had come to the wrong room when he tried to find his way back. And presently he thought, That party might have been the one the sailor went to in my story. And a nice girl, a girl nice enough for him, might have been all set up for him. And then he might have had to go out—to take a leak or something, the slum apartments on the Hill wouldn't all have bathrooms—and have been so drunk, so eager, that he couldn't find his way back. And that sailor might have been me.

That was the way he was going to write this story. This one, at last, was going to be really his own. He knew the way things went for those with irreconcilable hearts who always, always lost. That is what all his stories, heartbreaking and glad, would always be about.

* From Clem's notebook, dated two years after his first meeting with Wadleigh: "The Marxist-regionalist—he despised The Rape of the Lock because, he said, people who went around stealing hair couldn't amount to very much."

# 7

HOW DOES ONE DIVORCE? Doctrine and discipline for it there may be. Thought-stopping anguish there must be when the roots to the past are clipped at ground level. Shoots that loved the earth must learn to become air plants or die.

Like suicide, divorce surely belongs to that order of human possibilities where moderation, equivocation and middle-of-the-road prudence are well-nigh unthinkable. I suppose that one may marry tentatively, with reservations, without a full commitment, for marriage is a multiple involvement among multiple involvements, while the absolute act of divorce is single. Surely the shears of Atropos are borrowed for this work. It is an act that has no dimension in time, that great solvent of absolutes, and therefore one tends to consider it, like self-murder, the easiest or most nearly impossible of steps. Either one says, like Milton, That no covenant whatsoever obliges against the main End both of itself, and of the parties covenanting (which, after all, is like Mike Hammer saying "It was easy," after he gut-shot his blonde) or else it must be said, "How does mortal man dare divorce?" Even with the warrant and permission of Almighty God signed, sealed and pocketed, how can a man or a woman dare this mutilation of flesh and spirit?

Thinking of Clem, I thought it was easy:

By not leaving well enough alone.
By submitting to learn of the dog.
By the propinquity of skin.
By his gift of infernal quickness—that power of instantly discerning the honey secrets that most people draw out in a slow lifetime. The quick are a prey to change.
By his maddening incapacity for consolidating his gains. (Clem was born to be the first fireman down the pole—without his pants; the gold-rush leader who arrives at the diggings without his pick; discoverer of islands with no flag to hoist among the palms.)
I thought he wouldn't dare:
Because his life was ruled—almost made real—by language. Marriage was the subtle word in which were summed up all his contacts with reality.

Because the happiness of his marriage to the world had been consummated through the one venereal link the word allows.

Because Sheila was eponym for all the joys he found in excess of the common good.

Because there were no incoherences in his true life.*

Because he was Daddy and Sheila was Mommy. It pleased Clem to play, however secretly, the patriarch of a tribe that would someday take the world back from its spoilers.

And then because the past was the tyrant against which he never rebelled, though he might be in rebellion against everything else. The past had made its commandments clear to him—clearer than to any of us, I think—and the one who watched the inscription being delved in the stone could not be in the forefront of disobedience.

One thinks—but thought itself is swept away on a tide of circumstance. Whether divorce is easy or impossible, the New York State Supreme Court fulfilled that iota of the law for which it is responsible. In August 1953 Aaron Clement Anderson (defendant) and Sheila Golfing Anderson (plaintiff) were pronounced flesh of neither's flesh; emancipation of their bones was proclaimed henceforward and forever; the mythical rib was mythically restored to the side from which it had been torn; the helpmeets were rendered helpless. What the court put asunder, let no gods or recorders of fact presume henceforward to join.

The heavy news came to Janet and me while we were vacationing in Colorado at our usual resort in the mountains, under skies of such amplitude as might lead one bent on biography to imagine that the gods may go about their lawful business undeterred by New York's decrees, lead him to resift his facts and marvel at justice.

For Janet, the children and me this was our fifth year together at that little resort north of Leadville. We were already nested familiarly in the sentimental values we had lugged west like furniture. (Bourgeois values, as Wadleigh would have once, so aptly, called them.) We had not only our comfortable little "ranch house" cabin among a dozen other "ranch house" cabins scattered up a stream from the—well, really, it is pretty silly—"trading post" where we bought gasoline and groceries and took our electric blankets or mixers in for repair. We had our painted screen of mountains and sky—our puny little canvas of "nature" to shelter us like an Abercrombie-and-Fitch wigwam from the granite and the snow and, sometimes, the blue-black glimpse of interplanetary space above us. We never had to look at anything except the denaturized nature we brought with us, portable accidie, cut to our measure and decorated by Technicolor.

Beth, Jill and I hiked across the meadow in the mornings, or up the stream. We looked for beryls, chalcedony, arrowheads, flora and fauna from children's books or any other form in which beautiful meanings might appear under our lazy feet.

I taught my gangly Jill how to cast with a fly rod and had some fine simple talks with her about life and literature while we dawdled on stones half a mile up the trout stream from the valley floor. Beth fell in love with a fat mare named Sugar Belle and an obnoxious little boy from Chicago who used to further his suit by firing on our ranch house with his air rifle very early in the morning. Finally he broke a window. His dad took his air gun away. Beth fell out of love. I don't understand this.

Janet and I played undemandingly at renewing our college-day passions for each other. Lost heroisms of the flesh. Between our bodies, too, the decorated skrim of familiarity, almost as palpable as a nightgown or a contraceptive. But what we had was enough for us.

We had our afternoons together. (The children were obedient to the fiction that "in the afternoons Daddy works" and left us alone together in peace.) By tacit agreement we did not discuss (1) university politics (would I regret supporting Mason Forsberg's promotion to associate?), (2) the hydrogen bomb tests in the Pacific ("I wonder if the Pentagon is mad and I wonder if it means to kill, And I wonder if the world will die, for assuredly it is very ill") and (3) Clem Anderson.

Even in love "there is a world dimensional for those not afflicted with a love of things irreconcilable." We had it. We could not keep even this much forever. In the luxury of the pine-smelling afternoons, with a golden slice of melon lying between us on the veranda table, books in our laps and a bottle of Vouvray staying chill while we drained it, we felt no obligation to pity or envy anyone. No obligation to look up and see the shadows climb like a counterfeit tide of living stuff on the snow fields.

And yet the point of the place, the reason we brought our comforts and our blinders here was surely so that we could look beyond them when we—or should we—choose. It was not altogether the satisfaction of protecting our minds with labels that we sought when we called our resort a "foreign" place, meaning foreign to this settled planet. We said it reminded us of the peninsula at Sils Maria where Nietzsche had his joyous and awful visions, or of a Chinese landscape painting—and even in the coziest museum in the world one may stare at such a painting, or a carving in lapis lazuli, and see, if he chooses, the tragic dimension undiminished.

There to our "little halfway house" came one afternoon a missive from Sheila. A brief, perfunctory note covered the enclosure of an article that had been torn from the pages of a popular men's magazine.

"Are Eggheads Better Lovers?" was the title. Among several pictures of Cindy Hunt solo on the edges and ladders of a kidney-shaped swimming pool, there were three pictures of her with Clem. A text answered the crude question of the title in the affirmative. Beyond that scientific affirmation there was no reliable data. It all meant nothing much beyond the fact that someone (no one? she herself?) was busily promoting better things for C. Hunt (nee Butterfield, alias Beauty Bear). Eggheads—permit me to summarize—are better lovers because "they are more sensitive to the way a girl may feel."

I had a horrid suspicion that Clem had written this copy. (It was signed "Henri Ranker," a not too devious bilingual pun on Harry Rinehart, I noted.) If he had, he had succeeded in making it exactly as opaque as everything else in the magazine, had perfected this mask.

The pictures that included him were quite another matter. I felt they exposed him more shamelessly than Cindy's bikini exposed her. The most startling of them had been taken at the home of Clem's family in Boda. Around a picnic table on the lawn were Clem, his father, his sister and her husband and Cindy (with hiatuses of space to set her off like Our Saviour in "The Last Supper," L. da Vinci, color by Kresge). Clem's mother, in a pose of conscience-stricken artificiality, was serving them apple pie from an oversized pie tin. As the sheet lay before me on the veranda table and melon juice dampened into it a form such as one sees in an ink-blot test, I had a nearly irresistible impulse to draw a comic-strip balloon up from Mrs. Anderson's mouth and write in it, "How come you've brought this stranger home when you never brought Sheila but that once?"

Cindy looked like the only one of them all who was at home. She was dressed as demurely as ever a Boda schoolgirl might have been, in a sleeveless white dress with a collar broad enough to cover the shape of her breasts. She was showing enough dentalia for a Kwakiutl potlatch. She was happy to be home with the Hunt consumers in the farm belt.

Clem looked less happy. No camera could any longer hide the alcoholic bloat of his jowls. If he had been in childhood one kind of stranger in the midst of his family, he was another kind now, more than faintly resembling the gangster who has brought his moll home from the city for a visit with Maw and Paw. His eyes, above the pouches, showed an amusement as cynical as anything I have ever seen in print. The photographic editor of a better magazine would only have used this picture out of malice.

It was something of a puzzle to see him pictured with Cindy "at home in their New York apartment." This was the first concrete statement we'd had that he was remarried, and, even aside from the unpleasant thought that it had been very quick, the dates did not seem to jibe. In this picture Clem, overwhelmingly upstaged by a Cindy in lounging pajamas, was holding off a dachshund with a familiar animal hater's expression of mixed loathing and dubiety. Was this, I wondered, the other animal he had bought for fifty bucks to replace the pup he had kicked to death?

The third picture showed them together at a Hollywood première. It meant only that he had become a New York-to-Hollywood commuter now, whether for his own ends or as the tail to Cindy's kite.

When Janet and I had clicked our tongues over all this sufficiently I threw the piece away.

It came back to us. Next Jill found a copy of the magazine in the "trading post" down by the highway. She brought it home like a well-intentioned puppy bringing a rotten bird, proud of its contribution to the family larder. When her mother explained that such magazines almost never told the truth about anything, Jill evidently believed that it was we who were trying to mislead her. She carried the magazine to the Morrisons in the neighboring cabin to prove that she had glamorous connections in spite of her dull and bourgeois parents.

A nice boy named Roland Berge had entered Jill's life in the spring, and one sleepy afternoon while she was composing her weekly letter to him she came to my hammock and said, "Daddy, I know about eggheads and love and sex, but exactly what is a lover?"

"A person who loves."

She snorted impatiently. "But what do they do?"

"Libidinal impulses may branch and bloom in a variety of ways," I said. "It is well known that lovers may turn to hymn singing or even to a practice of the arts. Eros has been called 'the builder of cities.'"

"Sho 'nuff?" she said. Then with gravity, "I guess you don't want to talk about Mr. Anderson to me."

I was tempted to pass on Clem's wry advice that if you wanted to know about him you had to think about him. But plainly she had been thinking about him. Actions and facts were important in spite of his disclaimer, and all the facts she had to go on were a few brief

153

unprivileged meetings with a man who had hardly noticed her, plus the trash in that article. I wanted, even then, to draw a larger picture for her of the man who teased her imagination. But where would I stop once I had begun? It seemed like no task for a holiday, and I put her off, saying, "You know Mr. Anderson is a good man. Don't believe all you hear." No doubt I should have told her to believe that too, though.

Finally Clem sent us an odd little packet: a note, the reprint of a story just out in a literary quarterly—and "Are Eggheads Better Lovers?"

In the margin of the article, near the photograph of the family group in Boda, he had penciled, "Who says you can't go home again? It was not in another country and the wench is not dead. Worm wench never dies." An unpleasant, disquieting brag—perhaps his return with Cindy had been such a brag, too. Look, Jack Wagner, look, Margaret Shea, look up, Doc Wickham from your grave, look, you Grabers and Olsens, I've brought back to you the one sign of my superiority that you're willing to recognize. If I had written A Winter's Tale or Tintern Abbey you still would have thought me too short-peckered to be a man among you. Even if I had been the littlest All-American. But now set up a Maypole around which all your virgins will dance in honor of Phallic Anderson, father of your tribe. If one isolates his ancient grudge, one cannot blame him too much for this kind of brag—only, isn't it strange that he should still care so much what they thought in Boda?

Of course, as he recognized by sending the story along with the article, it is not possible to isolate the justice of any quarrel from all its surrounding conditions. The price of justice is always injustice, but he was not quite cynical enough yet to pay what was asked by Boda. He would not pay them off at Sheila's expense. For her and us he still had some stories that they had refused.

The story he sent was called "Like Sampson." By the title he had penciled, "Not new. I'm cleaning out my drawers these days. It's surprising how easy it is to publish what once was so hard to publish— now that I'm a better lover married to a better mousetrap."

I have talked to friends and admirers of Clem's who think that "Like Sampson" should have been left in his drawer or else polished up—polished as his new life was, I suppose, freed from the impertinences of love and truth by some divorcement in the style or the form.

The story strikes some as a ragged slice of life. Why is the senile landlady given so disproportionate a space? Granted that her speech is amusingly grotesque and colorful; granted that the anarchistic rooming house she runs permits the atypical college situation in which young writers, dilettantes, student nurses, Communists and innocent coeds can mingle, fornicate, and booze away the nights as if they were in a Left Bank hotel rather than in a Midwest college town. But what does she represent?

I would think the answer to this question is that Emmy Polk (you have already seen that this was another of Clem's stories from life) stands as the primitive of the way to poetic speech. She used to say, "You can lead a horse to water and why not?," "Many's the slip twixt the cup and the saucer," "Mr. Herzing is not a mill-of-the-run genius." The two young writers of the story are fascinated (or guided) by her according to the law enunciated by Valéry when he said, "The mind of an idiot is more beautiful than the productions of genius." As she was distorted they must distort.

Why does the author adopt so flippant and disparaging a tone in establishing the character of the narrator (who must be himself when young) and contrast it with the bitter gravity of his friend, who might indeed have had the potentialities of being the superior writer, but whose self-destructiveness, even before his suicide, canceled out the best of his promise?

The answer to this (aha, I have an unfair advantage) is that the narrator is not Clem jeune at all. I am the narrator of that little story. I mean that I have been fictionalized into the not altogether wise or lovable young man who tells the story after his friend's death. The lovable frozen sea, the young suicide is (was) Clem—outside looking in.

Yes, he could have invented us all and all our opinions and emotions toward him, that hive of subtleties—and did so for the space of that story. But even if you only wonder what happens to people in stories after they're done, I owe it to you to say, as Sheila said once, "Here I am."

There I was that summer in Colorado, still in the midst of the Anderson riddle, with another part of the truth on my hands to decipher.

I read it thus: That in fictionally recording a suicide he didn't literally commit he was nevertheless recording with autobiographical exactness what had happened to him that last year he stayed at Emmy Polk's. He hadn't killed himself literally, but figuratively he had. Ruthlessly and recklessly he had smashed the self that had groped painfully up to identity by his twenty-first year. Killed it. Not for the first time nor the last he had faked a death and profited by a genuine rebirth.

High and snug in our place in the mountains, I reminded myself that however self-destructive his new involvement with Cindy Susan might be, this time too he might come back a better man. We had waited a long time for Clem. We could be still and wait some more.

What do lovers do? I told Jill that sometimes they were moved by Eros to write. And that is what our egghead lover was doing with some flamboyance when our paths first crossed.

Ses ailes de géant kicked a breeze in my face before I met him. In his second college year I began to hear about him. Of course a writer in college does not make the kind of name that an athlete does, but in the small, gossipy and hell-for-leather serious literary circle on our campus we found (if not yet a Baudelairean albatross) that a creature resembling an upstart crow was among us.

Each year in the spring a couple of hundred-dollar prizes were given for the best short story and the best poem produced by undergraduates. Normally the prizes were awarded by a committee composed of the head of the English department, old Henry Powell, who taught the advanced creative-writing course, and some other cautiously venerable member of the staff. Now, it happened that this year I was counting on winning the fiction prize. The results were not exactly fixed in advance, but Henry Powell (the decisive voice on the committee of judges) made it plain that the award was to encourage the most promising writers in sight rather than to signalize the merit of a particular story. My whole clique knew well that Henry valued my prospects highly. He was always on the lookout for someone who might carry forward the torch from the failing hands of his friend Hamlin Garland or write a Winesburg for our state, and Henry may indeed have thought that I had the capacity to do so eventually. What is more, I had a story that was a likely contender. As I remember the story, it was a beautifully modulated blend of Hemingway prose, regionalistic subject matter and the kind of moral optimism specified as desirable for American fiction by the donors of the Pulitzer prizes. It had the almost overwhelming recommendation, I thought, of having been published on the eve of the contest by a respectable literary quarterly. Some of its competition was either already in print or scheduled for printing in our undergraduate magazine, but that was a lesser distinction. At any rate Lillian Esterman, who was editing our magazine that year, was under Henry's suspicion for being an Easterner, a pessimist, a Jew and an outspoken admirer of many works that Henry considered lubricous. It was a fairly sound bet that he would award no prize to anything she had chosen for publication if he could help it. My story offered him a convenient alternative. I started to spend the prize money when I turned it in, all neatly retyped, for the contest.

The major flaw in my calculations was that the judging of the contest was turned over that year to the poet and critic Nathaniel Bentley, who inopportunely visited the campus for a lecture and a week's consultation with graduate students. Bentley confounded us by awarding the fiction prize and the first honorable mention in poetry to one Aaron Clement Anderson. Lillian Esterman won the poetry prize.

Stunned and suddenly discovering myself in debt, I called at Henry's office to find out (putting it bluntly) what had gone wrong.

"Well," Henry said, "de gustibus." I still remember his fingering Clem's soiled and dog-eared manuscript as if it were a poison-pen letter he had found stuck under his door. "There seems to be a fashion abroad for the merely grotesque and macabre. Bentley, granted, is an exceptionally keen critic. I'm an honest admirer of his Order and Revolt. But just this once the critical Homer must have nodded." The weight of a world in which standards were shredded to the winds sagged his shoulders. "War's coming," he said. "I worry about it a great deal, wondering if we've got the stamina to face up to old Hitler when I read such defeatist whimpers as this. If you please, it's all about some spineless young sailor who lets himself be picked up in a bar and led along to what promises to be an orgy. Then we're supposed to feel sympathy because the poor boob loses his way and never does arrive at the scene of the carnage. He kicks down a door—he has strength enough for that!—and finds it's the wrong room he's come to. God pity the United States Navy if it hasn't any better navigators than he, is all I can say."

I left the office assured that I was still Henry's pet and assured, if I wanted to be, that next year the prize would certainly go to a story with spare Hemingway prose, regional subject matter and a morally optimistic tone. But I left also with the clean conviction beginning to re-establish itself in my mind that there were some qualities more valuable than these, and that Bentley and Anderson knew as well as I what they were.

Calling on Lillian Esterman, I found her naturally smug about her own success, and nearly as disturbed as I about the intrusion of a squatter on the terrain we had staked out as our own. We weren't in any real sense professionals, but we had managed to develop something of the professional's scorn and fear of the amateur. "I thought when I first heard it that it might have been Balaam Hoyt who'd turned something in under a pseudonym," Lillian said. "You know Balaam's sneaky, and with a name like his who could blame him for changing it? But there is an Anderson in the student directory, all right. A sophomore only. I don't know whether this thing he won with he did for freshman composition or what."

"Why don't you call him up and tell him you'd like to see a copy of it to consider for the magazine?" I suggested.

Her eyes went wide in speculative, reminiscent awe. "I did," she said. "He hasn't got a copy, because nobody ever told the lamb about carbon paper yet, and besides, when Mr. Powell returns it to him he's going to send it off to either Esquire or The Southern Review, and the poetry to Poetry. He made it plain enough he wasn't interested in whether we would print it or not."

I said, "Oh."

"And what's more, he apparently had a conference with Bentley and he says Bentley told him he was a better poet than I and should have had the poetry prize too, but he, Bentley, didn't think it was the right and proper thing for a visitor to break up old customs and give both prizes to the same person."

"Oh," I said. "O modest youth."

"But I have a date with him for Saturday night. We're going to the moom pitchers and I do mean to wheedle until I've seen what he's done that witched old Bentley."

"Don't tell me who asked for the date," I said. "Don't tell me who's going to buy the tickets and popcorn."

Wadleigh Hertz, with whom I had shared many a dialectic hour in Hopper's Tap, provided me with the next thumbnail preview of the poet and lover who had been, thus far, blushing in the desert air of the rooming house where Wadleigh lived. Until Clem won a prize, Wadleigh had served as his proxy in modesty, never mentioning while he talked to me about my literary fortunes and rosy chances for winning the fiction award that there was a kid of his acquaintance who called himself a writer, too. I was so much more respectably a young writer than Clem in those days.

Now Wadleigh unlimbered and, over a few glasses of beer, sketched the freshest, oddest boy it had ever been his privilege (Was it a privilege? he squinted) to have run into in all his college days.

"I thought first he was only the dyke of this fruity character we've got in the end room this year and he merely advertises he's a writer because they're always calling themselves writers or dramatic-otts students or sometimes they say they're dilettantes, like that was a decent thing to be. Imagine claiming you're a dilettante? Well, Anderson's buddy does. Except they are not any more buddies and who saw to that? Me. I mean, I took it on myself to have a little talk with the kid and put him right about a few things that maybe helped him, like the books he ought to read—he'd never even read Man's Fate, for example—and kind of edged him away from the fruity tastes that H. Warwick Lloyd had built up in him. And then I lined him up with a girl, but he flubbed it and for a long time held it against me that I'd presented her to him under false pretenses. See, the contradiction is that while it is true this girl wouldn't put out for him and maybe I had implied that construction on her character, still he kept on seeing her and still never making out with her and going on acting as if it was my fault he couldn't just because in the first place I'd halfway promised him he might. The human mind is a strange thing, Dick. And whose is strangest is, well, his.

"And now, to make matters either better or worse or maybe both, he's making out like crazy with Lillian Esterman, who you and I know doesn't put out for anybody, and they're down in that miserable little cubicle of his at the end of the hall all the time and whether they're composing terza rimas or playing stinkfingers who could tell without listening at the door? And Lillian being in the house all the time sets up quite a situation, with old H. Warwick racing out into the hall all the time like he's heard somebody calling his name and he thinks they want him in on their private sewing circle and when he doesn't hear a peep he eyes Clem's door like a mad coyote and I wouldn't put it past him that he had knelt down to listen at the keyhole as kneeling is probably his favorite position anyhow and someday, if I can overcome my revulsion, I am going to look at him in the bathtub to see if it is true or not that he has calluses on his kneecaps. But anyway Clem will hardly pass the time of day with him now and it's driving him wild.

"And now he's seeing this kid Sheila all the time and having a Dante-Beatrice relationship with her, since she won't even cross Emmy's threshold again, while at the same time Lillian and he are most likely making all the time the beast with two backs and we know Lillian is not the kind of girl that would do such a thing lightly—it makes for entanglements."

I said it surely must and wondered when, if ever, Anderson found time to write or study, since Wadleigh had said he also worked a board job at the Hamilton Hotel.

"The kid's determined," Wadleigh said, with undisguisable pride and fondness, and then a wraith of gloom crossed his forehead. "Jesus, he takes it all too hard. I mean, he's always ready for whatever comes along, whether it's this girl, that girl, writing or coming into my room for a beer now and then, and he gets so high up you'd swear he didn't have a care in the world. But then something comes to bring him down. He suffers about everything. I happen to know he's all torn up about having two girls when what the hell, he doesn't owe either of them anything and a normal person would just say it was up to them. He got drunker than a sonofabitch in my room one night, or rather he came in drunk. By God, it was just the night he'd got his prize money for his story and he still had half a bottle of rye on him and he was going to share it with old Wad. And pretty soon he starts to puke and cry and talk about these girls. You'd think he'd ruined them instead of just a little normal two-timing, though it might just be that why he weeps is that he's not getting it from either one or the other, since, as we know, Esterman is not physical.

"Then another time Emmy Polk, who, you know, can't tell day from night and is always coming with pail and rag to do her cleaning in the rooms at three in the morning, was on our floor before the break of day and she came and woke me up and said, There's something wrong with Mr. Anderson come look. And I gumshoed down the hall with her and there he's just sitting in his underwear at his desk like in a catatonic fit and it's true he doesn't notice us as we come in until I shake him. And, man, he was tight like a wire pulled tight, but not for once from drinking, and not asleep with his eyes open either. He came out of it in the creepiest way, like still in a kind of trance, and he said to me, dead serious, that the foul fiend had come for him. 'What?' And he said again, 'The foul fiend,' and man, language like that when I've just woke up I can't bear. So I slapped him. He seemed, you know, grateful. Then he laughed a little and said he'd been sitting there reading Light in August and he'd heard the milkman's horse came clopping along the bricks—you know it was a nice night and the window was open—and then, 'I suppose I imagined it was coming for me.' Which, I said, the horse or what? And he laughed some more and told me and Emmy not to worry about it and he and I dressed and went down to the Solon Grill for a stack of cakes—on me—and he was as merry as a chipmunk. But I did worry.

"I think he's like a lot of people we know. He thinks nothing's good enough for him. If he could maybe immerse himself in the class struggle and forget about his own problems he'd be all right, but I say

160

this to him and he's apt to come back, 'I don't know which are my problems and which are other people's problems,' and then he starts to twist the perfectly common-sense things I say to him and it goes nowhere. I tried to persuade him to go see one of the head doctors I know at Student Health who's helped a lot of people get interested in social things, but he's afraid somebody's going to tinker with that pretty pink brain of his, and he goes along flirting with the idea that maybe he's at heart a Nazi."

"Just to plague you," I suggested.

"Just to plague himself," Wadleigh said, "because I know better, since he's not only from a working-class background but soft as mush about, you know, lynchings or roughing up a Jew. I tried to get him interested in the Veterans of Future Wars and he wouldn't go because he claims he believes in war, but then when those turd R.O.T.C. colonels ganged Jack Miller, Clem tore a banister rail out of Emmy Polk's stairway and was going for them right then, though of course he was drunk when he did it and had no idea either who he was looking for. I caught him clear down by the library bellowing for the bastards to come and fight, and it's lucky I got there before the campus police. It's too bad he won this prize, in a way, because he doesn't know how to drink and he's trying to drink all the money up before he maybe loses it, because the little bastard never has any bottoms in his pockets and I don't think he owns a billfold but carries his folding money loose in his coat pocket. Not just to plague me. He fights himself."

"You'll take care of him," I said.

"Like hell," Wadleigh said. "I can't stay ahead of him. I've tried, but if he won't listen to reason what can I do? I'm not his keeper. In such a world like this it's infantile leftism to worry about one single individual, anyhow. Only, if he stays through the summer he's going to room with me and maybe I can line him up with some no-nonsense girls and get him unaddicted to those neurotics he's fallen into."

"You'll take care of him," I said. "He sounds like he might be worth it, too."

Wadleigh said, "Nyaaa. There's a billion odd characters in the world. Too many. Too many contradictions today. When the revolution comes things will be easier for people like Clem. Nothing's going to help him very much now."

Before I left school for that summer's vacation I heard more of Clem from Lillian. I don't think that Lillian was in love with him then, and according to Clem they never had an affair. I have always been inclined to guess that she, like the rest of us who knew him at greater or closer range in those days, was bemused, shaken and drawn to him the way floating leaves or chips are drawn toward and then involved in the vortex of water draining from a pool at the end of a season. I cling to this figure advisedly, for Clem was in those days pre-eminently a naysayer, a still adolescent nihilist, if you like, and one who should have had little influence on those of us who were better oriented socially and to the large values of the world. Nothing was good enough for Clem, from Wadleigh's pacifism and faith in "the socialist sixth of the world" to Lillian's avant-garde literary efforts (she considered our undergraduate magazine in the direct line of Broom, Seccession, The Exile and transition) and my academically oriented humanism—to say nothing of the stuffy values of the great university itself, the R.O.T.C. and the football team.

We might, correctly, have pointed out to Clem that none of these things seemed good enough to him because he was ignorant of them. In experience, including intellectual experience, he was still a boy from a very small town, a hick inhabitant of the outer fringes. We could have refuted him on the majority of counts that might have been raised in argument, and yet, because it was the end of a season, because we all felt as he pre-eminently felt, that all was in question before the imminence of the war, we were fair game for his not always eloquent refus.

Lillian spun to him—because he depressed her so much. She said so and I believed her. He had depressed her originally by what seemed his offhand ease in winning the fiction prize and almost winning the poetry prize as well. "He wasn't even going to submit anything," she said, "until Felix Martin badgered him into it. He didn't think it was worth bothering about or he hadn't heard of it or something. Only, he had it in his mind that if someone from outside of here—and he'd heard of Nathaniel Bentley, all right—could see his stuff, there ought to come in the next mail an offer from a New York publisher or he might win this year's award and publication in the Jansen Younger Poets series, since Bentley is on the committee of judges for that too."

"But his stuff isn't that good," I said, who had not yet seen a single word of it.

"It's good. Anyway, his fiction is good," Lillian said. "His verse—well, he writes lines like 'Dog men down by the anchor's bite' which are both too old-fashioned and melodic and at the same time too cryptic. I mean, if you'd ask him what 'anchor's bite' meant and if it meant the way an anchor bites into the bottom of the ocean he'd just laugh at you as if you were stupid. Sometimes he merely likes the sound of words. And I will say that the poem he claims Bentley liked better than mine is, on the other hand, a pure steal from Lawrence's 'Ship of Death,' which Clem has memorized parts of. You sort of wonder whether Bentley recognized the similarity or not. As a matter of fact, all Clem's poems sound like somebody, either MacLeish or Hart Crane or Lawrence. If you charge him with this, he'll either say, Why not? he only wrote them for the hell of it anyway, or else he'll get so upset about it that you're sorry you asked him."

Clem depressed her, also, by insisting that her verse was no good at all and that, if it were, there was no point in writing it, because the academic and publishing worlds were so rotten that no one recognized good stuff when their noses were rubbed in it anyway. "You'd think that he'd be 'way up in the air over winning a prize when no one ever heard of him before," Lillian said. "But all that happened was that Bentley dropped greatly in his estimation. Then when Esquire rejected his story and Poetry lost some of the things he'd submitted to them, he decided that literature was all in the hands of the fruits who hated new talents. I told him that I've sent out dozens of things dozen of times and haven't had anything published. Whereupon he took their side and said he could see why."

"He must be impossible to get along with."

A very painful frown wrinkled her forehead. She said, "Well … no."

I think the reason I never found out if she was in love with Clem was that I asked her.

"Clem's got a girl," she riposted with chattering briskness. "Or he thinks he's got a girl, and there are some psychologically very interesting overtones involved. I mean we've talked it over very intensively. That's how we get along. We talk wonderfully, Clem and I, if that explains what you're so curious about. But this girl, he thinks she's like Miriam in Sons and Lovers and he's like Paul Morel, and my greatest hope in life would be to make him understand how unwholesome it is to act your life out as if it was something you read in a book. But he does that, you know. I don't know what he'll do with the poor girl. I guess he'll persuade her that she is Miriam—he's got her reading the book—and then sometime he'll 'crucify her into sex' and—'

"Crucify? Is that his phrase?"

"Actually Lawrence's, of course, from 'Tortoise Shout,' but Clem uses it and I think the poor devil believes it. It sounds good to him. So he'll drag this basically wholesome girl down with him and I hate to think what he'll do when he's proved his point with her."

"Find himself a nice earthy Clara Dawes," I said, remembering the events of the novel. "Hello, Clara."

"Don't be silly," Lillian said. "I'm not so earthy. And of course he can't carry the analogy out too far, because reality does impose some limits. It's merely that I would like to help him ..."

"All the world would," I said. The poll certainly tended so far to show this.

"... because he's going to blow his brains out someday if he doesn't learn to separate life from literature. I mean, he's too involved."

She wanted to help him. To an extent and otherwise than she may have intended, she did help. She gave him another mirror in which he could watch his ego put out its pseudopodia. But Lillian was graduated that June and went home to New York. She wrote Clem long, witty, mothering, literary letters for the next year and a half, none of which he ever answered.

What did the lover do during that summer when he was separated from both his new girls? He did not go home to Boda, but, with some excuse to his parents about needing a special course that would be offered only that summer and never again, stayed at the university and roomed with Wadleigh.

According to Wadleigh, Clem became the terror and delight of the student nurses that summer, was among them like a miniature, feckless stallion in a herd of heavy mares, setting up factions and jealousies that would persist long after graduation had scattered them to hospitals across the state and the nation and in the armed forces, so that years later on Guadalcanal or in Marseilles, in Chicago or San Francisco, the operating rooms of great hospitals would be disrupted by hair-pulling, face-scratching brawls and "You double-crossing bag, Anderson was mine and you stole him."

It can't have been literally like that, nor can Wadleigh's description of their Falstaffian consumption of liquor be trusted as literal—if for no other reason, simply because Clem could neither have afforded nor lived through the excesses that Wadleigh attributed to him. Be that as it may, Clem must have been pushing himself—once again and in another direction—very near the limits. I know that he was jailed twice that summer, for drunkenness, and the police of our college town were inclined to be lenient with intoxicated students. Once Clem provoked his arrest by shouting "Cossack!" at a policeman who was mildly and innocently discussing the weather with his sister-in-law.

The policeman gave chase to the car in which Clem was riding—it belonged to and was driven by a med student at least as drunk as Clem—and forced it to the side of the street. It is probable that the policeman had misunderstood Clem's epithet. However that may be, he let the med student drive on in peace after extracting Clem from the car. While taking Clem to the station, the policeman beat him up rather savagely. The next time Clem was arrested, he had thrown a beer bottle at a policeman and had plainly called him what the first policeman thought he had been called.

One of the first stories that I heard when I returned to the campus that fall was of Clem and Wadleigh's publishing venture. They had acquired an unexpurgated edition of Lady Chatterley's Lover. They extracted and printed—on a mimeograph machine in the psycho hospital, available to heaven knows which student nurse, or on what conditions—the explicit sexual passages. They had printed an edition of three hundred copies and were offering them for sale at five dollars each. So far they had sold fewer than thirty copies. The majority of these had gone to younger faculty members, mostly on the English-department staff or the staff of the medical school, where, I understand, they were much talked about.

One morning to Emmy Polk's had come a brash young interne commissioned by his wife to acquire a copy for the family library. Man to man he quipped about what he was buying, ohing and ahing and smacking his lips in smug superiority over those dirty words as he leafed through the mimeographed sheets, giving Clem and Wadleigh to understand that of course their merchandise was only a species of dirty joke, and didn't they think five dollars was a little high for a laugh?

While Wadleigh bargained, Clem started to pace the far side of the room, his eyes red (from a hangover) and his face black (with a rage that even Wadleigh, who was growing used to him by now, could not comprehend).

Suddenly Clem burst out, "It's tragic and it's beautiful." He leaped across the room and snatched the booklet from the hands of the astonished interne, called him a fat swine and ordered him out of the house.

"I'll go, but nobody calls me names," the interne said. He got up and started for Clem. "Take it back," he ordered.

"I call you names," Clem said. He broke a beer bottle on the edge of Wadleigh's desk and with the jagged remnant in his hand stood his ground. "I call you a pusillanimous garter snapper."

"Man!" Wadleigh said in reporting the incident. "I thought I was going to faint dead out and away. I guess the interne did too, and so did Clem. After the interne slipped away, we sat for a while in silent meditation. Boy, I could hardly breathe. Finally I said to Clem, 'I didn't know you felt that way about our book.' He said—do you know what he said?—'I don't.' And I said, 'What's so tragic and beautiful about pewtang, after all? You've been knocking off enough this summer to know better than that.' And he said, 'There isn't anything.' 'Then why'd you have to set upon a customer?' 'I didn't like his looks,' he said. Well, it ruined a beautiful business, because this interne was exactly the type who'd turn around and go to the police about our product. So I took them to the lake and sank them.

"I asked Clem again why he'd done this to us, and he said, 'It's what Lawrence would have done to a garter snapper.' I said, 'Not over what we'd left of his novel. He'd probably have gone for us, but not with a beer bottle.' Oh, he said, a friend of his in the Navy had written to him about a fight he saw in Honolulu where they'd used broken beer bottles. That damn Clem just wanted to try it to see what it felt like. I asked him if he would have really used it. He got very white and said, 'The guy was yellow. I could tell. I knew he'd back down.' What do you make of that?"

I made out that Clem Anderson was a pretty wild boy.

I didn't mean to make friends with him, but I did want to get acquainted. Being a generous liberal by principle and in my own eyes, I must have intended that it should be a friendly acquaintance. Being a type of prig, as well, in my determination that "no man who is a fool would call me friend," I had pigeonholed him in advance as an oddity, somewhat vulgar. I came from an academic family—I had still not come very far from them. As far as I could see, he came from nothing much, and nothing can come from nothing. (The more I saw of what he came from the more I was convinced of that almighty but treacherous truth.)

I knew he had enrolled that fall for Henry Powell's writing class, and I recognized him from Wadleigh's description when we met, a select fifteen or so of us, in Henry's big office. I think I expected him to say something—something quaint but ridiculous, rebellious but unsound—after Henry had finished his introductory remarks to the new students.

Henry had begun comfortably to drone off his platitudes, which I had heard the year before. Henry loved to say that the only definition of a short story was that it was a story that was short—and wait for appreciative snorts or giggles. Clem dug in his ear with a pencil and scowled. Henry said that we must hold the mirror up to nature, but not too close. Clem dropped his chin behind his left shoulder. With his Gene Tunney haircut he looked for all the world as if he were getting ready to counterpunch. Henry said that every short story had a beginning, a middle and an end, though it seemed the fashion these days to write stories that were all middle.

At this point Clem got to his feet and walked out. Exactly seven minutes of the class had elapsed. He had learned all he was ever going to from Henry Powell.

I remember that Henry pretended not to notice his departure. Why should he have? He was far too venerably established in his trade to be disturbed by the affront of an unpublished youngster.

But as the hour went on and I sat half listening, half busy trying to incorporate what I heard with other preoccupations, I was already wondering if I shouldn't have followed on Clem's heels. That very morning, as it happened, Chamberlain had said, "I have now been informed by Herr Hitler that he invites me to meet him in Munich tomorrow morning." In Spain that fall the Loyalists still held the gains they had hammered out along the Ebro, but the Negrin government had announced that the International Brigade would be disbanded and all foreign troops would be sent out of Spain. I thought anyone should be able to read the horrible prophecy of these signs. But Henry, as he began to ramble from his technical pronouncements, made it clear that he could not. He told us that he had been in Europe that summer and had talked to a good many academic people in England, France and Germany. They were sound, intelligent observers and they had assured him there would be no war. I should have known before that a man who would speak of "that great white bore, Ulysses" and quip that Faulkner's characters should have met a psychiatrist instead of a novelist was not fit to teach writing. When he said that Chamberlain was "about to blow the whistle on Hitler," suddenly Clem seemed vastly smarter than I who had stayed to listen.

From pure outrage at myself and Henry I called Clem that evening to congratulate him on his walkout. We had one of the murkiest telephone conversations I had ever engaged in. (No one had told me yet that Clem did not, for all practical purposes, use the Bell telephone, an instrument that he believed brought sourceless voices from the ionosphere and distorted by its own whim anything he might speak in reply.) I tried to invite him to have dinner downtown with Jack Miller and me, and only found out days later that his reason for refusing was that he had to wash dishes at the Hamilton Hotel. I hung up feeling that I had been soundly snubbed.

But he showed up at the Blue Antler Tap around ten o'clock with Jack Miller. They joined me in the booth where I was talking to a couple of graduate students and the editor of the college newspaper. We were deep in the subject of Chamberlain's flight to Munich. What else could we have talked about that night?

For nearly an hour Clem was silent—learning, we felt, as we no doubt felt he should. As the talk got more desperate in its frustration (what else could it have been that night, when it was so clear what Chamberlain meant to do?) Clem began to swill beer at a frantic pace and to turn red. It was not merely that he flushed. His clear skin got red as a bandanna, as if in sign of some terrible muscular effort of his heart. And all at once he broke in to say, "No, no. That's not right. You're wrong."

The editor stopped with as much politeness and patience as the momentum of his statement permitted and asked, Yes? Well, just what point was it that he was wrong about? Surely anyone could see that if Chamberlain sold out Czechoslovakia, the Little Entente was done for. The possibility for co-operation between France, England and Russia was shot to the winds. Only that possibility had fenced Hitler in thus far. Now Hitler would be in a position to ally with either England or Russia. The uncertain balance of peace was broken.

We were all well informed, except Clem. But what we felt that night was the uselessness of being well informed, the blindness of the powers that had so obviously begun to live our lives for us. You may know all about me, the State had said to us, but I don't know anything about you. Munich was a curious turning point—and seemed so then. Afterward faith would be demanded of us as never before, but henceforward the grounds of faith would be gone. An alienation was being forced, our lives were being made incoherent. "They" were obliterating our reasons for being what we wished to be, leaving us like wishful parasites in search of a new host.

I think it not unfair to say that it was Clem's ignorance of sound opinion that permitted him to see our dilemma more clearly than we. He was in the position of the barefoot urchin quick to recognize that we were walking on broken glass while we still had to point with pride to our shoetops, from which the soles had suddenly been stripped.

Red-faced, Clem said that half-Nazi Lawrence told us the ship of the American spirit went down when the Pequod sank and what came after was post-mortem effects presumably.

Well, Lawrence—but we wanted something from Gunther, Lasky or Walter Lippmann, something with facts to support it. And besides, for once it wasn't America that was to blame. It was the Cliveden Set; it was Unity Mitford; it was that yellow Chamberlain.

Chamberlain wasn't about to do anything we didn't want him to, Clem said, shaking his head like Emmy Polk at her worst.

Well, did he mean the America Firsters, the Coughlinites, the fascist brass in the Army?

Incredulously, somewhere between embarrassment and outrage, we learned that he meant us—the good liberal Hitler-hating chaps who were buying him beer—and "all men."

The editor put his face in his hands and moaned that it had been a long time since he had encountered the literary mind trying to deal with politics.

I said with lofty dignity that Clem's nonsense didn't represent the literary mind. (I meant that mine did.) I named twenty prominent men of letters and promised they would say they hadn't wanted Chamberlain to go to Munich and make World War II inevitable.

If they would say that, wasn't such false declaration proof that you couldn't trust anything they said? Clem asked maddeningly.

A statement is not and cannot be in itself evidence of its own unreliability, we corrected him in chorus.

What could be evidence, then, of the reliability of a statement so broad?

Many things, a million things, so many that there wasn't time to catalogue them all.

Ha, Clem said, with a sick, foxy grin. There wasn't time to marshal the evidence of man's real intent. So what made our faith in the intentions of "all men or anyone" any better than his?

Some evidence is better than no evidence.

Who's to say at what point you may stop gathering evidence without prejudicing your findings?

None of us knew. But we did know and said that this kind of argument was sophomoric.

No doubt pleased that the argument had become ad hominem, Clem said that ours sounded like whistling in the dark. We were trying to bludgeon him with facts, and who gave us any right to pick our facts the way we had?

"Look," I said, "if Thomas Mann said tomorrow he was sorry Chamberlain had gone to Munich to arrange for a war, what would you think? Would the fact that he said this be a fact you'd respect?"

"It wouldn't ring true if he said it."

"To whom wouldn't it ring true?" Jack Miller said, bouncing on his seat like a giant boy on a merry-go-round.

"To me," Clem said. On modest second thought he added, "And to everybody."

"I wish you'd stop using the formula 'all men and me,'" Jack Miller said. "It makes me nervous, like there was too many people at this table. Can't you break it down into maybe a few sheep here and a few goats there and tell us, just spit it out simply, who it is you know wants to go to war?"

"You," Clem said.

Jack sprang as nearly upright as he could in the booth. He blew steam like an overwhelmed safety valve, and he started to pull his pockets inside out for illustration. "Look," he said, "you just discerned a motive I don't think I've got. Please look. I don't think you'll find it on me. I want to live and screw and paint, though not necessarily in that order, at any given time. And anyway, I'm not all men, even if you are."

Clem stared at the extruded pockets with the cynicism of a man who has found that really important contraband will be hidden in the body orifices.

"Look, Socrates," the editor said. "All this is very amusing, and I'm sure you sincerely believe we don't see the light. Tell us the truth. What is it? You can have five minutes all to yourself without any of our boorish interruptions."

Clem's red face went white, not bothering to pass through pink on the way. He was ever a boy to jump over the middle ground. "I don't think about these subjects much," he said in groveling embarrassment.

We punished him with our wise and watchful silence, confronting him with his five empty minutes. His tongue crept out, naked and vulnerable, to make sure that his lips were still out there and probably in working order. When at last he spoke, his voice cracked as if he were about to cry.

"We want out," he said in an embarrassed, embarrassing treble.

"I see." The editor nodded gravely, speaking in a tone he might have used to encourage a handicapped four-year-old. "We want out. And?"

"The world doesn't satisfy the cravings it stirs up," Clem said, closing his eyes. Once later, at boot camp, I saw a stupid religious boy from Indiana run at the hurdles on the obstacle course. Time after time he hit the bar with his chest and flopped bonelessly to the ground and lay there with his eyes rolling, whispering to himself until the petty officer cursed him onto his feet and made him try again. Bang. Down again. "You goddam malingering Hoosier, you're going over. Look at them little runts going over. A big old shitpot like you oughta jump over the goddam thing. Now let's see you clear it." White-eyed, flopping wrists and ankles, the boy kept up his hopeless attempts until all of us who watched were shamed and sickened of our humanity. It was a performance in which there could be no dignity for either the boy or his tormentors.

Clem was like that on the night of which I'm telling. He stammered and lost the beginnings of his sentences. He was shamelessly foolish—and ashamed to appear foolish to us who listened. He was eloquent for moments with the wonderful fragments from his reading, or again with perçus of his own that crackled like a misfire of powder. He was knocked flat on his back when he tried to connect these things (and show us the matrix of coherence where they all fitted inside). And we goaded him to try again.

Among other things he said that mankind had used up all its tricks and knew it. Therefore (I supplied the "therefores" whenever there seemed a chance of doing so) they couldn't abide in the closed room of the Thirties, even if they had to kill themselves trying to find a way out. There was no longer any primary desire. People could only want "what they had already wanted," and this somehow wore out the virginity of wanting. They couldn't even want this war as directly as they had wanted the First World War, therefore they would rush into it all the faster, goaded to war by their mere inability to want it candidly. Once "all men and me" believed in something, even if it was "The Yanks Are Coming" and kings, emperors, glory and dulce et decorum est pro patria mori. But "we" had learned everything—all that nature apportioned for us to learn—in World War I. Now we had to pretend to believe in Hitler or Roosevelt or democracy or dictatorship. But we itched intolerably in our hair-shirt of pretenses. Therefore we had sent Chamberlain to Munich to get the big show on the road.

"What does Tolstoy mean in War and Peace if it isn't that war is the will of the people? Who are people if they're not all men and me?"

We goaded him by pointing out that Russian Tolstoy was on the right side and therefore Clem mustn't use him, whatever he might have said "here or there" in his bulky novel.

The obstacle he kept failing to climb was his own good idea of the truth—not our opinions. He wasn't arguing with us, but, as it were, before us. Vaulting on our opinions, we sailed slickly over the truth that kept knocking him flat. He convinced us of nothing, but troubled us, robbed us of dignity by the embarrassing seriousness of his failure. Against him we made essentially the old plaint of liberals, "Don't we have enemies enough without being assaulted from within by the truth?" Condescendingly we hated him.

"Well," the editor said at last, "we'll all meet back here in ten years and admit who was right. Only time will prove it."

Clem bared his teeth in what he may have intended for a smile. "There isn't time enough in the world to show who's right. You said that yourselves. If you don't know the truth when you hear it, you never will."

What can you do with a boy like that, who will let go of nothing, who won't accept the graceful disengagements offered him?

When Clem finally left—no doubt finding us uneducable—Jack Miller said, "The kid's got a lot in his mind."

All undigested, we agreed.

But, in the black days of depression following Munich, my mind kept going back to his incoherent pessimism as to a counterirritant I needed in all seriousness. My world was itching me, too. Better seek company that knew how to scratch.

I saw him a few times in the next weeks, argued with him, drank beer with him, agreed with what I could and kept the rest in my mind longer than I had expected to. I read Lawrence's Studies in Classic American Literature because he said it was "good common sense" and thereafter understood a little better what common sense meant to Clem. (Not quite what it means to me; still less what it is commonly taken to mean.)

In a few weeks, when Jack Miller and I arranged a party in Jack's basement apartment, I called Clem to invite him. I suggested he bring his girl.

"I don't have a girl," he said.

I remembered what Wadleigh had told me of the summer orgies at Emmy Polk's and in the woods behind the nurses' quarters. "Bring any of your girls," I said.

"I don't know any girls any more." Then, so that I wouldn't think him queer—I was a friend of Wadleigh's and Wadleigh was a personified threat of accusation—he said, "I'm too busy on a novel to worry about girls."

I invited him to bring his novel. He sniffled and hung up, leaving me with the impression that he might or might not come.

He was busy on a novel in the sense that he was worrying about it. He wasn't writing it, not on paper at least. Not yet. But the novel that he would finish building and then finish cutting just twelve years later was conceived on the day when he had his first serious break-up with Sheila.

I fix the day so precisely because he did. If I were to quibble that it was only his superstition that fixed a date so far in advance of any tangible evidence that a novel was going to be born as the exact date of conception, I would have to add that for him superstition was a means of knowledge. And then I would have to defend the queer proposition that superstition can be a means to knowledge. And there isn't time for that.

He never changed his story that the novel was conceived in October 1938, that it was the same novel he was to complete after the war ("How many novels can dance on the head of a pin?") and that its whole period of gestation was a point-for-point accompaniment of the fleshing out of his relationship to Sheila. (And was its eventual mutilation an unheeded sign of imminent divorce? I must not extend his superstitions with my own, and on this point I never heard him say anything.)

I have put in this caveat dutifully. You are warned that there is a frosting of superstition on what I have to set down now. But Clem saw the episode this way, and I must try to show what he meant.

The first gold-green of his love for Sheila taught him that the other is a person in whom the same mysteries before heaven existed as those that tingled his own nerves with guilt, hope, loyalty, pride and reverence. From the springtime when he began to woo he realized he was wooing those abstractions beyond sense which are yet so inextricably involved in sensuousness.

After the misfire at Wadleigh's party he had invented a patience sufficient to assure her that he was manageable, that she might safely have coffee with him at the Student Union, go to the movies with him and, when the weather turned benign, ride with him in a canoe during daylight hours.

By the time she discovered his patience was a sham, she did not care. Unconscious as females are believed to be, she had matched his conscious design, had used the days of safety preparing to seize the nettle danger. When she consented, at length, to go canoe riding by night, she was too far committed to be frightened by the importunate hand fumbling for the hem of her skirt. Nature in her suspected strongly what unnatural Clem took for granted—that the hand should touch the quick of its desire in the fullness of time. It was right and would be good, but not yet.

None of the canoes they rode in on those nights of the previous spring was tipped over by Clement Agonistes in the fervor of his physical onslaughts. (O Canoe, thou perfect Freudian symbol, how can any campus be complete without thee? You vaginal flotillas, bright-painted as an array of lipsticks on a dime-store counter, on what lakes and rivers of surrendered time do you not float, frustrating symbols of fulfillment! Already in thee, and aching pleasure nigh, our duckfoot paddles scraping thy sides like juvenile swans scrambling for purchase on the Ledean vessel! Thou grounder on the shoal mudbanks of the Ilissus, what poops of burnished gold bore more fitly Her of the rain puddles and Midwestern ponds and the morning surf on Cyprian beaches? Canoe, qu'as-tu fait de ma jeunesse?) Nor did any of them—nor Sheila—tip from the onslaught of his impassioned rhetoric.

As Lillian Esterman had correctly reported, he hoped to persuade Sheila that she must be "crucified into sex." (And was still trying to persuade her seven years later in Mexico, when they were married and she was gravid with his child, that she should have played the Miriam to his Paul Morel in the irretrievable spring of '38. Lazing on the shale above the surf at Acapulco, pretending to tell it all to Janet and me, he beat her tranquil ears with the ancient, unavailing plea. "Absolutely I tried to make her prestissimo, but it was not just for my own sake." "Ha," Sheila said, licking melon juice from her fingers and chuckling silently to the thing in her belly. Clem said, "We used to wrangle so much about whether I respected her, and I admit that most girls only use that word for tactics, meaning that you ought to wait for their choice of a propitious moment before you ravish and degrade them, hang up their nether scalps and depart like Joy whose hand is ever at his lips. But I will grant Sheila conscious honesty." "Thank you, Poppa," Sheila said. Clem said, "While any fool could see I was trying to ravish and degrade her—just as she claimed—I would have respected her in her ravishment and degradation." "Dostoevsky Anderson, broad and lusty as nightmares," Janet said. We laughed and Clem laughed, but there was a bug of seriousness burrowing in his brain as he went burrowing back into the past—"for his novel," we would have thought. Then, in Mexico, he was deep in work on it. Was it only material usable for fiction he sought? He said, "I was an overgrown infant in the way I looked at women. They were just trees to me. I got whatever bird eggs I could shake out of them, which wasn't much, because they sensed what I was and they let me climb around.

All right. I knew that wasn't enough. I thought what was enough was if Sheila would let me be a horrid, egg-snatching infant with her, instead of to her." "No wonder you confused me," Sheila said, with her whispering laughter.)

Without doubt he was the greatest riddle her eighteen years had asked her. "I always knew Clem was someone," she said. This one certainty aside, she knew nothing about him for sure. He jiggled and changed form like quicksilver held in her palm. She was not greatly impressed that he had won the short-story contest. ("I didn't see much future in writing," she said, whose damnation or salvation came soon enough to depend on the word.) Sometimes it seemed to her that he was truly giving language to her own nature. And then she was most frightened of him. Again she thought he was only a pest, a little crazy about sex, and talked so much only because he had "just one thing in mind."

But it was spring, and when the canoe trembled on the lake and the inshore waters felt already naturally warm as kerosene to her fingertips, she would have told him right out that she loved him—if he hadn't talked so much in his effort to persuade her that she did.

Now a summer had passed. They had been separated, hadn't even written to each other, but they came back together as if the summer had continued for them the process of refining each to the need and quality of the other—"so to one neutral thing both sexes fit"—as keys and tumblers are machined to the idea of lock. From the first day of reunion when the fall semester began, they sensed that they were closer. So Clem, headlong Clem, pushed to find a language that would hasten the process yet more. Hot for certainties, he applied the fatal knife.

They were walking in an October landscape outside town. He had suggested a "hike" and she had agreed with an unreserved "O.K." They crossed a flat swampy area, brown in the sun, and started to climb a hillside where burdocks and rank horseweed grew. Where the weeds thinned they passed an outcrop of granite, speckled black and pink and eroded so that its giant force, its hardness, the furies it had endured in melting or under the filing glaciers seemed all tamed, so that it lay by their path like a comfortable old dinosaur. Or it seemed a planet of their own, the right size to be alone on.

Brown-green moss furred its side. Very close to it, where no grass grew, an edge of standing water was set against it, making a natural imitation of that poetic conceit which tells of the sword found in the stone.

Pausing by the stone for breath and looking back at our toy town across a finger of lake, Clem quoted, "'All I could see from where I stood was three long mountains and a wood.'"

"A wood what?" Sheila teased.

"A woodshed, wooden head."

"Why quote things you don't like on such a nice day?" Clem had made clear that he hated Edna St. Vincent Millay. Like Longfellow, she was the enemy—in fact, the Enemy Dickinson of his times.

"A person has to talk back. I couldn't stand all this—" he swept his hand at the treasures of the landscape—"unless I said something to it."

"Don't put your mouth on it."

"I'll put my mouth on it."

Little games of words that he had coached her in until they became her delight.

They sat on their freckled little planet of stone. Clem stared at her in worship. There was so much to say about her—to make her endurable, not to die of her roses in aromatic pain.

She was not ordinarily pretty, any more than this landscape was as pretty as Yellowstone Park. Her nose was longish and thin, like that of the hypothetical Cleopatra, whose longer nose had changed all of history. The real Cleopatra's nose, having been just what it was, left the world no more than it is. Sheila's nose was the philosophic illustration of the exotic possible, the world that had never happened but might as well have. No historic Antony had died for a nose like Sheila's. No galleys fled across ses yeux larges et clairs, but the men who had applauded the histories and probably written them had lived with such a nose and found in its baroque imperfections the unspeakable romance of the commonplace. One saw in her eyes the fleeing freight boat of some grave Tyrian trader, not the pomp of a battle line of galleys.

Beneath her eyes there was always a faint puffiness. She had a way of opening her mouth widest at the side to expose the point of a canine tooth. Today she wore a red tam, and it sat squarely, beautifully, gracelessly on her straight yellow hair.

She was beautiful—not so much beyond comparison as summing up an infinity of comparisons, which he wanted to save by compressing them all into a single, overwhelmingly exact epithet, one that lurked tantalizingly on the tip of his tongue but would not let itself be spoken.

The color beneath her eyes was the wash of water-color violets, of bluing that seeped in the enchanted tub where he had first seen his mother rinse clothes. ("Bloo," had said infant Clem, "blee-ew, blue,

blue is my favorite color." Now he knew why.) The faint, crepy texture of her face was the dust of sanding on newly sanded pine. ("Manual training," said the poet, with seven types of ambiguity, "is the sexiest subject in high school.") The hairs of her head, those of the surface and those of the depth, lying denser and denser in their own shadows like the measureless wheat growing in a Kansas field, were an infinity to the delighted eye, and finitely they composed a helmeting sheath that defined the unimaginable curvature of her skull. God would love the beauty of women with His eyes on infinite variety and indivisible unity, and He would never need to compare one with another.

The sunburst of lines in the pupils of her eyes Clem discovered as he had discovered the same patterns in his own eyes at forgotten seven. The same eyes that had stared back at him from the powder-and-hair-spotted mirror he found in Aunt Carrie's bathroom, and yet marvelously different in color. By their difference ponderable. Lovable, and exempt from that original prohibition against loving one's own flesh. The crevice lines of her lips extending to smoothness on the exterior surface, the fleck of tobacco poised on its corner in the bright paste of her lipstick, the slender fingernails with their undercolor of flushed lavender, the cabalistic, feminine scrawl of lines around her knuckles (surely an unknown language, as surely written by another hand that we could only know as feminine) and the sunstruck fuzz on the back of her wrist—all seemed to demand time for particularization if he wished to praise.

Well, that was what he wanted. He wanted no more and no less, but the single word evaded oral formation, while time refused him the luxury of endless cataloguing.

He saw how the October sun brought out rainbows of unsuspected color on the down of her coat, saw the never-to-be-repeated accident of loveliness which this particular boulder enforced on tweed, corduroy, rayon, silk, skin, muscle and bone of her thigh. He smelled her—tobacco, wool, soap, cologne, sweat and some fainter effluvium just so intractable to the language he "needed to" master that it had to be abandoned with such corny impalpables as "spirit" or "soul." If such things existed he did not yet know how to name them except by his erotic appreciation.

He heard the "over-the-hill, down-the-dale" intake and expulsion of her breath. Hearing it permitted him the unchaste imagination that he was already as good as inside her, entering with masculine reverence into her ruddy cavities, among the clutching involuntary muscles and the wanton gushes of blood that fed the herds at pasture on her living sleep.

With thread-counting sensitivity he touched the lapel of her coat, let his fingers know the perfection of the ideal circle when he tweaked one of her dangling coat buttons. And he had only begun.

Impossibility snorted like a dragon about to swallow this realized moment. If he let the dragon have them without having "got this down," circle would, so to speak, eat the button, girl would eat this diverse female extravaganza now smiling loyally back into his rapt eyes, color would eat these rainbows and patterns. In a word either time or eternity (and he saw they were both enemies; there had to be a third reality) would pounce like Saturns devouring their best children. He had to draw the sword from the stone and strike. (There was no sword, only a knife-resembling edge of water visible in the lower left quadrant of his eyes.) He had to steal the day-perpetuating fire. (He hadn't even the scientist's bottle for preserving sunbeams.) The task for a god or a demigod was assigned him as explicitly as ever any assignment in botany. (But when he beat his chest and said, "Lo, Hermes, I!" something laughed behind his ear and said, "Not even the Strongest Boy in Boda, you.")

He had to do what Edna St. Vincent Millay had failed (however glorious her failure!) to do for him—find the words that would protect them from the brown, freckled Kronos on whose back they sat to catch their breath. Admitting the responsibility was as good as admitting failure. He sensed, not for the last time, that the core task of the poet is to accept the foredooming of a failure that would never touch well-helmeted scholars, insurance salesmen or soldiers. He was willing enough. (The Strongest Boy in Boda really was the strongest, after all.) But the incommensurateness of his weaponry and the task it revealed made all his heroic will into a mock-heroic echo. He wanted to seize the instant as a poet should, and as none ever has. To be master of his own slavery. Yes. To be the magician with his wand of art lifted between time and eternity. But the frustration of that lofty wish said, "Let's fuck. We'll go up in those pretty woods."

Her pained eyes swept him briefly and turned away to look back toward town. "You're been pretty good since I got back," she said slowly. "You haven't bothered me with all that."

"Did you think I'd changed my mind?"

"You? It never occurred to me you could change your mind about anything," she said. To him it sounded like an accusation that he never changed his socks or underwear—a point on which he was too guilty to argue, but he felt like replying that a man couldn't change his mind just because he wanted to. Might want to.

She said, "I didn't so much hope you would change your mind, but I don't like to be nagged all the time. I thought we agreed that you'd leave me alone until I felt the right time had come."

"We agreed," Clem said.

"Then why bring it up now?"

"Did I bring it up?"

"You—"

"It's up," he said, coarsely, subtly.

She ignored both coarseness and subtlety, as was her function, and pleaded, "It's been so much fun seeing you again, picking up everything. I wasn't happy this summer. My mind was all asleep. Foggy. Not me."

"Aha. I stimulate her mind," Clem said. Not to himself or to her. To something that ravened around their feet.

"Don't you know I'm your girl?"

"I don't want to own you. But anyway, you never proved it, and you might as well know I forgot it this summer."

"Did you?" she asked. Red spots glowed under her cheekbones. "I rather thought you had."

"So that's why you did what you did?" he asked.

"What did I do?"

"I don't know. You never told me. Maybe you don't have words for it. There aren't words for everything that's done. That's why poetry will never be any use."

"But you know what you did," she said, with slow misery.

"I suppose it shows on me," he said. "Why did you think such a thing?"

"Because you were so ... hot last spring. Because you never wrote."

"That doesn't prove anything. I was hot for you."

She shrugged as if the stone they were sitting on were matched by another on her back. "It doesn't prove anything. But you just told me. Did you ... have lots of ... girls?"

They seemed to be sitting there in plain daylight on his knees, like the nude imps in old illustrations of St. Anthony's temptations. Maude, Irene, Connie, Dolores, Evelyn, l'affreuse juive, and Swedish Janine, in maculate student nurse uniforms, holding in their rubber-gloved hands the sort of red rubber bone one gives to puppies. Clem, Clem darling. It

179

hurts so nice, they chittered demonically. How should he deny anything?

"I wanted you, though," he said. "I was serious when I told you I loved you."

"I was as serious as you," she said, touching the stone as if it would answer for her.

"You were afraid I would hurt you some way. I know. And you're still afraid."

She lifted mocking, troubled brows and said, "I'm not afraid of being hurt. Lots of things hurt and that's not it at all. Look. For you, Clem."

She had been smoking, rather hasty, gulping amateurish puffs while the talk got knottier. The coal of her cigarette was glowing cherry red. She held her hand up before him now with the cigarette lengthwise between her thumb and forefinger. The coal was pressed into her fingertip.

Perhaps she expected him to knock the cigarette away. Perhaps she had made the gesture thoughtlessly, intending it only as a brief illustration that could be terminated as quickly as it was understood. But he watched her finger burn without moving. Now they could smell her skin burning. The smoke turned a bright, acrid brown. A stunned and terrible surprise showed on her face, but she would not let go.

It was a contest of wills, and hers broke first. She let the cigarette fall and put the burned finger into her mouth. Her head sagged in the anguish of defeat and pain. Tears ran hopelessly down across her cheeks.

"It hurt worse not to be able to take it away from you," he said. He lit a cigarette of his own, debonair.

"Oh, you ... devil."

"Tricks don't prove anything," he said. "I'll match you." Showing all his teeth in a grin, he took his own cigarette between thumb and forefinger as she had held hers. At first he thought the pain was going to be too much, that he would be shamed even before her. But then all sensations seemed to go away. He knew he had rolled back his head so that he stared at the sun without blinking. He saw it like a white spearpoint aiming at his hand. He seemed to hold it for an instant.

Sheila knocked the cigarette out of his grip. "Don't you be so silly," she said. "If I hurt myself I don't want to hurt you. I'm not smart enough for you, Clem. Hasn't anybody told you that? That's why. And I wouldn't know how to let you go if I ... if we—Clem, I can't stand it. I don't want to see you any more. I—"

This time it was he who was crying. His head lay in her corduroy lap. He was kissing her burned hand, cooling it with his tears. "No, no, no, no, no," he said. "I take everything back. I really am too yellow to hurt you. I don't want you if I could only hurt you. You were right to be afraid. Something terrible is wrong with me and it never will be right. You ought to stay away from me."

After a long time she said, "It wasn't sex I was afraid of. It really was that I was afraid of you."

"Aha."

"I don't mean that just the way you're taking it. I'm afraid of what I'd do to you, too. Why me, Clem? Clem, why do you want me? There are so many girls who really are more your kind of person. We both know that."

He nodded agreement. "Maybe that's why I need you. I mean, there's already enough of me in the mixture, in myself. I need something against the grain. So I won't burn out too fast. I might do that, before I'm ready. I'm sure. I want to marry you. You know all that. Do I have to go through the ceremony before you'll take me?"

"That isn't so important," she said.

"Everything important comes down to that," he said, already unsure that he thought so, but knowing no other image or symbol on which to hang all the importances of time resumed. (It had resumed, all right, and he was vaguely inclined to blame her refusal that it had.) "At least knowing you're not afraid of that part."

After a long while she said, "It wasn't sex I was afraid of. I found that out this summer. Too." The "too" came like a cheeping second thought, some soiled rag snatched to cover her nakedness when her courage proved unequal to her wish. "I'm not good enough for you, Clem, and you might as well know it, even if it hurts for a while."

He wanted to be cool, so cool, when he understood what she had told him. He fumbled another cigarette out of his pack, lit the match with his thumbnail and smiled his old smile of fantasy. But then there was no cigarette in his hand and he was staring in stupefaction at the little red flame approaching his mouth. He blew it out.

"You lost your cherry," he said. He dropped the burnt match between his feet and ground its blackened head savagely with his heel. "Well, it happens that way, I'm told. I never popped one myself, but the boys tell me—"

"Clem."

"Sorry. I didn't mean to be vulgar, or to be smart-alecky, pretending I'm somebody else. I was surprised. That's all. I guess I don't understand, but that only proves I'm much dumber than I thought, which is very healthy to know."

"Clem, I'm sorry."

"No. I'm glad you told me."

"I don't mean about telling you. I'm sorry I'm such a slob. That it happened. I didn't tell you to hurt you. I'm not good enough for you, and you have to know it."

"You know I don't think that way. I don't care about conventions. So you laid somebody. So?"

"I got laid," she said with heartbroken parody. "I guess that's all there was to it."

"So you felt like it. So why not?"

"I don't know if I felt like it. I feel like hell about it now."

"It doesn't matter," he said. A balloon of grandeur soared in his mind. Up and up and above the bourgeois world it went. Then he cut the rope and let it go on. Beyond any intention to do so, he saw himself glad that things had turned out this way. Light-shot misery bore him up like a rising current of air.

"Everything that happens matters," Sheila said. "It was a terrible thing to do to you."

But he was sheltering in his own vast generosity. Its folds hung around him like a tent. The woman taken in adultery was his woman (the hardest test of all) and he was not about to cast a stone. Here was the ideal way to revenge himself on his world, by overcoming his need for its patterns of vengeance. Moral heroism was possible, though art was a grinding mockery.

Nevertheless he peeked out through the blinders of his moral triumph. He still (literally) had his head in her lap. One roving, tearless eye (the other was still dampening her coat) ranged down the clothed perspective of her thigh—and saw a new opening into what he most cared about, triumph though he might over conventional views. He was an artist and he wanted to know.

"Once?" he asked mildly, evenly.

"A few times," she said. "One boy. I've known him all my life and he thought, I don't know, that I was glamorous—" She broke down on the word, so edged with mockery in the present circumstances, and could not still her sobs for several minutes.

Clem sat up and patted her shoulder encouragingly. "Several times?" he prompted eagerly.

"He thought I was gla-a-amorous—" and this time she laughed bitterly—"because I'd been away at college for a year. So had he. At

Cornell. And we were kind of showing off for each other, how smart we'd got. I took to saying some of the … witty things I'd heard you say about sex. The first thing I knew I was in over my head. All right, Clem. Don't say it. That's just what you can expect of me."

His woman taken in adultery was forgiven, but, strange to think, demanded stoning as her right. Recognizing this, it was as if his whole perception of human motive opened on a new dimension. Not with unmixed gratitude. It still hurt like hell, as he supposed knowledge must. He could not abstract himself from the pain he shared with her, and he said brutally, "You were so easy to push over, after all."

"Yes."

"And if I were anyone else besides someone you happened to love, we could be up in the brush now."

"I don't know. I can't think about it that way."

"I was a kind of highbrow pimp, giving you quotations that worked you up for someone else."

She pleaded, "I treasure everything I learned from you. I learned so much. I suppose I'm not to be trusted with precious things."

He groaned and chuckled, raw with pain, dazzled with laughter as he saw how her story paralleled his struggle, once upon a time, with Margaret Shea. Of course he was the groaning bearing on which the irony of similarity turned. He was the patsy—and had been given the patsy's incomparable vantage point for watching the ironic relationships of experience.

He saw that and, seeing, saw for the first time the novel that turned its axle in the wound of experience gaping in his own side.

This, one might say, was not the moment for such detached reflections. He had a girl and a wounding problem on his hands. But the truth must be that it was not a moment at all. It was what he had lamented lacking a while before—a place to stand against the twin enemies time and eternity. However painful, a place to stand. His inhuman heart rejoiced at his human pain.

It hurt and, it seemed to him, it need not hurt that she had given her virginity to someone else. In no trivial way it made her more desirable, as mothers may be for some sensibilities more desirable than virgins, for having harbored a child in their flanks and keeping some residue, even if only of experience, to which succeeding lovers may stand in loco parentis. Fictionally he might father this unnamed boy in Indiana who had undone her virgin knot on the floorboards of his father's Chevy. (He did not know that was how or where it had happened, and yet because the experience had somehow become his, it was to share those appurtenances that memory brought. In the parallel vision of irony would he not re-create the night of her abandonment, and in re-creating it establish for all that was given there a permanence not without compensating value?)

"In a parked car?" he asked her, sneering.

Sheila nodded in mute dignity. "I don't want to talk about it. I owed it to you to tell you. But you don't think I'm proud of it, do you?"

Yes. He was monstrous enough to think that her body must be proud of its rending. He was a monster and would pay for his vantage above her merely suffering humanity. It seemed to him, for a minute, that he did not care if she had suffered and might still be suffering. For that minute it seemed to him that that was what both of them and both together were for. She was (he did not use this epithet for her, but he might have) experience beyond his senses, and that, above all, was what he hungered to marry.

"Come over in the woods with me," he said in a stony voice, as if threatening a punishment to cancel her offense. But if she had come … Crazily, artfully, he anticipated that he could there take over the parenthood of the occasion that belonged in other lives. Would know, in the hermaphroditic completeness that his artist's rage required, the hands lifting his skirt, parting his thighs. In his ecstasy it seemed to him that the price of being violated was not too high to pay for the privilege of violating experience that nature had never intended him to penetrate. The semantic confusions of tumescence repeated themselves in the ambiguous libido of language. You screwed me by being screwed by him—art and life beat their terrible round as he grasped what he was doomed to want more than a faithful and mortal wife.

"Come," he said harshly. Let his visionary prod find in her an unresisting child named Margaret Shea and he would hold her no grudge for her unresisting lapses. Let personality be melted away and recast. Let him breathe (oh, monstrously) from her panting mouth the air of the deserted picnic ground in Indiana and hear in her moan the vowels of someone else's name. That was the most he could ask of his woman. All that.

And of course she would not go with him on this strangest of excursions. He could not have begun to explain the formal insight that had exploded in his mind, changing everything between them. She would not have understood. Would have put it down as mere highflying talk.

Still, as the excitement faded back, not to be lost, into the realities that she defined, he knew that the wish beyond the wish in his mind was to use her monstrously for her own sake, to bring her back to herself transformed and invulnerable. He had passed that strange transformation point from which life appears too immense to be mastered merely by living and whence the re-creations of art alone offered a chance to head off the prodigal stampede of brute events. He knew—intuitively at least; the knowledge was too sudden to be articulated in a reasoned structure—that he could reach to her only by going all the way back, to the beginnings and beyond, to cross the trivial and almighty gulf that separated them here, mind from mind and soul from soul. He felt the paradox of being in a tearing hurry to get where, apparently, they already sat—now an almost anxious willingness to re-enter time, for time was the course on which he must pursue her.

"I can't go with you," Sheila said, nodding to the gold-leafed woods. "Not the way I feel now. It would be so terribly wrong for both of us."

He believed her. She and the aching nearness of never-to-be-seized pleasure both seemed to echo his own new comprehension. And yet, at the same time, her scrupling sounded so much like Marienelle's Lesbian principles that he laughed in cruel self-mockery. The natural world, around and within them, was singular in appearance, but he understood its awful doubleness, as if he saw every tree in relentless conflict with itself, every atom of the air hurled against its matching enemy—a collision of worlds where the innocent eye saw only natural peace.

"There isn't much hope for us, then, is there?" he said to her.

She shook her head.

"Then why should we waste each other's time?"

"I don't want to waste your time," she said. "I think what everyone else does, that you'll do something great. I don't want to keep you from it."

"Then don't," he said, musingly, without inflection. "Go away. Start walking. Leave me alone."

She winced as if he had struck her. Without a word she got up and smoothed her skirt. Unaided she scrambled down the side of the rock and took her way straight through the burdocks that lashed at her face.

He watched her come out of the weeds onto the flat of the swamp, and then he went scampering down after her. He cut ahead of her and blocked her path.

"God damn you. God damn you," he said.

185

Her thin neck arched back like a steel spring. This she would not take, and he loved her unbearably for refusing his curse—as if her stubbornness had caught him, at the last possible minute, when he was about to fly loose from the gravity of the earth. The line of her mouth bent, trembled like a bow too strong for the archer.

"How can I get to you or help you when you don't trust me?" he shouted. He saw the spray of his spittle soil her face.

"I don't ask for your help—if that's what you call it," she said. "What gives you the right? Who do you think you are? Who? Who?"

"This isn't the end I imagined for us."

"Imagined! Clem, your imagination has done enough damage, and I'm tired of it. Get out of my way."

"Walk around me," he said. He folded his arms on his chest and forced her to leave the dry path to pass him. He turned and watched her until she scrambled up the embankment of the highway that led back to town.

Then he went back to the stone on which they had been sitting. Went on talking to her. Began to spin the immense length of the answers to her brisk, angry questions.

Who did he think he was? Uninhibited by her presence he told her what he was beginning to accept: I am not myself alone. I'm all of them and all of you that I'm obliged to re-create. Persons are never the persons they were, because that is all already lost, but they are those artifices that I have to find and shuffle and make over in order that they—you—will have been anything at all. Since her presence was his modesty and without it he had none at all, he answered that he was something more than one among the shades that had to be freed from the dragon by his reincarnation. He was, he told her, at least Orpheus, fumbling through the carrion dead to raise her, in particular, up to life with him. He smelled his fingers to see if the smell of decay was literally upon them. Only tobacco smoke and powdered moss.

The shadows were getting longer. As he sat exposed on top of the rock his was the longest he could see, a finger of blackness rummaging in the woods that faded with the day.

Who am I? I'm the bastard who misses everything, who had neither Margaret Shea nor you. Or spoils what he hits—Irene Lacey and you (for yes, I know I had you in a way, just as you said). At the same time, I'm the rightful son who knows how the error of circumstances can be recombined as it ought to be.

When he had satisfied Sheila by accepting this definition finally made of himself, he began to satisfy the rest of us—Jack Miller, the

186

editor, Wadleigh, Felix Martin and me—and to show us how it was that he had become this artificer who would make everything all right in spite of our folly and blindness. He had certainly begun on his novel and it certainly was looking like it would be a long one.

All his usable past began to march on him, like the soldiers carrying trees to Dunsinane. He saw that he would have woods enough and answers for us all. For instance—a tiny detail in the swarm—there'd been the time Jack Wagner was going to whip his father, so he could tell us what it meant that Chamberlain had flown to Munich and danced like a scared clown while Hitler fired .45 slugs around his feet and laughed; he could see how in imagination and then in fact his father might triumph over Jack Wagner, and therefore how Chamberlain might yet triumph in this war.... He could imagine us howling down such feeble analogies. Yes, he could see us better than we saw ourselves, and confidently tell us to wait until the grains of analogy began to pile up. Since we required him to go into all this at novel length—well, that was what he was doing.

Sunset came. Sheila was long vanished, disparue, as if she had never existed, and that was just what he had been trying to warn her against. But if Sheila did not exist, he would invent her. Or if Sheila did exist and was hurting too much—he supposed she was hurting like hell now—he would invent a Sheila who was beyond and safe from pain. He would take the pain of her existence onto himself. Impudently he thought that now he knew how he might.

He sat there while full dark came on, watching his novel begin to envelop and secure the past, burning his fingers with matches so that he would forget how much other things hurt. One, two, three, four, five, six, seven, eight, nine, ten. Not enough. Not quite enough. Never enough.

* I want to stress again what Felix Martin called Clem's "mad conservatism. Later the psychiatrist Gorman would characterize Clem's hold on reality as "an intense integrative effort." The phrases, both illuminating, come to the same thing. He was a string-saver of experience, from beginning to end tying bits of it together to make a continuous filament in a continent sphere. Not all will be unwound here, but readers who find the knots will know more than those who consider only the shape of the ball.—D. H.

# 8

FROM THE "UNSPEAKABLE DAY" when he had broken with Sheila, Clem fell burning on our party.

He came with an animus against absolutely everyone there, as if he meant to scorch us all out of the way to make room for his imaginations of what we should have been. Or, probably, his hostility was more general than that, for he seemed most willing to pick on people he had never seen before. He came, that is, like a corrupt little Jesus attending a party where everyone is named Judas.

Mostly the guests were Jack Miller's friends from the art department and mine from the English department. Felix Martin was there, unbending enough to come for the talk but drinking nothing stronger than Coca-Cola. There was also a man named Wallace Rogge who had fought and been severely wounded in Spain. He had been evacuated across the French border somewhat in advance of the disbanding of the International Brigade. His date was Shanah Beckstein, who brought her guitar. If any were anticipated as the special guests of the evening, it was these three.

I remember that most of us (even Felix) were singing "Los Cuatros Generales" to the accompaniment of Shanah's guitar, while Wallace Rogge, somewhat detached, smiling an aloof, tired benison on us who had not known the fire, watched in silence.

Then Center-Stage Clem came down the basement stairs and through Jack's door, attended.

H. Warwick was with him, and the poor homely Lesbian Marienelle, late of Barnard. They flanked him, smirking, while he swayed through the door, peeling off his sheepskin coat to display his new clothes.

He had on a bright bow tie which he contrived to make look like a mortal gash in his throat, a white balloon of a shirt and a black suit which I would not believe, for the next two years, he had intentionally bought for himself. He could have buttoned a girl inside the jacket with him. And above his pink-as-a-policeman's face, his pompadour seemed to have been erected by the horror of such unearthly presentiments as one encounters in Poe.

When I advanced through the crowd—few of them were too jaded to stare at Clem and his companions—and greeted them, it was H.

Warwick who explained that the trio had been shopping all afternoon. "And imbibing," he said with that pratfall archness only he could affect so well. "We've gone on the town to celebrate Clement's success."

I congratulated Clem and asked what had happened.

"I got a new suit," he said. He put his thumbs into the jacket pockets and pushed them forward. His arms were too short to draw that vast garment taut.

I said that a man had to look the part. What part?

"He's sold to The Southern Review," H. Warwick announced.

Antistrophic Marienelle said, "He's placed some poems."

The alternate announcements continued like a parody of a play for children. "He's got a New York agent," H. Warwick said.

"And an inquiry about a novel from a very good house," said Marienelle.

And must be the lost dauphin, I laughed. But somewhat shakily I repeated my congratulations.

"It's all shit," Clem said. "Where's your booze?"

"Clement can't stand to be praised," Marienelle chittered.

"But Nathaniel Bentley, who put him in touch with the agent and mentioned his work to the publisher, wrote him an extremely laudatory letter," H. Warwick said, teasing with a fingertip the pearly head of a pimple near his mouth. "Perhaps a touch fulsome, but nevertheless in excellent taste. I don't suppose Bentley is hot for his body, do you?"

It seemed to me that Clem's pink eyes were begging me to crunch these two companions underfoot, but he was so drunk with them and all he had imbibed on their shopping tour that he could not resist gloating, in a tone that simpered like H. Warwick's, "Bentley greeted me on the threshold of a great career."

"He must be hot for you," I said shortly. "Come on. The beer is under the stairway by the furnace. Help yourself and I'll introduce you around when you're comfortable."

But then Shanah, standing spraddle-legged and beating the guitar as if it were a fascist enemy of the people, her jaw clenched and her tongue hard as a railroad spike, began singing "Freiheit." Some girl caught my arm and dragged me around to join in the song. In doing so I lost track of Clem.

First he made his way through the crowd to patronize Felix Martin with the tale of his success—news of which, I would learn, had all come in one single morning's mail, like the wages of sin paid him for what he had done to Sheila. Felix was more than willing to be proud of him, would have forgiven Clem's inappropriate condescension more on humanitarian than on humanistic grounds. He knew well enough on what thin ice Clem's arrogance skated. But Clem, wrestling as with an angel, would not let Felix go until he had won a curse.

I heard a bit of their scene presently. Then they were arguing about great lines of poetry. In spite of Felix' polite equivocations, Clem was forcing him to take a stand. At length Felix declared his faith in Milton's line, "What is dark illumine, what is low, raise." He said that was the greatest line of English poetry he knew.

Whereupon Marienelle, still handmaidening it beside Clem, snickered and emboldened him to declare that Milton was no better than Longfellow. His line stank.

"Stinks? Stinks?" Felix said disgustedly. "I think you're talking to hear yourself talk."

"Tell him the greatest line, Clem," Marienelle pleaded. "'Come take a queen worth many babes and beggars.' That's what you were saying this afternoon when we were at Smedley's. Isn't that the greatest?"

"Clem fancied himself the queen—of the May," H. Warwick said, picking lint from Clem's shoulders.

"That's an excellent line," Felix said to Clem. "I'll admit—"

Clem did not bother to listen. "More, Foerster and Irving Babbitt have no more balls than a female rabbit. Did you ever read what Hemingway thinks of humanists, as in 'A Natural History of the Dead'?"

"I'm familiar with—"

"Well, 'What is low illumine and dark raise' might appeal to a humanist, but it's so dry. So dry." Clem poured beer down his shirt front in what may have been an attempt to get it into his mouth—or then, perhaps as an illustration of the virtues of moistness.

"Balls?" Felix demanded with an embarrassed glance at Marienelle, but an uncontrollable response to Clem's stupid baiting. "I suppose you must have a tiny pair somewhere in the crotch of your trousers. Yes, very well. Perhaps you have. Yes. Nevertheless ..." Then he shook his head and left the party.

I walked to the street with him, probably wanting to hear his censure. But I was disappointed in that. He said only that our "very lively" party had certainly made him feel his years. And when I said I hoped he didn't think Clem represented us, he said, No, no, that was not at all what he had wished to imply.

By the time I had zigzagged again through the tobacco-and-beer fog, I found Clem telling Jack Miller that it had been cowardly to change his name. If he, Clem, were named Goldstein or Beckstein, he would be too proud of the name to alter it for any Hitlerite sonofabitch. His balls might be tiny, but let the hammer beware that tried to crush them.

Marienelle giggled encouragement from his elbow, while H. Warwick pointlessly, foggily tried to explain that Clem was not truly anti-Semitic but that after all, as Jack Whatever-his-name-was would surely agree, Jews could not be truly gentlemen, though the Rothschilds and others—among them, for instance, Disraeli—had insinuated themselves into positions normally belonging to the upper classes and had, consequently, brought upon themselves whatever wrath the Anglo-Saxons were brewing for them.

Shanah, whose name had always been Beckstein, leaped into this fray on Clem's side. She attacked Jack in Yiddish for his disloyalty to the Jewish people. Then Clem capped everything by telling her she mustn't say "Jewish" but must say "Jew," because Jews had to get used to the word "Jew" just as everybody had to learn to accept the word "shit" to describe the holy natural function (Lawrence said it was holy, that's who) which they performed (if they were like himself, Aaron Clement Anderson, who had learned from the Boy Scout Handbook the importance of bowel discipline) every morning immediately after breakfast.

"I do not understand the logic of your allusive juxtapositions," Jack said, wide-eyed, sweating and hanging on to the edge of the bar we had improvised from two planks laid on barrels. "Whether you intend to imply that 'Jew' and 'shit' ..."

"No!" Clem shouted.

"... are, as the semanticists would tell us, words whose referent is the same objectionable correlative, namely me, in which case piss on you, or if, au contraire, you imply that shit is, 'spite well-informed opinion of many commentators, attar of roses and the anointion of princes, in which case let me state categorically that you are inexperienced, insensitive and underinformed, since, as your gentleman friend would agree—" here Jack seized H. Warwick's lapels and shook him so that his glasses slid down his nose—"the upper classes have what one might call dietary laws against it and even I whose old man is a janitor, distinctly do not like the taste of it, which is why I changed my name to Miller, but am too tired to change it back. And if you do not like it, we will, sir, go to the alley and maybe I will come back Herrick Lemon Anderson or you will come back Ripper Miller nee Moisevitch."

191

"You're purposely misunderstanding me," Clem said.

"You're purposely misunderstanding him," Marienelle said.

"So I'll fight you," Clem said.

"You will not," Marienelle cried, throwing her arms around him, pinioning his arms to his sides. She looked like a starved mother kangaroo trying to get its young into the marsupial pouch.

I think he stepped on her foot to make her release him. At any rate, she emitted an unnatural yelp of pain and let him wobble from her arms to the basement door and the stairway that led up to the alley.

H. Warwick went with him, muttering in a low soprano voice that there was no sense in this. After all, Wilde had fought the Marquis of Queensberry only with his tongue, and since Jack was a "brute" a person of Clem's station was not obliged.... As they passed the top of the stairs, Clem must have struck him, because when Shanah and I climbed up behind Jack, H. Warwick was sitting on the ground, whispering that his Adam's apple had been crushed.

In the remote, cold illumination from the corner street light, Clem was stripping off his oversized jacket, his tie and then his shirt. His torso looked thin and waxy when he had finally bared it. Jack was shaking his head in astonishment. It must have finally struck him how incongruous this battle could be, since he outweighed Clem by nearly forty pounds, was four inches taller and had a five-inch advantage in reach.

"Put on your tents and go home," Jack said. "If I misunderstood you we'll talk it out some other time."

"He wants to fight. Well, fight him," Wallace Rogge said. He had come up the basement stairs quietly behind us, slower than we because of the limp from his wounds. His face, when I turned to look at it, seemed too hard for compassion, but it was not cruel either, only watchful. "Go on," he said to both of them. "Fight."

Clem rushed Jack, and Jack hit him in the chest with the flat of his hand, lifting him rather cleanly off his feet and dumping him to a sitting position on the alley bricks.

"I shall call the police," H. Warwick wheezed, staggering upright and beginning to weave down the alley.

Rogge grabbed his arm and drew him back. "We don't need the police," he said, and it sounded as impressive as a slogan for battle in the strange whirligig of that night moment, as if it defined a we who transcended the society that slept around us.

Clem was on his feet again. He shook his head to get the hair out of his eyes. He rushed again. Again Jack hit him on chest or shoulder with a kind of stiff-arm that merely translated Clem's forward momentum into a backward-flopping sprawl. But when Clem came in for the third time I was sure Jack meant to hit him with his fist. In the drunken clairvoyance of the instant it was as if I knew that this must not happen, that here was a trial in which the very form of our future would be decided; here it would be either narrowed to "doing the only thing I could in the circumstances" or opened into the risk of a comradeship that might scorn circumstance. Ingenuously I believed that Rogge had foreseen this test and that he had been very wise to say, "Go on, fight."

But Jack would have hit him. And then, I suppose, H. Warwick and Marienelle would have gathered up the pieces on one side while Rogge, Shanah and I gathered up Jack's regrets.

Clem saved the situation. This time, just beyond the reach of Jack's cocked fist, he skidded to a stop and with a perfect deadpan (or with perfect seriousness) said, "I ought to warn you. I've taken boxing classes."

The dark moment was fractured with laughter. When Clem resumed his charge, Jack simply lifted him in his big arms, whirling him so his legs spun like a rag doll's, bellowing, "Crazy little bastard, crazy little bastard," and cackling as if his heart would break.

After that it was just a matter of the party's refining away to its essence, as noble parties will. When the lesser breeds had crept homeward there were Rogge, Shanah, Jack, Clem and I, exultantly drunk and at three in the morning determined we ought to drive in Jack's Model A to Chicago.

We stopped at Emmy Polk's to pick up Wadleigh, whom Clem had insulted earlier in his day of celebration, and to chalk "Defend the Soviet Union" on H. Warwick's door. (We heard him scamper on bare feet to brace a chair under the knob as we marched down the hall.)

With a tankful of gas, four quarts of extra motor oil, and a fifth of grain alcohol sold to us by a half-awake assistant at the hospital infirmary, we were on our way.

I remember that Rogge, Shanah and Clem rode in the back seat. Shanah leaned into the solid curve of Rogge's arm while Clem snuggled into a ball in her lap. A family group, a Flight into Egypt, I thought.

We drank the grain alcohol in soda pop or in near beer as we rode, and the long trip seemed to have no dimensions in either time or space. We talked rebelliously well and forgot what we said instantly. Somewhere en route Clem woke whimpering. I heard Shanah comfort him, questioning him in a low voice. Then she reported in a voice resonant with lupine maternity, "His girl's ditched him. No wonder he wanted to fight. Never mind, Clem. Plenty girls in Chicago."

"Never too many. Never enough," Clem said.

We meant to stay in Chicago until we ran down or spent our paltry funds, whichever would be first. All that day we drank in bars on the South Side with Negro friends of Rogge's, addressing everyone who had a turn at sitting with us as "Comrade"—but for laughs, as if the Party jargon were a kind of costume we had put on for this protracted ball. Far from our worries, we knew ourselves, and exhaustion came on us slowly, without a crisis.

I was the first to collapse. At nine that first night, I took a cab to my cousin's apartment near the University of Chicago. I slept right through until noon of the next day, when the phone rang for me. It was Rogge, informing me that he and Clem had moved to a bar on Clark Street. He thought that Wadleigh and Jack were sleeping in Jack's car in Lincoln Park. Shanah had checked into a hotel on Ontario Street, but he and Clem had "got their second wind." Why didn't I join them? And if I had any money ...

I borrowed thirty dollars from my cousin and joined them within an hour. They were in a booth behind a silent jukebox. Through a glaze that could not entirely hide his excitement, Clem was listening to Rogge's account of the Battle of Teruel. Coming upon them thus, listening a little, it struck me that Rogge had found in Clem his ideal listener. Nothing was being lost between memory and the scene recreated.

... going into line before dawn, we had to cross down through this bare field and the grove of olive trees, over walls of piled-any-whichway stones, you couldn't see the comrades but the little puffs of steam their breath made blossoming under the bare trees. The soil is brown you know the color of an old sweater. We passed a battery of the French comrades and they were all sitting draped with blankets like sick chickens the French will fight but there's no soldier in the world who hates more to be uncomfortable when he doesn't have to. We were on a knoll above a farmhouse and could see the fascist sentries down among the outbuildings. They were cold, too, huddled against the wall like you know flies on the first cold day of fall, and I was lying there with my hands in my crotch trying to keep warm. The first thing I knew it had begun, the weeds beside my face whipped a little. I saw that before I heard the battery we had passed and all the batteries back up the valley firing over us. I got on my knees and thought Jesus Christ I hope they don't hit the gasoline I'm carrying. There was a machine gun in the upper window of that farmhouse and I could see the flame of it going like the needle in Ma's sewing machine....

Outside in the Chicago cold a Clark Street bum paused to stare in at us. He may have been envying us only our beers and our youth, but it seemed as if he envied the far-off battle and nerves that could twitch like weeds when the batteries roared behind them.

At four that afternoon, when Wadleigh and Jack had caught up with us again, Rogge faded and left us to go to Shanah's hotel. That night we four were on the South Side again, the south side of reality where dark people did not so much approach as loom. In between wondering why Clem did not wilt from sleeplessness and drink, I wondered how anyone could. It was as if we were preserved in smoky crystal or under museum glass, so that we and all we said were set apart from the world where change was measured by hours. Everything I saw seemed heightened. I noted seven types of ambiguity in the signs advertising beer or wrestling matches. Even the penciled inscriptions in urinals seemed like those ideograms to which Pound attaches such importance. When the jazz horns blew, one felt a brave soldier in the army of concupiscence, called to duty.

At ten o'clock the next morning we made four out of eight people in a bar just south of the Loop; besides our party there were the bartender and three whores. The youngest of the whores looked about fourteen years old and must have weighed, for her five feet two, nearly two hundred pounds. Her skin had the dull luminescence of a frosted light bulb. Her eyes, deep in their dimples of flesh, were melting brown as those of an Arabian mare. She was pure vision, an end-of-the-rainbow, unworldly creature. Both Jack and Clem were fascinated.

They started calling for and adding up our money. Among us we had two dollars and eighty cents left. There was some unreliable accounting of what we would have left after one more round of beers and one only visit by only one of us with that human balloon swaying on her spike heels near the bar. I maintained that we would not have streetcar fare to wherever the car was parked if anything was spent for her. I was overruled on the grounds that we no longer knew where the car was anyway. So two dollars was appropriated for the cause. Straws were to be drawn. When it came to this, only Jack and Clem wanted to draw.

Clem won. With our last two dollar bills in the pocket of his enormous jacket, he went floating to the bar. The marish eyes sized him up. The tiny rosebud mouth puckered disdainfully in the center of that globular face. Pertly she shook her head.

Clem came back to us with slow, high, dancing steps, as though he were picking his way across a floor littered with basketballs. He put the unspent bills down before us on the table, said sweetly, "Her name is Rose. Rose. Rose. She don't like college boys. She gets three dollars. Worth every penny."

Slowly then he wilted, dropping below table level like someone being drawn into quicksand. With a smile of brute bliss he collapsed at our feet under the table. He was so sound asleep that the three of us had to carry him out.

We lived through our marathon of gut-rotting debauchery and came home the better for it, purged of certain evils by having committed others, stripped of energy and of money. We even had to hock fountain pens, wrist watches and the tool kit from the Model A to pay for gas to get us home. I have always been warm to the idea that this flirt with self-destruction was an attempt to immunize ourselves against the war we now expected. It adjusted us to the status of soldiers in waiting, which, after Munich, we were.

And in some indefinable way we all recognized Clem as the champion of our collective gesture. It was not merely that he had stayed on his feet longer than the rest, or had pulled the straw that won him the chance at Rose Rose. It was more as if he had been the Isaac we took with us to Chicago to sacrifice on the altar of rebellion. Yes, it was really as if we had hoped he would drink himself to death, just to show somebody what we thought of them. But we were, all the same, mysteriously gladdened when Rose Rose Rose corrected us. She said she didn't like college boys. She said, Not this one. Spare him.

I find it sadly amusing to note how easily the names connoting father-to-son, older-to-younger-brother relationships re-establish my attitudes toward him after that—Abraham and Isaac, Judah and Benjamin—and how truthful-seeming it is to think of him as "spared" by those days as by the war that followed.

That he belonged to us in some irrefutable sense after the Chicago junket none of us who had gone along ever seemed to doubt. The bond was for us—who didn't care much for the idea of family, but had its pieties ingrained in us, looking for an object more imperative than a family one. And yet, because he was both ward and leader for us, not quite so clear or easy. He was our idiot and wise man, goat and counselor, lamb and shepherd—not in readily evident terms, for we all seemed to go our own ways minding him very little, but in terms of some felt polarity of our responsibilities and his. He would creep into our conversations when we had not seen him for weeks. From that time forward we used him endlessly to illustrate our propositions. Sometimes we made him simple as a chalk diagram showing the intellectual as social misfit, the writer as antifrat man and sartorial buffoon, or the unimportance of habits. Clem had none whatever at this time. He was punctual-unpunctual, given to sleeping eighteen hours at a stretch or going without sleep for days. He went for a week to the gym for workouts in the pool or on the vaulting horses—and for the next three weeks courted gout, stooped shoulders, alcoholism and smoker's fag. One time his nails would be clean and squarely trimmed and his ears would glow with scrubbing. Seen a few days later, he would be wearing a week-old shirt and exuding an odor that combined urine, toejam, wet wool and stale pipe smoke. He yielded nothing to systematic study. At the semester's end he came up, for once and once only, with straight A's in Shakespeare, the Victorian novel, philosophy from Kant to Dewey, medieval history, and botany. But neither Wadleigh nor anyone else had ever seen him study for more than an hour on end. His only explanation for success was that the botany instructor hated him so much he had given the A as a furious insult, somewhat as an angry Japanese might commit hara-kiri on your doorstep. The other courses? Who could tell what had dazzled his teachers?

Still suffering along in Henry Powell's class, I liked to use Clem as the example of the futility of writing classes. Excepting Jack Miller, who had sold some lithographs in New York and had a commission to paint a WPA mural, Clem seemed farther up the hill of success than any of us, and he had spent only a few minutes in a writing class.

But more fascinating than all the stereotypes of the artist as a young man that he dramatized was our learning to read the peculiar scrambled code of defensive lies and unreserved confession by which he showed the constant self beneath. It was my uneasy privilege to become a sort of confidant during those following weeks when he was trying to patch up his quarrel with Sheila. He went so far as to practice the use of the telephone in order to re-establish verbal communication, but when he dared to call her she refused to speak to him. He found her in the library once. The meeting was briefly concluded by the library attendants, who ejected him for, as he said, "trying to reason with her." (He was trying to explain in so many four-letter words why she should have gone into the woods with him on that fateful Sunday. She was trying to shut him up by every means short of promising to see him again. When they pinioned his arms and dragged him away, he went insisting that he hadn't "even got to the point yet.") He called one afternoon at the sorority house into which she had moved soon after their break. A pledge, whose eyebrows met, dubiously admitted him to the parlor while she scampered upstairs to tell Sheila that some "crazy-looking boy" had come asking for her. Clem had worn his new clothes for the call and, spacious as they were, felt no more at home in them than in what he took to be the "whorehouse atmosphere" of the soft-carpeted, dimly lit parlor. He felt that the sisters who stole behind him on silent feet had come to get a good look and (like barbers standing behind him to marvel at his ridiculous hair) have a good laugh. He was prepared for an attempt to put him out as he had been put out of the library. First he would fight. Being (whatever they thought) a gentleman, he would not use his fists or strike for their bosoms when the sisterhood advanced on him. And so they would beat him. Yes, he was prepared to go down under the phalanx, but when they tossed him onto the sidewalk he would have such epithets prepared as would brand them forever with infamy.

Sheila, for her part, came down the stairs prepared to send him away with a statement so final, so evidently full of careful reasoning and sad coldness that he could stop troubling himself about their ill-starred affection.

She found him turning his head like a betrayed wild animal, and his first words to her were, "Aren't my clothes all right to come here?"

Preparation vanished like a bubble. "Clem, of course they are," she said, and she sat down to tell him he was not betrayed. She had reasons for sending him away, but she would not let him go for any reasons that compassion forbade her. If he had come here wrapped in a blanket and wearing a bone through his lower lip, he was not going to be driven out for that reason, not while she stayed.

So they sat on in that parlor through the dinner hour while her sisters passed, hiding their smiles and asking, "Sheila, aren't you going to eat?" "Do you want cook to save something for you, Sheila?" "Sheila, you're not forgetting the dance at the Phi Psi house, are you?" They sat on while the tuxedoed Phi Psis arrived to pick up their dates, while the dates came down in their formals, until they were surrounded by crew-cut chivalry and the self-assurance bred of good corsetry.

What were they talking about? It doesn't matter much. No doubt Clem was telling her how he saw her in the mirror of his novel and how she might step through that mirror into a world more real and less painful than the one she might think she lived in. He may have said, in effect, that he was going to make her a self which would fit her comely spirit better than the gaudy ready-made that "these jerks" sitting around them were trying to foist on her.

It doesn't matter—because she wasn't listening. She was straining every nerve for poise and control enough to keep him from being shamed by sleek haircuts and rented tuxedos.

When her date finally appeared, a blond youth, all gum-developed lower jaw and blue eyes alert to every movement and nothing else, she tried to manage a smooth explanation, a socially graceful passage à trois. She stood up to introduce the young men, resting her hand on Clem's shoulder so that he would not rise and show off the jacket that hung to his knees. He stood up anyway. He reached to shake hands, proffering, in actuality, the tip of his sleeve.

Yeah, yeah, yeah, her date said, showing off his splendid mandible with a series of muscular quivers. He unnerstood all right how these misunderstandings came about. His quick eyes swept Clem's hair like a bird dog's searching cover. He held on to Clem's sleeve while Clem tried to work his fingers out far enough to jerk it discreetly back. Yeah, he unnerstood that Sheila might have had a previous engagement with another party which she had clean forgotten about. But he wanted them to unnerstand that he really, see, felt sorry for her, was she blind? Tugging at Clem's empty sleeve end he said, "Get it shot off in the war, buddy?"

This, in free translation, is how he and Sheila came to resume. But this is not the way he was reporting such things to me at the time.

He said that the pledge who let him into the sorority house was covered with hair like a female gorilla. That when two of the sisters had snuck up behind the couch on which he was sitting, he had scared the hell out of them by turning and shouting "Boo!" That he had worn his new clothes only to give Sheila a laugh and to "soften her up." Or, alternatively, that he had worn them to épater les frat boys, and if he ever went back to that "nunnery" (pronounced with a sneering inflection that all Shakespearean scholars should understand) he was apt to go leading a turtle on a pink ribbon, with a roll of nickels in each fist for any gumchewer that dared laugh. That once he had worked his hand out of the enveloping sleeve, he had applied a jujitsu grip to the frat boy's hand that had forced him to his knees whimpering with pain.

And from such splendid lies he would pass into analyses of his feeling for Sheila that were grotesque only by their extreme frankness. "I have to persuade her that it's all right for her not to be good enough for me in some ways, or to try to match me in everything, because being imperfect for my perfections to fit into is the female of it."

His perfections? I would ask with an eyebrow cocked.

"Some of my ideas are perfect. You want to say I'm a grotesque, awkward bastard, I know that. But some ways, relatively, I'm complete and she isn't. For instance, she's not like us in intelligence, but by being ignorant she knows a lot of wonderful things I don't by being smart. She's like a beautiful crystal, or like a prism. You know, while we were sitting in that whorehousy parlor I could just look at her face and see everything that was happening in the whole room, like how Schmoe Blifil came in full of oxygen and dirty thoughts, asking for Doris, settling in a chair and crossing his legs carefully so as not to devalue the dollar-and-a-quarter press in his pants, then suddenly spotting Sheila and me, doing a double take and beginning to figure what he can make out of the fact that they let such funny birds into their high-class house, like he's figuring how he can punish Doris for it later and knock down her price a little after the dance when he's got her in the car, and how she's not going to like that and will take it out on Sheila by making some pointed comment on me at breakfast or whatever they eat in such a place. Sheila knows all that, and I wouldn't have dared turn my head to look over my shoulder, because Blifil would have turned me to stone with his gaze. Every time I'm with Sheila she does the same thing for me. I can see the world. But it takes the two of us, because she can't see it and I can't except through her.

"Or, I say to her great, complicated things" (I'll bet he did) "and she comes back with just making her eyes shine—as if she knew and caught what I was trying to say better than anyone else could, but at the same time didn't understand a word."

I asked in what way these special properties of hers differed from her being just plain dumb. Maybe he was only projecting qualities on her mind that she did not, in any real sense, possess.

He looked at me with a disgust that said I was being dumb in a useless way, while she was creatively dumb, and if I didn't understand the difference there, he couldn't help me. Well, I had caught a flicker of movement in the branches. Something showed in the beautiful crystal of his illogical arguments.

"Sometimes I see things happening to Sheila and me like they were happening to someone else. She lets me get back away. I even get a funny kind of pleasure out of watching us make each other unhappy, as we always will."

Masochism, I guessed, was a taste like another. But wasn't he concerning himself with differences that didn't make any difference? (I was a great hand with Occam's Razor and other positivistic cutlery that semester.) Basically here was a girl whose whole orientation—merely reflect that she was a sorority girl; intellectuals should no more involve themselves with sorority girls than Zionists should marry into the Hitler Youth—whose family, tastes and objectives were worlds away from his. With the war coming, did he have time to waste in pursuing her when catching her would probably waste even more of what he had left? Why not a more intellectual and pliant type? I had thought, for instance, that he and Lillian Esterman ...

No. Something had been committed between Sheila and him, and it was "too late" for either of them to take it back. If he could shape her as he knew she ought to be shaped, they would "get through." Desperate the gamble, all right. It was "the only chance" that either of them had.

Well, it seemed to me (who did not know Sheila yet except through his artful distortions) that his little sorority girl was taking him for a ride, and after all the anguish she put him to she would probably marry a commerce major. She might seem special, but when you looked at her sub specie aeternitas (my view, naturally) was she any different from thousands of other college girls who were saving their second-growth cherries for the highest bidder? In a spirit of counsel and consolation I told him the story of Jack Miller's pursuit of just such a girl for months last year. (I could see the fatal vulnerability of intellectuals to the common, the typical. I could. I had read Tonio Kröger, too. But what we had to talk about was American reality, not German fiction.) Jack Kröger Miller had wasted money, time and peace of mind on this pure type of American girlhood without getting to first base. Then, to impress her, he took her to a party held by some of his fraternity friends. Getting a little gassed, he lost track of her for a while, came to with his eyes wide on the spectacle of her unzipping the fly of a man she had met less than two hours before, hauling forth and wetly kissing.

I thought Clem was going to explode when I gave him this anecdote. But he was just bullheaded enough to cap me by saying that even if Sheila did something like that it would make no difference in the way he felt about her. Nothing can hurt a good girl, as Socrates said, and it was in her goodness, not her frailty, that he wanted to take Sheila. Who knew just what he meant by that, even if I was too impure to know. She was right not to let their present difficulties be complicated further by sexual ones. "I got her in trouble last spring," he said, groaning.

"In trouble? You said you'd never—" Then, belatedly, I began to realize that "trouble" was some sort of psychometaphysical state in his lexicon and did not mean pregnancy. Before I could apologize for misunderstanding, I'd hurt Clem's feelings and his guard was up. I suppose he thought I had considered him juvenile for misusing a common expression.

After a bit of reflection I was sure he meant chiefly that he had misprized her, that his awkward soul had too hastily affronted her tranquil one, tripping the serene and bridal shape he had adored in her approach across the field of his love—but I dared not trust myself to such more proximate language in those days, however reckless he sometimes became.

He was already regretting his confidence in the truth and swung back to lies when he wanted to communicate a sentiment to me—or test my reaction while forming his secret judgments. The only straightly reliable thing I heard from him about Sheila in the next many weeks was that she had bought him for Christmas a handsome brown sport jacket, on condition that he burn the monstrosity he had been wearing. I thought this little fragment of information meant quite a bit and began to wonder if Sheila wasn't a good, moderating influence. I also thought it meaningful that he did not burn the other, but merely hid it away and told her he had.

Like magic, lies are reasonably divided into white and black. Lies of the poet that grow, however indirectly, into literary forms might be called, like magic, prescientific forms of cognition. Clem's progress to a knowledge of what he came from (nothing in all his menagerie of visions came from nothing, but what it came from was not so easy to discern) must have been speeded by the lies he told, as if he were testing the appearances of memory until he found something that rang truer than the first facts falling to mind.

I never knew of any lies tending toward self-aggrandizement, though with a curious inversion he liked to make himself out worse than he was, boasting that he was louse enough to cheat Emmy Polk of rent now and then. (Actually it was Wadleigh who performed these frauds, no doubt to punish her for the charities she inflicted on him in the form of hot breakfasts, coffee when he studied, or laundering his shirts.)

Usually Clem seemed to lie about details that made no difference one way or another. He told me, for instance, that he had been in San

Francisco during his childhood. I caught him in this fib, because he spoke of crossing the Golden Gate Bridge some years before it had been built. And he told me that he had an older brother who had hitchhiked to Colorado with him the summer before last, then had gone on west and signed on with the crew of a tramp steamer, and was now settled in New Zealand. Later, when he told me correctly that his sister was the only other child in the family, he became very flustered and insisted that it was his cousin Mark who had been with him—and only at length admitted the harmless truth that he had been alone.

But the lie which appeared to have the most fruitful consequence was that two of his uncles, both brothers of his mother, had committed suicide in recent years.

He was working, that spring, on a story he called "Spider on a Rope." Shortly before the time when he would submit it to this year's short-story contest, he gave me the manuscript to read. In his letting me read it there was something, no doubt, of an implication that once I had beheld it I might save myself the embarrassment of competing with him by submitting a story of my own. I'm proud to report that I too thought it superior to anything I had done.

It was a relentless bit of nerve-banging horror, beginning quietly enough with a boy returning from his Sunday-night date. When he sneaks into his bedroom illuminated only by moonlight, he sees in the bed where he is accustomed to sleep alone "an indistinct mountain of blubbery shapes, phosphorescent and obscene in its palpability." It is his mother's brother, who has come for unexplained reasons to stay a while with the boy's family. Wakened by the boy's return, the uncle climbs out through the window to "go piss in the yard," since the flush toilet in the house makes him nervous. While he is framed in the window, "for a second Walter saw his fishbelly-white torso in the moonlight, like a sail hanging limp in the calm of a murderous latitude, wasting in its strength." A few days later, when he has returned to his farm downstate, the uncle hangs himself in the corncrib. The boy Walter, trying to find refuge from the intolerable shock and grief of the event in a masturbation fantasy, discovers himself unable to distinguish between his girl's imagined nudity and the visual memory of his uncle's body. Either the girl's pretty parts are dangling like a white spider at the end of its filament or his uncle's revolting body invites him to love.

That would curl the hair on Henry Powell's fat neck when he saw it, I thought. But I told Clem sincerely how fine I thought the story was, how skillfully he had managed the language at the end to give the effect of the contradictory but interchanging images of flesh.

At my praise, Clem blushed and turned pale in a swift succession of changes, responding like a chameleon that finds itself on a jukebox. Marienelle was right—he couldn't handle approbation. But beyond that he seemed troubled that I was concerning myself with its technique.

Without any prompting from me he began to insist that if the story was any good, its merit came from its re-creation of "the way it was— except in some places I combined Uncle Cole with my other uncle that shot himself."

He wanted to insist that the language served only like "the developing medium that makes the dark and light show up on a film." And all at once he was spilling over into a fuller account of the two suicides than he had given in the story.

Uncle Cole had hanged himself because of the drought that ruined his corn, because his oldest son was beating him in a contest of wills for the management of the farm, because "he couldn't sweat any more, even on the hottest days." Cole had been his mother's favorite brother, and Clem had suffered the estrangement, this once, of touching no response from her when he tried to comfort her. This had been the worst thing that happened to his family, worse than the quarrels about his father's investment in the Drake Estate.

But the other suicide, that of the unnamed uncle who shot himself "for no reason at all," seemed to preoccupy Clem more. Uncle Nameless had been young and fairly handsome, though small. He had a job in Minneapolis managing a group of filling stations, and everyone thought he would have a better future than anyone else in the family. So one afternoon he had calmly stuck a pistol into his mouth—Clem lifted his beer bottle to his mouth and drank—and blew out the back of his head.

Everyone who had seen him just before his death thought he looked extraordinarily cheerful. He had left no notes "giving silly reasons."

An acte gratuit, I contributed sagely. It is easier to speak of horrors in a foreign language. Anyway, Clem was beyond hearing my interjections.

Though there was no note, Clem had understood "perfectly" how his uncle had reasoned. "He believed that he would never have things so good again. He loved everything pretty in nature and women so much. It all seemed to stretch out before him longer and longer, like a shadow while the sun is going down, and he knew that things would be less and less fun, whether he succeeded or not. By the time he got something he wouldn't want it any longer. 'You have something, nothing. Be absolute for death,' he must have thought. You know it. 'Hast nor youth nor age but as it were an after dinner sleep, dreaming on both.' I don't mean that he was literary, but other people think exactly the same thing as we do and Shakespeare did even if they don't have the words to say it the same, and he didn't say anything. He did it because it was reasonable and it made him happy to be reasonable about life. You have to manage it somehow.... But I wouldn't ever tell my family what I know, because nothing is harder on a family than a suicide anyway, and it's easier for them if they believe there was some bad reason for it, like the drought or all that."

I don't know when I became certain that Clem was lying about his second uncle. I suppose that before we had talked our way through six bottles of beer that afternoon I knew that the man was an imaginary projection of himself that he was trying out on me. But I fought hard to resist those terms, finally appearing to convince him that the story he had written ("Let's stick to that, Clem, for pity's sake") was a fine synthesis from reality, that he could afford to take my praise of its craft and that he needed nothing else from me. I'm sure that I was sincere and sure that I saw how he used his lies as preparation, stretching his muscles as innocently as a dancer at a practice bar.

For twenty years I excused Clem's lies for reasons I have tried to make evident. And now I have to turn against the current of my special pleading (I recognize all I have to say about him as special pleading, all right) to admit that they have always bothered me. I never quite bought Clem's eventually perfected excuse that lies may be, as well as preparation, a shorthand for the truth—a code made of symbols that, after all, might be as useful as any others. There remains the question of the right to use such a code.

Granted that nature speaks its truth through a man's lies, and that specialists—I am thinking of psychiatrists, anthropologists and such philosophers as take on themselves the task of defining man in gross measures—assume a special privilege of disregarding what individuals intend in favor of discerning what nature means by them. I am afraid that those privileges have been assumed at a risk that only nature could ultimately assess, and the findings of such specialists are still, at the other end of the spectrum from our mean fibs of fear and self-seeking, nevertheless lies. For is it not the primal quality of truth to be a declaration of faith in the limited universe discernible by traditional knowledge? Our good old apple-counting mathematics, our engineering and star-plotting geometries and the fine orders of semantics all begin to lie for us when we breach this faith. Pascal avait son gouffre—and we have ours. We no longer see it represented by the spaces between the stars but in the infinite separation between the thought of specialists and common sense. The limitless universe of their discourse is one of anomalies recklessly accepted, of position-less positions, of nonserial numbers and a rakehell disregard for what we need to be told. I cannot convince myself that a writer should be of their league rather than ours. However difficult his language, it ought to ground on what any of us, possessed of common sense, might recognize as the truth.

If Clem's lies and his fake suicides—all in the mind—seemed harmless for so long and even abnormally productive, wasn't nature merely saying, Wait a while and see what they come to?

And we can't wait long enough. The end of every attempt to know the truth is speculation (as Clem and all men always knew). I will go on to the end of my speculations arguing, as I always have, both sides of the question of the writer's "responsibility." I see the commitment to destructiveness in those who choose to stand with one foot always outside the circle of their common obligations. But also I see in their very disloyalty to life and its values the half-holy chance to go along with the ruins, the wrecks, the might-have-been loveliness that a good life ruthlessly dumps in its wake. Where possibilities die the writer lives, and where he dies they may live, on the terrain to which the heart hot for salvation must leap in the very despair of immortality—to imagination's not easily won foothold on eternity.

I am stopped when I recognize the irreconcilability of these two postures.

When I won the short-story contest that spring, I was nearly ruined by Clem's grief and by the air of one betrayed that he put on. This combined all too readily with my awareness that the judging had not been ordered as it should have been.

He avoided me for two or three weeks, and that wasn't so bad. I put it down partly to brattishness. Hadn't I already made it clear what I thought of his story and what I thought of Henry Powell's decisions? Further, the poetry prize this year had gone to Marjorie Rangel for a bit of free-verse enthusiasm called, I believe, "The War-Cloud Frieze." Her series of poems (frieze) had to do with the Indians who trod our campus hills long before we white men came with our fevers and frets, our "airless books." Henry Powell called it "a small-scale, Indian Spoon River." Its level of sentiment can be indicated by the fact that one of the poems from it ("Laughs-with-the-Hemlocks"—an Indian maid's soliloquy) was later printed on the menu of a downtown tea shoppe. Surely Clem knew I wasn't comfortable in being bracketed with Marjorie.

But Clem! I swear that he was acting as he might have if Henry Powell and I had come upon his uncle's body swinging in the hot corncrib, had clicked our tongues and said, "That man's linen is soiled." It was my fault that I had praised his "Spider on the Rope" before the contest, since clearly I had been less than candid in my praise. Had been tricky.

When at last I stopped by Emmy Polk's to find him and offer what might be loosely categorized as an apology, he sat hunched at his study desk all the while we were talking and would hardly meet my eyes. Stubbornly I recited again all the virtues I had found in his story. Quite uselessly. If it had been as good as I claimed, it would have converted Henry Powell. Twenty minutes' reading should have transformed that turgid taste thirty years in formation, and at the end Henry should have cried out, "Credo!" Or so Clem's sulking implied.

I pointed out that I was graduating this year. Probably that fact had carried some weight with Henry and the other judges. After all, I said, this was my last chance to win, and I had needed some encouragement for my work, too. Clem's oblique glance suggested he could not see why. Nature's purposes in man are accomplished by a few individuals. I was of the many.

No, he said, the game of pretenses was finished. He would never be able to say what anyone else could hear. For a little he had been tricked into believing that what he meant had been seen and recognized. But the truth of the matter was probably that even his sweep in last year's contest had been a freak. "They gave Bentley this pile of manuscripts to read and he was in a hurry. He thought, Oh Jesus, I don't want to go through all this. So he tossed them down a stairway and the one that landed at the bottom was the one he gave a prize to," Clem said.

But he had published other things since.

So? A few more accidents. And being published wasn't the same as being understood. He supposed that if an inkling of his meaning soaked through, no one would ever publish him again.

"You're being pretty juvenile, aren't you?" I said.

"Oh, I'm just a boy. Just a boy." There was a silly glitter of tears in his eyes. I felt he was going to be permanently angry at me if I saw him break down and cry. So I left, nothing repaired, but knowing better than ever that I would never attach so much importance as he to anything I wrote.

Then I heard from Wadleigh that Clem had burned all his manuscripts in Emmy's garbage incinerator. "He's sore at everybody," Wadleigh said. "He had a big fight with H. Warwick the other day in the bathroom—I heard part of it—and called him a phony and a fairy. So H. Warwick is moving out of the house at last. I saw Clem carrying this stuff down to the incinerator and moseyed down to find out what was happening, was he moving out too. When I saw what he was up to I tried to reason with him."

"And he said no Marxist could possibly understand the ritual of religious self-immolation, crucifixion, Empedocles on Etna, or Heautontimorumenos," I guessed.

"Words to that effect. 'Lard-ass pinko' was his exact term for me. I don't know why I put up with it."

"Love."

"None of that fruity talk! I have to admit I was moved to see all he's put so much into smoking down in the weeds. I went down later to see if it had all burned, you know how paper doesn't sometimes. But he'd stirred it until everything was just ash. The last thing he said he was going to do as a writer was this big long letter he wrote to the student paper denouncing you and Henry Powell and all the 'false litterateurs' in the writing classes and the literary magazine. He had a point there. But Jesus, it would have done him a lot of harm. He referred to the whole English department as 'asses, apes and dogs.'"

"You have to admit that education sharpens invective."

"But he's got to graduate. I persuaded him not to send it."

I really began to bleed when Wadleigh said that Clem had been intending to use the prize money to live on that summer, staying at the university and finally giving up his board job at the Hamilton Hotel. Since he had won nothing, he was going home to Boda to work on a farm. He was talking again of joining the Navy, Wadleigh said.

Something had to be done to persuade Clem back into the fold. As a victim of injustice (so we thought him) he had got a punishing hammerlock on our feelings. We talked over ways of getting him some money—including a reissue of the digested Lady Chatterley. None of our ideas seemed very practical, but even so, at this point they seemed easier than getting Clem to accept them in the present state of his feelings.

The best thing we could think of to do—this was frequently the best thing we could think of to do about the crises of that spring, like the occupation of Czechoslovakia, the superfluous abundance of signs that Munich had been just what we impotently knew it to be—was have a party. Facetiousness aside, it wasn't the worst thing to do. As it turned out, once again a party marked a progress of the very greatest importance to us individually.

I said I thought a sweet, year-end, bang-up trip to the quarry for all of us who had been to Chicago, with some girls to keep the edge off us, was what we all deserved even if we were about to go our separate ways henceforward. I wasn't even sure Clem was speaking to me, but I wanted him along.

"He'll come," Wadleigh said confidently. "And don't take any shit from him. That just makes him feel worse."

What seemingly casual accidents make our fatalities! And if this were my story there could hardly be a more crucial moment in it than the almost accidental assemblage of eight of us on that May evening at the abandoned quarry east of town. It happened that Rogge and Shanah could not come with us. It happened that the girl I had been going with most of that year was in the hospital with a mastoid infection. I asked a girl named Janet Morgan to go with me. I had got acquainted with her some months before when she was working as a secretary in the dean's office. I had admired what I guess I'll call her firm tread, but I had never dated her before.

Until that evening everything had been arranged for me to go to New York after graduation and work until I was drafted. About the time the moon came up full I found I respected no arrangements at all except the wonderful symmetries of day and night, water and shore, of stone, coolness and heat, and male and female. So, as it happened, I stayed on at the university that summer, married Janet a year and a half later, got children by her, and—That is enough about us except for what we did to Clem and what we know of him. That night we furthered him.

Janet, Ginny Price, who came with Wadleigh, and a girl named Daisy, whom Jack Miller brought, were maids for a bridal night; Jack, Wadleigh and I, the wisecracking best men. By this I do not mean to say only that Clem and Sheila had intercourse for the first time that night, or that our wanton talk encouraged Sheila to give herself, though those things are certainly true. I am trying to insist, by this fashion of announcing it, that there was a formal paradigm of myth and ritual in the circumstance. There was a sharing of sacraments. Those elements of the law confided to nerves and memory—now that church and court law are unwilling to define them—were not scanted. What intended us to be what we would become was not mocked, though we might have intended to mock it by our informalities, unawed still by the awful commitments we were making.

I remember sizing up the girls when they first came out of the brush in their bathing suits to join us on blankets spread near the water. I still knew Sheila chiefly through Clem's reports and confidences, and just then I believed her the poorest of our lot. Ginny Price had long black hair and a way of running barefoot on the grass that made the grass spring up and grow faster. Jack's Daisy was a phys.-ed. major. Not stopping for the blankets, she came soaring over us like a female zeppelin, paused in mid-air for an apocalyptic moment, then tipped toward the water. Her splash fit her like a calyx. I wondered (and wonder still) what physical thing a mere university could have taught her. Janet came toward me with a smile that suddenly made her familiar as she is today. But among them there was something unripe and shy about Sheila—in her earnest diffidence. Even the way she laughed at my jokes struck me as overeagerness.

She was very slender then. There was nothing remarkable about her figure except the hard symmetry of the lines on the upper and lower slopes of her breasts. I remember a sun-slowed thought, merely tolerant—She may be just the right size for little Clem.

The late afternoon was hot as a bonfire, but the water in the quarry was still cold. Only Daisy, who came from someplace north of Duluth, could stay in it long. I think all the rest of us must have wet ourselves, but we climbed out quickly to eye and josh each other and enjoy the sun. We were in that nice equilibrium of desire which hopes the sun will stay up forever, that wants the dark to come quickly.

Wadleigh started his phonograph. Jack, Clem and Sheila leaned over the square-cut edge of rock to haul up a sack of the beer bottles we had lowered at rope's end to cool in the water below. I saw it jump dark and dripping like the corpse of a drowned man given the illusion of life by the hands that hauled it up. Thought, Full fathom five thy uncles lie, Clem. Drank, watched Jack throw a beer bottle cap into the quarry for Daisy to retrieve. She surface-dived as if straight for the depths of his lecherous pride in showing her off, surfaced again, white suit and gold hair rising from the murk of green to hold the cap aloft, threw it at us; dived again and came up with both hands streaming doubloons.

"I like your friends," Janet said.

I was lying flat on my back, admiring the way her face was stamped in profile on a hilltop tree, like a milkmaid's on a green coin. I winked agreement.

"I like them very much," she said. "I like Clem and his girl more than any of them."

"Yes. Why?"

Like a good wife she told me what I already knew. She put simply what was elaborate and difficult in my thought, cluttered as it was by experience and some undeclarable grudges. She took to Clem because I had already staked some irretrievable wagers on that puny body and that giant chaos that hummed between his ears. She had not my need to quibble. He was her boy, her grief, her charge, her underprivileged knight, her seeing eye and her jester almost from that day forward. Once, in the months following, I charged her with being in love with him. Honestly and plainly she did not know what I was talking about. "Of course," she said. "I love him. A person should." I think, too, that she carried Sheila along from that day in the same secure affection. It was as if she had come on us all there in certain relationships, had clicked a camera and stared faithfully at that one photograph for the rest of her life, simply unable to believe that what was could change. She saw Clem and Sheila kneeling together on the altar-shaped stones. For no reason at all she decided that this time must end there—they would never have things so good again. She would, if she could, have sacrificed them there, garlanded as they were with May and the colors of twilight, uncorrupted yet. (How do I know what my wife would do if she could? I put my ear to her chest sometimes and listen.) And if she couldn't literally leave them there in their blood for the flies and the coroners, she would do the next best thing—believe in the moment of her vision and refuse even what they might do that offered to degrade their essences into mortality.

She watched us and talked. I heard a little more than she was saying, considerably less than she meant. I figured that she had us, that I would have to have her.

I came awake presently from the sweet drug of afternoon to find Wadleigh and Ginny struggling in from the woods on our left with armloads of dry branches. We built a fire, and the girls went to the brush to change out of their suits. Coming back, Janet and Sheila were walking together, trailing the other two. They looked as if they were already plotting something. I felt as if I were being kept out of a secret when they sat down by me and went on gabbling about shampoos.

We warmed beans and roasted wieners over the fire. Ginny Price said we all ought to drive to the town eight miles west, where there was a dance that night. All of us who had something else in mind began cagily to undermine her wish. Was it only a rumor that there was a

211

dance or was she sure? Did any of us know exactly which road to take? The car was low on gas. You couldn't get there from here.

The moon came up deliberately, and when it was full it showed only three couples left around the freckled embers. Jack, Daisy and one blanket were gone.

Clem was restless. He began beerily to recite "Laughs-with-the-Hemlocks," which, out of pure malice, he had memorized. Then to parody. "I am she who swims beside your canoe, white lovers, she who steals dandylions from your garden before dawn, white gardeners, she who watches through the children's eyes the ice go in the lake, white mothers, she whose Sundays begin before the church bells, O white-man-on-his-knees. She who watched the moon you see, white moonwatcher. She who won a hunned dolla wortha mobbles, white mobble champion. How do you like that, Sheila?"

"Do 'looking at the moon' again and I'll look at the same time. You look at the moon and I'll say it."

"Look at a moon a squaw has looked at? I'd sooner lie dead at my mother's feet than mess with a moon some old squaw has had in her mouth," Clem said. "Look out," he warned when Sheila cuffed him, "you're messing with the Strongest Boy in Boda." He wrestled her down onto the blanket and nibbled at her throat. "Come on, Krivitsky, we know you, for we are the dreaded Gay Pay Oo."

She sat up, straightening her skirt, fending him away. "I am she who took boxing lessons, O white four-flusher." She turned to Janet and me and asked, "Did you ever hear how Jack kept knocking him on his silly prat? He was so proud of it. Clem's the only boy I know who can be proud of getting knocked down. But you know something? He can be proud of anything."

"I was there," I volunteered. "I saw it."

"Who'd have thought the old man had so much blood in him?" Wadleigh said amiably from the darkness beyond the fire before he returned his mouth to Ginny's.

"No blood," Clem insisted. "Jack was very neat. That's why I was proud. I take a friendly pride in his work. But I repaid him with evil. Miller? Where is he? He's gone, so I can talk. Dick, I cheated when we drew straws for Rose Rose Rose."

"Who is Rose Rose Rose?" Sheila demanded. "There never was a Rose like me, such as I. Look in my green eyes Clem and tell me you love another. Who was Rose Rose Rose?"

"Hyperion to a sorority satyr," he scoffed. "She was the white Pocahontas of North Clark Street. 'Cap'n Jawn,' she say to me. 'I am she who watches the limp go out of your writing wrist, white poet. I am naw fish nor fool but as it wuh an after-dinnah piece, redeeming you both.' The way I cheated—never tell Jack—was by tearing my slip of paper after I drew, thus making it shorter than his, and Rose Rose Rose might have loved him as she scorned me."

"Poor unloved Clem," Sheila said. "He never gets what he wants until after he's stopped wanting it. Do you know, Janet? Clem really meant to be the littlest All-American in the world when he came to college, but—"

He covered her mouth with his hand. She struggled loose and lay against his shoulder, purring happily. "You tell it, then," she begged gently. "They may be stronger, but nobody in the world is funnier than my Clem. Tell it, baby."

So he did.

We finished the beer while he was talking, and when it was gone Wadleigh was worried. Ginny was apparently not yet well enough primed. He could not quite make the grade where they lay nor persuade her to go far enough from our theoretical help to allow him to use proletarian force on her. He wanted to drive with her back to the last country filling station we had passed and there replenish our beer supply.

Dear Ginny had had enough to refuse to go with him. Wadleigh trembled with indecision. Rather, he began to make short runs in the direction of the car, only to come galloping back to the blanket where she lay to see if, in the seconds of his absence, she had seen her way clear to a change of mind. At last he ran down the hill, crying over his shoulder that he would be back in not more than twenty minutes.

I do not mean that all this was quite so explicitly clear as I have told it, but we all caught on to what was happening. And in the same general way we understood what was happening when Ginny moved around the fire and began to tease Clem.

We four who were talking had been perfectly tuned and happy with each other. I think Clem had even forgotten that he had a grudge left over from the story contest. Ginny upset this with her proximate invitations to a game of chase-me-up-into-the-brush-where-Jack-and-Daisy-went.

It wasn't that she really wanted Clem. Wadleigh would be back in a few minutes and I doubt that she wanted him to come roaring into the brush to find her with Clem. And it wasn't that she had anything against Sheila. She could hardly have cared about anything less than proving herself the more attractive. In her own terms she knew that she was. No one would have wished to argue that. Perhaps it is enough to say that she was overstimulated from her long session of petting with Wadleigh and the stimulus had to express itself. However, I have the feeling that it was not Clem alone she was after, that she had sensed a kind of nuptial readiness in the two of them that she wanted—the little witch—to trigger into action.

She flopped around on their blanket, pretending to be even drunker than she was, waving her legs in the moonlight, switching her mane of hair—well, dancing them a dance of the body, possessed for the time by some wandering nymphean spirit demanding human worship this night. She must have looked to Sheila the very personification of all those anonymous girls that Clem might remember if he forgot her. Clem must have seen the same thing and wished to hang on tighter to Sheila for protection against them.

I tried to discern whether Janet caught what was happening and whether she approved or disapproved. I think she was only angry at Ginny for seeming to intrude on something to which Janet, somewhat otherwise, had already given her blessing.

For twenty minutes there were some very mysterious promptings going on. ("I'm gonna tear off my clothes and run," the maenad chirped in Clem's ear, flexing her knees in front of Sheila. "No one will catch me. No one will ever catch me." "You'll hang up on the bobbed wire," Clem said in a slightly breathless remonstrance. "This country's all fenced in." He detached his hand from hers and put it where it should be, on Sheila's shoulder. Ginny slapped him across the face with her hair. "It's so hot tonight. I'm on fire." She exposed her white nape below his eyes, bounded to her feet and made a long orbit around their blanket to drop limp, whining, "Sheila, you'll come run with me. Men never understand how a girl feels on a night like this." "Clem couldn't catch me in time," Sheila said. "He's right about the wire. If we knew where we were ..." She swept a hand through her short hair with a gesture like Ginny's, bent her head between her knees. "I was also the speediest chaser in Boda," Clem said. "If the chips were down I could no doubt catch you both.")

At about this point we heard the throttle-on-the-floorboard roar of the Model A as Wadleigh returned. He drove it right on past the end of the road. We saw the headlights swing up and down like frantic beacons as it came bounding up over scrub, cattle tracks and stone to within thirty yards of where we sat.

"Oh, now I've got to run," Ginny said. She kicked off her shoes and headed into the silver-misted dark, slightly southeast of the moon.

A dozen seconds later Wadleigh came at a dead run up the rest of the slope to the dead fire. He had a case of beer under each arm.

"What have you done with her?" he yelled.

Clem pointed toward Florida, and, as if this was all the instruction he needed, Wadleigh dropped one of the cases of beer for us and with the other went plunging off in pursuit.

Five seconds. We heard a crash as if someone had pushed an automobile off one of the ledges of the quarry.

Immediately following the sound of smashing glass and sliding debris, we heard Wadleigh's voice shouting, "I'm all right. I'm all right!"—a reassurance meant for himself—"Ginny! Gin-Neeeeee!" We saw him reappear on a moonlit slope a hundred yards away. He was trying to combine a zigzag, searching course with his terrible anxiety to follow the shortest distance between two points. Like the fleeing figure at the end of a movie cartoon he passed the crest of the hill out of sight.

Presently Clem said querulously, "They really could hurt themselves, running wild like that. You think we ought to go help look for her, Dick?"

"No."

"Well. I'm not sure. They could trip or …"

"No," I said.

Clem whispered something to Sheila. When she nodded he helped her to her feet. "You're right," she told him. "It would be awful if something happened to them in their condition."

And away went Daddy and Mommy in search of the flying nymph. How gently the shadows welcomed them on their quest, dissolving their outlines as they left us, simultaneously hiding and advertising the purpose of their hearts. (Don't look where the moon is pointing, the shadows said.)

Presently Janet murmured, "Some of your friends are more literary than some of the others." She sat up to savor the amusement of this.

I said that while I could grasp her implication, it all seemed to come to the same thing in the long run.

She supposed that was so, in the long run, but, "I'm not sure you're the best companions for the young and innocent."

"You?" I asked fondly and aggressively.

"To an extent. But only. You don't worry me, Dick."

"Then who?"

She didn't answer, waiting until I was forced to name the person she had in mind. "Sheila," I said, and I was forced to add, "She's a very good girl, isn't she?"

"She's very good for him. They're like dancers. He leads and she follows. I hope he understands."

"I expect he's not easy to follow."

"I'm sure of that," she said.

Silently Jack and Daisy rejoined us. They had heard Wadleigh shouting his way over fen and brake, but a minimum of explanation sufficed them. They seemed to have little curiosity left. Jack lay face down on the blanket Wadleigh had vacated. Daisy—to express what? the human soul is infinite in its capacity for surprise—began doing pushups on an exposed flat of stone.

Twenty minutes later we heard mastodons advancing on us, and out of the brush leaped Wadleigh Bacchus Hertz, bearing a limp Ginny in his arms. His face was covered with scratches, but almost visibly aglow in the half-light. As he dumped Ginny onto the grass near us, he lifted his face to the moon and howled like the triumphant proletariat as they burst into the Winter Palace.

To which Ginny responded only with an infatuated, "Oh, you. Oh, you!" And covered her face with her hair, giggling.

With such forerunners to announce the capture of the nymph, the return of Clem and Sheila might have seemed anticlimactic in its quietness. They came with slow, half-shamed dignity, wordless, holding hands. Their faces were ever so slightly averted from each other, as if they no longer needed to look in the same direction, each trusting the other to cover an agreed-on arc of vision. Clem's shoulders were stooped. His head seemed heavy, and when they were near enough I saw immobile lines of worry on his forehead. Sheila, half a step behind him, looked incapable of speech; and I must say this for our delicacy, that there was not a single ribald mutter to question where they had been. Only, a little later as we sat having our last beer before going back to town, I saw Ginny, with her skirt drawn over her knees in front of Sheila, reach one bare foot out discreetly and with her toes touch Sheila's toes in a gesture of gladness and welcome.

It was strange how sure we all were of what had happened and how poignantly it seemed to have impressed itself, even on Wadleigh. He hummed with solicitude for Sheila, like a brand-new grandfather, started a dozen times to speak to her, stopped as if he could find no subject rich and delicate enough to offer her at this moment. Not even the myrrh and frankincense of Leninism seemed quite rich enough. From Daisy radiated almost luminous signals of assurance that the exercises of love improved the body's health—she strutted and twisted and did deep knee bends while emptying our last bottle of beer, declaring herself eager, if anyone would come with her, to plunge again into the exhilarating water. And Janet beamed her own secret signals that all was well in love when one had found the right partner.

And what did Sheila think of our happy-in-her-happiness addresses? I doubt if she noticed them at all. She only knew Clem was there. But on the ride back, of course, it came to her that tomorrow she would be going home. It was up to her to say tearfully that the eight of us would never be together again, that she thanked us, thanked us, thanked us for being so sweet to her and she would always remember us if we forgot her.

"Nobody's going to forget you," Clem insisted, being unnecessarily embarrassed for her in her outburst. "I told you I'm going to stay right where you leave me this summer. I won't stir a muscle. And what do you care if they throw Hertz in the dustbin of history?"

"Oh, they mustn't!" she said, seeming a little bewildered as we laughed at her remark.

We made our first stop at her sorority house, a rattling carload of liberty among the convertibles and slick sedans parked around for a night of goodbyes. The porch light was blazing, though it was nearly two o'clock. We heard music and movement inside—not our kind—and I felt a queer pang at seeing Sheila change herself, preparing to enter with the kind of dignity I valued least in her. Something seemed to dim her as she started sedately up the walk.

But just as Jack was putting the car in motion she came running back, her mouth round and desperate. She grabbed the door handle beside me and came scrambling across Janet and me to lean into the back seat. She kissed Clem in utter oblivion. "Did you understand how I love you? Did you, did you?" she demanded.

"All of it," he said.

Once again she was outside, standing beside the old car with her hand aloft in an ingenuously tender sign of one who believes that she who has deserted home and family is being repaid by suffering desertion in her turn.

"Take care of him for me," she asked without a smile. None of us had an answer for that.

# 9

STILL, we did our makeshift best for Clem that summer. To replace the money he should have won in the short-story contest, we got him a snap job as watchman at the power plant. That is, I helped Wallace Rogge arrange the job through his connections with the Young Communist League. Ordinarily the job was reserved as a kind of scholarship for out-of-state Communist students, much as other snap jobs served as scholarships for athletes. Many years later, I understand, there was an investigation at the university, which disclosed these facts, and they were publicized as evidence that Communists had been infiltrated to sabotage key functions in event of war. The deductions are too patently absurd to require explanation, but I might say that the truth behind it all is that the man in charge of student help there was a kind wounded veteran of World War I, not so much a sympathizer with Communism as a sympathizer with those he called "victims of the Behemoth State"—among whom he was as ready to include young writers as Communists. If the investigators really needed to worry about what might have happened—and they struck me as bad poets in their tendency to do so—they would have better expressed their ex post facto alarm over Clem than the Party members, for he was more likely than most to have flung a smelly tennis shoe into the dynamo. But actually he liked the place too much to harm it, even in a great cause. The refined, constant moan of machinery seemed to soothe him. For six hours each night he had a comfortable cubicle of an office in which no one would disturb him. He did a lot of fine work there—nearly all the poetry which was so much admired in the coming fall.

Since I had decided to stay close to Janet, I needed a room for the summer, and it seemed easiest as well as most agreeable for me to move into Emmy Polk's house, taking the front room that had been H. Warwick's, while Clem had to himself the big middle room he had shared with Wadleigh until Wadleigh's graduation. I don't exactly place my move under the head of "taking care of Clem"—I had too many interests involved to pretend altruism—but it came to that. One could not be close to him without finding that certain little chores had been delegated—sustaining his morale through depressions, pointing out the necessity of food and sleep, correcting his spelling.

Now that the picnic had put us on friendly terms again, I queried him about the burning of his manuscripts. I was more pleased than really surprised to find that it had been selective, for all the emotion he had put into it. It amounted to a major pruning of his first two years of writing. No one else would have pruned so recklessly close to the ground, perhaps. All he had left to show besides the story and the three poems committed to print in the previous winter was a half-dozen poems. It became clear that, now he had swung toward confidence again, no one else could have been so confident as he of how much more there was still to come from him. He left me no regrets except that "Spider on the Rope" had gone with other things of less value.

But, he thought, he could probably reproduce that manuscript word for word from memory. He knew it very well, he said with sly embarrassment. "Do so," I suggested. In a couple of nights of work at the power plant he did.

As we liked to say, Emmy Polk had a nest of singing birds that summer. The little room which had been Clem's in his sophomore year was occupied by Don Hazeltine, then editor of the college literary magazine and another "promising" writer—to use the epithet I first heard and learned to despise from Henry Powell. I hope that Emmy appreciated us as much as we appreciated her.

Poor soul, she was then nearly seventy, a tough, permanently tanned and sinewy old woman who had taught school for about half her life. Now her mind had become a placid Sargasso Sea in which floated a myriad unrelated details from the geography and history books she had used and from her life as maid, mother and grandmother.

"I'm Scotch, Irish, Canadian, German, English, French, Lithuanian, Russian and Dutch," she would say, leaning in through my doorway on her broom sometime in hot midmorning as I was trying to study or write. "Now, isn't that a pretty good thing to be?"

She wanted to talk—and mostly I put down my work for a little while to answer. Down the hall Clem would be asleep, and I could hear the irregular tattoo of Don's typewriter as he worked on his novel. They would get their visits from her later.

I had the daily privilege of responding first to her introduction. (And it always was an introduction. She told me her ancestry at least fifteen times in my first month as tenant. I think she assumed I was merely visiting in the room, that I had slept the past night there with H. Warwick, who might return at any moment to set the incense going. Why not? Even as late as the next fall my room had an unextinguishable odor of that incense, of something else that may have been the smell of calf bindings or of Balliol itself, though all summer the windows were left wide open. I was supposed to say—instructed by Clem and Wadleigh—"Do you speak the languages of these far-off countries, Mrs. Polk?"

She beamed like a complimented schoolgirl. "Yes. Oh, my, yes. Parlez vous. Sprechen sie Deutsch? Wee bawnie lassie. The ould sawd. Ay sah-ee theh, old chup. Bugfor oggly glubble—that's Lithuanian. Dingfeng the Slovvet Oonyoh. Russian." (And an obvious souvenir of Wadleigh's agitation among the handy proles.)

"Dutch?" I prompted.

"Deutschland über allies."

"Very good."

Beaming, unable to handle praise, she would fidget and peer down the hall, take a couple of heartless swipes with her broom at the dust on the linoleum. "Mr. Anderson is asleep," she said—as if before noon that was ever news in our house. "You know about Mr. Anderson? I'd kinda keep away from him. He has an Oedipal complex."

"No!"

"He surely has, and time must have a stop for him. Why, he's not allowed to play football any more because he's too erotic, which is his complex. And, I'll tell you, he was known in all America as the galloping ghost of the Four Horsemen of Notre Dame, and only that Indian, What's-his-name, was ever more of an all-around buck than Mr. Anderson before he got the complex. I could see what it did to him last winter, like sometimes he would throw up on the stairs or in his room. Mr. Hertz would call him a disgusting A-feet and threaten to call the wagons onto him if he didn't straighten up. But, land, it could hardly be called his fault, could it?"

"Not with a complex like that."

"That's what I say. And Mr. Lloyd told me that Mr. Anderson got it from his mother. Well, my boys were just the healthiest tads you ever saw, for I gave them every morning of their lives a hot steamy breakfast before school, and I thought maybe that would help Mr. Anderson. But when I asked him he said he was too far gone already and couldn't get up in time. You know, the Devil has come for him once, and even if it was a dream, that means something! He described how he had seen this Devil in his dream and no one could have done it so well if they hadn't seen him. The Devil was going to screw him into a light socket and then turn him on and off. Ooooh. I'd sooner have bugs than to hear about that again."

"Well, Mr. Anderson is a poet—"

"I knew it! I knew it! For he's the one, I'll bet a dollar, that's always writing things on the wallpaper in the stairway and I thought they were nasty words until Mr. Herzing explained them to me, but I scrubbed them all off anyway, just in case. 'Thalassa!' Now, doesn't that sound like a nasty word to you? And there was another time when someone had drawn all over the wall in the hallway in a big black line this picture. It was of an awful old fat man that looked like a pig riding on the back of a poor scrawny man on all fours that looked like a beetle. Mr. Hirsch said it was a capelist riding on the back of the people, though it more reminded me of the illustrations they used to have in the fourth-grade reader out at Spring Valley where it was a nasty old king up on the back of his slave, or maybe it was all a fairy story.

"Anyway Mr. Hutch said it was the work of a famous artist named Miller and that I better not touch it and someday my hall would be as famous as the System Chapel, but I scrubbed it off, too.

"Yes, I know you're right that Mr. Anderson is a poet and a genius, too. Oh, my, it seems to me I've had so many geniuses since I been here with this rooming house that sometimes I think, Wouldn't it be nice if I had a few ordinary boys. Mr. Lloyd is a genius, too, though he has very nice manners compared with most geniuses. You know, he read books that thick." She pointed to the Webster's Unabridged that Clem and Wadleigh had stolen last winter from the Lamb Reading Room and which was now a common property of our house. "Thicker. I don't see how one person can understand a book so big, but he read them all the time and strained his eyes.

"Mr. Anderson is the most peculiar genius I ever had, though. You know, a lot of times the other fellows have had their sisters up here to visit them, and I wink my eyes at them in spite of the university rules because their sisters just help keep young fellows going straight. But I'll bet you a dollar that some of the girls who came up to see Mr. Anderson weren't his sisters. So I asked Mr. Herzing about this and he said it was all right because Mr. Anderson didn't have very long to live with his complex and might run queer if he couldn't have his friends in to see him now and then. If I get in trouble with the university I suppose they'll understand that I acted for the best, because Mr. Anderson is queer enough already."

There was no easy way to get rid of her once she had begun to talk. After the penetrating comment and the parody of her roomers past and present, she was apt to go into some trouble she'd had with the school bad boy forty-five years ago in Spring Valley, or to explain what she'd said to the woman who stole her husband in Maple Springs. ("Your time will come as my time has come, for any man who'd leave one loving wife and two helpless children would leave another one as soon as spit on her." And by Joe, Emmy was right. Within three years that woman had come back all blubbery to Emmy and said, "Why didn't you tell me he was no better'n an old boar pig with a sore tail?")

When they wanted to drive her back to the first floor, Wadleigh and Clem used the strategy of walking naked through the hall to the bathroom. I hadn't yet the courage to try that myself, nor the strength of character to order her out of my room. From the doorway where her monologues began, she would generally advance until she was leaning on my desk, smirking and winking as she delivered her finest observations. My best chance at relief was to yell through the outside windows to waken Clem, then pretend to Emmy that I had glimpsed him in the hall naked as a jaybird.

It always worked. After she had retreated, mincing and abasing her eyes, I might have two hours left on an average morning to devote to my study before Clem came in to ask why the hell I had bellowed him out of a lovely sleep. (What he did in those two hours between my call and his rising always puzzled me.)

Frequently he brought his breakfast with him to my room. It might be part of a sweet roll that he had dug out of a dresser drawer or from the pocket of dungarees already stuffed into his laundry bag. Usually he had a cup of coffee that he had brought home from the power plant the night before. These breakfasts made an affecting show of poverty. The cardboard cup would be wilted like a week-old cut flower. The sweet roll would, more probably than not, explode in dry crumbs when he set teeth to it. So usually I would get my hot plate going to fix lunch for myself and breakfast for him.

If he was currently at work on a poem, the coffee would remind him of it. (Apparently it was not his work that he thought about as he lay abed preparing to rise.) Enthusiasm building to a head, he would presently rush to his room to fetch the latest draft of his work.

I remember him crouched on the trunk at the far side of my room, barefooted and bare of torso. His toes clutched at the knobs and handles of the trunk while his fingers were busy in his pompadour or ruffling the sheet he read from. There was a total physical involvement in his reading aloud. He strained like a dog trying to void a peach pit, or as if every word might be a cripple he was trying to help through an obstacle course.

Before the summer was over I heard, among other poems published in magazines later but never collected until after his death, "Rose Rose Rose," "Money Talks" and "The Deserted Wife."

*"The green enterprise of my youth was girls,"*

*Said the venerable folding money.*

*"I married the best and picked over the rest,*

*But there'll always be more coming on."*

*"We'll get them!" said the small change.*

*"Wheeled on the boardwalk at Usury,*

*With a black boy pushing my chair,*

*My greatest usurious pleasure*

*Was making the patriots stare*

*At the face of Ay-braham Lincoln," said*

*The greasy five-dollar bill.*

*"I'm Liberty. I'm a noble red man," rattled*

*the change.*

These lines from "Money Talks" seemed funny enough to me—as did "The Deserted Wife" (about Emmy Polk)—but Clem always came near to crying over his words as he read them.

He fought the loose ballad meter of this one as if trying to make it simultaneously a dirge and a mazurka. Sometimes he began to read the whole thing from the beginning again as soon as he had got through the last line. I suppose that thus I was privileged to see a reproduction of the way it kept sounding for him while it was still in process of being formed.

He was usually too impatient to let me find for myself the forms and themes that might lie under the surfaces penetrable in a single hearing. His exegeses, though, often appeared to be inseparable extensions of the poem itself.

"What I'm doing in 'Rose Rose Rose' is really photography," he explained, squatting on the trunk after he had read it to me.

Through the hot drift of noon in the quiet house we could hear the bells tolling noon or one o'clock down on the campus. Emmy Polk was clicking about her kitchen on the floor below. Clem bent to pick at the toes which had worked so hard while he was reading. "I don't want to add anything from afterthoughts," he said. "I only want to put things together again exactly the way they existed when I walked up to the old bar meaning to hop her. Absolutely nothing but what I saw at the instant."

"You couldn't see anything. You'd have tripped over a bridge if it had been in your way."

"Ah, I could. I could see Anderson's white false beard blowing like Whitman's and what he/they was/were saying is, 'I salute you with a significant glance.' I could have written the title on every foot of the floor I crossed: 'To a Common Prostitute.' I could see what old Wallace had been telling me about Teruel, the fire from the machine gun going in and out like a busy organ—not to mention that stupid ROTC sergeant who gave us the demonstration with the BAR, like a robin trying to jerk a worm out of the ground—little and tiny fire, but awfully fast in that big snatch of a morning where all those men were lying waiting. And she—you know, she was that morning, with the weeds and olive trees growing inside this big globe of her belly like the globe upstairs in the library. The—the—the—the—the—"

"Celestial globe," I said, supplying the words that I had just heard in his poem.

"Celestial globe." His lips tasted the words as if they were honeyed. "Celestial globe with all those wonderful designs in it. Scorpio, Andromeda, Taurus and the Ram. I could see how she would look naked. Like that, with the designs all over her belly like tattoos; and there, there'd be the horn gates and the delta for whatever or whoever was brave enough to—man enough to—enter this celestial other globe with his little machine gun under the noble signs and ... be there—looking out, looking in."

"All that for only two dollars."

"Three," he said without really breaking his trance of pursuit or vision. "She was dead as that glass globe on its spindle. Couldn't you see her skin and that dead little mouth puckered like a bullet wound? But otherwise more alive than you think, because of all the things that all the men have put in her, the seeds like little soldiers, and so much death. So she was celestial in living and not living. Total."

There was a long silence when he ran down. Outside the window at my right hand the leaves on a maple tree broke the light into a million details. I heard a boy riding past on a bicycle. The whir of his sprocket chain as he pumped was like the mechanically magnified sound of a pulse. My hand lay on a blue-jacketed volume called Milton of Christ Church College. Everything was like something and, in being like, merged substance—while I wanted it to. For a minute I believed in a universe of coherent meaning that laved me like uterine fluid—until disbelief said, Hand be hand, leaf be leaf, bicyclist be a boy on his way to the store for a loaf of bread. I said, "I like the way you've built up the connections and similes. You didn't see it as you've told it, of course."

"You think I could make all that up? I only picked out words and rhymes. Maybe it's more like a montage than a photograph, but it was there for me."

"If you saw all that in her you wouldn't have had the nerve to mount it."

"No. Absolutely I wouldn't," he said. "You know, Dick, when she said she didn't like college boys and wanted three dollars I felt like Dostoevsky when they were about to execute him but at the last minute the Czar sends word, 'Pack him off to Siberia instead.' My little heart was going pitty-pat for sure. Naturally I was scared of her. I'm used to thinking about everything, being such a coward, and sometimes when I get the hots—or used to—I think the easiest thing to do is go someplace besides a college town so there'll be whores and get rid of it, because when I get involved with someone I love I always … mislead them. Badly. And of course I agree with Wadleigh about women, that you should screw them as equals and not permit them to get the advantages they have when you feel sorry for them. But I can't manage it that way. So the best thing for me would be to go to some woman who doesn't count and who'll let you forget about it later instead of hanging around your neck like a poor albatross. And then, I always tell myself if I get siffed up, I'll merely knock myself off, put the old gun in my mouth. But I never have done that."

"Shot yourself?"

"Been with a whore. But when I walked up to Rose I was going to omit any precautions. It wouldn't have been right. Then I would certainly have got the malignant spirochete, and then there I'd be."

"Not necessarily."

"Not necessarily. But that's some more of what I was thinking about besides the poetry. I figured I ought to expose myself anyhow because of what I'd said to Jack about Jews and ... You remember that? It only came out of my mouth because I was drunk and I know I said it badly, which is as big a sin as having the wrong feelings, things being as they are. Christ, it's my profession to use words right and there I'd gone associating Jew and ... So ..."

"So you owed it to Jack to get syphilis and commit suicide?"

"Not only that."

"That's not enough? As a matter of fact, I'm sure that Jack has forgotten your whole silly bit a long time ago. He's your friend."

"He hasn't forgotten it," Clem insisted darkly. "There are words that people don't forget just because they forget them mentally. Words are dangerous things. No matter how many you use there must be some that count, like one poisoned piece of candy in hundreds of boxes of it, and there are some words that you'd better remember or they'll remember you. How could anyone write poetry if he didn't believe in at least poisoned words?"

"Or maybe holy words."

"Maybe. But the point isn't just that I remember what I said. You may be right that he knows I didn't mean to say it, which is like not meaning to push a baby out of a window. You shouldn't have done it."

"You've done that too?"

"I've done worse," he said cryptically—just because he could say so, I've thought; and evil is as finite as good, and I am just as skeptical of the champion sinner as of the champion doer of good. I challenged him to name the worse things, and when he wouldn't I said that he might as well forget his verbal injury of Jack.

"It's my duty to remember things," he said grandly, miserably. "But the other reason I should have had Rose was because of Wallace, who'd really been in Spain while I'd merely talked about going."

"You owed it to him," I said, nodding. "What did you owe me that you could only have paid by killing yourself?"

"Nothing," he said. "You don't take me seriously."

"Oh yes I do. I have to, since everyone who has had the luck to know you keeps repeating, 'Watch out for Clem.'" Then I remembered something he had said, making my own modest associations, and asked, "I take it that little Sheila is beginning to hang around your neck like the aforementioned albatross. You two ought to get it straight which of you is the bird and around whose neck."

He sagged morosely, enough of an answer. But to stop me from crude surmise again he hastened to say, "She isn't pregnant, of course. It's just that what's happened means so much more to her than it ought to. I knew it would, so maybe I shouldn't have done anything. I do love her, and that's partly why I don't want her forcing me to love her."

"You got a bad letter from her," I guessed. "Well, forget it. You'll get a better one tomorrow."

"I mean she's trying to force me through my own conscience," he said indignantly. "She wouldn't try to force me directly. It's merely that I know how she will feel about this, that's what I'm rebelling against. Moral pressure."

Clearly moral pressure was about to blow out of his ears, but I suggested he let her speak her own lines instead of trying to anticipate them for her. I meant it as a compliment to her when I said that she seemed quite able to decide for herself whether or not she wanted to push him now, but he took it as an oblique slander to both of them. She would not pressure him, but he would be less than her fit mate if he did not oblige her, positively, to do so.

But then—he spiraled fast when he got such a line of internal argument going—then maybe he wasn't her fit mate. "I'm not so much afraid of marriage for my sake as for hers. I know what she's like. She doesn't begin to understand what I'm like yet."

"What are you like?"

He spread his hands in the frustration of trying to make me see. "Maybe I wasn't meant for just one woman. Maybe I need twenty all at once—like Hart Crane smoked cigars and chewed chewing tobacco at the same time. Look. I can talk to you all day about how it was when I walked up to Rose. To you it's just words. But how far did I walk? Maybe thirty feet from the table to the bar and back again, and to me it was so important that it was worth having been alive all these years for, and at the same time everything else that I've ever known has been worth just as much—like I had everything in highly concentrated doses. I can have a lifetime walking thirty feet, and I don't know how to connect one of my lifetimes with another. I tell you seriously I'd have died for that whore just as quick as I'd die for Sheila, it meant that much. And on the other hand, maybe I wouldn't die for either one of them. I'd kill Sheila first, maybe not even knowing I'd done it. She doesn't see I'm capable of ... all this. Do you?"

"No, and I don't believe it," I said. But I did. Even then. As with the poem he had read and explained, there was a suspension of disbelief as I listened to him. Then it returned, as quickly as after the poem. I

227

saw him there in front of me, very corporeal, picking his toes. He looked healthy and young, as he must look to Sheila. Very nonmurderous. "If we went swimming it might cool you off and I could relax with some innocent dirty thoughts until I pick up Janet," I said.

We went to the pool in the park a great many afternoons that summer.

There, while we killed time in the dappled, chlorinated water, covered with confetti reflections of sky and leaf spots, my conventional resistance to his gloomy raptures seemed easily vindicated. He only had—as we say—dark moods. The water washed them away almost too easily. Half an hour after his most horrendous self-appraisal he could be sporting mindlessly as a dolphin—an awkward dolphin, that is. I never knew anyone who trusted the water more than he did at that time in his life, but he was a perilously poor swimmer. Lifeguards used to caution him repeatedly, pacing like nervous hounds when they noted his antics. But if they had had to rescue him and pump him out, I am sure he would have gone back in again as cheerily as when he first raced from the bathhouse. He might spend his nights and mornings contemplating death, but he could not seem to recognize it when it licked his face.

And out there at the pool he would talk of Sheila with reverent innocence.

"Her father's a contractor"—as if he had said, "Prospero, Duke of Milan."

"She has two older sisters—not so pretty, I've seen their pictures"—as if he had already tried the glass slipper on her and, finding a perfect fit, were offering me the chopped-off toes of the other two.

"She's letting her hair grow this summer"—as if for a ladder he might expect to climb.

"She's so much like me in spite of the obvious differences"—as if her name were Sieglinde.

And he could endure all the manner of dalliance with the girls at the pool—any female over the age of nine—without worrying that he might forget Sheila again. Early in the season he picked up poolside friendships with a girl named Midge (a fat thirteen) and Dawn (the wife of an alcoholic barber, a tiny, sinewy woman of thirty whose skin looked like freckled velvet. I guess she liked to be with Clem because his hair was such a symbol of disrespect for her husband's only skill.)

I used to wake from naps to see him on the high diving board, trying to get Midge onto his shoulders, pretending that he did not understand why the lifeguards were pointing and blowing their whistles. In a moment both would fall, shrieking like idiots, with Clem's hand perhaps still hanging onto her ankle. Midge would bob to the surface like an inflated mattress. A few seconds later Clem would come up near her, coughing out mouthfuls of water, admonishing her not to worry as long as he was there to take care of her. Then the dear little creature would let him hold onto her pneumatic calves while she rowed them to the safe concrete side.

From his familiarity with them at the pool, I kept expecting to see either Dawn or Midge on the stairs some night at Emmy Polk's. But when I braved Clem on this question he seemed genuinely shocked. "Why, why, Midge is only a kid. Why, why, Dawn is married. Why, why, Jesus Christ, Dick, you don't think I'd two-time Sheila the way things are between us now, do you?"

When I said that for all I knew he needed twenty women to chew and smoke at the same time, he seemed to think I had invented a bad joke out of entirely private materials.

"I talk to Dawn and Midge and the others, is all," Clem said. "It's easier for me to open up with girls than men. Sure, I pinch them now and then. Makes them feel like big shots. But I wouldn't do anything improper."

Which intended assurances served to make me wonder if he was pinching Janet now and then. He often went with the two of us for dinner or to a movie, sat with us in one or another tavern until it was time for him to go to work, or went—alone sometimes—to Janet's place. She had then what we considered a dandy job in the registrar's office (ninety dollars a month). She had a Ford roadster with a sassy little trunk, and her own apartment. She had a splendidly oversized easy chair that she had upholstered with a black-and-white striped material to which I became deeply and sentimentally attached. It seemed to me a kind of female throne (or the proper throne for a reigning female; it's curious how the adjective can slip over into the role of noun when I think of the lovely deep comforts that chair had to provide. What safe excitements I knew when I curled between its uplifted arms! How meekly I accepted the gentle yoke of the tyrant when Janet occupied its undulant striations. In the forests of the night I see that tigerish chair, couchante. Me it devoured). Although Janet was the only literal orphan among us orphans of that time (our mothering faith interred at Munich, our fathers deserted or dead, and stepfather Bloom only, after all, a fiction in default of reality) she had such talents for family as I had skeptically thought impossible. She fed me, body and pride. She arranged without seeming to arrange. She left me satisfied for the first time in my life that I knew the full scope and limitations of masculinity.

Now, my worries were not that Clem was on the verge of coming between me and all that. Janet and I had an understanding. But I suppose I was jealous of both of them, thinking both might "open up" with secrets to each other that, contrarily, I would not invite them to share with me. Of course I envied that which I could not, for myself, approve. If you have not already heard the voice of envy in these pages of mine, I must be more unobtrusive than I suppose.

At one point I thought he was making better use of her genius for being family than I could, and protested.

"He doesn't come to me for anything so grim or specific, as you think," Janet said, hiding whatever amusement she felt at my jealousy. "I suppose he's told me things about Sheila and his other girls that he hasn't told you, and now and then I've had to shut him up, too, because you just can't, the way he does, go around comparing … well, comparing."

"As if he were shopping for gloves."

"He's not shopping any more. But anyway, mostly he talks to me about the plainest things. He came in at five the other morning after he got off at the power plant and sat on the clothes hamper while I ironed some things, telling me all about his sister's learning to play the piano by correspondence. And, Dick, he makes everything interesting. I don't know how. By remembering so many extras, I guess. Not only the facts about the lessons, but the piano with the jigsawed scrolls on the front and the 'rose' varnish settling in little bubbles around the scrolls after his mother tried to make it nicer. The photographs of his uncles who were in the World War on top of the piano along with his graduation picture. The changeable-silk drape on it with the tassels, and this little girl hunching forward on the stool so loyally, trying to make music out of all those confusing directions they sent her from Chicago. See?"

I saw, heard and felt. That was all and was—nearly—everything. But I said, wishing I could growl, "If he loves his family so much, why doesn't he go home to them?" Having taken a position, I had to pretend I didn't know what angels forbade him to go home except as the littlest All-American, the littlest egghead ever to be the best lover.

Heaven knows I had data to support my occasional censure of his inconsistency. Loved his family, did he? That summer I discovered he would not even read the letters that came from his mother. They used to lie for two or three days on the hall table downstairs at Emmy Polk's. Then, maybe after I had told him ten times that he had mail, he would pick up the one (or ones) from Boda. I asked him now and then what he heard from home. "Oh, everything's the same," he would say. Or, "Oh, the folks are all right." So I thought for a while that he destroyed the letters from home without opening them.

At length he admitted that, while he opened them, he usually only glanced at the first lines "to make sure that nobody had died."

"Why won't you read the rest? Maybe somebody dies at the end."

"Na. They're always after me to come home. I can't stand too much pressure. I mean that I can stand it—I can stand anything—but it spoils my work. I can't concentrate when someone's around wanting to hug me or put cream on my cereal. Does Sheila seem like the type who'd do that? I want a mattress. When I get through working I want to run to the couch and wham."

For his own good I led him back to the subject at hand. "If anyone ever depended on his own experience to write from, you're the guy. These letters ought to be a gold mine."

He did not answer, but went to Janet to complain about me.

"Clem thinks you're trying to reform him," Janet reported. "You expect too much of him too soon."

"I expect him merely not to keep making himself lonely—as you say he is. He'd have all the mattresses he wants if he'd do the normal things to keep up his relationships with people. He reads the letters that come from Sheila—he goes that far—but he doesn't very often answer them. Not even that. If he wants to break with his family, he should start one he likes better."

Janet smiled as if I were talking about myself. "He says you expect him to write great poems and still dilute himself by writing dishonest, loving letters as people expect. He says you bawled him out for burning up manuscripts last spring."

"I flattered and cajoled," I said.

"He says you forced him to work beyond his strength on some poems you made him send to Nathaniel Bentley and still expect him to face bad news from home when he's spiritually exhausted."

"Bad news? It's got to be bad news? They can't all hang themselves up there in Boda. What does he come from, a race of victims?"

"'Spiritually exhausted' is his term."

"Don't you think I didn't recognize it."

"He says you think he needs more experience, but he had enough experience before he was sixteen to write the entire Library of

Congress if his hecklers didn't keep him spiritually exhausted all the time."

"Jesus Christ."

"I know," she said. "But really, he's so frail and so tough. You can kick him in the head, but you mustn't touch him with a feather. Not if you're someone he thinks counts."

When the reply to his submission of new poems to Nathaniel Bentley came, it was a different story than with the letters from his mother or Sheila. That one morning out of the whole summer, he woke me instead of depending on me to wake him. It was as if he had clairvoyantly known that the morning's mail would bring what he needed most. If it was not sheer clairvoyance, it was a calculation based on facts he couldn't have known. He would have had to know how Bentley was feeling if the poems came to him on a hot Friday afternoon, how Bentley would glance once at them and drop them into his basket while he went for a long weekend at Martha's Vineyard, meaning to read them more carefully on the following Tuesday, how Bentley would want to think about them after that and how he would be interrupted by more pressing considerations—as, his publisher calling from New York, as, spending an evening with a refugee professor from Germany whose contacts had told him It will be this fall, as, spending a long morning with a gifted young gentleman poet named Terry Burbidge—and how then Bentley would find a free hour on Thursday to dictate his letter to Clem. Obviously Clem couldn't know all this about Bentley. But there he was on Emmy's front porch to greet the mailman.

Ten minutes past eight he was banging at my door. When I saw that he had a letter in his hand, how pale he was and how he trembled, I thought another of his uncles had succumbed to the hot weather and hemp.

"Dick. You better see if this is on the level," he said. He thrust the letter at me and perched on the trunk.

I started to read aloud. "'I'm afraid that "Money Talks" is too boisterous in form or perhaps too spontaneous for my taste, though as light verse it carries a lively sting.'"

"It stinks!" Clem said, sparing himself nothing he had inflicted on Milton. "I'd never have sent it if you hadn't laughed when I read it."

To spare myself further abuse I read the rest of the letter to myself. In part it said:

I particularly like the tragic and parodistic vision of the prostitute in "Rose Rose Rose." It reminds me, at least in its central theme, of

Rilke, but it is still very much your own. The way you have worked in Whitman's lines updates them in a peculiarly shocking fashion and supplies a significant tension between them, with all they evoke of another moral order, and the present.

This poem seems so old, and I forget how young you are—perhaps because I am feeling so old myself these days and full of dread in this unhappy summer....

While nothing else you sent satisfied me quite so much as "Rose Rose Rose," I have been impressed beyond my former respect for your talents. I hope you will not mind that I have handed over everything you sent to J. Adler, who reads verse for The New Englander. I have just spoken to him by telephone. It may be that he will want to use one or more in the magazine, if they have not been previously committed.

... I wonder if you have made any progress with your novel. My offer to recommend you to my publisher still stands, so let me know when it is ready to be seen.

Cordially,

Nathaniel Bentley.

When he saw me finish reading, Clem demanded, "What novel is he talking about? I shouldn't have burned—Who told him I had a novel?"

"You did, probably. You told everyone else."

"That I had one in mind! Nobody knew that I had written any of it. It stank. What do they want a novel for? Could I send them 'Spider on the Rope'?"

I explained to him that the novel, a form recently introduced by Daniel Defoe, exercised a particular fascination on the minds of publishers, making them happy to lose money on hundreds of unprofitable novels each year, while at the same time they believed themselves victims of their own generosity if they lost somewhat less money on a book of short stories. As for books of poetry, publishers wear them with the mournful pride of a quadruple amputee displaying his wound stripes.

Why were publishers that way? I answered in a simulated Voice out of the Whirlwind that unless he could draw Leviathan up with a hook, it ill behooved a writer like him to ask such a question. "Get busy and write your novel if money is what you want."

But I could see he wanted nothing at that moment. Fame was the spur that had made him leap over the rooftops. Happily enough I resigned myself to waiting until he came down—and very gradual it was.

"You must have been right when you liked my stuff," he conceded. "I can see myself in perspective again. I've meant to finish my novel."

"Do it tonight."

"I see where everything I burned fits in my oeuvre. All those stories were my Poor People, or Werther, or Portrait of the Artist as a Young Man."

"You can write Faust tomorrow and we'll have a hell of a bonfire."

"Dick, I'm going to make it up to you and Janet and Sheila and my folks for all the shit you've had to take from me. I haven't been myself."

"Yes you have."

He looked at me for a long, blank minute, then softened into something nearly human. "I guess I have, at that," he said. "But I can be better."

He spun on his heel and went racing down the stairs. "Emmy! Mrs. Polk! Emmy," I heard him shouting, "can I use your phone?"

He called Sheila—and came back to my room fifteen minutes later looking as if he had been told she was married.

"Let's go to the pool," he said bitterly.

"At this time in the morning? Are you crazy? I've got exams next week. What went wrong?"

"Nothing," he said. "Nothing, nothing. She just wouldn't grasp how important this is. My life has been saved, but she couldn't see."

"She understands. You just don't get all you need out of the telephone, Anderson. Anyway, how important is this, objectively speaking?" Useless to ask that, seeing that no objects smaller than mountains were going to be recognized by his stimulated subjectivity.

"It means ... I'm a writer."

"You knew that."

"No I didn't. Honest to Jesus, Dick, I didn't know."

Honest he may have thought himself, but that very afternoon at the pool I heard him tell his playmate Dawn that he'd "risen from amateur to professional standing" quite some time ago and that he sold everything he let go out over his signature, "though I burn everything that doesn't meet professional standards."

It was only that evening, when we were riding along the edge of the lake twenty miles north of town, that he told Janet and me he'd asked Sheila to marry him when he called. I swear that he had forgotten it until that moment. It came back to him like another of those sunken but indestructible details from his long past.

"Well?" Janet asked.

"Well what?"

"What was her answer?"

"I don't know," Clem said. "I was so excited I wasn't listening."

Perhaps Sheila knew already then that it would be her task in their relationship to remind him of such details as whether she had said Yes, No, or Wait to his proposal. A missive came from her, special delivery, the following afternoon.

And once again Clem came to me for interpretation as he had done with Bentley's letter. This time I sadly suspected he did not quite want to know.

As reply, confirmation or emphasis of what she had answered over the phone Sheila sent two pages torn from a book he had given her. They were Pound's "River Merchant's Wife: A Letter."

"You'd think she could answer Yes or No instead of being so cryptic," he complained.

"She did when you talked to her," I suggested. "One or the other."

"Does this mean Yes or No?" he demanded, waving the sheets of poetry.

I took them from him and read in a pedantic tone, "'I desired my dust to be mingled with yours Forever and forever and forever.' I believe, sir, that this implies an affirmative answer. A yes, a yes, a yes. 'Yes,' she said. 'Yes, I will. Yes.' Do you understand? Yes."

This definiteness hurt him deeply. "She knows that the "River Merchant" is one poem I absolutely can't stand up to. It breaks me apart. I showed it to her. I read it to her. She wouldn't know there was such a poem if it weren't for me."

"She wouldn't be marrying if it weren't for you. There's a certain trustworthy chain of cause and effect involved here."

"How can I marry anyone? I don't have any money." I thought for a minute he was going to show me his smelly wallet as if I had asked for proof of this. "I'll never have any money. I'm a writer."

That consolation protected him until the end of the week. Then a letter came from J. Adler of The New Englander accepting "Rose Rose Rose" and "Money Talks." A small check came with the letter—about enough for a four-day binge, as I could see he was thinking. But a long letter came from Sheila in the same mail. She wanted him to visit her at home in Indiana, meet her folks and her friends, then return to school with her after two weeks.

"Shall I do it, Dick?" he asked.

"Don't you want to see her?"

"Well! So damn much."

"There is no impediment, no impediment, no impediment. Some people always come up smelling like a rose. You get a chance to see your girl and you get some pocket money at the same time. What religion do you follow that this doesn't satisfy you?"

He unfolded the New Englander check again, divided it mentally into railroad fare, whiskey enough to brace him for the ordeal with her family, a one-night binge before he left. "I'd have to hitchhike," he said doubtfully.

"Then hitchhike. Walk if you have to. Crawl, you stupid bastard."

"Dick," he said, still lingering toward the caution that made him hesitant, "what do you honestly think of Sheila? Would you marry her? Is she ... does she ... I don't mean does she excite you, but look—suppose I married her and did turn into a big shot. Would I ever be ashamed of her? I mean, would she go the distance?"

I blew up at this. "You should have kept your mouth shut until you were sure you were old enough to get married. That's my last word."

"I want to," he said dazedly. "O.K. I'll go see her."

"Thanks. You've just made me very happy."

But Janet and I felt, when we talked it over, that the uncertainties he was now voicing were a good sign, and there were some other signs of a summery new tranquility. He told Don Hazeltine that he had gone back to work on his novel because he wanted to make some money to get married on, and though I knew he had done no such thing, I took it as a sign of good intent.

He permitted Janet—or cozened her into—cutting his hair so that he would look "less abnormal." He who had never dared in his life dispute with a barber coached her up the sides and held a mirror on her while she was trimming the back. It came out pretty well, except for the part they tried to force into it. After all this time the hair simply would not accept a part.

He became more solemnly respectful of Janet's point of view when we talked together, as if it were occurring to him for the first time that women might have something cogent to say for themselves, were not intended by nature to be mere listeners. He began to treat Emmy Polk with a kind of insane courtliness, as if he were using her as a lay figure on whom he could practice the manners he wanted to use with Sheila's mother.

If all these tokens of reform had a suspect air of play-acting, no matter about that. Everything he did breathed the air of a performance, and this one was more promising than some of his roles. For Sheila's sake he was inventing a happier, more social self.

That self broke badly only once before he went to Indiana—on the night after Germany struck into Poland.

I had stayed late at Janet's apartment. She relinquished the tiger chair to me that night. I was sitting alone in it, she leaning against my knees, while we listened to the news reports coming in an unbroken series. The language of them was as quaint as if a malign Emmy Polk had been in control of communications. "Herr Hitler has ordered his legions to meet force with force in the Polish Corridor." Appearing white-faced before newsmen that morning in the Reich Chancellery Hitler had declared the situation "no longer tolerable." Hateful voices told us what loving ones could not—that at any cost humanity was breaking the dishonorable stalemate of the Thirties.

It was news that forced me to reflect what a good summer I had had. I touched Janet's hair, wanting to apologize for appetites and a heart too small to value properly the good that had been given me; and the terrible news seemed to light up our mundane inland landscape like a stronger light coming on behind a painted screen to show the venomous things coiled under our greenery. The gardens were mined, after all. In the depths of the quarry where we had behaved as if we knew no better, death lay like a slime separating water and stone. Even art—in which, reader, I put much faith in those days—had betrayed us by pretending it could be enough. Arts that had permitted this to happen were the arts of slaves.

I needed consolations that Janet did not have to give. I wanted to run from her quietness. Inside the camouflage of emotions I saw plain in myself the passionless wish to kill. I knew, with a knowledge that meant to have my heart for breakfast, how easy it would be.

For all the years between 1939 and 1945 I lived in a strange division from myself, knowing it was impossible for me to accept the war, but finding nothing easier than to do my duty to it. My recruiting officer said, "No covenant whatsoever obliges against the main end both of itself and of the parties covenanting." With a rubber stamp he freed me from the human covenants I had, not easily nor all at once, bound myself to. Let me assure you right now, lest you expect that my silent Angst came to anything, that I took the war in my stride. It was "easy" to pilot a landing craft onto the north beaches at Saipan with the long hair of the Japanese women who had killed themselves fouling the propellers—and all that kind of thing we like to read about for emotional purgation. I have never been terribly squeamish about the flesh. It lives and dies. It can do no other. I spent some time shepherding psychos, too, and I might as well put in here that their derangements never shook me deeply either, except now and then when they seemed to light up with matchless clarity the truth that I so easily ignored. What I pity in myself and in "all men" was the sane and orderly acceptance of what we had no right to accept. I think there was an irreparable dislocation made for which the hours will pay until time ends.

But you might well say that people thought this way about the First World War and the Civil War. No doubt about other wars. And look, there are more Germans, Russians and Japanese and happier Jews than in 1939. Yes, I know.

I can't lay my conscience open on the table to show it to you, and wouldn't if I could, and yet the rather pointless thing I have to set down about my encounter with Clem that night may, for once, have more to do with me than with him. He fought longer than I did, as you will see, and the image he then struck on my mind is of a surrender to horror which was only in my case unconditional, not to be reprieved.

When I came past his room after leaving Janet I saw his light on and stopped in to make sure he had heard the news. (He missed a lot of significant events that every newspaper reader knew. I had found that some days after the signing he had not heard of the Nazi-Soviet Pact.)

I found him lying on his back on his bed, staring up at the bare bulb hanging from a pulley contraption near the ceiling. He sometimes pulled it down close when he read. Tonight he hadn't been reading.

He didn't budge when I spoke to him. I saw the pupils in his eyes contracted to pinpoints. The double reflection of the light bulb moved lightly on the surface of his eyes, and the effect of illumination was such that his eyeballs seemed transparent. I could not hear him breathing or see any sign of movement in his chest. He lay stiff as someone poisoned.

I called from the doorway, asking if he was all right.

"I'm afraid," he whispered.

He was never a better poet than with those words. They're enough. We said some other things to each other that night before I went on down the hall to bed. Some of them were necessary and some were shrewd. Some were franker than we had known how to say before the liberation of the event. None of them had much weight for me in the times that followed. I knew what he meant when he said he was afraid, and, in knowing that my own fear was more circumscribed, I knew myself more evilly allied than he.

Finally I said, "We'd better sleep. If you need it, there's a little whiskey down in the glove compartment of Janet's car. She let me drive it home tonight. I'm going to pick her up for breakfast. You want to eat with us?"

"I have to think about it," he said, not meaning an invitation to breakfast. "I'd better not drink anything. There must be some way out, if we were smart enough."

He was sitting in Janet's car when I went down in the morning, waiting for me, ready to go to breakfast with us, as calm as I had ever seen him. It was apparent that he had been walking most of the night, but he said nothing about it beyond "I went up by the edge of the lake."

What he had known would come out almost as slowly, and just as surely in its own time, into the articulation of language, as the novel did. The actions that his knowledge might commit him to—assuming that he had a knowledge of what was coming superior to the silly pragmatism everyone could rely on—were at first indistinguishable from what any Clem in his place would have done. How should he be changed by the news that war had begun? How can the individual be affected by news from afar any more than the tides can be affected by remote celestial bodies? (Newton and Einstein agree that they can't. It's only poetry to say that the moon lifts the tides.)

He had found someone to go home to, Janet and I thought when we sent him off to Indiana. That was the major reality of the moment. No one was diverted from the local truth by the poetry about a war somewhere.

The night before he left, Janet ironed all his shirts for him, packed his bag and bullied him into shining his shoes. She had also loaned him money to buy a summer suit, going with him to the clothing store to make sure he got one his own size.

We drove him out to the edge of town, where he meant to stand until he hitched his first ride. Janet kissed him and said, "Now, try to be good, Clem."

"I'll go a million," he said.

"Sheila's family will like you. Everyone will like you if you try."

"I'll chahm them silly."

"You'd better, you little devil," Janet said, and she gunned the car and swung it in a slithering U turn as we headed back to town. She bet me even money that everything would go well on Clem's visit.

And she won—though I would not pay her until weeks later when I got confirmation from Sheila herself.

"He didn't uproot plants? Set fire to his mattress? Tell your father that capitalism is doomed? Make passes at your Sunday-school teacher? Get your family expelled from the country club?" I asked.

"We don't belong to the country club," Sheila said, "though Clem and I did go out there swimming with some of my friends. They all liked him. He had them in stitches most of the time—you know, pretending he can't swim and with his wit. And Daddy liked him very much. He was pretty dubious at first because Clem was hitchhiking to see me instead of driving, like a serious boy friend should, and Daddy was out washing our car in the driveway when Clem walked up right past him with his satchel in his hand and they didn't say a word to each other. Daddy was a little stiff when I introduced them after that, and dinner the first night wasn't exactly a ball. Then Clem began to gas with Daddy about building."

"Clem doesn't know anything about building. He was expelled from a manual-training class for striking at nails with the claw side of the hammer."

"Clem knows about everything," she said. "It comes to him as he talks. That's what he told me! He got along dandy with Mother, too. The first morning, before I got up, he went out in the kitchen where she was ironing and sat on the clothes hamper telling—"

"About how his sister learned the piano by correspondence?"

"No, no, no. About the war. She doesn't—or didn't—believe that we'd be dragged into it, even now. But Clem was explaining to her—to all of us—why it was likely. He quoted Walter Lippmann, Gunther, Mann, Churchill and people like that to show why."

"Clem hasn't read anything they've written this summer."

"He knows what they've said. You know what a wonderful memory Clem has and how he catches the sense of something so quickly."

"Yes," I said, watching her plain face warm to beauty with her enthusiasm and wondering if she'd caught any of the sense of Clem's doubts about their marriage.

She said, "I thought once he was going to make Daddy swallow his coffee cup when he said that after the war we'd take over the place Germany is trying for in the world because we're so much like Germany. Daddy hates the Krauts worse than anything in the world and particularly for what they're doing to the Jews. But Clem wouldn't back down an inch. Daddy sulked all day and then they started to argue again. Clem mentioned a lot of ideas that were the same here and in Germany and the way the Jews had been tolerated for a long time in Germany as well and how Germany had, in the Republic days, had about the same attitude toward Russian Communism that we have now. Finally he made Daddy very thoughtful, so that all he had left to say was that he hoped not. Just before we left to come back to school here, Daddy and I went for a drive alone and the, you know, Big Talk to Daughter. Daddy said Clem was very smart and very nice and that I ought to be very proud of him whether he was ever a big success or not. But he thought Clem was too intense about some things, maybe because he's still young, and that if I married him I'd be taking a great big responsibility on myself. Even though Clem has got a novel under contract—"

"Clem told you that?"

"We told Daddy and Mother that, so they wouldn't be too antsy about our being engaged. Clem wouldn't have lied about it if I hadn't encouraged him to. Anyway, he's going to write his novel this winter, so maybe we can get married in the spring."

"We'll count on it," I said.

And I think through that fall Clem had not yet stopped counting on it. There were days when he acted as if nothing stood between him and success except the drudgery of committing his story to paper. (And as for that, pouf! Had he not set the highest mark for speed typing in the history of Boda High School? No, he had not. But he had come close enough to license this optimistic fantasy.)

He was riding a tide of encouragement. It came from within as a new image of himself modeled after those writers who, in our century, have known popular fame early—Mann, Fitzgerald or Hemingway. And though nothing in the objective world measured up to such grandiose expectations, nevertheless the tokens of success began to accumulate.

Before Christmas he had sold (or "placed," in the case of literary magazines that paid nothing) three more short stories. According to the way he told it sometimes, these stories were parts of his novel. He had only to fit them into his over-all design. Two more groups of his poems had been accepted. This meant that his boast to Dawn was nearly true. Almost everything he had done that summer was going to be promptly published.

Irving Kinsman started his class in creative writing at the university that fall. In this group, which Kinsman's taste and force raised to a higher level than any which had assembled under Henry Powell's direction, Clem was undeniably the star.

The other students and Kinsman praised everything he did unstintingly. Beyond this, his natural bent for the theatrical gesture and phrase was coming into its own, and he ruled in the classroom like a junior Titan. He sparked away at the center of every controversy. He made the others angry and won them back. He drove out of class a bumptious fraternity boy who dared think (worse, he said it aloud) that the fiction in The Saturday Evening Post set a standard worth aiming at. Or, if Clem did not literally drive this young man away, he caused the fellow to trip himself so crudely before the rest of the class that he transferred to the journalism department to protect his dignity.

Kinsman, watching his prize student with mingled satisfaction and reservations, thought that Clem "sets them all an example of audacity, if nothing more." And—far better than any teacher's approval or disapproval as far as the other aspirants were concerned—Clem had "a hot contact with a publisher." This mark of distinction in a writing class is comparable to the blossoming of a bona fide stigmata on a girl in a convent.

Even Janet thought that everything was marching toward a triumph. She and I saw a very great deal of Clem and Sheila that year. There was hardly a two-day stretch when we did not eat together, go to the movies or a basketball game, drive to the country to picnic, skate or hunt.

Clem seemed to be on his way to domestication. He even went to a party at Sheila's sorority in a rented tux, though he came home in a blistering rage against the finks and phonies who he thought had been amused by his dancing.

He included Sheila in the rage, but she had—wisely and serenely, we thought—given up taking him seriously when he got angry at her or said painful things.

"Darling, I'm going to teach you to dance in good time," she told him. "Be patient. Anyway, you were handsome in your tux." Not like the others—she wouldn't have said that—but handsome.

"I have a natural sense of rhythm," Clem said. No doubt he must have had, as far as words were concerned. Since dancing was to his mind so far less demanding than poetry, he couldn't understand why the benefits of meter did not show on the dance floor. "What, exactly, was wrong with my dancing?"

"I loved it," Sheila said. "It's merely that they aren't used to seeing rhythms quite that natural. Like you say, this was a bunch of provincial yokels who have never seen how they dance in Boda."

Sheila went home with him to Boda for the Christmas holidays— his first visit home in about two years. As far as I heard, their trip went off smoothly. I believe that Clem's mother heckled him about getting a job if he intended to get married. She had no confidence that he would ever make any money by writing, though "he was the most imaginative child you'd want to see, Sheila. A lot of times I'd see him sitting by himself with his lips moving. I'd ask and he'd confess he was telling himself stories."

"I've always worked hard like that," Clem said.

His mother liked Sheila immensely. "'She's common and ordinary as an old shoe,'" Clem quoted. "Why should anybody want to marry a girl as common as all that?" But we were still convinced that he did.

It was the middle of spring when I sensed and then was sure that something had gone badly wrong between them. I believed for a while that his bad humor was coming from difficulties he had in getting his novel to move ahead. I knew he had been pushing himself hard to keep up with his classwork, and this was looking like it meant he could not possibly finish a novel before June. Therefore, there could be no advance money anticipated before fall, even on the shaky assumption that the first publisher to see it would buy enthusiastically. But such delays could be borne. As long as there was good hope, both Sheila and he could adjust to waiting a little longer.

But then I knew the novel was not progressing at all. Days, weeks and months passed when Clem did nothing on it. First he said he was "thinking it out." Then he said he'd put it aside for a breather.

The big shock came when I guessed he had put it aside because he didn't want the consequences of finishing it successfully.

One evening, in response to a casual inquiry from me, he let me know that he'd been over reading in the medical library.

"Going to be a doctor?" No answer, so I said, "I understand they have some gripping books over there."

"Reading up on pregnancy symptoms."

"Sheila?" I asked. Then I said I hoped it was Sheila.

"Sheila." He turned a clenched, angry face and nearly shouted, "I don't believe it. I simply won't believe it. She's overdue, but she hasn't got any other symptoms. There's no pigmentation and her breasts are the same. It's only that she wants it to be that way."

"You're swinging pretty wild."

"No I'm not. Oh no. If something has happened, it's her fault, not mine. I meant to be careful."

His unqualified bitterness against her made me angry in turn. I told him that he did not appear so great a catch that she would have to trick him that way.

"I know I'm not. That's the pitiful thing," he said. "She's trying to smother me. She keeps building up the pressure. When I tell her she's got to slacken off, she promises she will. But the more she tries to leave me alone the more actual pressure builds up, since I know she's hiding her real feelings. She's always asking—either aloud or not aloud—when I think I'll have my novel finished. Or why won't I read any of it to her any more."

"Why won't you?"

His eyes took on the mean desperation of a dog disturbed at its meal. "Maybe I don't want to read her anything until I have something good enough for her."

"And maybe it's because you haven't done any more."

"So whose worry is that but mine? You'd think I'd quit just to spite someone."

Yes, that's just what I did think, and I pictured a catastrophic tangle of injustices while it seemed that Sheila might be pregnant. If he was trickily paying her back for doing that to him … No, that wasn't the right way to put it, but there was no right way if what I suspected was true.

In a week Sheila told Janet, shakily enough, that she was all right. She'd been in great emotional torment, and Clem hadn't been much help. Perhaps she'd only worried herself into the belief that she was pregnant because she was so worried about Clem. "He insists I'm killing the goose that laid the golden egg. But I don't mean to rush him, Janet. I've told him that a thousand times. If it takes ten years to finish his novel, and if I get too old to have children before he's ready to marry me, I don't care."

"Yes you do," Janet said. "I'll have a talk with him. I want to see that golden egg."

Janet tried to provoke him into fighting with her, if he had to war with someone, if he had some irrational grudge to work out of his system. She would have been glad to draw the fire if that meant that he would stop blooding himself on Sheila. I suppose we felt even then that in some crucial, moral way disloyalty to Sheila was the worst disloyalty he could show to us. Our last emotional refuge against the imminence of war was a "let us be true to one another" despair of the world's promises, and Clem was increasingly repudiating what we wished to believe in. Increasingly we saw signs that Sheila did not bear the attrition well. She had no means to recall what she had given. It was pitiful to watch her trying to take for granted the elements of their previous intimacy that he would not let her take at all.

For Clem's part, he would not fight with Janet (or me) any more than he would openly and cleanly break with Sheila. As Janet said, he seemed to be freezing himself over slowly but very purposefully.

We who were close to his private life were not the only ones aware of a change in him, though I have felt, with all the weight of responsibility entailed by it, that I may have been the only one placed to see the terrible consistency in what he was doing. (Of course Sheila might have seen better if her already committed faith in him and her emotions had not prevented her.)

During the spring before Clem's graduation, Irving Kinsman began to wonder, first, if he had not spoiled Clem by overpraising him and permitting him his role as class genius, and second, whether he had not simply overestimated Clem.

Even Felix Martin had doubts of this sort. He remained convinced that Clem had showed powers of an absolutely exceptional kind, but began to wonder if the sudden emergence of these powers did not imply as sudden a consumption, as if Clem might have spent his whole force in a swift charge of brilliance across what was not, after all, the real sky. It saddened him to think there might have been more truth than he allowed in Clem's unchaste identification of himself with Rimbaud and Chatterton, for "it is conceivable that such Icarian flights as dazzle us depend more than we are used to admitting on the sustaining atmosphere. We laugh, somewhat too hastily I suppose, at the idea of the mute inglorious Miltons. But what would have happened to Rimbaud if he had been born in the American provinces and, God help us, for some reason had registered as a freshman here? I am not easy when I reflect on such things." He saw Clem's half-insane arrogance turning into a surly brash glibness. He would not make a judgment on Clem's future, but, on the evidence, he had become dubious.

Nevertheless, he and Kinsman did everything in their power that spring to bolster Clem. Felix now had taken his Ph.D. and was a newly appointed assistant professor. To the point of recklessly impairing his insecure position, he pushed Clem for every scholarship or grant where there was the slightest chance that promise might weigh more than academic record. His colleagues, depending, as most of us in the profession do, on recommending students who are faithful replicas of themselves, were irritated and amused by his persistence in Clem's behalf. Until it was clear that the Rhodes scholarships would be suspended for the duration, Felix did what he could to enlist support for Clem's candidacy. He approached the head and senior members of the department for support in getting Clem a scholarship at Harvard.

Finally he and Kinsman concentrated on getting the Blaine Award for Clem. This was a grant of seven hundred dollars to cover a year of graduate study, and the stipulation seemed broad enough to include Clem's achievements: "For literary and scholarly merit, this award is given in memory of Eleanor G. Blaine, wife, mother and poet." A small committee of the department sat to examine the scholarly attainments of nominees. Clem's publications, emphasized and by now overemphasized by Martin and Kinsman, gave him a certain advantage over anyone else in sight.

Certainly with any preparation for the oral examination, with any sign of honest effort toward it, Clem could have had this scholarship. Then he would have been bound to stay another year at the university, the other year it would take before Sheila graduated.

He blew his chance away casually. I think he did not (bother to) insult the members of the examining committee. He may have told them that Milton had spoiled the language for poetry for two centuries, but the committee would have accepted this heresy if he had only told them who wrote The Hind and the Panther and when. He told them instead that he didn't bother with periods that didn't interest him.

Sheila, of course, was most cruelly disappointed by this, though I can imagine Felix's heavy heart after his loyal, unstinting support of something he no longer truly believed in.

I remember once when Janet and I sat drinking beer with them while Sheila explained that now, of course, Clem would have to go to New York in the summer and get a job, maintaining himself somehow until he could finish the novel.

"Why don't you go with him?" Janet asked. "You don't have to finish school."

"It wouldn't be practical," Clem said.

"It wouldn't be practical at all," Sheila said nervously. "We've got to keep milking my parents as long as we can, the way things are, until Clem's appreciated."

"He's appreciated," I said. Clem had been busily peeling away and then repasting the label on his beer bottle. Now he lifted one of his eyelids to peer knowingly at me, as though we shared a really prime joke. I wanted to hit him. I wanted Jack Miller to have hit him. Anything to break the unbearable smugness of his defeats.

Nothing could. While we had been watching what seemed his still increasing emergence into our world, he had been all-secretly entrenching himself against us all.

He and I did not part on bad terms when he hitchhiked off to New York after his graduation. It would have been better if we had, for I had the feeling that he left his friendships and loves unresolved that year because he had already unilaterally resolved them—withdrawing himself—and merely didn't want the bother of fighting openly about them. It must have been that way that he had left his family in Boda, slipping away from them in spirit while they still thought he was there.

It took me half the following summer to build up head enough of anger to think I was glad he was gone—forever, as it seemed. But by the time Janet and I were married in August, I could say to her and she could say to me—no qualifications added—that we were not sorry to be rid of Clem. We would close no doors to him, but he had been swallowed away. By his own choice he had got lost.

He had promised to write, but he wouldn't write. That wasn't his way. If the war didn't finish him off—literally or as a writer—we might hear of him someday, but it seemed we would meet as strangers. We knew that the end of college brings such separations.

And we still had Sheila. We would hold on to Sheila, we promised each other.

During that winter we tried. With Clem gone, she had become a wraith to us. We had her to dinner a few times in our new apartment. She gave us the most optimistic accounts of Clem. Of course he wrote to her regularly—wonderful letters. He was sharing an apartment in the Village with a man from Michigan, named Henderson Paul, who had won the Hopwood Award and was also finishing up a novel. He had reestablished his friendship with Lillian Esterman. Lillian had so many wonderful contacts with publishers. They might start a little magazine together if Lillian could raise the money. Clem was working night and day—mostly planning his novel. But she … wasn't sure that she would see him at Christmas. Maybe, if she could get the money from her folks, she would go to New York for the holidays. Maybe … It hurt her and it hurt us for her to pretend that all was still well between her and Clem. But she didn't know how else to talk to us.

Toward Christmas time we began to see her—when we saw her at all—on the campus or in the taverns with an earnest, stoop-shouldered physics major or another fellow who looked like he might be studying for the ministry. We always spoke fondly, sometimes at length, when we met, but it became increasingly difficult, painful to all.

Then it was Don Hazeltine, not Sheila, who gave us our next direct news of Clem. Don had been in to New York at spring vacation and had seen him.

"What's he doing?" Don said. "Nothing. Trying to stay out of the war. It's my honest conviction that he's cracked up. You can sit with him for hours and he won't say anything, or when he does it's not as if he was answering anything you said to him but it was just a thought that had come to him. He's got a little job on a trade paper. That seems to take him an hour a day. I don't think he gets up much, otherwise. All I know about what he's doing otherwise is that he's visiting a guru in New Jersey once or twice a week."

"A ...?"

"Guru. He's learning Yoga or something like that so he can mentally resist the war or the war effort or whatever he may be trying to resist. That's what he told me."

"I see," I said.

"I tried to get a straight answer as to whether he means to be a conscientious objector, but he just smiles when you say things like that to him. He isn't eating anything that has a face, though he's drinking more beer than ever and I asked him if the rule didn't apply to anything that had a head."

"I don't suppose he laughed about that."

"Not a smile. You know, I don't think he'll have any trouble staying out of the Army. It's that bad. His people are going to have to come and get him pretty soon, I think."

So, with these fading images, he might have disappeared from our sight like a water color washed off the paper under a tap. But as it turned out, Sheila went and got him. For us.

The way they told it later was that, after her graduation, Sheila went to Washington to get a job. To Washington because she knew, even if she knew very little else about him at this time, they would surely try to draft him soon. She had to be there to make sure that they used him properly, once they had made a soldier of him.

She just happened to write him a little note, after all these months of silence, telling him where she was. And he came down to Washington and moved in with her.

He asked her if she thought he ought to go into the Army and she said she thought that probably he should. So he did.

248

Well, you can get such odd relationships in stories if the pace is suddenly changed (as you have just noticed me doing—though of course my hasty account of this time is a paraphrase of Clem's and Sheila's). The picture is like a map painted on rubber. Stretch it out and the space between co-ordinates is filled with variety. Squeeze it together and you get an image of homogeneity, of simplicity. Both pictures are true enough. Memory and whatever else it is we get from memory use both, stretching and squeezing according to our present need.

But then, of course, something that is neither memory nor private judgment tells us that there is an objective reality to which both subject and writer must pay its due. To pay its due in this case is not pleasant, for the squeezed-out gap of those years before Clem went into the Army seems to represent a pure loss, objectively speaking.

The life he might have had with Sheila—and those wasted years might have shaped the end differently for them—was willfully refused. What he might have written, in his novel or in other forms, was simply not written. The continuity of his life as writer was revealed to be not a continuity of progress but a series of waves separated with troughs so deep that one wishes not to follow through them—wishes desperately to glean only the unrelated fragments of high achievement. It seems treacherous even to suggest that the periods of falling away have their necessary part in the rhythms of creation. Why can't we claim the inexpensive privilege of appreciation and, since after all we are the paying audience, blame the individual or collective writer for what he might have done and did not?

Clem quit on us. He had, in the phrase current a while back, a failure of nerve. Self-pitying and self-destructive, he took the basest excuses that the time offered for a surrender of the spirit. By choice and not by the hellish circumstance that condemned so many, he enlisted in the race of victims. I can close the story of his college years with no other judgment. It does not matter one iota whether you or I or Sheila might wish to forgive him his willful failures. No one gave us the power to forgive, give back, the possibilities that inexorable time snatched away.

But because we have time left, may we not indulge in some plea for the powerless wish, what Sartre calls man, la passion inutile? We find our writer charged with self-pity, intolerable as cowardice in face of the enemy. The charge is admitted. But if, in himself, he saw the others? If what our imaginative coward was afraid of when the war began was the endless, innumerable accumulation of horrors it would bring, and, in the imagination for which he had not only a license of sorts but a supralegal obligation, saw himself as all the victims from Warsaw to Hiroshima, Dachau to Lidice, and Berlin and Coventry? I would be doing less than my duty to the imagination which was our one chance to find a way out if I withheld my surmise of what Clem saw dangling on the end of his light cord that night when the fear began. He saw his Uncle Cole, of course (not a soldier, only an economic warrior). And Eric Stein. Jack Miller machine-gunned when his parachute tangled in a tree on the Cotentin Peninsula. Harry Rinehart blinded on the Ranger. The once named friends of Wallace Rogge trapped in a French concentration camp near Perpignan, the never named millions hanging like human spiders over the horror that men without imagination invented for them. And the "child"—but we need not count this figment of mental disorder among the real who went into the earth. (Indeed, this figure is all too delicate for me to deal with, and when he must be spoken of I will let Clem speak, inconclusive as that will be.)

It may be that Clem saw the dead. People with a certain degree of imagination do not need to be given a tour through the crematories in order to understand. Perhaps there are among us sometimes those with the gift of pitying others in themselves, and where the question is dubious I do not choose to say it is they who break the human ranks. Perhaps Virginia Woolf had no right to yield (to mention one synecdochal figure) and perhaps some people find the Marshalls of the Crusade more gallant than she. And perhaps we need not pause to argue this point, for if God is just we shall all get what we deserve for believing individually as we do.

The boy who advanced on Rose because he thought she might give him syphilis, because he owed something to Wallace Rogge for not having gone to Spain and to Jack Miller for having called him a Jew, might have thrown away what he wanted most in those years just before we went into the war—not from personal weakness but for obligations not yet recorded on our tables of morality.

And anyway, if one plays the accordion of fictional time as I'm doing in these few pages that conclude one epoch and begin another, squeezing and stretching almost capriciously as my thoughts move, one can provide such startling variations. After this wailing discord (and the interjection of too many opinions that are at best a gloss for the record) I will play you a madrigal with some sweetness. A sounding of a theme that might well be repeated later on, even at the very end. Calm, long-drawn-out notes for an epithalamium.

Sheila and Clem were married in January 1946 in New York. See how all that was wrong comes right in time?

Clem was still in his Army uniform. By then he did have a signed and paid-for option for his novel in his pocket, and considerable parts of it had been written under circumstances superficially more trying than those from which he had failed to profit before. Stronger against the tide, our whale!

He would have a book of poetry in print that summer or fall.

The bride was no less fair than she had been five years before—somewhat more so, Janet and I thought. (You discern that, in spite of convictions that we had permanently lost each other, certain filaments of connection had proved surprisingly strong. We made a long trip so that we could see the end of what we had seen beginning, to pay our respects to formality, after all.)

The groom had lost his shifty-eyed uncertainty of manner. Though he had been but a sergeant and only once for a period of two months had commanded men, there was plainly the habit of command in his bearing. There was no trace in his speech or manner of his recent confinement in a psycho ward in Germany. (I thought if they had known him as I once had known him, they would hardly have bothered to treat him for the minor symptoms he had lately shown.) Plainly he had been eating many creatures with faces.

As we saw it—ceremony and kiss—the tale of lovers had a happy ending, just like the great war itself. The fated couple were married on a sunny, crisp day. It seemed to the few of us who gathered in their hotel room after the services in church that the long and painful equilibrium of their love had brought them together "like stiff twin compasses." (All right, I contributed that quote, drunkenly proud to do so, now soberly proud.)

They had found each other and themselves. The Oedipal complex had been mastered. They saluted each other in a propriety that no one else could have demanded of them. No time which brought this was wasted time.

And here, where they loved properly, I would like to write "The End." But even were I to end with that time, when peace loomed over the future like a gracious cloudbank just beyond a bird's-eye view of Hiroshima, I would have to end saying that an unquiet mind held something in suspense, would not let go its arms.

I remember remembering, as if it were a curse on their nuptials, the time Clem said to me, "She ought to get away. I'll kill her, Dick."

Like a blessing I remembered, "'I desired my dust to be mingled with yours Forever and forever and forever.'"

# IV

# THE GIANT WOMEN

*The huge doll roars for death or mother,*
*Synonymous with one another;*
*And Woman, passive as in dreams,*
*Redeems, redeems, redeems, redeems.*

—W. H. AUDEN, "New Year Letter"

# 10

SINCE NOTHING can come of nothing, the public figure of a writer must come from the mass of canned stereotypes available on the shelves and from the very limited cunning of those who blend and serve them up. This fall when *Death and the Devil* was scheduled for opening on Broadway a most amazing inflation of Clem's reputation as a poet was taking place. A purely quantitative inflation, that is, bearing no more discernible relation to his real achievement than the rites in honor of the Unknown Soldier bear to the unknown circumstances of his heroism, agony and death. To use a term from engineering, there was a tolerance so enormous between poet private and poet public that I felt the big new Clem might as well have been educed from any of a thousand male verse writers (provided only that they now had a marketable drama to offer) as from Clem's integral self.

For each single individual who had read Clem's verse, there were now thousands being sold on the idea that they should anticipate *Death and the Devil* as a special treat because its author was a well-known poet. (Remember, though, the distinction between "thousands" and "millions" in our land. Of course the publicity that projected the image of the new Clem on the white fogbank of national consciousness was of relatively small force. He was not competing for attention with the Korean War, juvenile delinquents, the Father of the H-bomb, or such Hollywood name writers as Fyodor Dostoevsky.) The "medium-large" public—roughly defined as those who live in the dark provinces and get the Sunday New York Times by subscription—were now being advised that a poet had written a play. With fair frequency one caught a reference to him as "poet" in the weekly liberal magazines or the women's fashion magazines. ("One of the best poets to be shaped by the war" or "curly, vital, bubblesome with wit, Clem Anderson was often visited by——'s editors on their trips to Paris"—take your pick.)

His marriage got him mentioned in columns where the names of poets since Longfellow and Bobbie Burns seldom appear. (This unnatural alliance of poet and cinemactress seemed to have some of the fascination of a beast marriage—maiden to swan, youth to lioness, depending on the orientation of the viewer.) His "credo" as a writer appeared in the theatrical pages of a great newspaper a week in advance of the opening of his play.

I, merely an amateur of the ways in which folklore is concocted, wondered why he was so rarely, if ever, called a novelist in this advance publicity. *Angel at Noon*, in paperback, had sold 250,000 copies (hard-cover, 6,183). I conjectured that in this age of digests the apparent brevity of the poems would appeal more to the (now interested) persons who had no intention of reading them than the lengthier fiction, which they had no intention of reading either if they had missed it when it was on their newsstands. But I could conclude only that if poetry remained unsalable in the republic, poets were a commodity. They have some aura of aristocracy about them, I suppose, and our republican passion for titles is too notorious to need further comment.

Somewhat vengefully I amused myself by considering that Clem's new physical girth was his accommodation to the new Anderson we had to get used to. Such a poet as I read about would have to weigh forty pounds more than the one whose work I respected. I did not bother with reflections that his acquisition of fat was of unconscious psychogenesis. ("There's not much unconscious left in me, Dick. I've been mining it too long.") No, the accommodation was intentional, just as the change of wives was—whether cynical or some form of self-torturing irony I was not yet prepared to say. Certainly both fat and wife were signs for all men to read that he was ready to profit from the years he had eaten locusts in the wilderness.

The public was profiting from Cindy's new connection as well. The skin magazines continued to show me rather more of her than I liked to see of my friend's wife. Still it was my daughters (Beth enlisted, too, in Jill's passion) who brought such pictures to my attention, smiling wisely as they dropped their garbage before me at breakfast or dinner.

There were no more pieces celebrating the amativeness of the intellectual. At least I saw none. But helplessly I recall one photo that showed Cindy in white leotard, gazing in more than rapture at the rapier in her hand with which she seemed intent on vaginal penetration. Underneath was the caption: "A poet's wife, Cindy Hunt has her Hamlet moments. (Above) 'Who would fardels bear when with a bare bodkin he can end it.' (Shakespeare)."

All this printed fanfaronade, plus the laudatory reviews of Clem's play, following in mechanical sequence, interested me on levels where neither memories nor any real emotion could be engaged. It was as if I were watching a movie so grotesquely removed from reality that it would tease me into curiosity about what the actors were experiencing as they moved through their parts. (I might mention that this mental displacement takes place nearly every time I am persuaded to go to movies, and it once led me to a real affection for those in which Bill Boyd appeared. He always looked before the cameras as if he had merely dropped into the studio that day to collect his wages and was filmed riding to and from the treasurer's window.)

I wrote to Clem that I would be coming in to New York during the Christmas holidays for the M.L.A. meeting, that I was very much looking forward to seeing *Death and the Devil* and that I hoped to see him and meet Cindy Susan. In the same mail I sent a letter to Sheila, in care of her parents, again mentioning my plans and the hope that I could see her if she was to be in New York then.

No answer came from Sheila in the six weeks before my departure, but Clem replied very promptly. He was glad I was coming, and, if I could come in one day earlier than I had planned, he wanted me to go with him and Susan to a party that he and Gorman, the producer, were giving for the cast "and friends."

In spite of Janet's nearly mute resistance—implications by deed and emphasis that I was withdrawing love from her and the children after thirteen years of marriage because, like my friend Anderson, I had whiffed blonde—I wrote that I would be there for the party.

"You can't resist seeing what such a party's like," Janet accused.

Stung by the accusation that experience, as such, had any irresistible attractions for one who had attained to my years, I barely refrained from answering her in detail—with the result that I was answering her not only in detail but with heat from the time the plane took off until it had landed at La Guardia. If she had only been along to listen to me, I would have won my argument cleanly. Yes, I would have shown her that experience always has a vital excess over any theoretical wisdom. However well one knows what is going to happen, it always happens a little differently. I was ready to call that little margin of surprise holy, and to point out that by it and it alone the generations could succeed each other with joy.

But she was not with me to be bullied and overwhelmed with the superiority of my thoughts, and in the cloudbank that covered eastern Pennsylvania, New Jersey and New York I experienced a worse melancholy than I could remember. My thoughts didn't stop when I had proved the superiority of liberty and experience, but went on to the next antistrophic level as I thought that the surprises of experience, holy as they may be, are of course, only conditional on our ignorance, and are—quite the opposite of representing an escape from limitations—the most dreadful confirmation of their power. It seemed to me I was going to Clem's party because I was going, just as I had come to his wedding seven years before. That it was all a dull mechanical grind, meaning no more than the monotonous groan of the motors beyond the fuselage window.

Fortunately for my state of mind I ran into Bessie Stoutamire in the airport bar. She is an old friend who teaches my period at the University of Utah. She had just come in from Salt Lake and was effervescent with enthusiasm for all she meant to see and do instead of attending the meetings at the Hotel New Yorker. A drink with her and a shared taxi ride into Manhattan refurbished my reasons for wanting to be in the city.

Bessie reported a terrible year. After a long siege of pneumonia, the death of her father, the discovery that her fiancé was homosexual and the failure of her prize student to pass his comprehensives, she had just been refused a sabbatical to which she felt entitled. But she meant to submerge all this by standing on Fifth Avenue "watching the well-harnessed girls and the beautiful old men," by going to the theater and the ballet, by calling dozens of people "who would do" while she was here. It sounded so familiar that I laughed and tried a line of Clem's on her, calling New York "the triumphant city where misery has found its company." When she asked me what my miseries were, I could suddenly think of none. The reasons I had for the trip seemed, if not sound or deep, sufficient unto themselves. We were here, I knew as well as she, "because the theater is here," because the circus animals of our morality emerge from our country dreams to a public display in New York.

By the time I checked in at the Wellington, the permissive anonymity of my hotel room was comforting me like a hot bath. I settled down with a bourbon to call a number of friends and my publisher. Between two of these calls, with my hand resting on the phone and I merely slow to lift it again, it rang for me.

"Dick?"

"Yes."

"Dick Hartsell?"

Then I recognized the voice, knowing with a guilty pang that my refusal to recognize it on the first syllable had been wishful.

"It's Sheila," she said.

"Sheila! I had no idea you were here. You didn't answer my letter. Did you get it?"

"I got it. Did you get mine?"

"No. When …? Anyway, I'm delighted to hear from you. It's what I would have wanted in my stocking. When can I see you?"

"Oh." I wished she hadn't sounded timidly surprised that I would want to, a little coy.

"I will get to see you, won't I? I'll be here until Saturday afternoon, and I'm free any time except tonight."

"Oh."

"You're not suddenly dashing out of town just as I arrive, are you? We have so much to talk about. The children … Janet sends her love, though of course she didn't know either—"

"No. I'm not going anywhere. I live here. I haven't brought the children in yet. But that's just what I wrote to you about. Tonight, I mean. There are some people I so much wanted you to meet and I'd arranged everything, but my letter didn't get to you in time, so what the hell?" There were lurking tears in the voice, a note I would never have expected from Sheila, unfamiliar—except that grief never is.

I looked at my watch to see if there was any kind of compromise possible. I was due to meet Clem and Susan at seven, in the Homesteader Bar, where we would eat before going on to the party. "Can I get in a cab right now and meet you for a drink?" I asked.

"No, but … Never mind, Dick. To hell with my plans."

There was a dead, mechanical click in my mind, as if the telephone had picked up the sound of a key turning in a door that I had entered recklessly. Plainly Sheila knew what my engagement was for that evening. I was being asked to declare abruptly whose side I stood on. I was being bullied by her, as one is bullied by a cripple flaunting his mutilation, and I resented it.

I was not being bullied. I was being overwhelmed, and I resented life for thrusting on me situations which I could neither approve nor resist.

"I want to see you," I said.

"Oh, we'll manage to get together. I don't want you to feel bad because … our plans got crossed." Her tone suggested that she was about ready to hang up. I knew she didn't want me to feel bad. Surely she knew I knew, but sometimes token acts are required as well as understanding.

"Look, look, look, look," I pleaded. "What's your number? Let me at least try to arrange things, see if I can break my date for tonight—it's only with Ava Gardner, after all—and come to your place if it's possible. O.K.?"

"Could you, Dick?"

"I don't know," I said. "I'll call back in twenty minutes."

"Do what you want to, Dick. It's my fault for not writing soon enough."

She hadn't written at all. I knew that as soon as I put the phone down. What had been resentment was, for a shocking minute or two, minutes full of demoralizing insight, a consuming rage. In a way I had considered inadmissible I saw how Clem might find love too difficult. For certainly I loved Sheila—the more for her disadvantaged state— and it was nothing but that love which fueled my rage. I am not a child to be played with this way, I felt. Love said, "My child."

Of course it occurred to me as I was cooling down that I might simply omit calling Clem. Allowing a decent interval, I might call Sheila back to explain that, much as I wished to, I could not cancel my conflicting engagement. But decent intervals have always been too much for me. I always use them to equalize the horns of a dilemma. I think.

Presently I found myself staring at the reproduction of a water color opposite me on the sterile wall of the room. By the time I had recognized the brook and the cottage, I knew the best possible solution was for me to go home at once. I was old enough, wisdom aside, to recognize a meat grinder when one began to nibble at my fingertips.

But brave. I rang Clem's number. Susan answered. Her voice simply and undisguisedly revealed the immediate emotion behind it as only the trained voices of actors and actresses can. There was no ambiguity with her as there had been with Sheila. Susan was disappointed. "I know how sorry about this Clem will be," she said. "Darn! I hope you'll join us later, though, if you can. You know where we're going, don't you? Let me give you the address. It will be going on until latish."

"You'd better not count on me for tonight at all."

"Sure, Dick, if you can't. Oh. Clem'll want to know. How are Janet and the girls?"

I said they were fine and was told in exchange that Clem was fine. "But you know how Clem is"—a remark I was left to interpret as signifying that he was hanging head down on a cross while being fondled and fed by houris.

"Can you come to the apartment for dinner tomorrow night, then?" Susan asked.

"Love to."

"That may be better, after all," she said cheerily. "Though I'm a teddible cook, it might be nicer to meet this way, just the three of us, or maybe some other nice people."

I bore down to express my faith that it would be better so. The effort we shared to make that conversation float must have got our friendship off to a good start. I admired her for leaving a wide margin around all the questions that must have been in her mind.

"I have a duck," she said with youngish enthusiasm. "Clem's mother sent us a duck, and I have a recipe and wild rice and all that delicious goo I've been saving. We'll eat it."

"Indeed we will."

I took some more bourbon to insure that my level of heartiness remained adequate to the evening ahead.

There was a smoky mildness in the streets as I rode down to Sheila's apartment in the Village that night. The air was damp and chilly, but tingling. There was a metropolitan benevolence abroad, unmistakable as the salt smell of the harbor. I thought it was the kind of night that should be crowded with trains bringing loads of boys to meet the girls home from Vassar and Smith or the South, where the girls' colleges are. It was the kind of night so protean and fleeting and yet so singular in its tone that it needed a girl's face to represent it, some wonderfully creamy face half buried in the collar of a fur coat. In a word, it was the kind of night when one could smell Clem's party in the air and wish—just wish—that one were going to it.

I pushed the buzzer at Sheila's apartment house a little before eight. There had been time for some quick shopping, and I carried an Italian coffeepot for Sheila, a model B-36 in horrid metal for Jess and a doll for Lulie. I had not wanted to come quite empty-handed.

Sheila met me halfway down the carpeted stairs in the pink glow of someone's electrified holly wreath. She kissed me on the mouth before either of us said the other's name in greeting.

In the benevolence of that dim holiday light in the stair well her face didn't look so bad. She had the kind of face that could stand anything except too much makeup, and the makeup didn't show until we had mounted to her apartment. Her hair had grown out long. She had bleached it almost white. It touched the tips of her shoulders on either side and swung like a ball skirt when she pivoted to take my arm and lead me up.

Fortunately I was not the first arrival, for in the full light of the apartment the ravages she had tried to mask showed through pitifully. Her new makeup and widow's mannerisms seemed to me not so much the sign of bravery as a declaration of her intent to disguise despair. The disguise would not have worked for a minute if we had met alone.

Bernie Masterson was there ahead of me. "He's a poet, you know, Dick. You've read his things. Dick reads everything that comes out," Sheila said. And then when I failed to match her advertisement of me— showed blank ignorance instead of recognition—she insisted, "He's one of the best of the younger poets."

"It's nice to meet a younger poet under forty," I said, sounding fatuous to myself. I kept trying to place Bernie by something I had seen in print, kept failing. Then Sheila jogged my memory by saying that Clem had picked him up in Kansas. I had been waiting for the first sounding of Clem's name. It came out with slurred emphasis, like a syllable either holy or dirty in these precincts.

The other earlier arrival was introduced to me as "a Trollopian from Columbia." Sheila made the two of them witness the unwrapping of the presents I had brought. She bullied them into a sentimental effusion that embarrassed us all—but made plain that we here were all still faithful to "the children" though we knew that there was someone who was not. Through the developments of the evening the mustachioed Trollopian (John B. L. Harvester) kept snatching the model plane (looking uglier and cheaper each time I saw it in his hands) from Sheila's mantel to show it to later arrivals—as if it were my token of membership in this company of shades.

Shades: Let me explain before I mention any more particular names that everyone gathered at Sheila's party was a former friend of Clem's. We were men and women whom he had abandoned or outgrown in his headlong trajectory. If, in other surroundings, we were habituated to feel that our lives continued on even and proper courses, still here Sheila had grouped us so that we must all feel dropped from the radiant presence into a perpetual night.

No doubt Sheila had burned to show us that she was constant. She was not tempted away from us by greater glamour than we had to offer. But her intent, if this was it, hid no more than her makeup did. And finally it showed us all how little faith she had in anything or any group not electrified by Clem's presence. It was as if she had meant us to see that without him we had no communion.

Barnaby Clyde and his wife came soon after I got there. They were both painters who had been part of Clem's New York circle six years before. They had been lordly then, in the confidence of their talents. But that very (justified) confidence had made them slow to "get into abstraction." They had been left behind in the land grab for reputations. Now they were querulous and talked spitefully of painters who had been even slower to "convert" than they.

Robin Stein came with the Kents. Robin had published three dismally unread novels. She had found in all her life not more than a handful of people with whom, in conversation, she could expose the cursed, crystalline, lovely menagerie of her mental life. One of those people was spectacularly absent from Sheila's wake.

The Kents used to talk fervently with Clem about bringing the theater to life outside the poison circle of money. It was strange and terrible to me to discover how such enthusiasts will come at last to a point where concern with money obliterates their happier interests. If Shaw or Chekhov had walked through the door that night, the Kents would have showered him with opinions about financing the off-Broadway theater.

I met George Creed again. Some years ago George had shared with Clem an enthusiasm for "the new short story." The story was to be a consolidation of the gains made by Joyce, Crane, Porter, Hemingway and Faulkner. As I recollect the eager theorizing, this new story was to be as compact as poetry, though without poetry's metrical devices, rhyme or alliteration. It was to keep the suppleness and reportorial virtues of traditional fiction while it added a range of subtleties unknown before the twentieth century.

George, I knew, had continued to write according to this excellent prescription. He turned out two or three stories a year, faithful at first to the hope that because they were truly superior they would presently find their due measure of respect. But in talking to George that night, in sensing from our talk the alienation that had come subtly on him like the thickening circle of ice that cordons off a pond's open water in the fall, I concluded (what was certainly implicit in Clem's demonstrative career) that the aim of art is no longer excellence. Excellence, I felt, was not enough. I had the devastating intuition that George, with his indubitable excellence, had missed the mark that dervish Clem still intended to hit.

Unlike the Clydes, George showed no trace of resentment that he had been bypassed while dozens of his inferiors had got some larger measure of recognition. Even his modesty seemed error. While my intuition lasted I would have preferred to find in him a calculating arrogance, for it seemed to me that art's function was always to celebrate what is sacred to the society. Among an arrogant people it could never do so by modesty, by blushing unseen. Perhaps the depressions of alcohol or the general hysteria of Sheila's evening worked on me unduly. Nevertheless, I felt George to be unmanly in his fortitude and devotion.

Next came Clay Feldman. Clay was a poet whom Clem had admired until unfavorable reviews had smothered his first book. To make a nice distinction, I did not feel that Clay was unmanly for having suffered at the hands of reviewers—I felt him unmanned. Clem had abandoned him in accordance with the terrible Deuteronomic principle, No man who is not whole of the stones shall be a member of the congregation of the Lord. Yes, there is something morbid about unsuccess, though conscience forbids us to admit it.

Came Marianne Luce, a big, handsome girl with blue eyes and taffy hair. She was also a young poet. Like Bernie Masterson, the Andersons had "got" her in Kansas. Marianne handled the model plane I had brought as if it were red-hot, and I read much into the glance of embarrassment she directed at me when Sheila and the Trollopian praised it mushily.

Came Venetia Pogorski, who had never joyed since Strom Thurmond got more votes than Henry Agard Wallace. She had gone to fat since her husband left her. Among the guests Venetia was the only one I had known well once before—when Clem was among us—and consequently I had more trouble being at ease with her than with the others. The taboo on mentioning Clem bothered us more. It seemed like a cork that floated inside the neck of a bottle, rising to block all attempts to pour.

I think I need go no further in characterizing individual guests, though there were more. Suffice it to say that the party was made up altogether of people whom Clem and Sheila had loved for cause. Everyone was what our generation meant by the heightened slang term "good people."

It may be prejudice to think that such as they were superior to their times. But I believe that such a prejudice is disinterested enough, and that it must have been shaped by all my learning, by whatever the civilized centuries lent to me, and by no light whim. These shades represented what history had pretended to us it wanted—and then refused. Oh, we were not wanted, and I took our not being wanted as a metaphysical reason for Clem's not being among us any more. He had to be wanted, even at the cost of making himself less. If these people remained, more than I, individually hopeful, still some daimon of hope had deserted them. I supposed Clem was off courting it among the dogs.

There must have been twenty-five people crowded into the apartment by eleven, when the buzzer sounded again. Sheila crossed to open the door and in came a man led by a Seeing Eye dog. He was stoop-shouldered, with graying crew-cut hair. I knew he must be the real Harry Rinehart. It was as if Sheila had calculated his arrival to climax her eerie celebration. Here now we had Clem's fleshly self, in a manner of speaking.

When Sheila introduced Harry and me and brought us drinks, we sat down together to talk. The dog lay at our feet. Harry seemed completely free of the undernote of embarrassment that all the rest showed to some extent. Perhaps he was calm because he was spared sight of Sheila's face or the extravagant tension of her movements. And he talked freely enough about Clem, as though completely resigned to the natural stretch and break of loyalty that time had enforced.

He had been even more recently disappointed by Clem than Sheila or the rest of us. He lived now in Florida on his government pension and had been working on a book for several years. "A sort of novel," he called it with a shrugging gesture of depreciation. Clem had known of it and had, at long range, been very encouraging. When the book was finished ("Or I thought it was finished—hell, I don't know anything about writing a novel, and Christ knows what that Cracker secretary of mine put on the pages; maybe she just put in blank paper and sent it off, though I used to hear the old typewriter going like mad") it had been sent off to Clem. Clem had acknowledged receiving the manuscript nearly a year ago. But that was the last heard of it. Harry had waited patiently to be told either that it was all a flop and a mistake or that it had been submitted to this or that publisher. Nothing. Clem had not answered his letters of inquiry. When Harry got to New York a few days before Christmas he had tried to call Clem. He had managed to speak to Clem's wife, but ... Wouldn't it seem that Clem was giving him the run-around? Finally he had got hold of Clem's agent. "The man gave me a lot of bullshit. I caught on quick enough that I'd been wasting my time. Only, I wish Clem had told me that himself," Harry said. "Well, though, it doesn't make any difference. I can see how he wouldn't want to." With a curious emphasis, as if he had to defend Clem anyhow, he said, "I ought to be thankful that I could write the thing. It cleared up a lot for me that I wouldn't have understood otherwise. And you know, I never would have written it if it hadn't been for Clem. I mean if he hadn't turned out to be a writer. Little old Clem."

He threw back his head and laughed. His dog looked up from the floor with eager uncomprehension. "Everything comes out all right if you know how to look at it right," Harry said. Which I could not help interpreting as a formidable argument for the blindness I was denied.

His stoical, just formulation did much to halt the precipitous decline my spirits had taken as I came to grasp what the party represented. It did as much as the fortuitous lift of alcohol. Yet I was glad to get away from him. And when, in a far from ambiguous state, I began to enjoy the swelling noise of the party, I kept glancing back toward where he sat with his dog near Sheila's Christmas tree. In a dream, he might have been a figure of terror. And, though it had seemed to relax into conviviality, the party had still to become more dreamlike before I would be released.

Moving between conversations (I had just been talking to the Trollopian when his pregnant wife arrived and came to swing on his arm like a spoiled parrot teasing for its perch, and I wanted to join Marianne Luce for no other reason than that I liked the expression of watchful benevolence she wore), I heard Bernie Masterson saying at my elbow, "She's ghastly, isn't she?"

He had caught me watching Sheila again and spoke with the authority of one who had counted the times I might have revealed my dismay. It seemed to me even that he had a shrewd impression of the weight I was giving to the detailed changes in her face since five years before. The delicate violet bulges below her eyes that had always been so much the distinguishing mark of her face were unchanged. But she wore an absolutely garish eye makeup that gave them a kind of reptilian glitter, their delicate tint shading into purple, green and black. Her cheeks were those of a Lautrec clown and her dark-as-dried-blood lipstick could only have been concocted by a cynical cosmetician who didn't mind saying what happens to women nearing middle life when their sexuality is maimed.

"Well, ghastly ..." I muttered evasively, seeking for a kinder and yet adequately compassionate word.

"I said ghostly." His round, gentle face and shrewd chocolate-drop eyes came into focus, appraising my slip. He laughed, "Ghostly, ghastly, geistly. They all amount to the same thing, don't they, as Jung says."

"Not quite."

"No, not quite, and I don't think she's ghastly at all. You know, I was close to ... them—I thought very close for a while—and I could never entirely figure out where the things came from until I got to seeing her without Clem."

"Did you?" Behind the conversational mask, spiders wove their sticky webs of conjecture and implication. One should not see ghastly ghosts and especially not alone, nor touch the shell of powder and paint that the Geist wears when the self has gone—as Jung would put it, reckless young Masterson.

"She was very lonely," he said with a frown of extenuation. "You have no idea." Then he recovered the line of what he wished to say. "I think the substance all came from her."

"Substance?"

He spun his plump hand like a lariat. "I thought ... Well, something happened to me.... It's hard to begin. You've known them a long time haven't you? Yes. Well, I was just dogging it in Kansas. I don't know what would have happened to me. I suppose I'd have finished my Ph.D. and would be teaching now. But—she wasn't with him there—I thought I'd never met anyone who seemed so exposed and at the same time so powerful as he was. You know?"

"I hadn't the privilege of seeing him in Kansas." Ambivalently I wanted to nod agreement—and resented this maggotish cozying-in to my attitudes. I thought he was going to declare that Clem was a saint, and I have a strong distaste for language that assumes the prerogatives of the college of cardinals.

"He seemed like a saint to me then," Bernie said. I was grateful for the qualifications of tense and simile. He laughed wholesomely. "Like the whole Karamazov family. I understood why old Zossima wanted to kneel and kiss Mitya's foot. He really set fire to the prairie. He ..."

Now comes the dirt, I thought—the revelation of those attributes of sainthood that particularly lend themselves to conversation at a drinking party.

But: "... he didn't say a single thing I believed, though there were times when he was loaded that he talked with more—more brilliance than anyone I'd ever heard. It was—You wanted to be near him. I can't explain."

Since echo is a form of explanation, it was enough for me to hear him echoing Bonnie Waller, daughter of Stein, and I thought, Even in their protected generations they have a sensibility and a taste for the sort of hysteria that the rest of us have to anatomize if we can. They are willing to take the heat with the light, this race of salamanders that has somehow learned to stand it and survive.

"I take it you caught him in one of his self-destructive lapses."

Bernie shook his head, almost in merriment. "I thought that then. Now I am sure—this will sound funny—that he was using Sheila up. I mean, she was like fuel, and he's hollow like some engine that has to be stoked. That's how I rationalize what's happened. And really, as long as they were together she was so much more than he was. More alive."

"I'm glad you have a way of rationalizing it," I said. "I feel we may have chosen an inappropriate occasion to—"

"Yeah, yeah, yeah," he said in sincere consternation, attempting to withdraw what he had exposed, leaving me in a fugue of embarrassment for having seemed more hostile than I would have wished.

We were standing shoulder to shoulder, silently, hiding our faces in our glasses as often as we could, when Sheila came to us. Surely, while she had kept her distance from me, she had been watching me as much as I watched her.

There was a sudden welling of tears in the corners of her eyes as she approached me. "We're boring you, Dick."

"Do I seem bored? Oh, no." I made some crazy motions with elbows and knees to indicate that I was stimulated indeed under my dry exterior.

"I drag you down here ..."

"I wanted to come."

"... and nothing's come to life. They're usually ..." She turned toward her guests, frowning. "No, they're usually like this. They come because they don't want me to be lonely."

"Oh, no."

"Yes," she said. "I know. They like me. But it doesn't go. Nothing ever goes. I try too hard. I try too hard."

"It's going. I'm about to bust my shell and be a butterfly," I said. "You just have to promise that no word of it gets back to the Administration."

"It's going fine," Bernie said earnestly. "What I think, we're all so noisy. Why don't you two mosey out for a walk? I'll keep the punchbowl brimming. I know where you keep the gin."

Sheila snapped at him like an owner. "Don't go meddling with my needs, Bubbie. Bring me a drink if you want to be some use."

Bernie flicked a glance of appeal at me before he went to do the errand. He wanted me to see that he was enduring the whims of one left an invalid. I saw.

"It will be lively," Sheila said.

"I didn't come for that."

"You could have got it better elsewhere? At Clem's party?"

Lightly as I could, I said, "Of course I'm counting on seeing the old boy. I was rather glad not to have to go to his party. It would have been only out of curiosity."

"Mmmmm," she said with crafty disbelief. She rubbed close against my shoulder and spoke in a confidential undertone. "I wouldn't have asked you down if I hadn't meant you to have fun. See that girl?"

I was uneasily startled to note that she was indicating Marianne Luce, since I had indeed been heading for her with somewhat plainer motives than Sheila had to recommend. "I think she'll play. She's just split up with her husband. She's ready for anything. You know how it is with women divorcing. They go a little crazy and anyone can have them."

"Sheila, let's walk out of here."

She answered with a gross cackle and nudged me in the ribs. "For heaven's sake, Dick. Don't play coy with me. You're away from home. It's Christmas. Help yourself. I won't tell Janet. This is Sheila, Dick. I know you."

Hurt and dumb, I let her tug me across the room and with imperious directness leave me with Marianne—with whom real conversation was thenceforward impossible that night. I stood with my feet anchored in the concrete of shame, explaining where I had taken my A.B., my M.A., my Ph.D., that my ancestors were Protestant, that I now held the rank of associate professor, that I had served three years in the Navy, was the father of two daughters, was fond of beagles, contributed in these days only to scholarly journals and was a very old friend of Mrs. Anderson's.

On her side, her natural candor and wisdom—which in time I would learn to depend on—were completely thwarted by the tension that Sheila had communicated. I remember learning from her only that she was teaching at a girls' college in Virginia, that she had taken her A.B. at Reed and her M.A. in Kansas, had been afflicted in recent weeks with a childhood disease (how mortifying! mortification transcending either pain or inconvenience) and rather preferred bassets to beagles.

My pipe was beginning to make horrid, gurgling sounds as I rocked on my heels entertaining the possibility that Sheila had prompted her as I had been prompted and that in the very midst of our stilted talk we should, in duty to Sheila, reach for each other's buttons.

Then she said, "I'm glad I don't know Mrs. Anderson any better. I want to blame her for what she's doing."

The odd clear ring of her statement seemed rather beautifully just. "I think you should," I said. I reflected a minute and said, "I gather from that that you know Mr. Anderson too."

She had a good smile. "From near and far. I don't want to blame her to exculpate him. But—maybe—sin is his medium. I don't think it's hers, and I'd like to kick her out of it. But then, I shouldn't say about things I don't know."

Before our recognition could be spoiled by too much examination, Bernie came to take my elbow and draw me away.

"She's in the bedroom crying," he whispered. His eyes were tragic. "I think you'd better go in. A walk would do her good, if you'd take her."

Sheila had seemed unnaturally aged to me, and now, when I found her lying atop the piled coats in her striped dress, she looked no more than fourteen—like Jill weeping for the monstrous iniquity of the world as some trivial or fancied slight would have revealed it to her.

I put my hand under her shoulder and said, "Come on, Mommy. You've got to help a little. I need some air, too."

Her face was streaked with black, green and purple when she twisted to sit up. There was a fleck of spittle in the corner of her mouth.

"Those people!" she cried in bitter general reference to her guests. "I go to all this trouble to keep them together when Clem won't, and they aren't grateful. They're spiteful. They talk about him. 'Our fine-feathered friend'—I heard Clay Feldman call him that. Envious and spiteful. As if he had to be run down for my ..."

I shook my head.

"I know," she said, clutching my hand. "I've got to figure whose side I'm on."

"And who's on yours."

"Why should they be on my side? For what I used to be?"

"That's not the worst reason, but—"

"I'll be good again," she said. "When?" Now she tried a smile. "I thought I could get through this evening, at least."

"I guess you didn't quite. But you surely have transcended it."

"Transcending's cheating," she said with a sobbing hiccup of laughter that blew tears onto my shirt front. "I didn't even take my tranquilizer, because that's cheating, too."

I nodded like Dr. Kildare and said that obviously the only way to come at a stone wall was head first, full speed. Only cowards went around or climbed over.

"I spent days figuring how this bunch might work together," she said. "Really, Dick. I didn't ask them here out of stupidity, though I know what you think. I can't make anything work any more. My parties were always good."

"You don't have to make anything work."

"Oh, yes. It's true. God exacts day labor, light denied."

"You're certainly a well-educated woman."

"Am I not?" she said. "Christ, Dick, have I not been educated? I'm so educated I don't know what anything means."

"Well, then, I'll cry too."

"You're not allowed," she said.

"I guess I'm not."

"Let me wash my face."

"Wash your face and we'll leave them to their gloom."

"They might cheer up when I'm gone. There's plenty of sauce."

"They can all take care of themselves," I coaxed.

"I know," she said. "I'm nobody's mama any more. It's only myself I have to think about, really."

On my arm she went out through the crowd of her guests with her eyes lowered—pausing only to run her hand over Harry Rinehart's gray crew-cut hair. He grinned and shortened his neck, nodding assurance that everything was, in his view, all right.

I think we knew as we turned onto Perry Street from the steps of her apartment house that however brief or extended our walk might be all the guests would be gone when we returned. All except Bernie, who had certain droits de maison and an anxious need to take care of Sheila that matched her need to take care of someone like him.

I don't mean that the party would all flee, its duty done, but rather that time seemed to have come unglued from its normal structure and had reattached to indescribable emotional realities, so that we could measure in our progress some correspondence to the cresting and diminishing of the party she had set going. Without calculation we would know when the way was clear for me to bring her home again.

I felt that though we had quit her party, we went out as its creatures. We went like doves sent out from a reeking ark, commissioned not so much to discover a farther shore as to scout, against hope, for the re-emergence of the familiar barns and arbors where our better years were drowned.

271

We knew what we were after by the time we had passed the brittle contemporary dazzle of Sheridan Square and were approaching the tall dark buildings where Varick Street begins. Sheila had asked—to settle the valueless present once and for all and get it out of the way—"I suppose it's plain that I'm sleeping with Bernie these days."

"Not plain."

"But you knew?"

I thought it honest to agree that I had guessed this. But Bernie had certainly not communicated it by implications I considered indelicate.

Of course he wouldn't, Sheila said with a visible show of ten fighting emotions and considerable obscenity. (Another reason why. I don't want to put this in dialogue form is that certain excesses of language, touching and perhaps beautiful in private converse, might entirely pervert the impression as gentleness I was so strongly aware of.) She said that of course young Mr. Masterson had not made the relationship obvious, because he was in many ways ashamed of it. He had been a protégé of Clem's (of the Andersons' as long as they were together) and could not reconcile his persisting sense of debt and, well, awe with his now privileged state. He really was delicate, and I must understand that the office he now performed had been undertaken out of hyperfastidiousness, not from any lack of it. It was she who had forced the intimacy on him, and his decent affection had obligated him to the indecent care of her rampant body.

The ingredient of moral pain was for each of them a strong erotic stimulant, satisfying further in that it helped each define himself in the midst of champion chaos as no mere allaying of the flesh could. "I obviously get something out of it," she said with a grin twisted to its barb like a fishhook. "Otherwise it wouldn't have lasted four months, as it has." The author of Beauty Bear, we tacitly agreed, need not pretend to a language capable of defining the suggested hypersubtleties involved.

And whatever else might be said of the relationship, I was to understand that it represented a degree of recovery from her behavior of last spring and summer. In a very short period, useless to remember, she had gone to bed with twenty or thirty men before she had settled down with Bernie. They had included old friends, many of them married. In fact most of the people (male) assembled back there for her party had taken the measures available to express the scope of their pity for her abandonment. She had "raped" them, she said. I understood that more than remorse spoke in her exculpation of them. She must have stated the moral, if not the literal, truth. She was trying to raise a monument to the departed hero. Yes, she must have seen his death beginning in his retirement from her, and all the deathless savagery of ancient female superstition must have kneaded the only material our time offers for memorials in a frustrate effort to make it stand enduringly. I understood her and was not much shocked—as one isn't by reincarnations of the truly primitive or mythic. The phallus had been raised on a headland above the empty whale roads, above the blue-black icy color of northern seas.

More shocking, because more sophisticated, was her attribution of motive to what should have been, I felt, merely "something that happened," motiveless, incomprehensible from the interior of the experience. She thought she had "whored" so busily because that would take the curse off Clem's whoring around. She thought, in parody of Adam, that the more common the sin the less chance that Clem alone would be found for punishment by those powers she never doubted must punish his unchaste presumption. "He can't get away with this," she said several times. It chilled me to my cold marrow to think that she was beyond contemplating any personal vengeance. I heard the accent of prophetic patience, that achieved willingness to disregard all appearances of immunity and then name the inevitable end of things as "punishment."

And yet, mercifully, her relationship with Bernie was bringing her back into contact with those quotidian realities so important to the other side of a woman's divided nature. Her time with Bernie was, she thought, approaching its end, too. And she would be glad when it was done. She could find enough to sustain her in the demanding lives of her children. It is almighty hard to surrender the personal will. But when it is done, something like life can begin again.

Presently she said that she regretted having encouraged me to make a trial of Marianne Luce. She did not want, really, to drag Janet and me "down into our muck." But I had already seen the vestige of a wish to strike at Clem by striking at one of his "faithfuls." Marianne had been one for years—like Bernie ever since that crazy time in Kansas. Sheila thought there had never been much between Clem and Marianne except a long correspondence. Did I know how extravagantly Clem wrote letters to some people "for no apparent reason" when he was so chary in writing to others?

"Clem's no respecter of persons," I said. "He can create a fictive personality by the mere act of addressing a letter to a name in a telephone book. Then, when the first letter has postulated a personality of a certain character as audience, listener, our Clem might very well

273

go on pouring himself into the imaginary receptacle he has created. Doesn't that sound like Clem? Well, anyway it sounds like Nietzsche finding his imaginary playmate. Or like Beth having the bodiless Snoober girl in for a tea party. Clem's still a child, isn't he?"

Not quite pleased with this attempt to divert her, Sheila growled that it might be so, and then she returned our attention to Marianne as she really was.

Sheila thought Marianne's recent marriage had gone to pieces because the girl wouldn't give up her hopes of Clem. "He'd encouraged her to think that if he ever left me he'd probably marry her." She laughed a vixen laugh and said, "Marianne's probably set to go on hoping through wives number three to seven."

Then in a more charitable mood she made it plain she held nothing against Marianne. As with "so many of Clem's women," there was something wonderful about her. Too bad Clem had the eyes to see wonder in a woman without the stability to resist. He couldn't marry them all.

We laughed together, and I said, "But isn't that just what the old boy thinks he may manage? Give him time and he'll do it."

We had spun, Sheila and I, like chips drifting in the periphery of a whirlpool down which they presently must plunge.

We began our plunge toward the sucking depths when I made out that all she envied Marianne was that Marianne had been receiving "the same kind" of letters that had come to Sheila during the war. That is—in the terms I had suggested—Marianne had supplanted her as that projection of Clem's self which he must glorify in its female objectification.

I sensed quickly enough how important this displacement was to Sheila and tried to rationalize away the special pain it caused her. The letters she had got were stuff of the past, I reminded her. However irrationally motives might be formed, surely envy of Marianne was inappropriate to her.

I said, "If you could, you wouldn't go back to those years when Clem was in the Army, would you? Back to all the frustration of his being away so long?"

Yes! That with all its mystery and impossibility was exactly what she wanted above anything else. The meaning of her life depended on something long done. She wanted (how vain, how silly, how destructive, even, of hope that their lives would continue at their fullest pulse, and yet how unmistakably true) to live over again her great victory, when she had snatched him away from the dark.

Being the recipient of those wartime letters was not something she valued for the sake of his absence then nor because of the frustrations and the unpleasant anxiety when he was in combat or "messed up with that girl in England." No, she valued all that in a lump because it was a lump with a victorious end. His return from the war, whole as we had seen him, was in her eyes a return from a cursed wandering that had begun when he left college. It was those years she wanted to live again, and if it meant never settling hereafter, very well, she would not settle.

"You've heard him talk about the 'first child,' haven't you?" she asked, beginning to explain. (I have to say that she explained. But of course one does not explain a thing so contrary to possibilities.) When I protested that I had never heard more than cryptic references, she laughed and said no one else had either, because while it was an important concept to Clem, it was also awkward, silly and generally subliterary. "Well," she persisted, "you know his poem about the stillborn child, anyhow."

I said that I did.

"What went into that wasn't made up out of the whole cloth. He never worked that way. But that poem's really obscure because Clem wouldn't come right out and say that he was the first child we had." She wiped her eyes. Impossible to label those tears, sprung from such a conglomerate of feelings.

I reminded her that to this day I knew little of what Clem and she were up to just before the war. For all I knew they might literally have had a stillborn child while they were living together in Washington. I could see reasons for keeping that a secret if it were the case.

"No," she said. "It was just when he'd feel he wasn't appreee-she-ated that he'd go sulking around and thinking he was stillborn. Imagine having that to deal with! And I'd like to see how she manages. Or when he sets up a tape recorder in the bathroom because he has his greatest thoughts shaving or moving his bowels. Ha."

Then she plunged into telling me something that, she said, might sound to me figuratively true. But, because it was Clem, I could understand that this was literally the truth. If I knew—as I did—how seriously Clem was able to take things that the rest of us dismissed, then I would be in a position to appreciate the truth of what she wanted, at last, to tell someone.

Like so many things "at last" revealed, after time has ironically changed their accent and isolated them from immediate concerns, her revelations struck me then as lacking force. They seemed more quaint than terrifying. The dragons were only dusty carcasses hung in museum cabinets—except that for her they had been quickened to life again by Clem's desertion.

She told me that Clem had been crazy before the war. Had "gone crazy" that last year in college. I thought, Uh huh, yes, he was. He certainly was. But nevertheless she meant something more than I had long ago granted and then ignored.

The principle around which he organized his insanity was that he intended no less than this: not to notice the war. Before he left college he had been turning this intention over, exploring what would be required to achieve such dissociation from something that the slogan makers were already enthusiastically labeling "total." He tried to foresee the values if he were successful. (It went something like this, a medley from science fiction, tales of the supernatural, and the children's fantasies that we are all trained to abolish before we reach ten: If he could sleep through the war, he might reappear afterward as the one uncontaminated male in the world. Uncontaminated? The contamination that he seemed to have guessed at was not the mechanical contamination of radiation, spoiled genes or physically hereditary mutations. It was some guessed-at essence which, he thought, the race had managed to preserve thus far in spite of assault. The conditions of the present war would spoil it unless its guardian psyche found a way of enfolding it deeply, preserving it against the exposure of the experience just then beginning. Whoever found this way—Clem had, naturally, never heard of anyone else who was even looking for it—would be among the few moral survivors of the epoch. Females were another matter, he thought. Either they were too lowly to count or too lofty to be endangered. He was never sure which. But he believed, at any rate, that there would be need of another Noah who could repopulate the earth with a human stock when the other humanoids had become the soulless debris of the aftermath. He was elected if he could find this way to seal himself and the human essence in, like jelly under paraffin, like a space explorer frozen in an ice block for the long journey from nebula to nebula.)

At some point after September 1939, and before Sheila found him again, he must have concluded that deep insanity, amounting to catatonia, would be required for his project, since, given his sensibility and the nature of those hectic times, it was impossible to notice birds in the trees, children playing in the green parks, beer in a glass or clouds driven before the wind without finding references to the war that had been set loose in Europe. As texts from Pascal or Eliot could make clear to anyone who chose to believe them, all action, even motion itself, led to the universal crime. "All man's troubles come from his being unwilling to sit still in one room," said Pascal. Clem took this to be truth instead of literature—and I knew it to be his one calamitous peculiarity that he never bothered to distinguish between them as the rest of us do.

He went to work at making himself insane. Though his purpose had carried him far enough to produce the superficial strangeness that Don Hazeltine and others had noticed, it had not produced the condition he required. He was crazy, but he could not achieve the ideal isolation. When he tried to reduce himself to physical immobility, itches and hunger beat him back from his wish to "go out." The Boy from Boda was too strong to be beaten by regressive wishes forced on him by the disjointure of the times.

It was then, in his need—as if the need were guiding him or perhaps even shaping objectivity to its subjective paradigm—he had found his guru. (Sheila referred to him as a "dirty old man" who had worked many years in an A & P warehouse in Newark until he got his "cult" assembled. But she had never seen him. I took it that the epithet "dirty" referred to his corruptive mysticism rather than to his physical state.)

The guru offered what seemed a practicable alternative to insanity. Rather, he offered two alternatives which Clem as buyer might choose between. Clem might get either a "breath body" or a "diamond body." For one who might expect presently to face artillery and small-arms fire, the advantages are obvious, for does the idea of an immortal "breath body" not correspond to and refine the universal dream of soldiers that they will get a million-dollar wound to save them from further exposure while it leaves the vital self unharmed? And a "diamond body"—is it not a child's dream of bullets glancing harmlessly away from the armor of consciousness? "Put on the whole armor of God," the chaplains prayed, or admonished. That armor would seem to be a more publicly available version of the diamond body that Clem sought for himself.

And yet, of course, the search for a diamond body had come to no more than the preceding imitatio Nijinsky. Instructions from the guru were only a phase in the psychological journey he was making—which, as I heard it and have reflected on it, so strangely resembles the journey of the soul after death on its way to a reincarnation. It was the first leg of his "night sea journey" from which he would return when, for him, the war was over. Following his symbolic death he had been for a while without desires, next had desired something that represented a personal immortality, and at last, in going to Sheila in Washington, had been lured by the "honey of generation" into a desire for rebirth, when his voyage should be done.

In those first months of living together in the winter of 1941–42 they must have been enacting a fantasie à deux. I don't really doubt Sheila's statement that she was "the sane one," and yet, clearly, she had been more than a little tainted by his crazy demands and convictions. At the time he came to her, a great many rags and tassels of his recent pieties still clung to him. He was not so sure yet that sitting together in catatonic silence was not the best way for them to spend an evening. When she fell on an escalator at work and was brought home with a badly sprained ankle, he assured her that if such a thing had happened to him his (partly finished) diamond body would have permitted him to go on without a murmur of pain. He would not work, because all labor advanced the evil on which the world had embarked. Further, he made it clear how much he disapproved of her job, which, nevertheless, paid their rent and bought their vegetables (she was not allowed, either, to eat of those living things which had features in common with man and God). Sexual contact or stimulation of any kind was totally outlawed in their apartment. Even the taking of a cold shower was regarded as a lapse from grace, since it might indicate the mechanical frustration of impulses that should have been controlled by mind.

How had Sheila put up with all this? Beyond the question of how she had endured was the question of how she had taken it seriously.

"Oh, it didn't last as long as all that. Maybe three months or four. The truth is, it was kind of fun."

How had it ended?

"I seduced him, of course," she said, with such a happy explosion of laughter that I could only conclude she had escaped briefly from the present to that strange point where memory can satisfy the bruised nerves and dishonored body. "After all that time it was great! Jesus Christ! But you know, for two or three weeks Clem kept pretending he didn't know what was going on. He'd break off a conversation in the middle and have at me, and as soon as he was dressed and back where he'd been sitting before he gave in he'd pick up the sentence exactly where he left it off. Oh, he was funny. And if I'd mention it he was apt to break into tears and look over his shoulder like he was remembering Paradise.

"Only, once I'd got him started it was funny how quickly he normaled up. It was spring, you see, and before you knew it I had a roaring boy on my hands. It was just like we'd picked up from the summer before the war began, but it wasn't like he'd suffered any loss of mind or memory in all this time between. It was, truly it was, more like what he said."

And what Clem had said—presumably known in some questionable sense of that word—was that a child had been delivered into the world in that wartime spring, an ephemera who was not so much his double as his echo, a kind of invisible imprint made by his energies on the essential stuff of the world. (All the terms I can muster are terribly uncertain, so much so that I can take them only as descriptive of a psychic state. But precisely that is what counts most in the development I am trying to trace.) The child had a sort of sexual origin. Its recognition, at least, had been impossible before the two of them resumed their normal sex life. The child lived in incredible peril. The massed cunning and fury of the war was, indeed, aimed at "getting it." At the same time it was invulnerable to everything except some magic betrayal that he sometimes referred to as "denial."

The presence of this immaterial child in Clem's thought was certainly not a hallucination, nor had there ever been anything particularly obsessive in the way he spoke of it. When it was mentioned between them, he was willing enough to label it a "memorable fancy" or disparage it as a notion—even to say that it was lacking in value to the extent that it was difficult to describe concretely. He claimed no communication with it. He did not expect it to be, in any way, a guardian spirit; rather, the shoe was on the other foot, he was obligated to defend it as well as he could. In other words, he seemed to reorganize his rationality around this irrational projection without conceding it any authority over psychic processes of an inherently different kind.

Perhaps the oddest thing about all this is that Sheila, who had categorized the rest of his mysticism either as an ominous nuisance or as fun (depending on where it seemed to lead practically), came to believe in "the child" very much as he did. The undescribed and questionably real thing was there, like an imaginary point in space where all the discernible hopes of their lives converged. She believed that the recognition of the child, whatever it might be, had permitted Clem's return to her, and naturally she was grateful to it.

In this phase he had come far enough to mock at his ideas of developing a breath body or diamond body, had socialized his opposition to the war sufficiently to consider registering as a conscientious objector. Actually he was already registered for the draft as "atheist," and attempts to change at this late date might have involved him in formidable legal tangles, which in turn might well have roused again his stubborn intent to become catatonic rather than serve. She thought it was the idea of the child that slowly eroded his resistance. Not that even here the idea worked directly on him, but under its benign influence he was reassembling the structure of a personality that at last wanted to engage with the given world. By the time he was drafted in January 1943 Clem was conscientiously "trying on" the commonplaces that guided so many others willingly into the services.

Only one virtue of the old Clem was conspicuously absent in the new man—he would not attempt to write, and he read only those things which, in his view, would improve his character. (The only example Sheila gave of this was Prescott's Conquest of Mexico, from which Clem derived the notion that he ought to be like Montezuma!)

He seemed to be afraid of writing, and, to the extent that this was a reasoned fear, his reason was that composition would require the psychic energies that now had been dedicated to "preservation of the child in the midst of war."

She had been prepared to hear nothing from him, once he had gone into the Army. Up to the day he left for induction he kept insisting that she go on with her life as if he had never existed so that they would be invulnerable to circumstances that might prey on them if they did not wholeheartedly accept their separation. She was to take up with other men—almost whether she wanted to or not!—and he would let old nature take its course. They would remain linked by purely "spiritual means." He would not trust mechanical communications, he said. Or that was what it amounted to. There was more danger to them in scrambled communication than in prolonged silence.

They had come to no agreement on that, though on everything else they had come to what Sheila remembered as a nearly perfect harmony. She had put him on the train to be inducted swearing that she would be true to him and would write. Sadly he shook his head and promised he would live the life of a soldier and never answer.

Letters began to come from him within a month. I must understand that they were wonderful letters. Taken in sum, they were better than anything else he had ever written. Clem had—always—thought so too. Wherever they moved after the war they had carted along the trunk full of his wartime letters like a kind of household god. Clem had never used them in anything he wrote later, though he had always said that he meant to someday. It had seemed to them both that it was enough that the letters existed. For when they began to arrive, first from the camps in the Southeast and then from England and France, Sheila knew that she had won. They were the personality she had brought to birth in happiness and against odds. Just because the odds were so great against anything of the sort happening, the victory they represented was that much more clearly defined. The letters were the sign that what he had required in the most extravagant and world-refusing excursions of the spirit could be made tangible—nearly tangible—in his relation to her. They were the sign of the great marriage that had, maybe, been poorly represented and finally ruined by the way they lived together after the formal ceremony had been performed.

Listening to all this, tucking much of it away undigested to ruminate on later, I believed her account insofar as one can be said to believe anything couched in unverifiable terms. And in my belief I alternated between pity and hope. On the surface it was pitiful to see her turning from the defeat of the present back to a victory no longer pertinent. I thought it would be even more pitiful if she were deluding herself that Clem's absence now was merely a repetition of his temporary absence during the war. But how can the spirit heal itself except by withdrawing before it attempts another leap forward? Wasn't it better for her to see the significance of her life in what she took to be its best moments than to dwell on the details that had led to their breaking up?

We had been rambling from bar to bar far south of the Village while she told me this, and I was, at the very least, glad to see that she was calmer than when we had left her apartment.

But there is no end to the degrees of suffering which seem to spin through consciousness like a great ring of endless light, segmented like a spectrum so that disparate kinds may be distinguished, nevertheless continuous as life. Passionate in her long talk about the abstract or mystical relations between her and Clem, she had to be calm, I suppose, to bear talking of a concrete act.

"I burned all his letters the other day," she said.

I can't recall without a shudder the moment she said this. It seems to me I have very seldom stood so perilously in the slippery places as while she waited for my comment. She had truly not meant to drag me into their "muck," but in realizing this I had made the error of concluding that she was not dangerous. If I had said the wrong thing then, or even an incautious thing, I would have been in the position of a man who is swung on by a very fine-ground blade, feels nothing and laughs, "You missed," then hears his attacker warning, "Don't try to shake your head." If I had said either "So what?" or "You shouldn't have," I would have stepped off into darkness and must thereafter have taken anything she said as diabolical. It was she who had phrased the considerations, drawn the argument of life down to a pinpoint and balanced it there.

"They were your letters," I said.

"They were mine," she answered—not diabolically, content to shoulder, since she had to, the load of guilt and love I had refused to topple.

"I had to," she said.

"I'm sure of that."

"It's not so great a literary loss."

"I'm sure of that too."

"I wouldn't have, even so, if Clem had let me have them around without reminding me that I had them. He called me about a month ago."

"Oh, dear."

"Yes," she said. "Oh, dear. He said at first he was only checking to see if I still had them. Something about this damn play of his. He's still rewriting it. It's ten million words long if they ever published all the scraps. If no one had said anything in the British Isles between 1943 and '45, he would have said it all for them by this time, GI's and natives. But he pretended that he wanted to check something he'd written to me once about Cecile Potter."

"So you said ...?"

"That I goddam well didn't want the letters degraded into anything he was writing now. So this started off some low-level comedy dialogue and I accused him of caring more about something he'd written than he did about the kids, and ..."

While she cried a bit I put my Band-Aid on the gut wound by saying, "It would have been unworthy of you two to bar any holds once you declared war."

"So I burned them. I didn't even read them over before I burned them. Just phweet—" she sprinkled her fingers upward—"they went into the fireplace."

"I suppose he knows they're burned."

"I called and told him."

"You had to."

"I did have to. He's got to break clean, this once. He's got to give up the notion I have anything he wants. I thought it would teach him—"

I shook my head.

"All right, I didn't think that. He's hard to educate, and she'll find that out. Wait until she finds the tape recorder in the bathroom because he has his great ideas when he's shaving. All that ..." All that which she was missing so badly.

"What happened?"

"The bastard came and camped in my apartment for two or three days after I told him. He sat in that chair by the window all the time and wouldn't talk to me, but sat all hunched up, crying. Day after day he sat there. Or he slept on the floor. I couldn't make him go home. Finally Cinderella got up nerve to call me and see if he was here, and Christ, I was so tired of it by then I told her to come and get him while I was at work. I don't know how she did it. But then, I've never known how she did it. Clem says she's got a great soul, and I think he's probably right. But how ..."

"How will she keep him?" I prompted when she fell silent.

"Oh, she won't keep him," she said peremptorily, as if that part of the future were a foregone conclusion. She smiled eerily. "He won't come back to me, either. That's what you thought I had at the bottom of my sticky little mind, isn't it, Dick?"

"What then?"

She shook her head, as if, knowing, she must not tell me. With a purposeful shift in tone she said, "You're going to dinner with them tomorrow night, aren't you? Cinderella is going to cook her duck."

"You're in very close communication."

"Or I wouldn't have been such a jealous bitch to call you down here tonight when you wanted to be with them?" I took what comfort I could from the lightness of her tone. At least some of the symptoms had been relieved in the last several hours. "Clem told me when you were coming and where you'd be staying. I was guessing about the duck, but Clem's mother always sends one at Christmas. I hope you enjoy it. I really do. I mean to enjoy things myself from here on out. I want my kids. The letters are gone. Clem's gone. That's the way things are."

Because there was nothing else to be done we clinked our glasses and drank to the way things are. Then she asked me to take her home. Purged with fatigue as much as with confession, we took a cab back to her apartment where Bernie was waiting. "Don't come up," she said. "I'll straighten up sometime and then ..." The street lights struck the whites of her eyes so that for an instant she seemed inwardly luminous. It may have been—it may only have seemed—that she had rolled the pupils up under the lid. Her fingernails were on my wrist, between cuff and glove. "I know I never learn from him fast enough to keep up, but wasn't there some other way for him to teach me?"

The old doubt, unchanged from college days in spite of all that had intervened and should have driven it away. A doubt that did not correspond with the facts, but was a fact of overwhelming importance. I couldn't answer her.

"Damn him. He's got to invent me some kind of a life from here on out," she said. "By myself I can't be sure."

Then she laughed and kissed me and went inside.

Afterward this evening too would take its place in the complex of knowledge that amounted to a judgment, not so much of weakness as of great strength still insufficient to its task. But even then I knew I would always blame her for burning the letters—blame her for doing that to herself and all she loved most. I saw in this act a portent of the way she would helplessly dehumanize the image of their father for her children. Unless they lived in that horrid mental prosperity that simply does not care, they had a chance to grow up thinking their father had been an excellent man, a writer whose books they could cherish doubly because their name was on the spine. That much was secured for them.

But the letters, which Sheila had made me see as a birth link between mute reality—"crazy" reality—and the unalterable forms of his published work, were perpetually denied them. This denial would change their father's truest voice into the voice of a stranger. Of their least corruptible heritage they might think "good" or "true" but could hardly think "ours" since they had no way to determine how it had become his.

For "the children" I unavoidably came to substitute the concept of the future or even the more inclusive concept of us—we who strain to hear. On the other side of a gulf we have heard voices telling us that greatness and beauty are eternal, that "one name shall not die," that neither "marble nor the gilded monuments of princes shall outlast this powerful rhyme," that the freshness of a girl's cheek or an old man's moral daring will have their immortality "in black ink." But we know this is only poetry. There is no bridge, so what should be an incessant dialogue becomes a fading monologue as the world burns behind us.

As I write now, a tormenting thought drums constantly in my mind: If I had all the letters, I could show you something more important than excellence—what we in frustration call value—in Clem's work; I could show you the silences from which it came, so that the silences in our lives might echo the same measures.

I have only fragments to show. After Clem's death Sheila sent me a packet that contained a few letters of his mailed to her from England and France and a few loose-leaf pages from one of his notebooks.

A very brief scrawl accompanied the package: "I wasn't altogether thorough. What's left isn't Our Boy in the Great War, as you'll see. Of course I want them back. Not so much for myself any more—I still go blind when I look at them—but for Jess and maybe even Lulie someday. They'll have to make what they can of them, because that's all there is. Only I'll tell them I was happy when I got them, however unhappy they may seem."

# 11

I HAVE CHOSEN to intrude as little of my own comment as seemed commensurate with minimum factual clarity on the following letters. I would not insist that they are any more of a "war story" than they appear to be. For the hypothetical person who has never read a novel dealing with the Second World War, I had better point out right now that here he will find no re-creation of how it was to be a soldier. The peculiarity of the author certainly overshadows any generalization about the quality of circumstance shared by so many and already documented so copiously in books of fiction and fact—in Clem's *Angel at Noon* among others.

At one point it seemed expedient to add a larger factual gloss to the episode with Cecile Potter in England, since that has so much to do with Clem's play *Death and the Devil*, but I chose finally to leave this bit of reality to be inferred somewhere between the letters and the final dramatic form. The letters and the Broadway production are both "ways of looking" at something that occurred, and again I would suggest that Clem's way of looking defines his fate in its progress better than any circumstances along the way. Because he was a writer, but only because he was a writer, the experience with Cecile had consequences that integrate it into his life.

I have not even taken pains to locate the letters geographically or in time. It is enough to note that Clem went to the European theater and stayed a little more than two years. The voyage depicted by these fragments is rather more like one of Gulliver's middle voyages than it is like the historic excursions of soldiers. Or it is like the Baudelairean travel where we go "berçant notre infini sur le fini des mers."

The first two letters were written at sea on the way to England, some nine months after Clem's induction.

## LETTER I

APO 927

STAINLESS WOMAN,

The riddle again, answered again, riddled again. This time they've set evidence of ocean around me as if something so big ought to do the convincing trick, but I'm still not sure the war exists. The fat ship and my fat captain (officers must have port) do not care whether I believe in them or their warlikeness or not. But something else does. I Am, says the War. And I recommend for strangeness the experience of standing in a gossipy chow line on B deck, inching your way through a slick of puke toward the big kettles, listening the while to Nobadaddy read the war news over the P.A. system, all the while silently arguing. The perpetual argument now goes something like this:

I AM: "I pinched that little gullie's ass so hahd she damn near jumped in front of the subaway train at Tom's Squaih. She was all prepead to take a strong dislikin' to me or maybe scream. Real cultivated gull, but shee-it, they all the same. You know that? You know they all the same? She so doggone little I could put her on and spin her like a piano stool. Crahd like she lost her Daddy when I told her shee-it I wouldn't marry her cause I got a better gull back home in Petal." "Thought you said they was all the same." "Sho. Told the gull in Petal the same about a gull in Biloxi."

HER PRIVATE, ME (in the guise of Pope Clement XIII, known to his cardinals as "Lucky," speaking ex cathedra on the occasion of his election): "Now that the votes are in I'll tell you boys a little secret. War does not exist. It is the opiate of the masses. As an illusion it has no future. It is no more than an anthropomorphic projection of man's primordial fears and aspirations on an essentially neutral cosmos. Universality of belief can no longer be taken as serious evidence of its objective existence. Further, the voice that has just spoken to us out of the whirlwind is in error. All girls are different."

I AM (whose jaw is like Roosevelt's, touchable father to the people): "The massed, angered forces of common humanity are on the march."

HPM: Could be.

I AM (in the voice of the P.A., which, with the eerie hooting of destroyers, sometimes pierceth my guard of skepticism): "Knock off all games. The smoking lamp is out."

HPM: That's a dandy iambic line. Wish I'd written it myself.

*"The smoking lamp is out and toward the dark*
*The convoy swings on azimuths of doubt.*
*On Hatch A shall worship the devout*
*As here below the profane M.P.s bark,*
*'Knock off your games, the smoking lamp is out.'"*

I AM: "How come an educated poet such as yourself did not apply for a commission or become a conscientious objector?" (No fancy, this. It was demanded of me by a hot-eyed type who has been hovering three feet above my left shoulder since we left Camp Shanks.)

HPM: I'd be the weakest link in the chain of command. Why should I object if this is what they want?

I AM: "Koomph, koomph, koomph, koomph." (This is the 20-mm. guns on our roly-poly ship, firing at flak bursts as they do every day before lunch. It is rumored that this firing is practice, but I have now learned just how strong the instinct of play is among the military gents. Perhaps there is even an aesthetic instinct, for I must say that the varied ranks of various black visible in sea and North Atlantic clouds invite the accent marks of flak and the chalky parabolas of tracer fire. I imagine that the Admiral of our convoy must regard this constant arch of sky as his Sistine Chapel and the guns his brushes.)

HPM: War is beautiful. If war did not exist, it would be necessary to invent it. "Some men there are who cannot hold their water when the bagpipe blows in the nose," and I'll admit I noticed a leetle drip myself the first time I took my, ha ha, battle station under one of the 20s, immobilized by a life preserver. That bang-bang compresses my prostate most pleasurably and if I were a millionaire I would certainly have some heavy guns on the estate. Do not underestimate the temptation war holds for your antisaint Anthony. Nothing is so lovely as to take these mighty guns in hand and send in the fire. "Take it, Comrade Voyager."* On the other hand I am (except in extreme anger or in alcohol) a greater coward than you know yet and I deeply want not to hurt anybody. Grant them diamond bodies, Lord, that my deadliest shots may ricochet upward to Thy Sporting Throne. It is a good thing I am a poet (as I seem to be, again), because my impulses are flatly irreconcilable, and if I were anything else—say the company clerk with marksman qualifications that they think I am—life would be impossible.

So much for the daily argument. I tell you, anyway, things you already know about me. Only I dare think that in the retelling they may have some silver edge of novelty which is more important than anything else. (Nobody in his right mind would read a book just to have it told them that somebody was doing things they could easily do themselves. They shouldn't anyway.) New surroundings make old stories new in some way I hope to understand. New experiences "open" old ones. I don't know how, but I can tell you now what you looked like the first night I met you better than I could have the day afterward. I have a notion that bugs like Dick and Felix Martin really may know more about Donne, Milton or Fenimore Cooper than their children did. The process of knowing is a long and spooky one, not at all solved by "seeing with your own eyes." (Who is you who owns the eyes?)

News? Hmmmm. The ship goes east. The propellers turn just the way you know they do.

All my love,

CLEMENT

## LETTER II

APO 927

### COMRADE GOLFING,

What is most characteristic of the American soldiers sailing to smash the Hitlerite in his lair? They do not mean to leave home. They have tied an end of their rubber band to the dock in New York, and they hold tight to their end of it.

What will happen? Unless dialectical materialism errs, the band will stretch past its maximum and break. When the too much loyalty breaks, how finds his way home from whale road the hero?

Rubber band tied to dock equals, you note, the cord of Ariadne held by Theseus as he descends into the labyrinth, and when this Percy among perçus caught me this morning I knew it was a poem or two. With it humming amidst my ears and with the intent of profiting from the languors of the voyage, I took myself up on the port side of Hatch A (for once not being used as a prayer platform) with a right hand full of GI stationery and my left clutching my Schaeffer white-dot pen. Flexing salt-air-uncreased O.D.s to place my butt between a sergeant reading Gone with the Wind and Ogilvie writing a nonstop letter (or prayer) to his wife, in mid-crouch, my eye noting the pomp of our destroyer escort feathering green waves to starboard, it occurred to me that my true insight had been not so much poetical as statal.

I saw at once it was my duty to write to our President, urging him to reconsider the cost of this expedition.

*Dear Franklin: Should the cord contact be broken between the American fighting man and his natural bride, the still virgin America, I shudder to contemplate the consequences. Ariadne will weep in the mountains, Mr. President, another in that grievous line of disappointed women that began with Pocahontas and Little Mohee. Surely, Sir, a man of your etc. must scruple etc.*

Mentioned my plan to Ogilvie as I sat down then, and he agreed it was a pity this war was not being managed by poets, but thought there was no remedy at this too late date.

The sergeant, overhearing, turned and asked me decently was I a writer. You cannot answer that honestly to a man who has Margaret Mitchell in his hand. So I told him, oh, that I played around with it a little. "I have trifled with the ambiguities, Sergeant."

That answer did not satisfy him, and he kept peering at my paper as I scribbled—a paper which in good truth began to look more like one of those lists that women make up before they go to the A & P than like the fixed, inevitable squares of verse that one encounters on the anthology page.

Be consoled that the military do not seem to bother me much for being a poet. I have such wit and bounce that they generally come to think I am a cute little rat, at least.

Later:

I can't finish my elastic poem. Something inside— neither heart, mind, nor gut, but more central—is still very weak, weak as a newborn baby. There are times when I tell myself that going without sex (the key archetype of poetic business) makes it unlikely that I will finish anything, but then I reprimanded myself with the reflections that such impure thoughts are not for one venturing on such an awful mission as I. I mean to win, now that they've got my Irish up!

You know very well that I have chosen this war. I could up to the last hour at the induction center have got out easily by accepting a "psychologically unfit" classification. But I chose it, and choose to be its poet and redeem it if I can.

Ever,

THESEUS

## LETTER III

APO 927

DARLING

it's

an

anticlimax.

While we were on that frigging boat amidst the pomp of destroyers, great guns, and battle wagons, running blacked out, everyone felt like it was the evening before Gettysburg, Waterloo, or Passchendaele. ("It is, it is! the cannon's opening roar!") Hotspur Anderson was prepared to bundle all the service records, directives and the Captain's hooch (my special charge) into a foot locker or burn them and lay wire in the very teeth of advancing Panzers. The War was just ahead of the lead destroyer.

And here we are, stationed not five miles from—— [Deleted by censor. For several months before and after D Day, Clem was stationed near Oxford.] A feeling goes around, well shared by me, that this was not what we gave ourselves for in the anxiety dreams of taking ship.

I am sore that my splendid image of Ariadne's thread drawn beyond the breaking point has been demonstrated untrue. We sit here on our bunks in a litter of mail with Ariadne's filament looped, looped, and relooped around our husband shoulders, and now I think that the Hitler Minotaur will be strangled by spare lengths of the Silver Cord. Surely *SS Panzerkampfwagen* cannot prevail against American Love. Ogilvie's mail, for example, contained a round dozen new pictures of his wife, though he saw her in New York the day before we sailed. Rommel, despair! Hitler, fugit! We hurl against you—Domestic Love.

Dragel, Burford, George, Sorel, and I have passes this afternoon and are going to scout for Lady Chatterley. We have heard already many funny stories about English girls. They are supposed to believe that nothing is immoral as long as they remain standing.

Actually, you know, I shall merely observe the quaint customs from afar. Fate having brought me to this spot, I will do nothing more reckless than raid the libraries, introduce myself to or as Mr. Chips, and post myself at the exact same spot where Jude the Obscure stood staring up at Learning's battlements. Forbidden by absence to press my curly nose against that breast which was the model for the left breast of Helen, I shall nudge it to the window of culture's candy store.

CLEM THE OBSCURE

P.S. My old New York buddy Henderson Paul has got a cushy job on Yank, though in the South Pacific area. He is one man who is certainly going to tell the truth about this war, because he certainly knows it. No one will ever shake that boy's testimony. I suppose I'll write to him, just to let him know the men with the net didn't get me, as he so freely predicted. He'll answer, "The game ain't over yet, Anderson." He loves to talk in baseball, a language that makes the truth about the war even truer.

CLEM ANDERSON

## LETTER IV

APO 927

DARLING,

Have I given up my great conceit of "the child"? I'd give it up if I could, but it won't give me up. I gather from what you say that you still suspect I thought I was the child. Never!

Not the child but a monk of the child am I. It is funny how military service has brought out the monkish in my nature, that adaptability to a strict regimenting of hours in which each day the soul performs its discreet functions. I ought to prepare a book of hours, not to follow, since I follow it anyway without exterior guidance, but as a testament. I have mentioned the Hour of Directive Dreams and the Hour of Bleak Rebellion. Exactly halfway between these (10:30–11:30, otherwise known as Second Piss Call) there is an Hour of Composition when messages sent from all over the celestial and terrestrial globes coalesce in my pentagonal nerve centers.

With coffee and cigarette in hand—the Morning Report completed, the Special Orders cut and dispatched, Sergeant Hinkel appeased and the Captain anticipated—I open the useful dispatches and, each morning, compose the skeleton of at least one poem. (I never finish anything at this time. It takes weeks for even short poems to finish themselves when, as is still infrequent, they ever do.) It is the grand strategy that is made then, the mental formation into which I will try to lure the wary, twice-shy stuff at my and its leisure. But as my rectum begins to twitch with the triple creative stimuli (le fume, le café, et l'ordure, as Sainte-Beuve should have put it) I compose with the authority of G. Catlett Marshall, author of North Africa, Sicily, and other works of the spirit. The nature of my dispatches? Not all of them can be revealed en clair, but I can tell you that lots of the best of them are censored newspaper stories, which I either unscramble by the Anderson Method or, more frequently, take straight. One of my major discoveries (one I was bound to make) has been that the truth about the war is exactly what people are being told about it. That is, the effort to lie on the part of correspondents and censors merely traps them into giving a

293

truth beyond their intentions. "I am the wings when me they fly," said the Real War. For instance, let me tell you that I have become a fan of Henderson Paul's dispatches in Yank and have even resumed a sly correspondence with him to tell him how valuable (I don't tell him half!) I find his on-the-spot tales from the South Pacific. He did a grand bit on the Kwajalein invasion. (Did you see it?) Well, there were no stained stones kissed by the American dead in Sergeant Paul's prose and no Bibles stopping bullets either! (One of the main things about the Second World War is that it is not the First World War.) This war took its inspiration from Stephen Crane and Conrad. ("There were five men in the rubber boat and none of them knew the color of each other's skin.") The second man in the rubber boat, according to the Paul dispatches and others, is always a black man, but you never find that out until right at the end. The fourth man is always a Jew with a name consisting of two iambs, and the iambs indicate his faith and racial origin at once, while color is still being held in suspension. The third man—the caesural pause between Negro and Jew—is from the Midwest, ordinarily from a town which he quaintly calls "Dee Moyns." The fifth man is from Texas or Little Italy, depending on whether a masculine or feminine ending is required. The first man is a coward and a salesman (probably of rubber goods, though sometimes this metier is thinly disguised by calling him a tire salesman).

Now, this undisguisable concern with number, place in series, suspension and synecdoche is clearly the very stuff of poetry and the stuff poetry is best able to re-create, and the only reason Henderson doesn't write it in verse is he doesn't know anything about verse. Numbers come through him (and his dispatches) like grease soaking up through paper. The basic pattern of numbers on which the war is founded shows with the reliability of certain key combinations that appear in the ranting of a spiritualistic medium. (I'm sure this is all as apparent to G. C. Marshall as it is to me. He knows that second man is a man of color, knows how to spring the rhythm by omitting him or moving him down to third or fifth.) The object of my work is to make this substructure of metric number perceptible to everyone, including Paul, if he ever wants to know; and this requires the bit of heightening that formalized verse can give.

I'm dead sold and enthusiastic about using only lignes trouvées (like "Knock off all games, the smoking lamp is out") in classic forms. (It became part of a villanelle, not a very good one, but that don't matter. If a man is serious about his work he should not all the time be trying to produce only good things.)

So far the main result of all the great insights that come in the Hour of Composition has not been much poetry I want to show anyone, even you. They (insights) are rather often sublimated into my first duty of the afternoon, which is to keep up to date the battle maps in the day room, which I have done in an inspirational manner. One afternoon I created near-panic by moving the flags around in such a way as to show that the Nazis had outflanked us in both theaters by airborne landings in Alexandria, Capetown, and Vancouver. In the next three or four days I had restored hope by a series of countermoves that would have left Clausewitz dizzy and had posted orders of the day on the Information Bulletin Board that managed to provoke considerable theorizing from all quarters. The whole company was interested and all went well until we got a visit from the I.G., who went mad when he saw the board and told me in all seriousness that I had risked the death penalty by acting as an enemy agent. Reduced to the rank of private, I have joined the company of Billy Mitchell, Charles de Gaulle and all such as have paid the price of being ahead of their times. Refusing to be embittered, I sent a letter to Marshall (copy to Eisenhower) offering to resume my rank should the adverse situation I have foreseen become a reality.

Later (2 days, in fact):

Another probable reason I have finished nothing adequate is my social life, which is now composed pretty much of visits to the Potter family. Brother Gerald Potter picked us up first—Ogilvie, Harlan, and I—no doubt because we are what his mother somewhat condescendingly calls "college men," though her idea of a college in the Midwest is almost literally Mark Hopkins on one end of a log and a student on the other. (And 'oo, pray, is this 'Opkins?)

Gerald, limping from a wound he got at Tobruk, found us in a pub one afternoon and asked us home to tea. We bicycled out, I'll have you know, coasting the last two miles among trees I recognized from fairy tales and illustrations in my fourth-grade reader.

I may have recognized the Potters' house and their way of living from reading E. M. Forster. (Every restrained gesture says, "Oh, I'm nothing; it's the inner life that counts." They truly rejoice at any successful raid on the ranks of the benighted.) But more than likely my sense of déjà vu results from the preparations made by H. Warwick Lloyd. Even the smell of the Potters' living room had been transplanted, I felt, from that delicate boar's nest that Warry once established at Emmy Polk's. He was such a fool that he became an artist.

The Potters specialize in a grand view and a vast amount of impeccably polished silver in relation to the pitiful amount of high tea or dinner they can offer. In manners whose chief beauty is their capacity to function in all circumstances.

When they found—I told them—that I was a practicing poet, they really clung hard to me, though in the course of things Harlan and Ogilvie have moved away in search of livelier fun.

Gerald and I have a perpetual mock-heroic game that goes oftentimes like this:

ANDERSON: Someday it will be said of the poet, "Anderson never read a single book."

GERALD: Would he had read a thousand!

Mrs. Potter considers me the voice of America, preferable to what she gets on her radio, and though I shake her by such devices as pretending to believe that Grey of Fallodon was (1) a hunting dog painted by Landseer or (2) the father of Tarzan of the Apes, she joys to sit with her stick between her knees and debate my jelling ideas of tragedy, which I have told you center in the idea of the child and which I won't give up for all her serenity and careful reasoning.

"Well, Clement," she says, "if it isn't the fate of the masses that is tragic and if it isn't the fate of individuals in this war that's tragic, what is it, then?"

And I, pacing around her parlor, striking the fringe of her chairs with my bloody ashplant, I say, "Man."

"How can we comprehend Man except as the mass or as the individual?"

"We'd better learn," I say, with prophecy darkening my brow. I squinch my eyes up very oddly and say, "It is the child, the burning child."

And Mrs. Potter says, "I believe that in America the child is venerated in a way unknown here." And nods sadly as if we all know something we can't tell her, which indeed is true, up to a point. I do know things which I can't tell anyone yet until I have distilled a language out of this war that we can all share.

I belabor her terribly with incoherences. The more I learn, the harder it is for me to speak so anyone can understand me. And I think there ought to be times when she would merely say, "You're talking nonsense."

At any rate, she and I love each other dearly. You know how I am always finding parents and substituting them for my real ones. That makes me just right for her, since I suppose she is always finding sons—besides Gerald, who is so good he ought to be enough for her but doesn't seem to be. One night on pass I stayed out at their house, and when a windstorm came up in the night Mrs. P came charging into my room to make sure I was all right. I have never seen such a ravenous maternal glare as hit me from under her curlers, and she retucked my blankets as though I were ten and needed to be soothed about the heavenly pother before she left.

There is also in the family a daughter named Cecile— very buck-toothed, or with a short upper lip, but also enormous breasts, nice eyes, and hair like Charlotte Brontë's.

She is very quiet while the rest of us spend all our time together jabbering a mile a minute. It is understood (by me, too—I am not slow to catch on) that she is Daddy's girl, though Daddy Potter was killed flying a glider in the German Alps back in the good days of the Weimar Republic. I think it is implied that her quiet stems from the simple circumstance of his absence. There are no complicated psychological knots in Cecile. She is the kind of girl of whom it could be said with perfect propriety that her "heart was broken" by this or that circumstance. Her heart is not broken, but the cat has got her tongue. She will never get over her loss, and no one thinks she ought to. A perfect spinster.

MONTEZUMA

## LETTER V

APO 927

FIT AUDIENCE,

I'm glad you liked "Country Matters" as much as I did. I wouldn't have sent it, even yet, if I had had any doubts about it. Now I'm nearly finished with another big poem, probably to be called, "It Was a Machine that Slew the City"—

*a steel-rimmed eye*
*That watched it die,*
*Not I.*

Anderson sings on every bough, in England now. I'm going a mile a minute, now that April is here, and every poem I did not write in the last three years has returned, crying in its frog voice, "Make me alive." Now I know that every pause and abstinence is good for me—in love, in work—bending a spring that spring will spring. Or perhaps the prosperity of my verse reflects the military prosperity of this island. From all my estuaries the fleets muster, and my meadows, too, roar with bombers preparing for the great invasion—of Europe, of the public world too long sealed from my commerce by Hitler guns. An indescribable erection of the spirit spreads indescribably from all this impatient military readiness.

I sent "Country Matters," "Festung Europa" and "A Bomber Called Vondalee" to Bentley, who, after all, remembers me. (This time I didn't need him to tell me the stuff was good, and I'm grateful for this circumstance, as I never wanted to approach him except man to man.) He offers to prod Gordon and Maxwell into doing a book of my things when they have saved enough paper. Cut the forests, there's a load of verse on the way!

Yes, of course "Country Matters" is "about" the Potters as much as poetry is ever about any specific thing. But if you read it for information you will miss most of it. It is also obviously about Hamlet and Ophelia and how a handsome prince feels about such a mousy commoner, and about

CLEM

[Stapled to Letter IV was the draft of a poem never, as far as I know, printed anywhere. Here it is included in its entirety.—D.H.]

## PILOT IN THE WATER

*For Lieutenant Waldo Monahan, drowned in the North Sea after a dogfight with an ME-109*

I

*A cup of air for that fish!*
*Stand back, give him water.*
*He's ripped the tide untimely, O*
*Death's the waste mold of our lives.*
*The airs have broken,*
*And—call it miracle if you will—*
*The water walks on him.*

II

*When I had gills for salt*
*Mother compassed me.*
*I'm lost in her long wave,*
*Drowned in her damp goodbye.*
*Baptize me in water faith,*
*Atlantis is worth a mass.*
*Convert me by immersion,*
*Make me a tuna or a bass.*
*My wind's the Gulf Stream.*
*If you ask me, keels are sails.*
*In Texas the WAFS went by*
*Towing target whales.*
*My shadow wiggles like fish alive.*

*Bubbles are tears, that crab's a gull.*
*Everything's reasonable here.*
*My face is the bone for my skull.*

### III

*I had a wild youth—*
*Breaking my nails on granite mountains.*
*My aunt's mother*
*Came from Los Angeles packed in ice.*
*That sun is violet—*
*The penumbra's yellow.*
*This button fires the guns—*
*They have dredged up sand, sir.*
*The flora of the sea*
*Is a vase, a buttonhole, a bed.*
*I am not I—*

*Patience, you'll soon be dead.*

### IV

*The spaces are webs between my fingers. I'm less optical than horizontal. When I was a child I thought in riddles of the air. A leaf or a bat could answer them better. Deride me fallen. Now I have the Kraut in my sights; he'll go up in waterspouts. Aqua-Ace Bags Deep Six.*
*Remember me.*
*Piccadilly knew me—not well. Amphibians, give rank its privilege. What are the war aims of Proteus? Brown-Eyes, why are you a fish? I didn't wait to be drafted. God meant me for something and I intend to find out why. It was a rebel that took the candy bait.*
*What will you remember, if it's me?*
*Through tourist deadlights, I'll marvel at your carapace of motion. We evolved from them, you know—and Evolution Counts! What would a beetle do in my place? Mice? Bats? Greeks? Cowards? Sinclair Lewis? It takes character not to die.*
*Forget me.*

### V

*Ambition needs breath.*

*Vocation needs breath.*
*I owe God a breath.*
*I'll stay awake in sermons for a breath.*
*I'll give my mess of pottage for a breath.*
*I'll trade two Commies and an agate for a breath.*
*I'll love Mommy and Daddy forever,*
*for a breath.*

*If you let me breathe,*
*I'll settle for half a death.*

VI

*This water's close as a phone booth in July*
*I want to call Betty, I want to call Lou.*
*My mind has scales.*
*I breathe you,*
*Sweetheart,*

*Sink me, Love.*

**LETTER VI**

APO 927

SHEILA, SHEILA,

*No. No. No. No. No. No. No. No. No. No. No. No.*
No to everything you say about my poems, my war. It is clear that I have failed to show myself to you (or, as you prefer to say, "was not honest")—as it was clear from before I shipped that I would not be able to. You never understood what I thought I would "accomplish" by asceticism or mysticism. It didn't help me write or earn a living or even "clarify" my mind enough to make a conscientious objector out of me. So then, in your book, it was all for nothing, like a disease. But I didn't want my mind clarified. I wanted it to work in its own ferocious way. It didn't work to any visible purpose, but at least I knew that its purposes were invisible. And now this.

301

This tangle of misrepresentation and misunderstanding had to happen if we tried to keep our holy communion and communication activated through the imperfect means that they left us—all their V Mails, artificial females among letters. Now, when it is too late, it has been demonstrated that I was right when I asked that you and I break clean until this war is over, returning then to each other as we chose to be, not as what they made of us. But you had to have it this way. We had to "try our best" in our letters, and now we have played their game of stretch and let them engineer through us a damned misunderstanding which I despair of ever straightening out. For the rest of our lives, maybe, we will have to favor the joint between us as one favors a wounded limb.

I despair—but who am I to despair? I have no permission to despair, and I am too indoctrinated now to do anything without permission. I have been appointed to watch while the happier apostles find their stones to sleep on.

Well, then, *watch with me*. I will tell you the truth on all the points you were reckless enough to charge me with. You asked to "share," dear Pandora. Then share.

1. Yes. I do seem to be getting egg in my beer while the poor devils are dying, and I cheer when no one should. And I sport me while you are wasting away sticking to a bargain you don't understand. I do not pretend to have chosen to be crucified upside down because the boys in the line are being crucified right side up. And I will not weep for you or anyone else to see because I know the child is burning. The child burns. Smoke by day. Fire by night. It is the child. I see him and will not cry. No, not for you, either. I will fiddle and I will laugh because he burns.

2. No. I did not tell you everything about Cecile Potter. If I told you all (or tried) you might think that in her I had found the burning child, and I have not found him. But could you stand what I know about her? Do you know what a stink women are when they lie in the hell at the bottom of their womanhood, unredeemed? Oh, I don't think I'm a redeemer with my little cock, but I can guess what a redeemer would have to be.

3. Yes. You were very clever to reason out that I had been able to finish a lot of work because I had started

sleeping with Cecile. More than that, you guess well that she was in the sack with me at their house that night when the storm woke us all and her mother came into the room so motherly fond to tuck us in. (And isn't that a scene, for you? Henderson Paul would know exactly what to do with it in one of the puky novels he is undoubtedly preparing to write when his United Nations have won the war. Lady Mother must either be shocked into squawking like a chicken or be a dandy pander who has plotted it all. But I don't know what to make of the scene, because I saw it, and I remember instant flashes so thickly coded with meaning it would take me forever to untangle—Cecile's ugly deformed mouth trying an Ipana smile of confidence from my pillow, and her mother, heartbroken not so much by discovery as by unwarranted hope that her chick was happy, spending in a flash the dignity they've been hoarding on this island a thousand years to try to make a look of blessing that would shelter the million wrongs she saw in the adjacency of our reclining heads.)

With your facts in your possession you have a case. What do you want with a "case"? This goddam life is to live and see, not to be justified in. The facts will not tell you much about the rich and sad relationship I have formed with the Potters, nor what a strange land the ships brought me to, after all.

"Country Matters" could tell you more about it, and you crack me near my diamond body when you appear to have read it merely to snoop for information. I am willing to confess what can be confessed, but you won't be much wiser, for if the poem doesn't tell enough of the truth, I can't believe that I can tell it in prose. Once more I'll say that I can't understand how you or everybody wants to think a poem is "just literature," while any old jabber in prose must be reliable.

The actual day on which I based "Country Matters" went like this:

Cecile and I had taken a train up to Coventry to see the bomb damage. It is quite the tour (I am not the only one who, to your dismay, regards the war as a spectacle staged for his entertainment) and on the way we fell in with other pilgrims who right merrily traded stories and C rations with us. Among them was a Catholic chaplain who would do for your

Pardoner and a good Marine colonel who would do better for your Gentle Perfect Knight than I would do for your Squire. (Though squire I was, with tender, short-lipped Cecile on my arm.) Not all (only most) of what we say about officers is true. The colonel called Cecile my girl, while the chaplain's pig eyes showed true his thought that such as I could be after only one thing with a girl whose face is so disfigured. Or was she my crip sister?

In the town Cecile and I wandered off by ourselves. The sky (you'll need the sky if you're really going to see this; sky helps imagine the machine that killed this city) was very densely clouded, but the clouds were high, seeming stretched like a tympanum to make an acoustic chamber in which there was no sound. (I did not invent the extraordinary silence that I said in the poem emanated from the ragged buildings; it exists, and the silence literally is their scream, awful spirit ditties of no tone. Anyone who looks at them will, as if automatically, find himself listening, and there is a uniform shock to all who hear nothing.)

What it did to Cecile and me, all this savage desolation—so much like the jungle Conrad describes in Heart of Darkness, those great and prophetic passages—was to make us hot. I think it was to us as if we were the only survivors, and all the death we knew not how to accommodate with our minds was crying to be celebrated through our genitals. Funeral games.

Now, there had been no thought of this when we left home that morning or ever at any time before. Maybe to the point of stupidity I had been considering Cecile my handicapped sister (the bad chaplain in his guesses was only morally wrong), my hurt and gentle one that I would take care of the way I had to take care of the stray dog I acquired when I slammed Jack Wagner with a rock.

Honestly, it was only in that suggestive rubble that the moral imperative became clear to me, and when it did I felt like someone had hit me with a sledge. I didn't want it. I felt like covering my parts with my helmet. My seed not for this fire-gutted island, I pleaded. But a pocked Venus rose from the craters and mastered me.

Hand in hand Cecile and I came to what had been a school building. It was of fairly recent construction, all reinforced concrete, and was practically intact except that some of the windows had been enlarged by the explosions nearby. It was totally emptied. No desks or cupboards or maps or pictures. You know, as if what was to be taught there was Nothing. Only the blackboards suggested human occupancy. I saw bits of Latin and mathematics under the swirls of erasure, overwritten with tourist names like Cpl. Al J. de Vilbiss, 8015 Huntington Road, Pasadena, California. "... the broken slate where some schoolboy had written 'boredom' and another written 'hate.'"

We climbed some flights of broad concrete stairs until we came at last to a small enclosed stair leading to the roof. Through a doorless opening we went out to get a bomber's eye view of the town around. It was raining a little, enough to make the concrete roof under our feet slick, and Cecile had the collar of her mac up.

Then one of my special states began to happen—the kind of preepileptic trance (I'm going by Dostoevsky's descriptions) that I've had a couple of times before, once in a silly cornfield, and once when Oom the guru almost succeeded in teaching me to stand on my head. All that I'd been discerning 'way out at the tip of my imagination moved in and became sensually real. I heard the houses scream aloud, a real baying and caterwauling, but lower in pitch than you'd think a scream could be, a sound like surf mixed with the voices of all the drowned men.

I thought that empty roof with the ruin all around us was our ark, with no Ararat in sight and no animals in the hold, either, except the tiger and the boar in our respective thighs. Our souls were right tempted then and there to go at it under the rain, though we could not meet each other's eyes or find anything to say. The brown nightingale, my sister, I took her hand and led her back inside, and after the business with underclothes she said in a piteous, wondrous voice, "If we did, you know I could never let you go."

I said, "I won't stay here."

She said—and drew away enough to smile that awful smile of hers, so much like a fragrant death's head—"I won't say No if you need me."

I would have needed her, too—so badly I couldn't have helped it—if the trance effect hadn't been fading so rapidly.

But I said that since I was the Strongest Boy in my country I didn't need her. Then all three of us bowed our heads and departed that place of death, nothing having been done—and perhaps I am guilty to those dead that nothing there was.

All the way home in the train she clung tighter to my hand under the sleeve of her mac, her hand so small and damp, and her eyes loud with that tongue-cut-out pleading for something I could not say. Practical thoughts buzzed about like flies going for the carcass of a dead lust. Did she want a GI husband? Sentimental love words? To be told her teeth were pretty and it's a good thing no lip hid them? A shilling's worth of deceit to lubricate her? Ah, well, maybe only something like that, I thought in great depression.

But I can tell you simply now that she wanted much more than any of that. She wanted me—as women often do, and that is why they come to me so often in my duty dreams—to give her back all she had ever lost, telling her that the Krauts had never come with their ravishing bombs, that nature had never raided her mouth and blasted the decent lip off her teeth, that her bird father was not dead but still went soaring off somewhere on the generous thermals of Europe in his bally glider. By the time the train brought us back from one psychological level to another I knew all she wanted me to say to her, but I could not bring myself to say it.

Enough to have borne and known for one day! But the days of revelation don't submit to laws of moderation—just the opposite. Only when the nerves are strained impossibly come those moments when they are strained more. It's very much as if emotional strain invented or caused the circumstances that will increase it—which increase in turn—and that alone produce something like "automatic writing."

Back at the Potters' for tea there was company waiting for us, a very old family friend, they said. I knew at once who he was—not just his name, though I recognized that from college texts, from hearing Felix Martin speak of him, A. S. J. Gilley, the philologist, but what role he had in that roomful of us friendly, civilized people determined to kill or be killed.

He was Cecile's fiancé—I guess that is the right word, though there are so many complications involved that no one epithet is quite sufficient. A widower for twenty years, a lifelong friend of Cecile's father, he was assigned to take her as the wife of his old age—as I thought, give her spinsterhood a gentle coloration it could not have had without their conspiratorial solicitude.

I was, willy-nilly, his rival, you see. (You don't see, and the fault is not yours but mine for being real invisibly instead of visibly as most people probably are. You think I could have declined the game, announced firmly that I was not, after all, playing. But I was playing. When someone pitches, I always swing, and had, in any case, earlier in the day, found myself at the wicket, at bat.) Unbeknownst to your knight, the Potters had been fattening him for just this encounter all along. I was to save the princess from this wonderful, kind old dragon, or yield my bones as dowry for their bloodless marriage.

My tactic (sic) was to fall in love with the old man the minute I saw that I had to fight him. He is one of those absolutely great men that I knew they had in this country securely tucked down in the national life like a garlic clove in a roast of beef instead of stuck up on top for dressing. He has a mind white and soft and supple as girls' bodies and then under this the firmness that comes from having Latin, Greek, and Hebrew as familiar as his native language. His mind is low-lying, superficially cluttered, and at points proud and high as one of their great universities, sloping down the hill to its easy river but sticking its chapel spires up high and white over the countryside.

Well, before the matchmakers said Jack Robinson, I bearded him and very aggressively tried to butt him down by arguing the genius of the American language against all those that he was shepherd of. Typically smart-aleck, I was playing the little barbarian for all it was worth, drinking Scotch instead of tea as if maybe when I got drunk enough I would begin to demonstrate with an Ozark dance or an Orchard Street windmill of gestures what I could not very precisely say. I recited Hart Crane to him, "O Braves, we danced beyond our farms, In cobalt deserts," and said the English would never have spunk enough again to hammer so much into so few words. I have never had so good a listener, one who seemed to hear in the apparently simplest combinations—my lignes trouvées—the same echoing complexity that I think I hear. I would have served him—my right father—in the same spirit that Ariel serves Prospero. We'd have made a dandy team if the stars and all had not set us in this opposition.

And then while I was ranting I got the notion—felt it all clear—that the Potters had not brought us together just so we could fight it out. They wanted me to win, drive him down. They were betting on me—yawp, splutter, slobber, drunkenness, beardless militance and all. Gently they hoped that I would down him—this wonderful old man—because in their bowels the English have lost faith in what he represents. They too want their Hun to free them from the doldrums of compromise.

I did not want to have the obligation of killing him for them. I began to feel Hamletish indeed when I realized that it was not I who wanted to do in their Claudius for them. Their I had to strike and my I said, Hold up. And all the while there was little Miss Ophelia-Cecile sitting behind me, ready to take my hot head in her lap.

All this was not so noisy or scenic, naturally, as I am making it out in this telling. I kept trying to outdo old Claudius in courtliness too (laughable as that seems), bowing and scraping and insisting that he made all the points, while he, from his throne, was giving me all the quotes and instances I was gasping for to hold my arguments together, tossing them down with ease as if he knew every word printed since Gutenberg.

On all technicalities he knew he had me. I was a foolish mouse in his wise cat hands. But then at last I knew he wanted to be beaten, too, relieved of responsibility of rule.

Our crazy battle went on through dinner, after which he went home, walking through the drizzle. He had almost ten miles to go and he is in his sixties and he set out so cheerily. God, I loved him and know him to be so much better than I in all ways, but they had taken me in by their game and I could not refuse to be in some sense their executioner. (Which suggested all the new interpretations of Hamlet. Was Claudius' real guilt in provoking Hamlet to kill him? Didn't Hamlet love Claudius more than his own provincial father? No, but these might be wondrous Rilkean variations on the classic theme.)

I had a tremendous headache when he had gone, and my face was burning—and it just happened that I was sitting with my head in Cecile's lap and she was running her hands through my GI hair. I think she said, "You are keen, my lord." But it doesn't matter if she really did or not. I knew that's what she ought to say.

I knew, by that time, what it all meant and how I would write it. But I wasn't free to go away and take pencil in hand at that moment. I went on with the game, twisting to joke at her that she could take the edge off me. She and I went on until bedtime playing our parts behind the knowing backs of Gerald and Mrs. Potter, me catching her in the kitchen to kiss her, or in the dark of the stairs and arranging with her how she would come to my room when the others were in bed. I had won her, and I could not just say, "No, thanks." On the other hand, now that I had been declared winner I was already beginning to wonder why I had competed.

I went through with it, all the painful farce, fooling no one, as I discovered when the wind rose and Mrs. Potter came in to see if I (we) was (were) all tickety-boo and comfy.

Lucky Clem, then—if you have to be bitter—who found not only an amorous nightingale but an approving, pimping top-drawer mother to cluck over his luxuries. But you could only say this by refusing to understand me as I understand myself—which is the only way that I can conceive of being any value to you. The truth is I lay with Cecile and I suffered more from that than I have ever known how to suffer before. It is non dulce et non decorum to discover the object of irresistible pity in an available crotch. All my body hair is singed by the flames I have embraced. It is truly through fire that Phoenix rises.

Rose, rather. The proper tense for all this (as for all truth) is past. The present is never true, though real. I am not going to the Potters' any more. I cannot save their Cecile or their future or whatever it is they mutely required me to save. I have kicked them out of the lifeboat and am alone again.

Gerald seems to know why I fled better than his sister. Cecile and I had a terrible parting. She accused me hypocritically of ruining her "chance for happiness" with Gilley. Though I can see that it might be happiness just to sit in the stilly presence of that man, she never could. Her "chance" with Gilley is lost only in the sense that she won't accept him now, after me. But now that it is lost, she believes in it, though she was skeptical when she could have had it. Now that she has psychologically put him beyond the pale of consideration, she can fancy that he might have been a composite of his own gentleness and my earnest eroticism. Gerald confirms for me that this is hypocrisy on her part, but we conclude together that people (like her, for all people are like her in this) believe in their hypocritical wishes as they could never believe in their unavailing honesties. And we conclude that this is very female, admiring it as we do not admire our masculine consistencies, but sadly refusing to countenance it as a fit view of life, for all its radiance. Better the desert than the social lie, says Gerald, lifting me to my feet for flight.

Their mother is willing to consider all that happened a "mistake"—which indeed it was not, but that is the best thing for those who muddle through to say. She asked Gerald to tell me that she did not consider I had "played the cad." I do not think I have, either. A cad could not have caused the pain I did. ("To play the cad" is a very rich expression, and you must not think I am mocking at Mrs. P when I quote her thus.)

I don't mock you either, ever, and I can tell you all this because I honestly think I did not do you wrong in my affair with Cecile. At the breaking point of what language I have, with desperate punning, I will still say that it was a soul I plunged for when I penetrated that long-preserved virginity. A soul and worthy—I could not deny it if I wished—all my love and more loyalty than I shall ever possess. Perhaps every woman always is and any fornication is as mighty a wrong as Tolstoy said. I know I would have given Cecile all she wanted if I could have. O monsters, your brother is here.

This target of paper, this scapegoat paper, has endured me patiently all these hours when I have been charging it with my sins. It has purged me well now, and the only question remaining is whether now to send it to you. You know I'll carry it a while before I drop it on you.

But I think it is likely that I will send it. It is not quite to be embroidered with gold thread and worn on your breast to the office parties, but I have this solemn feeling: If you accept it, you must cherish it and keep it safe forever. This scarlet letter has magic in it and it would be very bad luck to destroy it after you had once taken it as our own. (You would destroy it if you ever thought "it's not so bad." It may be, for all I yet know, the story of the man who through fog, brake, and briar and many perilles sought the holy child—and when he found it ravished it. It is a terrible story, but if we cling to its terror it may keep us safe. And if you did not know it, I could never put any of my real poems in your hands again.)

MAX M. CULPA

## LETTER VII

APO 927

DEAR MOMMY,

There are no coincidences. It's just laziness to think there are. Everything has meanings that grow like branches among other branches of meaning from the same tree (Ygdrasil). I have already told you how Gilley's dying at home on D Day set up such entanglements of meaning and association I could not doubt my mental storm resembled fairly the great storm of history.

It is the same when I grieve about Harry Rinehart, now that I have the news of him. I see a propriety, the propriety. For Harry blindness is the ultimate pensioning from a world he always dreaded to look at. Whatever is good in it is all secure in his decent darkness. Into Abraham's bosom went he when the gasoline flared in his face.

How can I talk this way? Because it was you who told me the news. Because gentle Harry wanted me to know what I have just said and therefore chose you for his messenger.

How can I anyway? My God, he's blind.

How can I say anything else? I'm not blind and I can't always stand what I see until I have remade it into words.

At night I say, like a little kid promising his toys under the bed, "Don't be afraid. I won't let this war get you." The dark shall not have any of mine. I carry everyone in a little nest I made for them up under the safe bones of my head.

311

(Where I should have left my brown nightingale Cecile instead of trying other means to save her.) I make up my mind again and again that nothing can happen to my people. When I lay me down to sleep, I set me up beside the bed with my Custer gloves and my best slingshot to keep the snakes away from the nest.

Love,

CLEM

## LETTER VIII

APO 927

SHEILA, DARLING,

I have been promoted to sergeant. No doubt on account of the affair at Verdun. Among the masks of Clem Anderson—Sergeant Aaron C. Anderson. I already feel myself a figure in a photograph album. Uncle Aaron Across the Big Pond. Or known to the family as

SARGE

[This is the first of the still existing letters written from France. The "affair at Verdun" was a small fire fight that took place after Clem and two other men in a jeep, trying to catch up with Division Headquarters, caught up instead with a rear guard of German infantry. According to the requirements of military duty, Clem acquitted himself well. In an engagement that lasted for about an hour, he managed to discharge several hundred rounds of ammunition from a submachine gun. After other members of his platoon had come up and Sergeant Henry Harlan had been wounded, Clem led seven men in an attack on a roadblock held by four Germans. Clem killed one of the Germans. The other three fled. His company commander recommended a Silver Star. The recommendation was not approved at Division Headquarters.—D.H.]

## LETTER IX

APO 927

DARLING,

Of course I'm sorry that my letters have been "unlike" me lately (as they have been; unlionlike they were) and especially at Xmas time. I should have been full of antimilitary hallelujahs, and pragmatic rejoicing, for it wasn't too bad a Xmas as such go. Now that I have been transferred to I and E [Information and Education Section of the XIth Corps—D.H.]. I am again enjoying the privileges of the gifted goldbrick. This unit is a real cell of writers—everyone has a novel or some short stories cooking, not to mention histories, dramas, or inspirational books. There is lots of talk at chow and in the latrine about whether this war will be followed like the last by a bunch of war novels, or whether it is so well documented while in progress that there will be nothing left to say when peace comes. I feel that by luck of war or complex fate I have fallen in with a bunch of professionals such as I never met while I lived in New York before. (These are nearly all New Yorkers. The term "professional writer" is almost synonymous with New Yorker, as they make clear with anecdote and knowledge of the inside paths. Most of them cannot write for bird shit, but evidently that does not so much count as we used to think. Connections, that is the thing, and their favorite tale is how Sherwood Anderson got his publisher to print Faulkner's first novel in exchange for being excused from reading it in manuscript.) They halfway condescend toward poetry, though they consider it good "background" for a writer. It is "learning his craft" so then he can go forward to doing something that doesn't require any.

In weak moments when I sit in the chimney corner listening to them, I dream of using the fairy-tale trick of the sparrow and the eagle on them—that is, learning all their tricks of how to succeed as a writer and then, at the top of this flight, launching my little sparrow of excellence to go beyond 'em all. Oh, 'twere an excellent stratagem—about like the plans I used to make for starring at football. And the truth is more like that I will end my life as a prairie poet, playing my

313

guitar for women's clubs while my long hair blows in their faces.

Your conjecture that I have been brooding about killing someone oversentimentalizes me, I think, though I have been considerably preoccupied with "my man" and cannot ever take the deed lightly.

There is some trick screen in my mind like an enlarged photograph of his face as it looked against the snow when we came pussyfooting up. It was a "poor" face, the face of a man I would not have liked nor bought a drink for had the circumstances been otherwise, with a ratty, old-fashioned mustache above the black blood still coming from his mouth. Sallow of complexion, and in life his eyes had evidently been shifty. All of which is mere data. I didn't kill him because I didn't like his looks. What, then, were my reasons?

I didn't have a reason. I had unreasons, many of which I have figured out, subsequent to the event, and which justify me at least as well as a reason would. In that peculiar kind of fasting and penance I perform—burrowed under seven blankets on the troisième étage of this yellow house, listening to the blue-green wind off the North Sea and sucking up on a bottle of Calvados I stole coming from St. Malo, I read the ceiling cracks for augury and made a private catalogue of how I had worked all these years killing what would eventually turn out to be a real corpse with a real mustache.

## ARMS AND CLEM ANDERSON

Under the bed that smelled like Grandpa's chewing tobacco, in Grandma's stocking the leg-shaped Winchester with slotted magazine. Down which, more soldiers than toys, the cartridges dropped like paratroopers in the attack. For targets I preferred tin cans to paper, and among tin cans the flat ovoid with a steel-engraving Prince Albert presenting himself black and gray as a mustache in a red frame. Grandpa's root-colored hands in my armpit and on my left forearm steadied me as I imposed my will across the brown pond where the tadpoles were. Loved the female pucker of bullet holes in tin. I was proud among the poultry for my noise, and in the afternoons, after experience, watching the sky wink its Kraut-blue eyes down through the fearful box elder tree, I began to compose my enemy.

Who was eight (little Otto Kleist) and I was four when Uncle Cole, from the pure generosity of Sunday afternoon and the bloat of a Sunday dinner tickling his prostate, shot me from the haunted rafters of the barn an Uhlan-helmeted and field-gray pigeon. From my candy-sticky fingers fell the seeds of something else's blood. Oh, hot little murderer, I trotted past the concrete horse tank with it—to hide the foreknown sin among rank weeds. Much of the deed was accomplished that day, and a terrible hand raised across the sun as the angel hid his eyes lamenting what I had become.

Over the barn went our shingle darts, among telephone wires and light fixtures our balsa planes searched. Arm them with nails; put pins in the wingtips—who told us that?

My enemy was twelve when I responded to the aggressions of Arthur Graber by dropping a cherry bomb into the car seat beside him. When reprimanded, I urged his racial untrustworthiness and the catfish smell of his mother's false teeth. "Force is the only argument the Grabers understand."

Followed two years of armistice when I put money in my purse and did not name my enemy's name until, for my good behavior, I was allowed to buy a Stevens Crackshot from Montgomery Ward. In gray October down from their pride of place in the mulberry tree, three spatsies fell in the first morning of my wrath. Godlike through gunsight (at last!) to watch the Kleistian sparrows fall. In the hieroglyphs of wingfeathers I saw the serrations of those triplanes Richthofen flew. I notched the stock. He was fourteen.

When I was a soldier at Boy Scout twelve, the Great War was on the piano top, where in the sworls of changeable silk Uncle Jeff in puttees like collapsible drinking cups or jointed wild onions, with the titty flaps of his pockets erect on cloth like monumental stone, a wooden-spoked Ford wheel almost retouched out behind him and beyond that a squad with a barefaced bass drum and a flag awkward as washing, under a sky tinted like sour medicine, stood. Beside him Uncle Mutt with his Jack Dempsey haircut, stretching the tendons of his neck as he learned the art of cold steel.

Sometimes the beast pretended to shoot at something high—'way high—in the cottonwood tree. No one else could see what was living among those ultimate branches when my pellet went singing through the leaves and sky, Hector, German Hector, take my tiny kiss. In the hour when we are trembling with puberty, guns that would kiss form prayers to broken bone.

Kleist was eighteen when Harry Rinehart, Jimmy Wickham and I cornered him in a deserted farmhouse west of Boda. We dug in above the farm, listening for division artillery to open up over us. Dawn, rosy-helmeted, leaped from the steeple of the Baptist church. General Anderson came by—tight-lipped, exhausted—slant-eying the farm. "Boys, they will not give us a barrage," he said. "Boys, we are going in now." Rapid fire until a faint warmth was evident in the Crackshot barrel. "Clem, you broke a window!" Harry said. "God damn you, this is war," I said, more truly than I knew.

In a zigzag charge we took that farmhouse, shot out all the windows—the carnage went on because it had begun—and the aerial down from the maple tree. We killed the straggling chickens, too—three lonely Barred Rocks, who might have been, for all we knew, spies affecting this harmless appearance, and who, in any case, poked their heads out of the weeds at the wrong time, hasard de la guerre. (I'd never have hit Kleist if he'd had the sense to sit where he was.)

If he had seen me knock that aerial down with one shot, he would have stayed out of the Hitler Youth. If he had seen me spin and kill the first Barred Rock with a shot from the hip, he would never have defended that roadblock.

After I got body hairs there was always something that had to be avenged. Krauts like Steve Baker would do unspeakable things to Margaret Shea as he walked her home from Christian Endeavor (broke her brassière straps). Letting the boys at Emory's drugstore smell his fingers after a date with Betsy George. We went to the hills to fight for purity. (Nevertheless we were punished for the attack on the farmhouse. The county sheriff spoke of reform school. I paid my summer earnings to replace the windows and that aerial. My enemy had escaped again, but the match was made.)

Or there was something to kill for killing's sake. Consider the sweet-eyed squirrels in a dome of November leaves. Little heart tight to the branch, an uncontrollable spasm of tail gives him away. Finer and finer the shape of the sights and the amorous tickle of the trigger. Instant of meeting, not unlike joy for us two when the slug touches— and then the generous anxiety as he drops.

Branch to branch, holding on to my life with his weakening claws. I, Clem Anderson, Boy Crackshot, commit my mortal body to thy death, little tumbler. Only hold on, hold on, thou, a little longer. Catch one more branch before the ground gets thee.

I never thought it was only animals I killed when I killed animals. I played as seriously as they did and therefore, as a child, killed innocently, and now, with Kleist, it was the child in me that killed him innocently. It was play.

That alone is what justifies me. The nations play and I play with them, and my luck—if I will accept it—is that I have been all my life learning the game. I have found out the verbal flaw in saying, "Waterloo was won on the playing fields of Eton." Waterloo was the fields of Eton, where the boys of history scrambled. Verdun was the great playing field of Europe with that old horse's ass Pétain making dumb slogans like a coach at half time. "On ne passera pas." No serious man would say such a thing seriously, for in real life no one can hold. They are always going by. Only in this ritual fun and games is the enemy thrown back, is there a breakthrough, a victory that you can show on a map or a scoreboard.

But—ah, there's the rub!—if it was the child in me that killed, it is not the child that knows now. And what in me knows is not so innocent, though what it knows is innocent. Huh? History always innocent, but our knowledge of it always guilty? How will I endure this paradox?

We apparently have to, and will have to, live in a world where everyone goes around protesting innocence. And shall I change my papal designation from Clement to Innocent? Not so, I think.

THINE

317

## LETTER X

APO 927

O MY DEAR,

We had to do so much, so roughly, to ourselves, you and I, to make ourselves fit for survival through the war. And we have done it now. The war is over except for disintegrating the yellow bastards or whatever they may be doing with that new bomb of theirs. And now it seems to be becoming clear to me that I should have been a conscientious objector to the aftermath though not to the war. The war seems to have been my health, and I am near a basket case now that it is over.

I have become a loathsome talker, preacher, and heckler. I know it. And those—not few—who liked me when I was halfway between my old silence and this now understandably cannot bear to have me around. They used to call me "Open-Throat Anderson" for laughs. Now no one laughs. I can't seem to begin a conversation without saying, "Let's start at the beginning." No one wants to start at the beginning but me.

So I mutter to myself and write you these letters, open-throated. You mustn't understand me, or you would be in the same leaky boat as I, but you must cock your lovely ear and listen.

All summer the word "liberation" has been mocking me with its ambiguous double significance. It has been also the liberation of a torrent of snakes against which the war slogans—my personal ones for me—have given us some mental defense but which now come slithering through the mind.

For example: I have just seen again, of all people, Gerald Potter. He was really here, but was really a ghost. He came as part of a civilian team of art experts, looking for stuff the Nazis looted.

He had, of course, news of Cecile, whom I "liberated" in my eccentric fashion. I really did liberate her, you know. She was a true sleeping beauty until I woke her with an ill-advised kiss. Gerald's news confirms this. She has now married an American sergeant named Harkness. She is pregnant and is hoping to go soon with Harkness to Nebraska, where he will teach in some cow college. Gilley is perpetuated in this new alliance by the fact that Harkness is a philologist, and I, I suppose, by Harkness' rank and national origin.

I was jolly glad she was married, said I to Gerald, glad that she should have come by however indirect a route to her happiness.

Generous Gerald emphasized my unintentional part in this. (How is he so sure it was unintentional?) Delicately he said I had played Pygmalion to his sister Galatea.

Then he added with genuine but limited pathos (the saving trick of the English, to look into the abyss and say, "Not so deep as one would have thought") that Galatea had learned to talk and walk under my sculpting hand. "When she does, she of course says to Pygmalion what has been in her mind all along—not his. Very disappointing." How kind of him to make this subtle alteration that implies she ditched me—and how subtle to pity me genuinely for what never happened!

I wanted (this is the way I am now) to break the politeness and sneer (?) shout (?) or howl (?) that I had not wanted her in the conventional sense, for his gentle hypocrisy stole away my private justifications for what I had done by giving me some sort of public ones.

I had wanted much of Cecile. I'd wanted her to say the right thing when I touched her imperfect mouth and gave her speech. I did not want her to say, "I love you." I wanted her to say, "I love."

How good if Gerald could have persuaded me that this was what she was these days saying to Harkness of Nebraska. And he might have done so adequately if he had not shown me a photograph of the happy couple. He tried to carry it off smoothly, but he winced when he took the picture from the envelope in his pocket—knowing what I would see that no one should.

The disfigured mouth, amounting almost to a harelip over prominent teeth, which is the undisguisable wound Cecile has had to live with all her life, is also—Harkness' mouth. In that feature they could be twins. And twins of what? After all the anguish and effort, after all, she went and married her own wound, "clinging to what had robbed her."

They will walk this earth looking like twins of misfortune, looking for—what? The limited parodistic, inverted happiness of the incapacitated. This is what I liberated Cecile to, so she could come out of the castle and embrace the dragon that had guarded her—tooth clicking on tooth when they kiss, the foetus in her growing everything but a lip to hide behind.

From the instant I saw Harkness' picture the myth by which I understood how my affair had turned out was not Gerald's comfortable old Englishy fable of Pygmalion making a comely woman capable of choice.

My myth was this: Perseus comes to free Andromeda from the rock where she is chained. As he has been told to do, he looks only in his mirroring shield as he approaches her and Medusa. In the shield he sees the writhing horror on Medusa's head. He swings his sword. Slays.

He drops the mirror and turns heroically to look upon the lovely Andromeda. And what does he see, there where hair should be?

Snakes, snakes. No wonder a person turns to stone in times like these.

Love,

CLEM

P.S. No word from Gordon and Maxwell on the book of poems I sent them. I don't care.

## LETTER XI

APO 927

Darling,

Why I went AWOL is very simple to explain, though I would not tell anyone but you. I stole the jeep and went back to bury Otto Kleist.

I know it is practically a year now since I killed him, and it is reasonable to suppose that someone long ago buried him or slung some lime on him. But when I thought it through the important conclusion to which I came was that I hadn't buried him, but had left him lying. Particularly I felt guilt when I was offered money for poems including one in which his name is mentioned without permission. ["Firefight at Verdun," later included in *Sugar Oboe*.—D.H.]

I suppose the alarm had gone out for me before I crossed the border into France, and no one knows quite how I got as far as I did. I'm not sure how I found my way there.

It scared the hell out of me not to be able to find him when I got back to where we had left him. Trying to orient myself near Vaubecourt, I took the jeep up to the turn in the road where they first opened up on us and hit Harlan. It was wintry then and golden fall this time. Nothing looked the same. The light fell differently on the houses and walls. I determined to wait until the light changed, in the hope that this would make things more familiar and I could see again how it had been.

The light changed. It did not become what it had been before.

I stayed on the road there for several hours. A fair number of godly folk went past me, on foot or on bicycles or horse-drawn carts. I wanted to speak to them but literally could not. I remembered that the dead do not know that they have died. So what made me so sure that I was alive? If any of them had spoken to me, I would have done something sensible like drive the jeep into Paris—as long as I had stolen it anyway—and try to see Picasso or Gide and talk things over. But no one did.

Toward sundown I was in a real sweat. The body wasn't there, the battle wasn't there and I was feeling ten times as guilty as when I pulled the trigger. I began to have dreams in the jeep, so I got out of it and crossed into the field along the road. The sun was like an eggyolk sac full of blood. I thought I must be just about where I had been the time before—going down a draw, guiding myself by some poplars along the road—but I had been strong then and I had no strength now. My knees felt like they were jointed to bend both ways.

Pretty soon I had to sit down and I had what might as well be called a vision, though I like to keep them separate from hallucinations, which this more probably was. I looked down at my chest and there he was. He was buried in me, like some dirty little gray rat that had half crawled into me and died.

Well, the thing to do was get him out. It was plainly an unsanitary situation. No soldier with a pride in his uniform likes to go around with a dead enemy protruding from his vitals. But I couldn't get ahold of him.

So what occurred to me to do was to get to Chartres as fast as possible. I don't know what prompted me, but it was right.

Something intervened to save me or I might have gone off. And now I have made this discovery: Whatever else there is or is not on earth or high heaven and whether there is any God or not or whether this tricky life is real, Chartres exists. And it works!

But what a race I had getting there. I drove all night thinking Kleist was about to hatch down there and the next time I looked I would see, well I won't mention who all could have been with him—my victims. There I went across those plump hills very early in the morning, humped over the wheel and whipping the horses like the old illustrations of the doctor racing the stork. Something was pretty close behind me. Whoosh.

All of a sudden, there it was, Chartres, like something growing and not growing, one tower high, one tower shorter, big as a zeppelin, comfortable as a barn, and I could breathe again as I came closer.

I left the jeep parked in the square in front of the cathedral and started walking around it, feeling it. The stones were still warm from the day before. After a while I went and bought myself a bottle of wine and some bread and came to sit down in the grass in front of it, watching the sun go up the towers. The great thing about this building is that it is exactly the right distance from the sun—neither too close nor too far, neither too hot nor too cold—and there seems to be a sort of endless trickle of light coming down the front.

After a while I went in, and the truth of this is that as I walked around I kept wanting to throw myself down and grab hold of the floor or anything fastened to it, but I was too proud. I think I was right not to do so, but it felt terribly lonely to remain on my feet. You know?

Where I belonged was out in front watching it. So I went and sat back down where I'd been and drank some more. Not a lot. Very slow and in measure. By noon I had got everything straightened out nicely. I understood very well that this fantasy of having nasty old Otto buried in me was merely a disorder of the nerves—which might or might not pass, but everything was all right whether it did or didn't. There are some circumstances when it seems to matter whether one is crazy or sane and others in which that doesn't matter at all.

Chartres wasn't indifferent to me, nor I tempted by any skepticism to doubt it. We got along wonderfully, that old woman of a cathedral and I, and I had made up my mind to stay there forever. I had all the practical details plotted—how I would take a room somewhere in the town within easy walking distance so I could come every day and watch. No doubt presently I would become an expert full of all kinds of the detail that tourists want to know about the measurements and weight of the buttresses, so I could make a living out of that and bring you here to live with me. There is no place else on earth, probably, where it would safe for us to have children—where it would be safe for me to have children— but here I could give them a good life.

Anyway, while it lasted I certainly wasn't worried about anything except continuing to sit exactly where I was. But the Frogs, who are a very irreligious race, could not comprehend my peculiar devotions. Some of them must have got ahold of the nearest M.P.s and the first thing I knew I was surrounded by about three jeeploads of them.

I think they are still convinced that I was engaged in black-market activities, since, when they began to question me, I put on the silly smirk you know so well and said, "Black indeed!"

There you are. That is why I have been in the stockade. My trial is coming up Tuesday and in the meantime Lieutenant Chisholm has sprung me, out of friendliness and because I am the only person who can find his way through the labyrinth of files that I, Daedalus, set up in just such a way as to make myself indispensable.

I don't care to predict what I will say at the trial. It would be too much trouble to tell the truth. I may get six months. If I do, you might as well go ahead and marry someone else. It's too long.

Love,

C

## LETTER XII

APO 927

Ariadne, I love you.

FRIEDRICH

[This V-Mail note was evidently mailed on the day that Clem was taken to the general hospital at Mainz to begin his twelve-week stay in the neuropsychiatric ward. Whether Sheila saved it from the fire because of some special sentiment attaching to it or whether it was spared by accident I cannot guess. Its particular interest for me comes from the light it sheds on the element of play-acting in Clem's life during the war. Later Clem would sometimes insist that he worked up a neurotic collapse in order to avoid trial for stealing the jeep and going AWOL. There seems little doubt, though, that the breakdown was real enough to those who dealt with him diagnostically and therapeutically. He was taken to the hospital by two men of his detachment after he had carefully swept the office—not one of his normal duties—and had begun to eat the sweepings. The first diagnosis was acute schizophrenia, and though this was later modified to "neurosis, unclassified," I am convinced that the onset was extremely severe and accompanied with real hallucinations.

Nevertheless, this announcement to Sheila of the onset of his madness is a deliberate imitation of Nietzsche's note to Cosima Wagner on a roughly parallel occasion. Such a borrowing is obviously consistent with his lightly playful identification of himself as Pope Clement, Esterhazy and others in these surviving letters. It is of course not evidence that he believed himself to be Nietzsche at any time. I suspect that from the visionary center, watching the helpless alternations of sanity and insanity, the writer in him went on recording images and notions that he could not then master with his practical consciousness.

And, malingering or helpless in the grip of mental disease as he may have been, his borrowed announcement remains what he called it later in full health—"Kind of an artful touch."

Needless to say, the letter that follows should not be taken as a reliable account of his illness, though it is probably a reliable statement of how it appeared to him as recovery progressed.—D.H.]

## LETTER XIII

APO 718

I'm still in the portable puzzle factory, but due to get out soon—unless those who have promised me I would are airy phantoms of my feverself. (They aren't. I have stuck pins in them and found them awake.)

Now that I am allowed to write you about it and correct the impressions given by the chaplain and those Red Cross girls, the lovely Red Cross girls, I can tell you that they have had a hard time trying to figure me out here. Dr. Gorman [Theodore Gorman, a cousin of Maxfield Gorman, the producer of Clem's play—D.H.] has by now indicated that he had me spotted for a very sick pigeon when I came in. And either he made a bad diagnosis or I made an incredibly quick recovery. Or there are other possibilities on which he and I speculate from our respective sides of the fence. He "presented" me to a board of convening psychiatrists the other day as a curious case and advanced the theory that it was really my having a bad cold that brought it all on, as I live normally by "an intense integrative effort" which became impossible when I was weakened by chillum vulgaris, the common cold. I tell you that the atmosphere of the board was that of a slave market, with me up on the dais alongside Gorman, and all the bidders down there eying me carefully. I wanted to show my teeth and flex my tiny biceps, yassuh! One of my theories is that I didn't waste my time with Oom after all, and that I really have a diamond body in there. Even when I was eating the sweepings from the office floor, it was in there shrugging and asking, "Why not?" Having that question clear—achieving an absolute indifference—was the margin that saved me. Maybe.

Since I've got my strength back Gorman and I play cat-and-mouse games with each other in all our sessions. He thinks, or suspects, that I know something about the way the mind works that he doesn't. This makes him insecure professionally. Also leads him to spend more time with me than with other patients—ha! I'm earning my luxuries again; now I see how I could have worked my way through college with something easier than dishwashing. He would certainly like to smell out my tricks!

I tell him straightforwardly that writers are different from other people and take different things seriously at different times. Things are not always most important to us at the time they happen. People who stay with us longest are not necessarily most important and their presence or absence is no clue to their persistence and power in our thoughts. (Viz. Kleist, viz. you, viz. Uncle Cole, viz. Baudelaire's Passant.)

When I say such things he gives his head a quick, touching little shake, as if he were trying to shake these septic words out of his ears. He frowns a tolerant Jewish frown at the idea that people might be truly, radically different from each other and therefore unpredictable.

That man needs predictability the way we (his patients) need our deliriums. His need mates ours, and thus his ward of loonies is a mental seraglio, with him the Daddy Sultan who will never know the secrets of his maniacal wives.

Granting that he has the advantage of some obvious (merely mechanical) skills—for example, he obviously knew the right things to inject in my rigid body to make me feel all cuddled and at home the day they brought me in, and the way he's kept me tranquil with his chats, drugs, diet, and regimen of rest is a mechanical marvel—but, granting him that, it is strange how barehanded he has to come into the ring for the final guessing game about the nature of my mind.

I have forced him to commit (in the military sense, as when a division or squadron goes into a chosen position or into a bombing run that cannot be modified again before the battle is joined) to the theory that, behind the bad cold, my crisis came from my original error of believing that I had to find a formula that could explain this too big, scattered war.

Why did a formula seem necessary to me? (He was sniffing for a Catholic taint in my pure, Midwestern mentality, you see.)

Because I was a poet. (They need formulas worse than the devout.)

For my work then? he asks.

It ain't exactly work, Doctor. It is to be.

(At this point in our usual dialogue he is apt to scribble something in his notebook, poor devil.)

Then (he's on the trace now! see his nose twitch!) how did I come to realize that the search for the burning child, the devout plumbing in Cecile, the killing, the impulse to bury, and the race to Chartres were not necessary, and that I didn't need to understand the war any more than the other happy citizens who endured it did?

I tell him the truth: I stopped being a poet.

Now he is sad. I will stop writing?

I cheer him up. That's not what I said, Doctor. I said I chose in this singular incarnation, avatar, essence, or function of myself not to be. I have buried my staff certain fathoms down. Have set my familiars free. I'll seek the child no more. (Gorman has pointed out that the child is a Jungian concept, and since he's down on Jung for sociopolitical, racial reasons, he's extra glad I've given it up, left it, as idea, stillborn.) I tell him I found it was too late in the world for poets. Ferdinand had already topped Miranda. Antonio had bombed the island and stolen the boat before I could get my gear set up. No future in the trade for the late-born.

Still he's sad. What do I intend to do, what will be my work (that obsessive concern with useful labor that I have often noted in him and chided him for) when I go home? Of course it takes an awfully nice man to consider making poetry as decent labor. But niceness doesn't, I believe, make for the truth here.

Oh, I say. I'll write poems, plays, short stories, and novels. I'll work, all right. But for the poems there will be less and less justification as time goes on. I'll copy out what is already there. But the wheels are coasting to a stop. Learning to write poetry was my journey to this war. The war is over, and I promise never to take my vocation so seriously again.

"You actually believe you could have prevented this war, sealed it off at least, like a malignancy arrested, unfused it, rendered it harmless, made it into a mere slaughter if you had got there in time?" (How his eye glitters as he poses this question. If I were to say, Yes, I could have kept it from being what it was, drawn its sting with white magic, he would joyfully throw me back into the deepest oubliette. Irrecoverable goods.)

So I say, No, Doctor. How could I, Clem Anderson, the Strongest Boy in Boda, mens sana in corpore sano, and medalist in the fifty-yard dash, believe anything so prima-facie absurd?

And yet you trifled with these delusions when, as you say, you thought of yourself—"styled yourself"—a poet?

Illicitly I may have trafficked with the Antiscientist himself. I plead only purity of motive.

My inquisitor sayeth, Ward No. 8 is paved with the pelts of those whose motives were, in a moral or wishful sense, unassailable.

Mine are now corrupt, sir. I am ready to commence a blameless life.

If you think that Dr. Gorman does not talk quite like this, you may be right. Yet I do not think he either is a mere shade. I think he is real, and if he lets me out on time I will accept that as proof of his existence. All I ask of the world is that it do.

Not only does he seem real, he is kindly concerned about saving every ingredient of me except that damned hallucinating poetic one. He urges me to concentrate on writing plays, since—who would argue this point by now?—I have "a strong dramatic instinct." And, as part of the continuing therapy he proposes, he has made a sincere offer to put me in touch with his cousin Maxfield, who was very big in Austria before the Anschluss and who is at this moment biding his time in Ozone Park, waiting for shipments of bullion, furs, and rubber goods from unfrozen Europe that will put him back on his feet. Cousin M. is eager to meet "young talent" and sweep again into show biz when the capital arrives.

Sometime maybe I will take them up on this. But now I am, I feel strongly and strangely, a novelist. I've written you before that many of the experiences of the last two years have "opened up" the more remote past. My life back there seems to be unfolding like a dying peony, with air space at last between the petals, and not yet too great an odor of decay. Now is my time. I have to catch it all before it fades. Within the next few years. Already there are pages of it accumulating in my foot locker, pages about Boda and me and Harry Rinehart (whose name I mean to take in the novel) and all the girls. What do you think of the title "I Marry Them All"? Now that I am ripe I can see that I have had a happy marriage to this world, and I want to honor the girls who have helped me.

One last comment about Good Doctor G. Poor man, he was horrified in his gentleness when he saw a couple of letters I started to write you a few weeks back.

"You don't want to tell your girl this kind of thing," he said.

And I said, That's what I've been telling her, in a million V Mails.

He cannot help thinking that it was very wrong to load on you all my bitterness, wildness, irresponsibility, grief, and hatred, as I have. He cannot forgive me for torturing you by writing about Cecile.

Now that I am a novelist, I agree with him. I cannot understand my cruelties either. But—oh, believe!—then I did. All these years and the pretenses were for something.

There were awful things, but if you and I have both survived them, then we have survived our war, and Daddy Gorman preaches that the one that's over is the only one we had to survive.

Almost he persuades me.

I had a "healthy" dream (classification by Gorman) in which you said, "I have put new yellow curtains at the windows. Come home and cry."

All right, I will.

Love,

LOVER

## LETTER XIV

18th Replacement Depot

DEAR MOMMY,

With a different kind of luck I might have been on the boat this Christmas Day, instead of being held over for the next one, which will "certainly" take me the day after tomorrow. And I am in that eupeptic state—all ruddy with health and verve—where every moment of delay has seemed a robbery from what is due the marital bed.

Have heard from Dick and Janet that they can come to New York for the legalization any time before Easter. Shouldn't Jannie be pregnant again? Having children seems so natural to them—they didn't have to invent the process as we have had to and will have to. The reason I have been tired so often (or rested so much, as Emmy Polk used to say) is that I have had to invent every simple human process—out of stubbornness in refusing what was given, I suppose.

I like the idea of being truly and statistically married before we bed again. Much more than the mere passage of time has changed us into what we were not, and it shall be these new, hopefully holier selves we join.

All this invites me home—and yet it is a kind of luck for me to have missed the boat and had this day here. Had it so. It has been the best Christmas of my life because:

1. The others were all lousy.

2. Its gifts, though measured, were ones I was perfectly able to accept.

The trouble with Christmas was always that I believed in the seasonal promises with all my hot little heart and took it hard when they only partially materialized. I was one of those who could never settle for half.

But I knew when I walked to breakfast this day, at the still center of the turning army, that the promise of peace would be made good.

There was frost in the early sunlight and the muted salt smell of the sea, motionless in air too chill to stir. The green tracks my boots made in the frost on the grass when I crossed to the mess hall. On my left was a row of pines, quite formal and shedding hoarfrost, while the crows, black rascals, went up, up, up from earthy nests into the genial harbor haze. Out there, a ship's horn fatly bleating, like a bourgeois's devotions. Laud we the gods, and from the altar fires of sacrificed Europe the crooked smokes (black rascals) ascend.

Coffee was exactly coffee to my hungry morning tongue—not since I used to visit Grandpa's at six, seven, and eight has coffee tasted so good to me. My thirty-one teeth were never, I will tell you, more efficient (I felt like I'd designed them myself) than on the sausage, eggs, and toast over which my heart said its thanksgiving, and I repented that I had ever bitched about army chow.

After the morning miracle, I walked far enough to find one of those good little cobbled streets, walled on either side, that has to veer a bit to come to its inevitable big house. When I saw it, peering over its wall like a belle turned old maid and still thinking she is fine, I began to chuckle.

Chuckling becomes me. I have always heretofore laughed, giggled, smirked, tittered, guffawed, snorted or tee-heed. But I think you will like me better now that I am a chuckler, though if it goes on too long I suppose it can become a bore and produce (chez moi) unsightly distortions of that abdomen which you have every right to expect perfect.

Back in the barracks a man named Kundry had appeared with kindling for the stove next my cot. Fortified all around with cans of beer, candy from the PX, paper and pencil for if I would have marketable memories, cigarettes, a few dirty pictures, I settled back and read Caldwell's Journeyman from beginning to end. Literature has many functions. Erskine Caldwell is exactly the right author to read on Christmas, and when we have children I will make a ritual of reading him aloud to them. From this day, family traditions begin. I shall found the House of Anderson. (Sounds like a distiller or shoe manufacturer?) Motto: We will drive the sonsofbitches from the face of the earth. Let the kobolds look out. I have warned them that if they come into town they had better come ashooting.

Truly, duck, this Christmas has been my best. Once in the morning when it seemed so beautiful I felt tears in my eyes, but like honey. It is indeed over. Consummatum est. And the void future says, "Come and sin no more." Ici commencent les lendemains qui chantent. "If after every tempest came such calms"—no, that one scares me.

All my love,

CLEMENT

P.S. I have no Christmas present for you—beads, fishhooks, yard goods or brass wire, such as you maidens are supposed to yearn for withal. When I get there I will buy you a hat so big you can wear it on your shoulders, with kissing room inside. For the time being I thought you might be entertained by this list of Christmases past I put together thinking it might be useful to my novel. You are supposed to love me for this as well as for anything else. How can you miss?

## PAGES FROM A NOTEBOOK—

## CHRISTMASES PAST

[A pencil note added to the top margin] "This appears to be a kind of autobiography of Christmas Anderson. There are twelve hundred ways to tell the story of my life; all of them could be true, none of them the same."

## SIMPLE XMASES

First: Borne to the tree. Recognized pine smell—how?
Second: Flight into Egypt. Father rode. Mother walked. Resolved to ameliorate this sexual chauvinism by art. Conceived a painting of Mother riding, Father walking, carrying me. Poet in his swaddling bands enforced peace on world. Armistice in my stocking.

Third: Went to the tree unchanged, swag still in my diaper. Mother gave me my First Anxiety. Father had built barn out of orange crate, detachable sides. Papier-mâché animals, color and texture of oatmeal inside the enamel, as revealed when broken. Cousin Mark broke horse and farmer. Excess of cousins. Poet uncomforted by parental excuse that damage was unintentional. Cousin Mark's fault thought to be not in opere but in esse.

Fourth: To Grandmother Clement's. Ford bucking in blue-orange snowdrift beside house. Inside, smell of sickness. Erysipelas (mythological Greek daimon unaccountably hostile to poet and vice versa). Insistent recapture of past of the grandfathers with sugar cookies and apple cakes, the best memorial is on the tongue. Poet had expected old lady to go for trike. Defrauded. Got cheap-looking large mesh red stocking instead, full of inoperative toys, walnuts and tin kazoo. Thorstein Veblen shed his first tears into poet's life. Whipped for breaking Sister's bisque doll. Intentional, of course, but how could they know?

Fifth: Sled. Supposed to be boy's dream. Detested being forced into two overalls and six sweaters and exposed on top of hill in park. Rude cries of older boys. Father, too, felt poet was sissy but refused to act consistently on this sentiment. Expected happened. Knees and mittens wet, soppy. Tears frozen on cheeks. Face burned by scraping snow.

Sixth: Poet disgraced by reason of sexual episode at school. Unforgotten on beaming Holy Morn. Presents offered as injunction not to repeat. Grandfather Clement's jackknife, honed thin while he lived. Poet's first act was to cut index finger to bone. Accused of carelessness by non-Freudian family. Knife put away until poet was "old enough." Broke Sister's piano, because it was cash purchase while knife was not.

Seventh: Entire family, including cousins, chipped in to buy poet violin because he was thought talented. (???Piercing treble in school singing? Tapping foot while listening to crystal-set earphones?? Renderings from The Magic Flute on his kazoo??? Poet had seen no evidence of talent, but they said so.) Poet immediately learned to produce sound like fire siren by caressing E string. Broke bow by striking at Sister. Bought Mother framed poem from dime store, "Only Mother in World." Touched her. Showed poet crudely cast pig-metal doll chair, claimed it was only store-bought gift she ever got as a child. Poet stood beside her chair embracing her while both wept over unassuageability of the past, wanted her to be child again so she could have his goddam violin. Later, felt disturbed by excesses of sentimentality and struck Sister with sugar bowl. Violin put up until poet was "old enough."

Eighth: Bought Father and Mother subscription to Collier's. Poet had come under spell of Sax Rohmer, featured in that magazine. Bought Sister six-note xylophone. Tried to teach her "Taps." Enraged by her lack of talent and threw xylophone into garbage pail. Mother ruined it by washing under tap. Poet given brown corduroy knickers with special pouch on leg. Inside—Grandpa Clement's knife, blood of the poet still evident under the folded blades. Also gloves with fringe and star on cuffs. During afternoon stood on the porch with gloves, shouting to Major Reno to commit his troops now or never as the damned Sioux had surrounded us. No help came. Poet attacked by neighborhood ruffians hurling snowballs and crying "Sissy." Even imitation of General Custer considered effeminate by present decadent generation. Complained of this to Father, who said Custer would have been a better general if he had known when to retreat. Ideology of compromise little consolation to poet.

Ninth: First Christmas in Milford. Move to Milford made under a running fire of talk about giving poet nicer friends. Smaller town thought to conduce to hitherto questionable manliness and health. But poet was sick for three weeks over Christmas. Carried to tree by father, promptly vomited on blue-figured rug. Sister vomited sympathetically. Received red-bound volume of Boy Mechanic, bought by mail from Sears, Roebuck. Later, lying in cocoon of fever heat and soprano smell of bile, heard parents discussing whether book was "too old" for poet. They implied lack of manual dexterity and recalled inability to construct simple kite. Poet hysterically grasped book between his legs under the covers. Determined to hold something against dissynchronization with time.

Tenth: Another, bigger sled.

Eleventh: Bought framed poem for Vonnie Searles, "Only Girl in World." Vonnie touched and touched poet in return. Mother prejudiced against Vonnie. Called her "dirty girl." Could she have known? Christmas gifts received: Books, Wonder of the War in the Air, Tarzan and the Jewels of Opar (already read), and Boy Scout Handbook; my own subscription to Collier's as Nayland Smith was already engaged in new adventure with Fu Manchu. Reproduction of painting "We"—with Lindbergh's ship high up in enormous clouds. All-steel savings bank.

Twelfth: First Christmas in Boda. No signs of manliness at Milford recollected by poet except self-defense with ball bat against Vonnie Searles's brother, after poet had falsely boasted in boys' toilet of intimacy with the sister. Boda was "real country"—no more than five hundred souls. In exchange of Christmas presents at school, poet gave Betty Otis small figurine in soap. Otis burst into tears at unwrapping. Claimed imputation against her personal hygiene. Poet snickered, though he had been unaware of the allusion until Otis found it. Father convinced that talk of Depression was merely "Democrat lies." To show faith in future and American Economy he bought poet bicycle and sister a fifteen-dollar dollhouse, both Sears, Roebuck. At Christmas dinner quarreled with Uncle Cole and accused him of being a "wet" for insisting that times were getting hard. Poet rode new bicycle into countryside on Christmas afternoon. So moved by snowy grandeur, efficiency of bike, and confidence in future of our economy, he dismounted in woods near Bethel church and masturbated on elm tree. On moss, indicating to any Boy Scout north. Afterward, hypocritical nostalgia for friends left behind in Milford and pangs of guilt for "unfaithfulness" to Vonnie Searles.

## REFLEXIVE XMASES

Thirteenth: Whole family shadowed by Father's melancholia, deepened by the Christmas season. Impression that Father particularly regretted having sold poet's bike to son of banker in nearby Murdoch. Reasoned that since bank had folded, banker ought to be as impoverished as we. Once had seen banker's son on poet's machine and had tried to run him down with Chevy. Had recently spent entire cold morning with razor in outdoor privy while Mother, poet, and sister pounded on walls and begged him to come out. Poet given model airplane, all balsa construction, Sears, Roebuck, $1.14, plus candy and nuts. After breakfast poet and sister went to pasture below Baptist church to fly plane. Poor thing lurched and leaped over frozen cow tracks, would not leave earth. Attempt at hand launching splintered right wing. Sister more disappointed of two, but poet boxed her ears nevertheless. On way home encountered Father. He had been watching from behind Olsen's cave and did not accept lie that plane had flown "keen." Snatched it from poet's hand and ran back to the house with it. Claimed later he was going to return it to Sears and Roebuck and demand a refund from lying Jews who advertised it as "capable of six-hundred-foot flights." Later in the day poet took jelly sandwiches and walked out into the country with Harry Rinehart. Harry extremely bitter over fraud of Christmas. Insisted he had never been happy on that day and it first occurred to poet that neither had he. "But you have to pretend you like it so your damned parents won't be disappointed." Poet had intimations of manliness from Harry's philosophic example. Marveled over paradox of being able to repeat annually disillusioning experiences with fervor of illusion. Sensed the magnitude, terror, and dignity of human condition. Remembered the previous Christmas and resolved to stop childish habit of masturbation, often accelerated by high feeling of this and patriotic holidays. Called self stoic.

Fourteenth: Stole two-dollar compact for Margaret Shea. Touched penis with powder puff before gift-wrapping. After school had resumed in January, poet was driven wild with guilt when disfiguring acne broke out on virgin's face. Consulted family Doctor Book. Transmission by such means apparently unrecorded in medical literature, but perhaps poet's whole life an exception?

Fifteenth: Built walnut gun rack in manual training for Father and family at large. Promised Father a double-barreled gun for next Christmas.

Sixteenth: Aunt Velma with us since Uncle Cole's suicide. Disgusting ritual of complaint that she can't eat, then stuffing herself. Her sidelong, knowing smile as the gifts were unwrapped. Et in arcadia ego. Later in the day more relatives in the house. Poet expected to recite for them. Instead took his football and headed across pasture toward Harry Rinehart's. Saw Irene Lacey heading out of town along the railroad tracks. Followed her at a discreet distance and saw her meet Jack Wagner. Spent the remainder of disgusted afternoon practicing forward passes into a railway culvert, alone.

Seventeenth: Drove to Moorhead to a movie with Margaret Shea on lap. Tried to feel her under the robe. "Later," she whispered. All the way back the same. Alone on sofa in virgin's front room she said she knew all about poet's troubles with Irene Lacey and henceforward would not even permit him kisses. Poet accused her of saving this ultimatum until Christmas, went out banging door when she admitted it.

Eighteenth: (College.) Worked the holy day at the Hamilton Hotel, bussing dishes besides regular job as dishwasher. Presents from H. Warwick Lloyd: a bottle of muscatel and leather-bound copy of Thus Spake Zarathustra. After work poet walked into country with bottle, sat in the snow on a hill overlooking lake and got drunk, alone. Thoughts reflexive to thirteenth Christmas. Time unrolling from its starry spindle, rerolling. Later returned to campus and lay down in the street in front of Chisman Hall. Puked on ice, constellations of vomit. Vague hopes of achieving poetic fame the ready and easy way à la Chatterton if truck came by. None came Poet caught cold from indiscretion.

Nineteenth: Worked all day at Hamilton Hotel. Under terrific pressure to come home because of Father's illness. Poet braced himself against such appeals by recalling examples of decadents. Would Rimbaud have come home from Africa, Gauguin from Tahiti, Wilde from Paris because of parent's strangulated hernia? Spent afternoon in art building posing for Morrie Solomon. Result to be milestone in two arts, like Stein by Picasso. Solomon flattered poet by remarking he had face of man of sorrows, though frivolous hair.

Twentieth: Successful writer, poet remembered how Machiavelli spoke of bathing, putting on fresh clothes, listening to music, and then, at last, approaching his true mistress—writing. Alone at Emmy Polk's, poet attempted this formula on Christmas Day. After bath and dressing felt it silly not to go somewhere. Walked past Sheila's sorority house, remembers sundown through black elms, snow, and the decent sparrows. Locked house seemed intact with secrets, as if girls had not gone home but had retired to essential chamber no larger than head of a pin to be female in ways poet would never know. Tormented by excessive imagination, poet fantasied orgies involving himself and entire sorority. Planned to stay all night by stealth in Sheila's room in order to find out what girls did in early morning. Driven away from premises by watchman, later followed by police car.

Twenty-first: Took Sheila home to Boda. Everything too reflexive. Poet felt essential hostility between woman and art, competitors in perpetuation. S. wanted to make love in basement of Baptist church, to "have" poet's first sex experience. Poet's refusal not understood, nor his term "holy" in relation to church. Poet's relation to family passed breaking point. Poet felt fraud for pretending not to notice Father's bad table manners.

Twenty-second: (New York.) Lillian Esterman, Henderson Paul and poet went to Brooklyn to visit Schoenbergs, German refugees. Poet sided with Schoenberg brothers in predicting Hitler victory. Invented and cited many statistics on German steel production, aircraft carburetors, bombsights, range of artillery, average training period of Stuka pilots, etc. Most of these statistics confirmed by Kurt Schoenberg, to Lillian's rage. She condemned poet as irresponsible. True enough. On subway going home Lillian denounced poet's theories of chastity and vegetarianism as "psychotic." She bought big steaks and cooked them in apartment in effort to demonstrate poet's fallibility. Poet ate lentil soup. After Henderson and Lillian bedded together, poet drove fist through kitchen window in remorse for dishonesty at Schoenbergs'.

Twenty-third: (Washington.) Faithful attempt with Sheila to reconstruct personal Christmas and unite in spirit with ordinary fellow man. Eclectic reading from Scripture, Sir Gawain and Green Knight, O. Henry, and Charles Dickens. Gifts to street-corner Santa Claus and elevator man. Careful selection of gifts for each other and families. Attended midnight mass. Long walk Christmas afternoon through

337

Georgetown streets and to Lincoln Memorial. Poet lachrymose over imagining Christmas in Army of the Potomac. Wrapped Sheila in coat and watched bombing planes heading south.

Twenty-fourth: (Camp Joseph T. Robinson, Arkansas.) Afternoon at the USO writing letters. Later, mixup with M.P.s who hit poet across face with thongs on billies. Poet taken to provost marshal's office at camp, where M.P.s were rebuked by major for treating poet like a nigger. Poet insisted he was nigger and was sent to hospital for psychiatric observation. There offered position on enlisted staff and asked to stay. Politely refused.

Twenty-fifth: (Oxford, England.) Christmas dinner with Potters. Poet careful to show he loved each member of Potter family equally. Cultivated Shavian dryness of manner for Mama P. Uttered barbaric yawps for Gerald and pretended to accept good faith of Roosevelt, Churchill, and Stalin. Gossiped about the royal family with Cecile. Played "Red River Valley" and other hillbilly songs on harmonica after dinner. Poet extremely touched by their gift of manuscript poem by Sassoon (though not impressed by poem).

Twenty-sixth: (Orléans.) Bad letters from both Cecile and Sheila arriving the same day. Poet depressed but refusing to admit guilt. At worst claimed military license and indoctrination in spirit of "if you can't fuck it or eat it, piss on it." At best insisted that apparently deep dishonor of acts would accrue "far-off interest of tears." Reminded self that first duty of soldier poet is to stay alive. Nevertheless in afternoon of Great Day rode with waist gunner of B-24 on a mission to Liége. Purifying cold. Land beneath tempting as candy in moist light. In evening composed verse describing how Me-109 had killed him on mission just flown. Santa in a B-24. Down your chimneys, Liège!

Twenty-seventh: Here.

* Hemingway, For Whom the Bell Tolls.

338

# 12

I LIKED CLEM'S NEW WIFE. I liked her without being prepared to, or without being prepared not to, I suppose, enjoying that neutrality of feelings that we bring to new experience after the exhaustion of wrestling with the dilemmas inherent in the old.

I had slept most of the day after my walk with Sheila. (M.L.A. meetings were in progress somewhere. Someone supposed I should have been attending them, and I would have gone to them, too, cool and interested, disjunctive as we all must be to survive, if I had had the physical strength.) It was just seven when I rang the Anderson bell on the seventh floor of a building in the east Eighties. A pretty gray eye appeared momentarily in the brass-ringed peephole of the door. I liked it.

With a swoop and a swish of her skirts Cinderella Susan swung the door open and, exclaiming, "Dick!" came lightly into my arms. I hugged her discreetly as if she were verily my old friend's wife, pressed my cheek ritually to hers, enjoyed her perfume and with a delighted eye followed her down the long hall to their front room. What eye would not delight in following her? It simply seemed she hadn't much to do with the burning riddle I had watched glow like a sign in the dark sky while Sheila and I walked toward Canal Street the night before. It seemed that this lively body, displacing air and reflecting light, hadn't much to do with the teasing photographs and the commands to love in the magazines that had given me prior acquaintance with her.

"Clem's been fighting a hangover all day," she said in that tone of intimacy that assumed, quite rightly, both of us knew from of old just what part hangovers played in his life. "Poor old boy. I offered him a martini when I got up at three. He said, No, by God, he was going to fight it out in the clean and healthy way until you got here."

"Tell him the reprieve has come," I said.

"Oh, he'll have heard the bell. He wasn't asleep." She chuckled, half to herself. "He's lying in there brooding about his enemies. It does him good to have someone to hate."

"He's got new ones?"

"Oh ..." If there were real troubles, she shook them off like water drops from her pellucid shoulders.

As she fixed me a drink, continuing to delight my eye with every movement and glad of it (as she had a right to be), I began to see her in the setting that Clem's prosperity had given her. The apartment had an air of loftiness and homely spaciousness—not of luxury, but that nice thing, the democratic grace of the well-off to which our taste inclines so readily. There were a few good paintings on the wall, and wholesome spreads of bookcases. There were comfortable easy chairs that seemed to have been placed by need and love in the ample dimensions of the room. It was a home where good children would have grown up well, it struck me—the kind of home that might belong to some aging and probably happy professor (probably in Classics) at Columbia or N.Y.U.

And so it did, Susan explained. Of course it was only theirs for ten months. It belonged to a man named Larenson who was in Germany this year on a sabbatical.

Nevertheless, the excellent touch that set off all the apartment's rather old-fashioned fineness was this year's Christmas tree. Its branches had been stripped of needles so that they had a kind of clipped-poodle smartness. It was a big tree, and on the splendid, phallic upcurve of nearly every branch there were varied clusters of real fruit— plums, tangerines, lemons and a few small, wondrously polished apples. A foot above the tree, suspended on a wire from the ceiling, was a white capital of angels, very discreetly touched with gold.

"Yours?" I asked Susan (not quite sure whether I meant the angel might be her sister—as in smartness it truly was—or her creation).

She nodded, flushing with pleasure at my pleasure in it. "I have a kinda knack for these things. I mean it isn't an idea I found in a woman's magazine or anything like that."

Under the tree there was still an excessive pile of presents, mostly unwrapped, though many still lay in their nest of wrappings, as if Christmas had been too much to use up in a single day. "Clem says The New Yorker laid those while we were asleep." Susan laughed. "It's certainly a storm, isn't it?" I saw a fine double-barreled sixteengauge, and a Deerslayer jacket with many pockets that seemed crazily, wonderfully appropriate to Clem's new fatness.

"God's plenty," I said of it all as Susan put a clear, sweating martini in my hand.

"What's left is mostly Clem's," she said, "though we had several things for the kids, too. Clem and I had so much fun shopping for Jess and Lulie. He's so great in a toy department. But—" with a swoop to snatch up a long, flat package—"there is something for Dick and family. Here." She put it in my hands and, sweeping her skirts up like

340

butterfly wings on either side of her, dropped through their upward motion into the chair opposite me, sighing. "It was so hard to get Clem started. He makes an issue of hating Christmas, and then he enjoys it so much."

"We know he's just pretending," I said. I busily opened the package with our gift. As the cardboard slide came out of its sheath there slithered across my lap a great, flat ceramic platter with a stylized design of a fish on it. "Wonderful," I said. With my forefinger I chose several spots of glaze or texture to admire. It seemed to me exactly the sort of thing Janet or Jill would choose for our house. How could Susan have known so well? Because our tastes are so interchangeable? And if tastes, why not everything else? If this platter resembled a Picasso and a Picasso was better than that which did not resemble it, and if the person who preferred a Picasso-type design had better taste than one whose taste was for realistic fish on a platter, wherein did it follow that love should not seek through resemblances of the best that ideal of which it is the earthly echo and scorn the singular individual? From the platter I looked up at Susan and saw the reproduction of a woman finer than any I had met in real life, then saw her as the reproducible girl, as much a feature of the explosion in population as this platter was a feature of industrial technology, nobly made and only a digit. If there are two million more girls in their twenties than there were in 1939, are they people, The People? Howso may one love them and howso not?

I saw that I was hardly strong enough, after the night before, to drink as much as I would have liked on this pleasant occasion.

Now she spoke in passing of a movie—or was it a popular song?—called "Easy to Love," and my ear sifted it out of our chaff of dialogue as the exact label for herself. If she was not veritably my old friend, she was very, very much like one—and wasn't resemblance enough for the requirements of one evening?

I assumed that she had stayed at the party last night as long as Clem, and I would not have been surprised to learn that she had drunk nearly as much as he. But there was no sign that last night—or any of the past at all—had touched her. If she was only acting out freshness, still acting seemed by itself to refresh her. I sensed that she knew I had caught her acting, and she even made being caught at it into part of her success.

We were getting along beautifully when Clem came into the room. He had on a red satin dressing gown, exactly as grotesque as some of the costumes he used to assemble in college, though considerably more expensive. He seemed to come into the room at an angle and a pitch, as if he were slipping across a comer while that featureless, pompous dressing gown marched straight toward us, as if he were the object and not the subject of hangover distortions. An Anderson trick if I ever saw one, a winning one. As he bent over to kiss Susan it occurred to me that, after all, there was some kind of inevitability and propriety in his mating with an actress.

He said to her, "Let's make it a rule, chum, we flush the stool when we've got company in the house."

Poetically, dramatically calculated—oh yes, his first words had that merit. Somewhere between thinking I ought to hit him or stomp out and realizing I was not the person who could do that—and wondering, Why take offense at this after so much that might be held against him?—I realized I would have to grant him credit for saying a great deal with terrible succinctness. He was making it clear to both of us that any tolerant illusions we might have about being friends were only illusions. He wanted me to see, even in Susan's reaction to his smashing cruelty, that she was not a fond little girl like my Jill who could be hurt badly by an unexpected rebuff. And in fact the blow seemed not to register on her, as his expression of patient weariness asked me to note. I was, to some small degree, his past and she was his future. He had paid a monstrous price to go over from one to the other, and he was not going to let the price be undercut by easy, ignorant familiarities. In sum, before any of us could think of the right thing to say next (and what is the proper sequitur to that one, Mrs. Post?) I had such an intimation of his pride and despair as never before or since. He had brought his smell of sulphur into the room; once we had acknowledged it we could play.

He said, easily enough, "I'm sorry you missed us in our glory at the party last night, Dick. It was apotheotic. You've never seen me dance like a dancing bear among the pale virgins of Broadway."

Susan was watching his mouth, absolutely rapt, like an eager child waiting her cue to laugh, or like a child enchanted by the fingers of a clarinetist performing with magic nimbleness. Now I knew she had forgotten all about me when he came in. Would remember me again when he permitted her to. Would re-create the scene. Would make us all easy to love. But when the scene was uncreated, there wasn't much in their house.

"I suspect you were amply appreciated without me," I said to Clem. He nodded in the melancholic manner of one acknowledging a hit, a very palpable hit, bent all his attention to his martini, talked to it a while, stared at the wall above my head. "No upper limit to appreciation," he said. "My good wife, my dear wife often tells me ..."

"I don't criticize whatever you do!"

"... that I am beyond criticism, but while that kind of appreciation tastes good, it doesn't stick to the ribs. If I had a big enough spoon ... Give me a spoon long enough and a place to stand and I will eat the world."

"When you sup with the Devil!" Susan corrected. "It's when you sup with the Devil you need a long spoon."

He was easier with her now, after a martini and a half. Indulgently he raised his eyebrows and pretended reproof. "You've told Dick that Gorman was coming."

"He's not—"

"No. He's not," Clem said, "a devil. It would be the devil theory of history to say so. And according to Aristotle the Devil is not in history, but rather is that final cause toward which all things tend. Isn't that what Aristotle said, Dick?"

Susan laughed. She loved nonsense.

"No," I said, standing foursquare for pedantry—for correctness—against the entertaining drift of mockery.

Again I feel that, as when I reported my talk with Sheila, I must characterize rather than reproduce the conversation. For the words actually exchanged bore so little discernible connection to their referents that a transcript of them would truly seem to be about nothing. Clem's wit—his toying with hyperbole and parody—seemed to run for its own sake, responsible to nothing but the effect it produced, and though it might be found entertaining, whatever virtue it possessed as entertainment would obscure its intended significance. The very tone of irresponsibility was an address to my conscience, a dare to listen—and not because my conscience was so fine or awesome to Clem, but, rather, because it was an instrument through which he could still carry on his abstract dialogue with Sheila.

(Is there anything so mysterious about this? We have simple machines into which we may speak, simple machinery for recording the written word. Once recorded, the message may be directly transmitted, like gossip, to the person for whom it is intended. Or it may be indefinitely stored. Two books which speak to and reply to each other [metaphorically speaking] may be shelved on the same library shelf, and, in a metaphor which I have not found to be beyond the comprehension of an average college freshman, we say that these books represent a dialogue. There is no mystery as long as we represent the instrumentality of this dialogue in mechanical terms of books on a shelf, or of recorded tapes; why should there be a mystery if I say that a dialogue took place through the medium of my conscience? Such modesty as I have does not incline me to think my conscience less subtle than the communication machinery of our time.)

Nor can I believe Clem so unsubtle as to believe that what we said that night was hors série, that it did not represent qualifications of a major sort, morally speaking, on ideas already stated in his passionate dialogue with the world—though the surface of his talk suggested that this evening had no antecedents beyond last evening.

He talked of the party the night before. There had been no episode in a stalled elevator to highlight this carnival, but I think he wanted me to have the impression that, had there been, Susan's presence would not have deterred him from mentioning it for laughs. There had been a couple of depraved blond twins at the gathering—"with Veronica Lake hairdos" which covered the left eye of one and the right eye of the other—and only decrepit age plus the geometric principle that states a body cannot be in two places at the same time, plus a macabre fascination in Gorman's maneuvering, had kept him from a "novel experience."

Susan laughed at his droll telling and so did I. What did we hear?

For my benefit, he sketched the recent production history of *Death and the Devil*. As I knew, the play had been "written, if that's still a term that means anything," nearly five years before. It had been "accepted, which is a term that means a leetle more," by Maxfield Gorman in the following year. Acceptance had meant that Gorman tried to sell the script to a couple of Hollywood actors whose names would carry it at the box office. Gorman meant to sell it to them on its merits ("lots of poetry in it") and on the strength of many promises that financial backers were eager to invest, promises that would materialize if the Hollywood names were brought in, but not otherwise. The first revisions in the script were made to "re-weight" the part of the man who was to star as the male lead—on Gorman's promise to Clem that as soon as the contracts were signed they would reinstate the original text. One of the stars signed; the other got a juicy part in a movie to be filmed in Italy, so one of the principal backers withdrew. The original text was—mostly—restored. Only Gorman's faith (Clem's word, used with no more irony than was implicit in the situation he was describing) had kept Clem from offering the play to Harold and Miriam Kent for production in "some grocery store they had rented on East Third Street." The Kents had introduced him to Joan Marian, who "had the great merit of understanding that Diana was physically ugly" (Diana, the character who originated as Cecile Potter). Joan had thereafter stuck with the play through thick and thin "until Gorman heard the voice of God telling him to take her to the land of Moriah and make a burnt offering of her."

It was Joan's success in another "sleeper" (it ran a year and a half on Broadway) that had enabled Gorman at last to pin together a fabric of backers and stars adequate to make a start on production. Joan had still wanted to play Diana. She had wanted to play it so much that she passed up an offer that would have brought her much more money immediately than she could probably anticipate from Clem's play. After rehearsals and the tryouts in Washington a year ago—when major revisions were made in the action and characters—she had still wanted to play Diana so much that she could not (or did not) shift her playing to meet the requirements of the altered script. She had not gone along with the team—as all the Washington reviewers agreed. If one could put his finger on any one reason why the backers had welshed last spring and let the play shoal up in a Second Avenue theater instead of opening on Broadway, that reason was Joan's inadaptability. The New York reviews had agreed with those in Washington, and though they had been generally very favorable, the finger had to be put on someone before the backers would unwelsh enough to try a Broadway opening this past fall. So Joan had been replaced.

Everyone hoped Joan's career had not been really damaged by the time she wasted on Death, by the bad notices she got.

"It was all awful," Susan said with a pretty shudder. She turned firmly toward Clem and said, "We're never going to compromise again!"

And the way he returned her bright, fervid glance—with a look of weary cynicism that said, Bless you, my dear, for inability to understand that I have not been describing compromises, but participation in evil! Certainly the story of the burnt offering made of Joan had a thematic parallel—almost an identity of form—to the larger story of the sacrifice of Sheila. Almost certainly that's why he had told it to me. (And wanted me to note that he was talking over Susan's head with his sly parables? I can't doubt it.)

"No, we'll never compromise again," he said. "We won't have to. We have money enough now so we won't have to."

Uncomfortably I asked what had happened to the play in all these expedient shifts.

Beginning as if he had misunderstood the point of my question, he said, "Oh, the play. It's closing. That's what the party was for last night. Partly. Gorman has been to Mount Moriah so often that he's reduced it to a science. He likes to create an atmosphere of benignity and relaxation to give God the chance to tell him either that he is not Abraham or that he doesn't have to use the knife on Isaac. That word has never come, but he still gives God his chance."

"You mean Gorman sold you—" I started to ask.

But Susan broke in, a little more angrily than I had expected, to say that he mustn't talk that way about Gorman. It wasn't true. Closing the play had become inevitable, a conclusion that anyone who understood arithmetic or dollars and cents would have to arrive at if he was reasonable. Out of common decency Clem ought to be grateful to Gorman for taking care of him when the debacle came.

Clem said, "Yes. You're right. It was ever in Gorman's thought that I should be so positioned that I would never have to compromise again, and he has fixed it so. My part of the transaction is that we've sold Death to the movies. It was on sale. At least the theater made a good showcase for the final purchase."

"You sold death to the movies?" My intonation made both of them laugh. I was holding my own in adapting to the tones and modes of this conversation. I said, "You mean Baby Death, the famous child star that sucks her nurse asleep?"

"I hope she keeps them awake," Susan said.

We put a long spoon in the martini pitcher, stirred and—still—waited for Gorman.

Baby Death, I learned, was going to keep the new air-rooted Andersons awake to what Susan called "the big life" as long as a hundred and fifty thousand dollars (processed and reprocessed by tax lawyers and internal-revenue agents) could be spaced out to provide an income of ten thousand a year. This jovial (Zeusial?) shower of gold meant annuities (futures!) for Jess and Lulie. ("And a decent alimony," said decent Susan, staring bravely into my eyes Apparently Sheila, like everyone else involved, was to be paid a percentage.) It meant travel!— for these poor pilgrims who had hardly ever done anything else. It meant, in case Clem should require freedom to write more poetry or another novel, immunity to the slings and arrows of outrageous editors. ("In case," Susan said. Clem gave no indication as to whether he was pregnant with such case.) It meant no more cheesecake shots of Susan. ("Those grisly skin pictures," she said, trembling her shoulderblades as if she were shedding the skin of corruption. It was easy to believe she could do just that. As Clem had said of her when we talked last time before, she had come through unscathed—poor child, what plastic surgery of the spirit was required to make her so immaculate within?) If she took a part again, she would do it on her own terms. And the present transcendence of earthly claims on her pelt seemed to mean that motherhood was now "definitely not ruled out." (I was not sure of the connection she made between staying decently covered and the capacity to conceive, but we seemed to be in agreement that posing with a rapier between her legs was, for a girl, to be something less than a fertility symbol.) All Danaë, she took the tumbling gold, conceived, turned lovingly to Clem and swore the child to be was his.

"But Dick asked a serious question and I derailed him," Clem said. "What happened to the play? You can go see for yourself, unless you want to wait for the movie at your neighborhood theater. It won't close for a week yet and I'll get you front-row tickets for any night you want to go and witness."

When I said nothing, he went on, impatient with me, "You don't have to do public mourning. It won't have died when you see it die. It died when I saw it die—so I'm still ahead of the game." He laughed. "You really think I'm a horseshit con man for writing the thing down to death in the first place, and at the same time you're honestly panged when the corpse stops making money. So! Everybody loves the Cinderella story after all, in spite of all their twaddle about the patient Griseldas. I knew that was so. Every time that inwit twanged—I have conscience like you, reverend sir!—and I had a choice to go ahead with things as they are or not to go ahead, I thought, Dick he'll believe, as well as he can, that 'Boy died for purity' if I say, 'No, you bastards cannot get me to do your dirty work.' But in the back of his mind he'll always believe that my play didn't make Broadway because it wasn't good enough. He'll never know what was lost unless I show it to him in process of being lost."

Susan laughed, "My, my. Don't be so solemn. I think if anyone, Dick would un—"

"What difference does it make to you what I think?" I asked him, more in embarrassment of the spirit than in social embarrassment. And then it came—once again clearly—that it made no difference. He had used my name illustratively, no more than that, to stand for all of those who had placed on him the obligation of resolving the contradictions that tyrannized over their happy lives.

"What? Solemn? I? I'm merely all things to all men," Clem said. "Solemn Dick turns me mauve, that's all, Chucky. Can't you tell when

I am in jest? Anderswer always. You wash your consciences in salt and I use the latest detumescent. No primal elder curse on mine. Let the damn play go, it tells me. Except for 'our bruited arms hung up for monuments,' in the second act, there's not a word of Anderson left in it."

"It was a very moving play," Susan said solemnly.

Then, to unwind us from an argument that would not be settled here (and to remind me that he wasn't the Devil—though the smell of sulphur stayed in the room), Gorman came.

Grave, impeccable, soft-spoken and gross, he came in with snow on his coat to be among us like a great mama, tolerant of any conscience games or games of communication the children may be playing, but knowing all too well that games are pointless attempts to outwit the insuperable authority of the present. A perfect soldier of life, as ready for feast as famine. A man who made his late arrival the right time to come.

This night Susan promised feast as soon as he entered. He rubbed his hands softly over all her promises and sent her off to the kitchen with an urbane blessing, turned to Clem and me and found us good—as he would have found either a pair of martini-liberated angels or a pair of rodents idling in a carcass. He was certainly a man for silver linings, and if the building had been on fire I think he would have remarked on how unpleasantly cold the night outside was.

He was, in his massive, peasant style, a very handsome old man, bald or shave-pated as a Prussian general, and I was particularly impressed by his chocolate-dark eyes, those eyes within eyes that one sees in good photographs of Picasso.

"I have good news for you if you want it," he told Clem, while every nerve in his relaxed body praised the martini shimmering between his fingers when he twirled the glass. "It is from Archie. Arch Orcup," he explained to me. "He loves Death, and in furtherance of his genuine admiration he meant what he said with a view to engaging your services in regard to the screenplay, Clem."

"Bully!" Clem said. "I have from the initial had inculpable respect for the artistic integrity and frenetic good taste of all the productions emanating under the Orcup imprimatura."

"Otherwise we might as well have sold to Billy," Gorman said. "Billy Stevens."

"Except that Billy was recalcitrant to unleash the old purse strings in a quid pro quo fashion," Clem reminded him.

"He would have seen fit," Gorman said dreamily. "The question always pervading uppermost was not whether Billy felt enough admiration for the play to see its tremendous potential in another medium. He liked it. But Archie loved it. He said this afternoon in our telephone conversation from the coast, 'Max, I cried.' When he saw it he cried each time, he said, genuine tears, and that is something for a man positioned as he. He wanted it."

"How about when he wanted me to do the screenplay? Were his tears pretty genuine?"

"Ha ha," Gorman said. "That is an extremely funny reference to the extent of his desire to do the artistically best possible. I see. He indicated no obstacle to twenty-five thousand."

"And we are positioned to assume that Arch Orcup's indication is his bond?"

A slight frown, like the shadow of a hummingbird crossing a polar icecap moved up the dome of Gorman's head. "For a few thousand he would be extremely unwise not to assure that the spirit of the original is not violated by some hack. He seemed to agree."

Clem laughed like a giant, liberated from the profitless quibbles that had lurked in his conversation with me. (And I was glad to see them swept away.) "I've always wanted to do a spirit play. Be the hack of the spirit. For a few thousand wouldn't I be unwise not to guard the spirit while they're violating the body?"

"I warned him, so it is off of my head that your integrity has had a reputation of being uncontrollable though not violent," Gorman said smiling. "I wish to repeat in so many words what Archie said to me verbatim. 'I love'm tough,' he said. Apparently he was not unacquainted through theatrical gossip and word of mouth about your intransigent attitudes toward not compromising. I was deeply moved to hear him instance, 'I need allies out here.' Archie is not of the Old Guard any more than his father was."

"Who is so mean as to compromise with compromise? Whole hog or none. No king, no bishop. Susan!" Clem shouted toward the kitchen. "'Our bruited arms hung up for monuments' indeed! Orcup and Anderson will go down together with their yellow banners flying! I've raised my yellow battle flag, Hollywood. Hooo, hoooo. Susan, we're en route again!"

Then his nose wrinkled as he smelled what I had been smelling for some time. From the kitchen (it must have come out in a blast when the oven door was open) an actual smell of burning flesh was drifting upon us, as if it were a purposeful counterirritant to the smell I had been imagining.

"My love's on fire," Clem shouted to us, and he galloped out to find if that was really so. Presently screeches and wails—in good-humored play, as far as I could tell—came in from the same source as the smoke.

In case this noise wasn't from good humor—and because I didn't dare risk an observation that might have seemed carping—I covered it by saying loudly to Gorman, "Well, your news seems to have made him happy."

Gorman measured me by that remark, silently said, Oh, dear, to himself, then seemed to decide I couldn't be quite such a fool. "No. He is not happy. Clement is a very complex personality, a true artist personality. Money cannot make him happy."

I said that nevertheless it seemed to give symptomatic relief. Gorman replied to me with a silence that said he knew very well that psychiatrists had their jargon, but since I presumably had one too, why didn't I stick to my own?

And in that silence we heard Clem's voice. "I told you for Jesus Christ's sake to get in a maid or a cook. He's an old friend."

Gorman said, "Clement takes things too hard. He told you we have been compelled by the circumstance of events no one's fault to discontinue the play? Yes? He took occasion to offer a heartbreaking scene to one and all the guests at my party last night. Revolting to such as fail to comprehend the artist nature or make all due allowances. Not as a man ought to behave. His levity is frequently superficial to hide the true hurt. Money may not be a boon to him as some people find it." Then he shrugged. "But he wants it so badly." And of all the things Clem wanted badly, that was one, at least, that he could be given.

Susan had done as well with her dining table as she had with the Christmas tree I admired so much. We were called in presently to a handsome and conservative display of bounty. Steaming vegetables, Technicolor salads, good wine and the handsome platter that bore the duck were all so tempting as to be almost vocal in their invitation to enjoy them. Tall candles waved their yellow flags. At the head of her table, for the crowning bit of décor she had Clement Anderson, pink-cheeked and sick of Christmas, tamed by all of us who meant to give him what he wanted, full of tremors and tics and memories of indignity, but able to go on. What Susan had assembled in her dining room had to be worth all it cost, I thought as I sat down. I could think of nothing to pray for except that this much felicity, at least, would endure.

350

We settled into our places with a counterpointed conversation about our individual memories of Christmas—how it had been in Vienna before the Anschluss, in Boda that first winter that Clem went home from college (he had gone with Sheila, but he told it now as if he had been alone), in Los Angeles where Susan had (quite literally like Cinderella) suffered from a cruel (but in this telling comic) stepmother, and my paling memories of boyhood in Buffalo. To the degree that was required we knew each other now, and it may have been some subtle recognition that we were all children of disaster which gave us a sense of belonging equally to a family where none of us had prerogatives over the others.

When she cleared away the plates and the wineglasses from the first course, Susan let her hand rest very briefly but warmly on my shoulder, as if she had felt from all the evening that had preceded that I was the one who most needed reassurance.

Then she asked Clem to begin carving the duck.

The knife and fork he took up were the latest, tasteful thing in Danish steel, with wooden handles. Costly Excaliburs among cutlery. But they would not penetrate that small, resistant carcass Clem had pulled up in front of him.

It appeared that his first effort to cut was in all good faith and confidence. But as his arm began to saw faster and faster without consequence, a look faintly querulous and sly spread over his face. He put one elbow on the table, cocking the knife up beside his ear. With the fork he poked here and there at the charred black spots on the skin. "Did you cook this with a flame thrower?" he asked.

"It's all right!" Susan insisted. "Stop clowning."

He tried to saw his way in again. He held the blade up and stared at its edge. "The brave man does it with a sword," he said. "Cowards with a razor. Susan, go to the bathroom and get—"

I saw Susan's mouth drawn back from her teeth, not in a grin but in an absolute, uncontrollable rage. "All right, funny man," she said with a tragic hiss. "You've showed off enough for one night at my expense. 'Flush the toilet!' Give me the knife. Let me do it if you can't."

"No." Again Clem started to saw. Our wineglasses all began to jiggle and presently to slop over on the spotless cloth.

"Give it to me." Susan reached across the table and grabbed one of the trussed legs.

"I won't." Clem snatched it off the platter and ran for the kitchen with it, Susan after him. And there they seemed to be fighting for it.

There was a wild uproar of threshing bodies, falling pans, crockery breaking, and sliding feet. Finally a slam as someone—and it would have been Susan—was thrown full length on the floor. Then sobs. Gorman and I did not look at each other.

They came back at last with Clem in the lead, bearing the platter on which lay the mutilated duck. He had hacked it apart with a butcher knife—or clawed it apart with his nails. It reminded me vaguely of a Japanese soldier who had committed hara-kiri by exploding a hand grenade inside his trousers. Clem wore an alcoholic smirk of triumph. Susan's face was locked in a smile.

He put the platter before us, saying, "Only my wife, gentlemen, could manage to burn it and leave it raw in one operation."

"It's not raw," she said.

"It's bleeding!"

"It's rare."

"Don't tell me that isn't blood. Only a cannibal would touch it. Let's all have something to drink instead."

"Please," Gorman said. "It's good food. Let us eat and be thankful." He and I served ourselves.

"I suppose that horse-face Sheila could have done better," Susan said.

No one heard her. At least none of us dared let her outcry strike full in the center of our consciousness. But in evading it we gave up the frail hopeful pretenses of sociability with which the meal had begun. We went on talking afterward. The cadence and volume of sound were not for more than a second abated. But after this I felt that Susan was watching the rest of us with the malign anxiety of a child who has understood that the threat of screaming will compel adults to do almost anything. Clem ate nothing at all, but drank wine instead, sneering at us, I thought, as if he were watching us eat mud.

Now and then I had the illusion that the wine was sobering him, or keeping up some constant, necessary level of combustible alcohol in his blood which in turn sustained his will to restore the eggshell surface of our communion. I believe to this day that when he began to talk about Susan he saw himself as her protector, redressing some grievous impression she had made on us.

Ever since he met her, he said, he had told her that she ought to write a novel about her life. It could be called The Darling, he had suggested, not because there was a Chekhov story of that title—though there was indeed, indeed there was, and Susan was very much like the woman Chekhov described in that she could remake herself into the ideal wife of any man she married—but because it would give a modern, or, one might say, a twentieth-century, replay of the Chekhovian idea, and in our time and place the requirements for a darling were interestingly changed.

He had bought her an enormous ledger in which he encouraged her to put down everything she could remember from her chameleon childhood and surchameleon days in Hollywood. She was to put down with utter frankness the pain she had felt from being considered so stupid in grade school. Actually she was not stupid at all, but merely reticent, as so many children are who suffer the handicaps of having worthless and stupid parents. Her teachers had not understood that her passionate interest was focused on going to Shirley Temple movies rather than the subjects to which they wished to force her. It bespoke her nature as darling to have found an elderly sea captain who shared her enthusiasm for Shirley and took her to every Temple picture not once but ten, twenty, thirty times. The children at school who knew only a runny-nosed, lath-skinny, tongue-tied little moron would have been astounded to hear her and the sea captain discussing at length and in incredible detail every bit of dialogue and every tinseled cliché from each of these films.

But the sea captain had died suddenly—no doubt it was a timely death, since it seemed he was working up his nerve to violate his little friend, but perhaps untimely, since he had many times promised to include her in his will. After the captain's death her stepmother had made inquiries, but had been told there was no will. The old gentleman's property had gone to three widowed sisters.

In Clem's serious view, a spark had been lighted by the glamour of all those movies. Miraculously, however you looked at it (and he could see that the story might be told with utter vulgarity or with supreme delicacy), the homely child had transformed herself—from the inside out—into her ideal. She had become beautiful from contemplating an ideal of beauty. As we knew, that sometimes happened, and right here at the table we had the living proof that the celluloid Shirley could be re-created in the flesh.

Well, not to go through the whole story tonight ("Thank God," Susan said with a half-flattered, half-hostile laugh) but to get back to his point of why her novel should be called The Darling, take the way Susan had transformed herself in the relatively short space of time that she had been his darling.

She had never read a book except The Brothers Karamazov before she met him, and even with that she had trouble. She couldn't keep

Brother William distinct from Brother Alphonse and never did know why the Devil should speak to Ivan in the language that Ivan himself had used. But since she had become the beloved of an egghead she had embarked on a task of self-education that would astonish Horace Mann and John Dewey themselves. She had been through the great books that contained all the great ideas ever conceived by the human mind and was herself a walking, talking synopticon. Not content with immersing herself in modern literature, she had looked into the literature of every major period, and though he would not claim she had read, say, Ovid's Metamorphoses, he was sure she was familiar with it, as with Wordsworth's Prelude or Horace's most important odes. Many a time he had come on her reciting, in full, great love poems by Alfred, Lord Tennyson, Christina Rossetti and Andrew Marvell, not to mention John Donne, in whose works she had found, marveling, that a man who lived over three hundred years ago could have had such a modern attitude toward love.

That was what he meant by insisting—and he would insist!—that her book be called The Darling. For once again, as in the case of the Shirley Temple movies, an ideal had been fixed in her mind and she was transforming herself utterly to comply with it. He hoped that she would not carry this to the point of transforming (again) her physical appearance. No, her darling trick there must be to preserve herself just as she was. But the spiritual woman who emerged at last would be as different as a butterfly from a larva.

I said that Clem began this awful description, analysis, whatever it was, with some intention of showing her off to advantage. And though his tone was impossible to interpret, varying as it did from the unmistakably satiric to the probably solemn, each of us was being given an interpretation. When he finally began to dribble off into incoherences and sleepy mutterings to himself, I was dismayed almost to despair to see that it all had mollified Susan considerably. The pages of the ledger he had bought her would, I was afraid, remain forever blank.

Still, he had got us through the meal with his ramblings before he passed out. But halfway through, something had seemed to go wrong with my teeth so that the invulnerable, bleeding duck flesh I chewed would not yield at all. Bit by bit I had to swallow it whole.

Then, like all genuine tortures, the meal ended abruptly. Susan said, as if everything were all right, "Would you gentlemen like to retire to the living room for your liqueurs?"

But once Gorman and I were on our feet we were both too smart to sit down again. We edged toward the entrance hall bubbling excuses, allying ourselves in a polite phalanx of defense that Susan could not penetrate. She wanted us to stay on. I thought she might be afraid of a physical assault from Clem, but apparently she was not. In any case I was not to be held by the promise of any more goodies.

Clem had not come from the dining room when we were putting on our coats. I was trying to decide whether or not to risk going back to say good night to him when he finally came trotting after us. His face was so distressed that he might have been afraid of being left with her. He grabbed Gorman's arm and mine, saying, "Don't go without Clem. We'll go down and look at Brooklyn Bridge. So much to see and every night."

"Some other time," we both said. We both asked him to call us in the morning.

"Too proud. I come from very aristocratic lines, though crossed. Hyacinth, chien de race. Screw you, buddies." He half turned to the right, lunged into and across the umbrella rack, driving his head straight into the wall.

He dropped like a poleaxed steer and lay there so ominously still that I bent to feel his pulse. It seemed strong to me, and I thought that both Gorman and Susan were smiling condescendingly at my concern. We got him onto his feet then and walked him into the bedroom like a surrealist wheelbarrow with rubbery handles and legs for spokes.

At the door he reeled away from us. With luck or weird dexterity he contrived to land plumply on his back on the bed. But all evidence of ability to take care of himself was annoying at this point.

He lay there snoring and seeming asleep. Susan, with a wink at us that was intended to say, He's just a lovable pranky boy and all's well, pulled off his shoes.

Then, before we turned away to leave them, she began unbuckling his belt. No doubt in wifely kindness, only ill-timed because she was a bit drunk herself, she opened his fly and began to pull off his pants.

It was awkward enough that she should have done this before we were quite gone, but I would have thought nothing of it if Clem had not suddenly, out of his apparently deep stupor, reached to seize her wrists, half raising himself and looking wildly from one to another of us. "Button me," he begged in what I swear was the voice of a child. "Button me! I'm writing a great poem. It cancels hope. Do you understand that, Dick? Button me, somebody."

Susan bore him back onto the bed, falling heavily on him, kissing his wet temples and the curling locks of hair plastered against them. "I'll button you, darling. Oh, I'm sorry. I'm sorry. I'm sorry."

Quietly Gorman and I took our way out of the house.

We stood on the curb together a few minutes later, pulling our scarves tighter against the increasing snow. Cabs were scarce at this hour, but we let two or three go by, as if we were waiting to find some formula by which we might excuse ourselves for what we had seen.

"You know," Gorman said at length. "Susan made herself a very dead pigeon for him."

"I suppose this isn't the first time they've had ... an uproar."

"Not the uproar. What she said about Sheila," he insisted wisely. "That was very—final."

"He won't remember tomorrow that she said it."

"Let us hope not," he said. "I hope our Clement will understand he needs her. But in my estimation he will remember."

Then a cab spotted us and pulled up. I insisted that he take it. I wanted to stand a while in the snow until I had some mastery over my own thoughts, some thread by which I could connect what I knew damn well I was going to remember of tonight with the judgments and prejudices I lived with on the other side of the abyss. I was trying to chew it the way I had tried to chew the duck at dinner, and my stomach told me I could not stand to swallow much more whole.

I remember the wave after wave of resentment that passed over me as I stood there, racking me like the convulsions of vomiting. And the promises I made to myself to blot out of my mind all I knew of Clem except the best.

So I consoled myself, without purgation. All of this experience in New York was still lying in great undigested chunks in my mind when I went home a few days later (without seeing Clem or Sheila or Susan again—I had only nerve enough to go see Clem's play).

Mere distance gave me some perspective on it—all that distance can, at any rate. Time let it settle. And Janet helped, as she always does in crises of doubt, by assuring me that no good lies in suffering over things that can not be helped.

Only—once when we were still talking about it in February—she asked what I had been gathering courage to ask myself. "Do you think it can't be helped?"

"How so?"

"I don't mean helped right now. And I don't think I mean helped by us, though if an occasion did present itself where we could do something I'd—do almost anything to help, including slipping arsenic to that Cindy Susan."

"Susan is good."

"You're very stubborn about that and you may be right and I'm not talented in poisons anyway," Janet said. "Nevertheless—"

"Nevertheless you think it would be better if Susan were gently removed, somehow erased from reality, canceled like God's error."

"I don't wish her any harm, in fact I'm willing to wish her all the best. On your say-so. Only, isn't the best, as we conceive it, that Clem and Sheila should get back together again? And isn't there—from all you've told me—every reason to think they will?"

"It's a possibility," I said. "If Clem doesn't drink himself to death first."

"It's more than a possibility," Janet said. "I have a secure faith that's what will happen. Barring accidents, of course. It's not so different from when Clem went to war and got mixed up with that English girl—got her pregnant or whatever he did and the child was stillborn and he came back to Sheila. He and Sheila are still very much linked. You've dwelt enough on that impression. And I think Clem wants to come back. Wants to dump his showers of gold in Sheila's lap."

"The English girl was never pregnant," I said. Furthermore there were a thousand uncertainties that Janet's theory skipped over blithely. And yet I found increasingly that the possibility Janet liked to dwell on was coming to seem a likelihood to me—was beginning to show where all the inscrutable signs I had noted at Christmas were pointing. I was sure enough that it was not merely what we wanted to happen. Surely both of us still knew enough of Clem to know that he wanted it, too.

And then, in March of that year, Jill (that faithful hound of superficial facts) found a piece in the paper that told us Cindy Hunt was dead.

She had died (poor Pseudonym) of an ectopic pregnancy while vacationing in Mexico with her husband, "screenwriter Clement Anderson." Pseudonymous death had caught her all unexpectedly, this graceless announcement said. When the couple left Hollywood a week before the tragic mischance, she had appeared in "radiant health."

The report was, like all the trashy prose in which Cindy Hunt had lived and charmed us, so shallow and unreal that the one absolutely accurate fact of death seemed hardly to contrast with any of the testimonies that she had lived. Where life is reduced to glamour, the glamorous fact of death hardly seems a change worth mourning. I remembered my half-drunken intuition that she was of the "superfluous population," a mere number. The brisk falsity of the story in the paper tended to confirm this as one bad dream confirms another. But she had reached for life, this neverborn one, and I had intimations, too, of the cruel ironies involved in her wish.

When Janet heard the news she was silent, lost in a maze of guilt that may have made her envy those born with a talent for poison. We would not discuss the guilt we knew, for it lay too far from the center of our lives, like the low-lying cindery clouds on the horizon that, on a sunny day, bring storm to some other city. We had no language to express directly our responsibility.

But I asked, after allowing time for the immediate shock to pass, "Do you think Clem will go back to Sheila now?"

Instead of answering directly she said, "I didn't want it to happen this way."

And it seemed to both of us that what we hoped for would be harder now that the visible obstacle was removed.

# V

# KNIGHT RIDING BETWEEN DEATH AND THE DEVIL

*It's only real success that wanes, it's only solid things that melt.*

—HENRY JAMES, "Greville Fane"

# 13

THESE INLAND YEARS of my life, the enjoyment of an academic sinecure, have sheltered me from a great deal and spared me nothing. In my privacy I have heard the muttering of the sea that means to have, in its own time, its own. At noon on a windless day I have heard the trees shake and, at the cocktail hour, among undemanding, respected and respectful friends, have known without warning—as if the very absence of warning were the symbol of its profundity—what the elder Henry James called "a sense of vastation." Sometimes that primal dream of loss, of something being over before one quite knows it is happening, has come on me in the comfort of lethargy, as palpitations come on a day of supreme health, or as thoughts of Peter seeking his inverted crucifixion come to terrify one on Easter morning.

I always told curious or interested friends that I had enjoyed Clem's *Death and the Devil* very much when I saw it performed in New York. I told the truth. I had enjoyed it, just as at first meeting I had enjoyed the company of Susan. In lengthening perspective I was not more shaken by my glimpse of Clem's second marriage than by my awareness of what he had done to his play.

In saying this I do not suppose I am venturing into the field of theatrical criticism. That field, like every other compartmented aspect of our present life, has its experts. They in turn have support in depth from those initiated in the present taste. For all I know such people may have unbeatable stratagems for demonstrating that Clem's play in the form eventually produced on Broadway was "better" than his original drafts.

I would have to concede that the stylized and disciplined action I watched that night won such an authority over my emotions as to disengage them effectively from thoughts awakened when I had read the play some time before in Paris. In the theater I did not think of the "real" Potters on whom the characters had been modeled, and, more significantly, I found in the central female character no allegory of the creative imagination wakened to the point of vulnerability and then ravished (though Clem had once intended the action to suggest this much, supposing Cecile to be an objectified representation of the mind, baited beyond its safe shell of innocence by the promises of the natural and social worlds).

361

Like a visitor in a well-appointed hospital waiting room, I was made to feel in the theater that what passed before my diverted eyes was all that was real of tragedy and death. The past—the human condition, our war, our betrayed youth—was only this doctored spectacle, and of its timid "Boo" no one who could afford the price of admission need be much frightened.

The central character of the play—still like Cecile in this respect—had an insuperable wound. But in the version I saw this had been transposed from Cecile's short upper lip into a psychic preoccupation with the house in which she and five generations of ancestors had been born. ("We stopped old Boney at the Channel, and we've stopped Mr. Hitler," says an old retainer who might as well have been named Firs.) The girl's enchantment with the historic house was confirmed and touched with a hint of evil by the suggestions of incest yielded by her recollections of her father. No more hint of incest than a lady would carry from spraying some into the air and walking through it; nevertheless, a fashionable scent. (The play was Cherry Orchard Becomes Electra, as Clem had so precisely characterized it. "You can't sell the money men on art unless you can show them where you invoked Chekhov or Old Gene," he said.)

The aging friend whom Cecile intends initially to marry is not depicted as a philologist. (If he were a philologist the audience would expect him to be doing something with words.) He is a titled neighbor who resembles and wishes to resemble the girl's dead, amorous father.

The American soldier who comes to waken the sleeping princess with his playboy kisses and brash irreverence is an oddly scrambled version of Clem as he might have appeared to a sociologist with the troops. (Given that any sociologist who had been with the troops in England in 1943 and 1944 would probably, in ten years, have altered his findings to conform to intellectual fads. I do not mean to set them above playwrights in responsibility to their subject.)

The soldier, at any rate, is just so much of an idealist as will expose the danger represented by idealists to an audience schooled to mistrust "true believers" in anything. He believes in Freud's task of liberation ("If the girl needs a lay, lay her"), the Four Freedoms ("Think of it. Freedom from fear! Never to be afraid again. Don't be afraid, darling, I won't hurt you"), les lendemains qui chanteraient ("a better Coventry will rise from the mire and ashes"), Romanticism's divinity of the flesh ("I believe that my body in yours is God in God"). He believes in Free France, equality of the races, sexes and faiths, and when he mentions a group of men the third name is Jewish, the second probably that of a Negro. For a cheap laugh, he is represented as believing in the Century of the Common Man. Now, given his own interpretations, these were all things that Clem had believed in when, once upon a time, he fell among the Potters. He had believed along with many of the rest of us, who probably had our own interpretations of them as well. But these beliefs had plainly been salted into the character as ingredients to prepare the audience for his untrustworthy behavior, to make them laugh with the slightly uncomfortable recollection that Back Then they had trifled with such foolishness, too.

Cecile's mother comes across as an oddly proportioned figure of comedy and tragedy, presiding over her daughter's seduction by the handsome stranger very much like the stock figure of Mom in the anti-Mom literature of our societal critics. She means to pay off everyone, including her dead husband. She is not a woman to take incest lying down.

Most illuminating, though, was the transposition that had been made in the character of the brute who replaces the hero in Cecile's life, after the hero, with fake idealism, deserts her for battle, the girl at home and country.

In the drafts I had once read in Paris, it had been a Negro sergeant who plucked the awakened Cecile, got her pregnant and was senselessly murdered by her in her final retreat into the darkness from which the idealistic soldier (the Devil of the title?) had pretended the wish to free her.

Harkness, the buck-toothed educator of reality, had gone through the avatar of a Negro Young Man Carbuncular to become—under the exigency of offending no ticket-buying or reviewing liberals—a gross Southern proletarian, come to England by way of a Detroit assembly line.

(When the work was restreamlined for Hollywood—not by Clem after all; he never reported back to the studio after Susan's death—this character would appear as an underprivileged and misunderstood youth, temperamentally inclined toward rape and therefore eminently forgivable because of inadequate recreational facilities as a child.)

On stage they were an altogether likable and easily understood lot. And, as I said, their simplicity consoled me while I was in my seat. While the snub-nosed actress tore Cecile's goblin-haunted silences to tatters and with a definitive pistol shot disposed of the boorish intruder in her sexual garden, I felt protected from the host of unborn possibilities that I once thought were Clem's real legacy from the war, shared with very many of us who had less promise of articulating them.

Charmed and comforted in the theater, I felt how much better were the lightly hidden secrets of the past which the post-Freudian theater can display with a prestidigitator's sweep of revelation than the fatal obviousness of the actual Cecile's ugly mouth. We would pretend not to notice her mouth in social life. You can't tell a lady to her face that her irremediable skull has determined the conditions of her unhappiness. And the theater is a social institution, where all raging material is made conformable to social usages. In a well-doctored play, like Clem's, motives are served up like the courses in a formal meal—and how much more consoling to the social instinct that is than Clem's poetic notion that "motives are nothing much, God reads the event."

Once upon a time what I had most admired in Clem's discoveries as a writer was a kind of Calvinism that had nothing to do with the schema of psychiatry or the social sciences, a candor at once ruthless and benevolent in its discriminations, a persuasive sense of the value or weight of every kind of circumstance, which seemed to me the superlative gift for a writer. Grace of this gift and by its grace alone a writer can point out what is beyond redemption in our lives and what is not—that is, write in the tragic vein, establishing some contact of awe between us and the mysteries that live us. Once he repudiates his gift, he descends to the pretense that anyone and anything is redeemable, if and if and if. He descends to the social lie that, with its pretenses of explaining everything, shelters us so briefly from reality.

I had come to the point of feeling satisfied that he should use the theater to deny the nature of tragedy, and perhaps my reflections on that night in the theater brought me to face Clem's willful betrayal of the past and to the question of why he had done it.

To answer the question of why Clem himself had abstracted the play from its responsibilities—rendering it truly into a "nonrepresentational" work, in some ways like the paintings that were the fashion of the epoch—would be no more and no less, I have thought, than to answer the question of why he left Sheila. For more than once I have thought that Clem's divorce was a literary artifice manqué, either tried in the wrong medium or an accidental byproduct of the theatrical medium he was then assaying. I suppose it is often the case that a writer—if he is a good writer and unless he is a very great writer or is supported by a conservative religious faith—is apt to cut his literary images with the same scissors he uses on life, like a child who cuts an admirable paper star but cuts a ragged hole in the tablecloth at the same time. The immediate and personal life may be involved in the creative act because there is nothing else to feed the imagination.

However detached the artist may wish to be, he will learn sometime that the world on which his imagination acts is singular and indivisible. His discoveries, if they have any value, are always going to be over determined, as Freud says dreams are.

But, I am told by all those who wish to admire the products of the artist and ignore his life, we do not ask of the imagination that it involve and compromise the private life of the artist.

Well, of course not. Nothing is asked of the imagination originally, for only the unsummoned imagination can conceive what it might be asked. And then, in the tragic denouement of an artist's life, in that period when the admirers of the work wish to avert their eyes, the imagination discovers nothing to be worth its attention except that cruel process from which it was born. Then the dissolution begins. The relation between the man and the work is seen to be not spurious, but fated.

I was told by both Clem and Sheila that the period in which he was rewriting the play to fit the requirements of the new public coincided remarkably with the period in which he was, so to speak, getting ready to publish word of a divorce ripening to its term. Line by line he labored to transpose what he had first wrought into its marketable equivalent, and tissue by tissue he simultaneously transposed the responsibilities, joys and agonies of his marriage into annoyances, impediments and obstacles holding him back from the immolation his imagination had begun to shape.

One might, I suppose, still argue that this coincidence of times is meaningless in itself. There is nothing inevitably mantic about a decision to make money by pleasing the customer. And I would concede that the servility with which he followed the coils of fashion in the theater is only part of the overdetermination for the dream in which he died. It is only when one assumes a chosen and deliberate—an expressive—irony in his public exposure of dissolution that one is permitted to say that all of it expresses the same terrible mockery, and the same love.

I think he corrupted and disfigured himself—life and work— because he was ours. As if, by divorce and the castration of his play, the same statement in different modes, he were to say, "I gave you my wife and my enjoyable play because I owed you explanations. You were addicted to saying, when you were literate enough, that always Time's wingéd chariot behind your back you heard. But who except yourselves did Time's work on your generation? By the kindest-seeming and most tolerant of frauds you sold yourselves for the sake of selves you never meant to become. Saturn had no appetite for his children more savage than your wish to swallow down what children you once knew yourselves to be. You were still unconquered when you came home from your war—and what you were then you consumed to make into a race more convenient to its inventions and better tuned to its self-lies than it had ever been before. What you had learned from the war at near-bankrupting cost you translated into an alien tongue. I thought you were in Rats Alley, where the painters lost their subject matter. You made yourselves alien in your own land and lives. You went 'abstract' to escape the concrete weapons you had to manufacture. Then—look!—so did I, because I was a writer and as a writer I was nothing if I did not go with you into your wilderness."

But the rest of us have outlived him? For a while.

I believe the vulgarization itself of his play is part of the code by which he expressed what he knew, that the play, in his ironic hands, became an inscrutable mirror that shows us what we have become with the same mocking efficiency as it hides what we might have been, as if it were the ultimate trick of the technique for a period of decadence of which Cyril Connolly speaks.

I have no keys to its code. I would like to trace back the process of the play's transformation, step by step, to its pure genesis, and I can only make a gross leap back in time to show the vacated camp where the visions were hatched. The play serves only as a device for contrasting one kind of literary success with another.

Against the opaque banality of the play I set a few years of Clem's actual life when he clarified for himself the tragic view required to make him accept it. If all too much of my account will seem a lament for talents missing the mark they might have defined for themselves, still I can now report a time when he truly reigned as King of the Hill. In the first years after the war he had what he deserved to have. He became what, from the first, he had intended to be.

I think that during the period of this success he took on Promethean debts (to use Jung's grateful phrase). He would go on paying those debts to the end of his paradoxical life. The powers would at last say to him, "Well, you wanted to be a writer. What does it matter that you have forgotten why? Go on. We'll let you rub your nose in it."

But the profit of his bargain depends on the angle from which it is observed. If one goes back to the high plateau where he taught himself how to love fate, one can feel that he must then have loved even what he foresaw of the topsy-turvy descent that his generation's innocence and sloth would require of him.

# 14

IN THE SUMMER of 1946 Clem, Sheila, Janet and I shared a house three miles north of Acapulco. We lived on the ocean side of town, where the breakers were too high for swimming. Our little house sat in a lush nest of trees surrounded by shale and scrub. The sun bore down hard all day long, but the mornings were good for work.

Clem and I both had "studies." At least, we had places to which we could retire alone. Mine was on a palm-shaded north veranda. His was in a little barn on the lizard run of gravel just below the house. From our worktables both of us could see the beach where our wives spent the morning—leather-colored girls against the fantastically glittering wall of surf.

A mile down the beach was the Pogorskis' shanty. When we refused to talk to our wives at need, they went there for refreshments and passionate conversation, and for such news of the world recovering from the war as came through Claude Pogorski's treble indignation.

Overhead there were always vultures. No doubt they fulfilled a purely symbolic function, since I never, to my recollection, saw one of them stoop to pick up food.

Sheila was in the early months of her first pregnancy. In figure and character she displayed the heart-knotting exuberance of a woman who has seized exactly all she wants. At noon she would sit half drowsily at the table with us, smiling at flies and lizards, stuffing herself with melons and the fish delivered by a boy who bicycled out from town. Now and then out of sheer inability to contain her satisfaction she trailed her fingers on Clem's bare leg or the neat little potbelly he had already begun to affect—in imitation of her, he said.

"How're we going to persuade her home?" Clem would say with a pretense of worry, balancing a seed on the tip of his tongue and spitting it onto the stones between his tennis shoes. "O.K., then. I'll build you a stone tower here and become the spic Robinson Jeffers."

"I'm worth it. I breed good," Sheila said. "I am what the poets labored for."

"That's one of my titles. Don't get it soiled before I write something to go with it," Clem said. Lowering his lids against the unfaltering glare from the sea, he explained that he had spent the entire morning in his study making up more titles. "I'm going to write a book that's made up of nothing but titles."

"It won't pass the time," Janet said.

"No. But it will be language charged to its highest potential with meaning."

"Gee!"

"People won't have to reread a lot of filler that they've already read," he insisted. "Imagine a reader who's got a thousand novels already under his belt, and in every one of them somebody runs out in the street at some point and hails a cab to take him to some important place. Who wants to read about that after a thousand times? And, as far as important places go, how many are there? The home of some ginch fuming like nitric acid. One. Bars where significant or nostalgic rendezvous take place. Two. Hospitals where people have reconciliations after near-fatal accidents. Three. Now, who wants to read about those things over and over again?"

"Put in new adjectives," Janet said.

"There are no more," Clem said. "So I merely mean to take account of the fact that my readers have read other fiction and give them a list of evocative titles. They can imagine for themselves all this stuff about fuming pussy, nostalgic rendezvous and the accidents. Now, wait. Don't criticize until you understand. Let me try some on you."

"I am what the poets labored for," Sheila said.

"Be quiet," Clem admonished. "'Bad Cat,'" he said. He looked at us expectantly and we looked at him expectantly. He seemed disappointed. "You don't see the story?" he demanded. "'Bad Cat!'" he shouted, as if shouting might prompt us to have the complete fictional vision.

Then, more in disappointment than in anger, he said, "I can't hear those syllables without at once visualizing a depressing city landscape with someone like John Garfield coming along kicking a can. He looks up and sees this forty-year-old woman peering down at him through the slats of the fire escape. He hails a taxicab, goes to a bar where the beer fumes like dry ice—All right. This heat has flattened your brains. Let me try some more."

He pulled a list from the pocket of his suntan pants and began to read, pausing now and then to see if our imaginations came panting after him.

"'The Bleeding Sculptor,' 'The Little Toy Friends,' 'Girls at Their Play,' 'The Fair at Tula,' 'Hair on the Moon,' 'Maid by Courtesy,' 'No Deposit, No Return,' 'The Saint of Boda'—"

"Oh-oh," Sheila said.

He glared at her. "That's not a reference to me. You don't get it, stupid? On a terrible, hot day during the drought years this bum drops off the freight train that twice a week goes through Boda. Later it emerges that he was once a successful boy evangelist in Los Angeles but has become a cross between an existentialist and a psychotic. No one knows what to make of him, but they need something, with all that sun boiling down on them and the earth spinning like a nasty little cinder—"

"Now the taxicab?" Janet asked.

"There are no taxicabs in Boda," he told her loftily. His expression changed to gratitude, and with an Anderson pencil (a chewed yellow stick splintered at both ends, sometimes producing only indentations when he wrote) he added something to his list. "'No Taxicabs in Boda,'" he said in awe.

"I get that one," I said. "Someone who looks like John Garfield is walking past the Baptist church. He looks up and sees a forty-year-old woman peering down at him from the belfry. It is his mother. He tries to hail a taxicab, but ... but ..."

"You're a fit reader," Clem acknowledged.

"No taxis, but plenty of fuming girls," Sheila said. "Clem's been remembering all the girls in Boda for three generations so he can use them in his novel. Whenever he remembers another one who frustrated his boyish pride I have to plead my condition."

"Let me go on," he said loftily. "'The Sticky Wicket,' 'Playing Doctor in Chesterfield and Boda,' 'The Throne of Oedipus,' 'The Boys with Their Light Summer Carbuncles,' 'Widow's Might,' 'Finger in the Pie,' 'An Image of His State,' 'The Girl with the Freckled Back,' 'Frost and Sun,' 'The Fields Are White'—that's from the New Testament and about a detachment of eight Negro sanitary troops who were attached to us once. The question was whether, being sanitary, they might or might not have access to the German cat-house patronized by my copains. Opens with a character looks like Paul Robeson coming along the street kicking a knackwurst. He looks up ... Take it from there."

Janet said, "Harrumph. I heard your typewriter and thought you were working. Is this what you did this morning, Clem?"

"Only a part," he said. "Let me go on. *Death and the Devil,*' *The Ascent of Pride,*' *Batter My Heart,*' *Batter My*—' What do you mean, is this what I did, Janny? Don't you realize that everything I do is work? I'm working now," he said in sudden astonishment, pausing to stare in wonderment down the relaxed, banana curve of his body, disposed in utterly indolent torpor over the cushions with which he had fattened his chair. He stared significantly up at the vultures, an indication and a gesture designed not at all to carry our gaze upward but to demonstrate the process of his toiling.

"He's working on a poem about vultures," I said. "Clem, when I have fears that you may cease to be before your pen has garnered up these daily treasures—"

"Gerald!" he said, staring at me.

"What?"

"You reminded me of Gerald Potter, who used to bat my lines back like that."

"And you're writing about him, too? At this very minute?"

He would not deny it. "About everything. About everything that has ever happened to me at every minute of my life. You ought to read what I'm doing, Dick. 'Modesty aside, it is something like The Iliad.'"

And if modesty were not put aside?

"It would be just the same," Clem said. "And it's going to go on forever." He stared up contentedly at the vultures and finished his wine. "We're going to stay here until I've remembered every awful thing that ever happened and put it down. Jesus, a vulture is a lovely bird. He eats everything. Dick, isn't there some culture where the vulture is a god?"

I quoted "Une Saison en Enfer": "'I bury the dead in my belly.'"

"That's very like The Iliad, too," he said. "I wonder if I can work that in somewhere? I've done just that, you know. In my belly."

Through ten weeks of that prosperous summer we were treated to some such dwindling eruption of his mind every day. This lunchtime jabber was, of course, his way of unwinding from his morning's work, a playful scattering before his grubby fellows of the gems he had that morning unearthed without finding a place for them in the opus at hand. But after a while, beyond the plain profusion of gauds and trinkets that seemed to mushroom into his head—which would not distinguish him from a run-of-the-mill master of ceremonies or anyone else with a gift for patter—I began to notice the way some of his throwaway ideas would reappear, enlarged or given a fresh nuance so that I could feel we were overhearing what he heard down in the barn where he was making his novel. That is, there was a constant sifting and sorting detectable even to me. He was finding out which of all that mighty sum of fragments under review were sterile and which might, properly tended, grow. And I got some idea of how his immediate circumstances and whatever people were around him were the soil into which he thrust his growing shoots, trusting them to mature. His method—blind enough, I am sure—was not so much to recapture the past by an almighty concentration on it as to get it going again, on however miniature and distorted a scale, in the visible present. He was constantly fitting us as characters, as he might have hung costumes and masks on us, requiring of us only that we make the costumes wiggle and the masks speak.

I think it came as a surprise to all of us how steadily the rhythm of Clem's work increased while we stayed there. Actually the trip had been conceived as a luxurious escape that we all owed ourselves whether we could afford it or not. We all had a little money saved up from the war. We were at the same time tired and restless. A friend of mine had suggested that Acapulco was attractive and out of the way— which at that time it was, though in the course of the summer we seemed to be visited often enough by other Americans in much the same situation as ourselves except that they were alighting nowhere, while we had settled with a thump.

We would run into them downtown in Acapulco in one of the bars or at one of the public beaches. As often as not they would drift out to our house for an evening before they went on their way, always a little curious that we were not taking advantage of our brief vacation to see Mexico.

They were answered that it was because Clem and I were working on novels, but the real truth is that only Clem was working well. And we were probably immobilized because he had got his wheel turning faster than even he had foreseen. The rest of us had no heart and finally no wish to interrupt him. Let Mexico look at itself. We would sit and look at ourselves.

On the surface of it I should not have been content to stay. My own work—my attempt to get started at it—was going badly enough. I even toyed with the notion that Clem's busy presence was sapping the force from what I might have done in other surroundings. Whatever our relative promise had been in college, it was clear enough now who was the natural and demon-driven writer as between the two of us. And if a great many of his ideas and conceptions were chaff, I was not so foolish as to think that all of them were to be dismissed lightly. It would have taken a real literary factory to carry out all the works he projected then—but I half believed he might turn into just such a factory. I would hardly admit it to myself, but the truth is that I was mightily content to see him moving with such surety and speed into the dimensions that I would never attain. Maybe even then I was afraid of going where he was headed.

I have no idea of how many pages of his novel he wrote in those weeks we were there. The number was high, but in any case that is no proper measure of what he did. The crucial fact is that in that one freakish burst of energy he conceived or made the major decisions on the poems, fiction and drama that constitute the bulk of his achievement. It would be years before these things, for better or worse, were shaped to their final form. But to count only those intentions that were carried through is enough to indicate that this was "such a summer as had never been" in his life.

The whole book of poems to be called The Throne of Oedipus announced itself as a by-product of the novel on which he worked so assiduously. *Death and the Devil* was first shaped in his mind, though at that time he meant to make it a dramatized section in the novel designed to "contain everything." I had more than one indication that summer that behind a surface of relations apparently candid he was exploiting me as a kind of model to round out his conception of Gerald Potter—the tolerant and pimping brother, impotent by his tolerance, more than faintly guilty in his feckless wish that "everything would turn out for the best."

It is true that there had been a day years before when he had thought that he "got" his novel. And while he was in the Army he had made vast catalogues of narrative bits, dialogues, descriptions and not-to-be-labeled fragments which he meant to use. What counts is that there in Mexico he discovered the form in his heap of treasure and scrap. At last he settled on a style and a principle of selection that would obtain until he encountered Plankton.

But with his flabbergasting capacity for overdoing everything (his astonishing ability to overdo, on occasion, what no one else I have known could even get done) he wanted to depict himself in process of discovering his form. We heard a great deal, at lunch, on the beaches, over our beers as we sat commanding the zócalo, about the astounding interrelationships that he found to exist in a life that was, after all, very much like everyone else's. (His wasn't, really, but at that time it seemed less different than it would seem later.)

He was obsessed with the notion that he ought to be writing an analytical work, taking his creativity as subject. If only he had time, wasn't working on an endless novel, poems and, probably, a play. There wasn't time to write it, so he threw it out in polychrome flashes that we tolerated as clowning.

To discover a form, he thought, was to unsettle or dissolve the forms hardened by earlier learning. So, for instance, finding a form for his novel that superseded the one he had been given the day he and Sheila sat on a big granite rock was to find that he had been "given" the novel even before that. Several years, as a matter of fact, before he thought of himself as a writer or even as a potential football player. To discover the way patterns repeated in one's life was to discover that nothing would ever happen to one that hadn't been intended by the very earliest choices. At least from puberty on he had been haunted and very frequently annoyed by a déjà vu quality in all his experiences.

Take for instance this landscape before his very eyes. (We were sitting on the patio.) As soon as the real-estate agent had directed us into the yard he had recognized it. As what? As the Forbidden Land. He was not supposed to come here, though at the same time it was exactly the terrain for which he had always been searching. Even as a very small boy when he used to run up and down along the ditch at the edge of his yard, pretending that the sundown clouds were mountains and dreaming that he would raise the cash to take his mother or some other girl off to live in them, he had known they would look just like this when he got there. Just these mountains, this beach and the endless ocean beyond.

When cautioned that he was going too far, he said, "No sir. It is not I who am going too far. Something has gone too far with me."

"Roll your eyes, Clem," said Sheila, hugely enjoying his prophetic mood.

He did just that, and then announced, "Something terrible is going to happen here."

We said, All right, something terrible was going to happen everywhere.

"No sir," he said. "Only where I am looking. Everything would be all right if I didn't look into it and see the flaw. Le dent," he said. "I see Baudelaire's dent and I always have."

Joking aside (when was it ever? when was it not?), he wanted his fattening Sheila to know that he had recognized some fated bearer of his earlier experiences in her and in Cecile Potter before he had recognized them as individuals.

"Why didn't you tell me that the first night?" Sheila demanded.

"You'd have thought I was crazy."

"But I did, I did, I did," she chanted.

"See? That proves what I am saying," he announced. "I am not the only one who has experienced the power whose law I am at present literarily defining."

If this foolery had about it much that was familiar from our days in college, there was something else to it, too. "I learned things from the Army," Clem said. And so he had. There was a certain confident aggressiveness to his apparent whimsicality.

It may be that his present success with his novel—and he knew he was being successful in just the same way a mother delivering knows that she is successful—had also bolstered his confidence to the point where he could believe quite calmly that he had always been a visionary with powers outside those we are conditioned to think natural. The experiences of his childhood turned out, in the proof of writing, to be exceptionally rich in the meanings he was now co-ordinating in his novel. Did that not mean that he had chosen and undergone these experiences because they would one day turn out to be elements in the form he was, in this new cycle of progression, creating? Did he know anything in the animated retrospect of writing about his past that he had not known in the thoughtless events of ten or twenty years before? "I used to be clairvoyant without understanding what my clairvoyance saw," he said—to our outrage and amusement.

"As a child you knew me, but you didn't know it was me you knew," Sheila mocked him gravely.

"That's right," he cried eagerly. And we swarmed in with our lighthearted logic while he fought against it like a bull calf tangled in the ropes that will lead him to market.

"But you see I know how I was and you don't!" he would cry grandly. And we thought that if these mad hypotheses helped him with his real work, at least, then they were doing all one could ask of them.

We challenged him, of course, to prove his clairvoyance by predicting the future, any part of it—his own future, for example.

"Well, now," he said. "Well, now. I can't do this as well as a fortune teller, because their language is designed for it and mine is designed for something else. And everything is a matter of language. Yes, that's the point. Everything is a matter of language. But I'll tell you roughly that after having put out my eyes I will wander the earth, poorly led by my dearest daughter, and then I will die in a grove and where I am buried will be holy ground."

The amusement value of this was low. We thought we might as well let the hum of wasps fill the hot hollow of the afternoon.

374

And then he said, "Of course, anyone can claim to be Oedipus, and you think that the real one was H. Warwick Lloyd, as I know. But I will write a book to prove that I am the McCoy. But then, books don't prove anything. They are a matter of language, but nothing else is. Very well, then. Come on, Sheila. Let's go prove our reality by killing something."

After the idle arguments of lunchtime had purged him of thoughts or the wish to think, Clem and Sheila often went hunting in the afternoons. They carried Clem's old singleshot .22. With a pocketful of gold-colored bullets to spend, they trudged into the warm hills behind the house or up the beach in the opposite direction from the Pogorskis' shack. Clem's great ambition was to down one of the vultures that he admired so much. Often when we heard the distant crack of his gun it meant that he was lying on his back on the sand firing up vainly into the majesty of the sky. Or sometimes he had led Sheila into a thicket on a hilltop from which he meant to ambush the great birds.

He never hit one. But when Sheila and he came sauntering back, looking like twins in their grubbiness, the color of their skin and their sun-faded rags of clothing, he was seldom empty-handed. He brought rabbits, lizards and small birds—sometimes a few fish, if they had gone by an inlet or one of the pools in the hills.

I think none of this game was ever eaten, and I suppose Clem never expected that we would eat it. The hypothetically edible creatures were apt to lie with the inedible somewhere in the general vicinity of the barn where he worked, until maggots finished them off or a stray dog got them.

Once I found a three-foot lizard tacked by its tail to a rafter more or less above Clem's worktable.

"A model?" I asked. "Do you always work from a model, Mr. Anderson?"

Clem said, "Wouldn't it stun the hell out of you if I brought it back to life one of these days?" And I suppose that meant he was working too when he hunted and watched the disintegration of his kills. Destroying for the sake of re-creating quick life in the motionlessness of art. Needing a model for death—a vulture, if possible. Yes, just that.

But he had a subordinate motive in this indiscriminate (though modest) slaughter of small creatures. He liked to plague our neighbor and sometimes visitor Claude Pogorski. Whatever breathed was holy to Claude, and when he saw Clem's miserable trophies of the hunt hanging on our fence (or heard Clem say that he had fired on a doe rabbit running but had probably led her too far) his whole vocabulary of indignation would ignite, sometimes burning until he claimed to see a connection between this petty slaughter and the monstrosity at Hiroshima.

Claude was one of those Poles in whose face one may recognize the white likeness of an Aztec warrior, a face without the meliorating plumpness of the Mediterranean races or even the grossness of urbanization that makes German faces look civilized. He looked like a tribesman from the Far East, a real Steppenwolf. We found some irony in his presence on this coast at the opposite end of the world.

The irony of his appearance was enhanced by a thoroughgoing softness of soul. He was a sensitive plant if ever I encountered one. But he had been in the war. He had been a ward attendant in some station hospital and had spent more than a year with it on a miserable island in the South Pacific. He had ministered to the sick in the wards and taught art in the Red Cross hut attached to the hospital. But even these benevolent, noncombatant duties had seemed like a degradation into militaristic aggression.

He despised himself for having been a soldier and held a permanent grudge against the powers that had drafted him and sent him off to take part in their butcher schemes. Sometimes, to hear him talk you would have thought he was a drafted SS man, forced to take part in the massacres of Lidice or Oradour, instead of the benevolent GI he must have been. I had the distinct impression that Clem baited him into some of his self-accusing, world-accusing tirades—perhaps using Claude to refresh his memory of what he himself had talked like in college.

Neither Claude nor his wife, Venetia, had been much out of Brooklyn before the war. Claude had studied art at the Brooklyn Museum. He had won student prizes for his work and later had been shown by one of the reputable galleries in Manhattan before he was drafted. After he was discharged from the Army in 1944 "for the good of the service" he might have returned to a teaching job in New York and the prospect of increasing note as a painter. Could have—if it had not been for the iron of guilt and antimilitarism festering in his soul.

Claude and Venetia had been political since their cradle days. As a matter of fact, they had met—at ages eight and six, respectively—when their parents took them to a Communist picnic up the river from New York. While they were in grade school they had marched with tiny red banners demanding freedom for Tom Mooney and after puberty they had thought of themselves as professionals of the revolution. Throughout the Thirties, guided at first by their families, they had sifted through the meshes that separated extreme leftist factions. They became Trotskyites, then splinter Trotskyites, then splinter-splinter, and so on until there was merely a two-family enclave of Pogorskis and Smilens banded together in the true faith, considering all Brooklyn around them as the enemy camp of reaction or traitors to the true cause. We said sometimes, to clear our heads of the doctrinal precision by which Claude defined his politics, that he and Venetia considered even their parents to be inclined either to capitalist greed or to Stalinoid repression.

Claude's discharge from the Army had come as a consequence of firing a .45 slug through the hut of his commanding officer. No doubt this was a decent action, considering the character of that man as Claude saw it: "Pure Southern fascist. He denied the enlisted men everything and diverted the patients' ration of fresh eggs to the officers' mess. He was responsible for the death of three patients because he refused to let the doctors set up a quarantine ward for our diphtherias. Set a trap for a Negro boy in the nurses' quarters, meant to machine-gun the boy when he came. Forced the nurses into whoring with the island brass. Humiliated doctors who'd been on the university staffs at Michigan and Louisiana. Wanted to chain the psycho patients. Claimed that psychiatry was a Jewish fraud." One thinks that if the Army put such a man in a position of authority and kept him there, he should have been removed by a conscientious citizen soldier with an issue pistol.

Claude had stalked him all one evening, from the officers' club to the nurses' quarters and to his own hut—and then had missed the great opportunity by firing wildly from a range of fifty yards. "I should have been inside waiting for him," Claude said.

That he was not court-martialed for his attempt was due, in a fairly direct sense, to the C.O.'s undisguised anti-Semitism. The hospital psychiatrist and the board of psychiatrists that was finally convened from all over the island bore some resentment for having been labeled a "bunch of kike phonies." They did not find Claude responsible for his deed—and in fact wrote a report that cast some doubt on the mental fitness of the C.O.

Which, taking it all in all, represented a degree of triumph for Claude. But he refused to admit that poetic justice was justice. (Clem, whose obsession it was to seize upon single words or hoary phrases and hold them up to all possible lights, delighting in the complex of meaning concealed beneath their superficial simplicities, made much of Claude's objection to poetic justice. At last Clem concluded that only justice courte deserved the name of poetic justice, and what is usually called poetic justice is an antipoetic fraud.)

As Claude saw it, he should never have fired—or he should not have missed. He was not one to leave either justice or mercy to the hand of God. All the unjustly slain, from Abel on, cried ceaselessly on the name Pogorski.

In the second or third week of our acquaintance he began to ride his bike into our yard on almost any day. Usually he came late in the afternoon, for he scrupulously respected our working hours and it would never have occurred to him that he had any right to intercept Clem on his way out to slay God's little creatures with his Crackshot .22.

No, Claude would not interfere, but he meant to await the returning hunter as a hellfire preacher would await the spent patrons of a brothel. When Clem appeared—perhaps carrying a rabbit, a lizard, or whatever—Claude would launch, with friendly anxiety, into his picture of "the web of life."

At about the same time his parents let fall on his infant ears Marx's theory of surplus value, it had come to Claude that insects depended on plant life, plant life depended on insects, and birds, those worthies of the air, depended on both. Nature might be red in fang and claw. No doubt it was. But there were niceties in the way nature adjusted balances between eaters and eaten, harmonies that only perverse man could destroy.

Claude drew, I must say, an appealing and artful picture of the natural kingdom, just as he drew an appealing picture of human society when the state should have withered away. He did not deny that if the lion and the lamb lay down together the lion was very apt to eat the lamb when hunger moved him. But he could discern the smile of innocence on the leonine chops, gory though they might be. To nature he could say, In la sua volontade e nostra pace. To man, who broke the peace, he could only offer the hope that reason might someday return him to his place in the natural kingdom.

But, Clem said—Clem unshaven and dirty, Clem swinging his useless trophies of the hunt like the stupidest young hunter from Boda, Clem spilling down his chin the Bohemia beer that Sheila would have fetched him from the cooler when she saw that Claude had buttonholed him and meant to have an answer—but what if man's destined and ordained place in the web of life was to be the perverse animal? Reason, Claude spoke of reason, but wasn't reason itself the symptom or even the springboard of perversity? Of course it was a different thing to peer through machined gun sights at a rabbit than to stalk it barefoot and barehanded, and it was a different thing to fire-bomb a city of strangers than to break a zebra's back from instinct. But was it not indeed conceivable that man's role as king of the beasts was harmoniously expressed by what Claude called the perversities of state and war?

Listening to the two of them, I used to marvel at the undress informality of their arguments, but marvel also to note the neoclassicism that Claude—and God knows what of his own experience—had brought out in Clem. Pope in undress, I thought, half expecting him to belt Claude with a quote from An Essay on Man. Borgias or Catilines or atom bombs—an Augustan would not say they broke the great design, but only that Claude was a victim of pernicious enthusiasm.

Nonetheless—I worried about this and I worry still—Claude was serious. Clem had merely assumed a position, as if he could have none of his own.

On Thursdays Claude usually brought us a mimeographed newssheet, sent out from Brooklyn by whichever faction of ex-Communists it was that he considered the least contaminated. (They would not, of course, seem pure to him. They would be rendered suspect by the very taint of organization that could have assembled funds to buy a mimeograph machine and assembled workers to sweat over the mailing.)

The wonder was that from this tiny newssheet—in wordage it compared to the New York Times as a clod compares to a mountain—Claude could read so much that no Times reader would ever suspect. He read it as if it were a condensed code—or was like the work Clem wanted to do, made up altogether of titles. Claude knew what followed all the titles, and if we didn't he told us.

China, he said, had been double-crossed by the American generals unleashed at the death of (that reactionary capitalist and double-dealer) Roosevelt. The airlifting of Chiang's troops into Shanghai and the supplies of American arms turned over to him was so cynical a betrayal that the Communists were bound to retaliate by building armies in Manchuria and Korea. The people (always, always!) were in the nutcracker.

The Baruch plan for atomic control was such a barefaced attempt to perpetuate the American monopoly on atomic weapons that Russian acceptance of it would be tantamount to unconditional surrender. On the other hand, Secretary of Commerce Wallace, who opposed the

379

Baruch plan, was a notoriously softheaded muddler who, if given his way, would turn over all of Europe to the commissars.

In spite of the million-times-repeated promises made as recently as a year ago, the United States would rebuild Germany as a dominant military and economic power in Europe. France would not for very much longer maintain her position as a mediator between East and West, but would plop solidly into a Western military alliance, while in the French colonies there had been a runaway massacre (hardly reported in the capitalist press!) of natives in Madagascar. The Vichy admirals were preparing to double-cross the new governments in Paris and Indochina and reconquer that country.

Russia was busily undermining the coalition governments in Rumania, Hungary, Czechoslovakia, Bulgaria and Austria.

There was going to be a long, fierce fight for the oil of the Middle East. Colonel Schwarzkopf's coup in Iran was only the first big-power move in that area. The English would play a dangerous game of flirtation with the Arabs for the sake of oil, and Palestine was likely to be stamped out in the process.

There would be no disarmament. Though no navy in the world could conceivably challenge the American fleets, the American Navy would be expanded and modernized. The staggering budget for arms that we had considered an emergency measure through the war years would be dwarfed by peacetime military expenditures. (In a choked voice Pogorski said, "Do you know how much they'll spend on silver service alone for the new ships? The czars never dreamed of such ostentation and waste.")

Listening to all these predictions that seemed so dire in those days, I sometimes thought that Pogorski was among us like a spreader of the plague. It's not easy for people just home from a war to hear that, willy-nilly, they are in the midst of a continuing one. Especially it is hard when one is out of his home country, deprived of the common opiates that help us believe our geese are swans. A time may come when, as Pogorski cried with such solemn emphasis, one feels an obligation to "do something."

When I was sure that Clem was leading Pogorski on to paint the world's prospects in the blackest of colors (including predictions that by 1960 there would be somewhere an arsenal of rockets with atomic warheads capable of blotting out life on earth) I grew anxious for all our sakes, lest we should use this pessimism as an excuse for slackening our work that seemed now only well begun. God knows I used to spend mornings, when I might have been working on my novel, worrying about what Claude had said the evening before, going to lunch with nothing but a bad conscience and half a page of hasty dialogue to show for the hours spent in my study.

But I think that Clem was only using his talks with Claude for ballast. There was a time of day when Claude was likely to be there— maybe re-creating for Clem the pessimism he had felt in 1939. But Clem could now swallow the poisonous predictions with a detachment that said, Why, yes, if we did what we did in the last six years, then of course it must follow that we will do the terrible things you predict.

He was learning to enjoy and use what made Pogorski suffer so. It amounts to something as good and as awful as that, and even then I guessed that hardness of heart in the face of the event might be the curse ordained for those with responsible imaginations. Nothing surprises them into adequate pity or adequate charity.

He led Pogorski on, as if Pogorski were persuading him of something by citing reasons unknown. And from the beginning there was not the slightest chance that Pogorski could persuade him of anything. After weeks of Pogorski's fond attempts, Clem said to him with facile cruelty, "You aren't going to ever change this wicked world, Claude, and you ought to know that. You missed the colonel. That was the task the ages had been preparing you for. And you missed. You won't get another chance." Unhappily Claude was shrewd enough to guess that Clem might be right.

In the evenings after Claude's missionary visits, Clem was pepped up as if Pogorski's message had been a tonic. He took it like bad medicine needed to tone him up for tomorrow's work on the novel, but as if it had no pertinence beyond that for the world in which he and the lizards did what they must according to their respective natures.

He was more interested in talking about the coming fall and his personal career, though these things too were clearly subordinate to the main, reckless drive of his writing.

He had been offered a teaching job. During the war Felix Martin had become head of the English department at a good university in Kansas. He wanted Clem to come as instructor. Clem wrote back accepting the job, and when he talked to me about it I was at first conned into the belief that he seriously meant to take it.

Sheila was opposed. She knew Clem well enough to know that he would be unhappy with the snail's pace of an academic community. "We're going to New York and we're going to live on the GI Bill," she insisted. "If you want this child to call you Daddy, you've got to live up to him. We're not going to wait until you're forty for anyone to hear of you. If you want to teach, wait a few years. Something better will come along."

But he didn't want to teach—except in the general sense that he wanted to do everything. Of course, I shouldn't minimize that. There was something forever embittered in his nature because he had to inhabit just one skin. In sum, however, he had never really believed he would live up to his contract with Felix.

It was a position he took, from which he sucked the goody, caring more about what might have happened to him (for that was potentially usable in his book) than about what would.

Basically he was far shrewder than Sheila in calculating the advantages and necessities of succeeding as a writer. Odd, remote or even crazy as he may have been while he was in New York before the war, he had nevertheless seen enough of how careers are made to understand the importance of being near the fountainheads of power in the literary world. If he had to be an upstart crow, then clearly it was better to be one where upstarting would be noticed—resented and fought, if that was what it would come to. He was the more eager to compete as his novel satisfied him more. It wouldn't hurt to be in New York, where he could talk to Nathaniel Bentley now and then. It was always worth while talking to Bentley. And Bentley had connections.

Lillian Esterman had been heard from again. She was married to a refugee with money, and she had plans for a magazine that would naturally welcome Clem as a contributor. There might be a place for him on the editorial staff. Clem's friend Henderson Paul had brought out a successful war novel in the previous spring. From a peak of good feeling he had written to Clem that his editors would certainly like to read Clem's manuscript if, for any reason, Gordon and Maxwell did not offer him a royal advance.

These conversations among us that always seemed to turn to the excitement of Clem's prospects naturally increased my professional uncertainty. The wish to write fiction was dying hard in me, but dying. The false spring of relief that came when the war was over had brought me back to trying a novel I had given up years before. For the sake of the novel, I should have stayed away from Clem. I was beginning to see much too clearly that I didn't want to shoot lizards and hang their smelly carcasses over my desk as Clem did. Even if I had been willing to do it, the crazy hope that someday the lizard would live again—with a life I could give it—was lacking in me. I might have finished the novel and I might have sold it. But day by day I found myself less able to believe in it.

So, with considerable inner crisis, I quietly gave it up for good and began to work on some critical articles. When Clem found out that I had done so he reacted (1) as though I had deserted him on the firing line, and (2) as though I had finally come to my senses and followed a course he had known all along was more suited to my arid talents.

I resented his attitude on both counts, of course. One afternoon as we were walking home from town, we had it out.

We had been swimming in the rollers of the afternoon beach east of town. Clem had made us late by dallying to eat some of the clams that diving boys brought in superbly fresh from the offshore rocks. Since company was expected for dinner—a touring couple named Benson, as I remember—I was annoyed by his irresponsibility in this small circumstance and then angered by his implication that he had a right to it, being more responsible in his work than I.

"Responsible, hell," I said. "You're just lucky. Everything you want is right in your grasp. All you have to do is close your little baby hand around it now."

"Everything I wanted," he said morosely, flinging a stick at one of the large spider webs hung like a sail between palm fronds on the roadside. "What you want isn't separated by so much time from when you want it. Hell, what I have now is what I wanted in college."

"So be thankful."

He shook his head. "It's hard to feel myself here with it. The way you are. The way all the rest of you are. I could run, run, run sometimes when I get to thinking. When I'm not actually working, I'm scared. It's so far from what I am as a being."

"The more to be pitied," I said, "for your Midas touch."

"It is like being Midas," he said immodestly. "I made a mistake. I should have stayed in Boda. I shouldn't have wanted what I did."

"Nor I," I said, thinking sorely of the novel I would never finish.

"It's different with you. With you it's a reasonable choice. You simply quit."

"Yeah."

"I'm not allowed to quit. You know, I think sometimes I didn't come back from the war. Like when you're a child you cross the road in front of a truck racing toward you, and when you get across you think, 'It got me and I don't know it.' Well, in the war I went outside— it was because of what I wanted—and I can't really get back in where I could make choices like you. I couldn't give up my novel just because I decided to."

"Holy, holy, holy."

"It's true. I'll never be able to touch anything again. Not Sheila or the kid, or—"

"Or clams and tequila and rock candy? What the hell were you doing this afternoon? I never saw such a glutton. So now go home and have the big dinner and knock off a piece and feel sorry for yourself. Clem, there were people who really didn't come home from the war."

"I don't feel sorry for them," he said. He threw another stick into the purple tropic shadows. "Yes, I do. That's part of why I'm willing to go on working—for everybody that lives and dies, even if I can't do it myself. I admit I can't have a life of my own now ..."

"Because your nuts were sawed off. Hi, Jake Barnes."

"... but I want to be a healer, to make everything all right for—"

"—us! Clem, what are you doing? Are you writing a manifesto or talking to me? Cry to me across this bitter air."

Suddenly he planted his feet in the road and would go no farther. "Go on!" he shouted tearfully. "Go on back and tell the ladies what The Wings of the Dove means. It's so easy!"

I kept walking for a minute, then turned and shouted back at him. For five minutes we roared back and forth at each other, using only the two all-expressive words we had learned in the war years to encompass and reduce all meaning to the level of expletive. We made a subhuman comedy routine of it, particularly grating and grotesque in the lulling Pacific silence around us and the tranquil sundown.

Then I walked stiffly home, determined to head for the border in the morning, and Clem went back to town to finish getting drunk.

In explaining to our guests his absence from dinner, we used the simplest banal jokes about the temperament of the artist, and in using them I tried to reduce the episode to something merely insignificant. Sheila would not hear of our going to look for him. And, sure enough, he came rolling into our place some hours later in a taxi, glad to see us all, sorry we had not been with him. In the morning there was no hint from any of us that there had even been a quarrel. But the substance of it, the essential mystery of who should envy whom, had been revealed to consciousness as mystery. He never took me as seriously afterward, I think. Against the drag of my own stubbornness, I took him more so.

The morning after that shouting match he was badly hung over. From the nature of that hangover I got a confirming insight into the price he was paying (and was to go on paying in hypochondria and delicacy of balance) for his good fortune as artist. His hangovers seldom appeared in the form of headaches or nausea or loss of appetite, but, rather, in a sense of precariousness almost metaphysical. They spoke to him like the sermons of Jeremy Taylor, insisting on the frailty of the spark that animates this clay of ours. It was as if the very denial of pain in head or gut were the ultimate torture, so that the terrorized consciousness went throughout the body like Diogenes in search of one honest nerve that would report a pain to prove that life was still going on.

That morning I found him in the yard below the house with his thumb on the pulse in his neck. He was rigid and staring out to sea. He had not moved when the shade grew scanter. The sun was blazing full on his back.

A beer would help, I suggested. "It cools the blood, it cools the brain."

"No!" He didn't really turn to notice me, but there was such an anguish of supplication in his tight posture that I brought him a beer anyway, and a few aspirins.

Before he would take them he asked in absolute seriousness what the human pulse rate ought to be.

Around eighty, I told him, though I had read somewhere that Robinson Jeffers had a pulse of forty in the morning.

"Mine is ninety-one," he said in grief and anxiety. "Ninety-two." His eyes were fixed greedily on the bottle of beer I had put in his hand, but he would not trust himself to sip it until I had explained that my pulse frequently rattled a hundred to the minute after I had been drinking. At this he drank the whole bottle, relaxing visibly, like a dampened paper doll. Wiping his mouth, he said, "That Jeffers is the luckiest man alive." I believe he saw his pulse in the image of a little hammer chipping away at the rock of life.

On another occasion Sheila came running for Janet and me, insisting that I drive into town for the doctor. "Clem lost consciousness," she said.

He was, as a matter of fact, sitting at the table in the barn where he typed—looking vital enough, shamefully energetic—when I had brought the doctor and we were all gathered around him.

The good, calm doctor refused to be impressed by Clem's account of the attack. He told Clem that aside from a blood pressure slightly below the average, there was nothing whatever physically wrong with him. He said, "A little fellow like you shouldn't try to drink up all the alcohol in Mexico. Now, if you lost consciousness for a moment, that is nothing to worry about. That is only nature's way of returning you to the cradle of life. Sometimes the consciousness obliges the body to go beyond its strength, and you ought to be grateful when the blind process of unconscious life takes over."

To which Clem said later, darkly, "He doesn't know. I haven't got as much unconsciousness left as most people. If I wasn't watching it all the time, it would go out." What would go out? Well, it. Whatever it was he thought of as life, I suppose.

I was always impressed by the way he could get over his attacks of hangover or hypochondria (and once, to all appearances, he healed himself of an attack of food poisoning that kept the rest of us out of commission for two days and more) by going back to work. Work was the health of his condition and, conversely, he could be made physically ill by being interrupted before he was ready to quit for the day.

For an example of swift recovery let me point out that on the morning when I gave him the beer and aspirin, his mind was already churning productively by the time the beer had uncurled his toes. Out of the hangover (he used everything) he was beginning to compose a war story that he would call "Hangover." It had to do, he said, with his voyage home, when the troopship came upon a floating mine. For more than an hour the unescorted ship had circled it, firing the five-inch gun, the three-inch gun, the forty-millimeter and the twenties. Finally the troops began to fire carbines and tommy guns in an effort to dispose of this floating remnant of the war.

"They couldn't sink it," Clem said, with a malicious note of knowledgeability in his voice. "We sailed away and left it floating. And the trick I would use to get the meaning in the story would be to reverse subjectivity and object, ve-e-e-e-ery delicately shifting the language until the reader thinks the blue sea is his own blue eyes and that the dynamite mine is really floating inside 'em."

He was jumping in his chair as if he had been wired in when he finished telling me this.

"So go write it," I said.

"You don't mind if I write?" he asked with a caustic edge to his voice. I didn't answer, and that was all there was to patching up our quarrel of the night before. But after he had trudged down to his barn to work, I sat in the chair he had occupied, staring out at our Pacific. And of course I was thinking of that figurative mine his story suggested. He had made me believe it existed, floating at large in the blue, all-seeing, biding distances—internalized but nonetheless malignant, a hazard to navigation left over from the war.

And it seemed to me that I was little by little becoming more susceptible to Pogorski's brand of despair. Nothing I had of faith kept me from believing that the world had been poisoned like a poisoned well.

But of the four of us who were preparing through this summer to go back to our cold-war lives, it was Sheila who eventually caught the virus from Pogorski most seriously. Maybe because she was pregnant, but more likely because of the straight-grained honesty of her character, she came strongly to believe that "something has to be done" about the public iniquities that Pogorski sketched for us.

She began to intrude Claude's arguments into our lunchtime or evening talk. Clem accused her of waiting for her shot in the arm when we were expecting Claude to come with his weekly bulletin from Brooklyn, or of going for her "vitamins" when she went down the beach to the shack where the Pogorskis lived.

"Not that exactly. But what's the use of what you're doing—of having children!—unless there's going to be some kind of decent future for the world," Sheila said. A part of what had sustained her during the war had been the optimism of her boss, a China expert in the War Department who had liked to talk about "TVA's on the Yellow River" and "a thousand years of peace." Word had come to us during the summer that this man had been picked out by a New York journalist as a fellow traveler of the Communists and had been forthwith excluded from the government. Sheila was taking this hard—and as all too explicit confirmation of Pogorski's predictions.

"There's no use being alive," Clem told her, evading her passionate concern, withdrawing his mental energies from the grim disintegration she predicated, like a cat cleaning its paws before it retires to curl in the sun. And it seemed more than a little unfair that he should have a fictional world and his work to retire into while he left her outside and, as it were, unsheltered. For though she was reading his manuscript approvingly as it advanced, still she was excluded from the vision that welded these fragments into a whole.

Then, for a while, I thought that Sheila's emotional involvement with Claude was verging into something more than a shared political passion. When he sat with us, it was to Sheila that he more and more frequently turned for support. The nods she gave to his indignant denunciations were far too gentle, I thought, to have been elicited by the substance of his protest.

More and more often she went by herself down the beach to the Pogorskis' when Janet was bored with them or wanted to read or had somewhere else to go.

This in itself was innocent enough. Claude painted in a thatched shed behind their shack. The shed consisted merely of a roof supported by poles. If Claude sat down with Sheila when she arrived, they were both clearly visible, even from our place. Besides, Venetia was always there, though she did not always join the couple in the shed when Sheila arrived.

To look at Venetia you would have thought that her appearance alone would have kept Claude's affections from straying. She was twenty-eight that summer. Her style was that plump, hot comeliness we used to admire in Italian movie actresses. She had a stridently powerful thorax on which the large breasts stood with remarkably little sag. (There is a figure by Maillol called "Action in Chains" which indecently resembles Venetia as she was.) Her belly was ridged with muscle just above the mons, and her wide pelvis made one feel that she could have carried a minotaur in that bushel-sized shell of bone. Her columnar legs winked dimples around and above her kneecaps. Her pale skin had a tendency to burn and peel, so after she had been in the sun she looked faintly raw. For all the political dismay she shared with Claude, she was characteristically quiet, sitting at the fringe of our talk with what we called a "spayed-cat" smile on her face. (We didn't mean the epithet. Clem and I meant, indeed, the opposite, thinking it rather a smile of righteous pride in her bodily secrets.)

It seemed reasonable that a man who had such a wife and the outlets of painting and politics to burn his energy would be not at all likely to invite the attentions of another woman. And it never occurred to me that what I was noticing was the slow preliminary to an affair. For Sheila that would have been unthinkable—if she had been able to think of what she was doing.

Yet there was something in the very atmosphere of those long hot days that seemed to invite vagrancy of the soul. When you looked at the shadows and felt the blaze of the sky or heard the absolute repetition of surf boom—out of forever, into forever—you felt how much time there was, as if the sun said, There is time for every sin and every repentance. Insidiously the light promised that it would not fail, that it would go on showering its benison on whatever the senses demanded.

I think it likely that I projected a part of the erotic coloring which I saw in Sheila's visits to the Pogorskis. I used to sit in semifrustration at my worktable and watch the tiny, remote figures meet under the thatched roof. It was like watching a microscopic puppet play for which the heat working in my own loins supplied the script—might have supplied a dialogue of love, of proposition, if I had allowed it to.

There they were: the tall, restless man before his shrill canvases, picturesque and more than picturesque in the white native trousers he habitually wore, a mat of fierce blond hair on his lean chest, she, feeling her body enriched with pregnancy, satisfied with the satisfaction that demands to be multiplied, that makes the rich vulnerable to desire as the poor can never be. And around them the aura of encouragement spread by that fleshy Venus who lies abed inside the shack, nude, stretching her arms and smiling about what she knows, and who may silently speak to them in the same language and with the same amoral intent as the sea beating on the other side.

No, I did not think Sheila and Claude were verging toward an affair, but I fretted to think that Sheila might carry some marring dissatisfaction away with her from the very fact that what was begun with Claude had never been consummated.

As it turned out, my intimations were beside the mark, but I owe to them and their erotic tint a comprehension of what Sheila and Claude sought in their familiarity.

The scales fell from my eyes and I knew. What did their love talk come around to? What subject made their eyes glow softly when they sat close to each other on the bench in Claude's unwalled studio or ambled back toward our place gesturing in the emptiness of light? Clem.

"You know, Claude has a terrible crush on Clem," Sheila said to me eventually, with a veiled, crooked look, as though she meant to hide something by this partial revelation and pick my brains. At least find out if I had guessed their secret. (I hadn't quite. She gave it away.)

"I don't mean it's sexual," she hurried to add. (A little too late. At least I was shrewd enough now—taught by my own fantasies—to see that the sexual element was fused oddly into this abstract love.)

"Do you mean it's better or worse than if it were sexual?" I asked.

She ignored the question as unanswerable and perhaps beside the point. "It's more that he admires Clem so much, expects so much of him. I think he really suffers to see that Clem isn't more concerned about things, that Clem can seem so lighthearted."

"Why doesn't he simply believe that Clem is irresponsible and live with that belief?"

She shook her head, impatient with my heavy-footed ironies. "It's that Claude is … sensitive."

I laughed at the word, so unavoidable in describing Claude. It was a cliché that took its revenge for our general scorn by appearing here as the mot juste.

"He feels what Clem could be," she said.

As if to show how considerable were the obstacles to such a perception, just at that moment a burst of mad singing came from Clem's barn, and then we heard him "trying words" aloud, as he not infrequently did. "'I spit on you. I spih-ut on you,'" he sang.

"Obviously a trifler and vulgarian," I said of him. "Sheila, Clem's seldom been known to undervalue himself. I don't think he needs Claude to persuade him of what he might be. The other night on the road he propagandized me on how he meant to save the world, be a more-than-poet healer and all that."

Such a look on her face! She could not have looked so caught in nakedness if I had found her actually lying in Claude's embrace. And by this limitless embarrassment I finished smelling out the indulgence she and Claude shared. I had trapped her with a metonym for that word which she and Claude must actually, in the license of their admiration, have used in speaking of Clem's potentiality:

*Savior!*

I can't say how deeply touched I was (and, of course, embarrassed too) by my discovery. But at any rate I dared not inquire any further at the risk of profaning those real-unreal intimations that Sheila and Claude had, with greater innocence, sounded. I know I was choked with emotion for a time, wanting to laugh at them for their childishness, wanting to laugh to rid myself of the oppressive awe I felt (not for Clem, as they did, but for that immanence and power they had known how to see personified in him).

Matter-of-factly I said, "Clem has to shut off certain distractions or he couldn't cope with a sustained demand from his work. It's all right for Claude to stew about the atomic bomb if he wants to. Right now, Clem has other fish to fry. If he has something to say politically, his time will come."

"I don't think so," she said. "Clem's so strong, but so terribly weak at the same time." Her manner had again become the oblique evasiveness of someone with a secret as important as a hidden disease or, literally, a vision. "They'll always find ways to keep him penned. We will. Dick, I find myself doing it all the time, just by being what he loves. I want to turn him loose."

"Loose? Mankind cannot stand very much Clem Anderson."

"Don't joke. Claude thinks—Well, we've talked about whether I oughtn't leave Clem."

"So Claude could marry him?" I knew that wasn't it, wasn't fair to the elusive and irrational purpose of their devotions. But it would have been intolerable to encourage their madness merely because it might be tinged with superhuman grace.

"That's idiotic," I said. Mournfully she shook her head in agreement. "You're good for him, Sheila. It may always be your function to protect him from enthusiasms like Claude's instead of ... I don't know. But wouldn't it be a shame for Clem to burn himself up in some useless gesture of protest? And I don't think he would. Any more. He's become canny in a way that Claude will never be."

"I know," she said dutifully, as if she were letting it go at that.

As if such a tangle of fanaticisms could be discarded so offhandedly! No, the irrational dialectic had to throw its coils around our uncertain feet until there was a heroic resolution, or a fatal one perhaps.

There was a nearly fatal stop to this queer business one Sunday while Janet and I were away from the house with the Bensons. We had driven inland to see an Indian village. Because Clem had a hangover and would not get out of bed, we left him and Sheila behind.

When Clem eventually got up, he was sullen and fragile, feeling his pulse and trying hopefully to belch. He began to smoke too much, weighing each cigarette as if it were, like arsenic, a deadly poison that might save a life in special circumstances.

He had just lain down on the stone patio and covered himself, head and all, with a blanket, when Venetia and Claude walked into the yard with a picnic lunch and two bottles of tequila in a sack. Venetia also had her guitar slung on her shoulder.

Some time ago Claude had mentioned a fresh-water pool beyond the ridge, in the jungle. It was his inspiration that they might all go there for a picnic and a swim.

Clem was rude enough about the invitation at first. He wanted to lie under the blanket until he had strength enough to go down to the barn and revitalize himself with his work. But to please Sheila he let himself be talked into going along. He drank a bottle of beer to beef up his strength for the hike and also filled a canteen with it and slung it on his belt.

The pool turned out to be farther by almost a mile than Claude had said. There was some considerable climbing to get there. "I could tell how awful Clem felt," Sheila said later, "because he kept insisting that I ought to sit down and rest. Or that we ought to idle back home on account of my precarious condition. He kept feeling himself all over and had that pleading look in his eyes."

By the time they reached the pool Clem had drunk the beer in his canteen, but was feeling even worse. While they were all changing into their bathing suits—Claude made such fun of the girls for wanting to go into the brush for this that they changed together in the open sun— Clem didn't even look at Venetia. "By which you know how he felt," Sheila said, "considering all the things he's had to say about her. And I must declare the sight is even more than you'd expect."

However he felt, he extended himself so far as to wade out on the rocks in the shallower water, splashing himself and making a few halfhearted pretenses that he was not only swimming but enjoying it. He kept announcing to Claude, who was a much better swimmer than he and who had already swum out to the middle of the pool, that he couldn't be responsible for him today, because of his condition—a warning by which everyone was reasonably amused.

The food Venetia had prepared was ample and good. Among a profusion of feminine talents, she prided herself on making special delicacies out of the cheapest of local foods. Avocados and lime sauce, cevice and corn bread can be a wondrous luxury and, supplemented with a limited amount of tequila, can be healing to the worst hangover. So when they had eaten at leisure Clem really seemed to feel better, but again announced that they would be fools to swim, "since we all feel so lousy."

After lunch Sheila dozed. Claude sat with knotted brows, tossing bits of shale at the nibbling edge of the water. Clem lay near Venetia's knees while she played her guitar and sang to him. Embracing the guitar and touching the strings in her lap as if she were congratulating her genitals with a fond patting, she had the air of a carnivorous plant swallowing a matchbox.

On two sides of the pool confronting them jungle growth came almost to the low wall of volcanic rock that dropped to the water. The shadows of foliage were lambent blue, gold and green, chuckling with birds and whispering full of secret movements. Generous and fecund. Cool enough, even though the day was hot. On the side of the pool opposite the picnickers a single, flawed slab of stone ("Gethsemane-red" as Clem described it) rose a hundred feet or more from an underwater rubble of black, like the decayed root of an immense tooth. The fourth side was a piling of fractured boulders, common enough on that coast subject to earthquakes.

The water was almost perfectly transparent, except that in its extreme depths it seemed to assume a kind of colorless darkness like that which one imagines to be the color of outer space. A number of trees had fallen into the water. In the course of time their leaves and smaller branches had been dissipated so they lay stark, projecting their thornlike shadows onto the sandy bottom or losing them in the inane of the greater depths.

A good place for a picnic—Edenish, though with a view of wasteland rocks across less than eighty yards of water.

None of them could quite recollect afterward how Clem and Claude began to argue. It is sufficient to say that their conflicting positions were well enough established by now. What was the right thing for a man to do in this postwar world? Oppose it or hope (on thin enough grounds) that it might be redeemed from within?

No doubt the pond by which they lay had its influence on the course of their argument. "If Walden is a good book and reading it is a good thing and I wanted to promote the good, I would favor making a movie of it," Clem said. "With Gary Cooper as strong, silent Henry Thoreau, Misunderstood of Concord, Mass. And a cast of thousands to represent the people he's misunderstood by, but who, in the triumphant finale, turn to a love of nature in the raw and all run out to Walden Pond flinging their clothes in the air as they strip for the plunge. A movie like that would at least promote the cause of conservation and many would buy the book."

Venetia chuckled softly over her guitar, crooning, "'Hi, said the little, leather-winged bat. I'll tell you the reason that ...'"

Claude, Indian-rigid, tormented and impatient, sprinkled salt on his left hand in the crotch of thumb and the forefinger that had once pulled a trigger in mortal earnest.

Clem went on baiting him. "I see a scene in which Cooper makes his famous plea for Captain John Brown—collage shots of Lionel Barrymore (whiskered, and the wind machine blowing his beard in Ethel Brown's eyes), patting a nigger boy on the head—while all Concord cries, 'Commie!' except for Ralph Waldo Emerson, who says, 'I never yet met a man I didn't like.' And there's Bette Davis as Harriet Beecher Stowe, who is hoping to plant a few roses on the Walden cabin. At the finale you could have the Pasadena Glee Club singing 'Ballad for Americans' while Misunderstood is appointed Secretary of Labor in the cabinet of Franklin Dee, played by Spencer Tracy. That way you've got the whole paideuma on one life raft, Claude. We can march into the future lightly loaded, Claude."

"You make us laugh," Claude said.

"At your service."

"But you're not a fool. Why won't you talk to me?"

"I'm talking to you," Clem said idly, trying to peer under Venetia's lowered eyelids.

She ripped the jangling strings of the guitar and said, "Clem's talking to you, honey. Nothing's going to be settled today."

One thinks it would have been so easy to take her advice. They were all friends, really very dear to each other. Surely there was an imperative commanding idleness in the sweet, hot afternoon breeze raising its thunderheads out over the ocean.

But Clem said, "How can I talk seriously to anyone who takes the attitude you do about killing bunny rabbits, Claude?"

"I think you're not being faithful to your best when you go around slaughtering things. Pretending to be the white man with the gun. Bang, bang. Life is holy."

"Not unless death is," Clem said. Lying on his back he swung his arm to catch a grasshopper bending a stalk of grass under its weight. Deliberately he began picking the legs off it. Then the wings. He tossed the stripped thorax into the water.

"Oh," Venetia said throatily. "Why'd you do that?"

"Because he can," Claude said. "Only because he can. He's so proud of his power to do in grasshoppers."

"You can't make an omelet without breaking eggs," Clem said. "I don't want to waste my breath talking to someone who likes to chatter about politics and can't stand pulling the legs off a grasshopper. Did you kill anybody in the war, Claude? I killed somebody."

"And are suffering for it," Claude said, putting all his tenderness into his inflection. "That's why you won't let yourself be honest."

"I'm honest. And why shouldn't I suffer?"

"Glib, glib, glib, glib," Claude said. "How you have the gall to bring a child into a world like this when you won't seriously concern yourself—"

"I'm not bringing the child. God left a little baby among our roses, that's all."

"Funny. Ha ha. Because you don't think I'm worth talking to."

"It isn't that, Claude," Venetia said wearily. "Why don't both of you swim? I've never heard either of you sound so stupid."

But when Sheila awoke a while later the two men were still harassing the question of children put abroad in the pain and evil of such a world. It was Sheila's impression that they were by this time both equally but not overwhelmingly drunk. Oppressed by the twang of hostility in their voices, she joined Venetia in demanding that they change the subject. Clem said nastily that he was willing if Claude would let go his ear. He put his head in Sheila's lap and began to sing folk songs with the girls.

Claude continued to drink, muttering to himself. He began to pace up and down the rock shelf in front of the pool. The others paid no attention until suddenly he dived in.

Clem lifted his head and said uneasily, "Shouldn't swim while drinking."

"He's a good swimmer. It'll cool him off," Venetia said. She did not even turn to look at Claude.

He took off with a hard, clumsy crawl, heading straight across the pool. He was past the middle when Clem became convinced that he was in trouble.

He had been watching out of the corner of his eye, and when he raised his head to look squarely he saw that on every second or third stroke Claude was sinking a foot or two beneath the surface.

Getting to his feet and beginning to dance nervously, Clem shouted to him.

"For heaven's sake," Venetia said. "Don't be so antsy, Clem." But little by little she was getting alarmed too.

Now Claude was making hardly any forward progress. He was less than fifty feet from the glaring rock wall on the far side of the water, but his strokes were unmistakably impotent with fatigue, and his face—they could see it plainly enough when he came to the surface after each floundering—showed no sign of consciousness. They were sure he did not hear them yelling.

"He's finished the whole bottle of tequila," Venetia said. "Oh, that fool."

Clem put his thumb to his throat to see how his pulse was responding. ("I could see myself from the outside," he said later. "If I hadn't stopped to feel my pulse I wouldn't have been shamed into doing anything at all.")

There was a moment when Claude seemed to have given up. He sank several feet under the surface, almost down to the shadow area of the depths below the big tooth of rock. Then, very, very slowly his arms and legs began to move again with the boneless fluency of plant tendrils animated by a current. He surfaced a few yards away from the sheer rock wall and blindly swam to it.

It seemed to the watchers there was nothing he could possibly cling to on that side. It was too sheer and water-slicked. But they saw him hang there nevertheless. ("Like watching a barnacle trying to suck itself onto a metal plate," Clem said.)

The three of them started to run around the pool toward him then. They scrambled over the jaggle of boulders and climbed the overhang. Actually there was no way for them to climb down its face and they had nothing to lower that he might catch hold of. They were only trying to get as close as possible to him, thinking if they could get him to hear he might be able to take care of himself. As they got halfway up the slope of the big rock, they saw him let go his hold and begin to swim toward the center again—that horrid, subfetal, plaintive flutter aiming at nothing.

Later Clem would accuse himself of not having gone into the water immediately when he knew Claude was in danger. The fact remains that he did—at this point—dive forty feet down the rock wall into the corner where the boulders were scattered.

("Boy, I stood there a minute thinking what a loss for American letters before I jumped," he said. "All the way down I kept telling myself that, after all, the Nobel Prize was just a material gaud and they'd probably have given it to some Icelandic bard or Southern queer anyhow.")

He landed almost on top of Claude. Claude rolled a little to one side, muttered, "Mo Kay," and began to sink. To keep his own nerve up, Clem plied him with questions all the while he was dragging him to the side where they could climb up the boulders.

Clem found a foothold on a shelf of rock and boosted Claude halfway onto a flat slope above the surface. But altogether the grips were too precarious and Claude too heavy for Clem to plant him securely. After they had rested a minute, Clem asked if Claude couldn't climb a bit under his own power. Again Claude insisted that he was O.K.—and promptly slithered out of Clem's grip. Feet first he sank straight down, like a magician's silk whipped through a ring. Clem went down among the rocks and pulled him out again.

By this time the girls had picked their way down to a ledge from which they could reach Claude's hand, and, in a scene composed like the deposition from the Cross, the three of them hoisted his sagging body up and dragged him into the shade.

For a long time Clem lay alone on his back, feeling his pulse (a hundred and twenty) and getting a more familiar perspective on the omnipresent vultures circling above the peak of rock. He stared at the high point from which he had dived. Thinking it out.

Later, when they had all come safely back to our house and were telling Janet and me about it while we sat in candlelight on the patio, I happened to use the term "episode" in referring to what had happened. Quickly Clem caught me up and said it wasn't an episode. It was a total, he insisted, without antecedents, without sequel. It was complete in itself and therefore without any relation to time. It was not one in a series of events.

"If you saw it that way," I said agreeably. "All right. Dramatically complete. But not tragic, thank God. Thank God no one was killed."

Clem replied with arguments to this attempt of mine to soothe everyone with a platitude.

"If you count us, we're all here," he said. His voice had a peculiar brazen note that I would have thought hysterical if I were not inclined to believe that it was, in sober truth, prophetic. "That's a good way to be—realistic," he said furiously. "But how do you know your count was right before it happened? There was someone else with us who didn't come out of the water."

Sheila was watching him with anxious astonishment. "Don't fight with us now," she said. "It's all over. Let's have a thanksgiving nightcap and a bite."

"I know," he said. With no tolerance for the lingering mood of fright the others meant to tame and dispel, he began to insist that in spite of appearances there had been "a death and a birth" equally terrible and fraught with consequences while he had been under water looking for Claude.

"How do you know?" Sheila demanded. She was losing patience with him.

His lids lowered with an expression strangely compounded of suffering and cunning. I thought I had never seen him treat her with such calm and cruel contempt. "It doesn't matter how I know things," he said. We might almost have mistaken his tone for sympathy. "What I saw fits with everything else. You'll see."

Did we ever see the birth and death that fit—symbolically at least—with all that preceded and all that followed that plunge of his?

Yes, I think we saw a hero reborn in archetypical circumstances. We were soon to have, in weird and comic parody, a disciple's testimony of the rebirth. Reborn from the water, returned from his night journey through the war to a place in the desert heaven of our new age, henceforward Clem would shade us like a colossus. There is no doubt about the identity of the hero reborn to us.

But the death he saw down there in the pellucid green and mineral-tainted water—whose? I can believe that in the moment of crisis he may have had a perception exempt from time, a truly prophetic knowledge. But was it an individual death or that communal shade which inhabits all of us impersonally? Was it Susan's death he foresaw, so that someday he would know where to bring her to find it? Was it his own? Bentley's? What of the Strongest Boy in Boda?

"There was another who didn't come up," Clem said, glowering at Claude, who nodded in shame, as if he understood exactly what Clem meant.

# 15

ALL SUMMER we had been anticipating advance copies of Clem's book of poetry—each of us in his own way sensing the need to take the physical thing in our hand, as if it would be the charter that justified our being where we had been, working as we were. Half a dozen times letters from Clem's publisher had come to tantalize us with promises that our wait was nearly over.

Now, a week and a half before we were to head back toward the border, the representative of the local post office bicycled into our yard with a special-delivery parcel that had to be put into the very hands of Señor Aaron Clement Anderson.

Señor Anderson, surrounded by well-wishers, opened the parcel as if it might be a time bomb sent by one of his considerable number of enemies. "*Sugar Oboe*," he read, from the carmine letters on the dust jacket. Plainly he did not understand what these obscure words meant. He flipped the book open and felt the paper for quality. Good quality, it seemed. He thrust a copy at Sheila and said, "Here."

She began to cry, turned to the dedication, read it and cried louder.

"Stop that," Clem ordered her. He jerked the book out of her hands and turned it over suspiciously to read the testimonials on the back. "It says, 'Anderson reports a war that newspaper readers may not have heard of.' I wonder what war they're talking about, hmmm? Look, Mommy, what old Bentley says. Stop this caterwauling! It's only a book. He says I'm a winged two-headed horse. Mommy, be quiet."

"I can't help it," Sheila said. "It's such a little book and there's so much in it."

Now he flipped it open to see if she was right about that. There were all the titles at least, transformed into bold black type. In the front the poems he had written in England, France, and Germany: "The Great War on the Piano Tops," "Firefight at Verdun," "How We Brought the Good News to Ghent," "Country Matters," "A Bomber Named Vondalee" and the rest. In a separate section at the back were the poems he had published before the war.

"It's not so little as all that," he said. "You want it carved, for God's sake?"

We had the feeling that if he could have he would have put a rubber band and a propeller on the little book and flown it, put a stick

399

of mast on it and sailed it, or equipped it with a string to make a yoyo of it. He so visibly wanted it to do something now that it was here in physical reality.

But what can a book do? Clem, who must have known most of it by heart, presently slipped down to his barn to read it all through again by himself. He read the thirty-nine poems in something under twenty minutes and returned to us with a look not so much disappointed as just plain lost. We knew that down there where the dead lizards lived this book had died for him. All these years of work, with so much of his salvation hopefully staked on the outcome—and the little machine of a book turned into paper, ink and glue almost as soon as he got it in his hands. For a similar investment a scientist would have been able at least to blow up a city.

Obstinate against his disappointment, Janet and Sheila and I determined to make a festivity of this day. We started planning where we would have dinner that evening and how smashing a party we could afford. We knew, at least casually, eight or ten Americans who were in Acapulco that week who would have been fit celebrants for the birth of a book, besides, of course, the Pogorskis.

But after much driving around through the day, announcements and offering of invitations, it was only the Pogorskis and two other couples (one couple homosexual) that sat down with us for dinner in that restaurant on the north side of the zócalo. Some others had promised to catch up with us later.

Claude, with his cactus-thorn hair slicked down for once, meek in a lavender bow tie and a white shirt, was clearly trying to be on good behavior for that night. Or, since he customarily phrased his internal fury and despair gently, it might be more exact to say that he had made an enormous effort to analyze what about him was offensive to Clem and was overconscientious at first in his efforts to suppress it. The waiters who brought our drinks and dinner did not remind him of the oppressed masses—at least he didn't say so—and the head of a fighting bull, hung in the gloomy dining room where we ate, did not remind him of the evil aggressiveness in man commemorated by Picasso's "Minotauromachie" or of rabbit hunters who "broke the web of life."

He merely beamed and fawned and nodded and bit his tongue to keep from uttering his obsessions. And got enormously drunk while the rest of us were still in the lofty first stages of alcoholic euphoria.

The first we knew of his condition was when he rapped on the table with his knife handle. Shakily he got to his feet. There was a drooping leer on his mouth while he bobbed his head and nerved himself to speak.

Bob and Merton, the two homosexuals, nervously moved their chairs closer together, and I had the impression that under the table they were holding hands for comfort, sensing the strain. The other couple, George and Helen Gantner, beamed encouragement and anticipation. They were very well adjusted. Venetia smiled. I wonder if she knew what Claude had to say.

"Not forget the occasion for which we are here," he said, blistering us all with an accusing gaze, as if we had forgotten indeed. "To speak in all honebly have ordered more wine, much wine. Some are the same and some are different. Shit. I myself am a little man, given mysterious talents of air I cannot cope." Here he made a scribbling gesture, as if he were painting, and then shook his head in self-deprecation so fierce as to suggest that painting, for him, was pure mortification of vanity. Angels snickered at every brush stroke. "Not so with Aaron Clement Anderson, gnome to his wishers true poet, Dichter. Casts no bread on waters. Shhhh!"

He was cautioning homosexual Merton, who had giggled and muttered, "It's a love song. Of J. Alf—"

Venetia said, "Clem doesn't need flowers, darling."

"Sssssssh! Onto the occasion have something to read for humanity." Then he began to recite, not read, one of the poems from the new book that had been lent him in the afternoon when the invitation to dinner was given, no part of which he had ever seen before. The poem was the one beginning with the line, "When I was a soldier at Boy Scout twelve." Claude recited all twenty-four lines without a hitch or a pause, in a clear, boyish voice. There was something uncanny in the performance; maybe we sensed that this was, or Claude thought it was, his true voice, breaking momentarily through the incoherence and cursed impurity of his dogged attempts to persuade mankind to live at peace.

At any rate, when he had finished it his tongue thickened again. His mind relaxed into an unstructured fluency that revealed only the currents of his drunkenness. "Known to all, the secrets of man and married life," he said. "Many times to sleepers, words unsuspect their meaning and elect. Father and child instruction in power where I kneel, blessing marriage vows in my house. Reading Anderson is to know, like it happened to my long life. My father was a little man, swell. Big giant to me. Called me Buddy and such love. Saw him pee his pants the night Sacco Vanzetti …"

"Good Lord," Bob said, moving closer to Merton. Merton smiled apologetically at the ladies.

"Anderson control of passion kills grasshoppers to break an egg. Belief. Anderson speaks us faith in art, purity. Good work. Cheers."

"Thank you, Claude," Sheila said, with an effort to stay somehow balanced between dignity and compassion. "I'll drink to that. Let's drink now."

George Gantner was looking rapidly back and forth from Merton and Bob to Claude and Clem, thinking he had not been let in on one of the cardinal secrets of our company. Helen Gantner was laughing sociably, as if one of her mother's guests had spilled a cup of tea and she meant to assure the offender that it would not stain the rug.

Only Venetia seemed to be enjoying this. But Clem, at least, did not appear shaken by it. He sat watching, something quite cold about his attentive gaze.

In spite of attempts by Sheila, Janet and me to divert him, Claude did not intend to be stopped until out of the spate of verbiage his tongue stumbled on the one statement his frustrated passion required of him. "Jealousy beside the point in the differences of races, creeds, nationalities, people and naked is a tribute to admit that Anderson the superiority of the native-born white. My hero," he said to Clem. He swayed and leaned forward over the table as if he meant to reach its entire length and plant his congratulatory kiss on Clem's cheek.

"My hero."

"Sure," Janet said coaxingly. She was sitting beside Claude and had been listening with bowed head. Now she put her hand on Claude's arm and tried to pull him back into his chair. "Clem pulled you out of the water. We understand."

Claude gasped and sat down, nodding a desperate gratitude to Janet and fumbling over the table top in search of the wine bottle. Even he, at last, had to climb down from his apotheotic belief by way of some easy misinterpretation. But we all knew what he had meant. He had simply meant what he said: "My hero."

And how did his hero respond to this costly adulation? (For whatever else may be said of it, it had required that Claude sell all he had of self-justification for his exiled life and give the return as tribute.)

Within an hour and a half, when we had all moved into the open air of the zócalo and had been joined by more friends, Clem disappeared with Claude's wife.

I don't know exactly how or when they ditched the party and went to attend to their more urgent calls. I remember Claude, a little more sober than he had appeared at dinner, leaning into an argument with the Gantners—urging them, of course, to "stand up and be counted for peace," while they came back with the faint, educated, tranquil worries of burghers who intend to wait and see whether anyone really meant to change Boulder, Colorado, into a cloud of atomic ash. In need of a supporting statistic or quotation from Einstein, still sure that he could persuade them to fight for their lives, because they were surely good people, Claude turned to call for Venetia's support—and Venetia wasn't there.

He seemed to think at first that she was inside in the ladies' room. He even asked Janet or Sheila, after a while, to go in and see if she might not be sick and in need of help.

They pretended, not without some grim reserve, to do what he asked and in their turn disappeared from our happy midst. Of course they knew what was happening, and they took what was no doubt the wisest course, slipping out another door and taxiing back to our place.

I sat long enough at the heartless, noisy aftermath to watch the truth dawn on Claude. Though he returned to his argument with the Gantners, little by little he was losing steam. He began to admit to them that the American occupation of Japan and Germany might turn these rascal nations into something closer to a democracy than they had ever been. (Claude!) That nations not so confirmed in love of peace as America would have pressed the military advantage of the atomic bomb until they had conquered the world. That little children all over the world would be given an unexpected bowl of mush by the Point Four program. And then, conceding to their optimism, he sank into a mean silence.

I was afraid to leave him and tried to persuade him to share a taxi home. No, he said with a wintry, dead-sober smile, he thought he would walk out and sleep on the beach. Admitting to myself that it was better for him not to seek his own bed that night, I left him there and rode home alone. Clem, of course, had taken my car. To conclude this sordid business in style.

Superficially nothing was seriously fractured by this exercise of Clem's droit du seigneur, any more than it had been by the fiasco at the pool.

Sheila stayed out of sight all the next day. Clem came in after daylight merely to pick up a blanket and some beer before he walked north up the beach alone. All day Janet and I snapped at each other, maybe as our only defense against probing a situation we preferred not to examine. We had been so ready to go home feeling the summer had been good. Now this.

The following day we were back in our routines—even of attitude—again. If I kept some irritation, it now turned toward the Pogorskis for continuing to come around as if nothing had happened. Oh, sure, they implied, Claude had got a little too drunk to remember what had happened in the course of the evening, but then we were all drinking people. They hoped we could all still sit down to a happy dinner at their place before we left. And we did. It went off not too badly.

In fact, the Pogorskis behaved as if the incident had created a new and special bond among us all—which, in a way, it might be said to have done.

It seemed so natural to us not to let anything disturb us that did not physically harm us. I wonder if that is not something we learned from the war—to accept any stain or insult with gratitude that it did not break the skin. In this case even indignation served more as a balm than an incitement. When Janet said indignantly, apropos this confusion of wives, "We're not Eskimos!" I laughed at her quaint phrasing until she laughed, too. Since we could laugh, it seemed that nothing crucial had happened.

Each time after that when I saw stout-thighed Venetia I thought of her as Venus in a bearskin parka, and thus I was able to say goodbye to her with a good humor that more than tolerated the perils of the summer. In a way we proved that nothing serious happens except to those who take things seriously. Frivolity is the perfect defense against atom bombs or adultery or other annoyances of this life. Even Claude would have to learn that.

We were in Mexico City when the Pogorski theme was sounded again. We had come over the mountains into the perpetual, surprising autumn of the highlands. The weather was pleasantly crisp up in the city. The change out of the T shirts and suntan pants in which we had spent the summer seemed by itself to change the emphasis of our thoughts. It was as if wool clothes and neckties gave us a different vantage point to look at the tropical anarchy from which we had come.

Clem and I had gone one afternoon to a bullfight. He slouched beside me on a concrete seat in the Plaza México, preoccupied, drinking beer and munching a taco. The lunar curve of shadow moved with the pace of an eclipse across the sand of the ring. Every bull that came out seemed like a new chapter in a continuing story of dangers that, happily, we had a proxy to face. Our proxies down there in the ring with the bulls faced them manfully and skillfully, as far as I could tell—judging by the response of the crowd as much as by the thrill of approval in my lower nervous centers, and by the crude fact that each bull was eventually dragged out dead.

Each chapter of the afternoon ended with triumph for the fighter and beer-swilling satisfaction for us watchers. Then how account for the intimation that each successive bull came blinking into the light with the last one's death already incorporated in his power? Could that be the meaning of the programming itself, of the institution of bullfighting itself—to show the fighter at best transcending his fate, but to show the bull as eternally victorious within his own realm?

So I was thinking when the fourth bull came out, running close to the ground with a reckless, absolute commitment of destiny to strength. He came almost directly across the center of the ring, out of the curve of shadow into the diminishing orb of light. He stood there a minute, for no apparent reason, with the crest of his horns lifted like a heraldic emblem. I yelled my Midwestern tribute, "Olé, olé!" as if I had indeed, for an instant, seen the god plain.

I certainly did not glance aside to see what Clem was watching, but he chose just that moment to say, "Venetia was like an animal."

"What?" I yelled disgustedly into the noise of the crowd. "What?"

The bull was lured around the ring a couple of times by the cuadrilla. The novillero came out in his pink suit of tights. He blinked a bit as he turned his face to the sky, studying the movement of clouds and paper scraps in the air. He shook out his cape, adjusting the folds as if he meant to put it in a trunk. Then he came pussy-footing across the sand to invite the charge.

The head of the black brute went down. The muscles of his flank bunched and the white thigh curve of his horns leaped to embrace the pink wisp. The black head socked up, and missed its vital, withdrawing target.

A dozen charges through the taunting swirl of the cape. Then both man and animal, as if exhausted and seeming to fall away from each other, separated for a while. The novillero took shelter behind the barrier and washed his mouth with water.

And now the second act, in which the picador took the bull's socking charge against his stout pike and the padded flank of the horse, merely leaning his weight down while the black thing bobbed and danced in its frantic effort to kill. You could hear from where we sat the impact of horns and bone against that padded caricature of an armed knight, and once the horse lost his footing. The cuadrilla came in to take the bull across the ring, where it charged the other pic.

Finally the resolution, when the novillero returned to kill. This one was a brave boy and he killed clean finally, but not before he had been knocked down twice and the bull had split open the leg of his trousers from the knee nearly to the crotch. He put the sword in with a strong charge of his own. The tip of it was visible below the bull's breastbone when it fell. The novillero wrapped his exposed leg in a lady's scarf before he made his triumphal tour of the ring.

The last fight was over and Clem and I were being swept out into the chilly lavender dusk of the streets around the plaza when I asked— thinking that this suspension was just as silly as it sounds in retelling— "What? What did you say Venetia was?"

He answered as if the death of the bulls and all the scamper and roar of the fighting had not interrupted our talk at all. Indeed, as if it had been an expository part of it. "I only said she was like an animal. It was like topping an animal. Which Deuteronomy forbids. Though sometimes there are excuses."

We found a little café on one of the nearby side streets and ordered hot buttered rum. It tasted like something we deserved for having endured the fight. Excuses?

"Claude challenged me," he said with his lip-chewing expression of search for the right word. "As soon as he knew how much I agreed with him he saw he was in a position to challenge. To drag me down. He kept cutting his green knightly head off, since I refused to lop it for him, and then he kept ragging me because I wouldn't match him."

"So you paid him back by knocking off his woman."

"No, no. That was the biggest trap of all. If I'd really taken his woman Claude would have had me."

"You mean you and Venetia merely wandered hand in hand in spite of all indications to the contrary."

"I penetrated. But I was true while I did it."

"You put someone else's blocks to her."

"That's a way of describing it," he said with an impatient grin. "Ah, Dick, you know there are different ways of doing the same thing."

"But if you weren't there—I believe you, Clem, I always believe you when you say that you were off contemplating your diamond body while something else was using your corpus—how did you discover the lady to be Morgan le Fay?"

"She told me," he said mildly. "You know them to be good people, Dick, but between them they'd laid the goodness-badness trap for me. They can't stand what it costs to be in this world and they don't want me to make it, to really make it, with Sheila. They can't stand ... Venetia has had her tubes out. For the highest motives. They won't bring any grasshoppers into Clem's world."

I said nothing. I was thinking too hard about those awfully bad jokes we had made on the subject of her spayed-cat smile.

"Don't you see?" He wanted to make sure I did. "It's a pledge of her love, never to have children by anyone if not by him, and not by him because his beautiful conscience forbids it." He was looking at me with calm eyes, not particularly wearied, but—in a new way—hopeless.

"Then to break that pledge with you, Great Enemy. I'm afraid you've clobbered them, Clem."

He shook his head. "Why is that the worst? They put great faith in the act of love. Logical consequence—get and give as much as possible. Why should they grieve over my taking of nature's bounty? Only, I'd have been clobbered if I had. It was a good thing I was true."

"You said she was not good—"

"I didn't do it for pleasure. You know, I thought what you must have, that it must have been Claude who was sterile and that she was trying to get me to make her pregnant the other night. Came as quite a shock to find things were the other way around. I was lucky to get out of the trap. You know how such things are."

I knew and I didn't. Not in detail and not with any concreteness. But then, he seemed to be taking it for granted that the bullfights we had just seen were incorporated enough into our thoughts just then to furnish images that would adequately substitute for detailed attempts at analysis.

Presently I asked, "Did she tell you that Claude had persuaded her to have the operation?"

"Who knows who persuaded her? Claude? Good sense? The ditto-machine boys? People who can't hold their water just because the state fries a couple of wops? 'He called me Buddy and such love.' There are lots of persuasions to stay out of this world."

"And they may be right," I said. The bullfight mood was still imperatively controlling my mind—the secondhand but persuasive fear I had felt when the bulls came out the gate, lifting up the ancient horns of death for my worship, the wop-frying triumphant horns of all evil. It might be better not to look at them.

"We'll find out someday," Clem said. "All I plead is, I don't know yet—now—though I used to think I knew. I haven't mentioned this to a soul all summer, but the truth is that every time good green Claude stuck his lamentations in my ear—how wicked is man and given to evil and torture all his days—I could hear myself back in Germany on that bed in Ward Eight explaining to my pillow why I couldn't come out and say good morning to Herr Doktor Gorman. Claude gave me the same words and the same facts I gave myself. Why should I argue with them? How can you argue with them? On balance this world isn't a success. But maybe there's more to it than we say. And you know, if there isn't—" he cocked his ear as if he were still listening—"I like the sound of that goddam horn. How was it?"

Hearing nothing—since there was nothing to hear any more—he tried to whistle the rise and splendor of the trumpet blowing the paso dobles in the bull ring. Though the imitation was poor, I heard it well enough. Defiance that remains itself in spite of all it knows. We had that left at the end of the war. For a long time I relied on the faith that Clem (and all the others who wanted to help) would define it, broaden it, perhaps make it a continent where we could live.

# 16

THE STORY GOES ON WITH DIFFERENT NAMES. It is just these words, so often rising of their own bidding when the scene or the epoch changes, so difficult to suppress, and yet so contradictory to our good old idea of what a story is, that seem to me at once the key and the lock of the Clem riddle—at once my chance to illumine and the darkest of enigmas.

Already, as every reader has seen or sensed, I have had to compromise a good many times between the sheer multiplicity of people who were important in Clem's life and the need to keep the story within manageable proportions. Already I have tried to make an impossible marriage at some points between what a story is and what Clem's story was. All this effort to simplify might be more forgivable if I were giving the biography of a simple nature that recognized itself in its core simplicities.

Evidently that is not my task, and I am as guiltily uncertain about every omission as I am about the misleading inclusion of too many names. For instance, when I included with Clem's letters the unpublished poem dedicated to Lieutenant Waldo Monahan, I was keenly aware that I had not identified Monahan in my account of college days. Of course he and Clem were acquainted then. Monahan sat next to Clem in old Silas Waters' class in the English novel, used to lean in front of Clem to court a perfumed Pi Phi with a mixture of fraternity name-dropping, bullying innuendoes and childish pleas that moved Clem to both envy and contempt. He and Monahan used to mimic Waters' speech habits automatically when they met each other on the campus. ("Tooooo dayuh w' will 'zamine Jay-uh Naus-tin," "Jaw-udge Mare Edith's caw mic spit ...") A dozen times I saw them meet, deliver their identical parodies like ritual Aves, clap each other on the shoulder in the midst of uncontrollable laughter, and then part, with each quizzically marveling that they had nothing—absolutely nothing—else in common to say. In time Monahan became Clem's stock example of the brainlessness of football players (Waldo was a second-string halfback). But Clem always knew when Waldo had gone in as a substitute, and through Sheila he kept track of Waldo's reputation in sorority circles. He met Waldo again once in London. They had a beer together. For conversation, even there, they could only bay "Jay-uh Naus-tin" at each other. And then briskly Waldo was dead in the North Sea. Outwardly he figured very little in Clem's life. But the testimony of the poem indicates, I should think, how vividly he inhabited Clem's mind. Very well, I think I should have given him more breathing space in my account of the times when we knew him. I am sorry that I omitted him and scores of others back there.

Nevertheless, it is in trying to come to grips with Clem's second stay in New York that I am confronted with such a plethora of names as threatens to smother continuity and coherence altogether.

New York, indeed, is a kind of synonym for that multiplicity of acquaintance—even a multiplicity of brief loves and hates—that we find so hard to accommodate to our notion of ourselves as singular individuals. (What? I had a thousand friends? They must have been the friends of a hundred selves more or less mine.) That triumphant city confuses me to the end with its replaceable human parts.

I would not know at all how to account for the sheer multitude of actors in Clem's story from 1946 to the end if I did not strongly suspect that he kept them in their place—and at their distance—by assigning them roles already firmly established in other times by other names. If the new actors surprised him a little by their individual variations, he loved that and learned from them. If they surprised him too much, as many did, he simply forgot who they were. For there was a core of continuity in his life at this time that no one really shared except Sheila, and he knew, quite as well as he needed to, that the confusing surface multiplicity had little relevance to his fate. He was a power among powers now, lonely and terribly lonely amidst abstractions, but win or lose it was with them he must grapple.

If the names of his friends and enemies that follow will seem a random and arbitrary selection from among many who helped or hindered a little. I have this strong excuse: that he selected people at random and arbitrarily now. He did not think, nor do I, that what would happen to him henceforward would be influenced much by the chance of selecting this person as fate's agent rather than another. A time had come when he needed people but not persons.

He went back to his first substantial measure of fame when he and Sheila settled in New York that fall. As much as any of the books of verse that came out of the Second World War *Sugar Oboe* was received as a testament for the citizen soldiers still trying to weigh their responsibilities for events beyond their control. Parodistic to an extent that made it first seem a mere junk heap of traditional poetry, reslanted by the violence of new experiences, its values illumined from another side by the burning cities of Europe, the majority of these early poems were distinguished by their formal excellence and by their unmistakable—but undeclared—dramatization of a personality, an "I" in whom the need for parodistic revaluation was keenly felt, a compassionate first person to order the magnitudes of experience by imposing a human measure. The poem about a bombing run ("How They Brought the Good News to Ghent") establishes in astounding series concentric circles of meaning around the apathy of the bombardier who takes over control of the plane for the duration of the attack only. "Death of a Waist Gunner" and "Country Matters" might have been, in another, hypothetical age, truly popular with such bright young men as flew with the Eighth Air Force and sported with Amaryllis in the chill English shade.

Sales of *Sugar Oboe* ran to about eleven hundred copies. It was well and favorably reviewed in the pulp-paper liberal weeklies and in five little magazines besides Poetry. One of the slick-paper fashion magazines published a full-page photograph of Clem pushing his bicycle out of the Bleeker Street apartment house where he and Sheila lived. ("One of six young writers you'll be hearing more about.") On the campus where I went to teach that fall there were a dozen younger instructors and graduate assistants who read the book, and we recommended it successfully to perhaps twice our number of students—all of them hoping to become poets or critics, it goes without saying. And this small, firm wave of success gave him the status that would support all the new friendships he was making without requiring an extravagant outlay of affection.

But whatever else may be said of the book's effect, it must be noted that it provided nothing directly for Clem and Sheila to live on. The small advance he had got for it and the somewhat larger advance against his novel had been too little to cover the cost of the summer in Mexico. They were in debt, and in her condition it was out of the question for Sheila to look for work.

They were enabled to float through that next year largely by the benefactions of Lillian Esterman's new husband, Rudi Leed. "Rudi was a cross between Dostoevsky's Myshkin and Lillian's Idiot," Clem said pettishly. Rudi's help came not as outright charity, but by an indirect complex of expedients channeled through Midway magazine.

Her hour of destiny come round at last, Lillian was on the verge of launching this magazine as "simply the best, most advanced and most widely circulated little magazine anyone ever heard of." It was to have the good qualities (but not the defects!) of The New Yorker and The

Kenyon Review. As proof of her high intent, she had forgone the post of editor, confiding it to one Collis Maitland. She observed grandly, "I'll be content to do the secretarial work or even scrub the office floors if I can gather enough better people to staff the mag for me."

She didn't see just yet where Clem would fit in. ("We never did get it straight just which of us was going to scrub floors and which be the poetry editor," Clem said.) But, plainly, he was a Midway man, to be groomed as such against the day when the first issues would be offered to the public and the editorial needs clarified in the trial of circulation.

This was her general position, and her husband took it as excuse and encouragement to shower bounties on the Andersons that had no conceivable connection whatever with grooming anyone for anything.

Rudi was above calculation. Clem was a poet, ah? So much the better. If he had been a pin setter or bell ringer it would not have mattered to Rudi—except of course that he liked to have Lillian's approval for his generosities. Were Clem and Sheila not, as Rudi liked to say, "on the threshold of life"? Were they not about to have communion with the holy mysteries in producing a child? Had Clem not given his best years as a soldier? Did not the soldier father deserve a roof over the head of his little artistic family? Rudi would do his best.

In the terribly tight housing conditions of that year, Rudi unearthed a landlord cousin who would rent them "a modest apartment. Actually, it is rather ratty and not fit, but for the time being ..." Rudi said humbly. At least this apartment was on the ground floor, "So the Mother will not have to climb too much." Behind it there was a small court paved unevenly with bricks. There was a single large elm with a solid armchair beneath it. "We can put up a wall of high boards," Rudi said, "so the Father can meditate without the lousy distractions and the Mother can sit in the sun with the Child." Then, burning with embarrassment, he took Clem out of Sheila's presence, to a neighborhood bar "for a talk of man to man." To Clem alone he explained that because of certain irregularities that would cause trouble for his cousin with the Rent Control Board, it would not be feasible for Clem to pay any rent "until it is all straightened out."

Without embarrassment Clem said that he understood and would most gratefully accept these conditions.

"No gratitude. It is business," Rudi insisted. "All business, and for what you are doing for Lillian it is too little. All too little."

Rudi's first wife was dead somewhere in the European shambles, and in the great void left by her absence Rudi tried to concentrate on

Lillian and tried to understand what the young lady was up to—and in his anxiety neither to overshoot or to undershoot the marks she set for their lives, he tended always to discharge a blunderbuss of tolerance and funds.

"He was only a fool by choice," Clem said. "He must have known, when he wanted to, that Lillian was never going to get the magazine going on anything like the scale she talked about. Surely he saw early enough that making Maitland editor was asking for trouble. He must have known she still had eyes for Henderson Paul. But none of that mattered to him. He wanted everything to be what it had to be, only more so. With love."

Rudi provided housing and "little loans" to piece out the GI allotment Clem earned by registering at Columbia (in the classes of a friend, who marked him automatically present for every session and sent his regards downtown in the form of A grades). Lillian got her return by worrying with Clem over whether she should also cling to the post of fiction editor (after she had decided Clem was not catholic enough in his taste for anything but poetry) or whether she should let Maitland appoint one of his friends. She also urged Clem to line up Nathaniel Bentley as a regular contributor of criticism. Wouldn't it be slick to have a monthly letter from him covering "the broad aspects"?

Clem put her off by agreeing that it would be nice indeed. Because he would not advise her about the fiction editorship, she got a little bit hurt and let Maitland give the position to his protégé Cohn.

The first major crisis came soon after Cohn was given access to the office files. Presently it came to Lillian's attention that Maitland had returned a novelette, some criticism and a dozen or more poems that had already been accepted for publication. He had not told Lillian that he planned to do this, and she discovered it only in a letter of complaint from one of the contributors, charging that Maitland had been abusive in the note that covered the return of the manuscript. With poor Rudi in tow, Lillian went to the office by night, pried the lock off Maitland's files and found the extent of his manipulations. Maitland might be editor, but it was still her magazine.

Or was it quite? Since no magazine really existed yet—they hadn't even printed a dummy—and since Maitland might after all have been within his rights as editor in whatever he had done, probably the thing to do was have a staff meeting and thresh things out definitively. So Lillian decided. And since the outline of the staff was still ephemeral, it was her thought that "interested parties" should also be included in the brawl. She numbered Nathaniel Bentley among those and proceeded to interest him, since lazy Clem wouldn't. Poor, unwarned Bentley replied to her letter with kind wishes for the magazine, said that yes, he would be in New York the following week and would be happy to call at her home the night of the staff meeting—not as an adviser, of course, but as a respectful observer.

Among the twelve or fifteen potential staff members whom Lillian assembled, Maitland dropped his bomb. He was not at all exercised, he wanted them to know, about the pilfering of his files. He seemed to accept that as a natural part of the literary life. But he did want everyone to consider very carefully that the contributors whose manuscripts he had returned were "known Communists."

Cohn immediately sided with him. The two of them took the lofty attitude that they were among a bunch of innocents (presumably so, at least) who would very soon be cat's-paws of the Communist Party unless they were protected. Smiling Cohn seemed to know not only the publishing history but the ancestry of all the offending contributors, including Californians and Midwesterners. He felt strongly that it would be wrong to put the Midway seal of approval on writers who had erred in thought or deed. Midway should deny them intellectual responsibility.

In the following brouhaha even Bentley was drawn to express a firm opinion. He had not come for any more substantial reason than to see Clem and bestow his elderly blessing on young enterprise, but he said now, with an unmistakable effort to remain calm, that he thought a decision might well be based on an examination of the texts of the offending manuscripts. If they were seditious, then probably they should not be printed. "It would appear inexpedient as well as ungrateful for you to bring down the walls of the Republic with your first issue," he said.

Of the people that Lillian had brought into this mess, only Clem and Rudi took no position. "All I felt obliged to give Maitland by then was my name, rank and serial number," Clem said later. "Poor old Nathaniel had never looked an adder straight in the eye before or he wouldn't have unlocked his word horde either."

The decision finally devolved upon Rudi—the one person who was constitutionally least capable of discriminating among "all you sincere people"—on the tawdry grounds that he held the purse strings. Maitland would not budge unless his salary and Cohn's honorarium were threatened.

After being instructed by Lillian in the kitchen, Rudi came back into the smoke-filled parlor. With hanging head he announced stumblingly that he "from my own personal point of view" could not see how the magazine was going to exist without harmony between sponsors and editors. "But," he added brightly, "it is my own personal view that the Communist issue is petty. Now it is much in the newspapers. But we are artists and are above that. In the spring it will have all blown over, and by the time these poems and novels are in print no one will care if the writers have been Communists as long as they are sincere."

Clem remembered, "Maitland licked his chops when he heard that. Anthropophagus Cohn barked. Maitland might have whisked out his notebook and written it down on the spot, only—you know—he could always remember more clearly what people had said after he'd let a few months go by."

The evening ended with Rudi flinging an arm around Maitland's shoulders, enveloping him in a private balloon of cigar smoke and telling him that, after all, in Germany he had known many sincere kindly people who were Communists.

Cohn was seen engaged in his inexplicable habit of pulling books from the shelves and knocking the ash from his cigarette onto the back of the shelves before replacing the volume. Months later Lillian was still finding behind her books the little mounds, like the droppings of a strange bird.

Why Maitland and Cohn remained on the staff of the magazine after they were thus overruled remains, at the core, a mystery. Just as I felt that Clem would have found his profit in those years regardless of the particular circumstances or people with whom he was cast, so, I feel, would Maitland and Cohn.

It is true that Maitland was drawing a salary from Rudi—something like two thousand a year for the minimal work he put in. And though he had a spurious sort of literary reputation, he was still, at that time, a poor man.

He had originally come from Ohio, one of that small, hardy crew that remained in Paris after the First World War. He had painted for a time in Fresnaye's studio. It was said that he had composed a symphony for tire irons and motorized street sweepers. Then he had turned purely to letters. He had known the great and famous expatriates of the Twenties, from Stein, Hemingway and Tzara to Brancusi and Joyce. He had once published an experimental novel and had been associated with the "Revolution of the Word." His contribution to that movement was that he had "abolished the conjunction."

Most of his notoriety (and most of it was still in store for him) depended on the fact that he had been there when it happened and could speak for the great when they chose to remain silent. He knew the chimney sweeps with whom Hart Crane had soiled the Crosbys' beds, knew the fundamental reason for the hostility between Hemingway and Stein and how close Kay Boyle's novels came to the real truth about many folk whose names we all know. His first wife had been a member of Emma Goldman's circle and he liked to hint that his marital situation had provided Hemingway with material for one of his more grisly short stories.

That is to say that he held a treasure house of gossip that even then could have been peddled under the label of criticism. And it is hard to look back and see why he was not living off it earlier, instead of drawing a pittance for editing a literary magazine and working on an endless novel that he promised would be the sequel to Finnegans Wake.

But the horror of Maitland's situation, as Clem believed, was just that Maitland was sincere and, for a long time, scrupulous. Of all the company sheltered by Rudi's tolerance, it was exactly and solely Maitland who was entitled to wear the badge of sincerity. All the carnage that he wreaked before he lost his scrupulousness came straight from his deadly integrity.

He had sold himself to Lillian in the first place by insisting that he would not let his name go up on the masthead of a magazine that was not chock-full of "the best." It was to be a long time before a diagram of what he considered "the best" could be correctly drawn. Until a series of events disclosed them, the dreams and lies out of which he had cobbled his ideal were simply incomprehensible to Lillian, Benchley and Rudi. Clem, of course, said that he had suspected all along. Through the hard times when the rest were denouncing Maitland as a liar and double-dealer, Clem insisted that they had merely been dealing with a conscience so peculiar that generations of savants had neither reported nor prophesied its like.

He did not even believe it a breach of Maitland's sincerity when Maitland acquiesced in publishing works by writers Cohn had fingered as Communists. He said that Maitland had not been jesting back in those days in Paris when he "abolished the conjunction." Somewhere in the lean years of exile, yapping always at the heels of fame that never turned to single him from the pack, Maitland must have thoroughly purged from his conscience the conjunctive relationship between himself and other people, so that when he rehearsed his stories of watching Old Ernie leap barehanded into the bull ring at Pamplona or seeing poor sick Crane getting slugged by some Philistine California heterosexuals outside Charley's Bar, he was no longer sure these things had not happened to himself.

"So another person either was himself or was nothing, was no more than a presumptive diagram traced through certain colorful facts that might as well be rearranged to suit the convenience—no, the imperative—of the present moment," Clem said. "It was impossible for Maitland to lie, because he had done away with that relationship between a man and the objective world in which either truth or lies are possible."

Clem saw Maitland as the fictioneer par excellence, the pure writer at large—where he did not belong—in life. That is, he saw something of himself in Maitland, and not only in their shared Midwestern origin. He liked to study the man as he would study his own reflection in a twisted mirror. And was fonder of Maitland than it was safe to be.

In the aftermath of the fracas at Midway, Sheila was bewildered that Maitland should begin to come around so often to their apartment on Bleeker Street. Either with or without Cohn in tow, he dropped in two or three times a week. They had many other unexpected or uninvited guests, but Maitland never called when anyone else was with them. Sheila thought he must keep watch on their door to make sure that he would find them alone. For her part, she could not stand to be long in a room with him and could not—or did not wish to—believe it when Clem said that Maitland came in envy "because I have you for a wife."

She understood, in fact, rather little of the peculiar charisma that she and Clem possessed just then. Their growing circle of friends she attributed to the fact that there were "so many nice people around New York after all."

She liked all who came except Maitland and Cohn. It would have been quite compatible with her generosity to like them too, even those, if Clem had not showed her so clearly that she must not. Behind Maitland's back he poured out the most venomous analyses and predictions, delighting in his subtlety when he detected some new strain of impending malice in them. He made the sign of the cross when Maitland came to their door and spat on the rug when he had gone.

So Sheila challenged him for inconsistency. "You say he hates Lillian and Rudi and tries to pick your brains for anything you know about Bentley. Why do you see him?"

"I don't ask him," Clem said. "He comes here."

"Why? I don't want him to. I don't want you to pretend you like him when you feel the way you do."

"My feelings aren't the issue. He knows what I am."

"That flatters you."

"Dear God, no. But he helps me understand who I am. He knows."

"It flatters you to think so, but I don't believe you. He knows a lot of people more famous than you …"

"Say it."

"Not more famous than you'll ever be. Probably. But more famous than you can be sure of being."

"It's uncanny he should bother with me," Clem agreed. "When I know for sure why I'm so important to him, I'll know a lot of things."

"He thinks you're on his side because you wouldn't stand up for what you believe in that night at Lillian's."

"I don't believe in Lillian's magazine," Clem said. Then he corrected, "All right. I believe in it more than anything Maitland represents, and I'll defend it if I can. But what do I have to fight him with?"

"You're good and he's bad."

Clem laughed. "Then there'd be no contest. No. I'm not good. You have to realize I gave up being good to get to be something else. And whatever I am is all I have to fight with."

The argument hung, relentless as the icy weather that seemed to immobilize the city. They could stay in out of it—as they did, softening to the warmth of their pretty little apartment, idling together forgetfully in front of the fire, tasting, talking, touching, waiting—but it was out there, waiting for them, too, in its own fashion of patience.

In somewhat the same way as their home, Clem's work received him. It was both a shelter (without which an emergence or counterattack was unthinkable) and an evasion that kept him from considering the ideological world into which that work would, eventually, have to enter. It would not and could not be enough that it would eventually go on the market, so much yard goods of entertainment, and yet unless the world was successfully kept off until it was done, there would be no work at all. The choice was strict enough, strict through all these years, too strict for Clem to permit himself to be advised on it. For better and worse he made it alone, refusing to be good at the expense of being a worker while his work was waiting to be done.

And through that fall the work was advancing with a bull-like health of its own. It seemed to consume everything, like a great plant with carnivorous roots, or like a big machine for which Clem had become mere guardian and fireman. He wrote us that the novel was coming along "like toothpaste out of the tube." He hoped to be finished with it by spring or perhaps by midsummer. It knew exactly where it was headed now. With perpetual fatigue and perpetual exhilaration he went each morning to serve it. Five hours a day, each day, he wrote. He discovered as each new section took form that it was "about something besides what it seems to be about." This other something became the by-product poem, which in turn was about something beyond itself.

The schema of literature, the beautiful relationships between various forms in which the same thing might be known and repeated endlessly without monotony, was opening for him. It took strength— continuous nervous and muscular energy, spent without thought that he might hold anything in reserve—to keep the darkness of experience from sealing itself again, but the effort itself seemed to renew his strength as long as it was uninterrupted. He felt like a man on a tightrope over a gorge—better not try to get off and rest.

He sold three small sections of the novel as short stories. Was remotely pleased but mostly just amused by this token of success. The money he got for them went unnoticed through his hands, fattening up their Christmas that year, buying a few things for the expected baby.

Before Christmas he finished that marvelous lyric section of The Throne of Oedipus called "The Child Wife." In these seven related poems he rounded off his statement defining the panoply of mysteries worn by his encounters with women, discovering the likeness of his mind to "the habits of the female body in light and air." It is a series of love songs that I have never tried to rank with other love poems, historic or modern, feeling it enough to know they rank with natural objects, as smoothly formed as stones in a creek bottom for all their veins of complexity. In them, at last, he had moved beyond the parody and wit required to support most of his earlier things. For all the difficulty these new poems presented to readers, most of them sensed that he had found some ultimately simple combinations of language that the language itself had been ripening under the screen of love clichés, as berries ripen under a screen of leaves and thorns. These he always called his "unbreakable poems." Like good sculpture, he said, they could be rolled downhill or run over by carts without losing their formal qualities.

Sheila remembered that they had their best Christmas that year. She was in her eighth month and feeling fine. Clem's mother had sent the usual duck from Boda, and Harry Rinehart had come in from the veterans' hospital on Staten Island for the midday dinner with them.

Harry was then being trained in the use of a Seeing Eye dog, and it was typical of his alert serenity that he could tell them a funny story about getting excited when he and the dog passed a bitch in heat. (Typical of Clem that he would try to run this anecdote out into a complex thicket of meanings, trying to articulate the meaning of knowledge in blindness by a series of analogous transfers of sense— postulating the Man Who Was an Automobile Hypochondriac (had the hood up every time he got gas on the stomach), the Man Who Liked Birdseed (could feel his arms strengthening in Icarian anticipation), the Man Who Wore Shoes for Mittens (had the perfect intuition for singling Yahoos out of the human pack) the Man Who Smiled Only When Monkeys Smiled at Him, the Man Who Tangled with Ropes— wearing out the line of conceits until he seemed to satisfy himself that blindness was only a costume of the soul, to be chosen at discretion like any other.

None of this offended Harry, but it bored him. He wanted to talk more practically, to tell them about the course in stenotyping that he hoped was preparing him to make his living as a court reporter.

It was this afternoon that Clem sprang on him the idea of using his name for the autobiographical character in the novel.

"No, by God," Harry said. "There are still some people in Boda who don't know who knocked up Irene Lacey. If they get your book they'll think it was me." Why was it important to use a real name anyhow? Clem couldn't explain, but he very much wanted it to be so.

When he had time to think it over, Harry was deeply pleased. The use of his name seemed one last trick that they—as boys—could play upon the invisible world of their youth. "As long as you make it funny," he said when he at length agreed. "If you got too serious about it or anything else that happens it would spoil it all."

"I'll make it as funny as it was," Clem promised.

He read some of his new poems to Harry, explaining that they too were about Boda. The poems made Harry nervous. While Clem was reading he focused his attention on his dog. "You're degenerating," he said. "I remember reading some of the things you wrote in college and they were bad enough. This is too—" he paddled with his hand in front of his blind face until he found the obvious word—"too obscure. You have to give people what they're used to. Make them see."

Clem said mildly, "Anyway, the poems keep my hands busy and out of the devil's business."

"Speaking of whom," Sheila said suddenly, breathlessly. She had been sitting in the sun by the frost-rimmed front window. Now she nodded out toward a car parking at the opposite curb. Maitland and Cohn got out. Cohn carried a paper sack.

"Did they see you, Mommy?" Clem asked, peering around the edge of the window.

"I'm sure not."

"We won't answer the bell," Clem decided. It rang half a dozen times, insistently. "They'll go away now," Clem breathed.

But apparently the outside door of the building had been left unlocked, for in a minute they heard steps approaching in the hall.

"Clem? Clem? Clem?" It was Maitland's high-pitched voice. He knocked on their door several times. Then there was a whispered conference outside, sibilant on Maitland's part, soundless on Cohn's, as if Cohn were merely talking with his lips.

There was a tiny clink as something heavy was set against the door. The footsteps went away.

"You hiding from the law?" Harry asked. "I always knew you had the makings of a criminal."

"Literature is a dangerous game," Clem said.

"They left you three bottles of something. Bring it in and see if it's arsenic."

"Let me make sure the coast is clear," Sheila said. She leaned to the window again, cautiously, intending to peer through the curtain and see if the car was gone.

Then she squawked and jumped back on Clem's foot. A few inches from the glass the bushy eyebrows and stern, ascetic face of Maitland had risen above the window ledge to peer in at them. He was clinging with both hands to the worn brick ledge, and even when he knew himself discovered he hung on a minute with a determination to see who else was in the apartment with them. Then he dropped out of sight.

For a second Sheila wobbled as if she were going to faint. Then the color rushed to her face and she roared with laughter. "What on earth can he have imagined?"

"I'll shoot the bastard," Clem said. He ran to the bedroom and came back with the P-38 he had brought home from the war. Throwing open the window, he snapped the trigger at the disappearing car.

Then he began to laugh, too. "I couldn't remember whether I'd loaded this damn thing or not. But anyway, Cohn saw me. His eyes—

his eyes looked like a couple of manholes. If he kept a tight ass he's braver than I think."

Harry's dog at last began to growl excitedly. "What's going on? Explain," Harry demanded.

But it seemed too much trouble to give the elaborate background necessary to explain Maitland, and Sheila said only that they had an insane friend. "Now go see what he left, Clem."

"It's Rhine wine," Clem guessed, correctly. When he brought the sack of bottles in from the hall he said, "I'll pour it down the sink. I don't want to drink this cheap Kraut slop."

Harry said, "Don't throw it out. You can't corrupt liquor or money."

"Harry's right," Sheila said. "It seems wicked not to accept a Christmas present."

Clem brooded. "Why three bottles?"

"Don't try to read any great significance into it. We'll never know what goes on in that poor, poor sick mind," Sheila said.

Nevertheless, when Lillian and Rudi stopped by later in the evening both Clem and Sheila felt it better not to mention the incident. They thought Lillian capable of becoming hysterical over such things and inventing a host of improbable meanings with which she would trouble everyone involved in the magazine.

They talked about Maitland, of course. Her "responsibility" (to letters, to the unborn future) weighed heavily on Lillian and she was not sure yet that she had done right in giving Midway to Maitland's direction. (The first issue had gone to the printer now. It seemed to Lillian a compromise issue, and it seemed that it need not have been.) But she and Maitland had had a heart-to-heart examination of their difference recently that had ended in a new and loftier agreement.

"He'd been afraid I meant to castrate him creatively," Lillian said. "Really afraid. I hadn't seen the depth of his fear. It wasn't Communism as such that he was ever worried about, I find. It's just that honestly and sincerely he believes the touch of politics profanes the sanctity of literature. He knows so little about politics—really nothing—that he thinks Communism and politics are synonymous."

"For which you can blame Cohn," Clem offered.

"Oh, Cohn ..."

"Cohn is very sincere," Rudi said. "The boy has suffered." The reverence with which he mentioned suffering was a reminder to them all of his dead first wife, her death a kind of general infliction on all

Jews for which Cohn too deserved sympathy, tolerance and the benefit of every doubt.

"Maitland is Regular Army," Clem said. "The Regular Army of literature, despised and spat on during all those peacetime years, drilling with dummy guns and cardboard models of Joyce and Proust, stuck off in some Godforsaken outpost on the Rue Delambre, watching the youth of America go slack and forget how to salute from reading too much Wolfe and Farrell, never giving an inch, year after year begging for appropriations because he knew the Philistine meant to build a New Order that would last a thousand years. Well, you can't expect breadth from a man like that."

So they sealed Maitland outside with the harmless weather. They understood him, so how could he be dangerous? Sheila and Clem served his wine to their guests as long as it lasted. More people came in during the evening—the Guthries, Connie Firbank and George Creed, Morrie Braunheit, Henderson Paul and a rich Smith girl, Vincent Ford, Robert Hartman and Clay Feldman.

Rudi covered them with a parasol of love and cigar smoke. Sheila carried her unborn child among them like an ark of faith. Clem pranced and beamed his fatherly benison down on each one, finding an occasion to talk to each about his special concerns, knowing enough about them to bring a blossom of excitement into the talk—too adept now to let himself be trapped all evening with someone like Robert Hartman, who could get down to brass tacks on any given detail. (A milk carton would draw Robert into an analysis au fond of "the problem of milk in the city" and "the psychologically projected differences between milk that's been handled several times and milk.") Too content with his life to mind Henderson Paul's condescension.

The party, they felt, might have gone on forever if it had not been necessary to break it for Sheila's sake. Not that she was tired, not in the least. By some miracle—nothing quite supernatural, but quite definitely like what one thought the supernatural might be—everything that could have been grievous on that holiday had been transformed into pleasure, wit and comfort. This—if nothing more should ever come of it—was what art was for, Sheila thought. It was a way of life. The only good way of life. Her throat ached with thanksgiving that she had never been misled into doubts during the hard years before. This was what she had always known she wanted.

But when the guests were gone and she was making up Harry's bed for him in the living room, she found him unaccountably morose. Yeah, he liked their friends, he said. Yeah, he'd had a swell time. But

Clem had upset him. Clem wasn't "like himself"—whatever that meant, and it probably only meant that Harry's idea of Clem, established so long ago, had been jarred by the changes he noted.

Still Sheila couldn't get him to commit himself on that either. At last Harry said he hadn't liked Clem's fooling with the gun.

"Oh," Sheila said, "he wasn't really going to shoot at that fellow. He's never had any bullets for that gun since he came home."

Harry nodded. "That was always Clem's trouble, and I hoped he might have got over it. When I knew him he wasn't ever sure whether he was really doing something or pretending. That got him into all his scrapes."

"The scrapes have been good for him," Sheila guessed.

"But there comes a time when you have to act like a man," Harry said. "It seems to me that if a man points a gun at somebody he ought to intend to shoot. Well, that sounds like something out of a Western story, doesn't it? I never did go deep in literature, like Clem."

"I didn't either," Sheila said, hearing a tone of complicity in her own voice beyond what she had intended. And it suddenly occurred to her that she was afraid for Clem—the word "deep" rattled and echoed on her nerves. She realized how much she had been missing Claude Pogorski, who, like Harry, had shared her indescribable fears. "But Clem knows what he's doing," she said with breathless loyalty.

"I hope so," Harry said.

Before she slept Sheila had a kind of fantasy—not a dream—that it was Clem's very self she was carrying in her body. And she bit her lip, afraid to let him go where he wanted to go.

They had no chance during the next few weeks to thank Maitland for his gift of wine. It appeared he was out of town. Once Clem ran into Cohn in the sparse office Lillian had rented on Christopher Street to house Midway. Cohn was sitting with his feet on the desk, dropping his cigarette ashes into the top drawer. He was telling Lillian a joke, and as Clem entered he gave the punch line in Yiddish, making a sly face to indicate he knew Clem wouldn't understand and he was sorry for that, but some things had to be accepted as they were.

He said he had been very eager to see Clem. He had made a tentative selection of stories for the second issue and wanted Clem's opinion of them. He laughed at every joke Clem made and "he was careful not to turn his back on me," Clem said. But no mention was made of the episode at Christmas. Nothing was said of Maitland's whereabouts.

Maitland was in Washington. As if he really had a sense of humor, he had told Lillian that he had to go down there to "straighten out some painful family business." He spent the first three weeks of the New Year conferring with the FBI and a junior Congressman who had come in on the Republican sweep of the previous November.

What Maitland told them and how much they believed of what he told them is, of course, a secret forever buried in the untouchable files and the sealed memories of the agents. I suppose it is no longer worth speculating about the manner or most of the details of his revelations—though in the topsy-turvy spring that followed, Clem's circle speculated up to and perhaps beyond the farthest range of possibility.

Had Maitland said—sincerely, of course—that all American literature after W. D. Howells was tainted with subversion? Had he diagrammed the network of editors and critics who, during the Thirties and the war, had either prevented or minimized the publication of anti-Communist fiction and poetry? Or had he more airily theorized (backgrounding his theory with scraps gleaned from listening at the figurative keyhole for thirty years, from the disillusionment of Emma Goldman to the anxieties Nathaniel Bentley had expressed that night at Lillian's) that the taint of leftism had colored all our arts without the machinery of a clear conspiracy to spread it? Or had he begun his interviews with such theorizing to plain men who did not wish to bother with a semantic distinction between "coincidence," "concerted effort" and "conspiracy," discovering as the interviews progressed that he was only a crank to them until he had begun to invent concreteness in order to make them understand, lying about particular people and their particular acts merely for the sake of illustrating the ideal truth that he had divined?

Maitland was fond of using Pound's phrase to characterize himself as "one of the antennae of the race." In Washington he must have sat with the race itself in all its earnest dependence on facts, facts and more facts that a common-sense America could grasp. So, perhaps, Maitland may have had to invent a few shadow parables of the sort that Plato recommended in order to make himself comprehensible to those who had never come out of the factual cave. In charity one might assume that he never understood how his parables might be construed as accusations of purposeful treachery.

But—to shift the order of speculation—was he not simply a paranoiac in a time when paranoia assumed the stature of a national virtue? Or was he trying to clear himself for having served as a GPU agent? (The person who suggested this hinted that the GPU had fired him on grounds of general incompetence just before the FBI took him on.) Or was he simply evil?

This last is the question that I worry with to this day, long after the sensational details of our purge trials and hearings of the Forties have been filed away in newspaper morgues. Is there a better way of describing Maitland than to call him part of the residual evil still floating at large—like the mine Clem talked about—after the war that released it was formally concluded?

Well, then, was it the Devil's face that Sheila saw outside the window on Christmas day? Clem thought, "No, it wasn't the Devil's face that she saw. But that was what I saw. And what's a window to some people is a mirror to others." But who and what is which, in this riddle of wickedness? He wanted to leave it a riddle, and so must I.

Whatever the Washington people thought Maitland had given them, they thought, as the Congressman said later, they had got hold of "something."

On the day before Sheila went to the hospital to deliver Jess, an FBI man dropped in to see Clem. "A nice fellow," Clem called him. "We had a dandy chat. The only malapropism in the visit was that Sheila hadn't done up the lunch dishes and I kept trying to explain—ha ha—that usually she was a very good housekeeper. But he didn't seem to hear me and as a consequence got butter on the sleeve of his government overcoat."

Facts. All the agent was concerned with hearing were some facts that any fiction writer or poet would recognize as impertinent dross.

Did Clem know: Collis Maitland, Gilbert Cohn, Rudi and Lillian Leed, Nathaniel Bentley, Martin Lawrence, Irving Alpert, Wadleigh Hertz, any of the contributors whose manuscripts had once been returned after acceptance by Midway, and —— (everyone who had been at the Andersons' apartment on Christmas day)?

"He had all the names down except the name of Harry's Seeing Eye dog," Clem said. "Gave me the feeling we hadn't been alone."

Was it true that Clem had published poems and stories in such and such magazines? "A perfect bibliography."

Had he been at a meeting in the Leeds' house when —— (a complete list including the maid) were there? "Yes."

How long had he known Nathaniel Bentley? "Since 1937."

Did Clem own a pistol and any other weapons? Clem showed him the P-38 and discussed where ammunition might be found for it. The agent cautioned him that he had better register the gun.

Had Mrs. Anderson worked in Washington during the war? Her department? Her immediate superior? Where had she lived?

Did the Andersons know Claude and Venus Pogorski? "Venetia," Clem said. The agent made the correction in his notebook—one of the few corrections of information already compiled. "We had social intercourse with the Pogorski family last summer," Clem said.

When the agent had gone, Sheila came out of the bedroom angry and upset. "Who are they after?" she asked.

Clem had no answer. The one thing clear was that a wide net was being thrown.

He called Lillian to report the visit. To his astonishment she listened calmly and minimized its significance. "It's no doubt only about the pistol," she said. "Cohn reported it to the police and then he was ashamed, but it was too late to get them to forget about it or strike it or whatever they do. He realized you didn't mean anything by it, so that's why he's been so strained with you lately. Guilty conscience."

"Lately? You knew about the Christmas visit, then?"

"All about it," Lillian said gaily. "I don't see how I keep such a bunch of wild men working so smoothly."

Plainly—even Lillian would have known—the FBI would not have been called in because he had brandished a pistol. Clem became so suspicious that he abruptly cut off the discussion with her.

The windy night that Jess was born and the following morning were too full of common demands for attention and emotion to let either Clem or Sheila worry much about the web of intrigue into which they had been drawn. The baby was delivered normally at 3:15 A.M. Clem saw him first, through the glass of the nursery, at ten that morning, awed, shaken, jellified by "the knowing look the kid had, knowing everything I knew, only keeping it to himself better."

In a demoralizing moment of envy Clem pressed his face to the glass and tried to lift his arms in a gesture of supplication, as if begging to be picked up and held. As he stared, it came home to him as it had not for years that he too had a father, and his father and his child seemed to embrace him like a loving parenthesis, mute but indestructible. The weight of his peculiar responsibility seemed lifted from him, as if now, now at last, only now, he was free to indulge himself as a sensuous being. This evidence that he had discharged his physical duty seemed to render even his social obligations nonsensical. In this intoxicated euphoria he felt his loins charge with blood, and he was not sure, when he pranced away from the nursery window, whether he was looking for Sheila's room or for a nurse or a black janitress that he might drag into a linen closet and ravish.

"I never saw Clem so speechless as that morning," Sheila reported.

"I was never in such an erotic fugue before," he said. "Luxe, calme et volupté. Why do you think I held my overcoat in my lap while I was talking to you? It had just dawned on me what a marvelous tactic we had."

And it was as if the physical event had burst a whole new set of recognitions up from the fringes of his dreams into the daylight of his consciousness. While he wandered through midtown bars between the morning and afternoon visiting hours, the omissions from his novel, from his poems, from his awareness of what his life had meant swarmed after him like half-benign furies.

So this was what had begun so long ago in the Baptist church in Boda, begun the day of the immersion baptism when he had first longed for Margaret Shea. And this was the open end of the black wedge of time that he had seen figured between watch hands and between the loosening thighs of that other girl in the church. This was the child he had seen Irene Lacey holding in her arms as she prophesied, "Here's our boy." What he had dived for from the rock of his marriage that day in Mexico when he went in to save Pogorski's manhood. What he had killed Otto Kleist for, and what at Chartres he had asked to be forgiven for. This, after all, was what he had wanted to give Cecile Potter, all he had to give in his high-principled and poetic fornication.

The tiny, wise face of the infant mocked his thought, reduced all truth to affirmative or negative, the grunt of assent or the shriek of denial. Of denial he must think, too, before this particular clarity would disperse and fall back like a shattering wave into the common. This was also the gun in the furnace of the Baptist church basement, the black window of his room at Emmy Polk's that had tortured him into writing, the septic fear of the war, and the surrounding vacuity that obliged him to return daily to his work in fear of losing himself before he was done. This was the other body, perhaps, that he had flung off that rock in Mexico when his courage failed him.

This came to pass with having a son, did it? Nobody had told him how easy it was to sum up all a life might be by getting a child. He wept self-pitying tears into his beer thinking of all the painful roundabouts and delays it had taken him to come to this day. And everything could have been so easy, if this was all it was.

In the afternoon visiting hour he came back to Sheila's room carrying flowers, a huge and gaudy bouquet of gladioli that amused her to tears. When he demanded to know why she was crying, she could only splutter, "They're so ugly, darling. No one but you would have brought them, and they're just what I need."

She had put on lipstick and a lace-fringed bed jacket. She said it was time to call the grandparents, and they called her folks first. When Clem was put on to speak to them, he shouted, "I'm very proud of your little girl"—and wondered why Sheila again broke into sobs of laughter.

They called Boda next. Clem's father, hard of hearing now, caught little of what was said except the boy's name. "Jess," he said, "Jess. That's a good name. That's a fine name. Jess. I'll remember that. He ought to be a good boy, with a name like that." Clem's mother said wistfully, "We'd like to see the little fellow. When are you coming home?" Then the thousand miles of line between New York and Wisconsin trembled with boohoos from either end.

"I don't know, Mama," Clem said through his blubbering. "When they let me, I guess."

After he had hung up and wiped his face, Sheila asked, "Who's stopping us from going back? That was a silly answer you gave your mother." She pillowed his head on her breast and promised him they'd take Jess to see all his grandparents in the summer ahead. Since Clem returned from Europe each of them had gone back separately for a brief visit with their parents. Now they would all go together. Wasn't this maybe what they had been waiting for without knowing it?

With grandiose foolery, attempting to cover his own display of weakness, Clem said, "They do not comprehend the nature of my wound, woman."

"Hasn't this healed it?" Sheila asked, her new maternal pride smarting a little.

He was monstrously ungrateful to speak of wounds on such a day, Clem assured her.

"Then can we go back and show them?" she asked. "Show them all?"

"We'll see," he said.

Lillian and Rudi came in presently with the smell of snow on their coats, bringing flowers and candy and a box of cigars which they "knew Clem would forget to buy"—Rudi's cigars, expensive and dignified, appropriate gifts to celebrate the birth of a poet's son.

The women embraced and soon fell into the ritual accounting of statistics, those convenient formulas for speaking of an event about which there is at the same time all too little and all too much that might be said. How long a labor was it? How fast were the contractions coming when Sheila got to the delivery room? How many fingers of dilation?

Rudi beamed moistly as he eavesdropped. Two fingers dilated? A noble. Three fingers? A prince. Four fingers? A king with the brain of a Solomon, a philosopher king, his smile said. Now and then he slapped Clem on the shoulder, but it seemed he could think of no better compliment for the supreme infant than to express incredulity that he had required a breach four fingers wide to wiggle through into life.

Then, in the midst of this euphoria, Lillian suddenly said gruffly, "It looks like I've lost my baby."

At first Sheila thought this declaration was meant literally. And today she was pathetically vulnerable to such news. Which may have been why Lillian chose this particular way of announcing that her magazine, for which she had hoped so much, was defunct. In spite of all Rudi's admonitions not to mention "the mess" here and now, she evidently decided that Clem and Sheila were now secure enough to hear what she had been sparing them.

She had known for some days now, she said, what Maitland had been up to in Washington. Clem was by no means the only associate of Midway—or contributor—who had been visited by the FBI. An instructor at Bard College had called to ask for his manuscript back after an agent had questioned him. A poet teaching in California had written an angry letter denouncing her as a police spy and agent provocateur after being summoned before his dean and advised not to submit any more "polemics" to Communist-front periodicals.

Cohn had dropped out of sight, leaving only little piles of cigarette ash behind the books and in the drawers of the office. He no longer answered his home phone. A cousin of Lillian's thought she had spotted him wearing dark glasses in Brooklyn Heights.

While it was true that Lillian knew about the farce on Christmas Day, she had learned of it from the FBI man who came to interrogate her and Rudi. She had merely misled Clem when they talked yesterday, to keep him from worrying.

"This surely doesn't mean you can't print your magazine," Sheila said slowly. "Won't it be a better magazine without Cohn and Maitland?"

Lillian shook her head bitterly. "I'm afraid to get anyone else in trouble. They've even been to our printer, and he wants to back out. So ... We could get another printer, of course. There are lots of printers. There are lots of distributors. There must be lots of people with a quarter to spend for the magazine, only there won't be. We've been kissed. Rudi and I talked to his lawyer. I was going to sue Maitland."

"And?"

"Rudi's lawyer will sue anybody," Lillian said. "He'd sue Admiral Byrd for trespassing on the South Pole. But his advice is to lie low this time. He says, 'Don't forget you're Jews.' It's this kind of thing that reminds you."

"All this will blow over," Rudi said with gentle emphasis. "Next year, the year after, will come a better time." He poked his cigar at a ghost of smoke that hovered in front of him. "In a democracy ... personal opinions ... currents and tides ... sincere patience ..."

"I don't understand your reasoning," Sheila said to Lillian. In her weakened condition she was taking fright perhaps excessively from the unspoken implications in Lillian's decision. For decision it was, since there had been no force used or even directly threatened by anyone who might conceivably want Midway abandoned. Were the powers so mighty that they could work without even disclosing themselves? "If you're Jews what does that have to do with it? Surely the FBI doesn't care if you publish a little magazine. Who're they after?"

Rudi jiggled on the balls of his feet, and his pink-rimmed blue eyes begged Clem to help him arrange a sensible termination of such talk. Clem was no help. Rudi said, "Lillian, let us leave the Mother. I want to go peer at the Wee Child through the glass. Will he have the Father's handsome forehead?"

"Who knows who they're after?" Lillian said wildly. "We know how things happened in Germany."

"They may be after Truman, if they can nail him," Clem said. "However, he hasn't yet submitted anything to Midway. Maybe they want to pin a tail on Bentley, or Harvard, because he's going to lecture there this spring. They're probably still fishing to see who they can hook. I doubt if it's just Jews."

"It's always Jews," Lillian said. "Always, finally." She got to her feet and began pacing around the room in an effort to control her feelings—dramatizing them the more in doing so.

Presently Clem said, "Come on, Rudi. Lillian. I'll show you the concentration nursery where they've got baby."

"Wait," Sheila said. "Lillian, Rudi, why don't you and Clem stand up to them? Fight them right here. I know that Midway isn't a very big thing. But it's big to us. And if enough people everywhere do the same … Make Maitland retract."

Rudi, in his gentleness, did not want to answer, though he must have understood where she meant to touch him. He would have known that ruthlessly she was asking him what he was going to do for the sake of his exterminated wife. Not that Sheila would have believed Lillian's hint that the same thing was beginning here as had happened in Germany. But she would have believed, like all of us, that what was to be shaped of conscience in these years after the war would either hold true faith with the dead or drop them into a lime pit of dishonor by blurring out the name of what had killed them.

"I have faith," Rudi said, looking over her head. "Oh, all will be well."

"Because we're afraid," Clem said with ugly bluntness.

"If you two are afraid, then who is there?" Sheila asked, mouth trembling. She did not mean to compliment them for past evidences of courage so much, one supposes, as ask them each if they had not a special mandate to refuse their fears. She had learned too much from Clem not to understand how large a part of a writer's capital is simply courage, and though he might twist and turn and split hairs in averring that a writer's courage has specialized objectives (indeed, discovers itself in cowering and hiding from the practical snares as often as not), it had never quite occurred to her that it was useless for everything except its prime objective. "If you're afraid, why shouldn't I be?" she said.

A nurse came in then and said it was time for Mrs. Anderson's snack. Sheila closed her eyes and submitted. The others went to see the baby.

While Rudi was making faces at it and waving to it with his unlit cigar, Lillian said to Clem, "I didn't mean to get Sheila going, and of course there isn't any immediate danger, and yet I had to express my feelings, and it's all so subtle and complicated."

"It certainly is," Clem said.

"And just because nobody is holding a gun at your head is no reason to say there isn't any danger."

When Clem had said goodbye to them and went back to the room, Sheila was lying on her side, staring into the swollen lump of pillow.

"Mommy?" Clem called. But she would not lift her eyes to meet his.

432

"I suppose you think you can leave all your fighting up to him," she said.

"I could," he said, kneeling and burrowing his face in beside hers and searching for her lips. "The Andersons is only every-other-generation fighters, and he's a good boy. Your boy."

"They'll eat him," she said.

"What? What did you say, Mommy? Are you all right, Sheila?"

"I had a dream when they were taking him. I don't know. I'm tired Clem. Do you have to get after me now? I'm tired. Why are people such pigs, darling? Why can't we be somewhere else?"

"They won't eat him," Clem said. "It was only a bad dream, Mommy. You won't dream tonight. There isn't any use in it."

"Why couldn't Lillian keep her mouth shut just for today? Who cares about her lousy magazine? If she wouldn't fight for it, why should anybody?"

"Nobody will."

And that was the wrong answer, too, so she fell asleep in his arms, sobbing.

Always a peculiar part of his hypochondria was to "catch" dreams from other people the way most of us catch a common cold, and Sheila's parturition dream that Jess was being taken from her by a bunch of scalpel-armed and white-gowned cannibals became a part of the permanent slush that he carried in his mind. Sometimes this or that bit of the slush ripened into an idea that would begin a literary work. But a great deal of it never did. What was useless seemed to have an equal potency, an equal "reason" for sticking with him, and some of it would go on troubling him for years. In fact, what he could write down often went away and left him alone. The other, the never-written and compulsive fragments, remained as if they were a second, larger personality grafted onto his own and quite malignantly burdened him with responsibilities for which he had made no rational contract.

So it was with Sheila's cannibal dream. A time came when he was not at all sure that she had dreamed it in the first place instead of him. It remained a vivid chord in his memory, returning with such dynamics as to suggest it was rooted perfectly in some ancient guilt of his—a guilt merely compounded (though by no means explained) when he considered that it must have been his fault, his unknown sin, that caused her to suffer the dream in the first place.

However that may be, and whatever might have been the mythic root of the dream, he kept it and always related it to the talk he had with Nathaniel Bentley on the following day.

433

Bentley at that time was in his early sixties, a slight, red-faced lath of a man, just beginning to stoop, as if the tip of a thin, rigid bow were giving to the draw on the bowstring. Decked for twenty years with academic honors and respect, he seemed still harassed by them, and the nervous habit he had of jerking his head back and to the left reminded one of nothing so much as the movement of a frightened colt unable to bear the touch of harness. All his features seemed extruded from his face—that is, his mouth, nose and ears as well as his faintly exophthalmic eyes seemed not to depend on being part of an ensemble. Each had to make its own way. Which each did, rather handsomely. His white hair usually looked as if he had slicked it down severely with water.

Though he and Clem had talked extensively on a dozen occasions, either alone or at some literary party, it had never seemed to Clem that they were friends. Besides the natural shyness that a lifetime of teaching had failed to break down, the old man gave the sense that his life was long ago booked full. He would have made a handful of friends in his teens and to them added one a decade, and besides the very few friends there were the literally hundreds of good students and colleagues and literary acquaintances to whom long ago he had assumed a fidelity which he did not intend to let the years erode. For the latecomers there was standing room only.

And yet he never gave even so keen an observer as Clem the appearance of skimping either his interest or his support. He did not need to be reminded anew each time Clem talked to him what Clem was up to. Once he had spread his cloak and done what was in his power to welcome young people into the comity of letters, he made it his business to follow their progress with all the professional keenness and decent concern that he could possibly exact from himself.

This time he had summoned Clem. And as they sat down to lunch in the dining room of a midtown hotel, he said with a tight smile that he did not quite know why.

There was, of course, the Midway affair, in which they were both somewhat peripherally—Bentley only by the slenderest of connections—involved.

No, it wasn't that which was worrying him, though it made a talking point; was, perhaps a definitive symptom of the goblin work that, increasingly, he was aware of.

After he had beamed and spoken his polite, elaborate formalities of congratulation on the birth of Clem's son, he suddenly demanded rather brusquely how Clem was getting on with his work.

With measured confidence Clem told him it was going fine. Another year, at the most, ought to see the completion of the big novel. Then there was the bonus of poetry, accompanying it at a steady rate, perhaps forming into a book. Knowing that he had the best of listeners, Clem expanded on the unfolding discoveries he was making as the big fiction work progressed.

"Yes, yes, yes," Bentley said, impatiently. "Clem, I'm sure it's good. But do you know where you are with it?"

"What do you mean?"

"How does it integrate with things around it? What does it serve?"

"It serves me," Clem said. But Bentley, who always listened, was not listening now. He had too much to say, too little time in which to get it said, so that there was already evident a waste in his intense effort.

It was his own intellectual life, nearing its completion, that had begun to slip its gears. Just when, according to all promises of reason, it should have been ready to stand like a monumental arch under which the legions of the future might march to fields never tried before, it seemed to have lost its pertinence, and everywhere he saw people willfully floundering into gulfs that he and others had so painstakingly bridged for them.

In the humility that only a man intoxicated with pride of the intellect can know, he had disciplined himself to serve what he believed to be a transition in American life and thought, only to find (or to be convinced that he had found) that his position was terminal. The "good old cause" for which he had relinquished all enticements to consider culture an account that Europe had opened and closed, could now show only himself and a few other "relics." The idea of America to which he had bound himself with the reckless optimism of a seventeenth-century bondservant had, without formal notice to its creditors, declared its bankruptcy and given over its stock to be sold—"To be sold," he repeated, as if the words were vinegar on his tongue—by the auctioneers.

And was being sold already—sold back in meaningless piecemeal to the people who owned it (if they only wanted it) title free as their birthright. Consider, he said, that the academic salesmen and the little magazine hucksters were already busy selling selected morsels of Henry James—Henry James glamourized and morally bowdlerized, to be sure, sold for his snob appeal to the hordes of inflation-smitten nouveaux-riches created by the snot-slick magazines that had, during the war, taken over much of the popularity of the old dull slicks. Only a few days ago, he said, a man on the staff of a New York university had sent him the reprint of an article on The Ambassadors. The reprint had come under the cover of a flattering letter, expressing indebtedness to Bentley for his book on James published twenty years ago. Flattery— and an implication that, while Bentley's work was sound pioneering, new discoveries had been made that invalidated most of it. "And the goddam fool hadn't even, apparently, read through to the end of the novel, or if he had he hadn't understood it. Or if he understood it, he took it upon himself to suppress the ambiguity that James intended to leave. The message he found was that European travel was broadening! That the rich are different from you and me! Chad Newsome was the hero, mind you, of this little fairy tale that passed for criticism."

Since Clem had not then read The Ambassadors, he had to take it from Bentley's tone that Chad Newsome was something less than the hero of the book and that European travel might not be, in and of itself, sufficient for salvation. In any case, he did not interrupt. And Bentley was so immersed in his own thought that an interruption might have broken the drama of his presentation.

"He even quoted James's devastating phrase, 'to drift on the silver streams of impunity'—offering it as evidence, mind you, of Newsome's election to grace. Pfui."

Of course—of course—Bentley had replied to the author with congratulations, had swallowed the toad of disgust like a gentleman. But too full a diet of toads was sickening him visibly. And everywhere he seemed to encounter the same kind of thing. His students increasingly showed a preference for "some smooth artifact that resembles an idea" over ideas themselves. More and more of them, even the "battle-hardened" veterans, thought of a liberal education as a social asset rather than an "arming for their war with God." They meant to be prepared to "talk well about what is being talked about" without regard to whether it was worth their time, without curiosity as to the mechanism that had made this subject or that one fashionable.

And old reputations were being manipulated like stocks. Granted that it would be monstrous to fix once and for all any reputation. Not even Sophocles, Shakespeare or Dante ought to be immune to the shift of interest. But what was beginning was not the normal shift of interest—it was trading. Just as there were bulls for Henry James running his stock up, so there were bears out to depreciate the Whitman stock. "And they'll sell him back, too, one of these days," Bentley said, with no more clairvoyance than an honest and experienced man needed, once the principle of the action had been revealed. "Just as is done in

Wall Street, they'll shake out the crumbs—the small investors in Whitman, the little scholars and the readers—and when everyone is sneering at poor old Walt they'll switch and 'discover' him. Glory to the discoverers! A corner in the dispensation of critical reputations! Oh, it's magnificent!"

There were bulls (just now) for Melville. Bears for Dreiser. Bulls for Donne and all the metaphysical poets. Bears for the romantics. Bulls for Madame Bovary. Bears for Thomas Mann. The whole literary history of the Thirties was being rewritten, largely by ex-Communists trying to dodge the public hysteria by the simple expedient of erasing ten years of the national conscience from memory. "And those years too will be resold when the price is right."

The infamous process was well begun now. Where would it end? Where but in the destruction of all that could decently call itself literary education? It would end with all discrimination vested in the staffs of publishing houses, they deciding, like Dior and Schiaparelli planning a new hemline, where to dip into the treasury of literature for each year's fashionable flood of reprints. "The presses will run," Bentley said. "They will run as never before, and the sheer mass of esoteric titles available in cheap editions will silence any criticism of cultural famine. Every poor booby of a student who finds Arnold's prose too difficult for comprehension will be carrying Pascal and Meister Eckhart in his pants pocket like a passport." When this situation matured, the teacher would be finally denied his library, would be at the mercy of the force majeure that the publishing industry represented, forced willy-nilly to "teach" the books they had decreed significant just as every small-town dealer in ladies' ready-to-wear was forced to straggle after Paris fashions.

And Clem thought what was galling the old man most—the toad among toads—was the ineradicable suspicion that he had helped set this pernicious tendency in motion. Bentley had, humbly enough, conceived of himself as a bearer, and twenty years ago when he published his book on James it had seemed to him that he was keeping alive something in danger of extinction. But had not the flattery from his New York colleague implied that he was a "smart bastard" for having sniffed out, so long ago, a profitable racket?

He had begun his career with a book on Whitman. It had been an attempt, as he saw it then, to prune away some of the pomp, turgidity and plain silliness of Whitman's work, to leave the glowing core visible to a generation eager to junk the heart and save the bawdy mannerisms.

437

In his shorter pieces on Dreiser, Melville, Twain, Garland, Robinson and Bierce it had been his intent to find the elements that linked them in a chorus voicing the American experience. Paralleling his purely literary concerns he had spent his critical intelligence freely in an effort to define the same center in political and social currents. He had assumed that the young whom he had encouraged were branches of that great root and bole from which he had helped to clear the surrounding underbrush.

And now, perhaps, he found himself mistaken for an ancestor of those who meant to vend the forgotten or the obscured as their own property. He said, "The bitterest confrontations one ever makes with himself are on those occasions when reason and rationalization prompt identical courses. Or identical views. I've faced that difficulty many times, but now it seems a perpetual, daily quandary. I find that the apostolic succession of writers is broken. I find that there is no dialogue between men because we have finally breached our deep commitments to consistency and there is no longer any unanimity of consciousness to which one can address himself. And I do not know whether my findings are reasonable or rationalized on this matter. It is a great sin to despair out of personal weakness, and if I thought my gloomy view of the current scene were rationalized I would find strength to try one more time to accommodate myself to what is coming. I could even find reasons to approve using The Ambassadors as an ad for the travel agencies. Yes, I could. But to support what one knows to be a bland inversion of the truth, to swear that villains are heroes and heroes villains, and geese are swans ... Surely it is better to withdraw into silence than to traffic in such nonsense."

"I take it I'm being lectured on my callow eagerness to contribute to Babel," Clem said uneasily. If there was one thing he was sure of it was that he was not being lectured, but now as two o'clock passed and he knew that Sheila was expecting him at the hospital he felt restless, anxious merely to break off this unprofitable listening. It struck him how little he was equipped for the one thing that Bentley seemed to ask—that he sit still in pity for abstract losses. If Bentley had said that the soul of the world had died and he had agreed, still he would want to be doing something. To go see his son. To go home and write. He had accepted the inertia of his life, and his health was to stay in motion until something stopped him. "It would ruin me to stop writing. There's no substructure to my life, financial or otherwise. Everything I am has been mortgaged so that I can do what every day I do. There's no way back out."

Bentley said, flushing, "I hope you don't think—" He broke off and laughed. "I'm not suggesting a writer's strike, young man. I can think of nothing less likely to succeed in a time like this. If every serious writer in the country struck permanently, the presses would not miss a beat. There would be exactly as many great writers in next Sunday's book sections as in last. As you well know. No. I know that you must go on—and go on in the awareness of how many bright young scientists there must be, or career soldiers for that matter, who must say to themselves what you just said, 'There's no substructure to my life.' And think what it means. That they dare not let conscience intervene, that they dare not pause to examine their reasons. Very well. Go on. If I had any advice to give you it was to go on, whatever the end may be. But to do so, I feel strongly that you should not—now— involve yourself in politics. I see no position now that would not be corruptive."

"I'm not involved in politics," Clem said, surprised and not quite understanding.

"Oh? No? Well, I thought with this magazine ... that it was intended to take a leftward slant, and that you ... Well, perhaps I got the wrong impression."

"And gave me too much credit," Clem said. He tried as briefly as possible to untangle the confused impression Bentley had taken of Midway and all involved with it. There was no way to unravel it quite, and both of them seemed to understand that his inability to state the situation patly was the mischief itself. The tangle grew with every attempt to straighten it, and at last Bentley raised his hand to stop the explanation.

"There was no need for anyone to be concerned with me," he said. "The political views I have are already clearly on record, and no doubt I'm too old and wily to be caught in such a small snare. If I am caught, it is in something else. Perhaps the spoiling of the people. And if such a thing is possible, how idle to point the finger at Collis Maitland or anyone else and say the blame is there. The blame is on all of us. 'Thus much I should perhaps have said, though I were sure I should have spoken only to trees and stones, and had none to cry to, but with the prophet, "O earth, earth, earth!" to tell the very soil itself what her perverse inhabitants are deaf to.'"

He jerked his head back hard as he finished the quotation, wrinkling his mouth in a wry twist of self-depreciation. "But I've said it to you, haven't I?" he asked. The moment had come for him to apologize, as we always do, when we have unloaded our personal despair on someone that we have no right to burden. He said nothing, only stared at Clem with burning, resentful eyes, and the agonized emphasis of his silence—like that of a man who means not to howl until he is alone—seemed even then to tell Clem that he had been selected to hear a unique outburst. It would not be repeated.

For a minute this realization burned across the table. Then, brusquely summoning the waiter to bring their check, Bentley said urbanely, "Of course, nothing can be as bad as I have made it out. There must be an unconscious bias forcing me to select this constant stream of negative symptoms, and since you haven't that bias, my conclusions will mean nothing to you. But don't be seduced into politics, young man." He ended so absently that Clem nearly laughed. That point had been well enough covered.

Bentley walked with him to the subway entrance outside the hotel, where they said a matter-of-fact goodbye. Clem turned to wave from the landing of the stairs, saw that Bentley was already gone. Clem actually started back up, prompted by an anxious feeling that he had left something unsaid that he ought to have said. What it was he didn't know, but it seemed to him that if they could only wait a little longer with each other he would find the right thing. It might spill out of the feelings that had poured with sentimental liberty through his mind since he first saw his child, as a hard line of poetry sometimes spills out of a mind free-wheeling through worthless clichés. Perhaps he wanted Bentley to see in him what he had seen in his child: some infinitely slight margin of miracle that might escape the determining conditions of the future. At any rate, a spasm of gratitude shook him—now that it was too late to express it.

There was no sign of Bentley on the street, and Clem turned in bewildered embarrassment, thinking he had missed again a crucial occasion that might have established the identity he had always felt. There went another of his fathers, and the fated sign of recognition had not been given.

As he went on down then, brooding, into the noisy hole of the subway, fingering his bow tie, the spirit of this lunch came back to him, totally recalled, but stripped of its verbiage. The train came chattering in and he had a moment of intense fright as he listened to the cutting edge of the wheel flanges on the rails. And then it seemed very clear to him that what Sheila had dreamed of the horrid presences who meant to eat his son had been repeated, in a sophisticated form, within the last two hours. The cannibal void of the world had been feeding while he and Bentley fed.

This by no means unusually morbid sensibility could be dealt with, and profitably, in the Oedipus poems he was writing. There he could articulate the tragic linking of parents, children and grandchildren as experience actually finds it. Within the poem success is a very different thing, almost the opposite, from what it might be in raw life. In poetry it is just the missed opportunity, the ironic crossing of intents, that makes the beautiful echo, enduring as a footprint in concrete made by a foot running to the gallows. The might-have-been that rings so brazenly when we look back on reality is nothing less than the joy of poetry. And eventually this last meeting with Bentley and its near-coincidence with his son's birthday would be converted into a promise in Clem's poetry and even whisper optimistically through his story of the young suicide in college.

That much would be saved, then, but when time went on to collect its longer-term debts Clem would remember that there had been only about twenty-four hours in which he had really been elevated by the faith that his son had freed him from the psychic obligations of being a writer. When he went back to the hospital that afternoon he found Sheila in completely rejuvenated spirits, but his own were (as it would turn out) permanently tainted. A slight ambience of fear had crept in. Not of anything in particular. Just a coloring.

"Clem was so frightened of Jess when we first brought him home," Sheila said. "He could hardly go to sleep in the same room with him, even when Jess was quiet."

It became a family joke, and it was Sheila's habit to explain fancifully that Clem was afraid Jess would steal his breath away. But I suppose the truth of the matter must be that Clem always saw Jess as a stunningly fragile being thrust onto the scaffold of fiction that his nimble father had invented. Clem could manage his way on that scaffold simply because he had disconnected all its perils from time. The scaffold was outside his time, but it would be—might be—the very trap of foreknowledge in the renewed time of Jess's life. He was like Daedalus, one thinks, at that moment when he realized that Icarus really meant to try the invented wings.

It is all right to say for oneself—and even one's contemporaries, once their chance is clearly missed—that the nature of life is tragic. It may even be imperative to bite the nail of tragedy for the sake of joy. The moral difficulty is infinitely increased by inviting a child to share the sky because you dreamed of flight. One may well pray for

441

shallowness, banality and conformity over a child's bed. But the price of earnestness in such a prayer—well, as Clem had said to Bentley, he couldn't pay it. He had to go on being what he was, even at Jess's expense, if it meant that. He had to endure the split between jealous art and careless life with no hope except that someday the breach between them would be closed, knowing that life could never close it.

And yet—artfully, I would say—he seemed to Sheila and others more humanized by his usual relations with his son than he had ever been by any relationship. Sheila thought the child was the final connection she had sought for him, and even long after things had gone bad for their family she used to look back fondly to the way Clem's interest in the theater had grown in those first few months of fatherhood.

Happily, the "writer at work" was generally indistinguishable from the father making himself useful around the house. It was laboratory business when he tried young Jess with "primitive experiences"—that is, sat holding him in his lap in front of the fireplace, or lowered him into bath water, or pretended to drop him, or turned lights on or off for him, or fed him—all those cardinal communions of the race which had the secondary merit of being very helpful to Sheila. Though Clem was not to be disturbed while he worked in the morning, Sheila found again that she was lucky not to be married to a man who had to go to the office to do his labor.

Jess was, naturally enough, uninterested in the fire. He refused to evidence any racial memories of cave days or to let on that he understood the centrality of the Prometheus myth in the human accommodation to the world of nature or the gods. He blinked at lights. He fought when the bath water was too hot or too cold, gurgled when it was right. He frowned at the pretense of dropping him. When food was put to his mouth, he ate.

He behaved like a good ordinary baby. But Clem, extraordinary father, insisted that he was making discoveries and verifications he could not have made alone. If, for instance, Jess would not declare himself squarely on his fear of falling (of being dropped), still Clem perceived a Gestalt of fear that embraced both the holding parent and the held child, a "community of fear," he called it, that did not have to be specified as originating in either one of them but seemed to pre-exist like a paradigm, to be an absolute ratio like Planck's constant, at which love was converted to anxiety. It was no less than a pretragic cognizance of the sort that the dance, among the arts, comes closest to expressing.

("You don't know anything about dancing," Sheila said, reminding him with fond sarcasm of those days in college when she had so vainly tried to teach him the rhythms that every bonehead fraternity boy acquired without pain. "If Jess has taught you the spirit of the dance, why don't you prove it and take me out sometime?" To which Clem replied loftily that he was always dancing. Did she not see that when he swept the hall for her, or carried out the garbage, or made love to her, he was dancing? In effect. "In effect!" she said. "Boy, the next time we make love I want none of that dancing stuff. I want concentration." "The dance is the supreme concentration," he said, and demonstratively made love to her at once, it being then two-thirty in the afternoon, an hour when the nondancing population was trying to decipher its postprandial dreams with business machines.)

At any rate, his nonverbal communications with the baby were powerfully seductive to Clem, especially in those hours of fatigue after he had spent the morning with words. The baby seduced him into thinking there must be an easier way of doing what he was trying to do. Easier and therefore better. "It's the intonations and gestures that mean something to that smart kid," Clem said. "If I tell him, 'Why that's my dainty Ariel! I shall miss thee; but yet thou shalt have freedom; so, so, so,' he only blinks. But if I put on my black hat and shake a stick, he thinks I'm really Prospero."

"Anyone would," Sheila said. "Why don't you give him his bottle now and pretend you're Lady Macbeth in her better days?" Which two useful things Clem did—and because they were not enough to keep him busy, he began resifting his novel to find what was in it that was dramatic, or what might be converted. Not, certainly, the passages about boyhood, for that was a period essentially narrative. Things happened, up to a certain age, like stories, not like plays, and must be written in a form that had some intimate relation with how they were. No wonder there was no serious drama about children. In drama children were only victims, viz. Medea, viz. Little Eyolf, viz. Macbeth. (He noticed that Jess's eyes were closed and jerked the nipple away from him to make sure, by his responsive howl, that he had not just been made a victim of his daddy's powerful thought.) Or else they were always hanging around the fringes of the action uttering pious banalities, while any storyteller (viz. Dostoevsky's wonderful boys in The Brothers Karamazov) knew that this was not at all the truth about children's lives.

But didn't the narrativeness of one's life start to branch out at a certain point and become drama? And therefore shouldn't his novel, since it was the book of everything-as-it-was, end in dramatic form? It ought to begin with the poems. And, hell, it ought to end with a dance, he thought. Hell, it ought not to end. Out of the dance, poetry ought to be born again, and the novel ought to be a self-renewing circle. Good. Decided. That's the way he'd offer it. That's the way he was offering it, by God—and let the publishers worry about how to get a cardboard cover around that.

"The bottle's empty and the baby's asleep," Sheila said.

"Good. I'm going back to work a while. I'm going to write a play. All the England stuff. I haven't come to that point yet, but I'm going to skip and start writing it the way it ought to be."

Sheila, who did not believe any more than he really did that his novel could conclude with a purely dramatic section, protested this emergent development only on grounds that he was already involved in two unfinished projects. "We have to think sometime about how we're going to eat," she said. "There's that. But there's more important things. If you get involved in a play are you sure you'll ever finish the novel?"

"I'm going to finish everything. I'm going to live forever," he said. And this, to someone who had watched for a long time his hypochondria and his fear that an extra cup of coffee might kill him when he was hung over, was satisfying news. She credited his optimism directly to the child.

But was it optimism? Certainly it had about it the quality of a choice, but no doubt Clem already suspected that it was a choice (again) to jettison the handicapping load of moral baggage that slowed him as a writer. Was he not preparing to curse God and live? Whatever ambiguities had been contained in Bentley's warning to him, what the old man had said could be simplified to "Take care of yourself." In Army orientation lectures one had always heard that "the soldier's most precious possession is his life"—and however one might giggle over this as a truism, it was a text hard to escape. Like a line of Scripture or poetry, it was capable of a large variety of constructions, and if one construed "life" in his private terms, then one was quite in agreement with the military. As Bentley had said, it is hard, in our times, not to enter such a basic agreement.

If he had got by without having to choose opposition to Maitland in the Midway affair, still choice is the burden of those who best understand that it may be made by default. He said, "I am a thinking reed, and what this reed thought was, It was time to get out of the way when Maitland tried to pin the red star on us all." But he must have known that the books were not closed yet on that fracas.

By April it was clear that it had been a beginning and not an end. Lillian and Rudi had gone to Paris, from where Lillian wrote that she had adjusted to her disappointment and would try again in the fall to revive the magazine. This time she would edit it herself, and if its fate was to remain "tiny," that was all right as long as it was good. She had learned her lesson and was not mad at anyone.

But almost at the time she wrote, Clem's editor at Gordon and Maxwell was being forced out, and when he left Clem was notified that the house wanted to buy back the contract for his novel.

In a fighting mood, he put on a clean shirt and a necktie and went uptown to the publishers' office to demand an explanation. He came home three hours later to tear up his copy of the contract. They had insulted him, he said, by offering a settlement of three hundred dollars beyond the thousand already given him as an advance. He told them to buy an ice-cream cone with it.

"I have too much faith in the novel to leave it with someone who doesn't think he can sell it," he said grandly—quite ignoring all the wishful plans he and Sheila had been making out of the expectations suddenly vanished.

"Yes, but ..." Sheila said. "Why did they change their minds? What did they say?"

"I don't know."

Sheila thought she was being given the run-around and insisted angrily, "You've just been listening, for heaven's sake. What did they say?"

"Oh, I heard what they said, but I didn't hear what they meant. It was all double talk, so I put it out of my mind."

"If they were unfair, I have a right to know."

"You won't let them get by with it?"

She let him hurt her to assuage his own hurt and let him keep silence. Anyway, it was quite true that he didn't then understand what had happened. Some weeks passed before he could see a coherent picture emerging through the screen of evasions and the inside dope provided by his friends.

The core of the crisis at Gordon and Maxwell, they were finally told by Henderson Paul (who was plugged in directly to the inside line of gossip in the publishing world) was a struggle for control between the partners. In it Gordon simply held a number of losing cards. The house was plagued with rising printing costs and a decline in sales that had been constant since the end of the war, beginning, ironically, just when government restrictions on paper were lifted. In the optimism of the last year of the war too many contracts for unfinished novels had been given. If bankruptcy was to be avoided, it looked as if the only way out was to rely heavily on resales to the movies or to paperback-reprint houses. And this meant different principles of selection in making up their list. What was controversial, too long, esoteric, experimental, or simply not engaging in subject matter had to be lowered on the scale of preferences. Gordon had bucked this necessity. The stockholders and the company's salesmen had sided with Maxwell.

And while this was coming to a head Collis Maitland had submitted his novel—five hundred thousand words, delivered in an iron-bound Civil War foot locker. In a month Gordon—or his right-hand man Lefever—had rejected the novel.

Maitland's response was definitive. Armed with a record supplied him by Cohn and/or the FBI, he had gone to Maxwell with the charge that Gordon and many of his stable of writers were or had been members, dupes, fellow travelers or inadvertent fellow travelers of the Communist Party.

"It isn't that Maxwell necessarily believed Maitland," Henderson explained, "or even necessarily thought that anyone else would, but you can see how convenient the allegation was for him. Gordon saw that he had had it. Right under the ear. If he was going to get any of his marbles back from the game, he had to sell out fast."

"I don't see what this has to do with Clem's novel," Sheila said stubbornly but not quite candidly. She was ready to believe that whatever Maitland touched with his magic curse was necessarily corrupted from the norms of decency and sanity. "If it's a good novel ..."

"Who knows whether it is or not?" Clem said. "They had never read any of it when they gave me the contract any more than when they wanted to cancel."

"It's a hell of a way to run a railroad," Henderson agreed. "But that's the way it's done. And anyway, you're lucky to be free of them. What a writer needs is a fat and happy publisher. Now, mine ... Clem, Oscar Parsons talks about you every time we have lunch. If you want a contract now on the novel, he'll give you one on my say-so."

"Tell him I'll have a book of poems ready first," Clem said, still grand.

"Why not?" Henderson said.

"And they'll take it? Just like that? Is that the way it's done?" Sheila asked.

"That's the way it's done sometimes. All the best things are done by sheer nepotism," Henderson said.

And that, finally, was about how Clem's next two major publications were arranged—but not until after Henderson's new novel appeared in the following fall, promising to make his publisher fatter and happier than ever.

Until those happy financial arrangements were made, Clem went through a period of mad financial duplicity that is not the least of the heroisms I would credit him with. Against the intractable mountain of debts they were accumulating he did not visibly bend at all. Neither Sheila nor he was going to work in anybody's office and that was simply that. Any man who calls himself a writer, he supposed, should not be too proud to apply his talents to writing someone else's name on a check if that was required. While he did not go that far, he did leave a trail of puzzlement behind him among his many friends.

To shore himself economically he arranged with Felix Martin to teach the next fall at Felix' university in Kansas. With his letter of appointment to show him solvent, he borrowed five hundred dollars from a bank to which Rudi Leed had recommended him. And simultaneously he was arranging to attend the Sorbonne that fall and live in Paris on his GI entitlement. He borrowed from every friend who had anything to spare, telling some of his small creditors that he would repay them out of his teaching salary while at the same time he told others that their contribution would help pay his fare to Europe. He sent Sheila and the baby home for a two-week stay with her family in July for the pre-eminent reason that she could raise some money from them by showing the grandchild—and begged off going himself on grounds that he would "seem more glamorous" to the old people if he didn't show his tricky little face to them. His own parents were deluged with photos of the youngster but given no promises that they would ever see him in the flesh—not even if they put up money to see Clem through the "terribly hard work that I am giving my life to finish."

When Clem learned through his friends in the theater that Maxfield Gorman was at last stirring out of his dormancy, he swiftly typed up the outline for a play and renewed his acquaintance with Dr. Gorman, then practicing at a downtown psychiatric hospital. There is no doubt that Gorman was proud and pleased to see his former patient full of ambition, diligence and the will to succeed—further, that he was impressed by the book of poetry that Clem could now put in his hands, though if he had read it shrewdly he would have found in it the very substance of the turmoil for which he had once treated Clem. What is greatly to be doubted is that Clem had any intention of writing then or ever the particular play he had outlined. (He even hinted that he got the outline straight from a play then running successfully on Broadway, merely changing details, names and locale.) He wanted an option—and the Gorman brothers cannily invested three hundred dollars in him.

Janet and I paid our tax to his determination along with a lot of others that summer. Not so much that we were ever anxious to be repaid. And even when we heard from him in the following winter that he and Sheila were established in a very expensive Montparnasse studio and had bought a car, we were not inclined to feel that he had overused his newly discovered talent for fund-raising.

The Throne of Oedipus came out that winter, and I could not feel otherwise than that any cost his friends and family had borne was trivial in respect to the return they got in this book.

As a matter of fact, I have never talked with anyone who was involved with Clem who felt that Clem had cheated him—though again and again I have heard the statement or insinuation that he cheated someone else. "At least he cheated Sheila," "At least he cheated Susan," "At least he took Lillian and Rudi Leed," "At least he beat the Gorman brothers out of a nice little hunk of money, long ago"—so someone or other has said to me. And I have the impression of an odd circle of fingers pointing around him, indications of nothing substantial, adding up, nonetheless, to a presumption that somehow he had made his way to the peak of his life less than honestly.

Well, and then there is his own oblique testimony that he felt this, too. Not that he worried, when it counted, about the money. Toward the end of his life he made some indiscriminate efforts to pay that all back to people who no longer wanted it.

It was rather that in his going to Paris at the time he did—an absolute necessity, he had thought, if he was going to finish his work in progress—he had not stood where he should have stood. It was a cheat to offer those he loved a writer instead of a man.

In June of 1949 Nathaniel Bentley jumped from a hotel window in Manhattan. His suicide was, as far as I can measure such things, a particularly demoralizing symbol of the demoralization of intellectual life in America. Later when those of us in academic life would kneel to kiss the rod of the various loyalty oaths exacted of us, I suppose that few who remembered Bentley did not see in their submissions a token repetition of his physical plunge. As one remembers, the late Forties was a time when this manner of suicide seemed almost a matter of form for political and intellectual personages whose place to stand was denied them by the postwar alignments of event. Masaryk, Forrestal, Matthieson, Duggan—the names of those who literally went out the window are a sort of epitaph for otherwise unrecorded losses, moral and intellectual.

And though Clem professed that he had come to a point where he was unshaken by the news of Bentley, it was in his character to accept a moral responsibility for the death of one to whom he was so deeply obligated. At least Clem would understand, better than most of the rest of us, that one must have both feet anchored to the stone foundation of the world in order not to be shaken when Bentley yielded to despair.

Bentley had been involved that spring in one of those endlessly widening investigations where the trick of the Congressional ringmasters was to inculpate the whole defense, and then all the defenders of the defense, and so on. Even the man in whose support Bentley had gone to Washington to testify was not originally accused of disloyalty, merely of improper association. Of course no charge was ever proved against Bentley. I believe that none was ever made in language that would be intelligible to a regular court. Nevertheless, as things were done in those days, the newspapers gave an impression to the raw public that Bentley had been tampering with its soft underbelly, had been manipulating its depths, had corrupted the barbarism in which safety was thought to lie.

The antipoetry of journalism had vaguely defined a host of crimes that never would or could be spelled out in the law. Bentley was put in a position of having to defend himself to the American people. The American people? Only an abstraction. Wherefore defend yourself to an abstraction when by ignoring it you might live safe? But "the American people" was an abstraction that Bentley had labored all his life to make potent and awful. He could hardly ignore it at the end merely for his own convenience.

So, by his mode of death, he had replied in language they would understand—as well as his friends—that he was personally indefensible. If they would not and could not tolerate the purity of his mind, he had no right to withhold from their justice his corrupt and aging body.

I was in New York myself, preparing to sail for a few weeks of study in Cambridge, when I heard the news over the hotel radio. The announcer spoke as if he were in a position at last to refute the angry mutters of support for Bentley in his recent inquisition. Of course the defense, whose very principles had some slight degree of complication, had not got much publicity outside the academic community, while the impression of his guilty complicity in something had been splattered far and wide.

Mr. Bentley had "denied," the announcer chortled. "But jump Mr. Bentley did!" That obscene chortle of glee shamed me that I had, like the speaker, an opposable thumb and walked upright. "Jump Mr. Bentley did!" All they wanted was proved when that old man hit the street.

"Jump Mr. Bentley did," Clem said when I saw him in Paris a few weeks later. "If a man is wearing pants, he certainly ought to wet them like Pogorski's father when he hears that said."

We were walking alone together that afternoon, Clem and I. We had come down the river, across the Champ de Mars, and were returning along the Avenue du Président Wilson. It was a beautiful, hot day, with running clouds coming from the north and such greenery over us that I could imagine we had, in a single continuous walk, merely come from a suburban to an urban quarter of Acapulco—or even imagine that we were continuing one of the talking walks of our college days. What had intervened of time and change was only subject matter. It might twist and weight our concerns. It had not changed them.

I remember that Clem flipped a piece of bark over the stone balustrade into the Seine before he went on, "But a man ought not to piss on those who said it if they were burning. You know, Dick, I'll never go back. I'd be afraid to now."

I said I envied him the opportunity to choose his exile so easily. I knew that money was no longer a problem with him. While his novel had been no great commercial success, it had given them more than enough to live on for a year at their decent standard. Clem was still drawing his GI allowance. Manna had fallen in the form of a foundation grant amounting to three thousand dollars. But of course I knew, too, that it was more than money that had established him here. The years in Paris had been his tenure in the great good place. The solitude in him had found its city, a city like no other, where the historic landmarks and the unhistoric weather would be a constant mirror of the historicity and the moods of his nature.

He had learned a new fashion of smiling in the two years since I saw him last, a smile of such tragic complacency as I associate with the late photos of Chekhov or the Khmer Buddhas in the Musée Guimet. (And there, I was told in a less solemn hour, was just where he had acquired this smile. One day he came home wearing it. Sheila asked if

450

he had eaten something he liked, and he told her that he meant to model his expression thereafter on the Khmer stones. The dignified candor of the Egyptian kings in the Louvre, which he had considered appropriate for a while, had finally seemed too "pretentious" for a little fellow like him. Further, they seemed to express a loyalty to the future that he could no longer duplicate. "Those Khmer fellows knew something had gone wrong," he said. So he smiled like them.)

Paris was the convenient center from which they had traveled to England in the previous summer, motoring to Coventry and Oxford, going past the Potters' house, though they did not stop there. (Gerald had been on the lawn. He probably recognized Clem, for he waved. But Clem stepped on the gas. He had Gerald securely placed in his mind, noble in the nest of memory. He was not going to risk the fine opinion by any further comparisons with reality.)

They had been to Italy, Germany, Spain and Corsica. They had stayed with their friends the Burbidges in the Dordogne, and another time had moseyed around the South of France, in the Gertrude Stein country. They had found the motifs of van Gogh and Cézanne in the Provençal sun.

Hopefully they had been to Chartres a number of times. For a while they had talked of doing a book on the cathedral. It would be a modest, unscholarly book, done lovingly for the tourists. Happily, Sheila could collaborate on this, as she had never done with his other works.

He had finished his play. He could afford to sit on the corner of the Rue du Bac and the Boulevard St. Germain in the café that delighted him so much, fingering his glass of white wine and announcing himself as metaphysically self-supporting. He could wait in happy confidence for his hour to arrive, wait for fame without caring too much that it was slow, wait for money, wait for the conception of new works, succeeding like new generations on what he had already accomplished.

"My happy marriage" was what he called all his life in Paris. Again and again while I was with him that summer I would hear that phrase. I knew it meant each day with its connubial circumstances, his marriage with the ancient trees and tempered customs of the city, as well as his relationship with Sheila and the children.

Yes, it was easy—it might even be obligatory—for him to stay away forever from the catastrophes of the spirit lit up to our gaze by Bentley's death.

451

But he would not let me make the point that it was easy now for him to stay in his Paris.

"You know, Sheila's never really forgiven me for coming here," he said. "For silence, exile and cunning, as the fellow put it. You know, for letting old Bentley go out his window alone. She's known forever how much I owed to Bentley. We'd taken him into the family. She knows that if he hadn't reached his hand down to me from 'way up there—a man has to be 'way up there to have a place to jump from—I'd have probably thought I was only a student poet like Esterman and have gone into the vault-bronzing business."

"Or back to an athletic career," I said.

He shrugged off my impertinence. "Given the demonstration, in my own snot-nosed case, of what Bentley meant when he talked about keeping the idea green, keeping the republic of the arts republican so a corporal like me would have some reason to keep a marshal's baton in his knapsack—knowing what he meant, just knowing, Sheila would think, enlisted me with him for the duration." His voice was suddenly trembling, though he did not give up his Khmer smile. "Besides, I knew what Maitland and Cohn were capable of. I know their names are legion. Dragon's teeth are dragon's teeth, and the genes of the conjunction abolisher are in every bloodstream in America."

"That's not your doing," I said.

"I know. But there is—to satisfy your literal cravings—one practical detail I have to reproach myself with, that Sheila reproaches me with: I wrote Bentley a bleeding-heart letter when Plankton was cutting the meat out of my novel.

"You know, Oscar Parsons and I got along so well in the publishing of Throne of Oedipus, and then after he died Henderson told me what a great fellow Plankton was—I wasn't altogether prepared for such a meathead. What I went back for—what Sheila sent me back for—was to 'fight' for the novel just as it was. And then I didn't. Somehow I didn't really care. It was done and I'd got the goody out of it.

"What fighting I needed to keep my system in tune I did with Henderson, who had the gall to tell me that the novel was a lot better after it had been cut—which shit you can take from people like Plankton because it is their economic function to dispense it, but not from personal friends just because their novels have sold over ten thousand copies and they think they know how. So I did throw a drink on Henderson, and that bitch Vassar wife of his came at me with their wedding-present fire tongs in front of a whole crowd in their apartment.

"But, just to have Daddy kiss the bump, I wrote a sad letter to Bentley, giving him some of Plankton's funnies and how everything had got distorted until the novel didn't fit into the old apostolic succession, et cetera. There was no excuse for sending such a letter except that I'd written it; that's where writers go wrong, thinking that's an excuse in itself. As soon as I'd put it in the mail I felt cat-happy and glad to be getting on the boat and returning to Paris. I divorced them all. I couldn't care less whether people got cheated when they bought my book. And probably they didn't, because Plankton had designed them one that resembled the real thing for three dollars, whereas they'd have had to pay six if all of it had got printed.

"But as soon as I landed here I found a reply from Bentley. He took it all harder than I did. He linked it in with everything up to the Hiss case—and generally wore himself down in the effort to wipe my dry nose."

Yes, I understood how he—or Sheila—might feel the anguish of remorse for Bentley's death, and even of personal guilt. And yet I thought his talk to be no more than a purgation of evil dreams.

In my envy I saw him too well placed to imagine he would bolt his good fortune for the sake of any regrets. I supposed that in ten years I might visit him again in his well-loved city and find little changed from what I saw this summer.

If the days of his happy marriage were not identical (and they had varying moods, as a good wife does) there was nevertheless a perceptible mating of equals between him and what his days now brought. They were days when "nothing happened and everything was."

# 17

HIS SUMMER DAYS in Paris might begin like this, while he was waking slow:

Out of sleep, where there need be no syntax to express resemblances because resemblances there are things, his first moment of wakefulness is a discrimination. Sheila's garter belt on the chairback beside the bed resembles an inverted white crown. It looks like the frail stylized headdress of a playing-card queen, but he can register the resemblance without mistaking what it is. The metaphor of sleep is mastered, reduced to a rational simile.

Noting the time, he realizes that Sheila has been up already to give Lulie her morning feeding. Lulie is in her crib across the bedroom, buzzing like a salon overheard across historical distances, like Joyce's prose and maybe like Joyce's mad laughter, but happily derangement is the fit order of babyhood.

Sheila is in bed beside him again and probably asleep. Her left arm is stretched above her head, exposing the armpit hair which he has insisted she grow to demonstrate their Europeanization. Perversely he has resisted her counterclaim that, hair for hair, he ought to grow a beard to match. The child in his nature would be falsified by a beard, he said, and at any rate one law for the lion and the ox is tyranny. In their household there are as many laws as there are situations, so the component of confusion amounts to a permanent anarchy. Adults and infants are free to be such noble savages as their impulse will permit.

Jess, at two and a half, often has impulses to be a dog, and this morning as Clem comes into the kitchen he finds the boy on all fours by the door listening after the concierge's Pekingese, which has just scampered by on the stairs. Child of a beast marriage, Clem thinks, canine heaven lies about him in his infancy. The track the flesh loses is remembered yet a while. Hawk and hound and bay horse are his, lost to us who tried to make them captive. He swings the boy up to kiss him, trying to read the inscrutable frankness in eyes which are so much like his own. He is the beast of me, Clem thinks, conjugating Good, Better, Beast, then personifying this trinity as the family group in which the child is father to the man and Mother Better's genes are printed like a monopolist's brand on every cell of husband-child and child-husband.

454

Yes, yes, yes, we are surely married to that woman, he thinks. We will marry her again today, and loyally beget each other through her.

"Do you want oatmeal?" he asks. "Jus d'orange?"

The child shakes his towhead. He frowns lightly, accusing the wrong guess exactly as he would accuse a moral flaw, provided that he saw any necessity in distinguishing between them. Grave initiate of Tao, he knows that meaning is not in things, but in the void between them.

"A bone? A boh-un?" Clem guesses.

Jess laughs aside his embarrassment and says (as he has been taught to), "Grrrrr." It is a joke and yet not entirely a joke that he wants to be a dog. He comprehends the joke from the stronghold of values that his parents have lost. In the year before his second birthday they owned a nervous, snobbish Russian wolfhound, afraid of its own shadow and completely disdainful of children. Through being scorned by it, Jess came to an idolatry of the corrupt animal. When the dog disappeared, Clem kept his memory fresh by telling all of Jess's friends the story of the unrequited love. Sheila complained that Clem had "made it all up" and had subsequently taught Jess to believe he wanted to be a dog like Oblomov. And there is no way to be sure, once and for all, just where the myth began. But sharing it now, for the thousandth time, father and son laugh together.

"I ate," Jess grumbles. He does not mean to be laughed at, of course, and like most people who have encountered Clem when his rash fit of irony is on, Jess retires to the fort of the commonplace, shutting the old man outside, where he is welcome to speculate all he wants about beast children and the nonsensical ambition to be a dog.

"Did Mommy fix you oatmeal?"

"Anuff."

"Enough? Or un oeuf?" (Sheila's French remains Midwestern. Very deep in her is the conviction that it is merely slovenly to omit final consonants. Yet she likes to talk to Jess in French.)

"Egg."

"O.K. However you want it, paysan. Whatever you say."

"Want to go with you."

"Where?" Clem asks, unaware yet, in his morning grogginess, that he is going anywhere. He is trapped in the realization that the boy has set no time limit, has not said "now" or "this morning" or even "today." He pauses to admire the clever expedients of ignorance (Tao?). It is only wisdom that binds one to a single course and a selection of times and things. Nature tries a thousand tactics for a single goal.

But Clem has learned to fight fire with fire and does not make the mistake of explaining that he will probably fix breakfast for himself, shave and then read a while in the front room—that he has not meant to leave the house before noon.

He says, "You don't want to go with me. You want to wait for Huguette. She's going to take you to the market." Huguette is their maid, who comes in each day to straighten the apartment, help with the children, shop and prepare dinner. The foundation which gave Clem his grant to pursue high-sounding objectives is really paying Huguette's salary, just as it paid the key money for this roomy apartment on the Rue du Bac. Of course it is only a manner of speaking to say that the foundation's dollars are going for these specific luxuries, since the household keeps no books except check stubs. But the fact remains that without the grant there would have been no Huguette to help, and the Andersons would still be living in the grand, drafty studio in Montparnasse. And still Clem would be writing exactly as much and exactly as little as he does here during the term of the grant.

"I want to go with you," Jess says. And here again, as in the matter of aspiring to be a dog, there is a question of where myth originates, but from his son's urgency Clem understands that he himself wants to go out into the June morning.

When he knows what he wants, he remembers reasons. For one thing, he is expecting mail. He has been getting a lot of mail, and this summer most of it has been good. Checks, commissions, praise— valued in that order.

But then he has always looked forward to mail since the war. It is one of the occupational distortions of a writer to believe that the mailman is a minister of fate. He believes that mail will lose its freshness, even that checks will melt to a smaller figure, commissions turn more speculative and praise grow faint, if it is left in the mailbox.

He will have to go down three flights of stairs to get the mail in the concierge's office. There is no point in climbing so many stairs again immediately. He will take the mail to his café on the corner. He will sit in the sun opposite the War Ministry to read it, breakfasting on coffee and a croissant. Of course, he would breakfast better if he ate at home. There are always eggs and poitrine fumée in the house—a good Wisconsin breakfast. And he has never had a sharper appetite than this summer. His appetite is keenest in the mornings, when his mind still tingles with that break-over of useless dreams into the sense from which his best ideas come—the surf, the faint thin instant of foam through which Venus wades into his verse.

But against this appetite for Wisconsin-type food there is the attraction of. "going to Paris." He never quite feels that he is in Paris while he is inside the house, and it is a treat that he owes himself to read his mail in Paris sitting in the historic sun, while he notes what they are doing and thinking and paying "back there."

Only, now he cannot leave his son until Huguette comes. He invites Jess to the bathroom to watch him shave. If mornings and a good breakfast are the preconditions for his best work, then shaving is the mechanical, symbolic art of harvest that yields his lignes données, the dictated lines, or the positive choices between scenes, bits of dialogue, or descriptions that have seemed at midday equally usable. This morning his clear thought, the donnée, is merely that this has always been so. Himself has been a mirror as innocent as the one that shows his sudsy face. "Gillette, reed-throated whisperer," he apostrophizes his razor, "that comes not now as once, but inwardly ..."

"The inward razor," he says aloud to Jess, who is balancing between the bidet and the washbasin, disgusted with himself that he had to come watch a procedure so essentially boring. "Just as my razor in that glass scrapes whiskers, so that glass, in my whiskers, scrapes the dead Muzak. Muzak, old artificer, I too am a twig that Eros bent."

Lee. In the mountains. Unfettered Lee bent. Bowed from his pride of place. The unfettered bow to Demos, and the head of Coriolanus popping like a dropped gourd at the bottom of the red rocks. Bentley's Razor. Bentley of Occam and Oxenford. Bows. So might I have done it. Why should the spirit of Whiskers be proud, when that great two-edged razor at the door scrapes once? Scrapes no more. Scrape no more, Grace, from my graceless face. The hand that holds the razor rules the world. If razors were common as blackberries, I'd not bow to them. The Bentley twig is a bow that's bent and drawn. Make from the shafting.

"Cut, cut, cut," Jess begs.

"No. I only cut myself when I want to," Clem says. He dries his face with approval. Not a scratch or a scrape. With diligence he has proved—for once—the safety razor really safe, even in his hands. And though this is a disappointment to Jess, who counts on a little blood to make the show worth while, it is a satisfaction to Clem.

When Huguette has arrived and Clem has descended, he finds that his premonition of mail is correct. There are four letters for him, and a fifth, from Sheila's parents, is addressed to them both. He knows that this one will be directed to her, including him in its sentimental effusion only by a kind of formal recognition that someone must be husband to their daughter and father to their grandchildren. In reading their letters he has often reflected that he would not be surprised to find himself referred to in quotes—"Clem"—as if he were a fictional excuse for her absence, for the pregnancies that have to be given a good color to their neighbors. Once they did call him a "writer" in quotes, and he is still wounded by that uncertainty.

It would be proper for him to take this fifth letter with the others. Yet he feels it unfair that he should get all the morning's mail, and he rocks on his toes a minute, debating whether to climb back to the apartment and leave the letter for Sheila. To spare his heart the exertion, he decides against it. He has been told by six doctors in the last four years that his heart would be perfect if he didn't drink and smoke quite so much. He believes them, but reminds himself that even a perfect heart can be worn out, and this morning he has appetite to hope for fifty more years of health. This hope is an indication that he is not at present engaged on any big work. When he is, and when the work is going particularly well, he is subject to an awed sense of impending death. No doubt he has at times attained intimations that the health of his worldly state is sickness indeed, but now he has forgiven himself them. He has been a sick eagle looking at the sky. The triumph of Parisian architecture is that it holds the eye low, keeps the eagle from knowing he is sick.

"Dites à Madame qu'elle doit me suivre au café," he instructs the concierge. Dogtrotting, glad to find that he can still run on his toes, though the days of the fifty-yard dash are far behind him, he goes down the Rue du Bac in the lemon-and-lime-colored morning.

The garçon who serves Clem is by now an old friend, almost his collaborator, since Clem did most of his writing in the café during the previous winter. Vincent worked at the Dôme for many years before changing to this more docile neighborhood. He values Clem and Clem's friends who come to sit with him here as a souvenir of the old days and a leaven amidst the bureaucrats who are his usual clientele. He likes to discuss politics, particularly American international policy and le plan Marshall with Clem, for whom he generally saves copies of Semaine and Le Monde. Vincent has been unreconciled to America since the death of Roosevelt. He refers to President Truman as "la vache qui rit" and is convinced that America intends to make Germany again the principal power in Europe.

But this morning he has other news. Another American friend of his, someone he has not seen since before the war, has made a name at last. Collis Maitland. Vincent has a long clipping torn from the book review section of Time. He reads English indifferently and is not sure whether the review praises or attacks Maitland's Passionate Decade: A Memoir of the Lost Generation. But there, in the center of the page, is a photograph of Maitland with his sharp eyes peering straight out at one from his saintlike, wolfish face. And from the size of the review and the placement of the photograph, Vincent draws the penultimate conclusion. "Il touche maintenant l'argent, hein?"

Everything is said when that is said, Clem feels, and he puts the review down on the table without reading it.

The first letter he opens is from Claude Pogorski. He has heard from Claude three or four times since that summer in Mexico, but he has never answered the letters. Whatever Claude has to say—and after the appearance of The Throne of Oedipus he wrote to censure Clem for "turning away from realism and anger" to the "obscurity and chi-chi that is all too fashionable nowadays"—is always spoiled by a note of sick fawning. No doubt the fawning is an attempt to be polite against the grain, but nevertheless it is repugnant when not redeemed by the ferocious mental suffering that one had to acknowledge in Claude's actual presence. Yet when Claude's letters come with other mail, Clem always opens them first.

And thinks, as he reads this morning, that here at last is the revelation that he has been anticipating in the others. Claude and Venetia are separated. Venetia is back home in Brooklyn, getting a divorce. "I knew you would hear of this, sooner or later, the world being such a small place as it is," Claude writes, "and I wanted you to know, before you heard from strangers, that I did not blame you." Blame me? Clem thinks with a start. With a part of his mind he knows exactly what Claude is talking about, but the more sophisticated part complains, I am not Abraham, even if he has decided he is, was, Isaac.

"I realize you did not think as we, and it would be against your happy-go-lucky nature to credit the idealism on which our marriage was based. You saw only an attractive woman and we were all somewhat under the influence the night it happened. I can honestly say I forgave you both, without any reservations, and though that is not the kind of thing one forgets, I would not have mentioned it again. But in frankness we have had to talk continually of you when I admitted that divorce was the only way. I do not mean she remembered you with enthusiasm. After she began to take up with others she confessed to me that you were small and unsatisfactory in spite of your usual animation. But you were the one who shattered her idealism to such an extent that I could not save her and now have had to let her go, with much anguish

459

and worries for her future. But I have thought so much about this and have concluded that it was not merely by sexual infidelity that you disappointed us."

Us? Clem wonders. Everyone? In the moral disparity of experience, it might be that everyone spoke for everyone, that nothing was canceled out, and one man wronged spoke for all victims. But that is his thought and not exactly Claude's.

Claude writes, "While all the terrible things were going on in America and only Henry Wallace's Progressive Party offered some hope, Venetia used to say that at least Clem would stand up and be counted, or else be silenced and go to jail."

The trouble with Claude was that he did not tremble when he thought that God was just. I was counted, Clem thought.

"You kept on publishing things in more and more servility to the right wing."

My left was tender, I had to favor it, Clem thinks. But he does not need to mock any more than he needs to defend. The balance of guilt and knowledge that Claude is stumbling toward was chosen long ago. The inner wounds are beginning to show, that is all. Let them, then, since they must, come out.

Clem sighs curiously and reads the end of the letter. "When I am most depressed about it, I think that none of us should blame ourselves, but blame the times in which we live. It was not you alone who disillusioned her. I am never going to return to the United States. I have arranged to take political asylum in India. I am afraid you won't hear from me again, but I wanted my last word to be that of friendship."

Clem drops the creased letter on top of Maitland's picture. The past is a poorer fiction than I have made of it, he thinks. If Claude could merely read what I have written without judging it, he could not be so wrong about what happened as he is now. He realized that for all Claude taught him, there was never a chance that he could teach Claude anything, and he knows the iron law that scales wisdom to impotence, He wonders if Claude is telling the truth in saying that he seduced Venetia, when all this time he has thought it was the other way around. Well, it was dark and he couldn't quite tell.

The next letter is from Clem's sister. Since, in writing his autobiographical novel, he "killed her off," he semiconsciously thinks of her as dead. When some reminder that she is very much alive crosses the threshold of his consciousness, it comes always like an unexpected bonus, as if a miracle has taken place about which he is the last to hear the good news.

Clem's sister is married to a schoolteacher in the county seat near Boda. Clem's career as a writer is to some degree an embarrassment for her—she is inclined to defend him to herself, and this gives her away—but, naturally, she is also very proud. To an extent she shares the conviction of Clem's mother that his memory is very poor, since his stories about his own childhood or Boda people never conform to what are called there "the facts." She knows it was only some kind of sly joke to have given Harry Rinehart's name to the character in the novel who "resembles" himself, and this reinforces her suspicion that if one had the simple key to unlock Clem's poems, out of them too would come pouring an avalanche of commonplace facts that other people could verify or refute from their memories of how it all was.

Nevertheless she knows Clem too well to think it is going to be easy to get the key from him, and she reports with amusement something Clem's father has said about The Throne of Oedipus. Mr. Anderson spent many evenings trying to "get the hang" of what Clem was talking about and finally grew quite angry at Clem for being so devious. "Well, he always did think he was a little king," Mr. Anderson said.

With a crow of pleasure Clem recognizes the justice of his father's dictum. Ironic abbreviations are dear to him and there is no more fruitful source for them than ignorance. But again he realizes, It is I who know—hear—what he said. The poetry of earth is never dead. For anyone but poets no poetry is ever alive. The street runs into Paris but never back again.

His sister has written, "I don't suppose you remember Margaret Shea very well." Yes and no. Of course Clem remembers the fictional Con Everling better, his fiction instead of theirs. "We saw Margaret's picture in the paper the other day. Her husband is very high up in the Shriners, and Margaret has two little girls. She never comes back to Boda since her folks moved away."

Of course she cannot come back. When Clem was a little king he banished her out. Now he sees that if he had been Dante himself he could not have punished her more exactly than by marrying her to a man high in the Shriners. A small, vindictive and poetic grin hooks the corners of his mouth. Time and he have paid her off for saying, "You think too much, Clem," for once imperiling his sanity by her positively aggressive chastity.

At every mention of the names from Boda or of his own family, he notes an artificial response in himself, compounded of wonder and gratified curiosity, replacing the emotions that once they could engender. By this sign he is comfortably reminded that the beasts of childhood are tamed and that they are, after all, the same beasts that wore the other names—Pogorski, Maitland, Bentley, Kleist. In mastering his art, he has mastered his vulnerability. There is no need to fear any of the crying ghosts that harried him up from Boda long ago. The victory over the past immunized him against the future.

Now does my project gather to a head: My charms crack not; my spirits obey ...

He asks Vincent the time and, because it is past eleven, permits himself to order a glass of white wine.

The third letter is from Felix Martin, once again inviting Clem to come as a lecturer to his university. Felix's department is prospering, and in a way that one would hardly have expected. A literary magazine is published under departmental and university auspices. This summer a writers' conference has been held on campus. It is to be made an annual affair, and Clem is invited for next year or "whenever you come back from France."

From the throne of his café chair Clem projects a scandalous future where his rambles will be stopped only by satiety. He sees himself the laureate of conferences, Alfred Lord Anderson careening into the picnics of literature in a sports car, a smile of condescension lighting his man-of-sorrows face. Young poets faint as they hear his tread ascending the steps of the podium. When he cocks his head and half closes his eyes a hush falls over the assembly, broken only by the sibilance of nylon whistling on nylon as two thousand literary coeds cross their legs.

"As Valéry has so well expressed it ... While in my own verse ... With your indulgence ... a little composition of my own ... on the back of an old envelope as my wife drove me to your charming campus. I may call it 'The Sermon on the Mount' ..."

Word of his charm, modesty and wit creeps, then flies, out beyond the literary circles of the campus. He becomes the idol of young athletes and their sorority doxies. (Was his marrying a sorority girl dictated by the remnants of his old dream of athletic glory?) The football team careens with linked arms down torchlit streets chanting his verses. He is called on to address a pep rally. It is not tomorrow's game that fires all hearts. The vulgar multitude is chanting, "Go, Anderson, go. A sonnet, a line, a word." He winds up, throws a long, spiraling trochee. A thousand hysterical throats answer him. The chariot of years grinds to a stop. Poetry has defeated Notre Dame in the

Rose Bowl. Knute Rockne and Clem Anderson exeunt into the west, riding Will Rogers' horse.

Yes, things will be better if he ever goes back to America.

The fourth letter is also literary business. He is asked to contribute "notes from Paris" for a women's fashion magazine. "No specifications or restrictions," the lady editor writes—and he knows this means he is expected to mention homosexuality among Americans on the Left Bank and to allude quasi-humorously to the "U.S. Go Home" signs chalked on the walls of the Rue Monsieur le Prince. The writer should sit behind Sartre and de Beauvoir at the Deux Magots, eavesdropping for something hilarious and profound. (He could send Viola.) One should describe Genêt hurrying past the Hôtel de l'Univers (any of the forty Hôtels de l'Univers) and the followers of Garry Davis. He should discover the formation of a new style of character in which jazz and petulance are the pylons of truth. Now that Collis Maitland has found his profitable vocation, the editorial search is on for a young writer who will do for this postwar generation what Collis has done (it being time for a revival) for the Lost Generation. The formula is easy and it will pay two hundred and fifty dollars. Enough for a trip down the Loire valley. He might get Viola or Sheila to write it, then sign it himself.

Still the dishonest offer of freedom to write what he pleases stirs him to ask what it would please him to write. Nothing. In his well-earned complacency it seems to him that he has spent all the coins that his experience has earned, spent them wisely, bought the homestead of his heart. He has nothing more to express—and cannot, quite, yet, bring himself to believe that he must turn over his sharpened tools of expression to be used for ends other than his own.

Surely there is an ample paradox in this, and, if he wished to worry it through, a very puzzling question as to which ends are his own. In all that he has written up to this point, following his own line purely, he has never really felt he was working for himself, however much he worked out of himself. And now it is as if he might ask himself what he has missed all these years that his art might get for him. Again, nothing. But put this way, the shades of very personal obligations dance at the corners of his visions, and the thought comes to him that it might be time to begin paying his debts.

Suppose, taking advantage of the offer to write what he pleased, he should write a version of Bentley's suicide, just as it looked from where he sat, drinking his wine. Let it begin with Sheila's dream of the cannibals when Jess was born. Let it end with a cry of shame on all who let this happen. Yes, he might write that. It would teach lady editors not to say, "Write what you please."

But he will not do this. The very nature of his day in Paris permits him to see what ought to be done without feeling the obligation to do it. Morality, and all the nightmares of history or sleep from which it is born, become aestheticized, matters for apprehension rather than action.

Now, in the cresting balance of his morning and his life, he sees a woman coming down the Rue du Bac. For a minute he watches her with desire. She is an American girl, wigged and shod with all the shallow, heart-weakening coed loveliness he scorned in college when he was so busy with higher interests. The eye—even the spirit!—is not swift enough to catch the transformation from illusion to illusion when he recognizes his wife, but he knows that in the metamorphosis the heart has lost twice.

Two losses—matched and compensated for by the perquisites of his condition. For just as his wife approaches wearing two irreconcilable disguises, there is a doubleness in him that can master the tragic division. The not quite dead Clem he has always been mourns each loss lugubriously. The Clem immortalized by Paris (like a fossil immortalized by its encumbering milieu of stone) joys in the transformation itself. He permits himself the thought that he has evolved from being a poet into being poetic datum. What luck!

He thinks, touching his diamond body like a prize fighter fingering his biceps, he is also lucky to go on breathing after achieving immortality. Not even eternity can stop the Boda master of time. If he has come to the end of life, he will have a new one, please, with the dear faces from the old.

All these years he has climbed up the ladder of his work. It has brought him to the "Paris" he anticipated when he left the house this morning. It is a Paris that could not exist without its history, its geography, its fluid subordination to fate and time—and yet a Paris that could not exist either without the contribution of his creative will, which has its geography and history as well. When Jess announced with such ignorant assurance that his father was "going somewhere," had not the boy too conceived this special sanctuary, privileged equally in time and eternity? Surely the child knew where the man had to go.

He has finished the trip from Boda. And he wants Sheila to join him here. He is immeasurably grateful that she is coming to keep him from loneliness in the condition he has worked so hard to achieve. But—he knows this too as he watches her from under sun-warmed lids—that loneliness is the price of invulnerability. If he shares his Paris with her, it will become another thing.

It is Sheila more even than his children who will subject him again to chance and change. She more than they is flesh of his flesh, who has shared the toil of his liberation with him—but who cannot share the full measure of tragic and comic insights that allow its claim of aesthetic justification. One person alone can come to his Paris. Not two. And if she crosses the street to him, as she is about to, the world he has outrun comes with her.

He wants her to come and break his revery again—and he does not. The traffic divides. White-clothed, she steps down from the curb. He sees the sun explode like shrapnel among the leaf shadows on the street at noon.

In the afternoon they are with friends.

There is Viola Lansdowne, who joins them for lunch on the Rue des Saints Pères. Viola is an English girl, the handsome spinsterish daughter of a parson. Two years ago she came to Paris to write, but was appropriated quickly by a school of Irish poets who took advantage of her ingrained servility, her bad conscience about the Rising, and her secretarial talents. Now she has a bad conscience about having let the Irish exploit her, and she works this out by suffering Clem's exploitation.

She types his manuscripts and keeps him informed on literary and artistic gossip. She is Clem's walking library. She has read and reads everything. When he wants references or quotations she pumps them out with a quick intuition of his need. She is better educated than he, altogether, and with her to serve he no longer feels like a private of literature, but rather more like a staff officer.

She also sits with the Anderson babies in the evenings when Huguette is not available. For all this she asks in return only that she be allowed to adore from close but not intimate range. Once it occurred to Clem that he ought to pay her by taking her to bed—or perhaps thus make firm the contract for her baby-sitting services. He found her horrified at his advance—not so much for her sake as for the sake of his talents, for Sheila and the children. Of course she slept with the Irish, married and unmarried, but that was all right, because she did not really respect them.

Frequently there are crises in Viola's life. For example, she will just miss finding an apartment where the Andersons could live rent free, or has just failed to get Clem a noble brown-skinned patron. Or has suffered an attempted rape at the hands of an Arab or a Fulbright student. Or she has found in Clem's play some misrepresentation of English life which she is loath to mention to him openly.

Today she must only be advised on whether or not to go to Provence to work in the grape harvest.

"It sounds very D. H. Lawrence," Clem suggests.

"Does it not? It might be such an adventure. We'd go on Roger's bike."

"You could trade Roger off for some brown, illiterate Provençal."

"And I should feel the sun strike deep, deep into the icy caverns within me," says Viola, who believes indeed in those icy caverns and in Lawrence's prescription for filling them, but has found that life is divided from truth so cunningly that the truth of the senses may be found and life still go on in its same exacting, unsatisfying way. "I daresay that would be pleasant and I might be the better for it. I say, why can't the Andersons come as well?"

"I have to protect my icy cavern from the sun," Clem says. "As an officer of American letters I have obligations to the corps. Anyway, we may be going back to New York."

"This summer?"

Sheila raises her eyebrows. "Well. I hadn't heard. See how deep he is, Viola?"

"Oh, deep."

"When was this decision made?" Sheila demands.

"Decision," Clem says, twisting. "It's only a thing that might happen. I go where I'm called. Maybe we won't go until next year. But no grape harvesting. Let them bring the grapes to me."

"I think I won't go either," Viola says. "After all, others have already been." Contemplating the lack of an untrammeled world open to experience, they fall into a discussion of the relative merits of going to Provence to tread grapes and taking opium to induce the illusion that one is there. During her bondage to the Irish, Viola was their chief procurer of drugs as well as the guinea pig to test the safety of the product, so she speaks with authority on drug hallucination as well as on most other subjects.

"It may be the ideals of my cloistered maidenhood," she says, "but I am temperamentally inclined to prefer the real thing. Even so, or perhaps therefore, I shan't go with Roger." Roger being, as they all know, a homosexual who prizes Viola only for the features she shares with boys. Now and then she shelters this Roger in her room on the Rue de Ciseaux, loftily mothering him at the same time she submits to his perversities.

In such a situation Clem sees Viola as reconciling nearly absolute contraries of chastity and degradation, and he is bound to her by envy, like Jess's envy of the dog. She seems to be truly immune spiritually, the moral salamander that he hopes he may become.

"Why don't you come home with us to America?" Clem says. "You'd be safe even there."

"Safe, I daresay," Viola agrees. "But that's not what one is waiting for, either."

"You misread me," Clem says. "I meant be safe and still have what you want." And he waves the thought off into the labyrinthine air, realizing it is himself he is trying to convince.

Later, with Viola, the children and Huguette—"the Anderson caravan," "the little artist family," "les saltimbanques"—they drive out to a place on the Seine that their friends the Burbidges have taken for the summer.

Terry and Tony Burbidge are the Andersons' first truly rich friends. (Everybody deserves to know the rich, Clem thinks. Like other colorful minorities, they are the toys with which humanity plays some of its prettiest games.)

Terry's money (his "American blood") has permitted him an ingrained seriousness and modesty that no one hoisted by his own bootstraps could readily attain.

He is a poet, but only in the sense that he writes excellent verse. Not a professional, but a great amateur. His trade is law, though this probably means, in the long run, government service rather than private practice. He had a small job in the ESC during the war, was taken in, he says, "to keep my family from stabbing the war effort in the back." After this summer in France he will go back to Washington as a sort of lobbyist "to keep the government from stabbing my family in the back."

One of the things that first endeared him to Clem was his show of spiritual immunity, not unlike Viola's but springing from radically different sources. There are no shadows in Terry's laughter, Clem thinks, nor any malicious giggles in his compassion. As Clem puts it, "Terry is the only man I know who doesn't snicker about the Bomb. He meets it head on, man to man—because he's the only one I know who isn't afraid that it can kill us."

Terry has, in a word, the barbaric and beautiful optimism of those who have never been humbled by economic impotence in a world where the economic flaw can lead to all others. In his achievement as a poet, Terry has never lived on capital in the way that Clem has always done. There is an economical deftness in Terry that only the rich learn, that the poor can match only when they are spendthrift.

In a sense Terry has enlisted Clem as Clem enlisted Viola, like a lord adding a minstrel or a jester to his staff ("someone to do the poetic dirty work"), but there is a question as to who has taken over whom. For Terry's life and his evident capacity for heroic roles to come are, perhaps, the extroversion of Clem's interior life, and it is possible to think of Terry as the servant who will sweat through the roles that Clem's base, imperial longing has conceived.

There is, it would seem, a balance of envy between the two men, so perfect that the symptoms of envy vanish. They have been easier with each other than either will ever be again with anyone else. Terry was once a favored student of Bentley's at Harvard. It was through Bentley's introduction that the Andersons met the Burbidges. On the subject of Bentley's death they are balanced in a disagreement so total that the circle seems to close. They even like each other's verse, Clem thinks, taking this as a measure of the antipodal remoteness that links them like sun and shade.

In the tableau vivant of this afternoon by the Seine, Clem sees with soul-delivering justice the relationship he wants between himself and—is it life or toys?

Clem wets his feet in the water that Renoir invented to flow through the happy landscape of this unhappy country. Somewhere upstream Terry is swimming in the full sweep of the current. Enjoying his strength as I enjoy my cowardice, Clem thinks. The episode in Mexico with Claude Pogorski ruined Clem's nerve for swimming. He panics in water over his head, but he no longer frets that this is so. All he requires of himself is to stay out of deep water.

Terry will swim for him. The thought is generally similar to the feeling Clem had—so briefly—when Jess was born. There is someone else to do all that he knows must be done. With Terry he is sure that there is someone else who can do it. He does not have to swim for Terry as he had to swim for Claude. He is not obliged to meddle with Terry's wife. And more, there is some deep shy notion of a life task that has always needled Clem, and with the Burbidges—knowing the Burbidges—he is inclined to give it up and be at peace.

Clem hears Jess shouting on the beach, where he is playing with the Burbidges' youngest boy. In spite of the fact that Jess is not going to put himself in danger, being a sensible child, Clem's thought about him is pegged to the question, What if the boy got into deep water where I would be afraid to go after him? Happily, Terry or Tony or

Sheila would save him. Or Viola would instantaneously teach herself to swim and haul him back. That is no longer his obligation, Clem thinks. It is enough that he has "saved" the boy by the eternal recognition This is my son. It was only this that he had to give the boy beyond what others could give him. And this was enough.

Standing waist-deep in the warm water and slapping little waves against his basketball belly, he stares at Tony Burbidge like a small-town boy of twelve ogling a cooch dancer at the county fair.

Aboard the houseboat the Burbidges use for a dock and guesthouse Tony stands with her back toward him. She leans, supporting herself with her left hand against one of the steel uprights that hold aloft the red-and-white canopy. Her left hip is thrust out by her posture, and from her wet red bathing suit a drop of water trickles viscously down the back of her thigh.

That is what my mind looks like, Clem thinks. (There is a game he played once on shipboard, where the question was, What does your mind look like? Like a nest of bluebird's eggs? Like the machinery of a clock? Like a hall of mirrors? Whatever he had answered then, here was his perfect image.)

A current which is not desire but like something induced by the magnetic field of transcended desire measures her sexually. He loves her because in the fulfilled prime of her privileged life, well husbanded and well fed, mother of two downy boys, she is beautiful as Cleopatra, and through her beauty he loves Terry's life, because Terry is beautiful as Antony in the colored theatric light of her sexuality. All the lewdness and chastity of his peculiar spirit integrate at the focal center of his visual field, the coursing drop of water like a universe seen from outside, the sterile globe which his watching fertilizes.

The marriage of true minds, he thinks, staring square. My vision. Her ass. There is nothing I am not capable of, but nothing I need to do. He needs and wants no more of them than, in the recognition, he has.

"Do you remember ..." Sheila asks when he climbs the ladder of the houseboat to join her (with Lulie perched on her bare knee) and Tony and Viola under the canopy. Listening, pouring himself a whiskey, he remembers Pogorski's attempt at making love to him through the medium of a shared wife and without revulsion or amusement notes how the theme repeats as between himself and Terry in the vision he has just had of Tony. "... that day not so long after we met when we went swimming in the quarries with Dick and Janet and Wadleigh Hertz and that pretty girl from Duluth?"

469

He bobs his head as if he means to say, Of course. That too is integrated in the perfect sphere of this afternoon, as it was integrated in the drop of water now dried and vanished on Tony's leg. All the personae are in the themes, he thinks. He can distinguish them, but feels no prosaic need to do so. The integration that wise Dr. Gorman once called so "vast an effort" has become automatic, nearly facile. His art has trained him, made him something. What? What follows creation in the cycle? Ecstasy? And is this it? And is it not a task heroic enough for the man he always planned to become—to be ecstatic?

He drops flabbily into a deck chair as he lofts the universe onto his shoulders. "Eternity certainly is in love with the productions of time," he says. He makes a Daddy face at Lulie and crooks his finger to coax her off her mother's lap. "Daddy loves you. Come, Miss Zwieback. My Miss Zwieback."

Breastless Viola leans from her chair and as if she knew exactly what he had been thinking says, "One of Zeno's paradoxes is that there is no difference between the infinitely great and the infinitely small."

"You certainly have to watch out for them both," Clem agrees, lofting his daughter and licking the tip of her ear as she burrows against him.

"What are you goblins talking about?" Tony demands. Tony is very bright, went to the best girls' schools and loyally believes that if she can decipher her husband's verse she can understand anything. Any conversation she does not grasp seems to her an interrupted one, in which she has been denied access to what went before. It does not occur to her that there may be coincidences or lucky times when things may enter into communication as if they were words registered simultaneously by two minds abreast.

But Clem says, "You invite a gnomic poet out to lap up your booze, you got to stand for some nonsense, lady." Still, he loves her too much to bait her—loves the environment she gives him ("I always feel like nothing can happen to me when I'm around rich people") so much that he owes her more than entertainment in return.

"I was thinking of how I came out of the nut ward in the Army by bearing down like the boy in 'Rocking Horse Winner.' I mean, it's hard for me to put everything together, but when I do—for myself—other people notice. Like Viola just did. You didn't know I'd ever been psycho? Well, that's certainly a tribute to me, isn't it, since I cured myself. They thought what was making me silly was that my energy was sapped by the common cold. True. They had that written on my chart, and how I found out was that when they locked me up snug I had a buddy for a ward attendant who let me go up to the office to read my record. 'My sea-gown scarf'd about me, in the dark groped I to find them out.' It seemed so ridiculous that straightway I got well. By an 'intense integrative effort.' It was a struggle then, but now I can do it easy. I've been integrating your social afternoon, good hostess. You've certainly got it all here."

Proud as a mother, Viola listens. Amused as she is supposed to be, Tony bats her long lashes and pulls up the shoulder strap of her suit. "It's often nonsense, and nonsense to explain nonsense, but it's sterling inlaid nonsense," she says. Her fine teeth flash, and he decides that she, with her exact degree of obtuseness and comprehension, is his ideal audience. She and Terry are like teak, which he can strike with the hardest blows and razor's edges of his mind without being afraid he will destroy what is precious to him.

While Sheila—he thinks that Sheila is pretending to be undisturbed by the fact that for the twelfth time in the last three days he has made some reference to his period of insanity. From that he goes on to think she does not approve of the jester's role he plays for Tony. And then: How different things might be if Sheila were dead.

With his fingers tightening ever so slightly on the skimpy flesh over Lulie's ribs, he thinks how different if she were dead. And Jess, and Terry, and Viola. And he were alone on this flower-scented deck with Tony, wooing her with jokes, hunting the goodies of her sex down inside that bathing suit the color of a Christmas stocking. He can think this now without passion. Only curiosity. And it must be a sign of health that every possibility can present itself fully to his mind without derailing his desire to have things just as they are.

Sickness of the man was health of the poet, he remembers, and knows that every poem he wrote after the war was a rung of the ladder he climbed to get here.

He goes to the rail and looks upstream. Terry is swimming down toward them, his arm swinging cleanly like a wave of reassurance. It happens, and is evident immediately on his return, that Terry has been swimming so far and long alone because he has been trying in all conscience to grapple with something Clem said a few days before. He was not ready yet to talk about it when the Andersons arrived.

Terry is in good appetite now. Helps himself to cold chicken and bourbon, then turns on Clem to deny that Bentley's suicide was, as Clem called it, "an act of despair," a choice in which the full mind at the peak of its powers refused to believe in the eventuality of human success.

With an artist's finicking, Terry has put together the reasons why it could not be so. His handsome, earnest face is drawn with intensity as he reviews his long acquaintance with Bentley. If Bentley was driven to his death by the twisted moral pressures of his time and country, why, then it was America that went wrong and not mankind. And it was one's duty to go back, in spirit or with a mace, and use America against America if need be to make what was wrong right.

"I don't say there won't be civil war," Terry insists. "How or in what shape or in how many decades I can't guess. But it may be that it's the national destiny to be the battlefield for the ultimate civil war that man fights for himself, with blood up to the hubcaps and the first Civil War only a miniature of what is to come. The insight of Lincoln saying that every drop of blood exacted by the slaver's lash might have to be paid back is not gainsaid by the fact that it hasn't happened yet. Nor would it be only the slavery of the black men before 1864 that would be included in the formula. Why not all the blood exacted by the economic iniquities of colonialism and economic imperialism? That is not to say that it can never be done, that sometime, somehow, a balance can't be struck from which people thereafter advance without the shadow—"

"But blood—I know you mean injustice—is just exactly what can't be paid back." It is Sheila who takes up the argument, not Clem this time, though she uses the fine deviousness of language that he has made for her, that she has got from him and Viola when Viola was making her reports of the existentialist position. She says that there is no debt to the dead except for what we have from them. Nothing for what they suffered or meant to give us. We owe our country nothing except for what it has given us. Bentley might have despaired and had perfect knowledge of why he must despair of God and man. Yet his despair lays no contribution on our ignorance of what he knew, and in turn our knowledge obliges us to no more than they who do not know that                anything                is                lost.

Clem thinks this true, but not as true as the day itself, the mystery in which the words sound. As he listens he thinks that each of them is saying exactly what he must. He does not pause long on the first apparent ad hominem argument against what Terry says: that day by day and country place by country place and drink by drink he is increasing the gulf of economic injustice that he dreams may sometime be not only eradicated but paid back. Nor the second, which is that Terry's passion for justice springs from guilt. But he is captured now by the idea that the only argument against any—and against all—reason is an ad hominem argument. So nature argues, by necessity, and if guilt is the mother of reason, then the limitations of reason are fatally established by its parentage. This passion among us is necessary and only necessary. Therefore worthless to itself. And yet, because it is passion, within itself there is the necessity that it be worth something. Therefore, in Paris it is necessary that one think even necessity is beautiful. We must be beautiful in contention as in peace, Clem thinks, my wife, my friends. I think so because I must. It is the last position. Ninety degrees north. From here the mind's direction is only south. All twigs bend south, if they are ever to bend at all.

He admits to himself that he can not distinguish between this very moment's immobility of passion, frozen at its very nadir, tight as a tongue frozen to a pump handle on an icy morning, and death. And if this consonance of nerves and mind is death, the sought-for terminal of all his anxious work and all the times he has made himself over from the original unpromising boy, then he is smugly satisfied with what he has done. This refusal to move or be moved is right for him.

But he does not quite like to hear Sheila using his language and his arguments. What in himself would be far beyond morality seems immoral and perhaps callous when she utters it. Almost worse, he is afraid that in her speech his justifications lose their valuable color and pattern, like some tropical fish fading to the color of a shoe when it is pulled out of water. (Just as his image of Tony and himself would go wrong if he should really touch her; even if he said what he knew.)

"Let the dead bury the dead," Sheila says. It grates on his ear.

"I have great hope," Terry says. Terry is a fact of hope, saying what he has to say. But it seems to him that Terry is merely announcing his assigned response in the Gestalt of fear where Bentley had another part. What Clem recognizes is only a larger version of the Gestalt he recognized when he pretended to drop Jess. Which was afraid? Both.

He says, "The only way to deal with his death is to understand that he left us exactly nothing but a clean slate. The fullness of time arrives when no minute owes anything to the past. That's the only way we can be free."

"Precisely," says Viola, who has read all the books and has nothing from them, nothing better than the loyal drudgery for the Andersons and her service to Roger, but who knows she need not wish for anything better.

Terry shakes his lion head. "When the hero falls he cancels, by accepting, all his flaws and defeats and the arrows and leaves us ..."

"Nothing."

"… the image of that victory. The sacrifice fixes it the way they fix dye in a cloth."

"You see him falling from his hotel window in a parachute of morality," Clem says. "Let me offer you instead the image of acceleration stripping the body as he falls—necktie, shirt, ethics, love and heroism—until what hits the concrete is nothing at all. Everything was on the ledge he jumped from. Nothing at the bottom. So what the tabloids show of the blanket over the remains is more true than all our pieties. As any artist knows. We may try to say "is" but all we can say is "was." It's a terrible thing to confuse them. Bentley's gifts were. Are not."

So serious, for once, and forgetful of irony that he has forgotten to watch for his effects, he wakes into the surprised realization that he has moved beyond the intent of Sheila's argument—so far that now she seems to be on Terry's side against him.

He feels himself the moral chimera among a flock of natural animals and, since it is so, resolves to enjoy it. "I remember once when my mother taught a Bible-school class in St. Paul and in summer the kids in it met in a bandstand in the park. While we good children sat prissy-calm around the circumference, one day the bad little boy who wouldn't keep his seat went around the circle, tugging his foreskin out, demonstrating to each of us in turn his strength, sign of the flesh. I must have envied him, and there it all began, or else I'd never have learned to say what I really think. Bentley's dead. O whitehead Humpty-Dumpty. It's only when the good are dead that you can laugh, y'see. The cat's away."

"Oh, no," they all chorused against him. All except Viola.

That night when they are back in their Paris apartment and the pretty children are asleep and Viola and Huguette gone, Clem and Sheila make love. The window of their bedroom is open, and what comes in on the July breeze is as rich in sensuousness as a night scene by Colette—the evocative odors and indirect lights that seem to come from a better century. In the way they can and must, Clem thinks, he and Sheila try to show again how much they love each other. Stout bucks and gentle exploratory caresses, then, as they try to yield two consciousnesses to a single sweet blankness.

But it will appear that the senses are no longer blind. Effort to yield consciousness merely scatters it, like a swarm of bees dispersed through a glade of nerves. What they achieve is not abandonment, as, perhaps, it should be if the flesh is to be healed from the desecrations of thought. But feeling thinks, and the sexual union is the most intense integrative act of all. The blind organ sees from its empty socket. It sees the rock-rimmed pool into which one time a body was thrown from a rock to save Pogorski, and sees the vulvar crease of Manhattan street into which Bentley stooped to save no one. Knows itself the inverted sign of Christian salvation, the fletched arrow aimed at where the soul hides in the belly. It marches on the rose of the world and for love and remembrance sacrifices its dearest. It pampers, pleads, and in a counterfeit of holiness blinds itself in a simultaneity of pride and despair. Knows itself in death and makes the Paris of the flesh for one instant identical to the Paris of the conceptual mind. Knows the pleasant laving of withdrawal ... O my darlingest. Has ridden well between death and Devil. Rides no more.

He chuckles and contentedly snuggles into Sheila's armpit.

"And?" she says.

"And time. Everything can happen to us now." Since nothing matters. "It will be different and we will go back home one of these days. We'll go to Felix' conference in a limousine. It's important to keep incentive before the young. I'll show them how to live." When the finally exhausted creative climb is finished.

"Do you really want to go this year? We can if—"

"Oh, hell. Not this year. Sometime. When my play is sold and we're rolling in money. We can't go back until we have something to show."

"You have plenty to show."

"Give it time to float to the top."

They are in agreement, relaxed. Nothing is demanded of them now.

But as Clem goes to sleep he feels, as he must, the double effect from the double aspects of their act of love. The senses always recognize two women, her before and her after, and in surrendering the function of the disciplined reason to the senses, one always gathers it back with a commitment to double thoughts and recognitions. Now the libido, freed of its immediate preoccupation, reveals its true inertia. Now there is Sheila herself—and the Sheila whom he must remember. Sheila who lies contentedly beside him and wants nothing more than to keep him safe in the Parisian globe of his contentment. And the Sheila whom he loves with the one passion that will not come up to the light of consciousness, who says, Come home. Come back to where we were—about the worst—innocent. Come back before our war.

So, divided in love, he had to say to me that summer, "Sheila has never forgiven me for going away and leaving everyone," although nothing was clearer than that the Sheila to whom I talked held nothing against him. He had let the dead bury the dead and she was wise enough to see the heroism of the choice. But tricky Clem was too wise.

So he could lead me around Paris to show me all he had found, his friends and the furniture of his life in this happy exile. We drove together down the Loire valley in the splendid ebullience of summer. And I told myself that the cynicism I heard from him sometimes was something he could afford now, now that he was on top, safe.

He was drinking very little that summer. The hangovers he had described in Mexico with a vividness that could arouse in all of us pity and terror were apparently a thing of the past. He had put on weight, without coming to that unhealthy fatness that he showed later.

He was not working much now. But from years of unbroken effort he had more than earned his rest. He had filled the granary. He was fulfilled.

Only, "Sheila wants me to go home."

# VI

## SLEEP BEFORE EVENING

*For the rest, he mixes everything—and with art. We are at Harar, we are always leaving for Aden, and he tries to find camels, to organize a caravan.... Quickly, quickly, someone is waiting for us, we close our bags and go. Why was he allowed to sleep? Why didn't someone help him to dress? What will be said if we don't arrive on the day named? His word won't be taken any longer, no one will have any more confidence in him!*

> — Letter from Rimbaud's sister to his mother as the poet was dying. Quoted in Elisabeth Hanson's My Poor Arthur.

# 18

SHEILA THOUGHT Clem came back to America in 1950 because his play had been sold, and in her opinion he came back expecting the perquisites (and the duties, too) of a writer who has arrived. She also thought that his decadence and final catastrophic disintegration began when he arrived in New York to find the play was "not exactly" sold. His last six years seemed to her an uninterrupted, accelerating plunge after that disappointment.

The second opinion seems to me less arguable than the first. Those six years—in the middle of which I began this account—have a certain undeniable unity. Every time I saw him or heard of him, he had broken more china, had mortgaged more of his chance at a good old age, respect, tranquility. In fact it is just the unity in his self-destructive phase that makes me doubt the superficial motives Sheila attributed to him.

It is true that in May of 1950 Gorman cabled the news that he had found backers for *Death and the Devil*, and equally true that Clem gathered his family and books for the return trip in the blossoming euphoria set loose by Gorman's announcement.

Of course he anticipated the realization of his fantasies of success. Sheila describes overhearing him, in a conversation on the ship, tell an acquaintance that "he would not be one of those playwrights always hanging around his director telling him what to do." He must have imagined for himself a position of dignified reserve, somewhat above the battle. And I suspect that as soon as he left Paris he began to practice a Dr. Johnson scowl of genial (yet potentially irascible!) tolerance to replace the Khmer Buddha smile. He would be above faction. Above criticism. The friend of the struggling young. The merciless (but suave) foe of entrenched pomp and merely commercial mediocrity. A man of letters who devoted his mornings to "the task in hand" and his afternoons to his not inconsiderable literary (and perhaps statal) correspondence. He would receive his peers on Tuesday evenings, and, separating themselves from the world behind a veil of cigarette smoke, they would enjoy the incomparable conversation of the elect. Attaching himself to no faculty, he would nevertheless feel himself a part of the academic comity, as accessible to educators as to his young imitators. Visitors would be received in his house with the announcement, "Mr. Anderson is, of course, in his study." After a suitable pause Mr. Anderson would emerge, pince-nez in extended hand, crumbs of still burning pipe tobacco falling from his dressing gown, his beard leveled like a lance, and the welcoming "Cher colleague!" exploding from his wryly merry lips. He would take solitary walks before dinner, like the venerable intellectuals in Thomas Mann's stories, and like them would have tragicomic reflections on his domestic life and the great themes as he tapped his cane along the street. On momentous issues, after the fanatic and desperate had expressed their contending views, he would compose unimpeachable letters to the editors of the New York Times to silence the dispute. He would, perhaps, take a little mistress—a toy, no more—to beguile those humors that sometimes come upon the responsible men of this world. He would arrange with a university library for the disposal of his papers upon his decease. He would remove all vulgar expressions from his style. He remembered Yeats's lament that Synge had died too young to enjoy the adulation and society of cultivated women and congratulated himself that he had outlived Synge.

One feels a twinge of the heart in recalling these fantasies of Clem's; something worse in reflecting how reality would caricature those it did not smash like froth. And yet, of course, they are the most superficial kind of froth—meant to be smashed, as Clem basically knew. He was always profligate with such projected wishes, and reality would have had a hard time smashing them faster than he could produce them.

Certainly by now he had gone through the wringer enough times to be wary of any promises. The fate of his novel should have—and had, I think—prepared him to expect disappointments with his play.

When he saw Gorman after the ship docked in New York, Gorman told him, weeping, that his cable had not meant exactly what Clem took it to mean. True, there were two backers ready to put up eighty thousand dollars on the play, if George Blake or Ray Carpenter would play the lead. George had accepted. He was ready to sign, but his commitments tied him up until the fall of '52 and one of the backers was unwilling to wait that long. This particular backer was very uneasy just now. Gorman was drawing the long crossbow with him, and from the other side Clem's agent was sewing him up with a pincers movement. But it appeared that unless Carpenter could be signed within the next few weeks, the chances were possible that the best-laid plans of Maxfield Gorman would go up in smoke.

.

Clem took this news quietly at first. "Too quietly," Sheila would always believe. He said they would buy a car and drive with the children to Boda, just as they had planned. When she reminded him that until some money came from the play they had nothing to buy a car with, Clem went to his agent and told him to get at least some option money on the play from the potential backers. The agent refused on the grounds that such a request might alienate those gentlemen at a point when negotiations were delicate.

Clem, working up a little steam, borrowed money from his friends to make the down payment on a sports car. Sheila thought he needed the car more than he would have if he could have paid for it himself. Buying it was a way of applying the body English of confidence to the pending fate of his play. "Anyone who can borrow money from my friends with no security can certainly sell a play," he said ungenerously.

He had the car, but he couldn't bring himself now to leave New York. Any day Carpenter might show up, preferring to give the word of his decision in person rather than telephone it from Hollywood. He might want to congratulate the author. He might want a drinking companion to celebrate a momentous cast of the dice.

Then Clem accepted Felix Martin's invitation to appear in Kansas for a writers' conference, even if that meant the trip to Boda would have to be a very brief one. Then he fumed and fretted for a few more days until the trip to Boda was out of the question and it seemed unlikely that he would even get to the writers' conference.

Finally his agent ordered him out of town on the ground that he would very soon be at the point of calling one of the laggard backers or the other and insulting him.

Yes, this particular period of tension and disappointment worked on him, and one cannot measure the extent to which it contributed to getting him off on the wrong foot at this last homecoming.

And yet I think that Sheila, in her need to explain what was forever inexplicable to her, attaches too much importance to Clem's concern with the play. I see a unity in those last years of his and believe it means something that, in the summing up, she refused to credit. She could not or chose not to see Clem's last dismaying period as anything but a waste, growing sillier to the very end.

There was a symmetry to their marriage and divorce that was not to be distorted by any final reconciliation of the sort that many of their friends hoped for. They had spun in orbits of mutual attraction for a destined time. To the end their lives retained the shape the other had, in each case, given them. But Sheila's sympathy for his visible progress diminished in almost geometric progression after their divorce. Her opinions and explanations of him are valid in measure to her closeness. Once, I think, she had known the truth about his destiny better than he. But did not know what it was eventually to be any more than she really wished to know.

I think it necessary to say that Clem came back from Europe for whatever happened to him in the six years remaining, and not for the play or his daydream wishes. To realize the unity of what he found and did will require of me a trafficking with the incommensurateness of things that may leave few shreds of the humanism or rationality I try to profess. But I believe that the intentionally silly thing he said in his TV appearance about his not being "the objective equivalent" of anything now has to be asserted like the cardinal premise of my theory. For his divorce from action, from moral deed and moral consequence, is the pre-eminent feature of his ruin and, as I will have to say, his salvation under the debris he pulled down on himself.

At one terrible moment Sheila had cried her minimum demand— "He's got to invent me some kind of a life from here on out." But he did no such thing. And eventually—sometime in 1955—Sheila married Bernie Masterson and went on living her own dilute but superficially faithful copy of the life she had lived with Clem. She and Bernie had the children. Harry Rinehart became more and more their friend, visiting them in New York once a year or oftener, and they visited him in Florida. They traveled. Back to France. Back to Chartres and the Dordogne. Bernie, I believe, is now writing a play. Sheila's parents mistrust Bernie and are awed by him very much as they always were by Clem. Which gives rise to familiar jokes in the Masterson house.

"Make real what you imagined me to be," Susan must have required of Clem. But he left her buried in Los Angeles. And then there were other women, quite a lot of other women serving neither as a sign of his appetites nor as a sign of their absence, signifying nothing much except his need for company.

He did no writing to speak of. I believe he made a small beginning on a novel to be called The Fair at Tula. The intense work he had done in five years after the war was still spilling out in magazine publication or in books that represented a profitable recombination of things that had appeared before in print. He signed contracts for the novel and for another play. ("Why shouldn't I?" he said about the signing. Since he was a writer making money with his pen.) But the intention of doing any more creative work was focused otherwise. It was never going to add anything to anyone's library.

And yet—the paradox is all that counts—I think he deeply believed that from the time he went to Kansas in 1950 until his death he was "working" on a major, extensive poem.

Well, working is always an equivocal state where a writer is concerned, and I will be reminded that he talked about his Prometheus Bound until it became a bad joke. He talked it away if he ever had anything to begin with, it is said, talked it to death, endlessly, with everyone. And where was the evidence, the goods?

Not, certainly, on mortal soil.

From Clem himself I heard that "the poem" had been begun in Kansas. For years I knew hardly more about his Kansas visit than that. When at last I had a chance to compare notes with Felix Martin, he remembered that Clem had dropped like Lucifer on their writers' conference that summer of 1950.

"I think this. We must anticipate a certain inertia in the career of a writer," said Felix, very gray now, but as willing as ever to extend his tolerance against what he knew to be the intolerance of the universe. "The wheel, set in motion, is going to keep turning, and we may not like where it goes. After creativity, no doubt it goes on spinning into a kind of exuberance—perhaps the word is ecstasy—which we never contemplated."

There was the tone of sympathy in Felix' recollection, but also plainly the wish was there that the ecstasy—or whatever Clem had come to—had manifested itself altogether in things of the spirit. Let there be burning—but why this offensive smell of flesh consumed? "I expect that Kansas has not had many such experiences since the days of the revivalist preachers," Felix said, with his gray smile.

Clem had arrived on the campus giving no special hint that he was tinder looking for a match. True, he and Sheila had made their appearance in a nimble sports car. They had left the children with Sheila's parents in Indiana, but if they did not give a first impression of being sober family types, they looked no worse than faintly collegiate, faintly expatriate still, as if they brought a welcome whiff of Paris with them.

If Clem was in a state about his play, there was no slightest evidence of strain when he gave his first talk to students at the conference. It was an altogether nonexplosive talk. Felix was somewhat surprised by the "scholarship" Clem displayed. He had forgotten Clem's magpie gift of gathering fragments without wide reading. Then, too, Felix had never known the encyclopedic Viola, from whose company Clem had come so recently. Clem's presence was intended to round out a panel where he and the novelist Woodward Cheney would represent the practicing writer, while a well-known Southern Lady of Letters and Thomas Wilder (neo-Thomist, author of The Veiled Lady: A Study of Hieratic Imagery in the Verse of Thomas Stearns Eliot and Eros Sublimed: The Allegorization of Ovid in the Middle Ages, former bombardier, father of six, ping-pong and chess enthusiast) would speak for discipline and the tradition.

If Clem took arms against discipline and tradition that first afternoon, he did it in a traditional, heartless fashion. He delivered the assembled students and faculty a pastiche of the enduring romantic concept of the poet as agonist, fated to fall upon the thorns of life and bleed, committed to suffer in his own person the irreconcilable contradictions of the world and to report—with the resources of art sharpening his truth—"the way things are." He wove with few interjections of his own a tissue of anthology, opening with Sidney's "Apologie for Poetrie" and Shelley's "Defence of Poetry," crossing the century of "the romantic agony" with appropriate allusions to Rimbaud's personal misbehavior and his decision to run guns rather than continue as poet. He mentioned the tragic-funny self-immolation of the poets of the aesthetic movement, the broodings of Tonio Kröger, touched dexterously and lightheartedly on Gustave Aschenbach's death in Venice and Hart Crane's intense habit of smoking a cigar and chewing a plug at the same time.

The poet is Cain, he told them with unblemished brow. And Woodward Cheney felt that this old-fashioned romantic lingo was just the ticket for the audience of "spinster schoolteachers and desperate housewives" assembled here for the summer session. It stimulated their rusty glands, justified the ache of their loneliness and the unnamable failure of their Kansas lives.

To top it off, Clem's own appearance, his very glibness, provided a happy antidote for the pessimism of his references. Shiny and scrubbed, wearing a Trumanesque sport shirt as he draped and dangled himself from the speaker's lectern, was he not, in his still boyish healthiness, a living proof that poets got by a good bit easier these days than in the black ages—before the days of miracle drugs—of which he told them the old familiar ghost stories? When he quoted sick Baudelaire to the effect that syphilis was "queen of the diseases" did he not, by the very allusion, remind everyone that penicillin has come to bless poets and bourgeois alike?

A pert Mrs. Fothergill—one of the "desperate housewives," if Cheney's epithet could be trusted—bobbed up from the audience when he had finished his talk and asked, "Didn't I see you and Mrs. Anderson drive up in a new MG a while ago?"

Love of things irreconcilable indeed! In a well-rounded American life there was time and place for everything. Here, yes, even in Kansas (no longer Bleeding Kansas), all the gods might be worshiped simultaneously, Mrs. Fothergill seemed to say—as much by her appearance as by her smart way of posing the challenge.

For Mrs. Fothergill was a dandy redhead with cobalt-blue eyes. If she might be called a "desperate housewife"—just to explain why so dazzling a creature might want to write—clearly she could have had her triumphs and her liberties in other fields as well.

Mrs. Fothergill had come to this meeting of the writers' conference loaded. In her white-gloved hand she held the printed sheet of biographies of the panelists given her at registration. In a clear, amused voice she said, "I read here that you've won a number of grants, Mr. Anderson. Society can't truly despise you. You've had a popular novel published, as well as books of poetry. You have two lovely children. Aren't they lovely children, Mr. Anderson?"

She bent her swan's neck to read from the authoritative sheet what, after all, Clem had submitted to describe his own situation in life: "'Two wise children, both wanting to be held at once.'"

She paused in her recitation of evidence, flushed with the joy of this baiting game. One white-gloved finger tugged winsomely at the corner of her bright mouth. Is all this comfort and coddling your idea of "the poet's agony," Mr. Anderson?

She had made her point. The audience comfortably stretched legs and inhaled the balm of midsummer air drifting through the amorous green of campus trees, cooling them in the handsome, paneled room where they were gathered in good will. Woodward Cheney leaned to his microphone, chuckling, "The lady calls a foul!" Felix Martin smiled his pedagogic benison to indicate the pertinence of Mrs. Fothergill's objection. In the rear of the auditorium Sheila was pleased to see her boy caught and exposed. She closed her eyes with satisfaction when she heard the temperateness of his answer, this temperateness that was so much her gift to him.

Openmouthed as an idiot boy, Clem gaped at Mrs. Fothergill. Nodded. "You know," he said in the tone of one who will not tell everyone but will tell you, "I've always thought that Rimbaud had a dandy time in Africa, kind of like Somerset Maugham on the Riviera, but was too much of a hypocrite to admit it. Or maybe his agent said, 'Go down there and wait for a rep, Arthur.'"

The terms of his retraction did not fly over Mrs. Fothergill's red head. Thus far, in her well-rounded life, she had majored in comparative literature at Radcliffe and was living out her desperate wife-hood with a physician husband who had taken her twice to Europe and would take her to Indochina in the following winter. No provincial she, but a young woman who had had and would have everything. A young woman impatient with the myth of the poètes maudits.

But anyway, to have spoken of the participants in this writers' conference as wives and spinster teachers, as Cheney chose to, was the grossest sort of poetic license. There were graduate and undergraduate students of the university among them—up to sixty per cent of the enrollment—and some of them were young poets who, like Clem a dozen years before, did not go home for the summer because something of great importance held them on the campus.

One of them stood up now from the front row, where he had been gnawing his fingernails. Bernie Masterson, a young man in posture reminiscent of the sharp angle of a comic-strip stogie, a young man who reaches for his revolver when he hears culture derided—as he has just heard from the immaculate lips of Mrs. Fothergill.

"It's all very well to be funny," he admonished Clem—not bothering with Mrs. Fothergill, but throwing his charge straight at the one who should know better. "It's all very well to say, 'Oh, I always knew Arthur Rimbaud had a keen time in Africa.' But suppose we consider seriously the idea of alienation and fear and trembling. Suppose we only consider seriously what Rimbaud said to his sister just before he died. He said, 'Deemen—'"

"'Demain,'" Clem corrected gently.

"'Tomorrow you will be in the sun and I will be in the dark.' There. It takes a poet to say that, and at the same time it doesn't. Anybody could say it. But a poet did say it, and I don't see the relevance inherent in asserting even for a yak that a person who could say such a thing was having a swell time. It's a confusion of jonners, of the spiritual life with was he enjoying the climate, or of knocking-off-Hedy-Lamarr-I-Make-Tiffin-for-White-Man stuff with the horror of the human condition."

Mrs. Fothergill shook her lovely head in a pretense of pure bewilderment at this "jonner" of argument. (Clem would find later that her favorite form of rejecting that with which she had no sympathy was to say, "I don't understand it.")

486

Clem stared at Bernie with the same idiot complacency, paused and said, very much for Bernie Masterson alone and for none of the seventy-five others in the room, "To hear that in Kansas—'tu seras en plein soleil'—is like Whitman's "Italian Music" in South Dakota. And you must write it down that way. Do you know his poem? 'Yet strangely fitting, even here, meanings unknown before ...'" Thus with his new glibness he seemed trying to blunt the young man's anger into something politely literary.

But, looking down from the speakers' platform at the stern Hebraism of this intensity, he knew that he was seeing—the memory made visible in flesh so unlike his own—himself as he had been. It would not have occurred to him to doubt that the root of poetry was in such anger as he heard burring the voice. He saw what would be confirmed two years later when he visited us in Blackhawk—what he had been, already accusing what he was. Irreconcilable things, and he loved them both.

He could only indicate his swift fondness and partisanship for the boy with a wink. Then he shrugged his shoulders for Mrs. Fothergill to interpret as she would. And yielded the floor to Woodward Cheney.

Cheney reassured one and all that writing was a profession like another. One practiced it as one might practice law or medicine, and in the evenings one was human like everyone else, though he might be during the day a writer "advocating rebellion." The main thing they (the young and the desperate) must concentrate on was learning their craft.

Good, bluff Cheney would also serve as compromiser, or the pincushion in the middle, that first night when the panelists gathered after dinner in the back yard of a faculty member. As always at an academic mustering of writers, there was plenty to drink and an opportunity to express latent hostilities through the mere assertion of differing tastes.

They sat about on a paved veranda under a festive string of lights. A red, bloated moon climbed slowly over the suburban black-and-silver landscape, accented here and there by the orange rectangles of open windows. Felix Martin was among them for a while, like a Spanish don extending courtesy for courtesy's sake, offering genuine but reserved compliments for the guests of the university, pausing longer with Clem and Sheila than with the others because he genuinely wanted some inkling of "where Clem had been" in the several years since college. But Clem felt, with a sweat of apprehension, that they held a dialogue of the deaf—that whatever they had been unable to say to each other long ago as teacher and student was still undeclarable. Only each had a more elaborate artifice for keeping his secrets now. That was Clem's first disappointment in Kansas.

There were the regular members of the university staff who taught writing classes during the academic year, and, whether of necessity or not, they assumed the role of apologists for the local talent. They set out to correct Cheney's insistent opinion that the students, who for the next two weeks would appear in small groups assigned to one visitor or another according to interest, were fairly called spinsters and desperate housewives. That had been a joke, of course. They knew it was and spiced their deferential rebuttals with humor to match. But wasn't it a tendentious joke, unpromising for the spirit of the conference?

Presently Clem, the Southern Lady, Wilder and Adrienne Solange, an author of children's books visiting for a few days only, were drawn into the loose circle of debate. Following the afternoon meeting, each of them had been given manuscripts submitted by the students in his group. It seemed a point of protocol at least to pretend they had looked into these manuscripts already and had formed a tentative judgment.

Cheney at bay repeated good-naturedly that he wouldn't be here if he thought that all the students lacked talent. "But you'll never convince me that writing can be taught. I was at a conference in North Dakota last month and I uncovered a lad who really knew how to tell a tale. Was he a writing student? He was not. He'd worked in foundries, bellhopped in a hotel, washed dishes, hitchhiked all over the country, done a stretch in the Marines, sold cosmetics. That's how to learn to write. And that's what I'm going to keep repeating to young people. They gotta get out of schools."

Felix intervened to praise him for consistency in his views, but then wondered whether young men who worked at a diversity of trades might not find their experience enriched by ordering it with the disciplines afforded by the liberal arts. "Take Mr. Anderson, for example. If I am not mistaken, he could base a song of occupations on his personal experience. And yet the tincture of learning has gratified me in reading his verse."

Cheney turned squarely to look at Clem. ("That man never saw anything out of the corner of his eye," Clem said.) He seemed to be measuring Clem—not for the first time that day—as if wondering how he might be fitted as a character into one of those substantial historical novels of the "real" West on which Cheney was constantly at work and for which he had already received one Pulitzer Prize. He still found no place for Clem, or none that could be inoffensively mentioned, and contented himself by saying, "It would be a darn poor world if there weren't exceptions to every rule."

An answer true and flabby as his prose in general, as the Southern Lady would put it later in the brief time when she considered Clem her ally against Yankee relativism and detumescent style.

For her part, she was not among the people who would enjoy listening to Woodward Cheney if he were reading Robert E. Lee's farewell to the troops. Rather than swallow his nonsense on top of three bourbons, she would reply, "I believe Degas has it. 'Anyone can be a genius at twenty. To be a genius at forty is what counts.'" She was forty. She was a genius. Felix Martin was politic enough to echo her feeling that these things counted supremely.

"Telling them they're geniuses is the one sure way to spoil a youngster," answered Cheney, who habitually heard (and read) only a few words, which he considered keys, in any statement. He generally missed qualifications or negatives, or perhaps dismissed them as effete adornment of the language. "If you want to make coterie writers out of them, that's the way to do it."

"I want nothing except to teach them respect for—fawm," she said, sizzling that word into his Yankee midriff like a Confederate bayonet, leaving him to puzzle out, if he could, that he was being rebuked for a lack of it in particulars vastly too numerous to mention. Perhaps, he would lament to Clem later, in that brief time when he believed Clem his ally against "pretentiousness and new criticism," perhaps she held him a grudge for making an ex-Confederate officer the villain in his last novel. (She had, of course, not read it.) "But I got the whole tale from documents," he would protest. "And, hell, if you read it close, there are no blacks and whites in Buford Lansing-ham's character. He's gray."

For the moment Clem was hiding his talents for inducing fission. (The better to blow them all apart, decisively.) "I always thought "coterie" was a perfume," he said, flapping his wrist languidly, "and if I catch any of my male students using it, I'll snatch the atomizer out of their wicked hands." (And for a moment it seemed that Cheney, the key-word catcher, had seen how he might fit Clem into the real West— as a disguised, smart-looking pervert. That would be something new among the wagons rolling to Oregon!)

"I got no use for them," Cheney growled, meaning faggots, coteries, atomizers—either or all three. The key word in his response seemed to be "use."

The moment was too fair for Clem to want to laugh or continue this particular exchange. The red moon floated like a cherry in the rich cocktail of his present life. It smelled like home out here in Kansas, and Cheney had gone far enough to remind him of the Boda postmaster and the way he and Harry Rinehart used to burlesque his speech. He moved back into the corner of Cheney's eye, out of sight.

"Dreams begin in irresponsibility," he said to the Southern Lady, who appreciated the source of his misquote. He assured her it was not a purposeful misquote, since, on such a night, so far inland from the menace of the sea and the "coastal spew," as the great Southern writer called New York, it seemed the mark of a spiteful man to have a purpose.

She agreed. She felt, she implied, that they might agree on very many other things. After her lioness gaze had located Sheila, she led Clem to the pretty table where their hostess was dispensing drinks, and presently the two of them were moon watching shoulder to shoulder from the fringes of the lawn, holding hands discreetly if not innocently—her hand squeezed his rhythmically and wetly, like an enormous mouth stripping a shriveled udder—sympathetically voicing their nostalgia for Paris, which she had not seen since the war.

Whatever this pumping at his hand implied, there was no reason why it should lead to anything, not even an alliance against Cheney. It seemed, in fact, to be an end in itself, as if, between imaginative people—highly imaginative people—all the positions and the effort of sex had been incorporated into an abstract and faintly gratifying synecdoche. Let the mental peasants grunt on the ground or the bed, this was for the aristocrats who had transcended straining. Or so Clem in his nervous exuberance interpreted it, feeling within himself a high-keyed laughter floating like the supreme intoxicant on the base of alcohol. He was (with himself, with what he made of things) happy, unbearably happy.

And it was out of this unbearable happiness dependent as it was on nihilistic laughter, that he must turn and claw down the human base of his happiness, re-enter the web of consequence where the tiniest trickles flow inevitably down the gulfward slopes and enter the flood.

There was only a small incident that night. When he and the Southern Lady came back from the moon because their glasses were empty, he found that Sheila had been cornered by poor Adrienne Solange. Adrienne had come straight to the conference from a two-month stay at an endowed writers' colony where the inmates had whiled away the boredom of summer evenings by such collective games as croquet, charades and murder mystery.

Even Sheila, who had to listen to it all, was not quite sure whether Adrienne was recommending that such games be instituted here among the guest lecturers or was merely trying to establish her identity within a group where she felt despised. But there was plainly a missionary fervor in the way she was explaining the murder mystery game.

"It has incredible psychological overtones if you play it seriously," Adrienne said. "With people like all of you there is more insight yielded than you would expect into the inner selves. Now, of course someone among us wants to kill someone else." She did not exactly indicate Clem as a candidate for murder, but her hyperexcitement suggested that since he had just wandered off with a woman not his wife, surely he would understand what she meant. "Plainly there are buried antagonisms in any group. Trivial, but splendid starting places if one uses them as a clue for what might be. You might like to kill Mr. Cheney," she twittered to the Southern Lady, who at this minute looked more as if she would like to crunch Adrienne underfoot. "Or I might want to kill Mr. Martin for inviting me here to a conference where I'd be among so many distinguished people."

"Shit," said Clem, rolling up within six inches of her sharp nose, and letting her see for one ghastly instant that he might mean her as well as her story, letting Sheila see the same intolerable contempt for a human being whose only offense was insignificance.

"Don't mind my husband. He's drunk!" Sheila flared. She put her arm on Adrienne's cringing shoulder. "Drunk and stupidly rude. Go on. For heaven's sake, Clem!"

"I remember at Hallow," Adrienne said with ghastly determination, referring to the colony from which she had come, "there was J. Morton Singer, who actually has, you know ..."

"This is an offense against nature," Clem said to Sheila. "Why are you standing listening to such crap? Nobody's paying you to."

"... published three successful mysteries under the pseudonym Vicker Webley, and Morton simply abominated a young poet thought to have homosexual tendencies." The part of Adrienne's brain that ran her mouth had slipped its contact with the terrorized part that watched Clem. When Sheila pushed him angrily, ordering him to go get a drink and lose himself, Adrienne grabbed his arm and babbled on, "Morton made up a splendid story in which the poet's body was discovered lying near a fountain on the grounds. And everyone was suspected of doing it. Morton laid him out so cleverly that all of us in the game were guessing for days after we had the clues who had done it."

"Morton did it," the Southern Lady put in, with a goatish "Haw haw."

"No," Adrienne said. "The handyman did it. Morton didn't do it. Oh, it was fun. It was educational, I mean as practice for writers keeping their hand in."

"For keeping Morton's hand in," Clem said gravely. And perhaps his gravity now offended Sheila, who knew, as Adrienne apparently did not, that it sprang from the same contempt as his overt rudeness.

"And everybody's," Adrienne said with a possibly genuine enthusiasm, reprieved now that the fire had swept beyond her and someone else was fighting the battle occasioned by her inadequacy.

She still hummed like a piano wire struck by Clem's coarse word, and she still needed to be told, once and for all, as the weak often do, whether she was loved or hated on sight.

Clem had approached with some idea of freeing Sheila from her. Now it was Sheila who had to detach them, for Adrienne had latched to Clem like a suckerfish on a shark, simpering and flattering, seeking the means to debase herself enough to win his approval.

This unpleasant business was grounds enough for Sheila to plead fatigue and headache and ask to be taken home. Clem sympathized with such pleas until they had got away from Adrienne, then wanted to ignore them in favor of one last drink. A light broad as the moon, but invisible, tantalizing, seemed to beckon him on, and he wanted Sheila to run for it with him. His whole day, his success in the afternoon—for it had been that in spite of Mrs. Fothergill's quibbles—seemed to have brought him within striking distance of a revelation. Only to go on in that direction ...

But Sheila was adamant. As they got in their car and prepared to return to the summer-vacated sorority house where they were quartered, it seemed to Clem that the fatigue she insisted on was more, must be more, than a matter of one evening. He was high. From a height one sees farther. What he thought he saw in her was an accumulation of fatigue, a bedrock beginning to show through the fertile surface of their life together. And whether what he saw was his own projection or a reality, he was hurt by it. If the reproach was not to him, it was to the life he had given her, and it was the only one he could have given.

As if they had to, they went on arguing about Adrienne.

Why did you let her monopolize you, since she was the feeblest excuse for a human at the party?

Because of that.

Why did you have to jump on her and humiliate her, since she was the most pitiful one there?

Because of that.

"Why couldn't you have been yourself with her, just yourself, instead of wanting to show off your claws for that Southern bitch?" Sheila wanted to know.

"That was myself, You just don't know me, lady."

Sheila snorted unhappily and crouched down to escape the hot wind that tore around their car. "You were yourself this afternoon. And I was proud of you. And you're yourself when you're with Jess and Lulie. We should have brought them along to keep you straight. I know you only hurt yourself by being cruel. And tomorrow ..."

It was myself who left Jess and Lulie behind, back where they're safe from me, he thought. But he could not bring himself to say this so that either of them would hear it aloud—and it came to him with a terrible blistering loneliness that always he had had to temper the ultimate finesse of his experience before he could share it with her. "No cruelty, no feast," he said, and he wished that Viola, who would understand that, were with him instead of, or as well as, his own good wife. He needed a multitude—in the instant of being reminded that he had no one.

"Furthermore, Adrienne will be sucking around me tomorrow and will dislike you."

"Only because you say that's how it will be," Sheila flared. "I suppose you're right. You make things come out the way you predict. But why do you have to always get there ahead of me? Why can't we go together on some things? I try and I'm so tired." Suddenly he knew she was crying, and it seemed to him she was crying for Adrienne, seeing herself as Adrienne, the fated object for the unchosen cruelty that had to spice his whole feast of life.

It had seemed to him as they rode that the fertile, inhuman smell of the night had been posing for him those ad hominem questions which alone seemed any more important to him. But with a great wrench of pain, like a crucifixion, it seemed to him that she was the one who posed them—she and his children from her loins. They were not with him against the world. They were the world. He knew. And the liquor in him did not protect—rather, made him more vulnerable to that

493

unutterable torture of the spirit when it finds that its highest achievement is to create a desert solitude around itself.

As he thought this, like a bad omen his penis lifted in a painfully taut erection. It was as if his body were crying out against its desertion.

He swung the little car onto a highway leading out of town. With nerves suddenly strained beyond their limit, he felt the car escaping his control as he accelerated to top speed. The tires screamed on a gentle corner and he slammed across a bridge without quite seeing the white rails on either side of him. Up a long grade and across a forested ridge he held the foot feed on the floorboards.

He took Sheila's hand and led it to his crotch, felt it clutch in fear at the upright support. He put his right hand on her legs.

"Shall I?" he shouted.

He could hardly hear her answer for the roaring of the wind.

"What?"

"Let's not go back," he bellowed.

This time she did not reply, and in a sidelong glance he saw her other hand clinging grimly to the steel door.

He lifted his foot from the accelerator. "Let's go home," he said. Almost with surprise he noted that his erection was gone.

With it had gone the dangerous lovely tension that, he supposed, had made him insult Adrienne before it dared him to put up his life and Sheila's in an absurd gamble where there was nothing to win. And with the tension gone, he hardly remembered that he had done these things. Once again the moment of ecstasy, one of those moments that had been not uncommon once but less frequent as he grew older, dropped out of comprehension like a coin dropping out of sight in dark water.

When he lay down to sleep he was relaxed as after sex—body and mind. But that was one of the funny things about it, for there had been no spasm.

"Good night, darling," he said to Sheila. "I'll be a better lad henceforward. Don't worry."

"It's too late to worry about you," she said, kissing him to make him sleep.

Unquestionably she needled him in the next few days—out of one anxiety understandable enough and another more mysterious.

His mere ebullience touched off the more rational anxiety, for she recognized in it an element of hysteria. They breakfasted in the sorority house next morning with Adrienne Solange. The Southern Lady was quartered there as well, but on this as on following mornings kept her bed until time to meet her students just before lunch.

As Clem had predicted, Adrienne was going out of her way to show that she bore no grudge for last night. And if that was not enough to ruffle Sheila, Clem did so by pinching the girl who served them their bacon and eggs.

Marianne Luce was earning her tuition for the writers' conference that summer by keeping house for the guest lecturers. Before long Clem would give her the nickname Little Employment, a name so rich in its assorted significances that it may serve better for a while than her given name. But she was a complete stranger to him when he lifted her hem, as she reached across the table to serve Adrienne, and set his fingertips keenly in her thigh. Merely to show himself and all the world he loved it still.

"Oh-oh," said Little Employment, who had been pinched before often enough to regard the sting with detachment. "You really meant it, didn't you?"

"Meant which? In the presence of my wife I don't mean anything, young woman."

"What you said in your talk yesterday. That poets can't help it."

"Mr. Anderson's bark is worse than his bite," said Adrienne, who had seen nothing below the level of the table top.

Clem frowned in a fashion that he believed to be professorial. "It? Whatever 'it,' most beautifully, means. Are you talking in Henry James?"

"I'll talk in Henry James if you'll, most splendidly, say something in Anderson," Little Employment offered, with her wise-girl smile. She was not flirting. As Clem would learn, she never flirted. She was engaging, for as much or as little as might come of it. This true candor was what Clem loved her for, from the instant the love began under Sheila's eyes. (And why not under Sheila's eyes? If anyone did, she understood Clem's capacity to love many women, and that would not have troubled her.)

Clem looked pleased. (And why not, when one is so suddenly and unexpectedly in love again?) "Don't let me out of sight or hearing all day long," he advised her. "I feel it coming on me."

"So much?"

"So much."

"So, as it were, splendidly early in the morning?"

"So early. This day, on the Philistine calendar, shall live in infamy."

"That, I allow myself to hope—and perhaps I speak for others among your students—it will."

"You're one of my students?" Clem asked, like a boy given a bicycle for Christmas when all he had asked for was a hoop to roll.

"Disciples," she said. "Bernie Masterson, Will Driever and I, at least, have been crying in the, as it not quite is, wilderness and predicting that the Second Coming was at hand."

"Sit down," Clem said, grabbing her arm. "I can't afford to lose you. It's worth helping you with the dishes for that, eh, Mommy?"

"It's worth it to you," Sheila laughed. Not jealously or with any hint of wifely spite. She would not be jealous any more than Little Employment would flirt. As well as Clem she recognized something fine in the girl from the first, and perhaps from the first innocently wanted Clem to have as much as he wished and could get from her. "My morning's dated full."

Clem did not help the girl do up the breakfast dishes. "I know my place in the orders, sir," she said, refusing his repeated offer—and he hadn't really meant it anyway. While he waited for her to finish her household chores, he read a dozen of her poems, told grinning Adrienne they were "wonderful, wonderful, wonderful," and forgot, in his enthusiasm, any notion he may have had of simplifying what he had to tell the writers in his group.

When he met them, presently, around an oak table in a chalk smelling classroom, it became clear at once that not all of them would measure up to his first lucky find. There was, among his assorted twenty, Fern Passavant, a red-haired, crepe-skinned woman who had written a play called Oil! sometime before the war and had been revising it ever since at the behest of this visiting lecturer or that one. (She had no use for the permanent faculty, nor they for her any more, but she wanted to be a disciple of Clem's, too.) There was Rusty Nims (who presently carried tales to Cheney of the unflattering things Clem said of him) surly and barrel-chested and inclined to measure all literature in terms of its "power."

And there, popped up again, was Mrs. Fothergill—far and away the prettiest woman in the group, but looking, in Clem's estimation, "like the FBI Auxiliary."

Still, as Little Employment had led him to expect that first morning when they ambled classward under the motionless elms of the campus, there were half a dozen splendid people who asked something of him.

They seduced him by their asking, by their excellence. He had never been a teacher before, and if there was one thing he was spectacularly unprepared for it was to find—of a sudden, in Kansas, of all places—that his talent was not the only rabbit running for his life. If he had grown more generous of late than he had been in college (when "someone else's talent" had seemed to him a pure contradiction in terms) he had never before confronted the glut of talent, that ocean not of mediocrity but of excellence, in which so many of this latest generation of Americans were, it seemed, going to get lost and drowned. If there were this many fine poets studying here with him, then, for God's sake, how many hundreds and thousands of others must there be between the coasts?

On the afternoon of his opening talk he had permitted himself the tolerance of seeing young Bernie Masterson as a reincarnation of his own young days. He was stuck with that. But now he found that did not make Bernie special. He was being reincarnated all over the place and either (1) that cheapened the treasure bought so dear by his loneliness, or (2) it laid on him obligations of leadership, of amiable counsel, that he thought his loneliness had freed him from.

Before he quite understood the choice that every teacher has to make between reserve and candor, it seemed that the choice had already been made for him, and he did not know how to hold anything back. These puppies had him by the scruff of the neck and were shaking him as if they meant to have his soul out. They had him for only two weeks. In that two weeks they wanted—worse than that, needed and had rights to—that fertile pip of truth that he had kept hidden from all his other lovers and ravishers, even Sheila.

I am not quite sure how this peril began to dawn on Sheila. Marriage, like any other stable institution, is the enemy of insights. So when Sheila first guessed that Clem was going to expose more of himself to these careless young than he had for a long time exposed to her, she must have been frightened. I opened my body and my life for him, and he held something back—it is hard for any woman not to feel the unfairness of such an exchange. And when she began to think that Clem might have—probably had—withheld his humilities and his fears for her sake, somewhere in her began the ache and terror of inadequacy.

In this trap she would turn again on herself, using the hints he could not help giving, with the accusation that she had, after all, lived all these years of their marriage in the comfort of protection, while she had assumed equality and honesty between them always. Surely if she had endured the shock of his wartime letters she had watched to the bottom of his anguish without being shaken. But no, there were caves under caves and endless series of recesses, immeasurably treacherous.

Like a spendthrift's wife on the day before the reckoning, she sensed the enormous debts that he should have told her about. She would guess now—begin to guess—that they had been willfully postponed until they had become nearly calamitous. She began to guess that the price of stability had been recklessness, not caution. She would guess that he had risked what must be most precious to him so that they could enjoy some outward show of bourgeois security. And what hurt most seriously was that now she must overhear things he might have told her if he trusted her enough.

If he had ever trusted her enough. Like most doubts, the doubt beginning in her mind was retroactive. She had consoled herself against the strain and trouble of being married to Clem—and had there not been nights when she woke to envy her older sisters the lawyer and the sporting-goods salesman they had married?—because it had seemed to provide the rock bottom of honesty that now she knew it to lack. Now to hear hints that it had been a fool's paradise worse than her sisters'. Too much. A fool's paradise ought not to have demanded of either of them all they had already paid.

The conference had been organized so that each of the visitors would have his own group of students. Once a day these met separately, though there were evening meetings open to all and to interested townspeople. Clem's students, as Sheila saw, began to coalesce into a faction with stunning swiftness, as if they had been partisans waiting for a leader so that they could show their colors. Quickly it was clear that Little Employment's word, "disciples," was not altogether a joke. Clem's young intimates unabashedly kindled from their first exposures to him—no doubt because he started dispensing genuine blood.

The first morning he met them in their designated classroom the talk swung to and came to a halt on Marvell's "The Garden." "The Garden" became their poem in a silly, wonderful way, and it appears that his mind opened in a kind of ecstatic relaxation to show them

*that Ocean where each kind*

*Doth straight its own resemblance find.*

I have often reflected—remotely—how a teacher's relation to his students verges on, or at least resembles, a sexual one. (There is more than propinquity to blame when one of our young instructors finds himself suddenly to be the lover of one or more of his charges. For

498

some temperaments there is no greater erotic stimulus than discovering a virgin mind ready to open to the caress of the intellect.) And in the case of which I am speaking I suppose that Sheila began to understand the sexual tint of the intercourse before Clem did. If he would eventually understand it more deeply than any of them, he would still have entered into it more naively. As he said, he often "came late to my own experiences," and when the mutual seduction of class and teacher began he would merely have been laving himself in its ambiguous warmth, releasing his hermaphroditic talents in sheer exuberance.

Sheila was, of course, not surprised to find him ganging with students rather than the other visitors. ("God made me an enlisted man," he said.) She was still rather more amused than concerned when he set up a kind of command post at Henley's U Tap, across the street from the main campus. She wouldn't have wanted him to turn into a pedantic sort of pedant. If pedantry there must be, a flow of beer and summery spirits could come nearest to redeeming it. Even when she was annoyed by not being able to find him, she was glad to think that he and some student might be crouched under a hedge or behind a flower bed on the campus destroying his schedule as he told what a stupid heller he had been in college or enjoyed with the student the goodies the latter had planted in the verse he offered Clem for criticism. It was a case of love at first sight, this affair between him and his students. She looked on for a while like a tolerant parent.

But who does not know that conscience comes from love? So it always was with Clem, and the revelations that grated on Sheila began to come faster when Clem began to feel his responsibilities to these young people. He began to feed himself to them, morsel by morsel. She thought, Don't give away what's mine.

When the happy shock of discovering how good his students were had lost its first blush, loving Clem began to worry about their futures as writers. He had reached a point—call it Paris, call it personal detachment—from which he could see so much better than they the awesome riddle presented to those who identify themselves to themselves as writers. While they never asked it of him, he took it on himself to try imagining a way through for them. It was all right for him to look down on a promised land he would never enter, but what's so promised about it if the led sheep can't get in, either?

They did not ask the loving anxiety he worked up in himself. For example, was it evident that Little Employment wanted more from him than to know if her poems were "good"? (Not evident to her. She did not ask to be told anything. She only wanted to listen, but he could not believe that.) She must know, he told himself, that the poems were good, just as she knew the excitement of the hours when they had emerged into form. Anyone who wrote as well as she must understand that the opinion of others is not a final—perhaps not even an important—measure. Fame certainly is not a plant that grows on mortal soil. But then, what soil? If he could not help her plant her foot on that terre arable, wouldn't her wandering foot be followed by a body tumbling through empty space?

She did not seem to think so. She understood a marriage of minds when she entered one. Asked nothing more.

He asked for her. "What are you doing here?" he asked insistently. The crude demand that only anxious frustration would be foolish enough to make.

"Enjoying myself," Little Employment said. "Enjoying, most splendidly, myself and passing, not too awfully, the time." It was all she would admit to, smiling from her wise blue eyes at him. It was not enough for him to accept for her. So he had to meet her and the gang for another long evening in the bar, mining deeper in himself in the hope that his pick would knock out the answer to the riddle.

He felt the same frustration with Bernie Masterson. Of course, part of the frustration could be worked out by tampering with, making suggestions for, Bernie's poems. But was this lapidary polishing of any real value? Perhaps already Bernie's poems had been carried as far as they should be. Many skills had already been incorporated in them. Bernie had read all the poets who counted for his time, including Clem Anderson. He had known how to borrow what was usable to him.

But why, Clem found ways to demand of Bernie, if he was all he obviously was as a human being, did he want to use all that in being a poet? Bernie saw no sweat in the question. Clem did.

It was about the third evening when Sheila sat in a beer tavern near the campus listening to Clem try to disillusion Bernie Masterson and Will Driever. (Sheila was "always welcome" in Clem's little gang, though she could not always stand the pace, nor appreciate the tendency of what she heard.)

Glib Clem was straining the seams of his glibness—trying to launch a sparrow of honesty from the back of the eagle—to convince the young men that poetry was both less and more than they could (yet) guess it to be. But that the poet's problem was not, as once, merely to write and love poetry.

Half in beery fun and half in beery anguish, as it seemed to Sheila, he defined "unscrupulousness" as being, in our time, a specific symptom of poetic power. He professed himself, again, a vulture-lover and insisted that such success as he had or would have came from willingness to eat anything.

"Even dog. The secret now dawning on poets is 'dog eat dog,'" he urged. "The poem defined by its most evident attribute is 'the thing not wanted.' Tut!" he said, lifting his hand in a professorial gesture he would never have used in the classroom. "The space of a poem, the smidgen it consumes of printed space that might be devoted to another poem is wanted, and the bibliographic testimony that a poem has existed is wanted. The occasion when your poem may be deluged down on the head of a captive audience is wanted. The fact of having written is wanted by a society hot with the instinct to do honor and having all too few scapegoats and kings; and the love's labor of writing is wanted by the sexed-up poet in his hours of tumescence. But the poem itself, that which comes of all this component of forces that try to drag it into being, is not wanted.

"Tut! Bad enough if Momma, Poppa, your girl and the editor of yon magazine—the space friend of poets on the make—do not want it. But what if nature itself, ultimately replete with verse, has no more room for it? Suppose that poets have used up their world before evening. It may be that the world did not last as long for poets, after all, as for atomic scientists, those notorious laggards. Are there so many poems possible? Nature said, 'Sing.' Did she say 'forever'? Nature has Keats's odes and Yeats's mighty modern song and all—one would think—the starry feys of lesser intensity needed for the train. Will you make those poems again? Will you pretend they do not already exist? Why are you needed if the job is done?

"Tut! I know you hungry generations are committing to paper that which we still call the poem. By the thousands and by the ream. To what throne will all this mail be delivered? It will not be. It is a basket of trash scattered in great space. But you tell me that there are still, multiplying also like flies in the shambles, readers."

"I have read Clem Anderson's verse," Bernie staunchly insisted. "I'll read it again."

"Flattery!" Clem beamed insidiously. "Yes. Now he begins to understand 'unscrupulousness.' Flattery, how I love it. Flattery, that gadget among the implements of intercourse, the wonder drug that makes us susceptible to diseases unheard of in the wholesome days of the Black Death. Flattery, yes! Now we have come, poets, to the Field of the Cloth of Gold where the myriad democratic singers will contest for the laureate's mantle, the verse emperor's new clothes, to be worn with the same distinction as the mantle of actorship is worn by the highest paid nymph or relative in Hollywood. For art must be aristocratic, in Hollywoodland or in next year's Little Treasury, and we have no longer, milling in the streets, outside the replete poetic granary, any better way of nobling the aristocracy than by payment. Cash, simple cash, and flattery. All arts approach the condition of wrestling, where the superior is the creation of consent engineers.

"Tut! Don't bother to point out the gravy-spotted tweeds and battered Chevrolets that are the nun-garb of even the most venerable or tell me that poets do not winter in Miami or Las Vegas. There are subtler ways of payment."

"Such as with honest respect," Bernie said. "Don't you honestly respect a lot of poets still alive?"

"When I am allowed to, yes," Clem said. "Stop throwing red herrings before swine. The true payment and coin for being a noble in poetry today and in the coming age is nevertheless flattery, which you may call respect and change nothing, for the only right payment is fame, which we are reminded is not a plant that grows on mortal soil, let alone on the rich black shit from which success henceforth springs.

"Therefore, young poet, youth in search, do not, I admonish you, read Longinus on the sublime, Horace on the art of poetry, Wordsworth, Coleridge, Valéry or the New Critics more than is politic. Read, for scripture and private guidance, Stendhal; read Père Goriot; read The Prince. For your success will be political, and the chairs of poetry will fall or maintain themselves by pure unscrupulousness.

"Put money in your purse. Think when the sun comes up tomorrow that this is only Kansas. Get you to a nobler school of English and seek preferment there. That way will lead to an acquaintance with the present laureates, who will be anxious to choose as successors those in whose verse and eminence their own names will be gilt with flattery.

"Learn that within the modern art of poetry there is the craft of ritual mention. If your preceptors mention black crosses, the Old Man or the Golden Bowl, you mention 'dun staves crossed' and 'him at the pickaxe crucifixion,' 'crystal with its thin veneer of gold.' However obscure the allusion, make sure the shibboleths are mentioned, for this will show that you have been admitted to the privacy and be your code sign.

"Be hygienic in your care not to mention proscribed things. Read Whitman through in order that, for the moment, you will mention nothing mentioned in his great mail-order catalogue. And if among the dogs running at your heels you find a violation of the code, however trivial or important, single it out for a review article, cautiously praising it. As, 'Alabastor Crinoline, whose two previous books were distinguished by eloquence and limpidity of diction, but unfortunately confined by rhythms all too often reminiscent of Hopkins or Fulke Greville, has in his latest work found his own voice in celebrating the Whitmanesque virtues of the Pennsylvania Quakers from whom he sprang.'

"There! You have caught him on the hip! Alabastor might as well pulp his edition. He's had the pink slip. You've caught him in Rats Alley, where the painters lost their subject matter. The next time he appears in print it will be with an outright steal from Wessex Poems, so pitifully plagiarized, down to the last substituted trochee, that you won't even have to do the dirty work yourself. Let the bastard go immerse himself in translations!

"Meanwhile, faithful to the motto 'Homo homini canis,' you will crouch closer to the Wall Streeters of poetry who are preparing for the time of the great shake-out, when the crumbs among poets will be scattered like small investors to the winds, and the bears will come down. Be prepared, young poet, to mention everything in Whitman and to disparage Hardy's roughness."

"Yeah," Bernie said, "but I don't want to."

"'Paris vaut une messe.' What are you, a yellow poet?"

Little Employment, who had been watching with love and belief, said, "Is that how you got your stripes, Sergeant Anderson?"

"My stripes," he said, wagging and lolling his head like a small lion wounded. "My stripes. Yes, my stripes. My stripes."

"I don't want success," Bernie said.

"What do you want, then?"

"To write good poetry."

"God help the deaf! Look, I have done some writing. It pleased me. Once it pleased me and I thought it pleased others. It was printed. Ugh. Nice things were said about it. In print. But is that a realistic story about a writer? Shit. The real story is always and is now at this bloody conference of ours that I was a poet who had such and such number of chips—things printed, spaces filled—so I could sit in on the game.

"Put it another way, as I did before. I ate dog some. I was a fierce competitor while young. But I tell you this: If I had eaten more dog I might have saved myself from eating human flesh. Which is the wrong that poets do."

By this time he was, as they all might have thought if they wished, drunk—high on the beer after beer he had been gulping like a hot engine trying to cool itself. Or if they had wished to see it so and keep it to themselves, since it was unexpressible, they might have thought him ecstatic, like an Indian making his war brag. At any rate, he was intensely with them and superlatively alone.

"Which is the wrong that poets do," he went on. "What do you mean to do?" he asked of Bernie, probably for no better reason than that Bernie was seated directly across the table from him. "Marry some nice girl who is innocent enough to want you to write poetry? And eat her up? Lean on some good, innocent old man who hasn't learned, cannot accept, that poems have become chips in a shoddy power game? And eat him up? You're young enough to take my warning. Don't do it."

Little Employment threw a veiled glance at Sheila, who seemed hardly nibbled at, certainly uneaten. Sheila was not very happy at the reference to herself, but was willing to assign it to many immediate vexations. She recognized the bigger part of what he had been saying as an extension of what he had once heard from Bentley—and wondered only why, since he had chosen to live, he should live with an extension of the old man's pessimism.

Bernie remembered later the impassioned tone—and that all the beer they had drunk had seemed to "elevate" Clem's language, though all of them by now were used to sudden shifts as if a score of lexicons were on permanent tap to express Clem's chosen inflection. He remembered Clem as sounding that night "like Timon cursing" and finally, when he knew more about the situation, attributed it to Clem's uncertainty about the fate of his play. No word had come yet from New York, and that was enough to exasperate anyone.

Only when they were alone together that night, undressing in the sorority house, Sheila said, intending comfort, "You haven't eaten me up, old boy."

Clem said quietly, dangling a sock from his right hand, "Then where have you gone?"

"Oh," Sheila said.

In the next few days, Sheila tried to coax him into relaxation. "You don't have to woo your students," she told him. "They're yours. The ones you want."

"I'm not trying to woo them."

"No. What are you trying to do?"

"To see something. Myself. I'm stretching my neck. It hurts."

504

"You mustn't worry about whether your play gets bought."

He looked surprised. "I'm not. I couldn't care less. What about you?"

She would not answer directly. "You deserve it," she said.

"We deserve it? I know," he said, hearing the note of fatigue in both their voices, in the turn the conversation had taken. Frightened by the implication that the trip of his life was done when he had not yet seen what he was ready to see.

She thought he was "hatching," hearing the first themes of a new work he wanted to start on. It had happened this way before—a remoteness, a superficial surliness, an outward lack of direction which would gradually turn to happiness when the project clarified. But when she had occasion to ask him if this was it, he said, "No. Nothing. That's probably what's scaring me."

Nevertheless, there were no open quarrels between them in the first week. To an extent they went their own ways—but no more than they often had. Sheila felt mildly put upon that she must be Clem's emissary to his colleagues. She had to sit agreeing with Cheney's eupeptic opinions of the literary scene when Clem failed to show up for the dinner that one member or another of the faculty had arranged. (While she and Cheney both knew that somewhere Clem was repeating the same opinions for jokes.) She had to accept solicitude from Adrienne Solange—and an offer to put her in touch with a publisher of children's books—until Adrienne left. Had to appreciate the hauteur of the Southern Lady. But she considered this her duty. Nothing worried her but Clem's malaise, his jumpiness, and if he wasn't going to explain that to her, he would have to work it out himself.

Through that first week her conviction deepened that he might have been much better off if he had come alone. She felt herself, perhaps for the first time since the war, a stone around his neck, and when she felt this it was as if a stimulating drug had been withdrawn from her. She had to pay with nerve and spirit for what had so long been easy between them.

Then, on the Sunday that marked the halfway point of the conference, there came a reason (or an excuse—neither of them would ever be sure which it was) for Sheila to leave him there alone.

A phone call from Sheila's mother informed them that Lulie was sick. Oh, nothing much. Evidently it was only a touch of summer flu. But the poor little thing had been throwing up for two days and her bottom was raw from constant diarrhea. Her usual vitality was gone and the change in her spirits had demoralized the grandparents. No, there was no need for Sheila or Clem to worry. The doctor had been in to give Lulie a shot of penicillin and paint her crotch with gentian violet. But apparently Sheila's mother needed bucking up.

It seemed to Sheila that her mind was already made up when she heard the substance of the call. She told her mother she would fly back to Indiana that evening if she could get a reservation. When she hung up the phone she turned with an odd, sly grin, confronting Clem with the fait accompli of her decision.

"We'll both go," he said.

"There isn't any need."

"Then there's no need for you to go. We'll only be here another week."

"I want to go. I'm tired of this."

"Then we'll both go."

"No. I'll stay if that's the way you feel," she said. But she did not mean to settle the argument that way. She had sensed now that he wanted her to go. He wouldn't have protested so much except to cover the guilt of wanting her out of his road.

"We ought to be together when we get the news about my play," he said.

She smiled. "The way to bring on good news is run from it. I always expect to hear my good news from you by telephone."

"Level with me. Why shouldn't we both go?"

It dug the gulf between them a little deeper that he should persist in the game when she was trying so hard to give him what he wanted. "You're needed here," she said, a bit sarcastically. "It's evident that I'm not."

"Oh ho."

"Oh ho what? Can't we agree any more on such a small matter?"

"We can agree on anything," he said then lightly, with a deep despondency and disgust with himself for losing his power to hide anything from her. "Let's call Wichita and see about a plane."

"Then you'll be left free to romp with your little friends, to pinch the girlies your own mental age." Was this something she had to say, something long latent, bursting at last through a small flaw in the surface of their lives? Or was it an extravagance of the moment, purely offhand? What frightened him more than anything else was that it didn't matter which it was. Like a loaded gun the accusation had been proffered them, dangerous to them both.

"Don't wear that one out, Mommy," he said. "What have I done? I pinched Little Employment. So. She's a good girl. We play Henry

James. I help her with the breakfast dishes. We talk high. Doesn't that leave her virtuous?"

"She's good," Sheila agreed. Then it seemed to her she knew what it was that was hurting them both. "There are so many good little girls," she said. That was it. A platitude and nothing more, but a platitude in which her pride must founder. The chariot of years had driven up to this trivial moment and stopped to deliver the message that she could give him nothing beyond what he could get and could have had from a thousand others.

And he wondered, more outraged than he dared admit, that she should have been seeing here in eye-opening Kansas so many "good little girls" while he had been seeing so many "good little poet souls"—he really had, and he could have told her truly that all but one of his erections had been of the spirit. He would wonder later if there was not an ill-omened parallel between her woman's relation to women and his writer's relation to writers. She is so much the body of my life, he thought. Her sex is my art. They are the same, but cast wondrously and terribly in different materials. And he would remember that first night here when he might have driven them off the road as the given moment when he might have forever wed body and spirit. But he had seen her hanging on, and he had let their moment pass.

"So there are," he said quietly, quietness hiding his rage.

"You never noticed?" she mocked. She had to make him share her hurt.

"I noticed."

"I don't reproach you, you know."

"I know." But he knew, too, or thought he knew, that the reproach was there, ad hominem, mute as an unfired gun, but waiting in the nature of things for a voice to speak it. Perhaps he already knew that the terms of his service, the pact he had signed long ago, obliged him sooner or later to become the agonist of such unspeakable disharmonies.

At this first apparent beginning of their estrangement, there was no more question of his loving her than there ever was later or ever had been before. His heart might cry out now, and a thousand times, "Non serviam," but he had never been more keenly aware that he was obligated to some truth that was not the heart's.

When she flew out of Kansas that evening, under a bar of pansy-black cloud that hid the sundown, she left him reproached, despondent, liberated, penitent, full of resolutions to be good, and full of whimsical zeal to break his resolutions as quickly as possible.

He drove back from Wichita to find, like a portent, that a telegram had come for him from New York. Carpenter had signed to play the lead in *Death and the Devil*. The money bags were slit, the loot would come pouring in. The backers would stand at attention. As far as he knew then, he and Sheila would soon be standing ankle-deep in money. One of the big breakthroughs he had probed for had happened, and— nothing. It opened on nothing, and he knew this then. The wall was down between him and fame, and his soul would not go through the breach. He could not drive it through. Like a perverse colt it bolted away from the gap, looking for a fence it could try to jump.

Whatever had been anxiety about his play's future became a kind of delirium. He called Indiana and talked to Jess and Sheila's mother, planting the "good news" so that it would be there to greet Sheila on her arrival. And knew that was not enough.

It was not exactly to share the news—for the real news that came to him that day was unsharable—that he hunted out Little Employment and took her for a ride. When he kissed her on a dark side street there was a moment of unastonished but questioning pause in which she seemed to be asking, Why are you doing this? He could not answer, because no one ever says it this way except to himself: because my daughter is sick and I've got to fight back, because my life is sick and I've got to fight.

Presently she said in a practical way, "It's going to rain." So they went to a motel.

While the unleashed storm spoiled the seat of his sports car and hammered hail against the siding of the motel, she took him on out of sheer good nature, because he seemed unhappy and upset when his wife left, and because it was a way of, most pleasurably, passing the time. When he mounted her, for a little while, it did not seem that he was fighting back at anything.

"Well," she said when they were through, "we have, most beautifully, done it."

"And now know what, all ambiguities aside, old Henry J. had, somewhere in his inviolable mind, when he, so frequently, beautifully, used that pronoun."

"Now we know," she said, sitting up beside him and shrugging her shoulders so that her small breasts quivered on her large torso like waking birds.

"And what are we going to do about it?"

The quality of her silence was that of a thoughtful child. "I suppose you mean to trifle with the exordia of thoughts tending toward marriage."

"I'd sure like to marry you," Clem said. "I'd like to marry them all."

Her laughter sounded more comfortable than sleep in the heat and the half-dark, the aftermath of the storm raised by Kansas elves. "Poor old man. You take things too hard. I knew you'd be this way."

"You've been, then, speculating?"

"Indeed. And I doubt if I'm the only one in your class who has."

"Name, if you please, others."

"Well ..." Her pause was the audible equivalent of a knotted brow. "The so superior Mrs. Fothergill has been wearing more eye shadow than, in this heat, sticks to a perspiring skin."

"You can tell by that?"

"That she'd go to bed with you?" Little Employment laughed again, melodiously. "Dear man, no. Heavens. I'm not that kind of prophet. I'm more like you as a prophet, always, always wrong about practical details, but always right otherwise."

"Have I described myself that way?"

"You've said so much since you've been here. You mustn't think it's not heard or understood. We're out there in front of you, whether you notice us or not."

"I notice you," he said. "Mrs. Fothergill?"

"Well ... I have the feeling that she packed her diaphragm in with her rhyming dictionary, you know. She left her husband in Wichita."

"You don't like her," Clem said.

"You're right, I don't. Bernie and I had, about her, a big powwow. We think she's, if the right word were used, a bitch. She means to have her cake and eat it. Best of two impossible worlds, to put it in Anderson."

"I too am imitable."

"You're not, really," Little Employment said, kissing him. "But I think she'd like you to kneel. She thinks of you as a sort of Father Zossima, and she's ... a venereal Karamazov, if you know what I mean. She'd use you—as, be assured, neither Bernie nor I, nor Ellen Noble, Gretchen Fife or Will Driever or anyone else good would."

"You're all supposed to use me," Clem said.

"Yes. But not up."

They dawdled in companionable silence, holding hands and listening to the whine of tires in the wet outside their cubicle. It was so brief, their garden moment—when before and after were only delicacies held by the mind like grapes and strawberries proffered by cupidons at the apotheosis of the flesh. Clem thought of telling her his "good news"—the latest news about his play—but saw that plainly it would seem an impertinence here. "How vainly men themselves amaze ..." The little time between one spasm and the next seemed, in the assurance that there would be another, time itself, the privileged sanctuary of survey without consequences; seemed like babyhood; seemed like death in those apprehensions that sense death to be a shedding     away     of     the     tormenting     will.

"You don't like Mrs. Fothergill, so you figure her as ready to bed with me. Don't you like yourself?"

"Oh, boy," Little Employment said. "Now I'm beginning to understand the older generation. You're the most explosive, inconsistent, unscrupulous bundle of idiosyncrasies I've ever seen. Notwithstanding which, you're a devil for consistency, and probably for loyalty too, and are chewing yourself for being, at this moment, where your good wife doesn't know you are. Provided she doesn't, which she hardly could, exactly. But, to answer your question, I am, in spite of inconsistencies, right now fairly fond of myself. And to answer your other question, What are we going to do about it?—you don't even have to give me an A. What we are going to do about it is," she said, "again."

In the unrushed repetition she found occasion to murmur, "You do it with, one must observe, relish."

"Doesn't everyone?"

She answered with a flattering laugh.

Driving her home through streets running tire-deep with water and under the street lamps still dripping the diamond aftermath of the rain, he said, "No one ever told me that adultery could be so consummately sweet."

"No one ever told you a lot of things," she said gravely. "In spite of all you know—and you know yourself, I think, in infinitely more detail and scope than anyone else I've met—there are such a lot of things more you don't know."

"I want to know them all," he said with a hoarse pain that shocked her. He slowed the car for a cross-street dip where the black water ran ahead of them lively as a mountain stream. In spite of slackened speed they sent up a drenching shower of spray as they crossed. He pounded the steering wheel with both fists. "You know something? They'll never drag me out of life until I know it all. I'll kick like a calf they're trying to shove out of a truck."

"Who's trying?" she asked, laying her silver-touch fingertips in the crook of his arm.

"You're not."

"Nor ever shall," she said. "Don't brood about tonight. Or think you were unfaithful, or whatever you might think. Remember, I don't ask anything. Say hello to me at breakfast in the morning if you want to. I'd be pleased if you did."

When he let her out at the white frame house in which she shared a room, she leaned down to kiss him once more and said, "Sleep well"— as if she had, just that simply, meant to give him the specific that would permit it.

Beyond any doubt he recognized this Little Employment. The silver stream of impunity had been described again and again in the stories his psyche told him of itself. Here, in wondrous flesh, was the "other bride," the Rachel of his years with Leah, the figure of shadowless light who had always lurked in the corner of his eyes when he walked to those other women whose demands goaded him to the torments of conscience and creation.

On the surface of things there is absolutely no visible reason why he should not have enjoyed in Kansas, with Sheila gone, a pastoral idyl, a garden interlude. True, his dalliance with Little Employment might have had a superficially shameful side, but the fears that made him reject it were the opposite of superficial.

The summer cup was held to his lips. He had only to take it, pro-merit, as it were, a little adultery as a reward for being faithful so long. Sheila might have been grateful if he had.

But he could not take it as offered. He had to—had to—make something of it. The fear of leaving well enough alone was too closely akin to his fear of psychic death to let him rest.

When he rose from the sweet sleep that Little Employment had given him, he must rush out on the small world of the conference like the Assyrian descending on the fold, like a sick man, sick with something beyond Little Employment's power to guess—beyond anyone's power at that time.

It was as if he had recognized her as goodness come once more to promise that evil lay ahead—or else he used her in that way, using the moment of retreat that she had given him as the recoil in preparation for an unimaginable leap.

It happened that on the morning following there was again a general assembly of all students and lecturers of the conference. And Clem took this occasion to offend Cheney gravely by referring, in front of everyone, to Cheney's heavily documented novels as horse operas. Cheney might have brought suit if he had been called an artist, but he did not want, either, to be called a hack. Considerably upset, he took his complaint to Felix Martin, who, in turn, spoke to Clem.

"Did we come here to mislead the young?" Clem asked.

Felix properly said that was not the issue. The lecturers had been chosen to represent diverse points of view in the hope that out of dialectic there might be some synthesis of light. No doubt common politeness would best further that end.

To which Clem replied that he could have invented Cheney, while Cheney could not have invented him, and that, somehow, this gave him the responsibility of clarifying Cheney's limitations. Whether he liked Cheney or not had nothing to do with it. All this talk about "synthesis" was fraud, as Felix very well knew. What happened when you synthesized truth with error was, plainly, error.

Gravely Felix agreed. Only it appeared to him that for anyone to claim possession of the truth might be dangerously close to the sin of pride.

Clem said distraughtly that it was the very opposite of pride. It was an agony of humiliation, barely supportable—supportable only if it could be shared, or to the extent that it could be shared.

But he would apologize—why not?—to Cheney. Which he did, stooping to plead concern for his sick child and his wife's absence in such a way that Cheney was put on his honor to forgive, but was left, as he slowly came to realize, with a stiletto handle protruding from his shoulderblades. For the last week of the conference Cheney dared not shift his eyes from those of even his humblest interlocutor for fear of catching a smirk when he looked again. He began to brag about the sales of his books. He philosophized more desperately about the "web of history" which he tried to depict in his writing.

In brief, he was driven to such foolishness that even mild Thomas Wilder got fed up with him and said so to his best students. The fire of faction was in the brush. Clem had put it there, but a surprising number of mouths were ready to blow on it. A small clique of homosexuals who had suffered in resentful silence Cheney's manly diatribes against the "homosexual clique" began actively to rumor that both Clem and Cheney were latently gay. The implication was that in Clem this was delightful, while on Cheney's part it explained his "confusion."

The Southern Lady, who had thus far veiled her humors behind a fan of elegant persiflage, sought Clem out before the day was over and poured into his ear her grievances against Cheney.

He had given out, she said, that she was still fighting the Civil War, while the truth was exactly the opposite. He had told some of her students that he couldn't read either James or Proust, as if that were a criticism of those masters rather than a sign of his own stupidity. He had been heard to speak of Faulkner's characters as degenerates. Well! On the night before the conference ended she was going to read a paper on Faulkner, and she would hurl that misprision back in Cheney's teeth. For her part, she might go so far as to say that she couldn't read Hemingway, whom Cheney was—still!—holding up as a model for young writers. She would say that as far as she was concerned, no subject in fiction, unless it was table tennis, was less rewarding than bullfighting. Clem must be there to witness the coup de grâce.

Did Clem really agree with her? Whether he did or not, he drank bourbon for bourbon with her through the hot waning of the afternoon and through the dinner hour. Presently he found himself with her at the same motel to which he had brought Little Employment the night before. ("I'm a merman," he explained to the gaunt Kansan who registered him in again with an inquisitive peek at the other occupant of the sports car. "Every man to his own religion," the fellow said.)

Of this encounter by night, Clem remembered only that the Southern Lady had nearly broken his back with a scissor hold and that they had whistled a duet of "Dixie" in a vain attempt to coax what she called, with Anglophiliac snobbery, a second "stand." They were expelled from the tolerant court sometime after midnight for practicing the Rebel yell.

The next day Clem sensed in the bleary air that Cheney and Thomas Wilder had been busy propagandizing while the irresponsibles left them the field. It seemed that one had said Clem was "on his way to the Cross," while the other had more than hinted that he was on his way to the asylum.

When Clem's group met in their classroom for their regular before-lunch session, Fern Passavant asked him to declare himself as between these two interpretations. (Her drama Oil! was an expression of her ardent materialism, and if Mr. Anderson's criticisms were papist in tendency, it was clear to her why they had helped her so little.)

Shakily Clem dodged. From the profundity of his hangover he began to decry all the minorities that dammed the mainstream.

And was promptly, smilingly attacked by Mrs. Fothergill, whose strong impression it was that Clem himself was very much the kind of cliquish, internationalist writer he was now pretending to oppose.

"Can't you declare where you yourself stand?" she said, tugging down the corner of her bright mouth to unsheathe a beautifully long canine tooth.

Feeling himself trapped, Clem's eyes sought those of Little Employment, seated far down the barren expanse of conference table. Those eyes were as unanswering as the blue sky of the Kansas morning, and he remembered he had not even, since their night, said hello to her at breakfast, for the not irreproachable reason that he had not since then been to breakfast.

Mrs. Fothergill pouted impatiently. "I've been listening several days with great interest, and I frankly don't know just where you are, what you represent. Are you on the way to the Cross? I mean, Where is poetry going?" She looked around the table for support. Fern Passavant nodded vehement approval, the two redheads looking like the crone and maiden versions of Morgan le Fay.

Clem tried to parry. But as if she knew she had him running, Mrs. Fothergill refused to give up. "We've talked about everything under the sun. Marvell's 'Garden' is running out of my ears."

Fern Passavant cackled. As if Marvell had anything to do with Oil!

Mrs. Fothergill said, "It would help us all organize what you've said if you dropped your mask and gave us a less ... shimmery picture of what you're driving at." Well aimed, then, the shaft that she had been withholding so long. Here, in the moment of weakness that he had brought on himself (oh, yes, perhaps intentionally) she was saying for all the class exactly what he had said, for their sakes, to himself. If he did not see his way through to a justifiable end for poetry, saw no longer a reason to go ahead, how dared he bid them follow? The whole class, even Mrs. Fothergill's detractors, seemed urgently to press for the answer he didn't have.

Clem consulted the three-pronged ache of hangover in his body, the too bright glitter of sun falling from high windows onto the desert top of the table, the unwashed stickiness in his crotch, the beak deep word of memory having at his inward lights, then sighed dramatically. "Presumptuous of me to say I am on the way to the Cross." There was a breath of laughter from Bernie and Will Driever, cornflower-blue approval from Little Employment's eyes. For them he went on, "But if that is the will of things, tell it in Gath and Ascalon that I was seen to be dragging my feet."

His people laughed because this was their Clem talking. Mrs. Fothergill laughed because they did. Fern Passavant resolved to restore Oil! to the state it had been in before Clem came.

In his lightest inflection Clem said, "My inability to answer is your answer, children. Remember that well. Look—you are looking at my strength and you see that it is impotence. Will the Veiled Lady prey on those who offend her? Is it the Hound of Heaven or the Hound of the Baskervilles that is baying on my track? Watch with me. If it's really worth it to you. I don't know where I'm going. You will know. But not until morning." He flung his hands out in a missa est gesture and called, "Bernie, let's get some beer."

His escape was not to be so easy. Between him and the door, between his need and the comfortable, beer-smelling darkness of Henley's U Tap across the street from the campus, Mrs. Fothergill stepped to ask one more question.

"My poems," she said. "I've waited with admirable patience to be summoned into the presence for my turn and a discussion of my work. Were they so bad you've been putting me off?"

He opened his mouth to say that the reason he had not yet conferred with her was that she had given him no manuscript. But as he stared at the precision of her well-cut jawbone and the relentlessness of her eyes he understood that she was the kind of person who certainly would have given him a manuscript on the day of their first meeting.

And had.

He remembered tactilely the heavy bond paper and then remembered the perfect typing. He had not read the poems, but he remembered the typing.

He had taken poems from her, all right, but now he had not the faintest idea of what had happened to them. He knew well enough they were not among the litter of papers and books on his table at the sorority house. Long ago, as a defensive measure against his habitual sloppiness, he had developed a trick of mentally photographing the wildest disarray of papers, so that out of a trash heap that anyone else would have burned forthwith he could usually plunge straight to what he wanted. Provided, of course, that what he wanted was there. He was sure this manuscript wasn't, and among the wayward possibilities that flocked into his mind was that Sheila, packing, must somehow have gathered up Mrs. Fothergill's poems and carried them off, leaving him in this way, too, exposed to the unforgiving young.

"If that's all that's bothering you ..." It didn't seem to be. She was staring at him as if she knew he had lost her work. He put his hand out to pat her shoulder. She drew away. Coaxingly he said, "You come have beer with us and a little knackwurst. We'll find time this very afternoon to go over them in detail. For the moment suffice it to say I thought there were some remarkable lines, at the very least, in each of them."

"Not too reminiscent of Stevens?" she asked with a coy, sideward twist of her head.

He thought it safe to say her poems had hardly reminded him of Stevens at all. But that was the end, the extreme margin of his safety. He tried to assemble his whole claque for a defense in depth around him. Bernie and Will Driever would come along. When he asked Little Employment she said, "I really, in the circumstances, mustn't." Then, seeing him look so woeful, added, "No one's mad at you. Don't believe that."

While the knackwurst and sauerkraut went down, washed with steins and pitchers of beer, Mrs. Fothergill sat with them in a kind of suspended intensity that was neither patience nor impatience but, rather, something like a cat's beautiful poise of nonchalance while it waits for the mouse to come out of the hole.

Three or four times in the course of the lunch Clem reassured her that "presently" they would go to his office and talk about the poems she had given him. But each time he began to yield to the comforting thought that the poems were about to be forgotten, he would start up with the realization that it was he who was forgetting them, not she.

Perhaps early in that afternoon, he entertained the hope that she would become fogged with the beer they kept on drinking when the lunch was over. No chance. He was drinking three glasses to her one. He might have thought the sheer good-humored laziness to which the others abandoned themselves would drive her away in disgust. She joined it. She appeared to join it. She laughed at their jokes and took part in their talk about movie stars they had each idolized as children. But she was waiting.

Will Driever began a story about his widowed mother, who, years ago had moved to this university town with the intent of continuing her studies and keeping her only son near "educational advantages." For years she had run a rooming house a quarter mile from the campus, and by now she was studying art, having finished—or, rather, had done with—child guidance, religion and political science in that order, each field having reflected an unquenchable determination that Will should have a better life than his father (who had fallen from a boxcar in '31 on his way to Kansas City to look for work). In his early childhood she had studied him as child psyche. Shortly after Pearl Harbor she had switched to the school of religion, where she stayed long enough to be remembered for having denounced the chairman when he would not take a stand against the fire-bombing of our enemies. When Roosevelt died, she took to political science on the grounds that there was no one to replace him and somebody had to understand what was going on. But perhaps all she learned in that discipline was the helplessness of the citizen, and when the cold war went on and the government tried to draft her son she turned to art.

Tried to draft—for Mrs. Driever had put her foot down then, going so far as to picket singlehandedly the office of the local draft board, bearing a sign that read "OUR SONS WILL NOT SERVE THE TRUMAN WAR GANG—Signed, The Mothers."

"I was simply too embarrassed to report to them with her out in front carrying that sign every day," Will Driever said, his simple tanned face quivering with a thousand wrinkles of amusement. "I used to lock my bedroom door every night so she wouldn't come in and cut off my trigger finger. I had to promise to report in as a conscientious objector to get her to stop picketing."

Since the Korean War broke out, Mrs. Driever had been busily painting canvases depicting mechanized monsters, flying and crawling, discharging pestilence and fire on a gaunt-faced, dignified peasantry. The art department had given her a studio by herself so that she would not distract the other students, more interested these days in imitating the abstractions of Motherwell and Pollock.

"Ma doesn't exactly do these paintings for propaganda," Will said. "Nobody sees them except the education majors who room with us and have to cross the parlor on their way to the stairs. And they mostly avert their eyes. It's more, you know, a way of satisfying herself, like drawing pictures in a public john, which she probably hasn't thought of yet—expressing immortal hatred. There aren't so many ways open to her except that and talking back to the radio. She turns on the news in the kitchen every evening and listens to four quarter-hour programs of the news, one after the other, and every time they make a statement she yells at them that they're liars. But she keeps the door closed so none of the roomers will hear her and be disturbed."

There was a strange wavering of delicacy in Will's voice as he told the story, a butterfly-wing fluttering between admiration and outrage, between love and repugnance.

It took a long time to tell it—as if they had all the time in the world and there were nothing waiting for them to be finished. But Mrs.

Fothergill was. Clem glanced at her, saw her readjust her elbow on the table, hoist her shapely breasts as a signal that enough time had been wasted.

"I have a feeling of missing, in your poems, some of the quality of Will's story. Something," Clem said to her. He held up his hand and made the little finger tremble.

"What do you mean?"

Rather than answer—and of course he couldn't have answered—Clem turned quickly to Will and asked, "Would you have gone into the Army if she hadn't picketed?"

"Well, I wouldn't have," Will said. "But it's very ticklish knowing what is your own thought in such circumstances."

Nodding like a wise old owl, Clem said to Mrs. Fothergill, "I'll bet you have family in the service."

"Why do you say that? Is this a sort of snobbism in reverse?"

"Just guessing," he said, just killing time, just angling for any little old advantage against the moment when he would have to confess.

"Lots of them," she said. "My father was in during the war, and my older brother. Cousins. Uncles. And not all of them officers, either. My father was a lieutenant colonel and my brother was a sergeant," she said with her faintly hostile, collected firmness. "Each of them did what he had to."

"Of course," Clem said. "Of course you know—I felt this in your poems—that it's not the facts that count, but the wonder of the infinite particularity of persons." Her eyes narrowed, and he felt he had said the wrong thing. No doubt all her poems were about animals. "Excuse me while I meditate that holy truth," he said.

In the toilet, leaning above the stool in the gloomy smell of urine, disinfectant and wood mold, he wondered whether he ought to skip, right now. Plainly Mrs. Fothergill meant to pin him to the wall.

A fly buzzed lazily up the whitewashed wood like a messenger. He read a few inscriptions, appreciated a few drawings. The quality was good. It always helped to have an art department or a writers' conference near a toilet, he thought. It occurred to him that the art in here could, with a sufficiently perfected reading and critical exegesis, afford all the meaning that Shakespeare and Chartres would likely afford to a crass eye. So it was not for the sake of a needed art that he was obliged to go back out there and let Mrs. Fothergill score her advantages over him. It was the act that counted, not her unnecessary poems.

CLEM ANDERSON

So for her sake he prepared to yield himself—but found when he returned to the booth that reinforcements had arrived. The afternoon crowd was coming into Henley's. Two friends of Bernie's from the drama department had brought a pony-tailed girl, emanating vacuousness like a seductive spray. With them in the booth, Mrs. Fothergill was squeezed to the wall, far opposite Clem. No doubt this was the calculation of Bernie, who was doing his best to protect him.

But nothing was going to wear out Mrs. Fothergill that afternoon. She sat on, listening now to questions about the New York theater. She watched Mr. Anderson get groggier and cruder as he kept on swilling the weak beer, while her hopes of a serious conference alone with him vanished utterly. And she gave no sign that that mattered.

She watched while at least a score of students came up to be introduced and to take their turn at sitting awhile and contributing to the babble that rose higher and higher in volume. Perhaps the most important thing she witnessed was that it made no difference to any of the visitors that Clem was getting piggish and that he began to make raw propositions to the girl with the pony tail, who ignored him and put him in his place by concentrating her vacuity on the lank young actor who had brought her in. When the girl took her turn at leaving the booth, this young man leaned down the table from beside Mrs. Fothergill and whispered to Clem, "Do you want Gloria? She's yours if you want her! Don't be put off by her manner! Pretend you don't notice her and you can have her."

"Pretend? How can I pretend?" Clem gibbered. "I am an honest open nature, a youth who throughout life had his nose pressed to the window of a candy store. What doth Gloria of man require?"

"You can have her anyway," the lank young man offered. "Only you'll get her quicker if you pretend not to notice her. She thinks you're immense. I know."

"I'm in the candy store at last," Clem said with a round, radiant smile. "Hence, loathed morality!"

And Mrs. Fothergill sat on, as if she were studying this gibber profitably. He gave her a run—if that figure is permissible to describe their intense sedation—down into the jungle of student life that afternoon, like a feckless wild boar delighting in the shadows, lights and windlessness of underbrush and open glade where nothing, nothing, nothing will ever seem to happen. She followed—if that is the right word to describe her watchful patience—like a hound at the head of a pack.

519

At any rate, whatever subtle stalking was being done while his attention seemed diverted everywhere else but to her, she swallowed her rightful claims to his professional attention. She pretended to be amused by it all until, suddenly, it was five-thirty and he suddenly remembered that he was due somewhere soon for dinner.

With Bernie and Will Driever standing discreetly by to catch him if he fell, Clem swayed at the end of the table saying his goodbyes. To Mrs. Fothergill he said, "Sorry about the delay. Wonderful poems. Maybe see you later in the evening if you stick with the bunch." He drew a wobbly circle in the air to indicate his discipular ring.

"Oh no," she said, still managing to smile. "Perhaps you'll feel better tomorrow." She looked around at the ragtag of followers and tried to remember if she had really heard him make an engagement to meet them later. "Oh no," she said, then rang the personal pronoun like a bell: "Not I."

At that moment of successful evasion it must have seemed impossible to Clem that the real princess of his quest in Kansas should turn out to be Mrs. Fothergill, just as it must have seemed impossible that after the excesses of the last forty-eight hours he could do anything now but sleep.

And when, now, a taxi delivered him back to the sorority house he crawled directly upstairs to his room and bed.

But his face was hardly on the pillow when a slight tap sounded on his door and in came the Southern Lady. She had slept all day. Rosy from a shower, she was ready, she said, "for a fight or a frolic." Clem's choice, as she plainly presented it by word and deed, was to rise and go with her to the dinner and the showing of a film to which the guest lecturers were invited, or to frolic with her here and now while they were alone in the big lubricous house.

Clem chose to rise. With her help and cackling comment he showered, dressed and, clutching at her hand for support, went to the dinner. His hostess, unforewarned, had seated him opposite Cheney. This circumstance upset Cheney so much that he began at once to go over from the beginning his speech about the "web of history." Under Clem's fixed stare he grew more emphatic, silencing the others at the table in his unnerved determination to show, once and for all, what he meant. Every time he got as far forward as Rome, he remembered something he had omitted and started again. He was talking about the Roman cotton trade with Egypt when Clem's head fell against his plate with an overwhelming crash.

Lifted up, his eyes still open, Clem said, "Very interesting. Who is that fellow speaking?" Then with a sudden, mad vivacity he began rubbing his hands, imitating Cheney's voice and repeating verbatim all that Cheney had said for the last ten minutes. The hostess suggested they all go to the living room for dessert. The host offered to drive Clem home, but he insisted that he had come to see the movie and "since boyhood" had made a practice of adhering to schedule.

During the movie, a homemade documentary of the life and work of the artist in residence, Clem broke in several times with additional, muttered fragments of Cheney's eloquence. The darkened room gave several of the guests the liberty to laugh aloud at these interruptions. And Cheney left before the screening was done.

Clem stayed for it all. He was, of course, asleep, with his hand curled inside the Southern Lady's, but his eyes were open frequently enough to take in some of the sharp black-and-white images—for use later, one might say, by his souped up brain.

At the end of the film the Southern Lady was going to take him home—appearances be damned—if he had not absolutely insisted she stay with the party and enjoy herself. He evidently convinced her with his pleas of utter exhaustion, but her last words were "I'll see you later."

Sometime during the ride home he remembered that there was no way to lock his door, so he told the driver to take him once again to Henley's U Tap.

His companions of the afternoon were gone—except for Mrs. Fothergill, looking as fresh as at noon, Gloria and her lank friend. These three were packed in a booth with a dozen others, but when they saw Clem they called and made room for him. He sat beside Gloria, who, quite according to prediction, had warmed to him during his absence.

When Clem and she and the young man who had offered her and Mrs. Fothergill left somewhat later—to "go dancing," someone had suggested—everything seemed to have been arranged for Clem to spend the night with Gloria. But wily Clem climbed once more out of the frying pan and escaped from their next tavern stop with Mrs. Fothergill in her white convertible.

He rather thought it was her suggestion that they leave together, and he still had the impression that she wanted to discuss her poems. But he had another impression that she had stuck her tongue in his ear when she suggested they ride away.

In any case, once they were out in the sweet night air, under the late redness of the moon, all the trivial questions of who had arranged for them to be together blew away like chaff. Their riding together seemed so inevitable.

"I don't feel the slightest fatigue," Mrs. Fothergill—Joanie—exulted. "I won't sleep this night. I know where let's go. Are you hungry?"

He did not have to answer, only relax and acquiesce, only wonder at the splendid force of girl and car bearing him to an appointed but still undisclosed moment of destiny. There was not the slightest doubt in his mind that Mrs. Fothergill, unfatigued, meant to take him with the authority of a young lioness dispatching a tired hare. The only surprising thing was his pleasure in the anticipation. In that mind where something had always held back in protest, nothing protested now. When, after stopping to buy them a case of beer and a box of fried chicken, she said they were going to the game preserve, he laughed with a kind of high hysteria at the perfection of this detail. Nothing had ever fitted together so well for him without being labored over.

In sober reality—which Clem always called the mere antonym of drunken reality—the game preserve was a six-hundred-acre tract established and managed by the biology department of the university. It was bordered on one side by the local river and was surrounded on other sides by a tall fence of steel mesh, designed more to protect the collected fauna from hunters and delinquents than to fence in any dangerous beasts. There were none of those. This moderate land had never bred them since the days of the saber-toothed tiger. The poor survivors locked inside the wire were none of them more to be feared than an elderly bison called Webster.

Mrs. Fothergill and Clem approached the preserve down a gravel road that wound through black trees. The moonlight was so strong that the dust cloud raised by the car was clear in outline, seeming to settle back exactly where it had come from in the windless night.

Joanie stopped the car in front of a high wire gate swung on a steel frame. Looking up, Clem saw that the top of the gate was strung with three strands of barbed wire. When he indicated it, Joanie said, "You're not going to let that stop us, are you?"

They pushed the beer and the chicken under the gate and started to climb. Joanie was the first over, leaping down in stocking feet from her last foothold on the hinges. She swore happily at the stones that bruised her soles.

Straddling the barbed wire ten feet above the roadbed (and surprised that he had managed the ascent unaided) Clem saw the pale lozenge of the convertible on one side and on the other a narrow, disappearing lane, tantalizing as the background of a dream, the virgin land of the psyche. Farther off, crossing the lane, there was a horizontal glade full of moonlight where nymphs and fauns (and he among them) were already prancing in bacchantic joy.

"Jump!" he was commanded. But still he wavered, swaying colossally with one foot still outside in the present world and the other wavering over the mysteries of the preserve.

He had been here before. He had come a thousand times to this steel barrier topped by the triple warning of the wire. He had peered through the mesh at the creatures and their habitat. Only once before—in a locked ward in Germany—had he stood where he had a choice of leaping down on either side. Then, at the last moment, he had come back. That had been the decision of his life, not to commit himself utterly, to keep some escape open.

But now, in the moment of decision when he was going to commit himself beyond his power to turn back, it seemed to him he was not alone there. An old man whom he did not recognize balanced there beside him. Though the night was still, a gale wind seemed to be whipping the old man's beard, and the wind tore the command "Jump!" from his lips.

I shouldn't be up here trying to think of reasons, Clem told himself. In any case, reasons canceled out as quickly as they came. Around his head the sublime and the ridiculous whirled, chasing each other's tail.

I'm the father of a family, he thought, and here I am balanced ten feet up in the air. There was no reason he should not be.

"Jump!" coaxed Joanie.

Being Clem, he would not jump. Nevertheless, he cautiously clambered down inside the preserve.

Strong and silk-skinned arms—above all, young arms—received him. He was kissed wetly, and the revels of the glade began. These revels were not entirely actual in nature. If they had been, what happened that night could not have had so profound an effect on him. He might never have known what thereafter he knew.

With Joanie in the lead and himself toting the beer and the food like a squaw behind her, they followed the lane down to its end. There they swung left and downhill along a path, finally pushing their way through a screen of willows out onto a sand bar that gleamed with sulphur nakedness in the moonlight. Joanie lost a shoe in the muck at the sand bar's edge, and Clem had to fumble in water the temperature of his hand to retrieve it. But then they were on the firm sand, dropping their caricature of provisions and seating themselves. Across the river they could see no lights of farmhouses or suburban dwellings. The illusion of a return to the primitive was total. Nothing was there to stop them from discovering what each truly was.

Almost wordlessly they rolled together and began kissing. Pliant as a serpent in her strength, writhing in ambiguous convulsions that might have been either attempts at evasion or incitement, Joanie permitted him to reach—and only reach—the tight, smoother-than-flesh elastic of her protecting girdle. On that boundary they fought for a weirdly silent half hour, threshing about on the sand like saurians unable or unwilling to release what each conceived to be a death grip.

They flopped into the shallow water at the fringe of the bar and rolled back, gathering grit, onto the dry mounded sand at the center. They smelled like catfish and panted like coupled dogs and came to no decision in their quibble over that sheath of elastic.

In the mental transpositions that accompanied the struggle, sometimes it seemed to him that this girdle was a caul from which he was trying to fight clear. Again it seemed that he was trying to break from her arms before she sank her teeth into his throat.

"Why are you laughing?" she demanded angrily.

"Nothing," he said. He had been wishing all his discipular students were here to witness the hero in epic struggle. Then he told himself he dare not show his face to them again unless he came in carrying her pelt. There was no quarter in the struggle with the Philistine.

Here was, among many other things, a re-creation of a test match in his youth. So once he had wrestled with Margaret Shea, been overcome, been sent on his pilgrimage by the significance of that defeat. Now in the plenitude of his powers he was matched again with the same scornful goblin, this trophy of the mundane world that poetry must, he felt, penetrate. Joanie was what's-to-win, he thought. Diana of the Parked Cars, Maid of America, Miss Exactly-So-Far-and-No Farther, Lady Hot-Mouth Tight-Thigh. The exact and worldly echo of his unworldly arrogance. He would have her or die. What, like this—to be found, Visiting Lecturer, Sex-Slain on a Sand Bar? Yes, let them report how I was slain, he thought, neglecting the flopping thud of his tired heart as he kissed her sandy lips.

But with this glee of sporting thoughts, he was aware of a simultaneous underconsciousness of horror. He was and was not an

524

independent soul, aspiring to be received, like Faust into the blessed choir of immortal youth and restrained from that only by her resistance. As if his fingertips were eyed and capable of seeing in the dark he thought, All's gentian violet down there. He felt the writhe and evasion of his baby daughter under his hand, as if he were diapering her—had been starting to diaper her when something broke in the back of his head and let in this horrid wind of impossibility. Consciousness had broken down the retaining walls between love and love, as if the bloodstream in him were no longer separated from the tracts of elimination. All was blended now into a kind of subamoebal paste and had to be mastered all together if he was to play the man.

Play the man he could not. And Joanie seemed to sense this, relaxing her defenses at the very instant he felt the cold of impotence spread down through his body. Oh, she was cunning as the censor of his dreams.

"Let's have a beer," he said. "As long as we're here we might as well enjoy ourselves."

"Let's," she said with ladylike poise.

As he ripped the cardboard and pulled two chill cans out for them, he said, "I thought we were all agreed when we came here. We're not children."

"I thought I wanted you," she said in the voice of a tragedienne. (Wonderful! he thought again, seeing her mundane artifice as the Everest at which his conquest had aimed—and might again if there was enough kick in this Kansas brew.) "I thought I wanted to, but … Clem, we're both married. I could do this to myself, but not to Buster."

"There's no Buster here. Is there?" He looked around and for an instant thought he saw a buffalo bearded like a Freudian father image, but that was only a trick of his nerves.

"I know." She laughed wheedlingly. "I know, but … May I have that beer?"

"As soon as I find the opener."

"Oh, dear."

"What?"

"The man asked if we wanted an opener, and you said no."

"I did?" Clem rolled onto his back, kicking his feet at the moon.

"What is it?"

"A high-school joke. 'What did he forget to take to the picnic? An opener.'"

"I see," she said gravely. Then disapprovingly. "Is that all … sex means to you?"

"You're asking if I love you. Of course I do. Now let's get at it."

"It wouldn't be any good for you. Not the way I feel at this present moment."

"Chacun à son goût," he argued stoutly. "I want it lukewarm. I couldn't stand it if it was too good." Now, catching his breath (a maverick bronco that he must rope and tame in the palisaded, seasick corral of his chest), finding in his head a great pattern of floating lights like a city seen from the air by night, he saw a single real light come on across the river like an answer to prayer (though he felt impotent to pray), and he imagined that it might be someone rising to tend a sick child. "All right, then. If it's no dice, let's go home."

"It's either-or with you, isn't it?" she asked coquettishly. Whatever she wanted, she did not want to go home yet.

"Aristotle," he said. "'What is the most certain of all certain things?' We either fuck or we don't. Law of the excluded middle. Absence of Northwest Passage. Permit me, love, thy Northwest Passage."

"Why do you have to use those words and turn nasty on me?"

"Trained all my life to use them. Disciple of Flaubert. But you say not, I won't. Serviam. Now I will get by miracle the opener required for/by you." And, suddenly springing to his feet, he went charging off through mire and willows into the dark.

Where he meant to find something that would serve as can opener in the artificially primitive confines of the preserve did not come to him as a question. Fox fires and will-o'-the-wisps (all of them projections of his physical derangement) led him. So Pan did after Syrinx speed, he thought. Apollo hunted Daphne so.

Perhaps in the sick, ultimate stages of his drunkenness his mind returned to some boyhood familiarity with the Midwestern countryside—a nearly instinctive knowledge of where one looked for crop-pings of sharp stones or the ravines where farmers dump their junk, old fenders, broken steel, fence posts, hoes and corn knives. But he would always believe afterward—and the truth is very ambiguous here—that he was "led."

Led treacherously as ever Trinculo, Stephano and Caliban by an intolerant Ariel, he stumbled through his share of foul-smelling marsh and stinging briars. The lights beckoned him through alternations of tall grass, wild onion and gooseberry thicket.

He came once to a looming wooden tower surrounded by the same kind of efficient wire that circled the preserve. Probably it was a combination water tower and toolshed, and it might have contained what he needed. But he had not quite the foolishness or the strength to climb inside. All was neat around the base of the fences, as if it had been swept by a broom. While he hung on the wire he believed that inside were the diamond bodies of the Hitler Youth, encouraging their German police dogs.

The tower vanished (no doubt simply behind his back as he reeled away), and he went downhill for a long time, almost back to the river. Then he came to a moonstruck clearing where he knew he was supposed to stop.

As he dropped to his knees he saw that for a hundred yards ahead of him the moonlight fell unbroken on undulant grass so sleek that it must have been trampled by innumerable feet. At the far side of the clearing and in what he thought of as the wings there were humped, rolling masses of elms. (It was a landscape by Ryder or Old Crome. A natural theater that never was included in the biology department's dreams of artifice.) All the trees were very dark except for a tarnished-silver trim and certain corridors that appeared to converge from them onto the central stage.

Out of the fabulous velvet of the woods—black as the lining of a cheap, old-fashioned jewel box—the animals came trooping as he watched.

Seeing them materialize, Clem thought, It's like something out of Old Mother West Wind. Something from the fables that he, like each child, made once out of the common fables, something early as that first consciousness of wonder to which one is recalled by a reading of The Golden Bough.

Something more than moonlight illumined them as, two by two, the animals came to take their prearranged places on the stage of the clearing. By its violet glow Clem saw what marvelous forms had been added to the biology department's prosaic stocking.

There were not only the squirrels, jack rabbits, martens, lynxes, coons and badgers considered native to this region, nor the common starlings, larks, blackbirds and hawks the recent generations had known. Along with them came all manner of exotic creatures from every continent. Bengal tigers and arctic bears sat down, in a manner of speaking—at least, they had not come here to prey—with the homely democracy of chipmunks and rabbits. Marvel enough in this, but after pandas, spider apes and elephants had taken their places and flying foxes circled with condors in the turmoil of the sky, all manner of chimera and such impossible creatures came out.

Lions with goat heads, dragon-winged horses, the bloated white bean-shaped torsoes of Berkshire hogs bearing the sensitive heads of collies and showing in their luminous eyes an almost human melancholy followed the more predictable types. Hippogriffs and unicorns and combinations never named came padding softly to their places. And waited.

After them came figures like Egyptian statuary, yet obviously of flesh. There were among them hawk-headed females with human bodies, cat-headed ones with an etched filigree of whiskers cut delicately around their mouths. In order of appearance that suggested greater eminence came the holy baboons with snaky, trailing phalluses. They looked blue-green in this light, as if carved from some blue, translucent stone. Yet they were flesh.

All these waited, too—the great lords of what the imagination has conceived to be the animal kingdom, more wondrous in their combination of animal features with human than a simple human would appear. And yet they were not the apex of the hierarchy being assembled. The order of their arrangement suggested that a place had been left open. Clem knew—the word is ambiguous but there is no other—knew that they were waiting for the King to come.

In a modulation of light the Great Bride appeared, essentially human in form as far as he could make out, swarthy as an Indian. She was veiled in stuff that looked like the down of cattails or the drifting silk from cottonwoods—one would say it was something of the substance offered by this flat, dry land to start the materialistic visions of pioneer children. Or it might have been the synthetic gossamer spun for a posing movie queen, and Clem would not have been surprised on her arrival to see a million electric globes burst out in light that advertised the price of the spectacle he was watching. Disney could have done most of this, he thought disparagingly.

Still, those animals … And the Bride was big. She must have stood twice the height of an ordinary woman, a giantess superior in every way to the beasts.

Now when all these were assembled, they simply waited. The mustering was incomplete. This was evident not only from some air of anxiety from the multitude. Something like a voice speaking from outside Clem's mind promised that the King should be among them and the harmony of ritual begin.

And—that was all. In a moment when all the spectacle faded, a transcendent guilt seized Clem. It came as an indistinguishable component of the knowledge that he was not going to be allowed to volunteer as King.

His desire—or its aberration, if this is what his vision had been—would go only so far as to define the King. Something as forlornly human as reason (though it was more like doubt than reason) held him back with the argument that it was impossible to be at the same time spectator and participant. He had known what the King must be. And that was all.

At the end of his hallucination he found himself kneeling in the grass. In his right hand—and how or when it had got there he had not the faintest idea—was a knife-sized shard of flint. He had a vague intuition that with it he had killed the Bride and the animals.

But nevertheless it was what he had come searching for. It would serve to open the beer cans. As he made his way to the river's edge and then upstream to the sand bar, he thought it would also serve to carve Joanie Fothergill's name on her trunk if that proved the course of justice.

She had put on her shoes and was standing like someone waiting for a bus when he waded out to her.

"I would have gone in another minute," she said. "I thought you'd deserted me."

"You know the way to the car?" he begged piteously.

Of course she did. But now, since he had been successful, they ought at least to eat and drink a little before they left.

While they shared nourishment, she began to tell him freely and proudly what she was "trying to get at" when she wrote her poetry. While she rambled on, he noticed that the light on the other shore of the river had been extinguished.

When she had lightheartedly unbosomed herself, given him the falsies of her soul, she began to question him. She did not bother to ask about his work. It was as if she knew as well as he that what was published now was dead, didn't count any more in this world of myth and flesh to which she had brought him, his ideal guide. She wanted to know how he felt most deeply about himself, his wife, his children and his prospects of fame. And though such questions, by their very nature and commonness, invite shallow answers or lies, when he responded he tried to tell not only the truth but the truth as he had never divined it before. If she was not the shrewdest of inquisitors, it must have been that Clem was ready to grasp her dull questions by the haft and sink them into his gut. He made her into what he needed her to be.

What he told her must be thought of as a version, in other terms, of what he had just seen in the woods, of longing and rightful expectation forever denied. He loved his wife, he loved his children. But the love they evoked from him ran on beyond them, was not quelled, became a monster that threatened them. His darlings marched from the hive of his loins and the hive of his head, assembled and waited for him to come and reclaim them. He was powerless to be even the king of his own family. His senses, which gave them to him, imposed the terrible prohibition against his ever approaching enough to give or receive the real kiss that the senses promised. He was in misery and he had wished that all he loved might die. That if he could not save he might be permitted to destroy. That because he could not have them, he might offer them up as a voluntary sacrifice to the great serpent.

All this was incoherent (except to him), of course. What she heard from the fragments of his incoherence must have flattered her. The trick played on both of them is easy enough to understand. Any woman who takes a man's prayers for his soul personally is bound to think herself adored indeed. And, thinking so, may sometimes, however briefly, become so. No doubt they achieved an artful counterfeit of understanding: she taking his need to be a need of her; using her, not as a nymph but for a reed.

And in his achieved flight of neural, moral degeneration he found another way of flattering her. Again, this part must have been delivered in incoherences that only time and labor could reassemble. She could not have quite understood. But the essence of the matter is that he praised her as the great serpent to whom he was willing to sacrifice.

*She was a gordian shape of dazzling hue*

*Vermilion-spotted, golden, green, and blue;*

*Striped like a zebra, freckled like a pard,*

*And full of silver moons, that as she breathed*

Dissolved, or brighter shone, or interwreathed.
In his passion, at the very threshold of death as it must have seemed to him, he created and lived in the illusion that she was this lamia, woman and snake.

Mythically he conceived her so, and (I must put it thus) mythically she understood him, accepted the flattery and rewarded him

530

accordingly. Before morning came she permitted him an act of intimacy which according to her calculations would not infringe on Buster's conjugal rights, Buster being no poet and therefore too wholesome for this service. According to her transformed nature she took the kiss that was promised to his natural loves.

*Her head was serpent, but, ah, bitter-sweet!*

*She had a woman's mouth ...*

"You do care for me," she said tenderly when he was done, before both of them fell into a kind of sleep.

It seems that sleep did not stop him from talking. After she was quieted, Clem lay in her sterile, unreceiving limbs like an eclipsed Silenus (or a baby coon who has raided a still) in the white, sleek branches of a poplar.

He babbled frankness he had never offered another human being, the total frankness of self-abandonment. When he had said "Serviam" he had admitted a condition more than he had declared an intent. The stiff spring of the censor had disengaged in his mind, and she was welcome to all the treasures of nastiness and fire that he had so long guarded, even from his conscious mind. The conqueror was over his gate. He had knelt and offered her every spoil.

But there was cruel comedy here. Like most barbarian spoilers, she had no idea what to lay hold on. His secrets spoken were as mysterious to her as they had been unspoken. She told him in the morning that he had gone to sleep in her arms. "You were like a little boy mumbling in his sleep."

He had not slept. He had reviewed again and again the trooping of the animals he had seen in the clearing and had told himself (trying to tell her, at least willing if she knew how to listen) how they represented the trooping of his sexuality in its stages of ripening and decay throughout his life. What he offered her was his renunciation of the faith that out of this ceremony a hero King of the Beasts could be shaped. At least he knew what he was talking about (though, strangely, he could remember only bits of what he said afterward). He would always half believe that that night in her sterile embrace he had dictated thousands of lines of his new poem exactly as they should have been written.

When at last he was totally emptied of images and blacked out, the blackness had no duration. It seemed that instantly he was awake again, and all that he had known was scattered like a fine ash over the beauties of the morning landscape.

The earliest dawn was showing. There was enough light so he could make out the form that had lately frustrated him, now rolled just beyond his reach. Joanie's face was resting on her sandy forearm. A beautiful tendril of her red hair lay damply on her cheek under her eye. Around her in a strange scribble there were furrows, no doubt made by some frantic wielding of the flint they had used to open the cans—as if the blind hand in its own will had been searching for her life. Of the flint itself there was no trace.

He heard an outboard motor and presently made out the dark silhouette of a boat near the opposite shore, higher up, coming from the town. A red lantern glowed in the bow like a fallen dying star in the low-keyed colors of morning. Evidently some fishermen were getting an early start. They must have seen him and Joanie longer than he had seen them. They must have decided to mind their own business. The boat stayed as far away from the sand bar as possible, as if its occupants knew they must shun a plague.

When the fishermen had passed, two hen mallards paddled their way downstream, they also emanating discretion, like two brown-clad, middle-aged ladies scorning human naughtiness.

Presently Joanie woke. She woke charmingly. Her rumpled clothes and the dirty sand on her skin were managed like additional graces. It seemed doubtful that since puberty anything pertaining to her body or its appearances had embarrassed her. Her confident eyes said to him it had all been a lark, hadn't it? And no harm done after all.

"Eden!" she said, shielding her eyes to look into the depths of the rising morning. "Oh, I love the feeling of freedom! Ugh. You've broken my straps, you brute!" She reached back between her shoulderblades to assess the damage, grinning as if she would not have wanted less to happen.

"Brute?" he whinnied pitifully. He felt his shoulders curl down and supposed he resembled nothing so much as a grub worm hit by a spade.

"I'll write a poem in which Adam and Eve look around them on the first morning and see—" she pointed with overweening amusement—"empty beer cans and chicken bones surrounding their bower."

"Do!" he said in a timid treble, meant to placate her.

Their walk back to the car seemed five miles under the exhausted light of day. Already there was a delicate smell of dust in the air, though they found the leather upholstery of the car moist enough to be unpleasant to the touch, like the skin of some dead monster of glamour.

Joanie, reaching to make an adjustment of her shoe, pressed face and breast against the steering wheel. From that position she said thoughtfully, "I wonder if I—you know, missed something last night by being too prudish. I … You must remember I wanted you awfully, Clem." There was a welling of tears in her eyes, those cobalt eyes that did not need to weep for anything.

"You did? That's the one thing I couldn't stand to remember," he said, knowing that he would remember it anyhow.

"It might have been so great!" she said with enthusiasm. "'Strangely fitting even here. Meanings unknown before!'"

"What are you talking about?"

"It's your line," she reminded him winsomely. "I merely repeat what Teacher says." Her brows furrowed. "I'll never repeat some of the things you mumbled last night, though. I don't believe you meant them. If I did, I'd …"

"What?"

"Worry about you. But you were just trying to persuade me. If you hadn't tried so hard, I might have—Well, no use talking about it now." She started the car. Like Proserpine with the carcass of Dis on her fender, she drove him back into the waking town.

Mail waited for him at the sorority house. A happy letter from Sheila, and a lengthy expression of condolences from Maxwell Gorman. After all the play was not yet settled on. True enough, Carpenter had signed for the lead. Carpenter loved the play, but almost before the ink was dry the backers had split. One of them remained "ready to go" if the play could now be scheduled for rehearsal within a few months. But the other, the man whose personal reasons must have been so good and consistent but whose part in the combination required to make the play a reality seemed such sheer caprice, now insisted that they wait for George Blake, since if George came in he was sure Carola Groves could be signed for the feminine lead. Gorman made some attempt to rationalize this organizational madness, adding the last and perfect touch to Babel.

The letter had been mailed straight to Clem's superstitions. He trusted Gorman indifferently to tell him the truth, and he trusted Gorman implicitly not to give up hope. Gorman never gave up hope. But all the references to the whims and financial caprices of theater business seemed a mere froth on the ocean that would or would not cast Clem up on a firm shore. As soon as he had read enough to catch its drift, the letter seemed to him unnecessary. He had known, had he not, when he failed to make out with Joanie that disaster was on its way? And both his failure on the sand bar and the letter from Gorman combined to sour the letter from Sheila. They shamed him before her confidence, her relief, her plans for settling down at last. The thing he must do, he told himself while Gorman's letter still dangled from his hands, was go back and get Joanie, polish her off and return—to find another letter from Gorman on the table, one which said that already thousands of ticket buyers were clamoring for opening-night reservations.

He heard Little Employment coming into the kitchen. It seemed to him twenty years since he had said to her that adultery was sweet, and it seemed to him as useless now to hope for peace and calm of mind as to wish those twenty years away and himself a boy—a boy too smart to get involved again with writing.

He did not want to see her this morning and merely resented her presence because she stood between him and his stock of beer in the icebox. He thought he had not even strength to climb to his bed without another beer. So he lay on a couch in the TV room and slept.

This time he slept long, but the sleep was empty, void, utterly black. His dreams were in his wakefulness now, and he woke to find them crowding the perceptions of his day.

He found a note lying beside him on the floor. It was from Little Employment and said, "All right. I will tell the class you won't be around today. Sleep long." And this, like everything else practical that his mind could perceive, seemed to exist outside a coating of crystal that he now realized had begun to form around him while he lay babbling to Joanie the night before.

He knew, even then, on that first day when he still expected some of the strangeness to pass like hangover uneasiness, that he had caught something from his night of exposure. Some men merely contract venereal disease from their playing around, he thought with despairing amusement, but I have caught a poem.

He still thought—even before he had adopted the habit of calling it to himself "the poem" and considerably before he saw enough of it to understand he ought to call it "Prometheus Bound"—that it would leave him alone in peace once he got busy and wrote it down. His other works had done that. But even so, from the beginning, he knew he had to find some place outside the poem before he could even start it, and he would have to go a long way before he got outside.

How damned odd, he thought while he headed toward the sorority kitchen for a beer. And when he thought, rather disinterestedly, I ought to call Joanie, he supposed he ought to call her for its sake and not because he particularly wanted to.

If I can push her over, I'll be able to start writing, he thought. Just like that.

She told him on the phone that she was entirely refreshed after sleeping all day. Then she told him, "Buster—my husband—is coming up Friday night, Clem. I got a telegram. I'd thought that maybe you and I ... But there can't be anything more for us. It wouldn't be fair to him."

"Never more?"

"Quoth the Raven," she laughed. What a silly bitch, he thought, but "silliness" had no pejorative weight. He merely registered the fact. "It's the conjunction of the mind and opposition of the stars," she said, "for you and me. We were sinfully close last night. But we've got to go on our own orbits."

"We still haven't discussed your poems," he pleaded.

"Oh. No. Of course we'll have to see each other professionally. But—do you have my poems?"

"No."

"I sort of figured you didn't. It doesn't matter. I'll give you some carbons tomorrow. Only, you were naughty not to tell me."

"We'll go over them tomorrow evening."

"Oh. Evenings.... Maybe we'd better not. I'm afraid of you. There're only three more evenings when it would be possible. And you have other friends."

"I'd like to see you. I won't expect anything."

"Well ..."

It turned out, to no one's surprise, that Mrs. Fothergill did not mind being courted as long as she controlled the terms of the courtship. Being courted was, if you like, the circumstance for which infinities of evolutionary time and the choicest myths of her upbringing had prepared her. She rather enjoyed the bit of notoriety it gave her at the conference to be seen as much in Clem's company as she was in the next few days. To live secure and unseduced within a cloud of speculation that you have been seduced—that's not the worst thing for a woman in Joanie Fothergill's position. To lead a bull by the nose and be the only one to know how steerlike his spirit has become—there is the height of triumph.

Not that she had any notion then or ever that he was changed and changed by her. How could she suspect any magic powers in herself when the magic had, after all, been endowed her by his crisis of vulnerability? She merely liked the way things had turned out.

Again, in this situation, he could not let well enough alone and merely make a fool of himself. He had to seize creatively on the possibilities for embarrassing his admirers and those he had recognized as his people.

He attended Joanie Fothergill like a moonstruck boy. Yet no one looking on could have taken him for a boy, or have thought this was a belated show of adolescence where he was intoxicated with the glamour of the inaccessible. Even for the least-informed observers, there was something perverse and wickedly artificial in his shift of personality. "Serviam," he had said, in a whimsical reversal of Joyce's great romantic motto. To serve more than he was asked to serve, to grovel, to repudiate that part of his own career which represented a search for liberty—this was the "task" he began in Kansas. And is the epitome of service not found precisely in serving a cause foreknown to be without hope? He could hope for nothing from Joanie Fothergill. She was his first helper in shaping the great poem of denial that was to cap his achievement.

All the better if he could hope for nothing from following her in a mock play of courtly love. He said to himself, "Follow thy fair sun, unhappy shadow, for there comes a luckless night"—amusing himself with the riddle of this superficially obvious verse, concentrating perversely on its implication that because night comes one must prepare for it by subtilizing the material life, beforehand, into unhappy shadows.

He had reached the plateau of his creative life through a summoning of those extra resources offered in the crucial moments of need by sexual resolution. The underside, the seams, of everything he had made from his poor boy's treasure duplicated in sexual terms the outer show of his verse and prose—so much so that his favorite true joke was that he had got, upon the language, a husky boy child of a novel and a fairy girl child of verse.

Then, was not the way down from his plateau—and he meant to go down now, or had already gone down when he jumped from the gate of the game preserve—to tie off deliberately the cords of his sexuality? For which Mrs. Fothergill was the ideal woman to help him.

First of all, he stunned his class by "discovering" Mrs. Fothergill's superiority as a writer. Two morning sessions were spent, in the chalk-smelling classroom where so many frankly good things had been said, with him uncandidly arguing the exceptional merits of her unexceptional work. Not that her work was bad. It might be—it probably was—equal in merit to that done by Bernie Masterson, Will Driever, Little Employment and a few of the others. In which case Clem's insistence on its superiority might be taken as his (much too) sly way of driving home to Bernie the argument he had made a week before on the subject of unscrupulousness.

Line by line they wrangled through Joanie's ample sheaf of poems. Clem's people were not going to let him get away with his assertions. They called on him to show cause—and he showed cunning, glibness and intemperate zeal to prove them all wrong to Joanie's profit. And presently, with the bad taste of dishonest arguments in their mouths—his trickery kindling theirs—they all of them sensed that the critical language they were using was only a cover language for the unutterable treachery that he intended to commit. Before their eyes he was deliberately wrecking that integrity which more than anything else they asked him for.

Through these sessions Mrs. Fothergill "sat festering," as Little Employment would describe it later—"sat as if she were trying to hatch a doorknob." The hook at the corner of Mrs. Fothergill's smile, and her eyes smiling straight down at the table top, told them all, intolerably, that she already had what none of them would ever get from Clem. And the best they could do was believe that she must be a lovely piece to be worth so much.

Even Fern Passavant knew that something untoward was going on in the little class. She cornered, one after another, those who had been Clem's crowd and demanded to be told what had happened. Finally she went to Felix Martin with the complaint that Clem had gone riding with Mrs. Fothergill one afternoon when he was to have his last conference with her on Oil!

Henley's U Tap saw Clem no more. Where, so quickly, he had become a kind of institution to be visited in the afternoon by students of writing and art, and where he had dispensed a Dionysian encouragement to all comers, now there were again the summer doldrums. The excitement he had brought back to them from the far places of the soul, not to say from Paris, had been carried off somewhere in a white convertible. One trembling youth who had been inspired by the mere recklessness of Clem's beery orations to "give all to love" (to indulge at last in overt homosexuality with his roommate) reportedly tried to hang himself with his belt, but such apocrypha demonstrate little except the feeling—needing a joke to illustrate it—that Pan had been and gone.

Clem's colleagues as well as his students and other followers noted what was happening. The Southern Lady, if she had known the full truth of the matter, would at least have understood it tolerantly. In the name of the Confederacy and Anglo-Catholicism she would have approved all the rejection of the normal world it implied. But knowing only as much as she did, she was naturally angry at being ditched for a dull chit of a young married woman. It was not given to the Southern Lady to perceive how in reality and by his own sinister choice Clem wore Joanie now like the albatross hung on his neck by superstitious comrades, a symbol of destruction and deliverance, dangling in sleek caricature of Peter's crucifixion, her fiery tuft burning under his chin like the beard he might have worn, red as the great thoracic wound of the Prometheus he was beginning to rehearse.

Cheney, witnessing the new development, believed at last that he understood Clem well enough to use him as a character. You will find in Wagon from St. Joe, Cheney's latest novel, a former Confederate officer whose pathological infidelity endangers the entire wagon train on a night when the North Platte is rampaging in flood.

On the night before the conference ended, Clem was to read a selection of his own poems. Among the cynical the betting was that he would show up for the occasion in the company of Mrs. Fothergill. But any type of cynicism was an underestimation of our Clem. He confounded expectations by showing up with Mrs. Fothergill and her husband, one on each arm. That is, the Fothergills apparently had to support him into the auditorium, though the injection of vitamin B that Dr. Fothergill had recently administered gave him strength for the reading.

Clem had been a little high, of course, that afternoon when the Fothergills picked him up, though charming and evidently at ease. "My teacher," Joanie called him as she introduced him to her husband, accenting the possessive enough to cleanse the epithet of any implication that he might be her master. Just so she might have said, "My superior," meaning that superiority itself was a beast on the leash of her regal democracy.

Dr. Fothergill (Buster) said he had read Clem's books of verse, sent up to Wichita by an enthusiastic Joanie. He certainly meant to read everything else of Clem's when he got time.

Buster's handclasp was firm and without reserve. His eyes seemed at the same time knowing and candid, as if in his profession as pediatrician he might be merely the craftiest child among the group of his patients. Well manicured and handsomely erect in his summer suit, he was reminiscent of Terry Burbidge—except for being young and seeming, as Terry did not, to have the stamp of the assembly line in his nice manners and intellectual scope. He was a perfected model frozen into production. He showed no scars of truing up, as Terry had.

Clem liked him far better than Joanie. There had never been a question of liking her.

While they drank together before dinner Clem ventured a few seemingly timid questions in the realm of Buster's specialty. His little daughter, Clem said, was suffering a most agonizing diaper rash back in Indiana, and her doctor had prescribed gentian violet. What did Buster think of that?

"Of course that is the great old specific for fungus growth in moist areas, and I've prescribed it now and then," Buster said. His brow knitted in a professional indication of thought. "But in summer usually I just say take the diaper off and leave it off. Expose the damp areas to the sun. Sun and air, they're the great old healers." He gestured with an open hand, as if it were he who had prescribed the continent itself, the cloudless prairies and the myriad beaches from Far Rock-away to La Jolla. "Of course, the kiddies may make a few messes, but that's not serious. Off with the clout, I say."

"That would be my prescription," Clem said, staring significantly at his love, who just smiled and rested her hand on her husband's shoulder. "It has its sanction in the art of verse as well as in the art of medicine. 'What is dark, illumine. What is low, raise.'" He lifted his glass and drank noisily. "Expose les petites taches humides to the sun."

"Well, now, in your book ..." Buster said eagerly. With authoritative brusqueness he shifted the conversation to his pleasures and bewilderments in reading The Throne of Oedipus. He, Buster, meant to specialize in child psychology eventually. He had taken courses, and if they ever got back to New York for a year he meant to resume them. Now, it had seemed to him that Clem's book, insofar as it dealt with childhood and the unbroken patterns of experience repeating themselves in later life, was, nevertheless, post-Freudian. And his, Buster's, own inclinations were to post-Freudian revisionism—call it eclecticism if you like. Well, wherever Clem placed himself, Buster had found certain extremely suggestive insights in Clem's work. "I feel that medicine has to draw on all sources, the fine arts as well as science, every facet of experience." Again he made that characteristic, openhanded gesture, but this time it was as if he were reaping, gathering back, the bounties that he had scattered so profligately on the land, snatching back the bread from the waters before it had time to soak and sink.

With the malice of the doomed, Clem heard his work, his flirtation with healing magic, all his discoveries, relegated to the level of "sources." Formed or unformed (terms that pediatricians nicely used to describe infant bowel movements), the arts were only the little messes on the American rug, made when the diaper was off and freedom was permitted. He wanted to argue (not with Buster, but only with Buster's proposition) that there were no more "facets of experience" for science or anything else to draw on.

For that was what he had learned in the game preserve—that the natural dream was exhausted. If there was to be more experience it would have to be made up willfully from sheer caprice. No need—perhaps no way—to tell Buster that. And perhaps no way to show him, though for his own purposes Clem had already made up his mind to try.

"Stop it," he said to Buster. "If the only way to beat you is to turn toward disease, we'll do it."

Buster laughed amiably. "I don't set up as a competitor. It isn't necessary to beat me. I only mean to take what I can get. Whatever is usable."

"Then we'll have to invent what isn't."

"Invent? Who?"

"Joanie and I."

"You mean ... writers." Buster dropped a possessive hand on Joanie's and said, "Joanie does invent some pretty useless conceits and extravagances. Some fairly morbid quirks. But better they come out in poetry than in intrapersonal relationships." He had his own devices of irony, this Buster, and to show that he had intended to mock the jargon of "intrapersonal relationships" he tweaked her bare arm concupiscently. "Or in bed," he said with a good-fellow laugh.

"No. It's worse if they come out in poetry," Clem said giddily. "You didn't hear what Thomas Wilder said the other day. He said that bad poetry is what we suffer from mostly, and he's right. I'm going to buckle down and write lots of bad poetry and you're going to suffer from it if you don't leave me alone."

Joanie laughed to her husband. "You see? You're tangling with a dedicated man."

"One that's a little hard to follow," Buster said in a tone so calculatedly humble that it was plainly intended to soothe. "Tell me,

Mr. Anderson, now that we're around to it. What do you think of Joanie's stuff?"

"She's too chary. I'm trying to persuade her to destroy," Clem said.

They were only patronizing him a little. Not enough, as he well realized, to account for the mad bitterness this talk was rousing in him. He was overreading the lines, hearing double meanings where none were intended and putting in his own. And he wanted this exaggeration, wanted what it could lead to.

He believed that the double meanings were there anyway—that they were, in a manner of speaking, much better understood than the glib surface of their talk. His one advantage against the triumphant, damning substance of their health was that he was beginning to grasp the sickness it concealed.

He needed a sign to confirm his intuitions—and produced it from his own pocket. It was the wishbone of the chicken he and Joanie had consumed on the sand bar, his sufficient souvenir of that night. Almost before it cleared the cloth of his jacket pocket he saw Joanie's eyes fix on it like a witch's beholding the cross. She did not lose her sprightliness of manner, or gasp, or visibly age like Morgan le Fay (or turn into Fern Passavant), but her attention was fixed where our boy magician wanted it.

She watched the bone while they went on talking about her chances of making it as a poet. Clem made it dance most nastily on the table top. Sometimes it was a white and graceful crutch supporting the weight of his hand. Sometimes he tickled it prone and sometimes he cushioned it wetly in the palm of his hand. Her recognition of it validated it as a sign, gave it the curiously homeopathic tingle he felt as it sprang against the pressure of his fingers.

"What is that you have there?" Buster asked with a forced smile.

"'S a model divining rod," Clem said. He touched with his lips the spatulate, dark flare of bone below the joining of the slender fork. "Here, feel it."

He seized Buster's hand from the back and into his palm pressed the bone. Buster jumped as if it were red-hot. Then he took a clean handkerchief from his pocket and began to scrub at the palm where the bone had lain. "Oily," he said. "I see that it's a wishbone, but why is it oily?"

"'S alive," Clem said. "Remarkable thing, unaccounted for in scientific literature. Refused to die when the chicken died. Constant exudation of life oil. When it dries up, the poet will die." He began to laugh a bewildering, subterranean laugh. "Touch your tongue with it, you become poet, hey, Buster?"

"No, thanks," Buster said.

"Joanie?" Clem offered.

Her blue eyes twitched from side to side in an uncontrolled frenzy. Then slowly, slowly, her stiff neck bent as she lowered her head toward the bone.

"Joanie!" Buster said. He put his hand out as if to lift her head.

Her tongue came out, narrow and vibrating, reaching. There was a kind of snap, as if of an electric spark, when the strawberry point of her tongue fitted the arch of bone.

"You did that with your fingernail!" Buster said to Clem. "Good Lord, what's been going on down here? Is this the way you teach creative writing?"

Joanie laughed and said, "Of course he did it with his fingernail." She clicked one of her long, polished nails on the edge of her cigarette case to imitate the snapping noise that had come from the bone. "Don't look so flabbergasted, darling. It's not magic."

Buster knew there was no such thing as magic. But, even so, he knew that something terribly odd had begun to happen when Clem pressed that bone into his hand. He could still feel the burn and twitch of nerves in his palm as if a new organ of perception—an eye perhaps, or something totally novel, responsive to a world simply unknown to the ordinary five senses—was budding and about to open inside his clenched fist.

During the hour he sat in the auditorium listening to Clem read he must have been yielding more and more to the mercy of the new suggestions Clem had forced upon him, with growing terror and rage coming to believe that Clem was master of some arcane method of vision which he was now afraid not to share.

So after the reading when the three of them were drinking together again in a roadhouse outside town, a moment must have come when he begged Clem, "Tell me." Or he may have asked, expecting Clem to catch his cryptic reference, "Show me."

I don't know how it went. I'm guessing, of course, for it was never explained to me. Perhaps no explanation is possible of what happened then, and conjecture may be the only justifiable way of coming at it, for only the language of conjecture is allowable in describing what happens to the mesmerized. They continue, of course, to inhabit a physical world in no way altered by their extraperceptions. But reality, we may conjecture, is altered by the altered perception.

Buster wanted Clem to show him what he had seen in the game preserve. At least, Clem understood the request that way. So a little after midnight, drunk as lords, the three of them found the road that led to the steel gate.

At the gate Joanie would have said, "Why do you have to go in there? There's nothing in there. Nothing."

Buster would have said, "Because I want to see what this fake, this charlatan, claims is there to be seen. He called my science in question, him. Let him prove ..." Trembling and laughing and dancing around, his white teeth gleaming in the moonlight, not quite daring to ask while his wife was there, however drunk she too might be, "Did you screw her there? Did you? Because if you did you might tell me how to. Not how to go through the motions, but how to reach ..."

Unable to conceive a language better than Clem's gibberish for asking what he truly wanted to know, unsatisfied with that, he would have made one last insistent demand. "What's in there?"

Clem would have said, "Nothing."

And then, beyond the gate, mesmerized Buster would have heard it beginning, too, the slow, overwhelming rustle of feet as the animals started to move toward the rallying point, the something like a whisper as they confided aeons of hope by the act of assemblage, and the faint murmur of their restlessness as they waited.

"You don't hear anything," Clem would have laughed drunkenly.

Buster would have said, "I hope I hear something."

Joanie would have said—from her illusion, vainest of the three— "I don't know why we're here. Buster, take me home. Buster, it's been so long." She would have tried to handle him physically then in a way that would show both men her power over them.

So Buster would have hit her first, knocking her down into the soft dust of the road, merely to free himself from the frenzy of despair Clem had induced in him. Then he would have climbed the gate, would have rushed down into the hot, empty glows and shadows of the game preserve.

Clem would have sat in the dust beside Joanie, thinking, This is all the trick I have. I can only bring a man like Buster this far. But I brought him—I am a magician after all. I am. If only that helped ...

And Joanie, while they listened for Buster, would have demanded, "Did you tell him anything? Oh, what did you tell him? You know there was nothing to tell him. Why did you bring us here?" But she would have desisted after a while—Clem wouldn't have answered, anyway— content to think that nothing could be done which would harm her.

But then Buster would have come back over the wire gate, raging because he had not found, either, the King who had to be there. This time he would have gone straight for Clem.

He had to refuse the spectacle of nothingness that Clem's magic had projected for him. The only way he could express his refusal was to beat Clem savagely.

He broke none of Clem's bones, though he kicked him several times when he was tired of using his fists. He and Joanie roared away in the white convertible while Clem lay there unconscious.

In the morning Clem had no clear understanding of why he had been beaten, nor even of why the three of them had come back to the preserve. He supposed, forever after, that he must have worked some genuine enchantment on Buster to re-create the vision for him. Clem was certain thereafter that he could work magic if he wanted to. He never did again.

In his soberest moments he could not convince himself that Buster had struck him for boasting that he had brought wife Joan to the post. No, he couldn't believe that he would have claimed such a thing, nor that, for such a reason, Buster would have struck. What had happened was more mysterious than that, but, as time went on, of less and less interest to him. He had touched the edge of metaphysical experience. Found nothing there. Why explore it again?

His best formula to account for events of that night was to say he had been beaten "because it was time somebody did it." With which many people found it hard to quarrel.

A maintenance worker for the university found him sitting by the roadside near the game preserve early that morning, half nursing, half ignoring the bruises and cuts on his face. This good man did not know how to suspect the worst and, since Clem was cheerful enough and sober and had no interest in being taken to the police, delivered him to the sorority house with an admonition to take care of himself.

Little Employment was sitting in the TV room waiting for him when he entered. When she saw his face, for once her natural gaiety crumpled. In pity her expression lost its serenity. She could not help running to him and folding him in her arms.

"Touchez pas," he said lightly, disengaging himself. "You're acting like a mother kangaroo that wants to tuck me back in the pouch."

"Or somewhere," she said. "Do you want me to go get my arms and take care of them for you, Boss?"

"Angel arms," he said. He shook his battered cranium. "It may be that the Philistine is slew. As Samson said when the temple fell on his neck, 'By George, I'm the one He wants after all.' Have acquitted myself like Samson, have left myself years of mourning."

"Don't do it," she said.

"I'll do what I have to," he said. "You come up and help me pack."

"I'm going to cry," she announced as she was helping him retrieve soiled underwear and socks and crumpled trousers from the odd corners of the impersonally feminine room and cram them all together into his bag, socks over toothbrush.

"It would be very much beside the point."

"You have to run to the few people who don't love you, instead of abiding with the so many who do."

"Don't stoop to psychoanalyzing me. You know better than to do that."

"I wasn't," she said. "If you have to, you have to. But I'll cry."

"Don't do it this morning. Let me tell you I haven't felt so good since I came home from the war. You know, when the old ship came into the harbor, all the whistles blew. Miles of whistles. That elevates a man. And this morning I can hear them again." He touched the cut above his eye made by Buster's ring. "Wounds are ways of being with people. Don't begrudge me mine."

"I'll do what you say," she promised.

He told her to get into his car with him, once he was packed, and they rode around town a while before he drove off toward Kansas City. At length they parked just beyond the city limits on a grassy shoulder of the highway. Between them and the railroad tracks a line of cylindrical grain elevators towered over them, windowless and majestic, like some temporary monuments thrown up by a wandering tribe of Egypt.

A troop of crows was flying toward the willows that bordered the river, and Clem thought he recognized beyond it the green of the game preserve. There he had fought his great battle, and though he could not claim victory he did not feel that he had lost.

"Do you know what a wonder it is that we are sitting here, us strangers?" he asked her. "It is wonderful," he said, of themselves, of the homely beautiful crows and whatever else of nature found in that moment its exquisite equilibrium between time and eternity. "The eye is an organ of worship."

She nodded. All right, if that was what she was supposed to believe. But through the veil of cigarette smoke she asked presently,

"Why, after all, did you do it, Boss? I suppose it was a good thing to do, but why was it you who had to do it?"

"It? It, it," he said absently as if reviewing all he had done, assuming that she meant it all, whether she knew of it or not. And he supposed she knew, already then, all that counted. That he had purposely spent his treasures of fidelity and passion on a worthless object. "It was less than madness, more than feigned," he said.

"Was it to show us?"

"Show you?"

"How hard it really is?"

"To find out," he said. "But to pleasure myself, too, in my own strange way. I don't think I've meant any of my life for a display. No one loves candy more than Clem Anderson, or gets more of it. I'll tell you how banal my secret is. It's to keep living my life over and over again everywhere I go and between whatever knees. There Sisyphus hoists his stones again and again. I like it to be this way. All I did here, if I may say so modestly, was act my life out one more time. See, I project it, too, a little beyond what it seems to have come to yet. So I can see the end. I see it now."

"And you like it?" she said, with a keen intuition of horror.

"I love it. I couldn't love this—" he pointed to the white, barren columns of the elevators, as if they and the insistent horizontal of the land were example enough of all he meant—"if I weren't so enamored of what it makes me do. I liked the way my life went here. 'Strangely fitting, even here, meanings unknown before.'"

"You found the meanings?"

"Be the one person in the world to do me the great service. Believe, believe. Never wish me any different than I am."

She nodded quietly, finally. After a little while he drove her back to the campus and let her out on the grass.

"I'll do one more undemanding thing for you," she said. "I'll love you forever."

"Do," he said, saluting with a forefinger to the scab on his brow. "It's all right to remember one was loved."

"Oh," she said, still playing a little within the game of "Henry James," partly saying what she wanted to say within the ironic guise of a quotation merely literary. "Oh, adored."

One other confirmation came to him that he had not been quite the loser in his wild gambit. A month later, when he and Sheila were settled in New York and the surface of things had quieted again after the depths were momentarily shattered, a note came to him from Mrs. Fothergill.

It said merely, "Don't play games with people's lives. Someday you may do incalculable harm."

It had taken her a while, but, yes, she had understood what he was doing. He was learning to communicate his meanings unknown before.

In a deadly serious caprice he set out to create personally a new barbarism, destructive and self-destructive, from which alone, he believed, might come language for the great new poem that demanded his services. Becalmed, he had destroyed the calm with his own puffing, set out once more to find the shores of violence wherein lie the holy straits.

# 19

"HIS UNTIMELY DEATH AT FORTY"—so we wrote of it with a bad conscience. Was it untimely? Or was decorum merely denying him the inverted dignity of his last scandal?

It fell to my lot in that summer of 1957 to write a rather extensive critical memorial for Clem. The piece was commissioned by an editor of a book review section who had been friendly to Clem's published work, who had often found copy in Clem by transforming his garish exploits into bits of literary color suitable for family reading. I suppose I was selected to write it because Clem and I were both, by origin, Midwesterners. But when the assignment first came through the mails to me, I was stirred by the outlandish possibility that I had been selected because I might be, for once, reckless enough to open the seals that decorum and embarrassment had set on his life and death.

No doubt the real explanation is the exact opposite. I had done a good many reviews for this editor, and I am sure he counted on me because I had always contrived some way to praise the most hellish books entrusted me for judgment. The editor wanted to be kind to Clem's memory. No more.

I remember the three weeks that I gave myself to prepare the commissioned article. Falling just after a commencement had liberated me from a tiresome and subtly depressing year, those three weeks were the hottest and stickiest that we had endured within memory. Day after day the colorless rain clouds sat close overhead and the wet greenery—the tended university lawns, the residential plantings, and weeds and willows—flourished equally and with a kind of arboreal savagery that led one to wonder what they were eating that made them grow so fast. On evening after evening lightning played among the clouds from dinnertime until the middle of the night, and a gradually swelling flood condition threatened not only our back yard but substantial parts of the poorer residential districts lying between our house and the edge of town.

I mention these meteorological phenomena not at all to suggest that there was some portent in the skies or in the unpleasantly clinging air to signalize Clem's recent passing, but merely to confess at last that my hurt imagination seized on the accidents of weather and gave to their neutrality that emotive coloration which neither rational thought nor routine circumstances would bear.

My family and I were scheduled to sail for Europe at the end of the time I had given myself to finish the article. And though I had some details of preparation for the voyage to attend to, this deadline had seemed easy enough to meet. I had only to write some four thousand words. I knew what I must say. Two days should have been enough for the work.

But I fought it all the way. Something mournful and reckless that I dared not quite countenance kept asserting itself, destroying my intentionally conservative and decent review of a working life to which, after all, some decent and conservative praise was due. It would be an exaggeration to say that I became impossible to live with while I was struggling to make what I knew or believed fit into what I ought to say. Janet is used to the sort of withdrawal from immediate concerns that I permitted myself. My daughters had their own farewells and preparations to make and perhaps compositions of the heart that I will never intuit as I had to intuit those of my generation.

We were going on a voyage! I longed for it to begin so that my unsatisfying task could be dropped behind and forgotten. And I dreaded the day when I would finally have to put an envelope of manuscript in the mail and close a relation that at closer or longer range had so subtly shaped my relationship to life.

"It's only an article you're writing," Janet reminded me from time to time. Quite unnecessarily. It was only an article, and it was my last chance to be just, and my best efforts to be just trembled like damp candle flames in the uneasy weather of my soul.

It was only an article. With it I could not restore one grain of the past, neither the agony nor the hour of achievement. Surely by this time in my life I knew how to write an article. One made a choice and placed the emphasis according to that choice. My choice would naturally be to emphasize the true and personal note sounded by his poetry and echoed here and there in his prose or his play. And then, in the little corner of space remaining, I would place, like colored stones bordering a mosaic design, the ritual phrases about "domestic tragedy" and "headlong impetuousness"—a sort of code that would remind his friends and well-wishers of what they already knew, no more.

But this was never a choice that I could make. I sat unnecessary and wasteful hours at the typewriter in my study. I drove with a distressed but all too empty mind through the banal, rain-gorged landscape near home. And I tried to reread some of Clem's things, only to find that their very familiarity had somehow emptied them of significance. They were used up, and I was tempted to say so in print, to say that they no longer counted any more than the body lying buried in Brooklyn.

I made a hundred false starts and destroyed them all with a feeling that "this wasn't what was required"—either by the tranquilly waiting editor of the book review section or by the untranquil dissatisfaction that actually increased with each harder try on my part. Without any feeling that Clem was, literally, sitting somewhere laughing at my discomfiture, I did often enough entertain the thought that he had once upon a time calculated my exact predicament. He had placed me, I suppose, as definitely as Dante had placed his contemporaries in the hell, the purgatory or the heaven of their own dispositions.

He had me on the pin, and I might writhe as much as I could, but there was to be no escape for me, I thought, until I could meet him on some ground where we would have a language in common to relate his death and my life. The notion came to me then of what that common ground might have been.

It was clear as day that the big poem (which he had never actually written), and nothing else, could have given us such a language. I did not believe in it as an actually existing thing, but I believed in it as an existentialist believes in God, discerning by its very absence the absolute mortal need for it and feeling the hopeless desire to imagine it. In my own image, if that was the best I could do.

Obviously my conscientious writhings were destined to come to nothing. Time ran out, and in a fake of conscience I wrote the article as I had known from the first I would have to do. I dropped my lead flowers on the marker of "an untimely death" (stilling my suspicions that it was untimely in a far different sense), paid my respects to the theory that it was, furthermore, accidental (though I knew it was the purest formality to label as accident anything sought with such determination) and, in the hectic hours of locking the house and hurrying after our luggage to the train, mailed off the manuscript.

I saw none of Clem's familiars that time we passed through New York. I had seen them, many of them, in April when I flew in for his funeral, and whatever they had to say of him had come fresh and copious in the pain we all felt then.

I did not see my article about him in print until we were in Paris. Viola Lansdowne brought it to me one day when we had arranged to meet at the Flore. In the fact that she had brought it to me I sensed some wonderfully refined intuition on her part. She knew that, though I had written it and let it appear under my name, still, really, I had not read it yet.

I sat there reading it with a trembling of light on the paper and a growing emotion whose nature did not reveal itself until I had finished.

"Well," I said after a while, tapping the article with my fingers and by the motion setting the flower-colored wine in my glass to jiggling in beautiful concentric rings. "Well, it isn't Clem, is it?"

"No," she said, quite flatly, calmly, without reproach or commendation. "But it's all right. It's true enough."

And she meant that it was true, but not true enough. And I realized that while the article was certainly not Clem, it certainly was me. Reading it was like the accomplishment of that childhood fantasy in which one imagines looking through a hole in the earth "clear to China" and seeing down there, at the end of the perspective, oneself.

I was not horrified or terrified by what I saw. I saw myself true— just not true enough. I saw a shell, well formed enough, and as if intended for some use, but by itself pointless. I was part of something, but if that something did not exist, total and complete, I was nothing at all. Or let me put it this way: If the literary art is what we need it to be, then I am a part of something that justifies my being. If it is not this, I am a bag of air. My modest, peripheral services to literature could be vindicated only by what they had served, and if they had served a mere echo of the real world, I had spent my life betrayed and betraying.

Don't misunderstand. I didn't see Clem, his life and art, as "that which" or "what" my professorial diligences were supposed to envelop. None of my remorse for his fate went so far as to represent him as more than a synecdochal part of the comity of literature. But I saw him as another shell enveloping the central mystery, a little closer to the center, so that I would somehow have to contain him in order for him to contain his trust. The reasons for the peculiar past began to clear a bit more when I comprehended that, and for the first time I began to feel that his death was not an end.

As I say, I had thought of the article as my last opportunity to be just, but now I saw that a new cycle had begun, and a new demand. If we all had set the seal upon the living abyss from which our lives came, while I lived I had the obligation to reopen it again. I had to put off the linen decency of academic criticism and be willing to take the chance that I would appear absurd in my disclosures of the absurd. Eventually I would have to be prepared to assert what I had glimpsed intuitively and put aside in favor of those conventional responses that have nothing to do with the wellspring of art. I would have to trust witnesses who would be quite out of place giving testimony on the discreet pages of a book review section.

"Write it as it was and take your chances," Viola Lansdowne recommended.

I believe that Clem had been imaginatively preparing his death since that night when he leaped down from the gate into the game preserve. Like a game and devout Southern Negro who pays for and arranges a funeral in advance, Clem had long ago chosen the tone and the form for his last theatrical performance.

It is hard to say who caught on first to the fact that these last several years were a long, uninterrupted dying. For most of us there was not so much a moment when we knew this was so as there was a moment when we understood that we had known for a long time. His desertion of Sheila, his brief, poignant marriage to Susan, the silly and shattering effort to succeed in the theater, had seemed merely signs of chaos—of that disorder which we sometimes gratefully identify with life—until such time as one sensed the great wind blowing deathward and saw all these signs of rebellious life hunger as weather-vanes pointing into the wind. They indicated not its direction but the very opposite, its origin.

In those last years his disengagements from all those who might have clutched him alive longer had proceeded steadily. As he had done with Sheila and the children, he set all of us aside, carefully out of the way, before he was ready to turn and accept the lightning's stroke. I believe he went on elaborating a design that was as conscious as any great design may be, and I suspect that he saw it fulfilled with serenity. He may well have found a continual peace at the center of the noise of strangers. That, of course, he went on provoking to the end.

We have to do here with the most delicate stuff, with a "tissue of improbabilities" quite untenable if anything but matters of the spirit were in question. But of course it is precisely these that are in question when the mind ravens to be satisfied with the meaning of a death.

Matters of the spirit, I might go so far as to say, were all that had really been in question since Clem began his perverse courtship of Mrs. Fothergill. He knew as well as any watcher that his Kansas folly could not have had a successful worldly consequence. And in matters of the spirit a remote perspective may serve better than a near one. My faith that this is so at any rate explains why I have relied so much for the interpretation of his last phase on the letters which, over a period of seven years, he wrote to Marianne Luce.

His first letter to her was written two weeks after he wore his bruises out of Kansas. By then he was no longer any whit disposed to regard the affair as a carnal meeting. Mrs. Fothergill (so he wrote) was one of the giant women with whom his wanton fancy had played since childhood. There had indeed been moments before he "recognized" Mrs. Fothergill when he had conceived other women as giantesses— perhaps Sheila in the time when he had been overseas and needed a stronger mate than a merely sexual woman could be. But Mrs. Fothergill, appearing as she had at a crucial moment of his life, had been the giantess who, by her cruelty as by her instruction, had shown him how to find in his nature—in its shy and virgin fringes—the hint of a sequel to the poems in The Throne of Oedipus.

("Only triflers write anything but sequels to what they have already done. I am too busy to repeat myself just because someone might like it.")

One might not—one skeptical Marianne Luce might not—think, to look at Mrs. Fothergill, that she was either giantess or mentor in the poetic school. All depended on the angle of vision. The Anderson angle had been from twelve o'clock low. Whence he had seen the White Goddess herself, Athena in the guise of Aphrodite, Medusa in the lineaments of Andromeda, the lunar face itself ringed with a serpentine darkness of hair.

Suddenly—in his letter to Marianne he set this down with reckless audacity—her cruel-seductive promptings had enabled him "to see what human history might have been if it was not what it was, if every crucifixion were an enthronement and every wedding feast a torment of infants, and all other imaginable circumstance inverted or made other than it was; and to see that if it were diametrically different, still it would have run the same course and would have come out the same; wherein lies all despair, as you will so shrewdly see, but also all hope. This is the symmetry of the moon and the appropriateness of its bush of serpents."

Just as should have happened to the Scholar Gipsy (and may have, and may have, he never came back to report), the fire had fallen from heaven and he knew what he must write ("in order to keep people from doing what they are going to do under the mistaken impression that there is a way out of what they have done; there is still no sense in calling yourself a poet unless you can justify God's ways to man, and we who have pretended otherwise are lunatics").

It should not seem strange to Marianne that the White Goddess should have appeared in such unlikely guise as Joanie Fothergill. After all, Joanie had had the notoriously bloodshot eyes of Clement Anderson to distort her out of all reasonable focus, and at the moment "when it happened" he was in radiotelepathic touch with every dead poet since Homer. (Very important, that contact with the dead, for it was the very nature of his new task that he must "prophesy the past," create an alternative world to demonstrate the unalterability of fate by circumstances.) Further, had not Marianne herself used the term "venereal Karamazov" in describing Joanie? A marvelous early insight, though it had fallen short of defining even her human dimensions.

In front of Clem's magic analytic lantern Joanie the female had also appeared to him as the ambiguous Ultimate Consumer (and that was why the poem he was beginning must be, in all senses, dedicated to her). She was the serpent who would eat the world. She was also the ideal personification of those consumers who were presently to be given an abstract identification as "the influential" or "the ten million who make success happen in America." As the latter she sipped, she selected, she voted, she invested, she bought, she held opinions the way Marlene Dietrich holds a cigarette, she drank the cream of the National Product. She had wings and wheels, and it was no wonder that the ships and planes of appearance should be given her ideal and heartbreaking name. Through her titanic bloodstream coursed the distillate of a thousand laboratories, a spectrum of biotics and antibiotics that reminded one of the Circus Maximus on a cool fall day when the Romans had come home from their mountain vacations, infinitesimal gladiators of all passions and origins among the African beasts of disease. Just so, too, the distillate of a thousand libraries coursed through her mind, informing her with knowledges she would never even have to bother to realize she had. Sundays her voice rose in a choiring of supercilious thanksgiving. (Thy service ever, Lord, was to provide an outlet for feelings too good to waste on the drone male.) In the rubber chalice of her diaphragm she caught semen enough to populate the stars as far away as the whirling universes of Andromeda. The released tension of her orgasm could propel spears shafted with oak logs, seed arrows of renewed longing such as Herakles could not even have lifted to the string of his bow. The planned bounty of her womb would produce a race immune at last to the siren call of the past. In her collectivity, in the insuperable fact that there were so many of her, she was immortal.

Abstract as that idea of woman before which youth kneels to spill its seed on the ground, Giant Joanie loomed. Would it not offend Aphrodite (a fierce little shrew who, as was well known, abided with the rest of the belly gods in the Anderson thorax) to withhold from Giant Joanie her meed? Since he had been the one to discover her in her collective aspect—he had heard of no other investigator reporting this new beast in quite the way he had seen her—it was his intent to follow, follow, reporting back. Like some lone scout pilot, gas waning, who has found an unsuspected carrier task force in the Pacific waste and must keep contact until course is determined and the defending fleets are mustered to bottle the straits, eating dry sandwiches and pirouetting through purple clouds, pinching himself to keep awake between messages, he must attend, attend.

Of course, he said, he would not, in probability, ever see Mrs. Fothergill herself again. After Buster had tried to settle poetic and mantic matters with his fists, it was just as well to keep away from that couple. But of course Marianne must realize by now that the Joanie of whom he spoke was the shadow of a merely substantial woman projected by his desire on some cloud bank beyond the world. Futile to try to embrace this projection, and yet "a man would be a damn fool not to try. What can the human heart love as much as the projections of its own desire? Desire, that is, will become subject and object at once, and if it is antisocial to admit this, and, oh, indeed it is," wrote Clem, "still, who ever obliged me to report that man was a social being?"

Quite properly Marianne would have thought this explanation of recent events (in themselves all too difficult of explanation) funny when it came to her in a fat letter in the summer of 1950. And quite properly she wrote back that she supposed what he was doing to be the dramatization of a theory of poetry, a quaint little chapter on the growth of the poetic mind. She had hardly been fooled longer than her friend and master into supposing that Mrs. Fothergill was real. Clearly Master Clem had found a giantess, but she wondered if he were the original discoverer, since his giantess seemed to resemble those in Gulliver's Travels.

The only violation of proprieties in her reply was for her to say that Clem shouldn't have thought that he owed her an explanation.

"I owed it to myself," he replied starchily. "Therefore wrote it to you who, as anticipated, had the wit to see that in my venery I was indeed trying to construct or discover a theory of poetry and of the mind itself, self-contemplating. It is a project that has long teased me. Now I am begun. Everyone else thinks I am a loving and harried father, right now breaking my ass in the attempt to produce a new version of my play that will fit the octagonal mind of my all too present associates. I am, of course, doing the play with my left hand."

Funny it continued to be, their correspondence, persistently mock-heroic in tone even long after it began to contain material not in any sense proper for comedy. His "pursuit of the giant women" was still serving as the mock-heroic tag to cover his subsequent devotions to Cindy Susan Butterfield Hunt and to "justify" his leaving wife and children for her sake. The comic note seemed (properly enough—she was reading him right and, without knowing when, had accepted the obligation to hear him truly, whatever horrors he might put in her ear with his jester's spoon) the cover for a wound as giant as the giant women of which he spoke, and just as unreal, invisible, ephemeral. Of the wound itself he would not speak—unless one is to think that "woman" and "wound" are, poetically, the same term.

Joanie and Susan were not the same person? What did it matter to one who was, by choice, by fatality, by falling victim to his occupational hazard, increasingly indifferent to persons? Susan would throw the same shadow of Collective Woman on the air for him to run at and try to embrace. In fact, as he wrote in that tone of treble comedy that was simultaneously camouflage and exposure, hadn't the projection of her shadow been effectively and materially accomplished by the wondrous Hollywood machine said to have been invented by Thomas Alva Edison or maybe the Russians? A modern artist would be stupid not to incorporate the assistance of machines in his creative design.

"The difficulty," he wrote, "of course presents itself when the lights are out on Susan and me. I rather miss the rest of the audience and the smell of popcorn, but it is some comfort to know that I am frustrating the desires of millions when I am unwilling or unable to do their office between her sheets."

This perversity—not so much sexual or even psychic as metaphysical—he had written to Marianne from Hollywood, just before his ill-fated excursion with Susan to Mexico. The allusion to his impotence in these circumstances might be taken as a carrying out of his warning to Buster that "we will run mad on you." At no point in setting down frightening or disagreeable material do I want to preclude the benefits that might accrue to Clem from the simple observation that he was mad. The question is only to what extent—and for what end—the madness and perversity were controlled by a will retreating in search of its ultimate redoubt. One remembers that it was at just about this time that Susan conceived a child by him—and if there was to be something blighted and cursed about that conception, nevertheless the fact that it happened is evidence that the bleak central mood of Clem's last years was not readily apparent in his acts. I like to think that Susan never found out how deeply indifferent he was to her.

His refusal to grieve after Susan's death amounts, as far as I can see, to a mad but consistent refusal to admit that anything was changed by her death. The projected shadow of desire did not vanish when the being who had, for a while, cast it was in the earth. If it winked dim for a moment, it could be restored, as huge and evanescent and meaningful as before, by another female stranger.

For a little while—and this would have been immediately after Sheila burned the store of his wartime letters—the letters to Marianne had changed their tone. They had become more personal, more insistent that she and she alone was sharing some immense and awesome pilgrimage with him. ("I thought he wanted to marry me," she said. Both were married at the time and nothing extrinsic could be done about their situation, whatever subtle shifts of allegiance might have been made, planted to bide their time and to burst eventually into the light. "I thought he wanted to marry me, because he kept saying so in letter after letter. I was very tempted to take him literally for once." That was why she had come to New York that Christmas to see him. But had gone home again with some sense that the time was not ripe to ask him what on earth he might literally mean.)

To her credit it must be put down that even under such tantalizing pressure, living through the failure of her own marriage and seeking some assurances from reality to compensate for it, she did not really mistake the nature of her peculiar relationship to Clem. With a certain uncommon but simple clarity, she had said to herself that it was a bit like Swift's relation to Stella, and that it might be very Andersonian for Clem, also noting the resemblance, to make it more so than by nature it would have fallen out. Her final theory, accounting for both the degree of intimacy they maintained and the simultaneous alienation, was that they were like a couple afflicted with farsightedness. They could see each other plain only if they respected the distance between their actual lives.

But that was her conclusion after her one attempt to alter this not entirely satisfying situation. Earlier she had thought her election to be his confidante came from the fact that she meant nothing to him. I'm no one who counts, so he can afford to tell me the truth. But from such an initial position can come a liberty that counts more than anything else in establishing a union between two people. So next she thought, He knows he can tell me the truth because, by some fluke, I was dropped into life more like him than any of the other foals either of us has ever known or ever will know. And she realized that this was no ground for making a claim on him. Quite the opposite. The very talisman of their likeness was their tendency to claim nothing from life for permanent possession. And finally she thought, I count more than anyone else to him because he has told me the fantastic heart of the truth that no one else would even bother to reckon with.

The truth she believed herself entrusted with was that all these years, when he had seemed to be doing everything else, he was constantly, happily, self-destructively working as the poet he had meant to become. The only time she doubted this provided the occasion for cementing her faith.

She was nearly thirty. She was alone, teaching in a girls' college in Virginia. And she was there, she felt, because Clem had put her there. Without going into the details of her divorce or her life as a teacher, it is enough to say that she knew these were not of her choice. She felt she had been planted there to wait for a summons. And when the Virginia spring woke that year, she made up her mind that the summons would never come in any overt fashion from him. Since things were done between them all topsy-turvy and unnaturally, she might as well assume that if the "summons" was ever to come, it must come in the form of an intuition that would provoke her own decision. Good. She had her intuition, decided to go to New York for a showdown.

She had to ask him: What have we been doing all these years, Anderson? Is it, after all, only an enormous and overextended joke that there is anything we share?

She wrote to tell him that she was on her way. He replied with a one-word telegram: "Delighted."

So she went riding up through the greening countryside with an amused pleasure in the power of her decision to move this tower of thistledown they had been so long abuilding between them. It was so frail, really. A firm hand could lift it and set it where it belonged.

Yes, she had decided—literally and concretely, in the least poetic of terms—to marry him. It occurred to her with a sort of terrible glee that he was no longer strong enough to resist her. Since Buster beat him up, he had absorbed an awful lot of punishment. She would marry him, carry him off, set him down and lock the door while they spent the rest of their lives finding a substance for their airy love. Some of it might vanish in their grasp. She wanted whatever might be left.

But he did not even meet her at the train on her arrival as she had asked him to do. He was not to be reached by phone. When she finally tracked him down by calling his agent and getting a list of the Third Avenue bars where, in the middle of the day, he was likely to be found, he seemed no more and no less than surprised to see her in the city. Staring at her from his fat-rimmed eyes, he might have been surprised to see her on this earth. It was as if he was having trouble connecting her with her name, and in his effort to do so he said a very discouraging thing—"A lot of students on their vacations are always looking me up." He smiled at her as if he were smiling at an endless series of the curious or admiring young.

She settled down to drink with him, thinking, It's worked both ways. If he hasn't really been writing to me all these years—as I guess he hasn't—then the man I've been getting letters from isn't really him. But should she find the author of those letters, then he and she would share a more than ghostly joy over this confusion of persons. She had been waiting so long, she would stick and wait a while longer.

In the first days of her vacation she followed him from bars to offices to parties, and to bars again when the parties were over or had ceased to feed his apparently urgent requirement to hear around him a note of ecstatic rush. "Little Girl Glue" was her own wry epithet for herself when she told me about it, implying that he had not cared very much whether she kept up on his endless peregrinations, since there would always be someone with him. That was what cities were for.

And the days and nights gave her not so much an impression of whatever personality he had by now shaped for himself as of the fantastically crowded spectrum of personal relationships that now made up his life and into which he was subsumed—as if an organ of consciousness should have become entirely that which it is conscious of, an eye become light and the relationships of space, an ear become the cacophony of a tireless machinery.

Her Virgil in the New York literary scene, then, seemed no more selective a guide than pure chance would have been. He knew where he wanted to go when they got there. He put Marianne in a hotel and she waited there until he came for her; once she waited for thirty-six hours. If there was a principle of selection left in him it was the idiot tropism toward mere noise, toward the last lights burning when the night shifts of the intellect went to bed.

His business relationships had no more point. She had lunch with him and one of his agents, cocktails with him and a publisher. "Clem talked to them as if he were something they had invented," she told me. His own percentages, expectations, demands, willingness to be translated into Danish and Italian for what those minor dominions could pay, were unaccented details in the flood of gossip supplied by his agent about the fortunes of his fellow practitioners. ("You know, Paramount's paying seventy-five for this piece of shit of Mona Bryson's." "Well, if they can make a movie out of Tristram Shandy they can make a movie out of anything." "And have. And have. But Sid Morrison, who started Mona on this novel in the first place and gave Willoughby's the first best seller they've had since 'forty-eight is out on his can because Willoughby sold out and Thorberg hated his guts, and Sid's wife wants to sue Mona's agent on the impossible grounds that Mona can't write a correct declarative sentence by herself and without Sid's idea would still be typing copy for Rand." "She's got a gift. You've got to say for Something Above that it's got pace and readability." "I haven't read it, either, so naturally I'll grant that." "Heh heh." "Heh heh." "There's going to be a first printing of eighty thousand of Katya Stahl." "The bore that walks like a man." "The worst European picaresque novel since Gil Blas." "But Edgar Himes has already plugged it on the Snack Wilbert show ..." "Edgar learned the compound sentence so he could read the New York Times in the original." "... and two of the book clubs are already after Wilma, and Zill is going to do it as a seventy-five-cent paperback." "Wilma should have to read it for her pains." "Wilma's had two good breaks in the past month. When are you going to finish your new novel, Clem?" "Maybe in the summer, if I don't land in the hospital again like last year. I may be going to France in June and I'll finish it then. Yes, I'll finish it." "Sullivan's been asking me, every time I see him, when there's going to be a new Anderson novel or a book of poems—if you're not doing anything for the theater, he says, heh heh." "Heh heh. It's never done me any harm to be known as a poet. Whenever I've been in Smollett's column he's leaned over to leeward to mention Sugar and Oed. I may print a section of my 'Promethe' this summer, in some good quarterly, just to keep me smelling gamy with the discriminatious reader, you know.")

Listening, Marianne noted that he did, literally, smell. "Gamy" might be the word for it, but maybe it was as if he had brought here to this dim-lit restaurant and this unillumined conversation the insulting smell of a small boy with a bad cold, some kind of offensive excretion through the pores that was the one sign he did not belong where he was.

But except for a generous interpretation of such signs she found no way to penetrate the superficial agitation with which he confronted her. Plainly the marketing of ideas and what he joyed to call his "properties" was become a game he did not want interrupted by any across-the-Hudson reflections from her. He played it with only a slight change of key, somewhat more alcoholically and more flagrantly "deep" with the publisher than with the agent, and it took her longer to hear his interjections of intentional travesty. He was playing with them, but this was one business advantage the more. The hint of recklessness in him made them so insecure that they had to serve him, though he asked only for playmates.

"I'm an artist, fundamentally," Clem told the publisher. "Nothing goes out of the workshop—nothing!—that I haven't put my solemn signature on. From the time I was a boy in the Midwest I've had a like, you know, Socratic daimon that not only told me what not to do but what to do! And if I've worked in forms that you and I wouldn't ultimately regard as the highest, like although I refused to do the script for Death I had a hand in Festoon, which is an absolute meatball, still— and I say this with all due humility, I think—there are exchanges and passages of wit even in Festoon that are pure! Did you see it, Dave? You did. You remember where the war veteran says to Bessie—"

"Wait. Wait, now. Which of the women was Bessie?"

"It doesn't matter. He's been taught to kill, and now society is getting ready to punish him for the thing that he's been rewarded for doing in time of great national emergency—very much like my own case—and this sandy gash looks Gish in his face and says, 'You're not a murderer, you're a victim.' And Cecil Hardy, being the jack-boots- and-shooting-stick type of director with his goddam 'weakness for the Anglo-Saxon, ...'"

"Heh heh."

"Heh heh ... wanted the veteran to say, 'I go to do a far better thing than I have ever done.' But to me the logic, the comic logic, of the situation was to have this overgrown athletic beast who's gunned down three candy-store operators after helping to raise the flag on Iwo Jima look at the girl from his ox eyes and ask slowly, 'I am?' That's all. Just 'I am?' Because, believe me, there're twelve-year-old boys out in Plattesmouth, Nebraska, who only go to these movies for laughs anyway, and for them you have got to bring in a little French-movie- style humor."

"That's what you've done in your best work," the publisher said with restrained impatience. "That's what I want you to say—"

Clem shushed him with a wave of his hand. "I guess I'm just an untidy kind of writer. I could never write a foreword to anything of my own. I can only take the chance of sounding pretentious and say to you, Earl—"

"Dave."

"Dave, that whatever I was trying to do had a sort of cosmicness or a relationship to something I want so badly to profess, to bring out in what I'm doing, but I don't really try to analyze it, because if I do I'm scared that what I'm analyzing either isn't true to begin with or isn't very good."

"Clem, the devil with modesty! Hasn't there been some particular flaw or evil in the social get-up that you're giving the main focus to that you might spell out better if you wrote a preface yourself rather than have a critic do it?"

"Yes. Yes, there is. It's mass self-deceit, I think I'd call it, manifested by hardtop convertibles and Peace of Mind and Togetherness, and the train that's called the express-local. Now, I've had an uneven life personally, and there are a great many people who feel I have been a sonofabitch in relation to my wives and children— Marianne here will tell you—"

"I didn't say a word," she murmured uncomfortably.

"… but I've always had my eye on these social evils and I've sacrificed my dearest for a chance to step up there and swing on mass culture and mass complacency. When I was a boy of thirteen I remember my father brought a copy of a national magazine into the house and I looked at it with misting eyes and said, 'If I ever get a chance to hit this thing, I'll hit it hard.' So what me passionne au fond is to kind of make people reveal themselves through the banality they've been drenched in. Just kind of seeing what's left after the deluge of advertising, you know."

"That's it," the publisher said hesitantly. "That's what I want you to say in this preface to your sto—"

"I want to say No in words of thunder to the conformity and amorality that's so rampant and the teen-age gangs and the poor enfants maudits with polio who are not safe in our public playgrounds. 'Destroy the destroyers,' I would say."

"Exactly."

"Exactly."

"Then will you write the preface? It doesn't have to be much. Just what you've said here. Will you write it?"

"No," Clem said.

"You are a wicked man, Anderson," Marianne said when they had afterward made their way woozily out of the Algonquin and headed toward the Village for dinner.

"I sleep in the tents of the wicked. Wherefore?"

"To tease him like that."

"Makes him feel like a big shot," Clem said coldly. "Earl is very devoted to fighting the evils of conformity and amorality which plague our present-day culture. It doesn't behoove you to scoff at him." And in the hour they were alone together he would not concede her the slightest familiarity.

"Your letters were so different from this," she said, making a neutral observation. He looked pained that she had mentioned the subject.

The telling glimpses she got of his business connections could hardly have alarmed her as much as the slowly accumulating insight into his relations with his court of women. She had assumed, with the glamourizing effect of distance to aid her, that his current women were sleek sexual objects that in some cavalier jauntiness he took to bed in his marathon pursuit. But except for one shrill little shrike from Bennington, who confided in an hour of drunkenness that she had taken Clem to bed and found him "totally impotent," the swarming women seemed never to swarm into bed with him at all.

Marianne had been in town less than a day when it struck her that she was there on sufferance, as Clem's girl for the duration of her vacation only, and that her coming had been well discussed by a clique of people on whom she had never laid eyes. At first she thought it was merely on the sufferance of a woman named Eileen who lived in Westport, some hard vavasor of local culture of whom Clem would say only that she had gold teeth, declining to explain why he must call her so often. The calls suggested he was keeping a fellow conspirator apprised of the step-by-step unfolding of an elaborate crime.

But then there were rendezvous, having an air about them unexplained and all mysterious, with a lengthening series of women who—whether they all had gold teeth or not—had something in common. They all seemed to know, or know of, each other. What they shared in common was Clem. The youngest was a girl named Bartle, a student at Hunter. The oldest was a Mrs. Croly, whose husband was a magazine publisher and amateur of deep-sea fishing. In between, aged twenty to sixty, there were actresses, women from advertising, from fashion, from publishing, a couple of novelists, and wives from the remodeled barns, the handsomely redeemed East Side lofts and the smart Village walk-ups. Such "young marrieds" as liven the pages of the fashion and architectural magazines.

What bound them together in this institution, attached them to him or him to them, was not very clear. In her bewilderment Marianne entertained momentarily the notion that Clem had become a secret vice like Lesbianism, drawing his initiates from a cross section of otherwise unrelated suburbs of the intellect and the arts. There was that peculiar knowingness and cryptic reference on the part of each which reminded her of Lesbians stylized in personality by their perversion. Or it was as if some highly specialized religious band were maintaining personal contact, receiving instruction and the charge of the spirit from their swami, when these women were with Clem. In some fashion of lordliness, he reminded her of Father Divine among his angels.

But then it came to her that what she saw was a kind of salon without walls, a modern version of an ancient social coagulation, bearing to the older style somewhat the same relation that TV bears to movies or the legitimate stage. The lion's court was dispersed rather than assembled, which permitted the courtly rituals to be all the more shamelessly similar, since each operated under the illusion (vapid enough) of singularity.

Whatever the precise mechanism of the relationships might be, the women had secure possession of him. For example, Bets, a painter long fugitive from Laramie, Wyoming, had heard in almost total detail his table talk of two nights ago, carried on in a bar adjacent to the Windmill Coffeehouse. (Clem would not and constitutionally could not pass time in the coffeehouses that were becoming the exchanges for the young practitioners of the arts. He needed liquor of one kind or another—at least he needed it in front of him, where he could touch the glass, though there were days when he drank comparatively little. This weakness for alcohol, though taken to be old hat and something for which a lesser entertainer would be put down, was tolerated in him, and his station next door to the Windmill was respected as a kind of cultural annex, or even an inner chamber to which the really elect could retire when the Windmill filled up with "people from advertising and Wellesley girls." The young still sought him. But he sought them, too, more anxiously than ever as time went on. There was something markedly shameful in his going out of his way to make himself constantly available.)

Bets would have been there in the bar, at least for an hour or two to sit at his table and pay her respects, but she had promised to paint scenery for Roger's Atheist's Tragedy over in an abandoned fire-house on the East Side. But why she had regretted particularly missing him altogether was that Lucille had told her Clem had hinted his intent to do a section of the "Promethe" in hipster talk. Did he think, really, it could be done?

564

But Yes or No is a pallid answer for such a question, as Bets had been around long enough to know. What she truly regretted missing was the point in the ensuing argument when Clem had reduced Robert Mingus to tears. Mingus had been formed in the Kenyon school of English and had borne his chalice serenely among a horde of enemies, for all his seven years in New York. He begged Clem not to loosen his line, and Clem had said he would loosen it.

The assault had come, too, from another quarter when Ken Verger maintained that Clem would have to go on "horse" in preparation for such a task. The mind of the poet is an engine, he said, to be tempered this way or that by the fuel fed into it. And Clem had risked—and then triumphantly regained!—the respect of all the group when he allowed he could get more tunes from plain old alcohol than any man or woman among them could get out of a peyotl sandwich laced with prime weed.

Grandly and characteristically he had refused to demonstrate on the spot. Instead he ordered black coffee, Bets had heard, swilling so much of it as to produce a visible convulsion of his limbs, as if to make clear to them that when he worked on the poem it would be alone.

Sometimes these days he offered readings, either at Eileen's in Westport or at Mrs. Croly's on Sutton Place. When he did, it was never from his work in progress, but always from his old work. When "Prometheus Bound" was given to the world, it would be given intact and complete.

That such intellectualized baby talk was Clem's daily sustenance, Marianne came to believe with reluctance. But believe it she did before she left New York. ("The worst of it was that he would talk about his poem—the great unwritten—with anyone. And all his gang spoke of it familiarly with a diminutive. I swear I heard one woman call it 'Prommy'—like a little ghost mascot they had all learned to be fond of. He made them feel that they were, by remote control, helping him write it.")

At any rate, the encounter with Bets was an installment in a continuing serial. For Bets had heard from Elinor and Carla that Lou Swethers was bringing Mingus to Mrs. Croly's party on Saturday. And Eileen had told Bets that Clem was bringing Marianne. Would the estrangement between poets be healed there? Would Mr. Croly be present, and if so would he invite Clem to go deep-sea fishing with him? If so, would Clem take this opportunity to interfere with Lou's plans to wangle an allowance from the Crolys for Mingus to use for another year in Rome? And after the Crolys' party there would be a new series of questions, equally trivial, equally passionate.

Then, when Marianne had been around for three days, it came to her that she was not only there on sufferance as his girl, she was one of two girls that he was "interested" in, was allowed or encouraged by the managerial company of women to be interested in.

The other person, she discerned from a scattering of hints, was one Bonnie Waller. Like herself, Bonnie was an old acquaintance of Clem's. He had picked up Bonnie when he was lecturing at some college in the Midwest. That is, he had dropped a line, Bonnie had bitten it and followed. She seemed to have languished at the periphery of his consciousness—at least of his life—almost as long as Marianne had. While Bonnie had been in New York, going to school and "writing," for the last three years, she had certainly never been close to Clem. Had never got close to him, though she had tried. Again Marianne was shocked to guess how exactly much so many people knew of Clem's relation to this other girl and herself. He was a sponge who had only to be squeezed and he would say anything he knew. A very wet sponge, and he loved now to gossip. His best subject, as ever, was himself.

They knew, or seemed to know, that Clem had never been to bed with Bonnie, though apparently he could have been, had he wished, at any time in these past three years. It was only lately—maybe the effect of spring—that some flicker of interest in this interesting possibility had been noted in their balloony clown.

The difference between Marianne and Bonnie was that Bonnie was beautiful. So there seemed to be a competition shaping up, an ugly little caricature of the judgment of Paris, staged for the edification of the Anderson salon. She was in it quite without having chosen to be.

There was even a question, she gathered finally, as to whether, when it came right down to it, he would take her or Bonnie to the Crolys' party.

When she gathered in the gist of this, Marianne knew she ought to go home. Only one thing saved her. "I have absolutely no self-respect," she said to herself sternly, with pride. She waited to see, uncertain to the very late moment when Clem called for her that he was going to call.

Like a galleon among galleons home from searching the Fortunate Fields across the Atlantic Main, the apartment house in which the Crolys lived glittered among the lights of Manhattan's eastern shore. Reflecting, as so many others have done, that people who lived within such splendors of the eye could not live petty or tawdry lives, and realizing simultaneously that they did, Marianne nursed the ache of contradiction as she and Clem came in from the street to the elevator and were lifted toward the party. It seemed to her that she had never asked for things to be better, only that Clem be willing to share with her the acknowledgment of the way they were and had to be.

But he seemed to be saving himself, like a performer about to go on stage. He chatted gaily enough with her. Since he had arrived, so late, to pick her up at her hotel he had been rattling on with excuses (no doubt invented on the spur of the moment) for keeping her waiting. He rattled gossip about the people she could expect to meet. He affected a concern about how she would like them, as if it were a foregone conclusion that they would all like her. And nothing he said engaged with anything she wanted to hear from him. He was slippery as a greased pig in evading attempts to find what he really thought of the thin glamour that had become his medium.

He accompanied her for not more than one turn through the rooms where the guests were crowded, and for a few casual introductions. Then she found herself seated under a grand piano, like a child in Plato's cave, within touching distance of Clem, but now excluded from his entertainment. He was seated on the floor, too, but reclined against a swan boat of a couch. Rapidly his women, some of them, mustered around and he lapsed into the imperious infantilism for which he seemed, here, to be so prized.

He lolled, obese and physically repulsive as a dwarf. One cigarette after another burned out in his mouth and the ashes scattered down his shirt front as he babbled endlessly. Even his head looked somewhat hydrocephalic, and the curl that lay against his empurpled brow was plastered down with sweat. His women crouched around him as if he were indeed chez lui in his own harem, though not so much in the office of a sultan as in that of the cutest fat eunuch in the guard—somehow a transformed creature who was permitted liberties that women would not endure from a man sexually dependent on them.

For just a moment, as if the surrounding faces had been mirrors, Marianne permitted herself to see his reflected image—and saw the infant Moses at the instant when Pharaoh's daughters uncover him among the reeds, saw an infant Pan, a prepubescent Adonis—and this seemed to her more obscene than his actual appearance. She wanted to say, "But he's a man." She dared not intrude on the spell and anyway wasn't quite sure.

She was not included in the conversation going on out there beyond the edge of the piano, though after interminable patience she found herself brought in as the subject of what he was saying. He was lying to Mrs. Croly, Liz and Tina about how he had spent the afternoon with her.

Except that it was a pure lie, his story was pretty good. It had an unmistakable lyric charm. (Partly, she began to suspect, because he was composing the heroine, given her name, out of Bonnie Waller as much as from herself. Had he spent the early afternoon and evening with Bonnie? In all probability, no—not with Bonnie any more than with her. Far more likely that he had loafed somewhere in a bar or at home on his couch, wasting the hours with an imagining of where he might have been and with which one of them.) His story exploited the awe and innocence of a young girl fresh in town, wanting to see the sights from the Cloisters to the Battery and to return by way of Third Avenue. As fiction, his account was improved by the implication that this country girl (herself) was rather more in the style of a Colette heroine than in those of Gene Stratton Porter. Sportive. She had been as delighted with the ancient lush mariner who seated himself at their table in Costello's as any of his listeners would have been, her laughter was the beautiful echo of the old man's gnarled wit and profanity.

Then, from a Colette heroine, Marianne heard herself being subtly and wondrously transformed into someone mentioned by de Sade. (Again the troublesome question was how much of this character painting was modeled on Bonnie Waller. That evanescent figure again threatened to usurp whatever identity Clem was willing to grant her. At least take us one at a time, she wanted to protest. But there was no avail in that, since she suspected sadly he was taking neither of them and the true subject of his story was merely himself reflective. As girls they were only his own emotions. The tranquility in which he reflected them was invulnerably coated by his alcoholism, his contempt for the literal truth.)

He did not say while he was using her name, while it still seemed to be her story, that the blue sea smells of the Battery and the April-shower gloom across the window of Costello's had so worked on her that by four-thirty she had insisted on their going to the nearest hotel. Nor that she had kept him active there until the late hour of their arrival at the party. But his story, even in its vagueness, was plainly As You Like It, and if they did not take a lubricous meaning from it Marianne would be very much surprised.

From under the piano it was hard to like his fiction. Particularly when she recalled that indeed it might have been just as he told it. There was a double cheat involved. Her resentment at being pictured as some sort of eighteen-year-old peasant was compounded by feeling that she looked her twenty-nine years. Worst of all was that as a storyteller he should still be getting all the mileage he wanted or needed out of something that had been only briefly real and that nearly seven years ago. She had been as scandalously overused as Joanie Fothergill by his endlessly re-creative mind. And feeling thus, she felt she knew at last what was really wrong with writers.

Robert Mingus sat down near Clem and broke his monologue long enough to change its direction. Clem had something important to say to Mingus—and it turned out to be the recommending of a fortuneteller Clem had recently discovered in a bar near his Brooklyn apartment. Priscilla was this clairvoyant's name, and Clem wanted Mingus to know that he had trusted this woman to the extent of engaging her to remove the curse that had been put upon him several years ago.

While Mingus shook his prematurely bald head and scowled, Clem pointed to his own brow and bade everybody look to see if they did not see a serpentine scrawl of pigmentation running across it. When Mingus angrily refused to look, Clem said that of course it was only visible in certain lights, but that they had his word it was there.

Priscilla had told him to get two eggs of pullets and place them under his bed. Sleeping with a certain charm she had given him taped to his forehead, he would feel the worm go out of him during the night, she had told him. So he had followed instructions. And—this is what he wanted Bob Mingus to particularly note—it had worked. In the deep reaches of the night he had felt something like a silver wire being pulled out of his body. The extraction had been accompanied with great pain, since the worm had had so much time to become fond of its host. But at this very moment those two pullet eggs, one containing the dread worm, were on the shelf in Clem's icebox. As soon as Clem got around to it, felt up to the suspense, he would take them to Priscilla, who alone was to be entrusted to open the eggs. She would crack them and, at last, kill the worm. "Priscilla has probably done this trick a thousand times," Clem said. "Of course, what she usually does is drag a burning match through the white of the egg, burning the protein so this long black wiggly thing comes out on the end of the match. This time she's going to find the real worm. Shock may kill the poor old gal. Or then, the worm may eat her. It's nothing to fool with."

"I think I'm supposed to understand something from that fable," Mingus said shrilly.

"Why you?" Clem asked, indolently hauling up his lids.

"Why me? Why me?" Mingus echoed bitterly. "Yes, why do you have to pick on me? You're trying to destroy me because you're envious, and you use every opportunity to bait me and when I try to be serious you try to make seriousness seem like a joke. There was no point in that little story you just told and you know it, but I suppose it will be held against me that I said so. You'll get people saying that I went to a fortuneteller that you recommended or that I didn't go, and either way it will seem somehow discreditable to me."

"Yes," Clem said, "that's the way it works. We know it's just as ridiculous as that, don't we, Bob old boy. So why do you stick around people like us? And anyway, you do need a fortuneteller, Bob."

Mingus shook his head and stood up. "I know what you're driving at."

"You're delicate, Bob," Clem said. "I don't know that I was driving at anything."

"But your story wasn't even funny."

"At least it was funny," Clem said.

Marianne felt merely that she had been witnessing an enacted dream. Something of emotional import was going on. It simply could not be expressed in these cryptic words and encounters. Beyond the quality of poisonous, frozen comedy no meanings rose. The scene seemed to her airless as a tomb. And nothing was improved when Mingus was replaced by Mr. Croly in the group around Clem. The husky and once athletic Mr. Croly crouched near Clem's shoulder as if to join in unlikely converse with a stranded pup whale.

He was a sandy-colored man with sharp-edged brows and deep-set blue eyes. One did not think him exactly the sort of man to have bought the great stained curtain of abstract impressionism that walled the room opposite the windows. Surely his wife was responsible for that, as she was for introducing Clem here. He was the sort of man who would catch game fish too big for mounting above the fireplace of any den or trophy room, so the evidence of his special prowess was a row of photographs in the entrance corridor. In them he stood with poles that looked like machine guns under carcasses of fish the size of blimps.

Mr. Croly was a member of one of the self-constituted select committees busying themselves in these years with our defense posture. He had just come from a dinner at the Waldorf, where the committee had been addressed by a ranking Air Force general among others. On his sharp brows sat the knowledge that war might be nearer than any of the others suspected. He was "distressed" by what he had learned this evening. And Marianne got the very strange impression that he was bringing the burden of his fears to Clem for some kind of mystic assuagement.

Rasputin, she thought. He's been elevated to the Rasputinship of these terrible people. This identification soothed her for a little while. But no epithets or categories seemed to contain him. If these upper bohemians were trying to use her amorphous drunkard as a kind of holy idiot, she felt they were hard put to get their money's worth of him.

For to Mr. Croly's worried reflections about "overkill" and "graduation of deterrents" now that the big bombs were getting so cheap, Clem responded only by launching into a reminiscence of how he had been in the Marines during the war and had been wounded at Tarawa. He had been hit by machine gun fire while wading in over the reefs, he said, and had pitched face down into sand "runny as undercooked Cream of Wheat." A photograph had been taken of him in this posture and was printed in a weekly news magazine over the (fortunately erroneous) caption, "Marine Dead at Tarawa." Later the photograph had been used in a national bond-selling campaign. It was on a poster that he had first seen it, recognizing his own silty body among the corpses by a copy of Thucydides protruding from the left rear pocket, where he had carried it throughout the early campaigns. That plus his high-school ring with the motto "Over the Alps to Italy" (in letters too small to be read, of course) on the hand so piteously loosened from the stock of his M-1 had made identification positive. It was while lying there, being photographed and bleeding from a shoulder wound, that he had begun to compose his poem "Marine." There he had heard its sullen rhythms in the lapping of warm salt water against his very eardrum. Oh, he had known what it meant to be a fish crawling up a beach to become a pioneer animal.

"Well, there'll never be another war like that, Clem," Mr. Croly said, with a glimmer of tears in his eyes. It was impossible to tell whether he was lamenting the fictive suffering of the past or the end of the age of chivalry, announced by the advent of "overkill" weapons. At any rate, he stood up and took his worries elsewhere.

And was replaced by Robert Mingus, slouching uneasily over Clem again. Bets Pomeroy stood just behind Mingus like a prompter, watching both the men's faces with steely eyes. Movingly, in a breaking voice, Mingus asked, "Will you talk to me and Bets, Clem? Alone?"

Clem said, "Maybe it's time." He helped Marianne from under the piano, promised to take her away soon and disappeared.

He was gone, she thought, more than an hour. A supper had been brought in for the remaining guests, and Marianne was listening to Mr. Croly tell of an expedition after marlin aboard the yacht of a millionaire writer—all of it sounding enough as if he had read it in a men's magazine to make her feel snappishly that he need not have left dry land, whether he actually had or not. Then Bets caught her elbow.

"You'd better come," Bets said, with a somehow triumphant lilt in her voice.

Marianne followed Bets upstairs into a vast bedroom, all dark except for the radiation (overshine) of that majestic dapple of lights sweeping out south toward New York Bay, coming through windows which matched those on the floor below.

Clem was sitting in an armchair, each hand clenched stiffly over the sleek end of an armrest, his head slightly bowed. Mingus was seated on a hassock directly in front of him. Mingus wept and crooned, and every few seconds he leaned forward to slap Clem. There was a kennel or nursery smell in the elegant room, as if untrained animals used it for play.

"Come out of it. Snap out of it," Mingus keened. For a minute Marianne thought merely that he was trying to sober Clem.

Then Mingus said, "He's the greatest of us all." He moaned. "And he won't say the word. He won't surface. 'Straight, straight up to thy apotheosis.'" At which point he slapped Clem again. "I grant him everything," Mingus wept. "Why shouldn't he talk to me? I won't settle for insincerity. I won't." Slap.

"Clem doesn't even hear him!" Bets said exultantly in her priestess voice, as if she had, after all, brought Marianne up here merely to see this supreme achievement of withdrawal. "Clem won't do anything but bait him."

"It's almost too late," Mingus said. Slap. "I say we've got to scream."

"Clem wouldn't lift a finger to save the world from mental holocaust," Bets said.

Mingus' hand was lifted for another blow when Marianne stepped forward and knocked him off his hassock. "Come on, Clem." She got her arm around Clem's chest, under his arms, and felt a hideous trembling. It was her own nerves gone out of control. He was tranquil enough. She felt that she was straining against her own fear as she lifted him to his feet, and that it somehow was appeased when she saw that he could stand. But he turned, once he was on his feet, and went to sulk with his face against the window.

All he said was, "Everyone betrays me."

Mingus turned with a convulsion of sobs and ran from the room.

Marianne's shock had turned to pure anger by the time she got Clem out of the house—without their coats, without attracting the notice of their hostess. Only, as they were getting into a cab at the corner, Mingus came running after them like a man hurrying across the surface of the moon to catch the last rocket back to earth. Behind him, at the door of the apartment building, lurked an anxious figure—probably his protector Lou Swethers, waiting to see if he was losing a boy.

Mingus threw himself into Clem's arms. He did not identify himself by a single word, and it occurred to Marianne that Clem was too sleepy to know whom he was holding. Clem said, "Don't worry. We're all together. I heard you."

Mingus' face in the street lights seemed suddenly smeared with bliss. "That's all that counts," he said. And went tranquilly back to the party then.

Marianne's disappointments of the last few days gathered to a head of disgust with what she had just been watching. And after a few minutes of stony silence in the south-bound cab, she was ready to turn and start slapping Clem herself.

"I guess I've finally got the moral," she said bitterly. "I'd be sorry that I overstayed my welcome if—oh, if I ever was, in any way, welcome. Never mind. Let me keep one shred of cleanliness. Let me not be one of those who fall into your trap of kicking you. Spider Masoch himself. But I won't kick you. I won't, you fat sonofabitch. You can drop me at my hotel, and that is the absolute end of my following you."

Only the taxi driver heard her. Clem was sleeping peaceably beside her, his hands folded, an expression of utter innocence on his face, round and dimpled in its dissolution as a baby's.

"Where do you want to go, miss?" the driver asked.

She had to look in Clem's wallet before she could answer. "Brooklyn Heights," she said. "I've got to get this slob home."

That night and in the morning while he slept off this latest installment of a perpetual drunk—hunting the flat fields near Boda, one would like to think, with his bow in hand and a quiver of homemade arrows on his back—she had her first chance to see where and how he was living.

"He lived in an empty apartment," was her wry phrase. That is, her strongest impression of habitation came from the character given it by former tenants rather than by Clem's presence. The little bit of furniture (it would have been abandoned by the last vacating occupants as

573

something that was not, in the hope of new beginnings, worth moving) showed the marks of unknown children and pets. Nevertheless, there was a kind of pleasant homeliness in the ample, uncarpeted rooms with their high ceilings.

Mainly what one could sense was the wear of plain sedentation. No drama of note had been played out in such rooms. The unknown and inarticulate had been there a long time. As Clem, evidently, would not be.

There were many books. Some dozens of them in their brand-new dust jackets were piled, discarded, scattered everywhere one looked. One was floating soggily in the bathtub, where it had been abandoned when at last he came to her hotel to pick her up. They looked neither read nor left untouched—rather, as if they had been "searched through," each one pilfered for a minute grain of contribution.

Beside the couch where she slept, after she had disposed him in the disordered waste of his bedroom, there was an upright typewriter set on a bare table of the kind that used to be called a library table—a Sears, Roebuck version of mission style. Around and over the table, trailing toward every chair and window ledge, there were sheets of manuscript and of correspondence. On a shelf that might once have kept dime-store bric-a-brac out of the reach of children, there were labeled boxes of manuscript, the bright boxes used by agents.

In the morning while she waited for him to wake she fought the temptation to rifle every page of the thousands evidently still here. She must find, once and for all, whether or not any of them were part of the Prometheus poem for whose sake he demanded so much tolerance. She saw from the labels on the manuscript boxes that most of them were drafts of his play—that hundred-times-rewritten abortion—and that others contained the ten-year-old pages of his novel. But somewhere in all of this detritus there might be what she wanted so badly to find.

If it were there—if it were there, not in all the majesty he pretended for it, but page on page of evidence of a vacated talent still sweating at the mill in Gaza, blinded but not utterly a lie and a fraud ("still having at least energy, still the will to make something," she told herself in those terms which the private soul is privileged to recognize as a form of prayer)—then such a world as she could visualize (la terre arable du songe) might seem to her still worth her faith.

It seemed to her she had a right, if she claimed no other rights from him at all, to know once and for all whether the great effort had been made. And as time went on and she waited, she saw that she was not going to exercise her right. Did not need to.

She was comforted—and, as she would think afterward, forgiven—for not prying. Not to look was to know it might be there, she thought in a kind of elation that she would describe as hysterical. Not to look was to deny the distinction between latency and fact. To keep alive the possibility that such a poem might exist was—well, at least it was her female function. Knowing where she must stop (and still wait) was her happiness, and gratefully she accepted it.

Accepting the limitation on what she was to know "for a fact" had a strange effect of liberation. The old romantic clichés about the figure latent in the block of stone, awaiting the discovery of the sculptor, about "the spirit ditties of no tone," were suddenly clean and new again, stripped of their swaddling cynicism. "After years in the wilderness," as she put it, she understood again the glory of looking over into the promised land which one may not enter.

She paced an hour while he still slept, her throat aching with the joy of her intangible discovery. Sentimentalities and great song rang in her head indistinguishably, waiting to be sorted. But waiting. Out there, somewhere beyond the walls of this house, the well-worn bridge still stood. Oh, not quite visible from these windows too far inland in Brooklyn, but there, not so much still to be sung as singing now. And the trash of the open road, the voyages to squalor, to conformity, to the erosion of talent, the death of passion, to somewhere else. All, all to be sorted yet. But there. Not done. And from here one might still go to India. To India. By God. Yes, by God, to India.

The future, somehow, was "poeticized." Was no longer for her different from the past, but stained with the colors blown from its all-mysterious crucible. And with the future, the immediate disappointment, into which she had been invited by illusions stretching seven years back, became itself tractable. I'm glad I came, she thought.

The poem that might or might not have been in one of the multicolored boxes on Clem's shelf sounded clear enough in her heart. For the time of her agony and delight, while, as she said, she "became a woman," she knew it.

Clem's bathroom with the dead book floating like a drowned fly and the medicine cabinet were (not sorted yet, not formed, but known) a part of the poem. The labels in the medicine cabinet were a catalogue of holy fears. The barbiturates, the dexedrines, and the Miltown were poppy for an Icarian life, the belladonna and the bromides not so much the craven evasion of belly pains won from excess as the appetizers for a great feast that one little belly could never accommodate.

She sat down in her rage of revery, put her arms on the kitchen table and cried, but not from despair. She heard children singing outside in the sunshine on their way from church, and she thought, "Goddammit, we're all risen this morning but him."

At length, toward one o'clock, she heard him singing from his bedroom. The song was neither cheery nor cheerless. It sounded as much like an asthmatic gasp for breath as like a paean to the risen day. And when it went on and on and she thought at last she must look in, she saw him staring up from his wet bed in fright at something on the ceiling she could not see.

"Did I wake you?" he asked, tugging at the covers like Noah uncovered by his favorite daughter. Clearly he did not want her to approach. "I sing to find out if I'm alive in the morning. I am. So bring me a beer."

She brought the beer and was gratified to see that it helped. She brought another beer with egg in it—the only breakfast he could usually stand, he told her. She brought from the medicine cabinet a trayful of drugs and a small apparatus that produced an aromatic mist when plugged into the wall socket. She cleaned and refilled the bathtub and sat by him so that he would not drown while bathing. She was glad to see that all these attentions had their effect. The man they re-created had the air of someone recomposed by a mortician, but even that was an improvement.

A third beer—on top of heaven knew what chemical combinations engendered by his mixture of medicines spinning their atomic galaxies in his veins and digestive cavities—worked the miracle of humanizing him.

For two hours then they talked. For the first time in five years, and the last time forever, they were with each other as she had wanted them to be. She realized at last that she had been wrong to expect that more could be hung on the fine filament whose opposite ends they held.

She remembered that he talked with "incredible sweetness" and that somehow he comprehended in such brevity all that he had to account for. He talked about his children and Sheila, was amused by the fact that the family reconstituted around Bernie Masterson had a thriving dog to replace the one he had kicked to death once upon an evil time. He talked about "the burden of being male" that his son bore—a burden which he thought, all things considered, he had left to rest as lightly on the child's shoulders as he could have done, "given the peculiarity of his being fathered by such as me."

"I haven't spent the whole patrimony of wonder," he said. The Drake Estate was inexhaustible, and Jess was its established heir. Jess would be small, like his father, but then to know him was to perceive that he had the brains to be the smallest All-American quarterback in the annals of sport—if he chose. Such choices had been left open to the boy; what could any father do more?

He told a wan little story about something that had happened to Jess at two, while they were still living in Paris. Clem and Sheila had already begun to coach the boy in manners, pleased to see how quickly he picked up the simple formalities and how he delighted in them as in other artifices. He learned when to say, "I'm sorry," "Thank you" and "You're welcome." Then one day he had been running in sheer exuberance to greet Clem and at a dead run had banged his head against the corner of a heavy table. Falling, dazed by the inert brutality of the blow, he had said to the table, "I'm sorry."

"If Jess remembers that, it won't seem quite as poignant to him as it does to me," Clem said, with a nod of satisfaction.

And now, with the simplest candor, he told her something about Bonnie Waller. Bonnie was a nice girl, he said, and really quite stupid. The whole point of her beauty—he used the word without inflection or qualification, intending it to be taken at its fullest weight—was not in its capacity to delight the eye, but in its significance, its representational function. He fancied that it might be a beauty which stood for all the Jews slaughtered in Europe during the war. No, not as a monument to them. Bonnie was the opposite of monumental. She was stuff of the modern, that very evanescence which shrewd Baudelaire had defined as the second aspect of beauty. If one could not see the transitory poise of beauty on her brows, then, he thought, one would not see that she was beautiful. At any rate, hers was not a fertile beauty. There was surely something terminal about it, and therefore it was entirely appropriate that it should be a beauty of the flesh rather than a beauty of the mind or the spirit. Perhaps one saw a doomed race nursing its infinitude on the finiteness of her lovely skin. She struck him as being terribly mortal, futureless, so merely there.

That was what attracted him to her, though Bonnie would hardly be flattered if she knew. The point was that Bonnie didn't want to know and didn't need to know. She called herself a writer, but that was merely an excuse for existing, for putting off demands that she do or be anything.

Nothing was going to happen to Bonnie, because nothing could. In a way he supposed he considered her to be not a product but another aspect of all those busy gas chambers of Hitler's Germany. He called her "unbearable," insisting that all true beauty was.

Well, that was the way he felt, and he would not wrestle with phrases to make his perceptions or his affection clearer than that. For the truth was that he had not the strength any more to fight his difficult intuitions into intelligible language. He satisfied himself with them and they gave a direction to his life whether or not that direction was apparent to anyone else.

Probably in a small way his inability to describe Bonnie more exactly was a repetition of his inability to master the poem. He supposed that he had really bitten off something too big for him to chew. "But bite I did. Bite Mr. Anderson did," he said. "With Sheila. With Susan. With the kids. With you. Bite Mr. Anderson did, and someone else will have to chew you all up."

He apologized elaborately and delicately for the evasiveness she had encountered after "coming so far" to see him.

"And waiting so long," she reminded.

"Yes. Waiting so long." He smiled. He had behaved thus not because he had anything better to do but because, these days, he was so seldom "ready" for the effort it would have required to give her her due.

She was about to respond, as Sheila and no doubt so many others had, that she had not come asking—rather, she had wanted to give. But she saw the impropriety of this, sensing that his view of her had frozen into something as fragile and complex as a snow crystal. That was all there was, and she had best leave it alone. If he chose to think of her as another demanding giantess, she had to let him.

Briefly he talked again about his poem, that "long look in a twisted mirror," calling it an "infamous thing" and admitting that it had become a source of shame to him, through his own fault, for having boasted of it so much without having anything to show. He asked her to understand that it had been real enough to him. For these several years he had nursed it like a wound that would not heal. Always before, when a creative work was preparing itself in him, the preparation had been marked by sickness, despair, withdrawal. Always before, something timely had intervened, like a good angel sent by the same powers that bound him to the task, to announce the turning point when everything that had been packed down tight was ready to be released. This time nothing had come. All he could say was that he had waited faithfully, whatever the appearances might be. And this time whatever forces in nature arranged such things had evidently passed him by. He had been prepared, but was not to be used.

"That's it," he said. "That's the poem of it. To be prepared and not to be used. You haven't—and only you could have—any idea of what that means. I don't mean you personally. I mean, women know."

As far as the poem as an existent thing was concerned, she might believe him or not, but once it had been complete in his mind and had required no more than the effort of putting it down. For it had, it really had, come to him in a flare of knowledge that had changed him. The irony that now teased him was that he was unable to remember much of it, though in a strange way it had grown by being forgotten. Since Sheila and he broke up he had not been able to remember things very well. "But that's all right," he said. "If I remembered them, I could only forget them. As it is, they're all here. I called them Buddy and such love." He put his thumb to his pudgy chest, not so much to indicate the figurative and literal heart as to indicate the fat, degenerating body to which he had entrusted even memory.

There was not, after all, so much to be said about things as professional writers liked to pretend, he implied. Why shouldn't the labor on his poem be to reduce it to the single and, if she liked, prosaic idea that to be human was to prepare oneself and then not to be used? One was obliged to prepare the edifice for love and then to disassemble it. All that went up had to come down, and man's life was merely to see this process through. Up to a certain point he had made things, then he submitted to the waste of what he had made. That was all.

How sum it up? There would be, by his terms, no summation. The argument fades into nothingness, neutrality. It is hardly worth setting down its vanishing moments.

Only, Marianne remembered that he spoke that morning with incredible sweetness.

To deceive her, she thought. To give her what he thought she wanted, just as he was ready, in his dissoluteness, to give anyone—anyone—else whatever was wanted of him.

A minute after he had been speaking so loftily and comfortingly about his resignation, the telephone rang. It seemed that others were privy enough to his habits to guess that by now he would be awake, would have taken beer, would be feeling ready to go on. The hardly inhabited apartment in the Heights became as public as a command post when Eileen's call from Westport was followed by calls from Mrs. Croly, Julia, Lou Swethers and Vivian Bartle.

Marianne's resurrected Rasputin was in business again, with her help, but not with her, she saw. The calls went on interminably. At four she interrupted him to say she would simply have to leave if she meant to gather up her things at her hotel and go to the Crolys' for her coat. She had not yet got her ticket, and the train that would take her back to Virginia left at seven.

"Take a later train," he coaxed. He was holding the phone against his chest. She particularly resented that he had not bothered to change, in speaking to her, from the oily simper with which he had been flattering Vivian.

"No," she said. Without another syllable she grabbed her purse and started to leave.

He came running after her, leaving the phone off the hook, his dialogue merely interrupted for the sake of her anger. Catching her in the hall, he stared beseechingly into her eyes and muttered, "So you're leaving, too? Everyone betrays me."

"I heard that maudlin sentiment last night. Don't use it on me."

He nodded in the simplest, most candid agreement with her. She felt he was pleased that she was not taken in. "I'd go with you now, but ..." He gestured down at the woolly robe he was wearing over a pair of flowered shorts. "I'll tell you what. You go get your things. I'll meet you at six." He named a bar near Penn Station. "Don't fail me," he pleaded.

And, of course, he did not show up there himself. Marianne sat there waiting for him, telling herself that, of course, it would be against nature and maybe fate for him to appear. She tried to console herself and stay her impatience—part of it just an impatience to be on the train and away from this triumphant city where misery had found its company—by re-creating artificially the hysterical gladness that had smashed her that morning when she believed that she had seen ... She could not remember very well what it was she thought she had seen. Some damned bridge that carried commuters in to work and home to sleep.

She tried, nevertheless, to think that this tawdry bar, with its romance of American ruin and all the spoiled lives, glittering around her in grimed neon tubes, spoke to her of what Clem knew, just as his apartment tucked into Brooklyn had in the moment of her true exultation. Here the lost desires whimpered. Here the broken endured the glamour of their defeat and panhandled with the slogan, "We were the last best hope."

One could think that if one chose. And hear hosannas from the jukebox if one chose. But the reason for so choosing had eluded her again. Her imagining of faith was consolation thin as dishwater. In reality she knew Clem was an alcoholic slob with no great talent left except a talent for sentimentalizing himself.

Toward seven she called Clem's apartment, thinking, Even if the phone rings unanswered, that will be something. I can tell myself he's on the way. She heard a busy signal. He was still otherwise engaged. She crossed the street to the station and took a train for home.

There she found a telegram waiting for her: "Black disaster. Missed you by three and a half minutes according bartender. Come back. Oh come again."

And this at last, this lying wisp of a telegram (certainly a lie, for if he had missed her at the bar by so little he could still have crossed the street and found her before she boarded the train, but certain to be a lie because he was a liar, a simple alcoholic liar), brought on the black, illusion-destroying fury that she would later believe had saved her, though what she was saved from it is not quite possible to articulate in a phrase.

It placed her again in the world that she had been side-stepping for five years. It showed her where attempts to evade must come out—as mere lies, whatever the gossamer of romance by which they begin.

Yet, following so hard upon the telegram that it must have been written that night after she left, and so long that it must have taken all night to finish, came a letter from him, without which the telegram and the harsh judgment it provoked would in their turn have been incomplete.

This letter was, in effect, the rest of the dialogue they might have had together. It was the might-have-been of the reality she had hoped for when she went to New York. It was like the story she had heard him telling about her at the Crolys', and it was like the sweetness of their Sunday-morning talk. And it filled in everything they had left out—as everything might have been, of course. And it came to just the conclusion that she would probably have reached if everything had (really) gone as she wished during her holiday.

You have seen us now [he wrote at the end]. Because you were shut out so often, it may be that you still think there is more. You found me singing in my infant bed and you were not exactly pleased by what I had returned to, thinking I had a truer note. Not so. It was I you saw in my empty

581

apartment. If you think I have other dimensions, you may be right in thinking so, but you will never witness them with your eye. You knew already that you were forbidden to come seeking them. What you could touch is not what you must have. There is a fastidiousness in you (which I never underrated when I soiled you with my life) which told you that.

Now you have seen. Now you know. It is your lot, like mine, to be content with that if you can. But I will not go content that you be content with this. After all, as the lady said, "It's so little." Ask more. They can kill us for asking, but they can't eat us.

It was April on the fire escapes when you came up here. In the rainy smell of the wet iron and the absence of lilacs I dreamed your coming. What could follow that? I can no longer rise beyond my expectations.

You won't come again. Thank you for helping me—all along in some way that doesn't show either—to order my life and be prepared. Go back and hide your white, white womanparts in April's smell. Now you know how much I love you, and though it has been told in Gath that Clem Anderson marries them all, thee I'll not. Henceforward to the elements be free, he said.

CLEMENT

She tried to live with this letter for three days, tried to convince herself that it was enough to live on—this nothing in lieu of the little bit she had asked for. Oh, she could have a life like anybody else. But the point was just that; she didn't want to have a life like anyone else. (But when she thought this, she thought, That's what they've all said, all the other women who've got their pink slip from him.) She fumed and reasoned and paused to consult her pride—and when it came clearly to her that she had no pride, that her last visit to New York had divested her even of the secret pride on which she had nourished her illusions so long, it seemed to her that exactly there lay her advantage. Someone had to get behind this tricky evader, she thought again, and head him off. Head him back, she thought. And since she knew of no one else who could, she went back to try again.

She left after her last class on Friday evening and arrived in New York early Saturday morning. At various hours through the morning she tried calling his apartment, and in the afternoon she searched the bars where she thought there might be some chance of intercepting him.

At nine that night, reminding herself that she had no pride, she called Bets Pomeroy to ask for a lead.

"Hadn't you heard?" Bets asked breathlessly, from that position of dignity that falls to all bearers of ultimate tidings.

With a ghastly sort of superior truthfulness Marianne said, Yes, she had heard. As if everything she had heard of or from him in the last seven years had been merely a variation of what Bets had to tell her, an infinitely varied sounding of that fatal sentence withheld from full recognition by a will power that must have been hers, since he had no will to hide it from anyone who really wanted to know. She understood that he was dead or dying.

"Only where is he?" she asked. "Where have they got him?"

Bets named the hospital. "Everyone's there," she said. "I'm going back myself, though there's nothing to do but wait. They let a few people in to see him yesterday. Sheila, you know, and some others Sheila designated. But he doesn't recognize anyone, and he's in an oxygen tent. I don't think you can see him."

"Is it …?"

"It's unquestionably terminal," Bets said, with her eternal facility for the right word. "The girl's already dead, you know."

The circus of Clem's death—for which Marianne was to be only a ticket holder, like so many others—had begun on Monday night. (As soon as he put that letter to me in the mailbox, Marianne thought grimly.) That night he had passed out (or fallen asleep, or just sat and waited—no one ever knew for sure) in Bonnie Waller's apartment. No, not even her apartment, but the apartment of a classmate at N.Y.U., loaned to her for the night. For if there was anyone who owned, possessed, clung to less of the world than Clem, it was she.

When they were found at midday on Tuesday by the returning classmate, Bonnie was stretched on a couch, nude as a statue. Even her rings and wrist watch were stripped off and her hairpins strewn on a coffee table. At the other side of the room (like an artist in a vantage point before his model, some romantic informant told Marianne) Clem sat (or slumped—it was hard to tell any more whether Clem's posture could ever be called sitting). The gas had been turned on (or left on by inadvertence, no one ever knew) in the Pullman kitchen. Both of them were still alive when the rescue squad of the Fire Department arrived.

Examinations on the first day made it clear that neither of them would ever again live as a human being. Only the deep centers of life remained to wage resistance against the encroachment of death. In both the neural damage from prolonged asphyxiation and from the raging counterfire of fever was massive. By Wednesday both had developed pneumonia and their already overstrained hearts were behaving unpredictably—flurries of pulse, followed by long, hesitant, shy tremors.

Thursday morning, in the presence of her baffled family, Bonnie died. They had not even been aware that Bonnie knew Mr. Anderson. They were particularly stunned by the indications, as hard to dismiss as to prove, that their girl had died in a suicide pact—a unilaterally decreed pact, it seemed to some, who pointed out that Clem had been drinking heavily, as usual, while the girl had not. The peculiar disposition of the bodies seemed, to those who cared about such things, an indication that Clem had been the victim of the girl's inexplicable dementia.

Still, if there had been a crime, it became perfect the morning Bonnie died. The act and whatever immediate motives it may have had in either person were sealed from every human apprehension except the spinal dream still flickering beyond the scorched earth of Clem's consciousness.

One felt that in his extremity he knew exactly why things had ended as they did. To justify this feeling, to give it any kind of communicable form, one had to—and has to—ignore what may have been the immediate motives and cast as far back as knowledge reaches to seize the thematic lines which converged in that mischance, so meaningless by itself. Meaningless or beyond meaning, which comes to the same thing.

One felt, as Marianne said, that Clem was "in possession" as he lay there straining to suck the sweet kindling oxygen into his stuffed lungs. And it seemed to her, that Sunday morning when she finally got her turn to see him, that she understood the common old tale whose point is that dying men relive, or possess, their whole lives. No doubt her feeling may be accounted for as a projection of her own knowledge on this gasping, hardly human thing. How could it be otherwise? But what she projected had come from him, supremely articulate, in the first place. He had written to her of his dream or vision in the game preserve in Kansas, and if, in imagining that now in his last hours he had recaptured the pointless wisdom of that dream, she was projecting, still in another sense she was merely restoring that dream to its proper

584

point in the chronology of his life. A proper enough function for the inheritors of a mind that had shaken free from the respectable bondage of time.

Through the plastic scrim of the oxygen tent he bared his teeth at her. His throat gurgled merrily. The stained whites of his eyes gleamed at her through the trembling slits of his lids. She felt his constant gaiety undiminished by the agony that had diminished everything else—as if, exactly as if, he meant to say, "Don't be shocked. You're not seeing anything that wasn't there before, waiting to be displayed. Nothing I didn't mean for you to see in the fullness of time." Like a demonstration contrived for children reluctant to learn, his death graphed the change from a subjective consciousness into meaning.

Yes, but what did he mean? One might very well believe him to be pulling the supreme trick of the artist, the old goldfish trick, in which the completed triangulation of reflection made him personally dispensable, and believe as well that no meaningful reality would be destroyed by his death. But how was that reality to be grasped? The mocking answer seemed to be that it was no more difficult to clutch him now than it had ever been. For his parents, his girls, his friends, his wives, he had always turned out to be elusive, while they always clutched for a mortal self they were not meant to have.

She half understood his trick when she assumed that now he was watching the animals of his psychic life troop around him in one more loyal pageant of disappointment. Rabbit and rat, chimera and holy baboon attended in the waning moonlight of his perception, and if he wanted to be—she thought he would want to be—he might be as happy with them as St. Francis in purgatory, waiting for darkness or the ultimate radiance.

This half-wishful fantasy, framed for her consolation, was encouraged by her experience with all those who flocked like the animals of his dream to the hospital to watch and wait while he died. Bets had been exaggerating only a little when she said that everyone was there. Not even all the personages of his life in New York came; not more than half a dozen got to his bedside. But there were a great many who entered the downstairs waiting room, milled for a while, demanded bulletins from the harassed staff of the hospital, gossiped together in little groups and went their wondering ways. There were rabbity girls and young male lions who seemed to have found some necessity to stop in here on their way someplace else. There were friends he had not seen in years and agents with whom he had long ago stopped doing business. There were chimeras of both sexes—among whom Marianne placed herself—who had come here as if there were no place else for them to go. She supposed that so many caught up with him here because "they finally knew where he was to be found at any given hour."

To be one of his trooping animals—that was her station, and at last it was incumbent on her to see what it meant to be thus related to him. She sensed in herself and felt in all the others a brutish anxiety, a restless unspeakable undercurrent of determination not to let him go.

There was Mrs. Croly, who had installed herself on the scene like a commander. It was she who called in the specialists—neurologists, heart men, lung experts, gastrointestinal sharpshooters—as the hospital's attending physicians discovered that one after another major system of Clem's body was succumbing to the invincible toxins. Marianne, of course, was not a witness to all the telephoning and demands, the consultations and the resolves to try the most exotic means to save him. It was general knowledge among the gossiping, faithful watchers that the Crolys' money had unleashed every effort.

There was Robert Mingus, prowling the waiting room or its marches at all hours like a juvenile, tuskless walrus. From his anxious watching at all the doors and windows, his searching glance thrown on every face that entered the elevator, it seemed that he was watching for Death to come—and when he came, Mingus barehanded would leap on the hideous figure, clawing, biting, scratching, to protect the one uncarnal love left in his overwhelmed life. If this is what the poet intended, it seemed at least as effective a defense as any the doctors were able to contrive.

To Marianne, Mingus said hysterically that at last he understood what Clem had meant by his parable of the fortuneteller and the eggs. The eggs were herself and Bonnie Waller. Certainly. Didn't she see the imagistic identity between eggs—he blushed as his hands described their shape in the air—and pure young women?

"Nonsense," she said.

Not nonsense at all. Mingus believed Clem knew that the dreadful worm which had left him was waiting with multiplied power inside one white shell or the other of the two, so to speak, pullet eggs. "He cracked the wrong one," Mingus said.

"Cracked? How can you pretend to be a poet when you do not understand heterosexual language?" Marianne turned her back and left him to resume his pacing on guard.

There was Claude Pogorski. He was newly returned to the United States, and he brought to the hospital with him his Indian wife and three dusky children. They appeared in the waiting room on Saturday night, and though the family did not return, Claude came back to intrude his presence among the others at each visiting hour. On his face was a horrid smile of accusation for all these others who had let things come to such a pass for his hero. In his smothered-volcano fashion he spoke to many of those he could identify as Clem's partisans. Identification was not so hard after one had sat in the waiting room for a while, watching the person who had come down most recently from Clem's bedside be surrounded by those clamoring for the latest word, the latest witnessing on which superstitious hope could feed.

When he buttonholed Marianne, she found that the main theme he had to voice was "Wasted." "Wasted, wasted," he said with something not far from vindictive glee. He did not at all mind scraping the sore wound of sensitivity that he found common to all of them. If Clem had only gone with him when he turned his back on America and went among the people, he implied, this great life need not have gone out in such a damply fizzling waste. Clem might have found his rightful children. And one wonders if Claude did not mean that those dark children he had brought home to show were really Clem's, Claude still imagining himself the servant through whom Clem's seed should flow.

As early as Saturday evening Marianne saw Sheila and Bernie Masterson and Clem's children there. Bernie kept Jess and Lulie in the waiting room while Sheila went upstairs to see Clem and talk to his doctors.

It seemed that, as old Kansas compatriots, Bernie and Marianne shared a perspective open to no one else. Each had retained and cultivated a share of profligate Clem that had been flung—like his knuckles and joints flung to puppies—all those years ago when he first came to them. Sotto voce Bernie told her how long it had been since Clem had seen the children—over a year now, though he had spoken to them on the phone at least once a month. Wasn't it odd how Clem had "moved back from people" so that many of his dearest liaisons had become those kept by telephone or letter? Behind this was the anxiously smug implication that Clem had kept his liaison with Bernie by some more substantial links. After all, Bernie had the very wife and kiddies.

Marianne, who had only some letters, replied that it was odd but understandable to those who understood.

Bernie stressed the point that he and Sheila still kept Clem's memory green "at home." In the strained inflexion he gave to "at home" Marianne glimpsed the extent to which he still believed it was

Clem's home. By a miracle he would never know how to trust, Bernie had intruded like a wandering spirit into vestments and a role—perhaps one might say even into a body—that Clem had vacated when he went in pursuit of his two-dimensional Princess Cindy. Put another way, Clem was still head of that house. His servant Bernie was about the master's business. Life, for all that it matters, was going on.

There was an accommodation for everyone around this death. In the battle now waging between civility and grief, plainly civility would triumph. Nothing would be interrupted. Nature, which abhors all vacuums, had already been mostly assuaged. The preparations for a change of tenancy had been under way for—a long time? Why not say forever?

Which did not mean that the recognitions of grief were not real. What nature abhorred was given its due as well. Beyond the ability of vocal expression, perhaps just because vocal expression and other natural communication had never trammeled the ground, living grief paid its tribute to the unspeakable.

Clem's son had plainly been grieving for something he understood no better than the others, something he would have to grieve for each year that he came to understand more fully why he had once apologized to the mute table that hurt his head. Mostly, while Marianne noticed this little heir to the Drake Estate, he sat gravely with his cap held between his knees. His round face—which resembled Clem's only about the eyes—was habitually lowered. But those resembling eyes were raised, less prayerfully than in some superstitious attempt at magic. She saw that he was breathing oddly. He held his breath long on every third inhalation. It was clear that he was trying to share its superfluous functioning with that struggling flesh upstairs under the oxygen tent. All he needed was the magic that Daddy had so recklessly promised to discover for him.

On Sunday afternoon Clem's father arrived. He had flown in from Milwaukee. Early in the week, when he and Clem's mother had been notified, it had seemed Clem would die before his father could reach him. Twice flights had been arranged and canceled. At last he and Clem's mother had decided he must come anyway. "If I have to bring him home in a box, she said, she wants him to come home," he announced—not only to Sheila, but to everyone he spoke to. The trip seemed kind of foolish to him. He had to justify it somehow. He was nervous—that is the only word for it—about the circumstances in which Clem had come to his mischance. It seemed to him the immediate consequence of Clem's high-school behavior, getting mixed up with Irene Lacey that way. Clem would have thought he had a point there.

Most of all—most significantly of all—Mr. Anderson was disappointed by what was left of his son, so nearly all withdrawn from life in his hospital bed. He could hardly tell, as he said later, that this dying man was his son. He had lost a son, somewhere, sometime, very long ago, and he could no more catch up to him in this agony than in the million evasions that had led up to it.

When he was shooed away from the oxygen tent after a half-dozen minutes beside Clem, Mr. Anderson went wandering about the hospital. In his old age he liked to visit with the sick and cheer them up—provided they were responsive. So during visiting hours he found his way into one of the wards, met a "real interesting old fellow" there, played a few hands of whist with him and then bought him a couple of cigars at the hospital gift shop.

On Monday afternoon Terry Burbidge visited the hospital. He was not allowed to see Clem, but had a cup of tea with Sheila and Marianne in a restaurant across the street. Listening to Sheila fill in the story for Terry and hearing Terry's grave summary finally rounded Marianne's view of what was going on.

What was there to say about Clem and this girl who had died with him, Sheila asked, except that for years Clem had used one woman to screen himself from another, giving each one less as he went on? This girl, Bonnie Waller, she supposed, was another of his "beautiful souls," which, of course, he had always preferred to find in a nice body.

"There's poetic warrant for that," Terry said, with judicious consolation. "That can be understood."

Understood or not, it asked something impossible of women. It asked them to be, she said angrily, figures of his imagination and nothing more. No wonder that eventually one of them had rebelled and had turned the gas on him. Sheila had no doubt that it was Bonnie's frustrated, outraged hand that had turned on the jets. "The man was just sitting there, looking at her," Sheila said with grating, not loud, hysteria. "Too goddam much." As to the question who Bonnie Waller was, Sheila said, "Nobody. Just nobody. I guess Clem had known her for quite a while. She came around to look him up. She just waited. Like the rest of us. Oh, I suppose she thought she was vaguely artistic, vaguely spiritual. He had a way of making women feel he was their destiny. By needing them so much, pretending to. It's the oldest trick in the world. He only managed to do it excessively."

Terry tapped his finger thoughtfully on the table top. "All these women. And the others. There are so many others over there, all concerned." He looked at Marianne and said essentially what she had heard from Claude Pogorski: "I think they can't stand to have him die, to let him go, because all these years they've been asking too little of him."

"I didn't," Sheila said. "He thought I was asking too much."

"I meant we might indeed have asked him to be many things that he wasn't. But we asked too little of what he truly was, and now we can't bear it."

That, Marianne would always think, was the note on which Clem died—the wail of deserted animals given its epigrammatic form.

When the three of them crossed the street again to the hospital they were met in the waiting room by Robert Mingus. Tears were flooding his thin cheeks. He made straight for Sheila and tried to embrace her. She pushed him away.

"He's gone," Mingus said. "He's gone and you weren't here."

Clem was dead. They saw Clem's stranger friends waiting to get on the elevator. The oxygen tent had been removed and all who had been waiting were going up to see the body.

As Terry and Sheila and Marianne got into the elevator they saw Mingus attempt to embrace a newcomer, crying to him, "He's gone. He's gone and you weren't there."

"All right, buddy," the man said. "I'm here now." He was an A.P. reporter, here to wind up the factual record.

In the room where Clem's body lay in the hospital bed, at least twenty people were crowded. It would be impossible for me to say what proprieties or what claims had brought most of them. Surely to each of them Clem had made some pledges of allegiance, some promises—all of which were here and now in default.

They couldn't eat the body (though someone had exposed the cold, yellowing feet, and when Mingus came in, Marianne saw him approach the bed and clasp one of them in his two hands in a gesture either of pleading or of farewell) and they had not asked, had not known how to ask, all they needed of the spirit that had been so long and lingeringly in process of vacating it.

They had asked him to descend from the Oedipal throne of his loneliness and art. He had obliged them one and all. He had given himself to them as their clown and their lover. Now they were shocked with a nameless horror that he had yielded to their request.

Now at last he was fully theirs. It was time for the rites of dismemberment to begin, and in embarrassment they could ask only, What shall we do with the perishable meat? Each of them, feeling the absence of Clem's power, had to understand at last that it had been no more and no less than the power of longing in each of them. It was the unripened dream of reconciliation between desire and necessity that Clem had, indeed, proposed to write out for them. But he had not written it. All the lines they had tossed to him fell back unattached and slack in their own hands.

Only Clem's father had a good reason for being with the dead poet. He had come to take the body home in a box, hadn't he?

Even this modest practical claim was denied. Clem's will specified in the most prosaic language—as if by calculation refusing to give any hint of why he would not return to Boda, even dead—that he was to be buried in one of the mammoth cemeteries in Brooklyn.

I heard his funeral preached in a dismaying, shabby Baptist church a mile from his Brooklyn apartment, saw him lowered into the earth among the innumerable headstones of strangers. The funeral sermon, though it mentioned his public successes in the journalistic fashion of our time, was as perfect a mask of anonymity as I could imagine. Through the clear, blue sky of April above the cemetery, the planes circled in for their landings at Idlewild, or took off for their well-charted travels. One was made to feel by this too that nothing was interrupted.

After the funeral I had time for long talks with Sheila and Bernie and for an interesting evening with Lillian Esterman and Henderson Paul (now married to each other, observing the proprieties of natural selection after so many years of trying to marry unsuitable mates).

Lillian remembered how, as far back as college, she had predicted that Clem would do himself in if he did not learn to separate literature from life. In her own terms she was right, of course, as we all were—in our own terms. But the chief legacy to the Pauls from Clem's death was a persisting debate about whether he had "used up his gift" before he died. (It sticks in my mind how sure they were that if he had a gift, he ought to have used it up. This seems to be the public-servant view of a writer, and I would think it implies an obligation to define that public which the writer ought to serve. But they never got around to that.)

Yes, Lillian thought, he had used all that was valuable. She recalled the open, almost theatric display of the artist turning his mill that Clem had given us ten or twenty years ago. Like everyone else, she had heard of the big poem he had claimed was occupying his efforts in the last years. She considered it a pathetic joke. Even if he had meant to write it, the intent was silly. Everyone knew or should know that the best things done these days were small, sharp and, I suppose, portable. She cited numerous critics and numerous poems I couldn't help admiring to cinch her point.

But Clem himself had never taken the "big poem" seriously, Henderson insisted. It was a boob-catching pretense, a kind of endless shaggy-dog story in the shelter of which Clem was marshaling the forces of his imagination to write a whopping novel. "Clem believed that poetry was used up. He said the language was saturated with all the valuable poetic combinations it allows. I heard him say that myself." Ah, yes—but then, what had Clem not said in the table talk of his last New York years? That, of course. And of course, to someone, sometime, its exact and unreconcilable opposite. With equal sincerity. So many blanket pronouncements had come from him that none of them could be taken as a consistent belief.

Sheila, as Marianne had noted, was angry. Clem's death had not softened the fierce and female resentment roused when she heard how he had come to be in the hospital. She would talk to me about old times—we talked in Bernie's presence, but without hindrance, as if he had long ago learned to accept even the homely commonplaces of the Anderson past as legendary, beyond the emotions of rivalry—but always her thoughts tended back to the ridiculous anticlimax of Clem's taking off, that fantastic tryst with Bonnie Waller, the comedy of the disciples in the hospital. She would not accept it thus. That there should be no longer any object for her anger was no more to the point than that there was no more object for the hopes, dismays and anxiety that all the rest of us had focused on him. Clem had become purely what we might make of him within the cells of our own lives.

"Is this all it was for?" Sheila asked, in so many words and in the effect of all she had still to say. Was this all that could be shown for loyalty and unfathomable patience? This waste, utter and ridiculous?

The question just as she had phrased it haunted my summer voyage to Europe and all my thoughts turning back toward the unredeemable promises of the past. But all the while, returning like a gay responsive echo to her question, came some intimation that the vanished past was persistently real. I began to sense that Clem's death had destroyed the handicaps of chronological time. Death had seemed a pin on which Clem's eventually desiccated figure must forever bear the study of eyes obliged to facts. But death was also a release from the tyranny of forms and factuality.

It came to me in those following months that the issue in my friendship with Clem had always been whether I could be just to a man I knew to be my superior. I had trembled often enough to think that efforts at justice would only reduce him to my smaller measure. Now, with his death, justice had been given its classic sanction to look back along the tracks of memory for the noble content of a life not at all comprehended by its shabby end.

I went through a period of quasi-religious exaltation. For a while I fell into the habit of thinking Clem had been as great as he might have been. But that was not quite justice, either. In the autumn following his death two things happened to correct my uncurbed impulses toward mysticism.

First Marianne Luce came to teach in our English department. Naturally and happily Janet and I made friends with her. At length I heard her account of what I have, near the end of Clem's story, set down. In those first months of our acquaintance she did not offer to show me any of Clem's last letters, but I have seen them since. They confirm my impression that Clem lived the years of his disintegration quite sure that he was still working out the creative task he had long ago begun. He whose life had been so polymythic in its circumstances had found a peculiar grace in his faith that he was living to its end the myth of the poet.

The other thing that corrected my view of Clem was the attempt Robert Mingus made to revive interest in Clem's poetry. Articles by Mingus and his connections began to mushroom in various literary quarterlies. They seemed closer to posthumous flattery than to criticism. Reading them sobered me; I might even say my teeth were put on edge, in spite of the value I set on Clem's work. The articles pretended that the Clem we had in print was of an order of greatness I felt to be only promised, perhaps only wished for. I do not intend to disparage Mingus' motives. But the whole revival smacked to me of promotion again, of distortion worse than silence.

So at last I prefer to rest my appraisal of Clem as artist on the poem that was never written. I assume the justice due his human failure depends on the value I place on that poem.

Irrationally I believe in it, but I am not so distracted as to affirm its existence, even in an ideal realm. It is uncreated, though the very nature of Clem's fall created the conditions for its existence, as some disturbance of the solar or atomic order might create the conditions for the emergence of life on a mineral planet. I have had some overwhelming glimpses into the processes of conception that were always misrepresented by his published work; therefore I can believe only in that which would be the true equivalent—in form and force, breadth and mass—of his immense desire. The monument conceived by hope must duplicate the magnitude of the abyss into which life tumbles.

Say that in his human dissolution Clem chose to serve the base image of Mrs. Fothergill, and you have already discovered a metaphor rich enough to keep up through our lives in awe. That metaphor is a cropping of the continental lode that he worked to the end of his strength.

Say, if you despair of his visible accomplishment, that finally he turned back one more time to repeat the formulas of his life from which holiness and meaning had already been exhausted. There, like a miracle, the search itself sowed meaning again.

If he had broken every other mortal commandment—and there were few he did not shiver by his recklessness—I think he obeyed the greatest: Do not betray the young. I find him true to the "first child" of his unworldly conception.

I have had intimations, thanks to him, of what a man may endure of the self-knowledge that nature seems to forbid us, and if my faith in that still unknown plowland of dreams were to mean my exile from reason itself, I would have to pronounce myself irredeemable.

In justice it is my duty to teach those whom I can that though the word may fail us, beyond the word is the word. The fact may fail us yet again, but beyond the fact is the fact. The Promethean legend is true enough, though we cannot, in this epoch, write it. The legend lives our lives, and it ends truly in a bondage cruelest for those who dare most. The vulture and the worm and the cliff overlooking the empty sea are not inventions but heritages, and the grief of the hero who risks them cannot be diminished or increased by the acclaim of any public we know how to define. If what I have been able to write of Clem is just, I care nothing at all about what it does for his reputation. In describing his bondage to the unreliable word, I have accepted my own deepest commitment to it and to all the humiliations we must suffer from time and appearances.

And yet by writing at this length—too long, not long enough—I have made some progress from grief toward the conviction that the bondage may be joyful enough for the creatures we are. By it I have been bound to answer Sheila's "Is this all it was for?" with a record which at least will say, "It was all this."

# About the Author

R.V. Cassill (1919–2002) was a prolific and award-winning author and a highly regarded writing teacher. Among his best-known works are the novels Clem Anderson and Doctor Cobb's Game and the short stories "The Father" and "The Prize," the latter of which won him an O. Henry Award. Cassill taught at the Iowa Writers' Workshop, Purdue University, and Brown University, and numbered many published authors among his students. He founded the Association of Writers & Writing Programs (AWP) in 1967 and after his retirement became the editor of The Norton Anthology of Short Fiction, a position he held for nearly a quarter century.

Made in United States
North Haven, CT
16 May 2022

19223540R00364